C000128504

Maxim Jakubowski is a [...] He was born in the UK and e[...] er in book publishing, he op[...] he bookshop in London. He [...] ed over thirty bestselling erotic [...] tic photography, as well as many acclaimed crime collections. His novels include *It's You That I Want to Kiss*, *Because She Thought She Loved Me*, and *On Tenderness Express*, all three recently collected and reprinted in the USA as *Skin in Darkness*. Other books include *Life in the World of Women*, *The State of Montana*, *Kiss Me Sadly*, *Confessions of a Romantic Pornographer*, *I Was Waiting For You*, and *Ekaterina and the Night*. In 2006 he published *American Casanova*, a major erotic novel which he edited and on which fifteen of the top erotic writers in the world collaborated, and his collected erotic short stories as *Fools For Lust*. He compiles two annual acclaimed series for the Mammoth list: *Best New Erotica* and *Best British Crime*. He is a winner of the Anthony and the Karel Awards, a frequent TV and radio broadcaster, a past crime columnist for the *Guardian* newspaper, and Literary Director of London's Crime Scene Festival.

THE MAMMOTH BOOK OF

Best
New Erotica

Volume 12

Edited by Maxim Jakubowski

RUNNING PRESS
PHILADELPHIA · LONDON

Constable & Robinson Ltd
55–56 Russell Square
London WC1B 4HP
www.constablerobinson.com

First published in the UK by Robinson,
an imprint of Constable & Robinson Ltd, 2013

A copy of the British Library Cataloguing in Publication Data is
available from the British Library

UK ISBN: 978-1-78033-789-0 (paperback)
UK ISBN: 978-1-78033-790-6 (ebook)

1 3 5 7 9 10 8 6 4 2

First published in the United States in 2012 by Running Press Book Publishers,
A Member of the Perseus Books Group

Books published by Running Press are available at special discounts for bulk purchases in
the United States by corporations, institutions, and ther organizations. For more information,
please contact the Special Markets Department at the Perseus Books Group, 2300 Chestnut
Street, Suite 200, Philadelphia, PA 19103, or call (800) 810-4145, ext. 5000, or e-mail
special.markets@perseusbooks.com.

US ISBN: 978-0-7624-4947-7

US Library of Congress Control Number: 2013915863

9 8 7 6 5 4 3 2 1
Digit on the right indicates the number of this printing

Running Press Book Publishers
2300 Chestnut Street
Philadelphia, PA 19103-4371

Visit us on the web!
www.runningpress.com

Printed and bound by
CPI Group (UK) Ltd, Croydon, CR0 4YY

Contents

Acknowledgements

"Grounded" © 2013 Nikki Magennis. First appeared in *Best Erotic Romance 2013*, edited by Kristina Wright

"The Tennis Pro" © 2011 I. J. Miller. First appeared in the author's collection *Sex and Love*

"The Copper Horse" © 2012 Vina Green. First appeared in *The Copper Horse* from *House of Erotica*

"The Reading" © 2012 Michael Hemmingson. First appeared in *Penthouse Variations*

"All My Lovers in One Room" © 2012 Kristina Lloyd. First appeared in *Stretched*, edited by Tinder James

"Saturnalia" © 2013 Vivienne LaFay. First appeared in e-book format

"Whore" © 2012 D. L. King. First appeared in *One Night Only*, edited by Violet Blue

"New Orleans When it Rains" © 2012 Maxim Jakubowski. First appeared in *Foreign Affairs*, edited by Antonia Adams

"Where I Can See You" © 2012 Remittance Girl. First appeared on the Erotica Readers and Writers Association website

"The Blood Moon Kiss" © 2011 Mitzi Szereto. First appeared in *Red Velvet and Absinthe*, edited by Mitzi Szereto

"Contract between Cazrina and her Submissive Anaïs" © 2012 Gala Fur and Véronique Bergen. First appeared in *Edwarda*

"Venus in Edinburgh" © 2013 Pat McStone. Original to this collection

"Exquisite Corpse" © 2012 Aimee Nichols. First appeared in *Little Raven One*

"Alice Before her Period" © 2012 Emma Becker. First appeared as a broadsheet from the UAE British Centre for Literary Translation

"Tourist" © 2012 Angela Caperton. First appeared in *Like the Hand of Time*, edited by Bethany Zaiatz

"Here There be Dragons" © 2012 Ashley Lister. First appeared in *Thrones of Desire*, edited by Mitzi Szereto

"Suffer for Me" © 2011 Teresa Noelle Roberts. First appeared in *Best Bondage Erotica*, edited by Rachel Kramer Bussel

"The Horniest Girl in San Francisco" © 2013 Charles Gatewood. Original to this collection

"Coucou" © 2012 Mia More. First appeared on www.cliterati.co.uk

"Marks" © 2012 Rachel Kramer Bussel. First appeared in *Cheeky Spanking Stories*, edited by Rachel Kramer Bussel

"Halloween in the Castro" © 2012 Donna George Storey. First appeared on oysters&chocolate.com

"Spar" © 2009 Kij Johnson. First appeared in *Clarkesworld*

"Romanesque" © 2012 O'Neil De Noux. First appeared in *Foreign Affairs*, edited by Antonia Adams

"Fleshpot" © 2012 Lisabet Sarai. First appeared in *Coming Together: Arm in Arm in Arm*, edited by Nobilis Reed

"The Pick-Up Artist" © 2011 Alison Tyler. First appeared in *Gritty*, edited by Sommer Marsden

"Come Inside" © 2013 Mathew Klickstein. Original to this collection

"Risk Reduction" © 2012 Madeline Moore. First appeared in *The Swap*

"Flesh and Stone" © 2012 Sacchi Green. First appeared in *Thrones of Desire*, edited by Mitzi Szereto

"Against the Wall" © 2012 Catherine Paulssen. First appeared in *Duty and Desire*, edited by Kristina Wright

"What Vacations Are For" © 2011 Thomas S. Roche. First appeared in *Best Bondage Erotica*, edited by Rachel Kramer Bussel

"La Belle Mort" © 2011 Zander Vyne. First appeared in *Red Velvet and Absinthe*, edited by Mitzi Szereto

"Suite 1226" © 2012 Michèle Larue. First appeared in *Secrets de Femmes*, edited by Franck Spengler

"Lessons Learned" © 2012 Jade Melisande. First appeared in *Cheeky Spanking Stories*, edited by Rachel Kramer Bussel

"The Graffiti Artist" © 2012 Amanda Earl. First appeared on the Erotica Readers and Writers Association website

"You Belong to Me" © 2012 C. Sanchez-Garcia. First appeared on the Erotica Readers and Writers Association website

"Into the Baptismal" © 2012 Peggy Munson. First appeared in *Stripped Down*, edited by Tristan Taormino

"Balancing the Books" © 2013 Lucy Felthouse. First appeared in *The Big Book of Bondage*, edited by Alison Tyler

"Hina, the Hawaiian Helen" © 2012 J. D. Munro. First appeared in the author's collection *The Strangler Fig*

"Hold" © 2012 Adam Berlin. First appeared on *Clean Sheets*

"Golden Hand" © 2012 K. L. Gillespie. First appeared in a different version in *The Erotic Review* and in the present version in the author's collection *Unlost*

"Stella" © 2012 Saskia Walker. First appeared in *Open*, edited by Alison Tyler

"Make Your Own Miracles" © 2011 Nikki Magennis. First appeared in *Steamlust*, edited by Kristina Wright

"Statues in the Snow" © 2012 Steve Finn. First appeared at literotica.com

"My Ass is Your Ass is My Ass" © 2011 Kristina Lloyd. First appeared in *Smart Ass*, edited by Alison Tyler

"Appointment Tee Vee" © 2012 Victoria Janssen. First appeared in *Morning, Noon and Night*, edited by Alison Tyler

"We Are Not What You Think We Are" © 2012 Michael Hemmingson. First appeared in *Fiction International*

"Something Twisted this Way Comes" © 2012 Kyoko Church. First appeared in *My Secret Life*

"New York Snow" © 2013 Elissa Wald. Original to this collection

Introduction

2012 was the year the erotica and romance literary map changed forever.

The *Fifty Shades of Grey* phenomenon, notwithstanding the intrinsic faults of the bestselling trilogy, has proven there is a strong appetite for erotic stories and tales explicitly depicting what I would term non-vanilla sexual activities and tastes. To the extent that we even hear sales of sex aids and toys have increased spectacularly worldwide as a result! And, of course, erotic books have also much benefited from the *FSOG* tsunami, with authors like Vina Jackson, Indigo Bloome, L. M. Adeline, Sylvia Day, Sasha Grey and Portia Da Costa following in E. L. James's footsteps onto the bestseller lists, while many of the contributors to our Mammoth series have also seen a significant increase in their sales and noted with a wry smile that publishers now looked upon them somewhat more favourably than before when the erotic field was still something of a popular fiction ghetto.

This is a well-deserved vindication of my convictions about the artistic and entertainment merit of erotica. After editing this series for now eighteen years I can only applaud this new-found recognition and hope that it is at least partly sustained after the wave of bad imitations and exploitative material that any new phenomenon generates abates and the quality authors rise to the top without being drowned in the sea of "me too" books that are currently flooding us.

Since I launched this series in 1995 (we featured five unnumbered collections prior to our now twelve annual volumes), I have been proud to introduce hundreds of talented authors, some of whom were and are still active outside erotica too, who have ably demonstrated that writing can arouse, fascinate and enchant. And year after year, they continue to amaze me with the breadth of their sometimes wonderfully twisted imaginations and the way they renew a subject – sex – that many wrongly think of as repetitive and not worthy of description, analysis and emotion. But if you've been reading our collections for years now, I know I'm preaching to the convinced.

Yet again, this year's volume features new names and talents as well as returning favourites. Never has so much erotica been published than during the past twelve months; not just novels with the obligatory BDSM background but also a record number of anthologies both in print and digital format and, as a result, I had an embarrassment of choices when it came to selecting this year's stories and was obliged to neglect many that could well have merited inclusion in a previous volume.

I am particularly pleased to be able to introduce for the first time writers I've long admired such as Peggy Munson, whose novel *Origami Striptease* I heartily recommend, Elissa Wald (author of *Meeting the Master*, which I was also delighted to include as a reprint in my digital list of *Modern Erotica Classics* from this collection's UK publishers) as well as French author Emma Becker, whose splendid (and realistically steamy) novel *Monsieur* I was privileged to be able to recently translate and which is now available in the UK and USA (and many other countries too). In addition, award-winning SF author Kij Johnson joins us as do Pat McStone (behind whom hides a rather acclaimed crime author), famed San Francisco photographer Charles Gatewood (who has featured in several of my *Mammoth Books of Erotic Photography* and some decades ago wrote the wonderful 1993 cult classic novel *Hellfire* as Charles G. Wood), and I. J. Miller (new to this series but a contributor to my *Sex in the City* quartet of anthologies).

With the increased visibility of literary erotica and romance on the bookshelves, I am hoping to welcome many new readers to our collections and can only repeat something I've said many times before: if you enjoy the voices, ideas, plots and characters you come upon within these pages, don't be shy and do continue your exploration by searching for other books and stories by the writers you discover here. You will find them not only rewarding but also liberating – even if it doesn't point you in the direction of the nearest sex shop for technical assistance!

And I can promise you that none of our writers have a need for handsome millionaires with helipads and naive, virginal students to be introduced to some of the manifold realities of sex. They are not only more subtle in their approach but so much more exciting, and as a matter of fact, closer to real life!

Until another year of brilliant sex on the page comes round, enjoy this one. Awaken your senses.

Maxim Jakubowski

Grounded

Nikki Magennis

Erin arrived first. Her red-eye flight landed hard and ground to a slow halt. She stepped out onto a flat grey desert of tarmac. The air was twelve degrees colder and everything was quiet, the airport still half asleep. Inside the terminal, Erin stashed her case in a locker and then walked circuits round empty lounges and past shuttered shops, trying to work the stiffness out of her legs. It was like wandering in Limbo. A space between destinations, a no man's land. Airports seemed to exist outside of any particular place, but she loved them, felt at ease in their anonymous spaces, unknown and free. Foreign voices echoed around her, as hushed as pigeons' wings.

She bought breakfast, a cinnamon wafer and hot, strong coffee, but her appetite dissolved, replaced by a swarm of butterflies in her stomach. Instead, she went to the newsstand and flicked through magazines on the carousel, looking at pictures until the colours blurred: a face painted blue; a crowd at a race; a map of Europe dotted with flags.

An hour later she watched from behind the plate glass windows as Mark's flight landed. It was like watching silent-movie footage on a vast, blue-tinted screen. He emerged from the plane into the Dutch morning light. The sight of him, six foot, tanned, lithe and weather-roughed, made her heart beat double-espresso fast. She got a glimpse of his two-day stubble and crumpled clothes before he disappeared into the walkway, swallowed by another passage, gone from her again.

She found herself finger-combing her hair and biting her lip, like a teenager.

"Erin." His smile was as wide as a sunrise. They crossed the last distance separating them as though drawn by gravity, and sank into an embrace so tight she could hardly breathe. She pressed her face into the coarse, air-cold folds of his jacket, inhaled all the smells that made her heart ache. Woodsmoke, cut grass, pine. He smelled like spring.

"God, I missed you," he said, talking into her hair, his words warm against her scalp. At the sound of his voice she felt her eyes prickle.

"Me too," she said.

"Oh babe. Where have you been?"

"All over the place," she said. There was so much to say, but then he held her chin and lifted her face to kiss her and it was clear they needed to touch more than they needed to speak. He tasted sweet. His body was hard and insistent against hers. His arms locked around her and held her tight.

She pulled away, looked around and saw where they were, on a polished floor, in the stream of traffic, taking up space. They'd hardly touched each other but she already felt like she was naked. She coughed.

"Got a bag?" she asked, her voice a breaking whisper. Did the question even make sense? She was fixed on his eyes, their blue gaze still shocking bright behind half-closed lids. He shrugged one shoulder.

"Just this."

"C'mon." Her mouth was thick from kissing him. The words bumped against one another. Now, they laced their fingers together and walked over the squeaky, shined floors, past the frag-mented groups of people wandering, dazed and sleep-scuffed, around the airport, weaving between knots of Japanese tourists, struggling families, scowling businessmen, cabin crew in their bright, tired uniforms, under signs and hanging curtains of LEDs and scrolling announcement boards and arrows pointing in so many different directions. His thumb brushed the pulse spot on her wrist, and it seemed to turn up the volume of her heartbeat. The ambient sounds faded, her pulse became as loud as their footsteps, louder than all the things she wanted to say but couldn't and didn't know how to phrase anyway, until it drummed in her head and all she could think of was his bare skin against hers.

They reached the doorway of the pod hotel where she'd booked a room. "Give me a minute," she said, pulling out her credit card and trying to find the right slot to swipe it in the check-in machine. Her hands were shaking. Behind her, Mark came up and rested his chin on her shoulder.

"Stop."

"Hm? I'm not doing anything," he said, scuffing her neck with the rough scrape of his stubble. Her knees almost buckled and she leaned against the machine with both hands flat on the screen. He laid a tiny, wet kiss on her hairline and she closed her eyes.

"I can't work the thing. Come on."

"I've waited six weeks," he said, his voice so low it sunk into the carpet. "OK. Do it. Get us in there. I need you in a room, naked, now." He backed away, holding his hands up, and she instantly missed the feel of him next to her.

"Don't go anywhere," she said. She typed in her number and got the key. They followed arrows, counting cabin numbers along the corridors, trying not to paw at each other, almost succeeding.

"In here," she said, tugging him through a narrow doorway and pulling it shut behind them. The space was so small a few lungfuls of breath would fill it. Against the spotless white walls of the cabin he was so vivid. So real and so close. At last she could inhale him and touch him and feel the different textures of him – his soft hair, the heat of his skin, his wet, hungry mouth.

She looped her arms round his neck and sagged against him, but he pulled away, placed a hand on her chest.

"Wait."

"More?" She almost laughed, but it caught in her throat. "Fuck, Mark." He wasn't smiling.

"I've got something in mind." He slipped his rucksack off his back and pushed it into her hands. "Open it."

Erin frowned. She didn't want gifts. They'd agreed. She had to travel light. "What is this?"

Mark stayed silent. She shook her head and unzipped the bag. Reaching inside, her hand met something cool and silk slippery. Rope. She pulled out a length of long black cord, wrapped around her hand like a waiting snake.

"Mark?" She looked inside the bag. At the bottom were a box of condoms and a small tube of lube. Nothing else.

She paused. She wanted to smile but her mouth wouldn't cooperate. Her hands swarmed with the need for him. "Drop it on the bed," Mark said, indicating the rope. She did as he asked.

"I'm going to undress you," he said, moving towards her and tugging at her buttons. Somehow, she was rooted to the spot. "Let me." He undid her steadily, tugging her arms free and throwing her jacket on the floor as if it was dirty laundry. "Good." He nodded, at her mute assent. Now he gripped her arms.

"If you want me to stop say so, OK?"

She opened her mouth but nothing came out. She nodded.

He continued to strip her: shirt, vest, chinos, roughly peeled off and discarded. Erin felt like her breath was too loud. She wanted to swallow but somehow felt embarrassed. "Mark," she said at last, "please kiss me."

He laughed.

"It's been so long. This isn't fair."

"Really? You ought to be used to going without. Told me to enjoy the anticipation, remember?"

Erin moaned. "You're punishing me."

"Not yet." Now he unbuttoned the top of his jeans. His cock sprang from his fly, thick and stiff. Then he pulled his shirt over his head, and she got a faceful of his scent – shower gel spice tinged with fresh sweat. He was beautiful. She hadn't forgotten, but the sight still left her reeling: his work-taut body, always restless, always in motion.

The drift of black hair that clung to his chest and crept down his stomach, spreading as it disappeared into his jeans. And his coolness, his ease in his own skin. Nothing ever seemed to faze him. As he came up hand's reach close, only a twitch of his pretty red lips showed any reaction to her proximity, or her near nakedness.

He lifted the rope and wound it around his hands. "Now, let me fix you."

He pulled her wrists behind her. The subtle pulse that beat between her legs intensified. Every muscle in her legs threatened to turn liquid, and she wondered how long she could hold herself up. The slight touch of his fingers as he secured her and checked the knots was like fine sandpaper. When the edge of his fingernail caught slightly against her hip it stung like she'd been lashed. Not painful, but a bright, dizzying burn, as if her desire was concentrated and written into that one thin dash.

"I'm going to fuck you so hard," he said, his mouth up close to her ear and so quiet she hardly heard it. But she did. Her body heard it. His words struck deep in her centre, and her spine curled.

"OK," she said, "Mark, please."

She held herself tensed and steady, trying not to rock back and forth. She'd wanted him for so long, his voice and hands and mouth and cock. The memory of how good he felt and how tightly they fitted together had been reignited with every phone call, every text and blurry phone video. Standing in the shade of a tall plane tree in Tunis, she'd filled a phone with dull brassy coins and stood listening to the unfamiliar dial tone, each unanswered beep like a castigation, a lament for travelling so far, for being elsewhere; a way of noting the uncountable miles that separated her from her lover.

Now, in this antiseptic little cabin, with the anonymous sheets and the empty corridors, with the endless flow of millions of strangers around them and the thought of how many others had used this room, used this bed, her heart started to ache like it might burst.

"I want you," she said at last, splaying her hands against each other, feeling the chill of the air-con roughen her skin with goose bumps, seeing the faint smudge of Mark's reflection in the shower glass and thinking how she so rarely got more than a brief taste, a furious, hurried embrace.

"Yep," Mark said, as if he was hardly listening. He looked her over, thoughtfully. Then he pulled the chair in close and turned it towards her.

"Sit," he said, tipping his head at the seat. Startled, she obeyed without thinking, and landed with a jolt. Now, he took another length of cord from the rucksack and crouched down, patting Erin's calf. "Shift your feet." He wrapped first one ankle, then the other, fastening them to the cold metal of the chair legs. Erin sat with her legs spread, feeling more exposed as her ability to move was gradually restricted. Mark worked quietly, as calm as if he were fixing a tarp to trailer.

When he was finished, he dropped his hands to his thigh and looked her over. "Test them," he said. Erin's eyes widened. She wasn't used to instructions from him – this was her warm, kind, laughing Mark, all business. There was flint in his gaze, an unsettling purposefulness in his movements. His want reached her as a force, so strong that it couldn't be deflected. Her hips had started to ache from being spread. Was he testing her? Trying to trick her into giving up control?

"OK," she nodded. "I'll play."

She pulled against her ties to see how far she could move. Not far. The ropes were soft, twisted cotton, and the memory of where she'd felt them before came back to her. Lead ropes. For horses.

She pictured Mark walking across the back fields, the rope running through his hands and the dew wetting his boots.

"What are you smiling at?" he asked, lifting his eyes to her face.

"Nothing," she said, "it's good to see you."

"You like that, huh?"

She shrugged, or tried to. "Not what I was expecting."

"Hm." He leaned forward and nuzzled at the lace edge of her bra, finding her nipple and catching it in his teeth.

"Ah."

He bit gently, until she cried out again, then nipped at the other one. His mouth left wet patches. "I could eat you up," he said, the burr of his accent softened by a whisper but still slanted with the Island accent she used to tease him about.

He gripped her waist, now, with both hands. He worked at her, kneading her flesh, rubbing down to her splayed thighs and pressing into the tender skin there. She could feel the heat of his breath against her belly and it made her want to twitch.

"Mark."

His thumbs hooked under her knickers and tugged the elastic away from her body. She felt the air-conditioned air on her, heard nothing but the motionless air in the tiny space, slowly heating up and growing closer. Usually she got claustrophobic pretty quickly. Right now she wanted the walls to close in further, to squeeze against her. The desire contained in her was turning almost violent, the immobility wildly frustrating. Waves inside her pulsed from her belly to her cunt and back again. She struggled in her seat. The tightness of her bonds was good. She fought against the rope, confident she would lose.

"You look good like that," he said, sitting back and leaving her with her pants half pulled down her thighs, squirming in her seat. He wet his lips with the tip of his tongue. She stared at his mouth, mesmerized.

"Don't make me beg you," she said, her voice cut back to a whisper.

"I won't make you do anything you don't want to do, you know that, babe" he said, a familiar, lazy smile hovering over his mouth.

Erin tilted her hips, trying to twist and press herself against the seat.

"Poor girl. You're in need," he said, dropping his gaze to her lap. "How long's it been?"

Erin shook her head. Her cheeks were flushed and her breath was ragged.

"Answer the question. How long?"

"We saw each other in ... April? Six weeks."

"Did you miss me?"

"You know I did."

"Answer the question." He reached out and pulled at her knickers, tugging the elastic against the back of her thighs so it dug lines into her skin.

"Yes. I missed you." Erin blushed harder.

"Did you fuck anyone else?"

"Mark. Of course not."

"Did you want to?"

They looked at each other. "I don't play jealous games, Mark."

"Who said I was jealous? I just want to know."

"I was working, for fuck's sake. Sweating my way round the Sahara. Sleeping in trucks, sometimes. No, I didn't want anyone else."

She looked away, biting her lip.

"Good." He slid one fingertip inside her, cool and gentle. Curled his hand against her, covering her pussy with his palm and a warm, maddeningly soft touch. She gasped. So slight. Her muscles tried to tighten around him.

"Not yet," he said.

She pressed her mouth closed. Held still and took a deep breath.

"More." She kept her voice steady. "Please. Give me more."

"Funny. That's just what I was going to ask next." Mark leaned in close, so she could smell his hair. Mint and seaweed.

"See, I've been waiting, too. It's taken me a long while to realize. I spoke to you last week, remember?"

Erin nodded, trying to concentrate on his words instead of his fingers.

"And you were talking about the fixer and complaining about the coffee and the heat and it hit me."

"What?"

He looked at her full in the face. "You're never coming home, are you?"

Erin shook her head. "Don't do this now."

"We only have now, Erin."

"And you want to know if I'm coming home? I don't have an answer. I don't even know what that word means any more.

Probably not the same as it does to you. The valley. The farm. But you won't leave, will you?"

"Leave my work? Let my parents struggle on without me? No. That's not possible."

Erin threw her head back and squeezed her eyes shut.

"Mark, *we* are not possible. We're the impossible couple. We always come back to this. But here we are. Let's talk about this later." She sighed. "I just want to touch you. Kiss me. Please."

"You know how much I want to," he said. "But this time, not without a promise."

"Don't do it. Don't you dare."

"What, ask you to give it up? Oh, I'd love it. For you to turn up at the farm in the breaking dawn one morning and climb into my bed and tell me you're never going to leave. We could just sink into each other." He worked at her now, slowly, his fingers describing a delicate curve over her clit before pinching her, hard enough for her eyes to widen.

"Take our time. See where we got to." He slid his fingers inside her again, worked at the sweet spot.

Erin closed her eyes. "There. There is good."

"That's what I thought. Here. Here is good. You know why?"

"Hmm."

"Believe it or not, a shoebox hotel room buried on the outskirts of Amsterdam is not my dream destination."

"It was the best we could do. Next time we'll make it somewhere sexier."

"Next time it's harvest, Erin, next time it's lambing. Next time I won't have any weekends left. But it doesn't matter."

"Course it does. But so does kissing me."

"Just stop for a minute." He pulled away suddenly, and Erin gave a sharp intake of breath. "Listen." He turned and rifled in his jean pockets, pulled out a condom and tore it open. He kept talking as he unrolled the rubber onto his cock.

"Here is good because a six thirty flight from Tunis can get you to within touching distance of a two-hour flight from Aberdeen. Here is good because you are here and that's the only place I really want to be."

As he talked, he manoeuvred himself so that the tip of his cock was pointed directly at her crotch.

"With you." He buried a hand in her hair. "In you."

"Yes." She spoke without thinking, and he entered her at the same time, sliding in in one movement, meeting the resistance and overcoming it until he was as deep as he could go. Erin opened her mouth but made no sound at all. She fought to inhale. As he started to pull back and fuck her rhythmically, slowly but decisively, the cabin filled with the sound of their scorched breath.

With one hand still holding a handful of her hair, he held her in position. Although she wanted to rub against him, to push all the burning points of her body at the taut, hard surfaces of his, Erin could only twist in her ropes. The plastic chair was slippery and her skin stuck to it.

"Please," she said, willing him for more. They were fixed together on his terms, his tempo, and there was nothing she could do about it. The imbalance made her want to scream, but then she looked at his face, the curve of his cheekbone and his slightly open mouth, the taut muscle of his arm as he tensed in position. His eyes stuck on hers. For once, she held still.

"Yes," she said, and gave in. At once her body brimmed with sensation. Pleasure flooded through her, sweet and hopeless. He fucked her faster and she could have cried with gratitude.

When his fingers slid between them and pinched at her clit, she ground her teeth together. Now they were tangled so thick and deep she felt the build-up start. It had the same force as a plane bowling down a runway. The sensation of irresistible pressure overtook her, and they were no longer just two bodies writhing together, no longer all clit and cock and cunt. He pressed hard against her, rough and desperate, fucking her with his teeth gritted, and then he was still. She called his name. Like a lucid dream, she sensed the ground fall away, and they were suddenly weightless.

The moment of lightness, then, as always, was shocking in its impossibility. It lifted her into another place, somewhere wordless and free. As Mark came inside her, she rested her cheek on his shoulder and felt the orgasm shake through her body and echo in his. He gave a low gasp. For a minute or two they stayed like that, drifting.

They laughed as they broke apart, Mark unfolding himself slowly, bumping against the furniture.

"What was the promise?" Erin asked. "I'd say yes to anything right now."

"Thank God for that."

Erin opened her eyes. Mark was kneeling in front of her, hunching his hands into his pockets. He held out his hand, palm up. A ring. A bright, glittering stone.

It was just a circle of metal and a piece of pretty rock. It couldn't weigh more than a few grams. Maybe it was just the unexpectedness of it that made her want to cry. Erin felt all the swimming emotion go out of her, flow down her arms and legs and centre on this brilliant point of light.

She wanted to reach out then, but the ropes held her steady. Suddenly she needed to be out, to be free. She tensed against the bindings.

"Mark, let me go now."

He looked up. "If that's what you want."

Erin's belly flipped as if she'd just hit a pocket of turbulence. "I don't mean us," she said, throwing a nod behind her. "I mean this, these knots."

"I do mean us," Mark said softly. "If you want, I'll let you go. Otherwise, take the ring. I don't care where you are, Erin. If you'll wear this, I'll know you'll come home again."

She looked up. Her voice was soft. "I don't know how we can make it work."

"Are you saying no?"

Outside, a group of women made their way noisily along the corridor, tried the door handle. "Sorry," someone shouted, and someone else laughed.

Erin shook her head.

"I'm saying I don't know if I can give you what you want."

Mark's hand closed shut. Erin stared at his curled fingers. "I don't want to lose you," she said at last. "But I know I can't ask you to wait for me."

She looked up. Mark's long, lazy smile was working its way onto his mouth. His eyes were sky blue, she thought, suddenly. How had she never noticed that before?

"Well, you know, I wouldn't be spending my whole time writing poetry on a lonely hillock in the rain. I might be able to function without you for – how long is the longest we've gone?"

"Twelve. Twelve weeks."

"Yeah. Given emails and a couple of naked video calls."

Erin bit back her own smile. "And what then?"

"Did I say I was psychic? I said I was in love with you."

"No you didn't. You said—"

"Don't split hairs, smart arse." He took her chin in his hand and held her face steady. "I don't know what next. I don't know where or how. I just know who. We'll work the rest out. Don't you think?"

Erin smiled.

"Is that a yes? A yes for the moment? A yes and we'll see?"

"It's a yes. A yes please. On one condition."

"Name it."

"Next time we're going to have a serious discussion, you're the one tied to a chair."

She darted forward and caught his mouth. He looped his arms around her back, loosed the knot at her wrists, and untied her while he kissed her. They both closed their eyes and for a while, forgot where they were altogether.

The Tennis Pro

I. J. Miller

He's such a beautiful man, she thinks as she sits on a cold metal bench by the net post of a tennis court in this dank, cavernous indoor club while the tennis pro gives her thirteen-year-old daughter a lesson. She is not thinking about the beauty of his spirit, the attractiveness of someone who is pleasant or funny. The tennis pro is just plain gorgeous, heavenly, hot, a hunk . . . beautiful.

To look at, of course.

That is why she sits on the bench in this drafty space wearing a winter coat. To look. That is why she is not in the warm, comfortable lobby, sipping coffee and chatting with the other mothers about forehands and backhands in front of the huge picture windows overlooking the courts. The view is too far away to truly appreciate the tennis pro.

So, under the guise of a concerned, invested tennis mom, she is at the side of her daughter, watching, occasionally looking over at her, nodding indiscriminately, legs crossed, thighs pressed tightly together, lest someone suspect, lest he suspect, that she – like the worst peeping Tom in a trench coat outside a bedroom window, the hungriest voyeur telescoping into the apartment across the way – is simply here to watch.

She has never done this before. She *is* a concerned, invested tennis mom, schlepping her daughter to obscure parts of the state to tournaments she is required to play, arranging practices with the other tennis moms who have the same aspirations for their daughters. She is also a skating mom for her ten-year-old daughter and a music mom for her eight-year-old boy.

"Nice shot," says the tennis pro as her daughter screams a forehand crosscourt. "If you take the ball a little earlier you'll knock the cover off." Her daughter nods, skips back to the center of the court, that bulldog look on her face, determined to show him that she can do just that.

Six feet, two inches tall, not an ounce of fat, early thirties, single. He is deeply tanned, as all pros are in the summer, but this is the middle of January. She imagines he went somewhere warm over Christmas and baked on a beach with nothing on his smooth body but a bulging, black, skimpy nylon Speedo, shiny and wet from a dip in the ocean. She uncrosses her legs, removes her winter coat. Her daughter hits her forehand crosscourt again and he does that volley move of his which is her favorite: racquet out in front, left leg stepping across the body, weight moving forward, and then, just at the contact point of strings to ball, all the weight falls on that front left leg and she can see the bulge and thick shape of his lower thigh, the quadricep, that's what she thinks they call it. He has beautiful, defined quadriceps integrated into a pair of long, sturdy legs, tanned as well, with many fine dark hairs streamlining down toward a perfect set of muscular calves. The face is not boyish, but manly, gentle – a strong chin, soft penetrating brown eyes, narrow cheekbones but not gaunt. On someone else maybe an average face, but on him – with the intensity of how he speaks, encourages, corrects, how he floats toward balls and returns them to his daughter with knifelike precision produced with perfect ease – beautiful.

But it's the hands that make him, the hand that first enveloped hers. She felt the tennis calluses, but the tips of her fingers touched the smooth, baby-soft top of his hand, his fingers so long they went up the inside of her wrist, as if she were a racquet handle, as if he were born to grip a tennis racquet. Gosh, she does not believe she is remembering all this detail about him. She is not a detail person. She is a routine person, dedicated to the routines of being an at-home wife and mother.

Details were lost long ago in the swamp of diaper-changing and car-pooling.

The hour, unfortunately, comes to a close. He beckons his pupil to the net and begins to talk to her, quietly, always holding his racquet against his chest, arms crossed. She wonders if her daughter – going a bit boy-crazy lately herself – has some sense of the aura of this man, his sexiness. But, as intently as she listens, after he is done, she is off scampering around the court picking up stray balls. No, the tennis pro is not one of the stringy-haired bad boys in heavy-metal T-shirts who stop by the house, who seem to be the subjects of multi-houred phone conversations with best friends. The hormones are definitely starting to kick in with her oldest, but the edges are still way too rough for her to appreciate such masculine fineness.

And what about her own hormones? She is sorry the lesson is over. She is already looking forward to the next lesson. She'd like to get on the phone and let her best friend know that at forty-one, just when she is sure an era of expectation, delight, intrigue – which began in adolescence – is officially dead, buried, gone, she has discovered that there may be a few out-of-control hormones remaining, leaving the pleasant thought inside her mind that she still has the potential to percolate.

On paper, of course. She had been bored enough during the sixteen years of her married life to contemplate an affair, but she was a little bit chicken and mostly too unmotivated by any of the prospects. Probably just around forty was when it occurred to her that in this crapshoot she had gotten what she settled for: a boring, hardworking husband who provided ample financial security and fathered three fantastic children. She can't complain. Friends are already experiencing drugs and unwanted pregnancies with their kids. Husbands have divorced for younger women, leaving behind single middle-aged mothers with few chances of improving their lots. Or they tolerate the affairs, trying to hold on at least until the kids get to college. She wants to stay married. Her husband seems too busy at work for affairs. She should count her blessings. There was a time, somewhere between getting engaged and married, when she felt there was an outside chance she could have it all. She remembered the flowers he bought for no reason, how attentive he was on their first trip to Mexico, how sweet he seemed when they lay in bed after making love and he talked about his business plans, the house he wanted, the future he expected for their children. But even those moments were spotty. She could see how easily work could distract him from her, how vacations only happened because she wanted them, how satisfied he felt with his performance in bed without any sense that it was something that should grow and develop, along with their love. His desire is need-based, then thank you. As they age, the reduction of need within him is directly proportionate to the amount of time spent on foreplay.

At somewhere around her eldest's current age she had dreamt of a grand passion, began believing in the school-girl crush stories she read, graduating soon to unbridled romance novels. She believed it could happen. She believed there was a man out there willing to kiss her with uncontrollable passion while rolling on the beach as the surf washed between their legs. She believed in two people tearing away at each other's clothes because their need is so desperate, making love under moonlight without worrying about being caught, sleeping a whole night through in complete embrace. She believed in it enough that she wanted to cancel the wedding with just a week to go, until her mother shook some sense into her. She played the dice and that's the way they fell. Be happy she didn't crap out.

She reaches for the racquet in her daughter's hand to put it away in the tennis bag. They walk toward the back of the court where a section of the large, heavy green curtain can be pulled back to exit. She fights the urge to turn around for one last look, perhaps something to carry her over to next Wednesday's lesson. What if he is watching them leave and catches her look? What if another mother is watching from the lobby? Nevertheless she can't help herself. She pulls the curtain and motions for her daughter to exit first, then glances back. He is moving toward the large shopping cart of tennis balls in the middle of the court. There is some sweat doing a lazy dribble from his forehead down to his cheeks, and, perhaps feeling unwatched, he tugs his white tennis polo out of the front of his shorts and swings the bottom end up to mop his brow. The result is a half-dozen or so mental snapshots for her to savor of his rippling, flat, hairless, hard body abs, neat quadrants of muscles lined up as sturdy and as symmetrical as any washboard.

It frustrates her when that night in bed, the children asleep, she gives her husband the signal that she wants to make love (she puts her hand on the pajama area covering his penis) and he says, "Not tonight, sweetie." It only took about a year of marriage to turn "sweetie" and "sugar" from terms of endearment to words tacked on when the other was trying to make a point, or a bit displeased. He had turned her down last Wednesday as well. She is not looking to use him as a surrogate. She has promised herself not even to think about the tennis pro if they do make love. She is merely interested in the positive results that would have to occur from some attention to a body and mind that has been juiced by more than its share of kilowatts. She jerks her hand away and turns the other way and must have let out a "hmph" or something – which must have surprised and irked him because they usually share the same apathy about their occasional "well, oh all right" bouts in bed – because he comes up with, "You know I work pretty hard and come home pretty late and get up pretty early. I don't have the leisure time to rest up for this sort of thing." Her first urge is to come back with something snide like, "Why don't you try running a kiddie cab service or cooking dinner?" But she holds back. He has a point. He always has a point, which on some level pisses her off. In the early years it was pretty hectic for her, but now the kids are in school full-time and a cleaning service comes twice a week. She has time for a daily aerobics class at the gym, though it has been ages since she's gone. As her figure goes, she is genetically a bit more blessed than some of her friends but has never dropped the extra weight after the birth of the boy, unable to lose the bulge in her lower abdomen. Nevertheless her husband is free of most of the wear and tear from the emotional turmoil of three kids: their needs that always seem so immediate; their moods that can turn lethal; the demands on time that start right when the first one gets out of school. No, maybe her husband doesn't have the time to feel sexy anymore, if he ever did, but he does have an occasional two-hour, two-martini business lunch, several wifeless trips every year to places that happen to offer golf, gambling, and strip clubs. Oh, she is becoming such a fusser. Comparing bullshit like this. When all that it's really about right now is that she would like to get laid.

"How many times have I given you a blow job in the morning to calm you down before a big meeting?" she asks. His head jerks toward her, surprised at her out-of-character language. But she's zipped, estrogen mamboing somewhere inside her. "How many times have you been up all night worried about something and come to bed at three in the morning and wake me up asking for one so you can fall asleep?" He coughs a little, choking on his search for a response. "How many times do you think I would like a little attention, but you're too tired to get off your back and I know it's not worth doing anything but finishing you off, rolling over, and saying goodnight?"

"Well . . . you know. It's not like. A blow job? Is that what you're asking me for?" Perhaps he feels that if he reduces it to the lowest common denominator he can shame her into backing off so he can get some sleep.

"Yeah. That's right. A blow job." Angry sex can be good, she thinks.

But who is she kidding? He lets out his own "hmph," makes a big production out of wading to the bottom of the bed through a tidal wave of sheets, comforter, extra blanket, hikes up her night-shirt and goes to work.

Who is she kidding? Even on his best days he is no good at oral sex and has little interest. He even fast forwards from the cunni-lingus parts to the doggie-style scenes in the occasional porn movie they've watched on a night as rare as Halley's Comet when all the kids are either at camp or on a sleepover.

He starts much too quickly and too rough and she tells him to slow down, which he does. There have been times he has gone all right for a while and she would start to get grooved, knowing she was at least heading up the mountain and there was a peak, maybe even a valley in sight, but then he would get tired and change the rhythm, or go from flicks to licks, or licks to circles, or sideways from up and down, or a stiff circular head motion as if compen-sating for cramped tongue muscles. The worst is when halfway up the mountain he simply stops for a second, to catch his breath, or because his nose is stuffed, or to remove a pubic hair from his teeth. It is supposed to be raunchy sometimes, sometimes sweet, sometimes simply intense, but it is never any of those things with him. God forbid she ever stops in the middle of a blow job.

She brushes some thick strands of wavy black hair (not the original color) off her face, away from her eyes, as she shifts posi-tions, tries to relax herself, tries to find the most comfortable position to make this work. The movement of her hand through her hair is involuntary and jolts her, as if she is receiving an erotic touch. Then suddenly it is all there, like a jailhouse break, a crack in a dam wall. She is on the tennis court, the entire club empty now except for her and the tennis pro. She is there for her own lesson, dressed in a white short pleated skirt with no underwear. He has stopped the lesson and is beside her to brush the hair out of her eyes, easily intuiting that it must be bothering her. But he continues brushing his hand through her hair – that long, sleek, gentle, strong hand. He runs those fingers right through the strands, the firm pull causing her scalp to send trillions of pulsat-ing tingles down to her aching clitoris.

Then suddenly the tennis pro slides that left leg forward, as if he is about to volley, and her legs part and they are an exact match; the flexed leg is lined up perfectly so that his bulging quadricep is meshed right between her legs in a fit that is all heat and pressure. She barely realizes that she has grabbed a hold of her husband's hand and jerked it right past his face, knocking his mouth out of the way and replacing it with the flatness of his open palm. She shoves it right up against herself and it feels exactly like the pressure of the tennis pro's quadricep. She barely hears her husband's protest; he even tries to adjust his hand, but her grip is so viselike it can't budge. All she hears is the tennis pro's deep smooth voice – as if he is beseeching her to take the ball earlier – telling her to hump his leg, that he is not going to do anything but keep his quad locked against her as his hand runs through her hair. All she feels is his hot breath bathing her lips, his perfect unchanging pressure against her pussy, the constant forward and back of her frenzied pelvic thrusts, the squirt of her juices that flow down his leg, the reassuring, electric touch of his hand through her hair. "Work it," he tells her. "Grind it," he says. "Give it to me . . ." She screams, perhaps waking her kids, certainly startling her husband, who tries to jerk his hand away, but she uses two hands to nail his palm down, to keep the pressure right where it is as she peaks and valleys, peaks and valleys, peaks and valleys the last three Wednesdays right through her and out, like giant, arcing, billowing pipeline waves exploding onto some way cool Hawaiian surf beach.

Done, she casts off her husband's hand as if it is an errant piece of driftwood and settles into the pool of sweat and juice her passion has created. He is speechless, looking at her as if he has found himself in bed with someone unknown. She closes her eyes. "Thank you," she mumbles softly. He moves away somewhere amid the tumult of sheets and covers, then quiet, covered, settled, snoring. She is half uncovered but she doesn't care. She needs to cool down once again. She needs to rid herself of the beehive frenzy in her brain that is asking, *What the hell is going on?*

She knows she has been a little ditzy with her voyeuristic outings to the tennis court, but she had no idea it reached this deep, that it could be more than the cheapest of thrills for a settled, forty-one-year-old, married housewife/mother. It scares her, scares her that she has just hung ten on a stranger's surfboard and rode the wave all the way in . . . scares her that now she is beached and not sure where it all could take her . . . scares her and thrills her all the same.

She is up before anyone the next morning, out of bed, showered, so much skip in her step she mops the kitchen floor even though it's cleaning-lady day. Her kids don't really notice. She makes her husband a hot breakfast. He tells her that's OK, he's fine with his usual bagel and coffee. But she plops down the eggs and sausages anyway, kisses him on the cheek. He eats. When he senses her watching him, he busies himself with some papers in the briefcase by his feet. He, seemingly, is ready to let last night pass, to accept it as something as aberrant as two moons in the sky.

When the family is gone, during the half-hour she has free before the cleaning lady arrives, she retires to her bed, and, for the first time in a very long while, masturbates. She starts with lingering caresses across her breasts, down her tummy, between her thighs, rehashing last night's fantasy, recalling the vibes. When she begins to finger herself with some real zest, she starts to remember every mental photo she has made of the tennis pro since she first met him, from the hands to the quads to the abs to the calves to the skimpy Speedo, finally to what's underneath the Speedo as she catches the last wave in just as the front doorbell rings. She quickly gets herself together and answers the door feeling so transparent that as the cleaning lady enters all she can do is babble, "I've mopped the kitchen floor," before hurrying off to the bathroom to pee.

For the rest of the week, during the spotty free time she has home alone, she masturbates. There were times in her life, teen years, when she was single, when masturbation was part of her regular routine: hard water spray in the bathtub, pillow crammed up between her legs as she lay face down into the mattress. A brief period, in her early twenties, when, like Bob Dylan, she went electric. But after the kids started arriving she rarely felt motivated for a solo roll in the hay.

On the next Wednesday afternoon, at the end of her daughter's lesson, she pays the tennis pro $100 and surprises even herself when she asks, "Do you think I could get a lesson from you sometime?"

"Uh, well." He drops the racquet from his chest to his side. "Sure."

"I'll call you." She turns to her daughter and nudges her toward the exit. She used to play once a week in a league, held her own, but has never been much more than a "B" player. She didn't even look at him when she asked and now she just wants to get out of there. Who cares if her daughter stares at her with that look she and the other kids have at bar mitzvahs and sweet sixteens when adults try to dance to hip hop.

In the car she finally catches her breath. Uncharacteristically, she lets her daughter fiddle with the radio, go back and forth between stations. He said yes. She knows for sure he doesn't teach adults. He has to know she's just a "B" player. Why would he say yes? Long ago, as a teenager, she allowed herself kooky perceptions of things: if she wrote just the right letter, Billy Idol would write her back; high school senior class president Dick Hanover would go out with her if she only had the nerve to call him and let him know who she was; her breasts really would get larger if she followed the daily exercises outlined in a teen magazine and when that happened she would find true love. As a young adult she dreamt of keeping her entry-level publishing job, even after having babies, and becoming an accomplished editor. But now she can barely remember when she hasn't been sensible Old Mom: "You're not leaving this house without an umbrella"; Practical Sweetie: "If we do the addition and go reasonable on the tiling and bathroom fixtures we can still get back what we're paying if we ever sell the house."

Can she even handle a lesson without making a silly, dribbling teeny-bopper out of herself?

She calls him. She sets up the lesson. It's three weeks before he can fit her in. She frets periodically during that time, feeling for sure she is making a mistake. Yet she still gets up early – her husband now pleased – to make a hot breakfast. She gives in, finally, to her eldest's request to allow text messaging on her cell-phone. She allows the younger daughter a credit-card clothes-shopping spree and her son to forego not one but two piano practice sessions. She lets her husband's up toilet seat slide in the master bathroom and has not initiated sex since that fateful Wednesday night.

The result of her new leniency is that both girls are helping her more around the house. The boy has been easier to manage. Her husband brought home flowers. She feels a lot calmer. "Nicer," that's what the younger girl said. "You're being so much nicer." She also starts up at the gym again and drops more than a few pounds.

Then it's time and she's there, on his court, in the morning, no one she knows up in the lobby, her new leaner self. She has ironed her pleated skirt and taken extra care to make sure she has on both underwear and tennis panties.

He asks, "What stroke would you like to work on?"

"What?" she stammers.

"What's your weakest shot?"

"Oh. My serve."

"Let's work on that."

"Let's."

He has her serve a few and stands to the side and slightly behind her to watch as they weakly bloop over the net. These skirts are stylishly short but she feels as if the back flies up as she hurls herself upwards for the ball. She wonders if he is getting a clear view of her tennis panties.

"Let's break it down," he says, all business.

He shows her how to position her feet with her shoulders sideways to the net. He shows her how to bring the racquet all the way back behind her head, as if she is scratching her back, then she must reach up with it and step forward with her back foot. She does all this and he explains that it will give her more power, because she is getting more body rotation through the ball. He makes her mime the motion a half-dozen times, pointing out little corrections here and there. He easily engages her while he speaks and seems genuinely excited when she gets something right. She comes to understand how that step forward into the court will empower her. For a second she becomes so intrigued with the prospect of having a harder serve that she almost forgets who she is with, forgets to steal a quick glance at his legs or hands.

Then he tells her she is finally ready to hit the ball, but when she tries to put everything together and focus on making a serve, the careful rhythm he got her into breaks down and the ball bounces meekly off the frame of the racquet before she even has time to step forward. She expects him to laugh. But he smiles kindly, says it takes practice, and if she's willing to practice, she will indeed improve her serve. He breaks it down for her again, has her rehearse each movement, and this time she does make contact but forgets to step.

"That was your old serve," he says. "It can take a lot to get rid of old habits. Let me show you."

With that he is directly behind her, so close she feels his breath on her neck, senses the tightness of his abs near her back. He is positioned exactly as she is, mirroring her. He grips her right hand and is able to go all the way around the hand and racquet handle with his fingers. His lips are close to her left ear as he repeats, "Let me show you." Only this time she feels his voice through her body, perhaps because he is so close, but also because of his change in tone. No longer businesslike, his voice is a whisper, cooing, beckoning. "You bring the racquet back like this and the weight will shift to the back foot." Her body is pliant and he moves everything for her. When her weight falls back, it is nearly nuclear as the pronounced arc of her butt cheeks presses against his crotch. She feels the outline of his penis and balls against her rear. It is such a pronounced feeling that she wonders if he might be the slightest bit aroused, or just extremely well endowed. He does not back off from her pressure, merely continues with the service motion as they step forward together. He extends the racquet, only now his weight falls against her, and she feels the pressure at her backside, his chest at her back, breath on her cheek, arms and shoulders enveloping hers as they put the final touches on the swing and follow-through around her waist, which leaves them in a momentary embrace.

Does he really teach serve this way? Does he know what's going through her mind? Is he playing with her or can he really have some interest . . . in her? The only thing she's sure of is that she's soaked through her own panties and for all she knows the tennis ones, too.

During the car ride home she feels ridiculous for thinking the tennis pro is even remotely attracted to her. While teaching her daughter he had simply been an object, the scantily clad model in art class, she the painter only able to observe from a distance and at best dally with the brush. That night with her husband, the tennis pro had indeed become touchable, as if he had stepped from his pedestal and come directly to her. But that had been fantasy. Was it her hyper-fantasizing that had her imagining he had been aroused against her?

In recent years she has become convinced that tennis players must be the best lovers. The sport requires the trimmest of bodies, great hands, extreme intensity, the intelligence of a chess player. Why else do all the pro players have the most beautiful wives and girlfriends? Pete Sampras is married to an actress. Andy Roddick is married to a model. It is not because of the money their men have, the glamour, the fame, or that their spectator reactions are aired over international TV during major tournaments. Brooke

Shields didn't need Andre Agassi's money or fame; she married him for one big reason. "A Zen master": that is what Barbra Streisand said after taking her turn before the marriage. She is sure Barbra wasn't talking about Andre's tennis. And now he has Steffi Graf, who surely has the inside track of what tennis players have to offer.

But what if the tennis pro is simply another beer-guzzling, sports-watching, channel-hopping, crotch-scratching, gas-passing man? What if he laughs at even the subtlest suggestion on her part that they take it beyond the tennis court, making her feel ridiculous, silly, and old? Or even worse, they somehow go to bed and it is rough, brief, or selfish and rids her of all this rejuvenated desire, breaks the tension of her need and returns her to the nervous mom, the disenchanted wife who just keeps putting on weight? Aside from her kids, when has the *having* ever been better than the *hoping*?

She remembers a long time ago reading an article about the sex appeal of Mick Jagger – someone she also had a major crush on. The writer had interviewed a woman who was obsessed with Mick and found that no matter who she slept with, at best, she found herself saying, "This is good, but it's not Mick Jagger." Then the time came when she found a way to meet Mick and go to bed with him, but in the middle of it all still thought, *This is good, but it's not Mick Jagger.* But what if, just imagine, how amazing would it be if the tennis pro *is*?

She finds herself calling him on a Tuesday at noon when she knows he is getting off the court for his lunch break. She intends to set up another lesson, perhaps this time work on her backhand, which would surely keep him on his side of the net. Yet she doesn't ask for a lesson. She asks him if he would like to go out for a cup of coffee on Wednesday evening around 7.30 p.m., which is the night and time of her monthly PTA meeting at the elementary school. He doesn't miss a beat, let out even the slightest inkling of surprise or shock. He simply says, "Why don't you come to my apartment. I have an espresso machine." She takes down his apartment address. This is absolutely the zaniest, craziest thing she has ever done. For she never did write Billy Idol, call Dick Hanover, find true love; and she quit her publishing job two months before the birth of her eldest child.

On Wednesday, she delights the whole family by declaring it favorite-food night. She serves her husband chicken cacciatore, her boy pizza, and her daughters a scrumptious salad with plenty of fresh vegetables and fruit, including egg whites and pieces of chicken and ham. They vote to have favorite-food night at least once a week. She laughs and says maybe. They all laugh with her, amazing as it seems, one big happy family.

Then she's gone, a special hug for each of her family. Her husband tells her to have a great time. She's soon at the door of the tennis pro's garden apartment, perfumed, ready, not allowing herself to think too much about what could happen. She has not masturbated since he agreed to the first lesson and just his touch might be enough for her to explode and get the hell home.

"Hello," he says, clad in jeans and a navy polo shirt, no socks, bare feet slid into soft leather clogs.

"Hi." She ducks quickly into the apartment.

He closes the door behind her, directs her to a couch in the living room, which is off the dining area, which is off the kitchenette in this modest but clean apartment. On the coffee table is a plate of neatly arranged butter cookies. She sits. He makes his way to the kitchen, returns with two mini cups of steaming espresso on plates also holding two little silver spoons. He places the plate in front of her, sits next to her, puts the other plate in front of him. He looks at her intently, doesn't say anything. Her palms sweat. She doesn't know what to say and fights back the impulse to bring up her daughter's progress as an icebreaker. She knew this was going to be awkward. She lurches forward for her cup and takes a quick, steaming sip of espresso, burns her tongue, says, "Delicious," before the flavor even registers. She knew this was going to be a mistake. He sits back, smiles, his feet sliding out of the open clogs, one leg crossing over the other. And she sees them: the toes on both feet, gnarly and bumpy from years of pounding on the court, one big toenail puckered purple from fungus. Her shoulders sag. Idiot! She could have gotten at least six months of mileage from simply looking forward to a once-a-week lesson with the tennis pro, with perhaps another six months if she could really be sure he didn't mind.

He gets up from the couch and goes over to the stereo, housed in a cabinet occupied mostly by tennis trophies. He picks out a CD, pops it in. She instantly recognizes Frank Sinatra and "Strangers in the Night." With a dimmer switch he lowers the living room lights. "Would you like to dance?" he asks. She wonders if he lowered the lights to be romantic or if he thought she would be more comfortable in the dark where they could not be seen from the street through the large, exposed living room windows. But then she realizes that he asked her to dance – a slow dance, a dance to a melodic song dripping with romance and the possibility of the unknown. She is alone in the living room of the tennis pro: the man with the body, the hands, the man who had inspired what has to be some of her all-time best orgasms, the man who just by pressing himself against her during a serving lesson caused her to moisten herself like a fifties schoolgirl at an Elvis concert. And now he wants to dance.

In the dark she can't even see his toes. Her "yes" comes out like a whisper.

He has her by the hand as she stands up from the couch. Then he pulls her close. Not too close so as to be impolite or presumptuous. Presumptuous? They both seem to be presuming way more than is safe.

They dance, slowly, seductively, she able to follow easily his lead. As they move, mostly in one spot in the center of the darkened living room, she feels the coordinated rhythm within him that she saw so clearly on the tennis court. She feels the same sensuous heat that bathed her during their serving embrace. He pulls her closer – another embrace, a close dance position only lovers feel bold enough to attempt. Then, as the song nears its end and slips into another Sinatra favorite, they look deeply into each other's eyes and he kisses her. It is a warm, full kiss that starts with the softness of his lips, then burns, like the espresso, with the fire of his tongue. When he is done she cannot immediately say what is on her mind because her breath, literally, has been taken away. He lets her recover, no rush to him at all, as they sway to the music. Finally, she ekes out, "Why me?"

He looks at her, seemingly confused, perhaps taken out of the moment.

She says, "Why me, when you can have anyone you want? Younger, prettier, more—"

"I don't think I can have anyone I want." He is a half-step back, though they still hold each other. "I find you attractive. And . . . well, don't take this the wrong way."

"Yes."

"But I got this feeling you really wanted me. I don't know exactly when. I became aware of you watching me during your daughter's lessons. And then it just kind of kicked in, maybe when we talked, or when you handed me the money and your hand seemed to linger. It became very clear that what I did, even the little things, affected you strongly. I guess I found such open desire in you very sexy. Our lesson was a real turn-on for me. Not that I power trip or anything, but you made me feel sexy."

She kisses him this time, steps forward into the court and embraces him. No it isn't exactly her adolescent romance fantasy hunk who hungered for the touch of her abundant, exposed cleavage, nor the grand passion she so desired that would bring about the perfect union of all her physical and emotional needs. He is turned on by her! . . . Which is enough to heighten even the normally fevered desires he inspires, enough to empower her to go after everything she wants.

He responds with the same. They kiss, all mouths and tongues, lips wet and moist. It is frenetic enough so that they don't make it to the bedroom and simply fall onto the couch. He does not hurt her with his rough kisses along her breasts. His suckling of her nipples is as gentle as she has ever felt. His hands are everywhere, wiring her body, and she feels absolutely no rush to direct them to her vagina. There is even an urge to allow the fury of his desire to overwhelm her, to lay back and to receive, but she does not let this chance to exercise her offense fall away. She has forgotten that a man's waist can feel this narrow in her hands, that a chest can feel this defined, that the earthy odor of his sweat – her body and the polo shirt absorbing it all – can be this sweet, that the taste of flesh can create such an appetite for more. Amazingly, after he produces a condom from somewhere and enters her moistness, easily, slowly, seemingly trying to control the rush that threatens to take over them both – as they make rough, throaty sounds in near unison – he takes his beautiful hand and runs it firmly through her hair while she slides her right palm down his thigh and cups his left quadricep. Shit, this is way better than Mick Jagger.

The Copper Horse

Vina Green

The interview was short. Aside from showing me around the estate and explaining the duties I would be required to fulfil, he asked me only one question.

"What are you most afraid of?"

"The dark," I replied.

I got the job, and he told me that if I was ever afraid, I should just ask him to turn on the light. And, I was to call him "Sir". Had any other employer said the same thing, I might have found it odd, or inappropriate. But there was something about him, a weight in his voice, which held me like a magnet and made my heart jump at the same time.

He liked the smell of leather. That was how it began, really.

I was employed as his cleaner and personal assistant. He'd been born blind, though you wouldn't know it. Despite his visual impairment, he was an artist. He worked with large, heavy sheets of thick white paper, and charcoal. His work was rough, full of flowing lines which didn't meet neatly, but combined to make a whole. Nonetheless, the portraits that I saw bore an incredible resemblance to the customers who left with them, and he had a steady stream of visitors to the house, each wanting to leave with their own small miracle, a picture of themselves reflected through the eyes of a blind man. One woman, who returned several times, told me that she wanted to know what a man, who couldn't see, saw in her.

I wondered the same thing.

It was only ever meant to be a summer job, but when term time came around again, I found that I didn't want to leave. I was paid well, and I liked the work. He had a big, old Victorian house, the sort that never really looks clean no matter how often you tidy it. There was a small greenhouse, and a stable, no longer in use.

He had converted almost the entire upstairs floor into a studio, where he spent most of his time. There were several large windows, so that light tumbled into the room all day, casting long shadows over his strange assortment of furniture during the afternoon. He had several chaise longues, a set of narrow, wooden, uncushioned chairs with tall backs, and a strange frame in the shape of a small horse, made from copper, which I supposed was some type of art. He had laid an old saddle along the top of it, complete with stirrups, because he liked the smell of leather, he said, and the feeling of the stitching. There were no curtains, but we did not have any neighbours, and until I arrived he had always worked in the dark. Now he left the lights on. The power bill, he said, was neither here nor there, and the environment was some-one else's battle to fight.

He was tactile, and meticulous. He'd lived in the house for his entire life, close to sixty years, and he knew precisely where everything was kept. I was to put every item that I touched back exactly where it came from so that he could find it again. He had a cane, black, with a white fox carved in quartz attached to the top, but he rarely used it, preferring instead to feel his way both through habit and by running his fingers gently along the walls to find his way from one room to the next. He always dressed well, in expensive clothes and fabrics that felt pleasant to touch. Down-stairs, the drapes were velvet, the carpet was bamboo fibre. He had cobbles in the kitchen, rather than tiles, which felt cool and pleasantly rough underfoot. Despite the impracticality, all of the work surfaces were made of thick, untreated timber, so that if you ran your hand along them you could feel the grain.

It was absolute murder to keep clean. None of the surfaces were easy-wipe, all of them were creviced, and required constant scrub and polish. I enjoyed the ache in my arms, and I found I could easily lose myself in the steady rhythm of the work. Increasingly I wanted to do a good job for him, although he couldn't see the degree to which I made everything gleam. He did, once, in feeling his way downstairs, notice that I had managed to beat all of the dust out of the drapes. "Good girl," he said. That made me want to please him more.

I spent a good part of each day on my knees, scrubbing.

Eventually, I began to find excuses to clean nearer to him, to dust the rooms that he was working in, hoover under his feet. He once commented on my perfume; he said that I smelled like cinnamon. I began to wear perfume every day. I leaned towards him as often as I could, handing him his mail rather than leaving it on the table, so that he might smell me. My heart quickened when I was near him, and I was sure he could hear it racing. I began to cook for him. I made food that felt good in my mouth, plates of oysters and smoked salmon. I made food with aroma, Thai soups with coconut and lemongrass, and soda bread that felt good to tear apart.

I started to wear lipstick, and nicer clothes, and gradually, fewer and fewer of them. First, a simple black dress, the sort I might wear on a date if I ever had one, and a long, heavy silver pendant on a chain that swung when I walked. Then, a satin chemise, black, short, without any underwear. I leaned in front of him as if to reach for something across the desk where he was sitting, so, had he been able to see, he would have seen directly down my front, my nipples erect, and breasts hanging down. I pretended I had dropped something and crawled under the desk at his feet, my bare arse in the air, so that he might smell me.

I didn't touch him, though I longed to. I felt that I couldn't, without his permission.

One day, I was naked, but for a pair of black high heels with red soles. I had walked into his studio, which was unoccupied. The door was open, and I had glanced in to check if he needed tea, or his water refilling. There was a large portrait on his desk, the size of a person. It was a picture of a woman, tall, with a full body and long red hair. He must have been working on it for some time, as it was unusually detailed, and painted in oil colours, rather than black and white. She was sitting in one of the tall-backed wooden chairs, completely nude, and bound, with a purple rope. Her back was arched, and her arms pinned, presumably with her hands tied behind her back. Her feet were forced apart, further than the width of the chair legs, with a bar, so that her vagina was on startlingly frank display. She had a thick bush of ginger pubic hair. Her breasts were large and heavy, and she had big, perfectly formed, coffee-coloured nipples and creamy skin. She was looking towards the sky, with an expression of dream-like bliss, like a woman who has seen God.

I heard the floor creak as he entered the room behind me, and I suppose he surmised, from my still presence in the room, that I was staring at the picture.

"Does it scare you?" he asked, gently.

"No," I replied. I envied her. She looked lost, in the peace of her stillness. "But how did you do it, Sir? She doesn't have any clothes on."

He had never seen a naked body in his life, not even his own.

"You don't have any clothes on," he commented.

I shifted from one foot to the other, startled by his observation.

"There's more to nakedness, you know, than not having any clothes on," he added.

I nodded, pointlessly.

"I'll show you."

I shifted awkwardly again, back to the other foot.

"What's wrong?" he asked. "You don't think I can see you, do you?"

Still, I said nothing.

"Sit down," he ordered, moving towards his desk.

"Where would you like me to sit?" I asked, cocking my head towards him.

"Where would you like me to sit, *Sir*," he corrected, authoritatively now. "Get onto the saddle."

I took off my heels. He must have heard them clatter onto the floor. "No," he said, "leave those on."

I swung a leg over the copper horse, hoisting myself up onto the saddle, putting a high-heeled foot in each stirrup. I left a trail of moisture across the cool leather, and was embarrassed by my sudden wetness. Later, I thought, I would come back and polish it. He pulled a chair up, and sat on it, facing me side on, with his mouth about two feet from the top of my thigh. He could have easily reached out and touched me, but he didn't. He held his sketchbook in his lap and a thick pencil between the thumb and forefingers of his right hand.

"Tell me what you feel," he said.

I felt increasingly embarrassed, each time I shifted my weight, the leather pressed against me pleasantly, making me wetter still, and wanting to shift back and forth, more and more. I gripped the saddle with my thighs, feeling the cracks in the leather scratch my skin.

"You don't feel anything?" he asked again, goading me.

I was silent, other than the creak of the copper horse, as I moved in the saddle.

"Then I want you to open your thighs further," he said, "and spread your pussy lips apart, so you can feel the saddle, properly." His face was the picture of calm, as if this was as normal to him as asking me to refill his water jug.

"Yes, Sir," I replied meekly, spreading my legs, and my lips, apart.

"Good girl," he said. "You can clean it later. With your tongue."

"Yes, Sir," I said again, closing my eyes, so that the sound of his voice washed over me, like a tide. I imagined how the leather would taste and the feeling of the stitches rough against my tongue. I would even lick the stirrups, so that he would know I was thorough.

"Lean forward," he said, and I did, so that the front of the saddle, the curve, rubbed against my clitoris.

"Now, describe yourself to me, tell me what you look like. And keep moving."

"I have long fingers," I said, because they were the first thing I could see, when I looked down at the saddle.

"Go on," he said.

"I have pale skin," I said, "and black hair. I dye it. I have a nipple piercing, just one, on my right nipple."

"Tell me about your breasts," he replied.

"They're small, smaller than I'd like. The size of an orange, cut in half, cupped in your hand. And I have small nipples. Each about the size of a blueberry. They're erect, always."

"Move," he said. "Move quickly. Harder. So I can hear you."

I ground back and forward, and back and forward on the saddle, pressing my feet into the stirrups so the metal bit into my ankles.

"I don't have a bridle," he said, "So I'm going to pull your hair back."

"Yes, yes, please, Sir." I was begging now, and grinding more. I could smell myself, the scent of my vagina mixed with leather. He put the sketchbook down on the ground, and stood up, touching my thigh as he reached forward to find the horse. I wanted to grab his hand, to feel him squeeze my breasts. He moved behind me, and pulled my hair back, hard, so my back arched as I pressed forward against the lip of the saddle. He ran his hand down my front, as I leant back against him, finding my nipple ring and tugging it gently. He moved his hand up, cupping my throat.

"Tell me if you're afraid," he growled into my ear, but I wasn't, I felt everything other than afraid. I moaned, and pressed against his hand. He squeezed my throat tighter, and I came.

"Good girl," he said, and let me go. He moved back into the chair and picked up the sketchbook.

"Stay there," he said, "until I tell you that you can go."

I sat, seeping come onto the leather until the long shadows began to fall across the room.

"It's getting dark," I said.

"Then I'll turn the light on," he replied. And he did.

Still, he did not let me go. We sat silently in his studio, me on the copper horse, and him facing me on the chair, for at least another hour, perhaps two. He did not have a clock in the room of course, and he was accustomed to sitting, sketching, for hours. His subjects sat still for him for hours and he seemed always unaware of, or unresponsive to, their discomfort. My legs grew stiffer and stiffer, until I feared that I would be too cramped to get off the horse when he asked me to. But still, I sat and waited, my thighs clenched tightly against the saddle.

Suddenly, he shut the sketchbook and stood up.

"You may go," he said, turning his back to me and placing the book inside his desk drawer.

Slowly, I unfurled, and slid off the horse, my legs nearly buckling beneath me as the blood rushed back through them. He did not turn as I left the room. He stood next to his desk, with his fists clenched, looking straight out through the window, as if he were staring at the moon.

The next morning, I woke to find a package next to my bed. It was beautifully wrapped, black tissue paper with a thick silver ribbon. I opened it slowly, careful not to make a single rip in the tissue, and I folded the paper neatly and placed it alongside the bow, on my dresser. Inside, was a black satin bag with a black drawstring, and within that, a deep brown leather corset, the colour of the saddle. It fitted under my bust, and was shaped to sit low on my hips. The front fastened with six gold metal clasps, each the shape of a crescent moon. It laced at the back with a long, thin strand of soft black leather. I put in on, lacing it as tightly as I was able to with the help of a mirror. I pulled the strings so tightly that the leather lacing cut into the palms of my hands, leaving bright red welts. I wore the corset that day, all day, cleaning.

I tried to clean his studio that afternoon, leaning over him so that he would smell me and know that I was wearing the corset, but he did not acknowledge me at all. I hoped that he would tell me to get on my knees, to clean the saddle with my tongue, but he didn't.

I barely saw him for nearly a month after that. He began to sleep in his studio during the day, while I cleaned the rest of the house, and then work at night, in the dark, so that I did not wish to disturb him. Sometimes, as night gathered, I would peer in through the door and see him standing in the same place, at his desk, with his fists clenched, staring out at the moon.

Every day, there was a new package. They were all beautifully wrapped, and I unwrapped each one with the utmost care, folding the wrapping paper, and placing it onto my dresser until I had a pile of neatly folded tissue threatening to topple over with every new addition. Each gift was expensive, and exquisitely beautiful, but not all were lingerie. One gift appeared in a leather box, about a foot long, with a weighted envelope-style lid and a metal stud that held it closed. Inside, the box was lined with velvet, and on the velvet lay a heavy black rubber penis, attached to a leather harness. The cock was attached to the harness with a metal ring, and it was double-ended. A small rubber attachment, not more than three inches long, slipped inside me when I buckled up the harness. It belted around my waist, with a leather strap between my legs, which rubbed against my anus. The dildo was tapered, and lifelike, with a large head pierced with a silver ring. Attached to the ring were two long silver chains, with a nipple clip at each end. The right chain was attached to a hoop, so that I could insert it directly into my nipple piercing, and the left was a clamp.

That day, I cleaned the bathroom.

I must have looked a picture, kneeling in the marble bathtub, naked, but for the black rubber cock erect between my thighs. Each time I stretched forward to scrub, the nipple chains pulled tight, biting my flesh sharply. When I leaned back, to release the nipple chains, the double-ended shaft of the cock entered further inside me. The harder I scrubbed, back and forward, back and forward, the more I imagined he was fucking me on the copper horse, pulling my nipples from behind. I scrubbed and scrubbed and scrubbed and scrubbed, until my nipples were raw and sweat dripped down my body, mixing with the wetness that had gathered at the base of the cock. I tasted salt on my lips. I wanted to take the harness off, to sit the cock on the floor and lower myself onto it, to grind myself onto it until I felt release, but that was not what he wanted. The gifts were for wearing, not for self-pleasuring. I wore the cock and the harness all day and late into the night, until my nipples bled and the leather strap chafed against my arse.

When I returned to my bedroom, I found a note, just two words written in charcoal, on thick white paper that he'd slipped under the door. The note read, "Clean it". So, before I put it back in the box, I licked the cock, from the bulbous head, down the shaft, to the base, which was sticky with cunt. I didn't wash my mouth afterwards. I went to bed with the taste of pussy coating my tongue.

Weeks went by, and those were the only two words that I had from him. If it had not been for the gifts, I might have felt that he was angry, or had abandoned me, and perhaps left the job. But the corsets, and the dildo, and the tissue paper and satin ribbons, and the wearing of his gifts every day made me feel as though he were with me all the time, giving me instructions. I began to spend more and more time at the estate, until in the end I stopped going home at all. I didn't need to go home for more clothing because Sir provided me with it, if you could call it that. Groceries were delivered. I didn't miss my studies or my friends, because when I was working for him, I felt as though the rest of the world was muffled, and I couldn't see, or hear, or feel anything other than the aching of my arms, scrubbing, and the rubbing of whatever device he had set out for me to wear.

My parents became concerned, and rang the house. I unplugged the phones. He became my world.

One day, the flame-haired woman I had seen in the picture on his desk returned to the house for another sitting. That day was the first day in six weeks that he had left me no package. So, I cleaned the house naked, and barefoot. He had left the door to his studio ajar, and when I had finished with the bottom floor and reached the top of the stairs, I could see straight in. She was sitting astride the copper horse. She was about twice the size of me, and it suited her. Everything about her was full. She had an air of ripeness, of heaviness. Her breasts were each the size of a cantaloupe, and they hung down, her nipples almost reaching her belly. She had thick thighs, outstretched over the saddle. Her skin was nearly as pale as mine and her hair bright red. She had hair under her armpits as well. She was rubbing herself against the leather saddle, and moaning. I could smell her scent from the doorway, a rich, almost overpowering odour of sweat and cunt.

He must have heard me at the door. "Come in," he said. I stepped into the room. "No," he said, without moving his head in my direction. "Crawl."

"Yes, Sir," I replied, and I got down on my hands and knees, and crawled towards him. I noted that I had not been able to clean this room properly for some time, as I felt the dust and grit scratch my skin.

"Lick her feet," he said, as I got closer.

She clenched her thighs around the saddle and moaned. I knelt, lifting my face towards her, and began to lick the top of her left foot. Her toenails were painted red, and her skin was soft, as if she'd recently had a pedicure. She tasted clean and sweet, and, to my surprise, I enjoyed it. The sensation of licking was not unlike the sensation of scrubbing, and I lost myself in the rhythm of it just as easily.

"Suck her toes," he said, and I did, as if each of them were a small penis. She pushed herself harder and harder against the saddle, bucking, and I sucked her toes harder and harder, until she came. When she came, she gushed, a fountain of liquid rushed down her thighs, some of the drips falling into my mouth.

"Clean it," he said.

She sighed, arching backwards, and I ran my tongue up her leg, gulping mouthfuls of her liquid. It was still hot. I licked it from the saddle, my tongue rasping against the leather. As I reached higher up her thigh I stood and bowed my head between her legs, to suck the last of it from her bush. I had only ever seen my own vagina in a mirror, and had the occasional glimpse of female friends dressing in the swimming pool changing rooms. They had all been trimmed, or shaved. My own was natural, but it grew softly and sparsely, almost like down, so I didn't feel the need to do anything with it. She had the hairiest pussy I had ever seen. After her orgasm, her lips were relaxed, like an open mouth. I pressed my face against her hair and ran my tongue around the inside of her folds, and she shuddered.

"Good girl", he said. "That's enough. Get back on your knees."

I returned to all fours and crawled towards him, until I was close enough to rest my head on his leg, if he would let me. He reached out a hand, and stroked my hair.

The woman got up, gathered her clothes, and left without another word.

When evening grew, I did not ask for the light to be switched on. I sat, curled against his thigh, as he sketched into the night, well after the shadows leapt into the room. The moon shone against his face, and as the dark gathered around us, he put down his charcoal and his sketchbook, and he held my head gently against his leg until we both fell asleep, each leaning against the other.

In the morning, he handed me the sketchbook. The picture was not of the red-haired woman, but of me, and as I had expected, it was a remarkable likeness. He'd drawn me on the copper horse, with my back arched, my head back, my breasts pointing into the air. But he had not drawn me in the throes of sexual ecstasy. Instead, I looked as contented as a cat stretching, like a person who has finally found their way home.

The Reading

Michael Hemmingson

1.

It was a short flight from LA to San Francisco and I drank as many of those little bottles of vodka as I could to get smashed: a needed condition for what I was about to go through. Yeah, I was nervous; I was informed that 200 tickets to the reading had been sold, and they expected many walk-ups. Two hundred? There was a time when I didn't even sell that many copies of a twenty-four-page chapbook of poems. My publisher had called before I left and said *Ugly Girls Are the Most Loving Creatures from Hell* was going to a seventh printing, 15,000 more copies this time, and we had sold 75,000 so far. "A miracle," said my publisher, "verse never sells like this."

"Two hundred plus," I mumbled as I slugged down my seventh vodka, one for each printing. Two hundred?! The most people who had ever come to my readings in Los Angeles were maybe thirty or twenty-five. Or twenty. The little cafés and bars, the independent bookstores.

"I'll have another in advance for the eighth printing," I told the sexy young stewardess. Maybe she wasn't that sexy or that young but I was at the point where every woman in the world looked like Venus to me.

She smiled and fetched me another.

"They say 200 pre-sold tickets," I said.

"Excuse me?"

"I'm doing a poetry reading to a big crowd of literary lovers, shovers and shakers and scalawags alike," I said. "Hell, I'm fucking famous, did you know that?"

She smiled and got me a ninth, and then a tenth, and then said she could not serve me anymore because we were about to land. I tipped her $10, the last money I had in my wallet. Those fuckers in San Fran better treat me well and pay what they promised.

A tall skinny fellow with a long beard and ponytail was waiting for me as I stumbled off the flight. What was his name?

"Mr Willis?" he said. "Danny Willis?"

"That be I," said I.

"Chuck Bellows," and he held out his hand.

"Bellows, yes, we talked much on the phone. I didn't envision you to be so tall. I saw in my mind a short fellow, a short Bellows, with thick glasses."

He laughed, and so did the woman standing next to him. Was this his daughter, girlfriend, wife, student? She seemed so young, wearing tight jeans and a halter top. Her blonde hair was cut very short, almost Jarhead style. Well, this was San Francisco.

"This is Cindy," Bellows said.

"I'm a big fan of your work," she said.

I grabbed her, hugged her, kissed her. "I *love* all my fans, especially the pretty and sexy ones!"

She giggled. "And the ugly and fat ones?"

"All of them! Bring them on! Brigham Young! I dig Mormon chicks, too, baby, the more the merrier!"

I was drunk all right, and feeling good about life . . . except for this reading.

"We need to get going, your flight was late coming in," said Bellows.

I had no idea what time it was.

"Can we stop off at a bar?" I asked.

"No time."

"We're in real time, my man," I said. "A liquor store?"

"Of course,"

I wanted a quick one at the airport bar, Bellows paid for the vodka tonic. I slammed it down, in real time all right, and off we went. I didn't care if we were late. Time was nothing to me. I was timeless and giddy.

He didn't have a car. No one drove in San Francisco. We took a Yellow Cab. He said there was a liquor store across the street from the venue where I was to read.

Both Bellows and Cindy had copies of *Ugly Girls* they wanted me to sign. I signed them while in the back seat of the cab, Bellows on my left, Cindy on my right. I put my hand on her leg and she let it stay there, smiling at me. Bellows put a hand on my leg and smiled and I started to wonder how this fellow Bellows swung. This was San Fran after all.

At the store, Bellows paid for a pint of vodka and a six-pack of Michelob. I had to piss something bad. Bellows said the men's room was not working at the venue so I took a piss in the back alley.

I went in. Back stage. I could hear a lot of voices out there.

"We're late by fifteen minutes but they are a patient crowd," Bellows said.

"What kind of crowd is this?" I asked.

"All kinds. Students, poetry fans, actors, professors, collectors, queer and straight, black and brown, white and yellow, you have some hefty fans out there, Willis. We sold 600 tickets total. That's the legal limit we can let in. We had to turn some people away and they were not happy."

I needed more vodka. "Six hundred?" I said.

"Pretty neat, pretty neat," Cindy said, handing me a beer.

"For me?" I said.

"That beer is for you," she said.

"No I mean the 600 lost souls out there, here for me?"

"You're famous, man," said Bellows.

So I wasn't lying to the stewardess after all.

2.

I was certain I couldn't do it, that I would choke up and run like a teen geek about to lose his cherry to a street whore with track marks. But once I got on stage and sat down with my pint, my beer, and my notebook of manuscripts, I eased right into the groove as I always did with an audience of three in a coffee shop. With the lights in my face, I couldn't even see all those people, those staring faces, but I sure could hear them. They laughed in all the right places when I read, and laughed in strange places where the words were never meant to be funny. Maybe they were laughing at me. They liked my comments between poems. "You're all fakes with your applause," I accused them, "and I should kick all your asses. I can do it too. I have enough vodka in me. See," and I finished the pint, "I can beat the fucking shit out of all you phony poseurs but what the hell, you paid to come see me babble, so I will read you some more of my shit," and they loved it, they cheered and urged me on and chanted my name: "Willis! Willis! Willis!"

I heard a woman yell: "I WANT TO SUCK YOUR COCK, WILLIS! I WANT TO EAT YOUR SPERM!"

"Well, c'mon up, baby, and do it," I replied. "Right here on stage, in front of all these fine people."

I heard a commotion, saw a woman in a short dress head to the stage. She tripped on her feet and fell face down. Some people helped her up and walked her out of the auditorium.

"She's drunker than I am," I said into the microphone. "And hell, under all these lights and after all this booze, I'm not sure I would be able to cum in her mouth for her."

Applause.

There was a big commotion outside. A group of skateboard punks who were turned away at the door, the max number of tickets sold, wanted in and were making a fuss.

"Let them in!" I yelled. "For the fuck sake of literacy among the young, let them in!"

I didn't see it, but apparently the cops came by and hauled the skateboarders away for public disturbance. If I could do it over again, I would've gotten up and opened the door and welcomed those little fuckers with open arms – and taken their cash for entry, of course. This was not just art: it was commerce, and my next meal and drink.

3.

It was weird, but I liked it. I signed books after. Moved 310 copies. The publisher would be pleased. Three women had me sign their tits and one guy wanted me to sign his cock, but when he whipped it out, Bellows and Cindy grabbed him and led him away.

"I have no problem signing another man's dick!" I told them.

4.

Everyone wanted to buy me drinks, dinner; they wanted to be my best friend and I never had so many friends at one time. San Francisco wasn't all that bad, and Bellows handed me a wad of twenties and fifties and said it was a grand, my take of the door as promised, two bucks for every ticket sold. I had expected $400. This was better. I had spent my last dough on airplane vodka and was broke, now I would be leaving with a grand. It was comforting to know my poetry could take care of me so well. I definitely needed to write more of the stuff, maybe that novel my publisher hoped I would compose.

5.

I demanded we go to Vesuvio's, across the street from City Lights, because that's where Jack K. and Allen G. used to hang and I wanted to be all literary and shit. First, Bellows showed me copies of *Ugly Girls* in the City Lights window. "I'll have to thank that Ferlingehtti some day," I said, "even though I can't stand the crap he calls poetry."

In the famous bar, Cindy sat next to me and I touched her leg and she let me. The hand went closer and closer to her crotch. She stopped me before I could cop a feel of her camel toe.

"Let's get out of here and have some private fun," I muttered to her.

"You should know something, Danny Willis," she said,

"You're married to Bellows?"

"I'm gay."

"A lesbian?"

"A bonafide dyke."

"Wow. The short hair, of course . . ."

"This is San Francisco," she said,

"But you've been to bed with men."

"Sure. That's why I went for the other side. Men just don't know what they're doing, when it comes to love."

"The hell with love."

"Don't worry, there are plenty of ladies here who will be glad to take you to bed tonight," Cindy said, patting my leg.

"Is Bellows a fag?" I asked.

"No. He likes to fuck his grad students, like all these men do."

I don't know about ladies, but our group consisted of a dozen young girls and middle-aged women who all bought me drinks and vied for my attention.

At some point, I vomited but I am not sure where.

6.

I woke up in a strange bed with a naked woman I did not know or remember, and had no idea how I got there and whether or not we fucked. Judging by the dried juices in my pubic hair, I assumed something interesting happened.

I got out of the bed and found the bathroom. It was a nice and clean bathroom. I threw up in the sink and took a runny hangover shit and painful piss. My urethra seemed to be clogged with pussy juice, or my own cum, or both. Maybe the naked woman was the one who offered to blow me on stage.

She was awake and smoking a cigarette when I returned. I put my pants on and she remained naked. She had drooping middle-aged tits with dark brown nipples, and a thick bush between her legs. Damn, she was one sexy momma.

"You OK, Dan? Danny? What do you prefer?"

"What did you call me last night?"

"Daddy." She laughed.

"Don't call me that," I said. "Danny is fine. I'm fine. Got a hangover but it's to be expected. I'm sorry, but I don't remember your name.'"

"Never told you it."

"Ah."

"Wanda," she said,

"Good morning, Wanda. Was last night memorable?"

"You don't remember." She laughed again.

"I'm sure it will come to me later on in the day."

"It was pretty good," she said, nodding, "you have a nice thick cock, just the way I like them. I don't enjoy the length if a man is that way, but I do get off being stretched."

"Where are we?"

"Professor Bellows' guest room."

"Professor? You one of his students?"

"Colleague. I am also a prof."

"Do say. What do you prof?"

"Postmodern American literature."

"That's a myth."

"Your book is on my syllabus for two classes."

"How kind."

"Would love for you to come to my classes and talk to my students."

"I'm on the spot, eh?"

"No need to answer yet, just think about it. Say, how about a morning fuck?"

"How kind of you," I said.

"I try to be a nice, accommodating woman."

7.

Wanda Merritt, Ph.D., was thirty-eight, twice divorced, no kids, and a tenured professor at the same university Bellows worked at. She had published some critical theory books with university presses, the titles of which give me a headache trying to remember, something about the virtual ghost in the electronic double of postmodern blah blah. She was a great fuck, though, and could deepthroat my cock, which made her a winner in my opinion.

So yeah, I returned two weeks later and read for her two classes.

8.

Deep down something primal and lizard brain told me this was a mistake, but I was just too damn curious to know more about Lady Postmodern and what she truly was all about. I figured the academic claptrap jargon and posing was just a role, and I wanted to see under that mask. I was the kind of guy always after the ugly truth, because then I could write a dozen poems about it. I was in the produce mode. That's what my publisher told me: "Produce, man, *produce*, get out enough for another collection and watch the money come rolling in!"

Was it really about the money? Where did the art factor in, the "fuck fame and riches" attitude most of the small press poets had? I realized, those days, that poverty was bullshit and the whole "I starve for my verse" was just a way of justifying the fact that 99 per cent of the poets out there made very little, if any, dough off the stanzas and broken lines.

I was starting to like the money, and this taste of fame. I was getting things I was never able to so easily before. I was forty-one and ready to give my audience more of what they seemed to want, and they did not want my old stuff, the terse verse and clean smooth words from when I was twenty-five and won the Bethlehem Young Poets Award, that first real collection in hardback and published by a university press that garnered much praise, good reviews, but moved few copies: 300 in hardback, 800 in paper. For the award, I was told that was common; for the university press, they said this was good, that most poetry collections seldom moved more than 500 copies all together, hard and soft editions combined, most of those sales going to libraries and die-hard collectors of first editions.

Speaking of first editions, I started to wonder how much the first printings of *Ugly Girls* I signed (I guessed 500 out of the initial 5,000 first print run) would go for down the road. I was told collectors were already starting to price them and some of my signed chapbooks of yesteryear were fetching upward to $100. I'd had one guy come by my place, just before *Ugly Girls* started moving, and pay me $500 for signed copies of all my chapbooks, letting go my personal copies. I needed the money bad at the time: I had an alcohol addiction to nurse.

I digress. Back to Wanda Merritt, Ph.D., the Postmodern Slut . . .

9.

Reading for the first class went well; there were about twenty students, ranging in age from nineteen to fifty, and they listened to me with academic intensity, occasionally taking notes. *Notes?* About *what?* About beer shits and herpes and abortions and saggy tits of old women I met at bars?

The second class was bigger, about forty students, and during my reading some fellow in a rumpled shirt and tie barged in, holding a bottle of tequila, and yelled, "YOU'RE NO POET, WILLIS! ALL YOU DO IS WRITE PROSE FICTION AND BREAK IT UP INTO LINES AND CALL IT POETRY! THAT'S *NOT* POETRY! WHAT *I* WRITE IS POETRY!"

"Yeah," I said, "prove it."

The students laughed nervously.

"I don't have my work memorized," he mumbled, swaying, "and I don't have my book with me – BUT WHAT YOU WRITE IS NOT FUCKING POETRY! I DON'T GET IT! WHAT IS THE WORLD COMING TO WHEN FRAUDS LIKE YOU GET LAUDED AS GREAT AMERICAN POETS?!?"

"Eugene," Wanda said harshly, "that is *enough*. Get out."

"Give me a swig of that bottle," I said, rushing to the drunken guy before Wanda could, taking his bottle of tequila and slugging a good portion down. It burned as sweetly as a lip-bite from a $20 Tijuana hooker.

Wanda ushered the guy out and I still had the bottle.

"Price for interrupting the Great American Poet at work," I said, sitting back down.

The students loved it. They applauded.

Wanda stood by the door, arms folded, looking at me with a grin, shaking her head as I continued to read and drink the tequila.

10.

"I'm sorry about Eugene," Wanda said. "He's what you call a tortured soul."

We were at the campus pub sharing a pitcher of beer with one of her students, a petite little thing with pink and purple hair and freckles.

"What an accusation he made," I said. "Perhaps he's right," and shrugged because I didn't give a fuck what anyone thought about my work.

"He is wrong," the petite student said. Oh, her name was Kelly.

"He can't get tenure," Wanda said. "I don't think he will. He isn't being published in any important places. Magazines that come and go. Nothing like, say, the *New York Quarterly* or *Ploughshares*."

"Both those places published me," I said. "*NYQ* recently, *Ploughshares* twenty years ago when I wrote a different sort of thing."

"I have both issues," Kelly said.

"Kelly is a big fan," Wanda informed me.

Kelly was playing footsies under the table with me.

"Kelly is one of my best grad students," Wanda continued, "has a bright future. She has already published critical essays in key peer-review journals. She wants to write one about your work."

"Compare it to Kerouac's verse," Kelly said.

"How nice," I said. "Wish Jack's stomach hadn't exploded and he was still around, I would've loved to meet him in the meat world."

"Kelly has agreed to something that I think you will approve and like," Wanda said.

"Yeah?" I said.

"A threesome."

"'You don't say.'"

Kelly had her foot in my crotch. "I do say," she did say.

11.

Everything went pretty damn good the first hour in bed with professor and student. Kelly was so fragile that I thought we might break her, with her skinny hips and flat chest and thin arms, but she kept up with us, going from sucking my dick to eating Wanda's hairy snatch. They swapped my cum, probably for my benefit, and I knew I had to write a poem about such a thing. I tried to fuck Kelly in the ass but her sphincter would not accommodate, no matter how much lube we used. Kelly was in tears. I said her pussy was fine. "No," Wanda said, "I want to see you make that little butthole gape."

Kelly jumped up and burst into tears. "I can't do this anymore! I said yes for you, Wanda, because I knew this is what you wanted but it's not what I want! Do you think I really *like* fucking men? And an *old fat man* like him!"

Old and fat? "I'm only forty-one," I said. Yeah, I guess I had a bit of a gut, expected with all the beer, wine and vodka.

"You like it when it's disgusting," Kelly said to her professor. "You're a *pervert*! I love you, honey, but you're *a pervert*!"

Kelly started to get dressed.

"You walk out that door," Wanda started.

"Or what? Or what?!" said Kelly. "Go ahead, *or what*?"

Wanda sighed. "Go."

"Have fun with your disgusting old drunk," Kelly said, and to me: "I'm sorry, Mr Willis, I think you are a genius writer but as a sex partner, you're too old and your penis is too big."

She left.

I looked at my cock. I was pretty impressive in girth, big veins and smelly of fuck, with a pulsing purple head.

Wanda groaned. "Never get involved that deeply with a student."

"So you're gay," I said, thinking of Cindy and the lost possibilities.

"I go both ways."

"Ever fuck male students?"

"Of course."

"And her?"

"She is in love with me."

"Do you love her back?"

"Don't be ridiculous," Wanda Merritt, Ph.D., said. "Come here and stick that fat ugly cock inside me.'"

"Yes, Doctor," I obliged.

12.

Kelly returned in the morning to apologize for her outburst and asked what she could do to make things right. Wanda said, "Get on your bony knees and blow him. I want to watch."

Watch she did, as little Kelly got on her knees before me. I was sitting in a chair in the kitchen, drinking coffee with a shot of rum. She did her best to get me fully in her mouth. She rubbed my balls as I jerked the base of my thingamabob.

"Swallow it all," Wanda ordered.

Kelly did not. She spat it out and rubbed my cum into my balls. I liked that. "You get over here and lick it up," she told Wanda, and Wanda did this, and everything now seemed to be right as rain between the two.

That afternoon, Wanda drove me to the airport (a rare person in San Francisco with a car). "Until next time," she said.

We both knew there would be no next time.

"My book tour starts in a week," I said.

"I bet you'll have *a lot* of fun," she said, "if you know what I mean."

I did, and I planned to.

All My Lovers in One Room

Kristina Lloyd

Yeah, that's right: all my lovers, past and present, and it's not a big room either. This could be a horror story, and maybe it is because I can't see the ending from here. There are thirty-seven men and two women but, even without counting, I know someone is missing.

Fancy him being late for my deathbed!

Ba-dum.

Baaaah. Dum.

I'm wired to a machine showing my heartbeat's on the wane. As if I didn't know. But I'm hanging in there, hoping he'll appear any moment. Besides, I have decades left to spare although my body begs to differ.

To stay focused, I check out the room, mentally putting names to faces: Lucas McGrath, Benedict Purcell (who lost the tip of his little finger in an accident with a glass), Joe Miller and the scruffy blond with the tattoo on his inner wrist . . . Dave, Mark, Mike? Some ordinary, monosyllabic name like that. He was a drunken one-night stand and I adored him for a whole weekend so I suggested we meet again, because you do, don't you, when it's been good, hey let's meet again, and he said, "Don't bother, I'll only fuck you about."

So I didn't bother. I can take a hint and I have no patience for games.

Jason Davis who made me squirt for the first time.

Saleem Hasan, a third-generation Asian guy with a tireless tongue.

A beautiful Dutch man on a beach in Sardinia at midnight, moonlight on the waves like this was the movies and sand in my asscrack like it wasn't.

Alec – surname escapes me – who declared himself a bondage enthusiast but used knots more suited to a parcel. Still, I couldn't fault him for his enthusiasm (ouch!) and he never claimed to be an expert, did he?

Daniel Marcus Frederick Thornton, aka Dan, Danny, Danno, sweetheart, darling, the love of my life for four and a half years, and proof I'm not suited to monogamy.

And look, there's Rob, another long-termer, poor sod. He was a competitive cyclist who shaved his legs more often than I did.

Still no sign of my Charlie.

Charlie King. King by name, king by nature. I'm concerned he'll pitch up late as per usual, horny but unhurried, tugging his tie loose and pulling plugs from the wall so he can recharge his BlackBerry and his laptop. And poof! He'll unplug the life support or whatever I'm hooked up to and it'll be all over for me, bar the burning or the burial.

You know that white light you hear rumours of? A glorious white light at the end of a tunnel, brighter than anything you've known; a huge sense of tranquillity and long-lost family members awaiting you with open arms? Here's a tip: avoid the family. Hang a sharp left before the exit and you'll find yourself in an ante-chamber with all your flings, exes and casual fucks. I realize it's not ideal (and some may prefer the family option) but if you want to buy yourself some extra time, it's a way to duck the point of no return and to avoid all those uncles you couldn't shake off at weddings.

The woman we had a threesome with (at Charlie's request – although to be honest, he practically begged me) is chatting to the chick I had sex with as a student because I thought it would make me cool. I suppose I used them both. I wonder if they're discussing me but figure I'm of little interest to either woman these days. If Charlie were here, he'd be hoping they were about to give us a floor show. He could be predictable like that, could Charlie.

But Charlie's not here, he never fucking is.

Oh, Charlie! He was the whirlwind I spun from; the storm who thrilled me; the fucker who kept me waiting and wanting. But this time, his rotten punctuality really takes the biscuit. Charlie, I'm dying here! Don't tell me you're stuck in a meeting and don't try texting me either. I'm at death's door, *capisce*? I can't get a signal. I need you here and I need you now.

I would never have said that to him in life, would never say "need" because I don't believe in need. There's only "want" unless it's life-threatening. But hey, it pretty much is right now!

Tick tock tick tock.

And then I feel him approach. I'm like an animal sensing an earthquake before the tectonic plates have shifted. Hairs ripple on the back of my neck and my blood sets up a pulse in my cunt. A thousand and one butterflies dance in my stomach. Oh Charlie, you divine bastard.

I smell him first. He smells so real, so intimate. He's the essence of life knocking for six the stink of sterility in my nostrils. I catch the scent of his neck, the aroma of warm skin spliced with muted notes of aftershave and the worn, laundered cotton of his collar. I get the tang of city traffic, fumes and hot rubber, then paperwork like linen and the metallic whiff of cheap, blue ink on his fingers. Maybe my nose is super-sensitive now the rest of me's shutting down but I think I smell the tabby cat he stroked en route to work that morning, the sun-baked wheat fields in the pasta he ate for supper last night, the heat of his cock in his palm, the spill of his come, the mountain breeze from the Alpine holiday we said we'd go on one day. Or perhaps that's his fabric conditioner. I don't know. I breathe him in, wanting to consume all the scents he acquired while he was busy doing other things, living a life I know so little about.

Tinker, tailor, soldier, spy.

No, he's not a spy. He just acts like one. "The name's King," I like to say, "Charlie King." If he'd been more available to me, I don't know what I'd have done. I might have lost interest but I doubt it. Time and again I tried to let go, move on, find a man who could topple him but how to let go when something's got you in its grip?

Ah, and there, now, the softness of his lips, like angels and feathers as he teases with his hello: kiss, murmur, kiss, his fingers sliding down my neck with a tenderness that's menacingly, enchantingly possessive. Those fingers say more than any words could: I own you, you're mine.

And already, I feel myself becoming small, vulnerable and blissfully free, disappearing into the magnificence of Charlie King's presence. Some people shape themselves to fit the world but where Charlie walks, the world rearranges itself like the Red Sea giving it up for Moses.

Confidence, grace, integrity, humility. Charlie has these qualities in spades. If he weren't so damn busy (too many ifs with Charlie), I might fall to my knees in permanent worship. But he *is* busy so I have to keep my distance. No, it's not game-playing; I told you I've no time for that. It's the art of self-protection. Nine years I've known Charlie. Oh sure, there have been others during this time, for him and for me, and years have gone by when we've never exchanged a word. But we keep coming back to each other because we can't *not*. He is my magnetic north, my lodestar, the brightest light in my darkest sky. He is the place I am rooted. From head to toe, he has me.

You know what they say about addicts? Once a smoker, always a smoker? It's like that for me: once I'd been fucked by Charlie King, I was forever fucked by Charlie King.

And that's why I run. I don't want anyone to have such a hold on me, especially not someone so elusive, so charming, so in tune with what I want. If I give it up for Charlie, I don't know where I'd draw the line. My fear is I'd give him my everything. And then what? Supposing he didn't give it back? Who would I be?

I run three laps of the park before breakfast each day. I do fun runs, 10K races and half-marathons. I put my earphones in and I run to find my strength. I run to get high. I run to get away. Treadmills don't do it for me. I need to know I'm moving.

But right now I'm going nowhere fast because Charlie King is with me. He's checking out the room, his black-brown eyes sweeping over the motley crew of assembled heads. A glimmer of playfulness lights up his face and I say, "Oh no, Charlie, why didn't I see that coming? No. But yes and oh God, I'm not sure it's appropriate with the Grim Reaper watching. Oh really, I can't Charlie but . . . How is it you know me better than I know myself?"

"Turn around," he says softly. "I don't like your hair that way."

I have my hair pinned up in a loose bun studded with diamante pins. Years down the line and I still put effort into looking good for Charlie, even when I'm practically a ghost. Charlie, patient, steady and only slightly rough, stuffs his fingers into the knot, starts unpicking its understructure. It takes him a while. He tugs and shakes. Glass beads rain down like cheap tears. I am being dismantled.

"Better," says Charlie. He fluffs at my hair and smiles. I can"t smile back because I'm dazed with desire. "So beautiful," he says and I believe him, in part because he's also so very beautiful to me. When he smiles, crow's feet crinkle around his eyes. He's ageing well but nothing dents that boyish sense of mischief. I look at him looking at me. Our mutual appreciation is like a mirror to a mirror, running into infinity. We're surrounded by people but there"s only us here, reflecting each other until the end of time. He winds his fingers in my hair, forming a fist at the nape of my neck. Slowly he pulls, forcing my head back, making my scalp prickle. He gives a sharp jerk of warning and his teeth are gritted when he murmurs in my ear, "So. Fucking. Beautiful."

Right back atcha, Charlie boy.

"Why do you always do this to me?" he asks. Another tug. "Why do you make my dick so hard?"

He does this, makes it seem as if his horniness is my fault and he's going to make me pay for it. As ever, I'm happy to pay. But I can see what's coming next and I've never paid quite so much. But then I've never been quite so close to death before.

Charlie undresses me and undresses himself. He's not a guy who needs to stay suited and booted to be bossman. If Charlie wants to be naked, Charlie strips. His thighs are superb, their big curves of muscle scooping in to meet the taut, succulent globes of his butt. They are the thighs of a gladiator and when he lowers my mouth to his swollen cock, I cup my hands to their bulk. I feel safe there, Charlie guiding my head back and forth, me clasping the power of those almighty thighs.

He sweeps back a lock of my hair, hooking it behind one ear. "Good girl," he says affectionately. I keep on sucking, gratified by his groans of pleasure. He never plays it cool, does Charlie. He likes to enjoy himself and revels in how willingly I provide for his needs.

"I'm doing this for you, you know that?" he says. Again, so gentle, so caring. I don't trust his tone one jot. I say nothing. My mouth's kinda full. Charlie squeezes his fist in my hair. "You know that?" he repeats, more demanding this time. I mumble an affirmative, nodding on his cock. "Good girl," he murmurs.

From the corner of my eye, I see them moving to gather around us in a ragged half-circle. Some of them are naked, fists slipping idly on their eager cocks. It's not easy to tell who's who. All I can say with any certainty is that these men, while not very organized about it, are forming a queue.

Charlie's tone changes as he addresses the room: clear, confident although not particularly loud. He knows they're all listening. He commands attention effortlessly. "Who's first?" he asks.

I moan around his cock. At my centre, I am simultaneously insubstantial and fleshy, a cavernous ache and a hard, thudding pulse. I break from Charlie and glance over my shoulder. It's the scruffy blond, Mr I-Will-Fuck-You-About. Charlie draws me back to him, filling my mouth again. "It doesn't matter who it is," he says, calm and self-assured. "Just keep sucking."

I'm not quite wet and ready enough. The blond's cock is blunt at my entrance. He nudges at my flesh, presses and pushes until he finds the right angle, then he slides into my tightness. His fucking shunts me onto Charlie's cock and, soon enough, we get a rhythm going where I'm swaying between them both, and where deep in my cunt means deep in my throat.

"You like that?" asks Charlie.

It's a rhetorical question.

Blondie grips my ass, pounding hard, making me wet, and when his grunts grow more urgent I remember how red his face turned when he came, how the sinews in his neck stood out. He withdraws when he's finished and slaps one buttock, a satisfied customer. I'm empty for a few seconds before someone else takes his place, slotting home and slamming fast. I am soaked. Charlie slips out of my mouth and drops down to my level. He tucks his fingers under my chin, lifting me so I look at him, eye to eye. I gasp and groan while the guy behind me comes too quickly, apologizing with a laugh.

Charlie's gaze is still fixed on mine. Another guy fills me, slowly this time, resting his thick length inside me, nudging and teasing until I can't bear it any longer. "Please," I gasp, half at Charlie, half at the ceiling. "Please fuck me, please fuck me hard." The man doesn't, of course, not until he's gotten his rocks off on me begging for it.

Charlie strokes hair from my damp face. "That's right," he says, "ask them nicely."

I start to lose count around six or seven. It doesn't seem much, I know, but either someone pulls out and re-penetrates or the changeover is fast and I'm suddenly confused. Also, my concentration is shot. I am too fucked to count. I barely know my own name. I try to recall it and for a moment I think I'm Charlie, Charlie King. But no, I'm Ruby, aren't I? I'm Ruby, Ruby, Ruby.

I think he's calling for me, I hear his voice. *Ruby!* Oh, but his lips don't move and as if Charlie would call for me. As if!

Ruby in the sky with diamonds. That's what he used to say.

Or Ruby Red, on account of my red hair. Sometimes, I was simply Red.

Ruby!

I'm on all fours and my arms are growing weak. I want to sink forward but Charlie holds me steady. At some point, he clasps my cheek to his belly, caressing my head as another guy drives into me. "Shhh," he says, "there, there."

Some finish fast while others linger. I can't be sure but I think my long-term exes and the two women sit it out. Strangely, in all of this, it feels as if Charlie is the one fucking me. He whispers in my ear, "We're going to keep going till you're exhausted, OK?"

I manage to nod.

"Who do you belong to?" asks Charlie.

My voice is made of ashes. "You," I say, "always you."

The final two guys penetrate my ass because Charlie tells them they can. I cry out. I am so high and lost. I feel there's nothing left of me but something is waiting, a place untouched, a shadow in the corner of a shadow. And here's Charlie, ready to find me in those shadows.

He flips me over and pushes my legs back. He sinks into my cunt, slow and controlled. I think his cock must be solid gold because somehow he is more to me than all the guys who went before him. He is harder, thicker, deeper, and with every thrust, he reclaims me. His eyes are locked on mine, watching how I melt beneath him.

Soon, there's only me and him, and I'm not even sure of the difference any more. My boundaries have gone. Whatever I used to have – my self, my soul, my psyche – is spreading beyond me into galaxies unknown. Then, for a single, pure point of impossible flight, the white light burns and I vanish.

I'm nowhere, existing only as ecstasy, transcendence. I am bigger than all the heavens and I'm coming so hard.

"Hush," says Charlie. "Everything's fine, take it easy."

He's holding my hand, looking down at me, his brow pinched with concern. His collar is open, tie askew. His dark eyes are black holes, my event horizon.

I try to smile but I can't find my face.

"Hello, Ruby. We thought we'd lost you back there," says another voice. A woman, brisk, efficient, cheerful. A nurse.

Oh, I'm in hospital, of course I am. Charlie's chopped my legs off. No, don't be stupid, he likes your legs, likes that you have them. The curtain around the bed is the same royal blue as the carpets in an office where I once worked. The reality of dying is so prosaic. I hate those fucking curtains. But I'm not here to die, no, I'm too young. I struggle to remember, then it comes to me, sharp as sanity: a routine operation on my Achille's tendon. Yawn.

Why all the fuss? Why's Charlie here? Do we have a date?

"They called me," he says, although I haven't asked. "There were complications."

Yeah, that's you and me all over, Charlie. Facebook status: It's complicated.

The nurse leans into view. "Your heart melted," she says, smiling. "We've stabilized it now so no need to fret. You still have some leakage around the left ventricle. Could be permanent but it shouldn't interfere with your quality of life. You need to take it easy for a while." She laughs merrily. "And since your leg's in plaster, you haven't got much choice!"

Charlie smiles. He looks beat, so tired. "At last," he whispers. "I caught you. I netted the wind." He gives my hand a squeeze, warm, reassuring and on the edge of painful.

I'm tired too. My head sinks into my pillow and everything becomes clear: I am Ruby, full of my own life, a jewel shining brightly, and fit for my king.

Saturnalia

Vivienne LaFay

XLVI BC

It was December the nineteenth, the Feast of Saturnalia, but Tullus Octavius was helping to fortify the boundaries of the Roman Empire against barbarians. Back in the capital it was a time of licence, when a carnival atmosphere would prevail with excess of feasting, drinking and sexual pleasure. But most of all it was a time when the natural order of things was reversed: masters became slaves and slaves became masters.

Tullus's wife, Claudia, knew what would befall her as mistress of the house. While her husband was there to protect her, Claudia had never minded the boisterous antics that the slaves got up to, taking it all in good part. She had watched her husband go through the rituals many times, but this time she would have to manage alone. There would be much horseplay and mockery, but she was confident that the slaves would not go too far out of respect for her.

As the winter evening drew in, the whole household was assembled in the hall for the lottery to take place. Claudia sat with her son, Gaius, and daughter, Virginia, on a dais but soon she would have to give up her seat to one lucky slave. She held a bag containing many white beans and just one black bean. Each slave must draw a bean. The one who drew the black bean would be crowned king and his word would become law in the household, his temporary power usurping that of master or mistress.

As the fourteen slaves filed past to take their chance Claudia smiled at each and mostly they returned roguish grins, already savouring the pranks to come. But then came the turn of Darius, the Persian, and Claudia felt her heart race with unexpected fear.

What if this man should draw the black bean, what then? The prospect filled her with dread.

He drew near and his dark eyes met hers. They bore a sardonic expression, as if he knew exactly what was going through her mind, knew how devastated she would be if he became the one with power over her, the one whose bidding she must obey without question, the Lord of Misrule. Of all the slaves his nature was the most proud and rebellious, and on several occasions Claudia had found it necessary to have him whipped. Once, she had even given him six strokes of the birch herself.

It had happened when she caught him in the bedroom of her daughter, Virginia, who was thirteen years old. No male slave was allowed in her quarters, and although he had sworn that he had only entered at the young lady's request to remove a poisonous snake from her room Claudia had felt it necessary to punish him. Virginia was young and vulnerable, promised to a Roman senator of good family and due to wed him in a year's time. However, if there was any question about her purity the alliance would not take place.

Darius, on the other hand, was a male stud of extraordinary strength and beauty, who was known to have sired several children while he worked as an attendant at the public baths. Virginia's reputation was not safe while he felt free to enter her room on such a pretext, so he had to be prevented from doing so ever again.

Claudia had not been able to call upon Tullus to administer punishment since he was away from home, so she'd decided to make an example of him herself. After assembling the entire household in the courtyard, she had forced him to strip and be tied up by a fellow slave. Seeing his magnificent body fully exposed she had felt an unexpected heat in her loins, but she had remained in control of herself and delivered the strokes with a steady hand. He had not once flinched from the rod. Lashed to the whipping post, his muscled back and shoulders had taken the worst of the beating, but she had struck him across the buttocks once, the taut globes marked by a red stripe that made her feel somewhat ashamed of what she had done.

When the other slave untied him at the end of the chastisement, Claudia had given an involuntary gasp. She couldn't help noticing that he had a full erection. His penis was large and well formed, the huge balls hanging heavily beneath, and after catching his eye Claudia had blushed deeply. An amused smile had flitted across his face, giving her the extraordinary impression that it was she who had received the public shaming, not him. The memory of that moment returned to haunt her now as she saw that same sardonic smile on his darkly handsome face.

There were not many beans left in the bag so the odds were shortened. Claudia held her breath as he plunged his hand in, making its cord tug at her wrist, and her heart fluttered wildly like a bird caught in a net. Slowly he drew out his chosen bean and held it up for all to see. Claudia's heart plummeted, now more like a bird brought to earth with a slingshot. He had the black bean. He would be crowned King of the Saturnalia. His word would be law in the Octavian household. A dreadful panic seized her and she wanted to cry out, "No, not him! Anyone but him!" But the entire company of slaves was cheering and shouting with glee and Claudia knew that there was nothing she could do to change Fate.

Slowly she stepped down from the dais with her two children, allowing him to take her seat and be crowned king. She watched nervously as the gaudy crown was placed on his head, a red cloak draped around his shoulders and a makeshift sceptre placed in his hand.

"All hail!" cried the slaves in unison. "All hail to King Saturn, the Lord of Misrule!"

They turned aggressively on Claudia and her children, forcing them to kneel before their new "master". Normally she would have done this with good grace, laughing as if at a comic play, but this time it felt different. The slave's dark eyes were boring into her with fierce intensity, making her feel decidedly uncomfortable. She held the hands of Gaius and Virginia tightly as they knelt in mock fealty beside her.

"What is your will, your majesty?" cried the crowd, full of jocular spirit.

Darius got to his feet, drawing himself up to his full majestic height. "Let there be feasting!" he declared. "And may the lady of the house and her two offspring wait upon us with due humility. Today the slaves rule, and those who were once set above us must now bow to our command!"

So far, so good, Claudia thought. This was the custom, and only to be expected. She led the children to the kitchen where they were to collect the bowls of ready-prepared food and carry them into the dining hall. Both Gaius and Virginia thought it all a huge joke. They looked forward to this time and playing the role of humble slave with exaggerated manners.

At first the evening went as expected. Claudia was kept busy rushing from slave to slave, serving food and wine, while there were many ribald jokes of a kind that they would never have dared to make while the master was in charge. As the wine flowed free, some even dared to suggest that "while the master was away the mistress might play". They began teasing her, suggesting that she might be having an affair with the oldest and ugliest of the slaves.

Claudia tried to take it in good part but she was aware of Darius's gaze upon her the whole while, watching her with an arrogant grin on his face that made her blood run cold. She was sure that he had some scheme up his sleeve, some act of vengeance that would give him satisfaction for the way she had publicly humiliated him.

To make matters worse, whenever Virginia came near he would reach out for her, grabbing her by the arm and pulling her towards him, trying to get her to promise to marry him instead of Quintus Publius. She giggled, thinking it a huge joke, but Claudia knew what was behind it and her anxiety increased. Maybe she should insist on her daughter spending the night on a couch in her room, just to be on the safe side. She didn't trust Darius at the best of times, and now he was even more dangerous.

The revels grew even more loud and bawdy, with some of the slaves daring to paw at Claudia herself. She tried her best to enter into the spirit of things, to slap them down with a wry comment, but her heart wasn't in it. If only someone else had drawn the black bean, she couldn't help thinking, but it was no use. What couldn't be cured must be endured.

"The King rises!" someone shouted. Everyone looked towards the high table, where Darius was waiting for silence.

"Honoured guests and humble slaves," he began, nodding first to the slaves then to Claudia and her children. Everyone hooted with laughter. "I think it is time for some entertainment. Shall we invite the lovely Claudia to dance for us?"

Claudia froze with horror. It would be such an indignity for a high-born Roman matron to behave like a common dancing girl, but the slaves were responding enthusiastically, clapping and encouraging her, so she could hardly refuse. To decline to carry out an order at Saturnalia was considered an affront to the upstart slaves, and if things got out of hand they could insist that she be punished. She would not give Darius that excuse.

"Very well," she replied, forcing a smile.

"You are not dressed for dancing," the "King" commented. "Sofia, take the slave away and find herself something more fitting to wear."

The girl came up with a broad grin, evidently delighted at the chance to deck her mistress out in something quite inappropriate to her real station in life. As they walked towards the slave quarters Claudia pleaded, "Do not make me look a laughing stock, I beg of you."

But Sofia, who had suffered many harsh criticisms from her mistress, only grinned.

"Take off your *stola* and *palla*," she told her, the minute they were in the room she shared with three other slaves. "I have something in mind that might do."

Claudia removed her fine embroidered robe and silk shawl with great reluctance. When she stood in just her breastband and loincloth the girl looked at her critically. "I think you should remove them too," she said. "Men like to glimpse a woman's figure when she's dancing."

Claudia was secretly horrified but to protest would be to risk exposure before the entire company of slaves. She wondered what Tullus would say when he returned if he discovered that his wife had been shamed or punished for being a spoilsport. He would never understand her feelings and, relying on hearsay, would be obliged to think the worst of his wife.

"Very well," she murmured.

"Say, 'Very well, mistress!' or I shall slap you!" Sofia insisted.

Knowing the girl would not hesitate to deliver what she threatened, Claudia did as she was told and then stripped naked. Sofia gazed at her body with frank curiosity, noting every blemish, every wrinkle. Claudia felt like a slave at a street-corner auction, and her shame deepened.

"Now put this on."

Sofia handed her a mere scrap of a garment in gauzy purple silk. When Claudia held it up and examined it she laughed in scorn. "I can't possibly wear this. It would show everything I've got!"

"Perfect – for a dancing girl!" Sofia said, smugly. "Are you going to be difficult? Because if you are, I . . ."

"No, no!" Claudia said hastily, pulling the shift over her head. It hung from her shoulders in loose folds, leaving her arms and legs bare. The proud tips of her nipples were clearly visible beneath its diaphanous sheen, as was her dark bush, and the material clung to the globes of her breasts and buttocks with soft sensuality, making Claudia painfully aware of the contours of her body. Every slave would be gaping lewdly at her in that attire.

"Give me something else to wear!" she pleaded." Or at least a shawl, for modesty's sake."

"You would not be able to move freely in anything else. Come, they are waiting for the performance to begin."

Sofia seized her hand and pulled her towards the door. There was a raucous noise coming from the hall, and another fear seized her. "Please, let the children retire!" she begged. "They must not see me debasing myself like this."

The girl hesitated then, to Claudia's relief, nodded her consent. She went ahead to have the children dispatched to their rooms and, when the coast was clear, announced that the dancing would begin.

Claudia had no idea how to dance in the suggestive manner of *hetaerae* but now that she was faced with the ordeal she decided to do her best. Four slaves who could play instruments struck up on the flute, cymbals, lyre and tambourine. Lifting her arms and wiggling her hips, Claudia started on what she hoped would be seen as a parody of such entertainment. The slaves gawped at her and Darius leered above them all, his black eyes taking in every curve and detail of her body.

At first Claudia felt exposed and ashamed, but as the dance proceeded she found herself growing defiant. She was enjoying the freedom of movement that the floating tunic was giving her, relishing the admiring glances she was getting from the assembled crowd. Far from proving an ordeal, the dancing was filling her with an erotic energy that encouraged her to shake her breasts and move her hips with sensual exhibitionism. The slaves were on heat, she could feel their hot breath fanning her body and smell the subtle scent of male arousal. The usual propriety that prevented a slave from regarding his mistress lecherously no longer applied, and they were staring at her with undisguised lust.

Then one of the men, fired with strong wine, leapt up and began mimicking her movements behind her back in a grotesque parody. The man tugged at her skimpy costume and managed to pull down one of the sleeves, exposing her breast right down to the nipple. Claudia stopped in shock and tugged it back, but the man clumsily tried to kiss her.

The audience roared. Claudia felt her cheeks grow red with embarrassment, and when Darius leapt to his feet and shouted, "Enough!" she was overwhelmed with relief.

But her relief was short-lived. No sooner had the musicians stopped playing than Darius got down from his exalted position and strode towards her, his face dark with fury.

"Evil temptress!" he snarled. "You have teased my men beyond endurance with your obscene dancing. Go to your room, at once!"

Claudia had never been spoken to like that in her life before, and his venomous tone horrified her. She scampered from the room like a frightened rabbit, wishing she had never agreed to dance. Remembering just how sensual and abandoned her dancing had been she felt even worse, her heart making painful thuds inside her chest as if it were hammering to be released. She fled down the corridor to her room where she tore off the revealing garment and pulled on her own robe, intending to go straight to bed.

"What will Tullus think, if he hears of this?" she wondered, knowing very well how angry he would be if he thought his wife had disgraced herself before the slaves. Things had gone too far that night, she was sure of that, and it was all because that Darius had won the lottery, provoking her into behaving in ways she would never have dreamed of before.

The sound of heavy footsteps was heard in the corridor outside and Claudia shrank beneath the bedclothes, praying that they would pass by her room. But the door was suddenly flung open and Darius appeared, his eyes flashing like hot coals at her in the lamplight. He slammed the door behind him and she noticed, with the utmost dismay, that he was wearing a short-handled whip in the leather belt around his tunic.

"So you thought to hide from me in your sanctuary!" he sneered. "Well, I have not finished with you yet. Come here, slave, and kneel before me! I, your King and Master, command you!"

This was no longer a game. Claudia knew that the moment of reckoning for the way she had disciplined Darius in the past had now come, and she was terrified. But there was to be no escape. When she hesitated he strode across the space between them and flung aside the bedclothes with an oath.

Claudia practically fell out of bed and onto her knees before him. She was trembling all over, the energy that she had worked up during the dance now transmuted into abject fear. He towered over her on his sturdy legs, a masculine scent of sweat and musk filling her nostrils as she crouched there in her white tunic wondering what he would do next.

"Stand!"

She rose painfully onto legs that would scarcely bear her weight, her knees half crumpling beneath her. The light in the slave's eye was keen and mischievous, making the most of his newfound power to torment and intimidate his tyrannical mistress.

He suddenly pulled out a knife and held it at her breast. Claudia froze, her eyes popping out and her breath stifled in her chest. A slow smile spread across the man's features, his wide mouth opening to show unusually white teeth. Somehow she found his smile even more alarming than his frown. Her pulses were racing as adrenaline coursed through every vein in her body.

"You are afraid of me?" he said, in hoarse whisper. "That's good! Very good!"

She felt the cold steel at her throat and closed her eyes, sending a silent prayer up to whatever god or goddess might be disposed to listen to her plight. The knife point travelled down her neck, right into the deep ravine of her bosom where it was inches from her heart. Claudia could not bear it. She longed to plead with him, to offer to perform any service he required providing only that he spared her life.

Then there was a sudden ripping sound and the skimpy shift she was wearing tore apart. Darius had sliced down the front of the garment so that it fell into two halves, hanging uselessly off either arm. He chuckled softly, and she felt his warm breath on her bare skin, giving her goose bumps.

"Now you know what it feels like to be a naked slave for any man to stare at, for the buyers to pick and choose," he told her.

She opened her eyes. Darius was standing back, surveying her with a sneer, but she could only see the length of rope that he held in his hand. Before she realized what he was going to do he'd tied it several times around her wrists, binding them strongly.

The thrill that passed through her was like a brief orgasm, a shiver that hovered between fear and pleasure, the strangest feeling. I am completely at his mercy, she thought. He really has turned me into his slave.

Instinctively she fell to her knees. Darius chuckled, looking down on her, his sturdy legs astride and his hands on his hips. In a flash Claudia understood how soul-destroying it must be for a noble creature like Darius to be enslaved. He was a fine figure of a man, intelligent and strong, yet he was deemed to be inferior to the meanest and stupidest of the Roman citizens. An accident of fate had cast him in the role of underling, but it was against nature. This man was born to rule, to command, to give praise and punishment according to his own lights.

At the same time, Claudia felt a deep desire to be of service to him. This was the man she had beaten, tried to subdue, yet she had not succeeded in crushing his spirit. He remained spirited and free, a natural master forced, through circumstance, to be an unnatural slave. She deeply regretted the part she had played in humiliating such a noble soul.

"What do you want of me?" she asked, humbly, her whole body thrilling to the nearness of him. She believed that he would not harm her, yet she held him in awe.

His drew his whip out of his belt. Claudia shrank from him. She knew she would submit herself even to that for there would be some justice in it, but to her surprise he threw it away and unbuckled his belt. She felt a tide of apprehension cresting within her, suspense feeding her with fantasies that she hardly dared consider. What might a man of his virility and lustful inclinations do when he had a woman like her at his mercy?

Still smiling, Darius flung the belt away and drew his tunic over his head. He wore no loincloth and his member reared before her like a beacon, huge and threatening. Claudia felt her womb leap at the sight of it and knew that she wanted to be taken by that rampant monster, forcefully if need be. It was alien to her, the phallus of a slave, and yet he was a man like her husband and might be forgiven for wanting to conquer her, his mistress.

Uncertainly she held up her head, and their eyes met. There was a point of light deep in the black pools that glimmered for her, made her think he would be merciful. He grasped his cock at the root and waved it at her like a weapon.

"See this!" he growled. "I want you to taste it, woman. I want you to lick and suck at it until my hot seed spills into your mouth as your husband's seed has spilled into your cunt. Do it now, or it will be worse for you!"

Claudia found she needed no coercing. Her head bent eagerly to the task and while she tasted the first seeping of his glans her fingers clutched at the heavy orbs beneath, tenderly cradling them. She took more of his organ into her mouth, licking first around the tip and then down the shaft, hearing his satisfied grunts as she abased herself with more enthusiasm.

This is I, Claudia, wife of Tullus Octavius, giving tongue to a slave! she thought, marvelling at herself, and a deep shudder went through her secret places, filling her with untrammelled delight. She could feel herself growing reckless again, as she had whilst dancing, and her little button was throbbing with uncontrolled pleasure, leading her to suck and lick greedily at the man's robust penis. She squeezed her thighs together rhythmically as she worked and her breasts felt taut and hot.

Soon she was imagining him taking her, forcing his way into her with brutal passion. Her pussy ached to be filled with him, unimaginable desires seized her for experiences that she scarcely dreamed of. The autocratic slave had awakened her dormant libido and now she would do anything for him, anything!

Hot and salty, his spurting juices filled her throat and made her gasp and choke, but still he thrust into her willing mouth and her body thrilled to the meaty solidity of his cock. He had opened her up, all the long channel from one set of lips to the other, and she was on fire with lusty fervour until she erupted with volcanic force. The spasms of her climax spread throughout her entire being, fiercer than the pangs of childbirth, sweeter than wine mixed with honey and perfumed with roses. Yet there was a dark edge to it that made her grunt and squirm, a feeling of total subjection to the will of a goatish demi-god.

Torn apart by her emotions, Claudia scarcely noticed his exit. When she came to she was lying on the floor in the moonlight, shivering. She crawled into bed and fell into a fitful sleep.

In the morning the Saturnalian revels were over, and the King had fled into voluntary exile. When the mistress of the house discovered this the other slaves were surprised by the strength of her response.

"There was no need!" she wailed. "He was King for one night only. Today, order would have been restored and all misdeeds forgiven and forgotten!"

But she had forgotten that, according to ancient tradition, the Lord of Misrule is ritually sacrificed after his brief time of licence.

Whore

D. L. King

The dress was red. Red with a restrained intensity. A deep, wet sort of red. A red that slithered behind your eyes and rubbed up against your hypothalamus. Just seeing it on the rack caused an involuntary shiver, a contraction of my pelvic floor muscles and made my pupils dilate. Seeing the price tag almost dissuaded me from trying it on. Almost.

It fit like it had been made by my own private couturier.

The fabric was soft, with a slight tooth to the hand. It draped with its own gentle weight. The dress had a high boat neck, brushing just over the top of my clavicle, but with a fitted bodice. Not too tight, just enough to enhance my small breasts and cling gently to the curve my body made from torso to waist. Long, fitted sleeves and a slight flare from the hips, ending just below my knee, completed the picture, or at least, the front of the picture. Simple and elegant.

Gazing at my reflection in the three-way mirror in the fitting room at Sacks, the physical responses I had on seeing the dress on the rack, multiplied exponentially. In the back, the dress fell from the center seam of the sleeves in a deep V to just above – and I do mean just above – the crack of my ass. I couldn't stop looking at the way it seemed to attach itself to my sides, following the curve in at my waist and then the beginning of the curve back out at my hips.

I turned and turned. I moved my arms and twisted my body. What made it stay glued to me the way it did? I guess you get what you pay for.

I have no idea what possessed me to bring it to the conference. What use would I have for a dress like that at a conference with a bunch of neurologists and neurosurgeons? But after three days of panels and presentations, and then finally presenting my paper, at the tail end of the last day, to a three-quarters empty room of mostly men, checking their watches to make sure they didn't miss their airport shuttle, I'd had enough.

Knowing my presentation would be one of the last, I'd decided to take an extra night at the hotel and return home the next day, which was a good thing because I really needed a break after the last attendee thanked me for my presentation and practically ran out the door. It was only three o'clock, a little early for cocktails, so I decided to have a swim in the hotel pool and relax before dinner.

Like I said, I don't know why I brought the dress, but I do know why I put it on that night. Once rejuvenated from swimming and a nap, I realized I'd exhausted all my conference wear and I didn't think jeans and a T-shirt would cut it in the hotel's restaurant. The dress felt unbelievably sexy and I found myself being extra attentive to my make-up. I clipped my hair up in a sort of messy bunch, to get it off my neck. I didn't want my hair to break the expanse of bare skin from neck to ass. I remembered reading somewhere that Japanese kimonos were worn with the necks dipping down in back because Japanese men found the back of a woman's neck sexually stimulating. Looking at the drape of the dress, I had to agree with them.

I made my way down to the hotel bar. I love beautifully appointed boutique hotels and this one, in Los Angeles, was no exception. The bar was beautifully designed in rich browns, platinum and gold and the low tables and upholstered furniture looked comfortable and inviting. A few of the tables had groups of people gathered round them, but I never felt that comfortable sitting at a table when I was alone, so I chose a seat at the bar and ordered a pomegranate martini.

The drink was perfect. I soon became lost in thoughts about one of the presentations on using electrical implants at the base of the spine to combat chronic nerve pain. I raised my glass to the bartender and he nodded. As he was putting my new drink down, someone took the stool next to me.

"I've got it," a masculine voice said.

I'd guess he was about fifty, with hair greying at his temples. He wore a very expensive-looking suit and red tie. His nails were manicured. I looked from his hands to his face and he smiled. "Thank you. Were you here for the medical conference?" He didn't look familiar, but there had been quite a few people there.

"No, I'm with the financial conference. I manage a hedge fund."

As I'd never completely understood what that was about, I asked him what he did and we spent the next hour discussing money, finance and his life. The conversation was interesting and intelligent and, although he was older than the guys I was usually interested in, he was dead sexy. So, when he put his hand on my back and slid it down to the top of the dress and asked if I'd like to join him in his room, I didn't have to think too hard. I probably should have opted for dinner, but after two and a half martinis, my lizard brain was more interested in the meat in his pants than the meat in the restaurant.

His hand never lost contact with the small of my back as he escorted me to the elevators. On the way to the thirty-fourth floor, I looked him over more closely. I'd never been much for one-night stands. Maybe it was the alcohol, but I couldn't wait to see what he was hiding under those very expensive clothes.

His room was about ten floors higher than mine and had a better view. I went to the window to look out and he followed me. He bent down and kissed the back of my neck. His hands stroked my sides, over the dress before sliding inside.

"You are gorgeous," he said, hands exploring under the sides of the dress, up past the swell of my breasts and back down to my ass. He placed my hands on the window and reached down, under the hem of the dress, to slide it up in back. His breath caught as he ran his hands up my naked ass. "I don't suppose this dress is well suited to wearing panties, is it?" he asked.

I turned around and began to undo his tie and he caught my hands. "We have plenty of time for that," he said, sliding my dress up and over my head. Once off, he turned it right side out and draped it over the desk chair before taking a step back to look at me. The only things I had on were my shoes.

"Do you like the view?" he asked.

"Yes, I do. It's much—" His lips covered mine before I could complete the statement and his tongue parted them to explore my own. He tasted of very fine Scotch, with a slight hint of expensive cigar. My hands reached up to explore his chest and he spun me around, facing the glass again.

"I like it too," he said.

Again, he placed my hands above my head, against the glass, as he stroked and kneaded my breasts before pinching and pulling at my nipples. My clit was buzzing and I could feel moisture begin to seep from my pussy as his hands stroked lower, over my ribs, down to the V of my sex. He ran his hands over the crease between my legs and my cunt.

"Spread your legs."

As I did, his hands snaked around my thighs to stroke the crack of my ass before pulling my cheeks apart. I could feel his hard cock, under his trousers, as he pressed against me. Keeping my backside open with one hand, he cupped and squeezed my pussy with the other before inserting two fingers inside my slit and spreading my lips open.

"Oh God," I moaned as I was left open, front and rear. "Please," I murmured.

"Look at the view. I'm told you can see Catalina from here, if it's a clear day. Although I don't really know where it is. Maybe you can see it now. Are there lights on Catalina?"

I felt his thumb pressing against my anus and an involuntary shiver shook my head.

"No?"

"I don't know,'" I whispered. I pushed back against his hand, but he moved with me.

"Now, now. Don't get so anxious. There'll be plenty of time for that later."

I could feel my moisture coating the fingers pulling my cunt lips apart. "Please," I murmured again, rocking my hips from side to side.

"You're so wet." He closed his fingers and rubbed them against my opening. "Is this what you want? Feel how they slide." He teased my opening with the tip of one of the fingers, still keeping my lips parted with the other.

I thought I'd go crazy with desire. I'd never experienced anything quite like it before. I'm no stranger to sex. I'm a very carnal person. But this guy was directing sensations I'd never experienced before. He removed the finger from my opening and again pushed my lips apart with both fingers. He pushed the edge of his other hand deeper, splitting my buttocks even more. This time, I responded with a full body shiver.

"Lovely," he said. "Now, spread your legs further and press your tits against the glass. Yes, that's right." He withdrew his hands and I must have made a noise because he said, "Don't worry, I'll be back. I just need to get something from the bathroom. Look for Catalina and tell me if you see it."

I fogged up the glass, panting through my open mouth. All sorts of thoughts went through my head but moving from the position he'd placed me in wasn't one of them. I saw what I was fairly certain was the Santa Monica Pier, but I still had no idea where Catalina was, or if it could be seen from here. I was just beginning to realize how inane that thought was when I felt his hand on my waist and the other rubbing between my legs.

"Did you find it?" My head shook back and forth jerkily while I felt my muscles begin to tighten pre-orgasmically. "So responsive," he whispered against my neck as he buried a finger in my pussy and stroked my clit with his thumb.

My orgasm was mind-numbing in the way all little orgasms are when what you really want is a fully body release.

"Just to take the edge off a little bit," he said. He backed up and told me to turn around.

Slightly dizzy, I turned around. He was removing his tie and unbuttoning his shirt. He had a thick thatch of salt and pepper hair on his chest and it was easy to see that he worked out. He had a tighter chest and abdomen than the last thirty-year-old I fucked. He opened his belt and pants and removed them, along with a pair of red silk boxers, as I watched. His cock was both thick and fairly long and my mouth watered at the thought of having him inside me but first I wanted to taste him.

Silently, I knelt down in front of him and gently stroked his shaft, feeling the weight of his balls. As my lips enclosed the head of his cock I could feel all the air leave his lungs. He was warm and hard and velvety. He smelled of soap and maleness and as I tongued him, all the air left my lungs, too. I massaged his balls as I took more and more of him inside my mouth. He was too big for me to get him all the way in, so I licked and sucked up and down his shaft, paying special attention to the crown.

His hands were on my head, massaging my scalp and hair, and as I drove the tip of my tongue into the slit of his cock I could feel his balls begin to tighten. He grabbed a handful of hair and pulled my head away from his body. I strained to get his cock back into my mouth before I realized what had happened.

"Not yet," he said. "I want to come inside you, not in your mouth."

"Condoms," I whispered.

"Yes, of course. Only a figure of speech, my dear," he said. He helped me up and we walked to the bed. He pulled off the blanket and bedspread, letting them fall on the floor, and picked me up, placing me in the center of the bed. I noticed his dopp kit on the bed table. He removed a couple of condoms and a travel-sized bottle of lube. "May I fuck your ass?"

I love anal, more I think than vaginal sex, so I smiled and said yes.

"You're sure?"

"Oh yes," I said, drawing him to me for a kiss.

He positioned me on my hands and knees on the bed and, with one hand on my back, holding me in place, he drew his other hand down my ass, gently teasing the crack. He repeated the motion several times before withdrawing his hand. "Your body is amazing," he said.

It's nice to be worshiped and I basked in the sensation of his eyes on me until I felt cold lube dripping into my crack. His finger spread it around and began to tease me open, slowly and gently. He obviously knew what he was doing. He was both sensuous and gentle.

"I love your ass," he said and he inserted first one finger, then a second into me, slowly fucking me with his hand. "I can't wait to feel that tight muscle gripping me." He added more lube and kept up the gentle finger-fucking. He slipped a third finger in me and I moaned. "All right?" he asked.

"Slower, please. Just give me a minute to catch up," I panted.

He stopped fucking me and held his fingers in place. When my breathing slowed, he began his slow in and out motion again. I hadn't felt this full in a long time and I was eager to feel his cock in me. My clit felt heavy and swollen but I kept my hands on the bed. I wanted to wait for his cock before touching myself.

He withdrew his fingers and I felt completely empty. I whined and he said, "I think you're ready for me now."

I heard him tear the condom wrapper and seconds later I felt the tip of his cock pressed against my anus and more lube drizzled over me and, I assumed, his formidable shaft.

He slowly began to press against me until my sphincter began to allow the entrance. He was an accomplished ass fucker. He took his time. It was minutes before he was seated fully inside me and I felt his balls against my vulva. I tightened my muscles against him and I felt, more than heard, him chuckle. He hung there, without moving, letting me get fully used to the pressure. I wanted desperately to touch myself but I waited.

"All right?" he asked.

"Oh, yes," I sighed and he slowly withdrew, only to slowly push back inside.

Each time he withdrew a little more and pushed back in a little faster until I was moaning, pushing back against him, fucking myself on his cock faster and harder.

I started to lower my head to the bed so I could take my weight on my chest and shoulders to free my hands but he told me not to move. He'd been keeping me steady, using my hips as handles. He slid one of his hands around me and stroked my cunt, only to find me dripping.

"You're one wet little slut, aren't you?" he said as he buried two fingers inside my vagina and assumed the same rhythm he was using to fuck my ass. My God, my muscles were convulsing wildly around both his cock and his fingers. I tried to get my hand on myself but he said, no, not to do it. "You want to come?" he asked.

A low, guttural "yes" spewed from my throat.

"Well, you can't. Not yet."

I growled and pounded against his body, his balls slapping against my flesh.

"I control this fuck and I'm not ready to come yet." His rhythm changed, became more syncopated but his fingers stilled. He used his thumb to circle my clit, without touching it, until I screamed. "Oh, the poor little slut's getting frustrated." He withdrew his hand, altogether, and slapped my ass. I jumped and my muscles tightened against him again. "Oh, yeah," he laughed.

His rhythm built back up to a steady pounding again and he slid a finger inside me one more time. This time, instead of fucking me with it, he began to stroke the ridge just inside my opening. His strokes became harder and harder until I was panting and whining. He was still actively fucking my ass, but the pressure on my G-spot was quickly bringing me to orgasm. Before I could even say, "I'm gonna come," I was squirting fluid into his hand, something I'd never done before.

"Good girl," he said. "That's the way."

His hand slowed and withdrew but his pounding cock never faltered. After my initial tremors slowed, his rhythm picked up until it began to break up and become erratic, with more strength behind each thrust, as if he were trying to force his entire body into me, and with a few more thrusts, he came.

He grew still inside me and I felt his last few contractions as his orgasm finished. We stayed like that for a bit before he slowly withdrew to my groans of complaint. We rolled away from each other, sweating and panting, giving our heart rates a chance to slow down.

"Jesus," I said.

"You're not so bad, yourself," he laughed.

"Fuck. I never did that before. I never – ejaculated – before. Jesus."

Once the sweat dried, I went to the bathroom to clean up. By the time I'd dressed and come back into the room, he'd put his pants and shirt back on. It seemed our tryst was over.

"May I have your card?" he asked. "Perhaps the next time I'm in town, I'll call you."

I was at the door. "Oh, I don't live here," I said, digging a card out of my bag. As I handed it to him, he handed me something in return. I gave him a quick kiss. "Thanks, it was fun," I said.

He closed the door behind me and as I walked to the elevator I looked at what he'd handed me. It was money. Two five-hundred-dollar bills to be exact. I laughed all the way down to my floor. While waiting for room service to bring my dinner I wondered what he'd thought when he read my card:

April Harriman, MD
Neurosurgery
566 Park Avenue, Suite 105
New York, NY
212-555-2170
Service: 212-555-8310

New Orleans When it Rains

Maxim Jakubowski

Some cities smell of diesel fumes, others of cats, and then there is the smell of the sea, or mown grass, or the sharp odour of curry cooking endlessly in basement flats, or again the acrid combination of industrial waste and low-hanging fog.

New Orleans smells of spices, the humid twang of nearby Mississippi bayous and swamps and, in early morning, the unpleasant waft of stale beer on the Bourbon Street sidewalk following yet another night of drunkenness and minor-league bacchanalia before the high-speed hoses complete their work and sweep away the detritus of the previous evening's boisterous excesses. Mardi Gras adds yet another dimension of smells and spills and noise, or the Jazz Festival or New Year's Eve when it can take almost a quarter of an hour to walk through the massed crowds from Jackson Square to the corner of Toulouse and Bourbon. A cocktail like no other.

Even the music rising from bar to bar on each side of the street, battling for your attention, blues against jazz, show tunes fighting hard rock, Broadway schmaltz wrestling with tentative folk melodies, all seems to hold yet more fragrant promise of sensuality unbound.

There is no place like New Orleans.

And, year after year, I kept on coming back.

It was a city that talked to me, whispered to me from faraway through to my European shores of melancholy and I would treat myself again to the long plane journey, with the customary stopover in Chicago or Atlanta (and once Raleigh-Durham) to catch the right connection, arriving at Louis Armstrong Airport as night was falling, bone tired but my mind on fire, my senses waking with a sense of delight to the smells and sounds of the French Quarter.

Some cities are male. Others are distinctly feminine. New Orleans was assuredly the latter.

The way it tempted you, caressed you, kissed your emotions, licked your soul, fed you with sumptuous plates of jambalaya, warmed your stomach with okra-sticky but succulent bowls of gumbo, and its raw oysters once split open made you think of a woman's cunt as you sucked on them with undisguised greed and swallowed their juice and spongy flesh in one swift and easy movement.

It was a city I had brought women to.

Often.

In a spacious twelfth-floor room at the Monteleone I had undressed a preacher's wife from the Baton Rouge suburbs I had met on the Internet. She had driven down in her SUV to join me and timidly tapped on my shoulder while I examined the shelves at Beckham's on Decatur, where you could once often find some interesting first editions amongst the morass of worthless book club editions. That was where we had arranged to meet. I turned round.

"Martin?"

"Hi . . ."

She was voluptuous, a lovely face, somewhat bigger than I had expected from the photos she had sent me, but I knew those curves and the demure clothes she was wearing concealed terribly guilty urges and a determination to be bad.

Once in the hotel bedroom I stripped her and buried my face between her high but generous breasts, licked and bit her nipples to gauge her reaction while I cupped her cunt with my hands. She was terribly wet. Her kisses tasted of cotton candy.

When I undressed, she looked down at my half tumescent cock and exclaimed that it was so big. Which warmed my heart of course, although I knew it wasn't particularly so, just that her husband's (she had known no other man, she had once confessed) was smaller.

I drowned in the folds of her flesh, my thrusts inside the cauldron of her innards setting of concentric waves of shimmering movement across the surface of her skin.

We fucked ceaselessly, between walks through the Vieux Carré in search of beignets and praline-led sustenance. She only had two free days before family duties required her to be home.

"Where have you told him you are?" My finger inserting itself into her anus, feeling her squirm with added pleasure.

"It's not important. I don't want to talk about him." Her regal thighs clinching me in a mighty vice, her hand roaming hungrily across my balls, nail extensions dangerously grazing me.

Even though she lived barely a couple of hours away, it was only her third time ever in New Orleans. A city of sin that represented everything that was evil in the eyes of her social set. Which made her brief affair with me even more of a thing of the night, and a temptation her frustrations had been unable to resist. Meeting a foreigner with a quaint accent for purposes of the flesh in such a den of iniquity somehow felt right. We would never meet again after those frantic two days but before we lost contact I heard that she had left her husband and shacked up with a pharmaceutical salesman who was happy to fuck her once a day at least, unlike the monthly diet her religious fanatic of a man had restricted himself to, and always in the dark at that. I had, inadvertently, lit the fire and set her on the right (or wrong) path.

Then there was Natalia, a Lithuanian waif and single parent who lived in Delft in Holland, who had been a regular fuck buddy back in Europe. My evocative stories of New Orleans and its sweet craziness had convinced her to accompany me across the Atlantic. She made it a regular habit to meet men she came across in chat rooms and I knew all too well I was not her only sexual companion (I was aware of the Korean business student she had been giving Russian lessons to; the English engineering export rep; the married car dealer who wanted to leave his wife and live with her; and the many others she had no doubt omitted to inform me about).

She fell in love with New Orleans. The hotel I had booked us into upgraded us to a suite and she wandered naked and free across the lush carpet, the angle below her pert white buttocks always just that touch apart, a sheer invitation to grab her and do my worst. She was playful, capricious, deliciously wanton. No post-coital sadness for Natalia: the moment I'd withdrawn from her following each frantic fuck, she was up and about, eager to go out and sample more French Quarter atmosphere, tiptoeing away from the bed on her heels towards the open window and looking out from the balcony in the buff, attracting whistles and cries from the street beneath on most occasions, and then rushing back with a cheeky smile on her face at having exposed herself and straddling me, or standing above my still exhausted form on the bed, her legs obscenely spread, affording me a voyeuristic close-up of her still wet cunt and her luxuriant and curly dark pubic thatch.

One morning, she had arranged for a local pen pal to pick her up from the hotel in his car. We shook hands, both introduced to each other as just friends. He was supposed to take her for a drive along the nearby bayous, but I suspect they spent most of that morning in his bed. No matter, it gave me a handful of hours to rest from the fucking.

In my memory, Natalia and New Orleans went hand in hand in perfect harmony. The fragrance of southern flowers, magnolias et al and the intoxicating smell of her cunt. The delicate curlicues of wrought steel of the Crescent City balconies and architecture and the cheerful curve of her snubbed nose and the gap between her front teeth. The Queen of the blow jobs who always insisted on going pantie-less when we went out for walks or to eat. I'm still in touch with her. She finally gave in and married the car dealer and had a son with him, although it hasn't worked out and they are now separated.

Another bittersweet New Orleans memory is the Finnish interpreter from Seattle. High cheekbones, square jaw and a monstrous tease, it took me ages to finally get into her bed proper (days of foreplay and petting until she finally agreed that having spent an eternity in bed naked together, we should finally fuck . . .). She knew of my attraction to New Orleans and suggested I join her there; she was in town for a conference and had a large room in one of the massive impersonal hotels on Canal Street, with a view of the Mississippi from her window.

By then, she was beginning to lose her looks and I was no longer as much attracted to her, I must shamefully confess, but the lure of New Orleans was too much to turn the opportunity down. I entered her from behind, her pale body squashed against the bay window, suspended above the void, like in a bad erotic movie (which is probably why I enjoyed fucking her thus . . .). Her plaintive voice endlessly calling out my name, invoking it in fear, in lust, as I dug roughly into her, slapping myself into her, against her. She liked it rough, made you know wordlessly that she wished to be manhandled, to end up with bruises across her arms, her rump after the deed was done, although in private conversation before or after, during meals, or normal social interaction, she would always refrain quite religiously from raising any matters sexual. She still sends me birthday and Christmas wishes every single year.

And then there was Pamela, who was married to a famous experimental jazz trumpet player. We'd met in New York at a party. She was a friend of a friend. We would get together on every trip of mine to Manhattan where she shared a flat with a girlfriend near the Columbia campus. Her husband was always away on tour somewhere. God, Pamela, so many years ago now! Dark, lustrous, long hair, sublime arse, heavy breasts, how we fitted together so well! She joined me for a Bourbon Street Mardi-Gras folly, walking up and down the alcohol-soaked road at snail's pace, screams from the balconies for women to lift their tops and show their tits and be rewarded with cheap, colourful beads. Which she did, roaring with laughter, on a couple of occasions. Her breasts so shapely. Dead drunk, we finished up in someone else's hotel room with a group of local acquaintances of hers, which ended in a fumbled orgy in which all present ended up in bed together; I even think her husband might have been there too and watched us fuck before dutifully taking his turn with her, while I was being indifferently blown by his blonde companion, my cock likely still coated with Pamela's sweet juices. New Orleans madness!

All this to explain the guilty attraction for New Orleans that simmers uncontrollably beneath my skin.

The spicy food, the oysters and crawfish diet I could live on, the voodoo fumes, the rumbling and heavy flow of the river, the fireworks off Jackson Square on New Year's Eve as all the riverboats on the Mississippi toot their horns on the stroke of midnight as the traditional glitter ball concludes its descent on the sidewall of the old Jackson Brewery; the drunks and druggies in Louis Armstrong Park, the endless causeway across Pontchartrain Lake, the antique shop windows on Royal Street, the antebellum mansions of the Garden District, the halting tramways, the diners dotted across Magazine, the sounds of every conceivable sort of music filtering like smoke from the bars and clubs, the noise, the warmth, the humidity, these have all become the foundation stones of who I am and entrenched New Orleans in my blood.

Why I always go back.

Even when I have no reason to do so.

No touristic urges.

No woman.

        ★   ★   ★

When it rains in New Orleans, it pours. The skies open wide. It's the climate, you see, a sheer avalanche of water. Within a minute or so, the streets are like rivers. It never lasts very long, and in late spring or summer, within minutes, it has all evaporated as if by magic.

But if you happen to get caught, you're drenched from head to toe in the blink of an eye. Best take shelter fast.

I was wandering aimlessly through the French Quarter, smelling the smells, drinking the sights, my mind both at rest and empty, although my soul, as ever, yearned for things unsaid. I'd already strayed beyond the main Vieux Carré area, which is always so full of bars and stuff, and was walking by mostly boarded-up buildings and all-night groceries. I recalled that there was a small park a few blocks further to the north. Maybe I'd sit for a while, collect my thoughts, read a bit from the old pulp paperback I'd picked up earlier at the Rue Dauphine Librairie Bookshop.

My short-sleeve shirt stuck to my skin and sweat painted a sheen on my bare skin. I took a sip of water from the Coke bottle I carried along in my tote bag and looked up at the sky. A mass of dark clouds was passing across the sun, and there was a touch of electricity in the air. A big storm was nearing. I knew from experience how quickly it could break and looked around for possible shelter. The park I remembered was too far, even if my memory of its location was correct.

A drop of water cascaded over the tip of my nose. None of the buildings nearby extended canopies across the pavement, unlike in other areas of the French Quarter. I darted down a side street, hoping for a bar or a store where I could take refuge. The sky darkened.

There.

A small neon light advertising something just fifty yards away on the other side of the street. I hastened my pace. Reached the door of the joint just as the heavens opened, water splashing against my loafers.

Inside, the smell of stale beer and centuries of cigarettes impregnating wood and bodies.

I'd thought it was just a bar but noticed the small badly lit stage at the back of the room. A titty bar! A strip joint away from the normal beat. The sort of place I'd never really cared for much, whether in New Orleans or elsewhere. Muted sounds of a Rolling

Stones song shuffling in the background. "Sympathy for the Devil", I recognized. My eyes were becoming accustomed to the ambient darkness.

Men along the bar, or at small tables, nursing drinks, hushed conversations. I found a gap at the bar. Ordered a Coke and was told they only had Pepsi. Fine with me. "No ice, please."

As the barman, a swarthy red-haired bull of a man, delivered my glass, the lights illuminating the stage area at the back were switched on proper. The music on the jukebox fell to an abrupt halt and with an asthmatic click the club's sound system came to life. Conversations ceased, punters shifted in their seats, glasses clinked.

Just as the new music took flight, I briefly heard the monotonous sounds of the rain outside beating against the pavement and the club's unsheltered windows. It was a major downpour.

As the sound of the echoing rain quickly faded into the distance I realized that the music now spreading like a wave through the room was not the sleazy sort I'd somehow expected. No sweaty rock 'n' roll, or brassy big band tune or jazzy effluvia. It was actually classical. I closed my eyes for an instant in an attempt to dredge some form of recognition from my memory. Lazy strings, shimmering beaches of melody lapping against each other, Ravel or maybe Debussy.

A spotlight appeared out of nowhere.

Highlighting a dancer who had also materialized from the undefinable contours of the surrounding darkness.

Again she was not some identikit stripper, all crude make-up, vulgar attitudes and gaudy minimalistic apparel.

She was clothed in billowing white gossamer material, a flowing dress or sheet suspended in an imaginary breeze. Reminded me of Isadora Duncan in photos I'd seen in books or magazines, or maybe from a movie. Her own face was even paler than her thin dress. Just a savage slash of red lipstick, like a still bleeding wound, highlighting a set of perfect features. Cheekbones to kill for. Eyes deep with ebony darkness. A luxuriant jungle of blonde curls like a royal crown, falling all the way down to her shoulders, framing her face in total harmony.

She was almost motionless at first.

I looked up.

Met her eyes.

An endless well of sadness.

Her face expressionless.

The billowing white dress concealed any hint of the shape of her body, just thin legs and delicately shaped ankles below her bare feet. Again skin of abominable pallor.

One shoulder moved imperceptibly to the rising beat of the strings carrying the melody.

I held my breath.

Hypnotized.

The next five minutes saw me transported to another time and place altogether as I watched the young woman's set. Similarly, every other spectator in the room had fallen silent as we all watched transfixed the spectacle of her dance and gradual disrobing, as her movements invisibly accelerated and she began to dance, sashay, sway, shiver, perform, display herself, lullaby of desire, conjugating the geometry of her sexuality to a factor of infinity, stripping, moving, flying even, suspended in the winds of desire, spreading herself with both grace and total obscenity and making the whole spectacle a thing of innocence and unashamed pornography.

Her slender neck.

Firm small breasts. Nipples adorned with the same fierce shade of lipstick. Fiery. Hard.

Her washboard stomach. The miniature crevice of her navel where the steep descent towards her delta began.

Her shaven mons.

The highlighted straight vertical scar of her cunt opening, again defined by the scarlet hue of lipstick. The coral depths peering with every other movement inside her as she floated between the billowing flow of the thin white material of the dress she had now shed and swam through a world of emptiness and gauzy material to the quiet, peaceful beat of the music.

Darker, brown inner labia, teasing our eyes.

An imperceptible tattoo just an inch or so along to the left of the opening of her cunt. Looked like a gun, or maybe more traditionally a flower.

The harmony of her thighs. The golden down in the small of her back caught by the spotlight. The symmetrical orbs of her arse. The darker pucker of her anal opening as she bent forward and spread herself wide for our edification.

It could have been offensive, vulgar, dirty, but it was anything but.

She was confident with her body. Knew how beautiful she was,
Remained in control of every square inch of her immaculately
white skin and she was gifting us with its vision.

At no moment did she stray more than a few metres from the
fixed spotlight. No need for wasteful moments or poles for acro-
batics or seeking tips from the audience. Not that there was
anywhere they could be tucked as she had been quite naked
underneath the white Grecian-like dress. No exotic lingerie or
suspenders or garter belts. No superfluous items of clothing.
Once she was naked, it was something so natural, the way a
woman should always be.

And her face, ever expressionless. Distant. At peace.

The melody began to fade, the strings shimmering as the journey ended. I felt as if my heart had stopped.

The young pale blonde woman's motion slowed.

Her legs open at a revealing angle.

Her arms spread wide in both directions.

Christ-like. Crucified.

I held my breath.

The spotlight sharply disappeared and the darkness that took
over the room was blacker than ever.

By the time our eyes adjusted, the dancer was no longer there
and the small stage was empty.

Every spectator present was silent.

I finished my drink and walked outside.

The storm had passed and the street was almost dry already,
thin clouds of steam rising from the gutters as the rain evaporated in overdrive.

It was late afternoon.

In the distance the calliope of a steamboat on the Mississippi
chimed.

Damn, who was she?

I walked all the way back to Toulouse and then, impulsively,
trackbacked to the small strip club. The stage was occupied by a
black girl with silicone tits and an over-prominent Jennifer Lopez
arse and the customers now few, as if all the previous punters had
known no one could properly follow the blonde and there was no
point lingering.

The barman glanced at me. His eyes twinkled with malice.

"She only dances once a day," he said, predicting my
question.

"Oh . . ."

"She's dressing right now. Should be coming out any moment," he added.

"I'll wait, then."

Away from the stage, she appeared even taller, straight backed, imperious if fragile, now that she had wiped the savage lipstick away, her whole face a symphony of whiteness. I was unable to recognize the fragrance she wore.

She seemed to be still wearing the white gauzy dress she had begun her dance in, under a floor-length transparent plastic mac. And was still barefooted. A large canvas backpack hung from her shoulders. It appeared to be full of books and silk scarves in every colour of the rainbow.

"Loved your set. Can I offer you a drink?"

"I just had some water in the dressing room," she said. "No thanks." Looked at me blankly.

"Going home?"

"Maybe . . ."

"Hungry?"

"A bit. Dancing does eat up all your energy," she said.

"My treat. Anywhere you want to go."

She agreed to share an oyster po'boy at the Napoleon House.

Even now, I remember very little of our conversation although we must have spent more than an hour together eating and conversing. She never told me what her name was or anything about her life. I recall discussing books, she loved F. Scott Fitzgerald and let slip she had once lived in Manhattan. Every attempt on my part to find out how come she was now a stripper failed. She wasn't rude or offended by my questions, just indifferent. The time passed quickly and I assume that yet again I must have done too much of the talking, and bored her stiff with my usual stories and feeble anecdotes and jokes.

We walked from the Napoleon House to the small Faulkner House bookstore in the alley by Jackson Square where I failed to find a copy of a book I had been singing the praises of and had hoped to buy for her.

"Sorry."

"It's fine," she said, with a faint smile. "So?"

"So?"

"Do you wish to come back to mine?"

My heart skipped a beat. "That would be lovely," I replied.

It was a walk-up in a decaying building that might once have been a mansion's slave quarters just off Dumaine.

She closed the door and took my hand in hers. "Kiss me?" she asked.

How could I say no?

It wasn't fucking. It was making love in the most absolute sense of the term. It could only have happened in New Orleans.

Her bed became our battlefield.

I knew how pale her skin was but never guessed how soft and pliant her body would prove, a feathered cushion firm and languorous, a perfect treasure offered up for plunder and worse. Oh, the satin of her skin, the marrow-like texture of her lips, the way her fingers caressed my cock with shameless impunity and coaxed it to full length and thickness before she took me into the oven of her mouth, nibbling, teasing, biting with kindness, her tongue delving into my pee-hole with exquisite, measured probing, riding my lust, controlling it.

Her cunt, a map of untold treasure. Yes, it was a tattoo of a gun there, no larger than a nail, a Chinese miniature in the heavenly pornographic landscape of her intimacy, inner and outer folds delineated with mathematical precision, a medical sketch where every feature was drawn with close attention to detail and colour. Beckoning me. Opening for me like a flower of the tropics, swallowing me whole, feeding on me, feeding me.

New Orleans night.

The sound of her moans, the tightness in our throats as we pushed boundaries and held each other in the darkness like orphans in a storm. Every single woman I had touched, loved, brought to New Orleans led to this moment, this epiphany.

Fuck! Why wasn't it always like this?

Morning. Lazing spreadeagled in a crazy geography amongst the tangled sheets of the bed. Our smells mingling, our sweat a potent cocktail of spent lust.

"Hello. Shouldn't I at least know your name?" I asked, a fingertip lingering indecently across the ridge of her cunt lips.

"Good morning, lover."

She rose from the bed, brushing away my greedy hands. Regal. Pale. Naked. My cock hardened again in an instant, despite its rawness.

She smiled and tut-tutted.

"Later," she said. "Offer me breakfast."

We dressed and walked out into the hesitant early morning sun to Jackson Square for traditional beignets and coffee at the Café Du Monde.

She still wore the white, billowing dress, a tall, pale ivory figure making her way across Decatur.

Wiping away the powdered sugar that had spilt across my dark shirt, I looked up to see the sun fading.

She followed my eyes.

"Seems like another storm is on the way," I said.

She nodded.

We began to make our way back to her apartment, hastening our pace as the dark clouds gathered menacingly above.

But we only made it halfway there before the heavens opened.

I laughed as the first drops fell on my tousled hair, turned towards her expecting a similar smile. But the look on her face was one of terror.

"It's only rain, water," I said.

And, one final time, I witnessed the despair that lingered deep down in the dark pit of her eyes.

The rain fell, implacable, surrounding us, submerging us.

Quickly soaking the thin material of her thin dress, instantly revealing the sweet contours of her body, the now transparent gauze sticking to her skin, betraying the dark hardness of her nipples and when she attempted to move, the cleft of her cunt. At any other time, I would have found this highly erotic and arousing. But not at present.

As soon as her total nudity beneath the dress was betrayed, she began to fade.

It only took a few seconds.

Fading.

Like melting in the rain.

Her contours losing their firmness, their definition. Her pale skin disappearing with every new drop of rain.

I stood there with my mouth open.

Her lips parted as if she wanted to tell me something but not a sound emerged and then she was gone.

The rain beat against the pavement with monotonous regularity, cutting through the air where once she had stood. And soon, as ever, the storm passed, and the water just evaporated and disappeared in little swishes of thin steam. Just like she had. And

I was left alone, on the corner of Conti and Royal, standing like a fool in front of the Federal Building.

I didn't know what to think at first.

Was this a joke? Was this illusion, magic?

My mind in a tizzy, I ran back towards her apartment but was unable to find it again. But then, in New Orleans, so many houses look alike and my mind had been on other things when we had first made our way there.

I tried to compose myself.

Went to my hotel to change clothes. Took a shower, reluctantly washing away her scent from my body, from my cock.

Then rushed out to look for the strip joint where I had first come across her. Half believing it also would have disappeared from the map.

But it was there. In the same place as the previous day.

Closed. It was still only mid-morning.

I found a second-hand copy of *The Beautiful and the Damned* at the bookshop on Dauphine. Hadn't read it in decades. It helped me pass the time until the bar opened.

Standing on the opposite pavement, late afternoon, I saw the blinds rising and the click click of the door's lock.

A short, greying man was wiping the tables clean with a wet cloth, and no sign of the customary barman.

My questions hit a blank wall.

No, it had been ages since they'd featured dancers.

No, they no longer had a license.

Elderly regulars slowly streamed in.

None of them had any memory of when if ever the place had been a strip joint. All it was these days was a convenient place to get a quiet drink.

Somehow, it was what I expected.

Made a strange sort of sense.

I finally sat myself at the bar and asked the middle-aged woman now serving for a drink.

As she bent down to get the bottle from the lowest shelf of her glass-fronted fridge, I caught sight of a fading framed photograph crookedly stuck to the large mirror that formed the back wall of the bar.

Squinted.

Recognized the pale features of my heavenly blonde stranger behind the sepia tones.

"Who is that?"

"Oh, that . . . Just an old photo taken some sixty years ago when the bar was a thriving private club for gentlemen," I was told. "Must have been one of the dancers."

I gulped down my drink and walked out.

Tomorrow, I will check out of my hotel, stroll down Royal Street and head towards Canal, leaving the mighty flow of the Mississippi behind me, and I will wait for the rain to come and maybe I will melt away and meet her again on the other side of the humid New Orleans curtain of rain.

For sure.

Where I Can See You

Remittance Girl

"Isn't she pretty?"

He pressed the flat, curved surface of the straight razor across her lower lip and drew it along. The blade so finely milled it slid as if oiled. On its journey over her skin, the steel leached the warmth it found there.

Suddenly she knew nothing. All her dark cravings, all the sensory yearnings for the cut and the bleed evaporated. Fear flared and burned her eyelids. She forced herself to ride the surge of adrenaline, to taste the tang of metal on her tongue, to let the dread sing in her limbs. As long as he was with her the fear could be forged into pleasure.

Slow.

She imagined herself as syrup gradually cresting the bowl of a spoon. No sudden moves. No twitches. No starts. Just breathe through it.

There were three of them in the room. Trust could take you only so far, but the blade was the blade – thirsty in its own right – it would cut what it touched.

Cold.

There was a subtle urge to anthropomorphize the razor. To give it more volition and power than it deserved. But doing so would deny both of theirs. So, no. There were only two of them – both with volition – and a tool.

Once she made certain, out of the corner of her eye, that the blade was well away from her face, she looked up at him. It seemed the steel he held in his hand had stolen all his warmth as well.

Freeze.

"She's pretty. But only because you're holding her," she said in a rust-dry whisper.

He levelled his gaze at her. She knew better than to blink or look away. He could read her soul, but that didn't bother her. If she couldn't have borne that scrutiny, she wouldn't have been there.

"Talk to me, please," she begged, sounding small and needy.

That was a mistake. He dropped down in front of her and smiled the terrible smile that wasn't a smile at all.

"What do you want me to say? That everything's going to be fine? That it was all just a joke? That I'm not getting hard at the thought of parting your skin with this pretty little thing? Is that what you want? You want out?"

Then she realized her mistake wasn't a mistake at all. It was the show of weakness he needed to allow him passage through the door of his conscience. Because unlike most of the other sadists she had known, this one had never sought to reason away his desires. He despised himself for what he wanted, and she loved him for his refusal to take comfort in lies.

"No," she said. "No I don't."

"Are you sure? Because if you aren't sure, then leave now."

"I'm sure," she lied.

But already he was pulling the buttons of her shirt open. Already she had started to cry.

Shirtless and on her stomach, her field of vision offered nothing but a bleak desert of crumpled white sheets. He touched her back, smoothed his big hand across it. Perhaps it was a gesture of affection, but she couldn't see him any more, read his face, or his mood. It felt more like a survey of real estate.

The moment she felt the swab, she knew where he'd cut. Wet at first and then icy as the alcohol evaporated. As hard as she tried to picture the razor touching her skin and drawing its hurtful little line, she couldn't. The image squirmed away, eel-like and the words to construct the image were equally indistinct.

Him. Who was he now? This man who was about to part her flesh with his sharp, shiny little toy? She said his name: consonants and vowels vaporous as they left her mouth, freezing in the air, falling like snowflakes on the sheets. Panic licked the hinges of her jaw.

He must have seen it, because he stroked her back again and made a soothing, hushing sound. "It's OK, love. It's going to be fine." And under the words, there was such a hunger.

It would be better that way, he had said: on her stomach with the cuts on her back. There weren't so many nerves there and she wouldn't see the cuts or the blood. At the time, it seemed logical and he'd sounded so definite – so sure. But now, with her hands fisted in the sheets, an awful sense of isolation rushed towards her like an avalanche thundering down the snow-white field of linen.

She had made a promise. Told him she could do this. Told him she wanted it. She wanted to know this part of him. She would love it. She could take it.

The next touch was not a caress. It was too sure, too firm. She heard him inhale as the tiniest chill touched her skin. That first tiny pressure and the skin tug. Not pain but wrongness. God-awful wrongness as it pulled over what seemed like a mile of back. God, she thought, he's fucking with my head. He's used the blunt edge of the razor. Then the sting came.

"Oh, Christ," she whimpered into the bed.

"Sh-h, pet. It's just a little cut. You did really well. Really well." It did not sound like him.

Her jaw locked, her tears brimmed over, and her chest would simply not expand enough to take in the air she needed to breathe. She tried to raise her head to look, but her muscles would not obey. They jumped and twitched and would not stay still.

The promise was a steel band around her skull. Pressing and pressing in. Like the blade. Cutting off the top of her head and slicing into grey matter. Shutting off the parts of her that could feel or care or reason.

Before he was through the second cut, she said it.

This was not about delighting in the fantasy of ravishment, or pretending to be unwilling. And so the safe word was not something obscure or quaint or quirky. She spat it out like a chunk of lead, black and hard and raw. "Stop."

And he did.

A warm trickle slid under her arm, over the side of her breast. Hot in the silence. Then another. The same temperature as the tears puddled next to the bridge of her nose.

She felt a touch on her shoulder. Tentative. Him. But she didn't know who that was any more. She would have known if it were really him, because he loved her. She surely would feel that. Wouldn't she?

"Love. Pet. It's all good."

They were the words he used for her, but somehow now they sounded sharp, brittle as the glass of a broken light bulb. There was an awful resignation in them.

It wasn't really "all good". It was all fucking bad. All just shit.

Where was he and why had he left her here with her promise and this cold, distant puppet of a stranger who sounded just like him?

Part of her knew it was him, of course. But she felt betrayed, abandoned. As if he'd let something of himself walk away when he'd picked up the razor.

She was too ashamed to look at him as she rolled away, and sat up. The cuts twinged as she moved and she felt the burn as another trickle of blood ran down the length of her back.

Her shirt was on the floor. Her bra was somewhere else. It didn't matter – she didn't need it. The shirt would do.

"No. Don't do that," he said as she bent to pick it up. "At least, let me clean the cuts and cover them." The voice was cold. Sensible. Reasonable. Formal. Not him.

He said her name – firm like a snap – reached across the bed and curled a hand around her upper arm as she struggled to do up her shirt. Her fingers were shaking so badly it was almost impossible and the goddamned button holes where swimming in and out of focus as she fumbled.

All she needed to do was to stand up and make it out the door before he felt compelled to show it to her. That is what he'd do. He'd told her so. Perhaps she wasn't brave enough to keep her promise to him, but she could leave without being told to get out. If he'd just let go of her arm.

He said her name again, breaking it into syllables. It forced her to look around.

It was him.

Him after all.

Him caught in a purgatory of cold and angry, scared and hurt. Stricken and sickened and kicked in the gut. All straining under a taut, thin plastic wrap of control.

The bubble burst in her chest and she sobbed. "I'm so sorry. So sorry. I love you, but then . . . suddenly . . . you weren't there . . . gone and . . . gone . . ."

He moved behind her, enfolding her in his arms, pulling her

tight against his chest. The cuts burned pleasantly in the press of his heat. His chin tucked into the curve of her shoulder and he tilted his head against hers. "Sh-h. Just be quiet for a bit."

In the silence she heard him breathe and felt his heart beating against her back. The beat prickled at the wounds. But that was fine. It was safe like this. Her organs could tumble out of her body and it would still feel safe with him holding her.

And in the silence she could think. Her mind cleared and she knew exactly what she'd done. She'd panicked. She'd lost her nerve and done what she'd sworn not to do – she'd clawed her way to the surface, past him, through him, anything to get to the air and the light.

He'd told her she didn't have to agree to let him cut her. That his love was not conditioned on that. But that if she did, if he showed her that side of himself and she balked, that was different. That, he wouldn't take. Those were the rules, and the rules kept him together. Kept him civilized. Kept him sane.

She had fallen in love with him for that. For his precision, his logic and his aching honesty. Yet in one moment of stupid, blind fear, she'd driven a massive truck through it all. There was no way back from that.

So this – these arms around her, this breath on her cheek – was not forgiveness or understanding. This was aftercare. What he felt obliged, as a matter of honour, to do. It was just like him to be able to do it with such sincerity.

"I'm so sorry."

"I know you are." He pressed his lips to her cheekbone; repeated the words into her skin. "Don't be."

She inhaled deeply and let it out in a stammering, rickety breath. "I'm going to go now. I know what I've done. And I remember what you said."

"You do, do you?"

"Yeah." A fresh wave of tears blurred her vision. "I'm so fucking in love with you."

"Hmm. Well, if you really are then prove it. Take off your shirt and let me clean and cover those cuts. Can you do that?"

It was as if he were speaking to a child. She nodded, childlike in return. When he withdrew his embrace, she looked down and realized just how badly she'd screwed up her blouse. The buttons were stuck in the wrong holes, some were missed and the whole thing was askew. Undoing it again was easier.

"Come on," he said. "Over here." He patted the centre of the bed and soaked a ball of cotton in disinfectant.

Warily, awkwardly, she moved into place. "I'm so sorry," she repeated inanely.

"This is going to sting like a bitch."

"I know. That's OK."

He gave a tight laugh. "And I'm going to enjoy it."

She looked back over her shoulder at him, unable to stop herself from smiling. "I know that, too."

"Good," he said, and slapped the dripping cotton ball onto her back at the top of the first cut.

The liquid streamed in a rivulet down her back, making it bow in the chill. Then, like a wicked skewer, the sting sliced through her spine, lighting up nerves all the way through to her chest.

"Oh! Fuck!" She was gasping for air, clawing her nails into her thighs and, the grin still stuck on her face. It was the shock of the pain that carved a hysterical giggle that interfered with language. "You . . . you fucking bastard!"

He clicked his tongue and slid the ball down the length of the wound. Just as when he'd cut into her, he did it with a slow deliberation. "You know I am."

"You are," she gasped, hiccuping, giggling, losing it. "Jesus, you are! And I still fucking love you."

"I love you too," he said, firmly slapping another soaking wad of cotton on the second cut.

She could hear the smile in his voice, just before she felt the pain again. "Jesus FUCKING Christ!" It came out as a screech. Her back bowed again, unbidden. The pain was far worse this time. Perhaps the second cut had been a little deeper.

"Shush your whining, woman." He swabbed his way down the cut. The room stank of rubbing alcohol. It hurt to inhale it.

"Fuck, fuck, fuck! It bloody stings!" But that was an understatement. Her whole upper back was on fire.

"That's how you know it's doing good," he said primly.

She turned and launched herself at him, wrapping her arms around his neck and although the urge to kiss him was strong, she stopped and met his eyes.

"I love you."

He tilted his head. "I heard you."

"Did you?"

He cupped her ass and pulled her onto his lap. "Yes. Did you hear me?"

His lips were so warm when she kissed him. And, even through the stench of isopropyl, she could smell his spit, his sweat, his skin. She tightened her embrace and kissed him deeper, waiting for him to open his mouth, but he didn't.

"It felt like you left. Like it wasn't you. I couldn't see you. Sense you. Where the fuck were you?" A pair of tears raced their way down her cheeks.

He nodded.

"I'm sorry I told you to stop. It was the fear," she said

"Fear of the pain?"

"No."

He nodded again, slowly. "The fear of me."

"No!" She furrowed her brow. "The fear of not-you."

Big palms slid up her back and came to rest just below her shoulder blades. She winced.

"Not-me."

She stared at him. "I can't explain it. This," she said, tugging his head against hers, "is you."

He gave the spot covered by his left hand a rub, then a slight squeeze.

"Ow!"

"Still me?"

"Of course. Still you."

The next squeeze was considerably crueller. It made her gasp. Not the pain – that was there and she didn't like it – but the odder sensation of the newly clotted cuts breaking open.

"And now?"

"Still you," she groaned, kissed him again.

This time his lips softened, his mouth parted under her petitions. One arm banded her waist and pulled her against him tight. The hand over her wounds felt warm and slick. He squeezed again, even harder, forcing a throaty cry from her. But he soothed her with his tongue, stroking it along hers, tempting her to suck it. And she did.

Between her parted legs, through the layers of her wadded up skirt, she felt his erection, hard and thickening. There was an instant rush of relief that streaked down from the base of her skull and settled in her groin, turned feral and hungry. Her hips moved, pressing into him, grinding against the cock that strained his pants.

"Cut me now. Can you cut me now?" she panted. "Like this?"

His hand skimmed over the skin of her back. So easily, wet with her blood.

"No."

"Why?"

His hips rolled, pushed back. "It's not safe."

"Oh," she muttered, worming her hand between them, tugging at the button of his trousers, trying to work down the kinked, distorted zipper. "Why?"

Her fingers pushed aside the remnants of his clothes and curled around his cock. It pulsed in her hand. This she knew. This she trusted. This part of him – sometimes all of him. She let her fingers graze the hot, soft skin, upwards, until the cockhead fitted snugly into the cup of her palm.

"You know why."

His hips arched, pushing himself through her loosely held grip. He cradled the back of her neck, grasped it tighter and pulled her back to his mouth. The slow thrusts through her curled fingers spoke to her of so much presence, so much intention. To be here. To be with her. To be in her. It made her cunt spasm with a needling ache.

When he bent her backwards, onto the bed, she didn't wait for him. She wrenched at the sides of her panties, tugging them down her legs, smearing her thighs with her own wetness and kicking them off one ankle before he settled between her spread legs.

It was then she saw his hand. The palm was smeared crimson. The blood had grown darker, tacky in the air. She reached for it and laced her smaller, paler fingers between his.

He entered her so slowly she thought she was dying by degrees. His eyes were open, locked to hers, but blind in that overwhelming pleasure of the first few moments of penetration. As he began to fuck her, she could not let go of his hand. Would not let go of it even as he slipped the other hand beneath her ass to thrust deeper into the tight liquid ache that constricted around him. Not even as they grew greedier and more frantic. Not as she shuddered and arched her body halfway off the bed, feeling the sheets stick and then rip away from her drying blood.

She half sobbed, half screamed his name as she came and felt him thrust with more violence, through her cunt's contractions, slipping into that strange pleasure hum of perpetual motion until he hilted, stilled, and erupted in thick heat against her cervix. She squeezed him fiercely – his hand, his cock – and the spasms of pleasure straightened his torso and locked his hips.

Afterwards, after he'd crushed her in mock collapse, after he pressed his face into the crook of her neck and groaned, after he'd smeared his face against her cheek and kissed her, he looked at the hand.

"I think it's stuck," she said, trying to disengage her sticky, interlocked fingers from between his. Finally they came free. "And I think I'm stuck to your sheet, too."

He kissed the top of her breast, just above a nipple. "We can fix that, love."

"I'm sorry," she whispered. "I broke my promise."

His dark eyes settled on her face and then darted away. He shook his head and looked at her again. "I'm sorry I wasn't all there."

"What do we do now, then?"

"I don't know."

She licked her dry lips. "Next time . . ."

"Oh," he whispered, dark and arch. "There's going to be a next time, is there?"

"Yes. Next time, cut me where I can see you."

The Blood Moon Kiss

Mitzi Szereto

Savannah, Georgia

The branches of a weeping willow caress the dark grass as gently as a lover's fingers. The artificially enhanced moonlight above illuminates the leaves with a silvery cast that's almost ghostlike as Christine moves into place, the cool night mist swirling around her bare feet and ankles. She's wearing only a nightgown, knee-length, pristine white, the fabric so gossamer that little is left to the observer's imagination. She's naked beneath it.

"Action!" shouts Mark Gaitzberger, director of *The Blood Moon Kiss*.

Strong male fingers reach out from behind, seizing Christine's long black hair and pulling her head back to expose the vulnerable flesh of her neck. An arm appears from the same direction, fitting her waist into its vise. Her nipples stiffen as she feels a hot mouth fastening onto her jugular, followed by the pricking of sharp teeth. At that moment she experiences the shimmering of an orgasm, which begins at her neck and moves down her body, exploding into a thousand fragments of pleasure at her groin. If not for the arm encircling her waist, she would have collapsed to the ground. The bodice of her gown darkens as wetness streams from her neck. She doesn't need to look to know it will be red.

How did it come to this?

Six Weeks Earlier

When you live in a place like Georgia and you get a call from your agent telling you he's just landed you a part in a hit television series that's being shot in Savannah – *and* you don't even have to audition for it, you aren't about to argue. I mean, let's get real: Georgia isn't exactly Hollywood. And for a Southern gal like me, this is home. Despite having no blood ties, I feel rooted here, a product of the soil like a Georgia peach. It's hard to explain, but something holds me here; maybe I was a Southern belle in a previous life, living on a big plantation and drinking mint juleps all day until some Rhett Butler turned up on my doorstep to ravish me. I just know that I don't want to be anywhere else, even if it means I'd stand a better chance at hitting the big time if I left. I'm happy enough to get the occasional role in a play at the Actor's Express Theater in Atlanta or in a TV commercial. By the way, that was me in the ad for Billy Bob's Burger Emporium. I was the waitress on the roller skates. You know, the one with the big beehive hairdo balancing the huge tray of food. I nearly twisted an ankle in those goddamned skates. I guess some things are better left in childhood.

I did wonder about the audition issue. It's practically unheard of to hire an actor without having that actor read for the part or do a screen test (unless maybe they're Johnny Depp or Angelina Jolie), but as they say, don't look a gift horse in the mouth. I've seen several episodes of the show and have to admit it's pretty good, as prime-time soap operas featuring a bunch of vampires go; I could do a lot worse. I also have to admit that one of the actors in it is really hot, and the thought of working with him gets me really hot as well. Not too professional, I know, but there you go. Not that I expect anything will happen – the guy's like the biggest heartthrob on television; he probably has women (and maybe even a few men) throwing themselves at his feet on a daily basis. Fred, that's my agent, said the series' producer had seen me on a public service ad for a battered women's shelter; I'd done this sort of one-woman performance deal, speaking directly to the camera as a wife who'd run away from her abusive husband. I realize it's only a TV commercial, but I'm proud of my work on it. I think I managed to portray just the right amount of fear and anguish. It was probably the fear component that got the producer's attention. Whatever, I'll be earning more money than I've ever earned in my life. By the time my stint is finished, I should be able to put a nice down payment on a house and maybe get a new car, too. Not bad for a few weeks' work.

Savannah

The night I first arrived on the set, seeing him for the first time . . . the entire planet seemed to shift. I was told in advance that most of the shooting would be done at night, so I'd already begun to prepare by sleeping during the day, practically living the life of a vampire before I'd stepped foot in Savannah. I'd met pretty much everyone in the cast and crew before I did my debut episode – well, everyone except the one person I most wanted to meet. I don't want to sound like some starry-eyed teenager here; I mean, we're all professionals, peers, and it's been a long time since I was a teenager, but I felt as if my heart would go bursting out of my ribcage, that's how excited I was to finally meet him.

Talen Dashkovar. God, even his name is enough to give you goose bumps.

We never got a chance to rehearse together before we came face to face for the first time. They'd used a stand-in for him, since he felt our debut scene would be much more powerful if we hadn't met yet. Apparently Talen's one of those method actor types who actually becomes the character he's playing, and being as popular as he is, no one's inclined to disagree with him. I also heard some of the crew saying that he was feeling slightly under the weather (*again*) and resting up for the shoot. Judging from last season's episodes, he did seem to have a rather fragile quality beneath the boyish masculinity, though that might've been down to his pale complexion, which I'd assumed was enhanced by make-up so that he looked more vampiric. I already knew from the script that I, too, would become paler with each episode, indicating that my life was slowly ebbing away, along with the blood in my veins. With my naturally black hair, the contrast with my skin would be made even more dramatic.

Our debut scene was brief, though that didn't lessen its impact. My character and his character share one of those fleeting-glance moments, full of lust and desire and the promise of more to come. It's late at night and Meridian (me) is walking past the fountain in a deserted Lafayette Square when Kyle (Talen) suddenly appears from the opposite direction. We both come to an abrupt stop, our figures illuminated by a full moon (with some added help courtesy of the lighting guys). Our eyes meet and hold; his are green and staggeringly beautiful, at times almost iridescent. I've never seen eyes like his before, not even on a cat, and they're not enhanced by any form of trickery from the make-up department or wizardry from special effects either.

Meridian is unable to move, she's so spellbound by him. After about a minute, Kyle smiles ever so slightly and steps aside, allowing her to pass. She awakens as if from a trance and glances around in confusion. Kyle has vanished from the square. A slow pan of the area reveals Meridian's lone figure standing by the fountain looking lost.

And Meridian *is* lost. Just as I am lost.

It's difficult to tell where he's from. His accent is like no other accent I've heard. At times it sounds Southern, then a moment later it sounds European, but it's always cultured, no matter which way it swings. My Southern accent has been beaten out of me by years of acting classes, leaving behind a generic North American one, which I can adapt at will, depending on what part I play. But Talen's a mystery. It's as if he came from out of nowhere and suddenly landed smack dab in the middle of a hit TV series. Before I left for Savannah, I tried to find out what I could about him from the Internet, but most of what came up was information related to the show, including some video interviews of him with other cast members. He always seemed to speak only if he had something of relevance to say, as though measuring each word's importance before uttering it, whereas his co-stars jabbered away with a youthful ebullience they apparently hadn't yet grown out of.

So when Talen invited me out for a drink on the first Sunday evening we had off since we started filming, I probably answered much too quickly. His mouth quirked up in one corner with what I came to associate as his trademark smile, as he named a popular place on River Street that overlooked the Savannah River. Apparently it used to be a cotton warehouse and was considered a place of historical interest, but one that served booze. I admit I dressed with a lot of care for the occasion, wanting to be sexy in an understated classy way – simple black dress, knee-length, bare legs, strappy sandals, lacy bra and panties, the latter of which I rarely wore (the lacy kind) since I generally had no occasion to, not being that big on dating. I guess it's safe to say I'm a loner – no surprise, considering my background. I'm not sure what I expected to happen between us, but the fact that *something* was happening between us was pretty obvious.

He was waiting by the bar, dressed casually in jeans and a long-sleeved black shirt, which had a couple of buttons undone at the top, revealing a discreet gold chain along with a tantalizing hint of smooth flesh like polished ivory. I wondered if the rest of him was as smooth and unmarred, since it looked doubtful he frequented the beach or tanning salon – at least not while playing the part of Kyle anyway. We greeted each other with a touching of hands, followed by a light kiss on the lips, which almost sent me reeling backward as if a current of electricity had been shot through me, though I managed to recover in time. "You're looking very lovely tonight, Christine," he said, his eyes looking more iridescent than I remembered. I nodded, unable to speak. He gestured to the bartender, and a moment later a glass of chilled white wine was placed before me. Whether I'd actually ordered it I can't say, but it is my drink of choice. How Talen could have known this I've no idea.

After a few nervous sips, I found myself talking all about my life, from my lonely childhood with foster parents who cared only for each other to my very first lover, who cared only for himself – a selfish young man I'd met at college who abandoned me when we thought I might be pregnant. I couldn't believe I was revealing so much about myself; it's not like me to open up to people, especially someone I barely know. Talen listened attentively and with appropriate sympathy, though he offered no private revelations of his own. I suppose I could have asked, but somehow it felt intrusive to do so.

No sooner had I finished my wine than another was put before me, and for Talen a glass of absinthe, for which the bartender performed that whole spoon and sugar-cube thing. I'd never tried it before, and Talen offered me a taste. I found it pretty vile, although he assured me I'd soon get used to it. I thought that a rather strange thing to say, but then Talen was . . . well . . . *strange*.

Sometime afterward I recall being in the back seat of a taxi, pressed close to him as the night flew past outside the car's windows. Then suddenly we were on a deserted beach among the sand dunes, the moonlight sparkling blue-white diamonds on the Atlantic, the scent of salt in my nostrils and the taste of it on my lips. It tasted like blood.

Her dress lies in a dark puddle on the white sand as she stands naked on the beach, facing away from him toward the watery horizon. His head is bowed into her neck, his arm crossed over her breasts, holding her firm against his chest. The nail of his thumb flicks against one nipple until it can harden no further, at which point he takes it between the pads of his thumb and index finger, pinching it lightly, then less so, varying the pressure so that she doesn't know what to expect, stopping just short of causing actual pain. She feels herself growing wet, so wet that it reaches her inner thighs, and she adjusts her stance, parting her legs to keep them from sticking together. The sand has retained the heat of the sleeping sun, and it feels warm and comforting against the bare soles of her feet. The moonlight makes her pale flesh look even more so, though with a blue tint that gives her an ethereal quality, like that of a ghostly angel. His hand leaves her breast to locate the V where her thighs meet. With a pairing of fingers he parts her folds, exposing the intimate pink to the sea air. The shock of what he's just done stops her from breathing. Her response is internal, all yearning thoughts and flowing juices. There's no movement from either of them, save for the gentle suction of his lips on her neck and the rhythmic sound of the ocean lapping the shore. The progress of the moon across the dark sky is the only thing that alerts her to the fact that time is passing.

They remain two silent figures on the beach, frozen in time and space, one fully clothed, the other exposed and vulnerable in her nudity. His fingers continue to hold her open, though he makes no move to stimulate her. It's as if he's tormenting her or displaying her secrets to some unseen observer – some nocturnal peeping Tom who got lucky tonight and, rather than spying on a pair of teenagers going at it with unpracticed haste and little in the way of finesse, instead finds himself being treated to the sight of a man offering a detailed exhibition of a woman's genitals. Through half-lidded eyes she looks around, expecting to see a figure crouching in the tall grass of the dunes. But there's no one, no one on the beach but them. For a moment she feels almost disappointed.

A breeze off the ocean kisses her exposed flesh, as if drawing attention to her wetness. It's bubbling from her now, frothing hot and needy. The sea mist licks at her like a tongue, licking that place the man holding her has forced into exposure. And when she comes, she weeps from the force of it.

They lie together in a small clearing in the woods, chest on chest, pelvis on pelvis. The camera moves in on them as Kyle dips his head to drink from Meridian's neck, his left hand tenderly caressing her face and hair as if he's making love to her rather than placing her at risk of being transported from one of the living to one of the dead. Meridian moans with what sounds like orgasmic pleasure, and her hands reach up to Kyle's head, her fingers twining in his dark hair. There's a brief moment when they tighten their grip and actually pull, though this moment quickly passes, making the observer wonder if it was ever there at all. The camera lens does not pick up on the fact that Talen's other hand has slipped between their two pelvises, or that his middle finger is wedged deeply inside her.

"Cut!" shouts the director.

Neither Talen nor Christine moves. He continues to lie on top of her, his face buried in her neck, his heart pounding hard against hers. Although Christine's eyes are closed, her lips quirk upward into a tiny smile, as if she holds a secret.

The crew collects their gear and moves off, chuckling among themselves good-naturedly at an on-camera romance that has obviously moved off-camera. Best of luck to them, they think, having seen their fair share of such things over the years. Christine and Talen make a striking couple. In fact, they look as if they're destined to be together. Why *shouldn't* they hook up?

When the echoes of voices can no longer be heard, Talen leaves Christine's neck and positions himself at her knees, where he draws up the hem of her dress, his earlier explorations having told him that she has forgone wearing panties tonight. He does so slowly, torturously, allowing Christine to experience the erotic shock of being fully exposed to him. The wounds on her neck bubble slightly with blood, but he has only drunk a small amount, all too aware that he's pulling her nearer and nearer to the life he has led for the last century and a half. She's almost ready to make the transition.

When the hem finally reaches her waist, Talen bends her legs at the knees and pushes her thighs apart, lowering his face to the portion of her that he has brought into exposure. Her positioning forces the lips of her sex to distend outward and he places his own before them, meeting their humid kiss. The taste and scent of her is such that he feels in danger of losing control and he stabs his tongue inside her, the tightness enveloping it, promising a pleasure so exquisite he fears he might not be able to wait for much longer. But wait he must.

Each thrust of Talen's tongue is met by a return thrust from Christine. She wants him inside her so badly; she cannot understand why he's making her wait. But the question's soon forgotten as Talen's tongue changes tack, applying dizzying swirls and circuits around her inner lips, teasing and tormenting and flicking over the flesh at the center. A warm shimmering begins to move along her body, starting both at the top of her head and the tips of her toes and traveling steadily toward her middle, sending electrical currents through every pore and hair follicle. These are no ordinary sensations, no ordinary precursors to the final moment of pleasure, and suddenly she can't breathe. She wonders if this might be it; that this time she really will die.

Christine has felt the breath of death before. It happens each time Talen drinks from her – that acceleration of the heartbeat followed by a curious awareness of things she never noticed: the rustle of insects in the grass, the distant sound of a bird's wings flapping in flight, occasionally even human voices murmuring in languages she can't recognize. His feeding on her has become more and more indistinguishable from her sexual pleasure, and she always believes she won't survive it – that it will finally be *the last time*.

The sound of Christine's wetness is amplified to her ears, and she pushes her pelvis into Talen's face, silently begging him to continue. She loves the sound of him licking her and wants it to go on forever. He seems to share her desire and never once falters; it's as if his tongue is memorizing her intimate terrain or perhaps even reacquainting itself with it after a too-long absence. When Christine's orgasm is at last brought to fruition by his tongue, she's pulled from this world and transported into another.

Afterward Talen rises up from between Christine's thighs, his lips shining with her moisture. As he looks down at her, he licks it away, his eyes burning in the night like emeralds that have been set on fire.

I have to smile whenever I look in the mirror and see the bruise on my neck with the two matching puncture marks located in the center. I touch the area carefully, though it isn't sore. Touching it gives me pleasure, as though the wound retains a memory of the orgasms I experience when the blood's being drawn from it. Not for the first time, I wonder why no one seems to have noticed anything unusual. There have been less and less instances of make-up having to come in and apply fake blood to my neck and any other parts of me it's spilled onto. Didn't they ever wonder where it was coming from? Or was the reality so unbelievable that their minds shut down until they neither saw nor realized what was in front of them? Do I even believe it myself?

Though it's been less than a month since I joined the cast, I know that I'm in love with Kyle. Or rather *Talen*. I get the two mixed up sometimes. Playing a character, particularly that of a woman who believes that spending an eternity as one of the undead is a better option than knowing she'll eventually lose her beloved by the fault of her own mortality is not exactly an idea I can't relate to. Having said that, I've never had such thoughts about other men. Envisioning myself with someone several months down the line, or even years, was as far as I'd ever managed. But eternity? No. I can safely say I've never entertained such a concept or loved anyone enough to desire it. Until now. I wonder if I'm mad, or if Talen is mad. Though if we are, then I'm happy to exist in madness with him, even if it means it might eventually kill me. If his artistic perfectionism has actually led him to become the person he's playing, so be it. Or perhaps it was him all along . . .

He knows I want him inside me. Want it so badly that yes, I'm willing to die for it, to let him take away what remains of my life, just like Meridian. But he's in control. There's nothing I can say or do; if or *when* it happens, it will be his decision.

So I wait. Patiently.

And at last I get my wish.

It's 2 a.m. on a Sunday morning when Talen takes me to the Bonaventure Cemetery. Although not the first choice on most couples' lists for romantic destinations, it feels right that we should go there – that it should be in this place where we consummate our relationship, at least in the biblical sense. I feel no fear being here among the dead. They don't wish me harm.

Like a fine Southern gentleman, Talen takes my arm and guides me through the darkness toward the oldest part of the cemetery. We eventually arrive at a moss-draped oak that overhangs a large grey tombstone. Despite its age, it looks surprisingly well tended, and I notice that a bouquet of flowers has recently been placed at the grave. He indicates with a nod for me to lower myself onto the grass. The blades feel cool and welcoming, soft beneath the thin fabric of my dress, and I lie back as if I'm in my own bed, stretching my arms above and behind me to create a pillow for my head. I smile up at him with a trust I've never given anyone.

Talen kneels down beside me, pulling my dress up over my thighs, my belly, my breasts, and then over my head. I'm naked beneath it. I only wear dresses when I'm with him, never jeans or anything constricting, and generally no underclothes, not even if he and I are shooting a scene. Ever since the first time we were together, that dream-night on the beach, I've stopped wearing anything beneath my dresses. I want to be available for him at all times, should he desire a touch, a taste, a scent. Sometimes he'll just pull me into his face and breathe me in, not touching me. Even this makes me come.

He leans down and kisses my lips, his tongue licking the top one, then the bottom, before sliding into my mouth to meet mine. His saliva is like a fine wine and I sip it from his tongue, savoring its herbal sweetness. I could spend hours like this, but when Talen breaks our kiss to straddle my chest, I suspect he has other plans. His fingers unzip the fly of his jeans and I open my mouth, pleased to be given still more of him to savor. The moment my tongue makes contact with the flesh being offered, my body begins tingling with that electrical current I always experience from his contact. I can actually hear it buzzing in my ears, as if a million bees are swarming around my head. I taste his tangy-sweetness and moisture fills my eyes. How can it be possible to love someone this much? Talen allows me a few minutes to indulge myself, and I lick and suck at him hungrily as bits of moss from the overhanging branch of the old oak drop greenish-grey tears onto my nakedness. Then he decides I've had enough. On this occasion my mouth will not be receiving the completion of his pleasure.

There's no preamble, no courteousness, as he jerks open my thighs and enters me with one thrust. His lips swoop down and fasten onto my neck, his teeth breaking through the fragile skin they have broken through so many times before. I arch my pelvis upward, swallowing him so deeply that it feels as if he's entered my womb. For a moment I allow myself to wonder what kind of child we'd have – would it be human, or would it be like . . . *him*?

The soft suckling sounds at my neck as he drinks from me cause my heart to swell with tenderness, and I cradle his head against me, stroking his dark hair and placing little kisses anywhere my lips can reach. It's as though I'm breastfeeding my child, giving it nourishment to allow it to live. Then I realize that yes, this is exactly what I'm doing, only Talen is not my child: he's my lover. He moves inside me with short hard thrusts that continue to increase in speed and violence, alerting me to his impending climax. As his pelvis grinds against mine, the steel of his zipper occasionally catches in my pubic hair or bites into the surrounding flesh. I welcome the pain; it's just one more element of the pleasure he gives me. I look up at the moss-draped oak and see an owl observing us with its large saucer eyes, as if it understands exactly what we're doing.

My hands leave Talen's head and slip beneath the seat of his jeans, fastening onto a buttock each. They are smooth and warm, and I allow my fingertips to skirt the crease, which is hot and humid and unexpectedly inviting. I can tell he's nearly there; the sucking at my neck has become more frantic, as have his strokes. Suddenly my breath catches as I feel molten lava shooting into me, filling me until I'm overflowing, pooling beneath me on the grass in a boiling puddle. As I imagine it soaking into the dark rich earth, deeper and deeper, until it reaches whoever lies beneath us, I cry out, consumed by an ecstasy that surpasses any I've yet experienced. With a loud flap of wings the owl takes off. The ground beneath me vanishes and I'm lifted up into the black Savannah sky. I too, have become a creature of flight, swooping on the currents and playing tag with the stars, my cries of pleasure like the keening of a bird of prey. Talen is with me, our feathered fingers entwined, offering a reassuring touch of safety in this strange environment. I know that he won't let anything happen to me; I'm safe with him. I will always be safe with him.

My eyes open and I'm lying on the grass by the oak tree. Talen's beside me, still exposed, the beautiful length of him glistening from our combined wetness. We're holding hands, our breathing perfectly matched, as if we share the same set of lungs. I prop myself up on one arm so that I can look into his eyes. They're completely iridescent now, and I feel myself being bathed in a green fire. "I love you," I say.

Talen studies me with a serious expression, and several moments pass before he finally responds. "But do you love me enough?"

The sky is starting to lighten, indicating that it will soon be daylight. Neither of us has slept, and we have another long night of work ahead. The filming of *The Blood Moon Kiss* will soon be reaching an end, at least for this season, and I've no idea whether

I'll be invited back for the next – or if there will even *be* a next. Talen helps me up from the ground and brushes the errant bits of grass from my dress. I laugh a girlish laugh, finding his gesture sweetly familial. This is when I notice what's been carved into the headstone at the place of our lovemaking.

Talen Dashkovar
Born 3 May 1824
Died 1 December 1853

Before this fully registers in my consciousness, I note another inscription directly below it.

Beloved Wife
Adelina Dashkovar
Born March 17 1817
Died 28 November 1853

He reaches up behind his neck to unclasp the gold chain he always wears. That's when I notice for the first time the locket that hangs from it. I can't recall ever seeing a man wearing a locket before, but then, Talen isn't like other men. He clicks it open and places it on my palm with great care. "Adelina," he says softly. "My wife."

A tiny black-and-white photograph of a young woman looks up at me. Her features are dramatic, the hair and eyes intensely dark against a face nearly the white of snow. There's something familiar about her, but I can't at the moment place it. "She died carrying our child." Talen's eyes glitter like minute shards of green glass. A few slide down his cheeks and he turns away, his face crumpling.

I take his hand and press it to my cheek, his heartbreak so palpable that I feel my own heart breaking as well.

Later that day while brushing my teeth before the mirror at the bathroom sink, I suddenly realize why Adelina seemed so familiar. The face inside Talen's locket is the same face that looks out at me from the mirror.

"The minute I saw you on that television commercial, even with the ridiculous beehive hairdo I recognized you." Talen smiles, the tiny lines at his eyes crinkling with affection. "I'd know my Adelina anywhere."

Talen's convinced I'm the re-embodiment of his dead wife. He's even admitted that he used some kind of mind control ability he has to influence the show's producer to get me hired for the role of Meridian. So much for my Emmy Award-winning performance as a roller-skating waitress at a drive-in burger joint.

I've never really given much thought to reincarnation. As a concept it has its appeal; I mean, the idea of never being truly dead, of having a second chance at life, or a third, or a fourth . . . who *wouldn't* want that? The fact that I know absolutely nothing about where I come from, or from whom, lends Talen's theory even more credence. I was a Jane Doe, a baby abandoned at birth, then later placed with foster parents. My past is a blank sheet of paper. Now Talen is filling it in, only with facts from a very distant past – facts that resound deep within me like an iron bell being hit by a hammer, making my acceptance of the impossible possible. For the first time in my life, things are making sense.

He grabs my hands and presses them to his heart, which beats hard and strong beneath his shirt. "I've looked for you everywhere. I never stopped looking, not for a single moment in the century and a half since you left me."

It's beyond my comprehension to be loved by a man to such a degree that he would look for me for more than 150 years. To be honest, I can't imagine *any* of the men I've been involved with even going to the trouble of walking around the block to look for me.

Adelina had died before Talen had been given a chance to transition her. They'd agreed that she would not relinquish her "normal" life until they'd started a family, believing it fairer on the children to decide for themselves whether they wished to change over. Of course, neither Talen nor Adelina knew if having one normal parent and one vampire parent would result in a vampire child, but they still felt the decision should remain with their future children, if such a decision would, in fact, be theirs to make. However, the couple hadn't reckoned on Adelina dying – and taking with her their unborn child, who'd been growing outside the womb. Talen had railed against the world, cursing everyone in it for killing the only thing that ever mattered to him, the only thing he loved. Adelina.

"I guess there were a lot of things I didn't know back then," says Talen, "such as the fact that vampires can't kill themselves by flinging themselves in front of a speeding carriage drawn by a team of horses." He laughs at this, but his mirth sounds hollow. "Clearly, I looked dead, or at least dead enough to be buried."

The conversation is surreal. But then, everything that's happened since I came to Savannah has been surreal. Even more surreal is the fact that Adelina died from an ectopic pregnancy. It had turned out that I'd been correct when I thought I was pregnant in college. My boyfriend took off, and a few weeks later abdominal pain and bleeding landed me in the emergency ward, where I was diagnosed with a tubal pregnancy. By then the fetus was dead. As I tell all this to Talen, he breaks down into sobs. "I can't bear to think I might've lost you before I'd even found you again!"

The following evening just before they are to be driven into the Georgia countryside for their final shoot, Talen takes Christine aside to once again show her the locket. This time when he clicks it open, she sees not Adelina as she was in the 1850s, but Adelina as she would be in the twenty-first century. Suddenly Christine realizes that the photo inside the locket is of *her* and she smiles.

And Talen knows that it's time to ask the question he's been waiting to ask.

Meridian lies on the ground looking up at Kyle, his lips shiny red with her blood in the artificially enhanced moonlight. It's a pivotal scene and the last one in the season, and the powers-that-be have left its filming till the very end rather than shooting out of sequence. They don't realize that the decision has not been entirely theirs, and that other powers have influenced the decision as well. It's the scene in which Meridian acquiesces to being turned into a vampire by Kyle so that she can be with him for eternity. He hasn't forced her or exerted any form of mind control on her; she offers herself of her own free will and with the full realization that there's no returning to what she was, no going back. *Ever.*

Epilogue

Actress Collapses on Set of Hit TV Series
                                                              – *USA Today*

SAVANNAH, GA – Cast and crew of the hit vampire TV series *The Blood Moon Kiss* were stunned yesterday on the final day of filming by the sudden collapse of actress Christine Emberson.

Emberson, 36, who plays Meridian in the popular prime-time vampire soap, had just finished shooting a night scene with actor Talen Dashkovar (who plays Kyle) when she collapsed. Paramedics were called to the scene, but by then the actress had recovered. She was later escorted off the set by Dashkovar.

"Ms Emberson has been suffering from exhaustion," said Mark Gaitzberger, the series' director. "It's not uncommon in a show like ours. We often work all night for several nights running. It was obvious to everyone that the schedule's been taking its toll on her. What she needs is a good long rest."

Dashkovar, 29, who's in a relationship with the actress, apparently agrees. He has taken Emberson to his secluded retreat in the Blue Ridge Mountains until she's fully recovered. "I ask everyone to please respect our privacy," said heartthrob Dashkovar. "I must look after Christine. She's my priority now."

Neither Dashkovar nor Emberson has indicated whether they plan to return for the series' third season.

Contract between Czarina and her submissive Anaïs

Gala Fur and Véronique Bergen

Translation by Noel Burch

In accordance with the terms of the contract drawn up at the request of her revered Mistress, Anaïs will live up to Czarina's expectations in every detail. She hereby undertakes to respect the lifestyle described below until expiration of the present contract, upon the death of one or the other of the signatories.

As defined in Clause 1, Anaïs's daily life will follow unreservedly the instructions dictated by her Mistress, which means she will have no other willpower than that of her sovereign.

Moreover, Anaïs will submit to any games, humiliations, ill treatment and punishments which will threaten her on fixed dates of each year, according to the rules of exception defined by Czarina on this, the twenty-second day of August 2012.

Mistress, would it be presumptuous to say that the clauses of the agreement between us resemble a quintuple wedding ring which commits this slave of yours from the moment when my life is bereft of all attachments, save to your sole person.

As I write down the words that will seal my entrance into servitude, I am overcome with delightful erotic tremors, for the juridical nature of this existential scroll constitutes a formalization of erotic power. The Law embodied by you and served by me is but the other name for the pleasures it produces.

The knowledge that the prescriptions of this contract of serfdom, of allegiance to your person, shall be tattooed on my body in designs representing these five rules fills me with voluptuous shivers which echo your own euphoria to come.

Many perceive in a contract of submission only the

rigid codification of the vagaries of life, failing to see that this appearance of immobility constitutes only the outermost surface of the pact. A trompe-l'oeil image for the uninitiated, a severe Apollonian veil, beneath whose steely, crystalline structure boils the Dionysian vortex, the body's screams in the night. Beyond the simplicity of the game, erotic spice or other adjuvant, the alliance sealed between Mistress and slave is a means of liberating demonic vapours in both. More than a mere dialectic of the reversibility of defilement and abjection, more than any paradoxical happiness in slavery, voluntary or involuntary, this is an exploration of territories where the very notion of limit becomes uncertain, where the body is rent asunder by the experience of the extreme.

The realization of this alliance will mark my rebirth, my accession to a civil status that abolishes the previous one, a status which is notoriously *un*civil, wild. The obligations of this pentalogue exist only to facilitate our entry into a state of depossession, the sloughing off of our old selves, our old gods, so we can jump sex first into the dance of atoms.

Please forgive, Mistress, my inserting here a plea on behalf of the revolutionary character of S & M contracts whose outward austerity is such that the observer may be deaf to the great song of chaos that they authorize.

I, Anaïs, the undersigned in her own blood, hereby swear to become the exclusive slave of Mistress Czarina.

CLAUSE 1

Each morning, upon awakening, submissive Anaïs will draw a scented bath for her Mistress and cook her breakfast. Sitting naked on the floor, in a position of offering, she will lay out beside her a range of accessories – plugs, geisha balls, nipple clips, intimate jewellery. Czarina will therefore choose the instrument of subjugation for the day. Wearing a dog collar tied to its leash, the slave must eat on all fours out of a bowl bearing her name. If she should happen to soil the floor, a series of punishments will ensue, distributed by her Mistress over the next twenty-four hours. The latter will be free to choose any form of discipline she pleases, as to duration and severity: an immediate whipping, in the course of which the impertinent creature is to count aloud the lashes biting into her skin delivered with a bullwhip, a riding crop, or perhaps a cosh or a lunge whip; bondage with straps, hobbles and muzzle; electrified collar; humiliation scenario to be enacted in a special evening, in private or in public; crucifixion or suspension in a cage; candle-wax calligraphy on her body; serving as a table, a hassock, a urinal for the Mistress or her guests; parading the streets as a pony-girl in the middle of the night, etc. In addition to the tattoo which she will have redone every five summer solstices or in keeping with a timetable dictated by her Pharaoh, Anaïs is committed to wearing, from dawn at least until dusk, an emblem of her Mistress's ownership, bitch-collar, O-ring, rosebud or nipple clamps . . .

During the morning, her sex lined with geisha balls, the slave will be expected to perform fitness exercises for one full hour prior to donning her sexy maid's uniform and turning her Mistress's home into a miniature Versailles.

Three afternoons each week Anaïs will be bound to make herself up as a bimbo to be tortured and fucked at will. Among the vulgar ploys required are hair removal, manicure–pedicure, tart-blonde bleaching and extravagant haircuts, teeth whitening, and other kinds of beauty-parlour care.

In order to educate her submissive, and inculcate over the years lessons of deportment which will earn her the Nobel prize for slave-training, Czarina will dominate her physically and mentally for one hour each day. Should these sessions come to be a burden, Czarina may delegate the task to dominators of her own choosing.

Any and every breach of discipline, impertinence, disobedience, minor or major transgression, will be punished with utmost ferocity. No limit will be placed on the cruelty of her punishments. To further chastise Anaïs, Czarina may hire out the bitch-whore to friends for a limited period of time.

Whenever Czarina and her pet girl have an evening on the town (restaurant, cinema, dinner with friends, S & M parties . . .), Anaïs will wear a dog collar and a sexy miniskirt with nothing underneath. She must not at any time lose sight of her Mistress's dark eyes and custom-made hats, on pain of being thrashed and left lying naked in front of some supermarket.

At nightfall, Anaïs will perform a dance in the living room, serpentine, lascivious, followed, if Czarina so requires, by a strip-tease. In most instances, the routine will be decreed by Czarina's plenary authority, and strict instructions laid down as to the scripts to be enacted and the appropriate finery to be worn. The basic cocktail of fantasies will involve Anaïs as a sophisticated vamp sheathed in leather or PVC, a Japanese Lolita with pink dreadlocks, an ancient regime chambermaid, a brothel star in heat, a doll stuck with needles, a gothic punkette with a screw loose, a young dude, somewhere between Genet's Querelle and Jean-Paul Gaultier, a four-legged canine.

During the evening and the night, after massaging her Mistress, Anaïs will be nothing but a sex toy, an erotic atoll offered up to Czarina's carnal appetite, which she is bound to satisfy by means of her unequalled talents for submission and her erotic virtuosity. The slave will display no reluctance to comply with any of her Mistress's wishes or whims and will thank her for every favour she is granted, from slaps to fist-fucking.

Lastly, each week Anaïs will be weighed. If the scales show a weight loss of 500 grams or more, she will be obliged to ingurgitate three times a day a special pet food for girls and boys, she will be photographed in black and white to reveal her protuberant ribs and other signs of skinniness. In the event of a second offence, betraying a guilty tendency to undernourishment, she will be force-fed with a funnel like a goose. Cigarette burns, vaginal lips stitched together for a certain length of time, piercings, branding with a hot iron, needles, water sports, copulation with a dog, being chained into a kennel or locked in a dark cellar – these will not constitute a mere array of threats but an assortment of available punishments to be administered according to Czarina's whim. Each day, upon rising or retiring, Anaïs must kiss the idolized hand which visits upon her the most piquant outrages and vintage specimens of the art of perversity.

CLAUSE 2

This clause of the contract can be implemented only on a rainy autumn or winter night, when the city is shrouded in mystery, asphalt glinting in the glow of the street lamps. Anaïs will submit unprotesting to a ritual of defilement motivated by a variety of offences, such as indolence, excessive chatter, failure to obey either a spoken order or some tacit precept requiring immediate compliance, as well as the memory lapses so frequent with this highly unpredictable female subject. But her Mistress's desire to dirty her may also simply be a whim, prompted by her eagerness to preside at the wonderful rebirth that will follow the purification of her submissive's sullied body, a ritual which often plunges Czarina into a state of erotic arousal.

As soon as she has been harnessed to the powerful house dog, wearing his own leather harness, Anaïs will accept uncomplaining a close intimacy with Orson for a nocturnal run through the city scantily clad in a wine-coloured miniskirt and a sleeveless T-shirt clinging to the curve of her small breasts, with spartiates to match the harness and strap that will join her to her equipage. Orson, Czarina's young Argentinian mastiff, coat as white as a Patagonian glacier, much prefers restaurant garbage to the contents of his bowl and the moment his Mistress removes his leash and opens the front door, he gallops off into the night, making straight for his goal.

Orson's gastronomic tour begins with a run through the puddles in the gutters, an exercise which opens his appetite and cools Anaïs's long legs, gazelle running side by side with the beast, adapting her stride to the gallop of her merciless coach, headed for la rue des Écoles. At the end of what will at times have been a freezing baptism, Anaïs's clothing, in the headlamps of the passing cars, will no longer conceal any part of her anatomy.

The great gastronomic halt in Orson's tour takes place a stone's throw from the art houses of the Latin Quarter, closed for the night at this late hour. The rubbish bins of the Brasserie Balzar contain the remains of the capital's most traditional dishes: black-sausage casings, grilled pig's trotters, scraps of tripe-sausage and half-eaten Charolais rib steaks. Trained to haul and driven by a sense of conviviality acquired by frequently sharing his rations with the domestics at Czarina's request, Orson will drag Anaïs smack into the middle of the food spread over the pavement, capering among the spaghetti, chips and ketchup; pressing his close-cropped coat against the belly of his companion in gluttony, steering her towards the choicest morsels with nudges of the snout.

The next halt in Orson's feast is the yard behind the McDonald's on boulevard Saint-Germain, obligatory even if the dog is already sated. Onions, vinegary lettuce and the remains of spongy burgers, devoured just for fun. Dragging Anaïs at his side, smeared with various putrid-smelling juices, Orson completes his invariable circuit, leading her to a tiny garden, open all night long, near the Cluny Museum. Scratching at the rain-soaked bed of medicinal plants, he rolls against her thighs, rubbing by turns his back and belly in the muddy earth, besmirching Anaïs's dripping hair with well-fed enthusiasm, gratifying his partner with joyful licks of the tongue.

Upon Anaïs's return, covered with refuse, Czarina will take pleasure in imagining the vicissitudes of the odd couple's tour, written on the flesh and torn clothing of her submissive as if on the pages of an open book. A soon as she is freed of harness and strap, Anaïs – normally clean and carefully dressed – will perform a languorous striptease, dripping water on the tiled entrance, her rags clinging to her skin as though they were the most expensive finery. After the thong has been discarded, Czarina will enjoy carefully washing Anaïs in the swirl of the Jacuzzi before carrying off to bed her renovated prey, a body whose miraculous rebirth and infinite gratitude will excite her enough for immediate consumption in its plain nakedness, breasts and rump offered up to her hungry fingers, with no need for complementary artifices of any kind.

CLAUSE 3

From June to September, after a good downpour and if Czarina so desires, Anaïs will cycle to the Bois de Vincennes, carrying in the bottom of her little basket a pair of short red leather gloves, a canteen filled with water and a roll of aluminium foil. She must find and pick stinging nettles, moisten them immediately and wrap the stems in foil so that the green leaves of those urticant plants may grace Czarina's champagne bucket in anticipation of the evening of the following day.

At the beginning of the nettle season, Czarina's wildest friends gather in the basement of her building for the nettle-fête, which will have five instalments throughout the summer, according to Czarina's whim. Leather and rubber gloves will be stacked in Anaïs's basket next to the champagne bucket planted with the splendid ceremonial bouquets.

Each guest signs the magic slate hung by the entrance to the cellar before the nettle-fête begins. Their written commitment will prevent some overexcited guest from lashing Anaïs's face in the heat of the action.

Guests of every persuasion will have a whale of a time taking out their aggressions on the bare, wriggling body of Anaïs, wearing only a red thong and collar, skipping about from the sting of the nettles, squealing like a panic-stricken doe, unable to escape for one second from her fervent pursuers as they chase her around the cellar. From the long legs to the small of the back, from breasts to belly, the bunches of nettles rub and whip her translucent skin till the beaten-earth floor is covered with shredded leaves and only the bare stems are left in the gloved hands of the guests.

When the party is over, Czarina promises to anoint Anaïs's body with Elizabeth Arden's Eight-hour Cream so that her submissive will be fit to be seen in a day or so.

During the height of the nettle season, the various seats on which Anaïs never has permission to sit – ordinarily obliged as she is to live at floor level with her bowls of food and water – will be lined with fresh nettles for her. There she must sit through dinners and home-projections with friends, encouraged on arrival to appreciate with their fingertips the sting of the leaves. Were Anaïs to moan or complain, she might well be whipped over her welts, especially in the crotch, the crease between thigh and sex, and even the cleft between her buttocks.

CLAUSE 4

On a fine day in the country, the Mistress may wish to go for an outing on the river, in which case Anaïs will have the task of rowing. Wearing a knee-length tunic of fine white cotton, and once seated between the oarlocks, she will be fitted out with tiny rubber-lined clips so that Czarina may regulate the pace. Clamped onto her slave's nipples, concealed beneath the tunic, these breast clips will be attached to a second pair fastened to the labia, this providing an additional and equally invisible element of control, the two pairs of clips being manoeuvrable together or separately from where Czarina sits on a cushioned plank. In the event that another boat should pass them by, Anaïs must display a permanent smile, even if Czarina, in a fit of ferocity, were to tug viciously at the clips to try and make her lose it.

In order to develop her muscles sufficiently for a long boat ride and a picnic, Anaïs will practise rowing for an hour or two with the rowboat moored to the riverbank, while the sun is still low in the sky, this in the event her Mistress is not in a mood to dream or to dominate with the flow of the river on that particular day. This training is meant to ensure Czarina's safe return, when her submissive will have to pull hard against the current. And this solo exercise must take place at least five times before the season's first boat ride. Anaïs will wear the nipple and labia clips, gradually tightened after the second session to develop the endurance required of her when hordes of tourists come flocking down the river in their rented canoes and kayaks.

CLAUSE 5

When Czarina is out of town, she will lock Anaïs in the cellar and have friends feed her and use her as they wish. In this windowless dungeon, she will wait for random visits from her jailers who will bring her food, basically dog biscuits, and chain her inside a cage if she shows signs of rebellion. No more will she resist the particular penchants of substitute master no. 1 – beating her to within an inch of her life with whatever incongruous object comes to hand, forcing her to perform the Carnival of the Animals – than she will shrink from the favourite scenario of no. 2, Mistress "Torquemada": a re-enactment, scene by scene, of *The Story of O*. Her torturess will have orders to play on Anaïs's phobias, to relish her fear of the dark, of asphyxiation, and of the canine race. In order for Czarina to enjoy the spectacle of her whore's debasement, key moments of the above will be photographed and filmed: Anaïs's striptease, her promenades on all fours at the end of a leash, with harness, feathers, animal skin, tail and muzzle, her acrobatic suspensions, ceremonial flagellations in the manner of the Inquisition, savage rapes and other gang bangs which leave her shattered and gasping for breath.

Apart from her educator's periods of absence, Anaïs will be handed over to other dominators on a variety of pretexts: as punishment for some serious breach and lack of docility, as a reward for having surpassed herself in servility, or merely on her Mistress's whim. High priestess of all these ceremonies, Czarina will orchestrate from afar each session and demand from Anaïs a detailed account of the punishments she has undergone, to be written with a fine paintbrush protruding from her sex. Manoeuvring her whore by remote control, she will dictate special punishments and humiliations that the masters will implement on request, she will specify the type and also the style of exemplary mortifications and abjections to be inflicted on her doll-baby. Penetrated at every orifice, transpierced, dildoed, fisted, abused, savagely fucked, insulted, slapped, spanked, strapped, gagged, cross-dressed, packsaddled, pilloried, straitjacketed, suspended, bound, diapered, electrically tortured, stable-milked, ridiculed, mortified, exhibited, impaled, the slave must cooperate with any and every idea that comes along. She will be spared nothing, in order to push her to her outermost limits so that the little sexual guinea pig which she has become will be conditioned to live henceforth only under her Mistress's rod. Her accepting and indeed requesting things that had once horrified her will attest to the success of the training. If Anaïs were to show the least sign of rebellion, Czarina's friends will bring her into line by crucifying her like an owl to the strains of Bartók's *Bluebeard's Castle* or Janáček's *The Cunning Little Vixen*, with an eye to improving her musical education. Mistress Czarina will demand absolute inflexibility of those in charge of defiling the submissive's body, for if Anaïs has violated her sovereign's law, she must be shown no clemency. They are not to be moved by any display of tears, any bitch's entreaties. Step by step, Anaïs will come to cherish her chains until she cannot live without them, will belong to Czarina, body and soul.

Venus in Edinburgh

Pat McStone

When I was thirteen, back in the seventies, I was sent to boarding school in Edinburgh, Scotland. It was a shock in more ways than one. I'd never been to the UK before, having spent my childhood in Bombay, location of the biggest hotel in my father's luxury chain. My mother, who died when I was four, was Scottish and I was sent to her home city, I've since realized, as an act of homage. I rarely saw her family, who weren't openly racist but had no interest in welcoming me to their home. Even light brown skin like mine was too much in the New Town's tall houses. Then there was the weather. I froze that first winter, the school seeing no need for heating in the dormitories. And there was the food. I was used to European cuisine from the hotel, but the slop we were fed would have tested the stomachs of the beggars back home. Then there were the prefects, older boys with something close to the power of life and death over us younger ones. Then there were the girls . . .

The school, one of those that the British call public, but which are in fact 500, had never accepted girls before. That year they'd decided to allow two members of the opposite sex to join the sixth form, though they didn't sleep in the houses. Think of it: 500 boys whose trousers almost permanently sported pyramids in the groin area, and two girls. Actually, one of them was not very attractive. In fact, she was tall, gangly, horse-faced and flat as an ironing board. I'm sure she still provoked a fair number of nocturnal emissions. The other one – let's call her Mary – was a stunner: of average height, with crinkly blonde hair that just reached her shoulders and well-proportioned legs (on the days she chose to tantalize us with knee-length skirts, minis no doubt being banned). What really turned our eyes were, surprisingly, *her* eyes. They were dark blue, piercing and ray-gun powerful. If her gaze settled on you, knee trembling and armpit drenching were immediate. All right, there was also the large matter of her bosoms, as my father used to call those glands. Mary's were big. Not water melons, but definitely decent-sized fruit of the yellow-skinned variety. There were days when she dispensed with a bra, the news flying round the school instantly. Lines of us would stand outside the dining room waiting for her, jaws slack and underwear concrete. She would smile regally, her shoulders back, and walk rapidly to afford maximum movement. Mary was definitely into adoration.

The school had seven residential houses, one of them being in the catastrophic combination of French chateau styles that was the main building. My house, Gladstone, was five minutes' walk away. By one of those quirks of fate that almost convinces me there is an Almighty, the girls were assigned to it. All that meant was they came to Gladstone for break and to do their homework in the afternoon, while we were out being rained or snowed on and balls of various shapes and sizes were thrown at us. But it still gave us bragging rights over the rest of the school, especially when Mary and our senior prefect, Dirleton – a handsome devil who was also captain of the rugby team – took up with each other. The other girl, Fiona, was an unofficial chaperone, but she was frequently to be seen alone in the room assigned to them, sad-eyed and hunched over her work. She went to Oxford and ended up as a government economist, sometimes to be seen on TV.

I had the misfortune to be Dirleton's fag. For those of you fortunate to have avoided public school, despite its unaccountable attraction to the makers of films and TV series, the fag is the prefect's personal servant – or slave, if he's a nasty piece of work. Dirleton was all right; prone to yell if the soles of his rugby boots didn't gleam and ungenerous with his tips at the end of term, but basically fair. Things began to get interesting in my third term, during what passes for summer in Edinburgh. The senior prefect had a bigger study than everyone else, with a small balcony overlooked by the dormitories, which were out of bounds during daylight. One evening, he sent word for me. I knocked on his door and tried to slide it open. He allowed only a small gap to appear.

"Ah, there you are, Patel," he said, his voice low. "I need my pillow."

I looked at him blankly.

"My pillow, fool. Bring it from my cube."

The dormitories for older boys had partitions between them, though they didn't go all the way to the ceiling. When the lights were out, they allowed those who played with each other a degree of privacy. As the school authorities must have been aware of such activities, I can only assume their tacit encouragement. But I digress.

"Yes . . . sir," I stammered. "But what about . . . ?"

"Tell anyone who asks that I sent you. My back's stiff after cricket."

Before I could respond, I heard a stifled titter, either that of a boy whose voice hadn't broken – mine had – or . . . could it be Mary? The thought sent a hot spurt through my veins. I raced to the stairs and got up to his dorm without anyone seeing me. A couple of minutes later I handed over the pillow. As I turned to go, I heard the sound of a chair being slotted into the gap between the door and wall inside. That made my heart pound like a steam hammer. Without thinking, I returned to the stair-case and went up, ready to use Dirleton's name if I was challenged. I wasn't.

I entered the cube with the best view of the study balcony. The light of the long Scottish evening was still bright enough – no clouds for a change – though the house walls created shadows. I crept to the window, then slowly inched my head past the window frame. Gods be praised!

Mary was lying on the narrow balcony, her buttocks on the pillow I had been holding. My cock strained like the mast of my father's yacht in the Arabian Sea, but I left it where it was, my eyes fixed on the scene below. Dirleton's trousers and boxers were round his ankles and I could see his tool waving over Mary. It was one of those weird ones that bend back towards its owner. She had taken her blouse off, but she was still wearing her bra. Not for long. Dirleton's hands slipped round her back and, after heart-pounding seconds, loosed it. I almost choked. I'd seen plenty of breasts in the magazines that did the rounds, the best pages stuck together, but never in the flesh. Nudism wasn't exactly the thing back home. Mary's tits, oh save me, they were magnificent. They stood up, somehow countering the force of gravity, the nipples dark and erect like the cigar stubs in the ashtray on the old man's desk.

Dirleton sucked them one by one, rotating the other nipple

between his thumb and forefinger. Mary's mouth was open, her hands gripping his back. Then she pushed him gently away and took his cock, looking at it with what appeared to be wonder. She ran her fingers up the bent rod, pulling the foreskin back to his evident but stifled delight. This went on for several minutes and I was amazed he hadn't come. Then he did, the semen squirting onto his belly and then dripping onto hers. Spatters rained over her tits and she smoothed the sticky substance into her skin as if it were a precious liniment. Then Dirleton, who'd presumably been told not to go all the way, got his head between Mary's glorious thighs. I couldn't see, but he must have been tonguing her because her face clenched, forehead furrowed, and she grabbed his hair. Her lips were opening and closing, but I couldn't hear anything. As well as everything else, I admired her self-control.

And then her torso started to undulate as she hit a rhythm that gradually increased in speed. She let her head drop over the metal railing, one hand moving between her long dark nipples and the other pressing Dirleton's head into her crotch. The end, when it came, was a blur of movement, and this time she couldn't restrain a high-pitched screech. It didn't matter; there were owls in the trees nearby.

Mary's body was still now, but her head remained back as the senior prefect stood up, running his tongue over his lips. That was when she saw me. A smile spread across her face and she winked.

Me? I wanked.

Mary and Dirleton were gone at the end of the term, he to read law at Durham and she to the Edinburgh College of Art. She's a well-known painter now. I have one of her female nudes in my den. It isn't a patch on her as she was that summer evening.

In my second year there were ten girls. Two were eye-catchers and the others ranged from average to any port in a storm. We weren't supposed to talk to pupils in different years and I was going through that awkward period when you prefer the safety of doing it to yourself than sharing with others. Several of my contemporaries had different ideas, creeping into each other's study when working late or slipping into neighbouring cubes. I never fancied male hands or other parts, and no one made advances on me. That was maybe one of the advantages of being mixed race.

Another of which was that I stuck out from the crowd. Occasionally I'd catch one of the girls looking at me in chapel or at lunch. I suppose I was handsome enough, I've never been able to judge my own charms. But those looks, which were followed by rapid turns away and red cheeks, were a good omen. They gave me something to think about as I brought myself off over the wash-hand basin or in the toilet.

Then the housemaster's daughter Morag – a sixteen-year-old who attended school and was definitely at the any port in a storm end of the scale – had a French penfriend to stay. She attended lessons too. I suppose it was some kind of exchange scheme. I'll call her Christine. She stayed in the other part of the house from us, the connecting doors strictly monitored. That didn't stop her. I was tall for my age and had good skin, both of which qualities distinguished me from my classmates. I caught Christine looking at me more than once. She didn't turn away, nor did she blush. You know what they say about French women, not that she was fully mature physically. But near enough.

She managed to slip a note into my pocket. I only found it after I'd finished sport, another dismal afternoon on the cricket pitch. It said, "Big shed 9.15". I couldn't believe my luck – or was it a trick? Maybe some of the bullies in the year above had written it. I was used to getting elbows in the ribs and shoves against the walls of the narrow corridors, as well as the usual racial abuse. I ignored it as best I could. But should I take the risk of going to the rendezvous? I thought about it, for about ten seconds. Christine wasn't a beauty, but she was fully equipped in all areas. And I was avid to have the benefit of the experience I could tell she had.

9.14. I slipped out the back door, past the room where fags were scrubbing shoes. The bigger of the two gardeners' sheds was about thirty yards away. I moved swiftly in the evening light, then turned the corner cautiously. She was there! What was more, her blouse was open and a lacy red bra caught my attention like a brothel lamp attracting a sailor.

"Hello," she said, moving her right hand to her breast. "What is your name? I cannot call you Patel."

Her voice was like honey and the French accent was balm to my ears. And cock.

"Samit," I said, stepping towards her.

"You like this?" Christine tugged the cup down and showed her tit. It wasn't as big as Mary's and the nipple was no more than a tiny pink pearl. I went fishing with my tongue, one arm around her.

She moaned and moved her hand to my groin. "He is *engorgé*." My French was just about up to that.

"You're delightful," I responded, kissing her on the mouth.

"You say this to all the girls, yes?" she asked, when our lips separated.

I shrugged, then tensed. Her fingers were deftly pulling down my zipper. I took that as a green light and slipped my hand under her thin skirt. It reached her upper thighs, which were damp, and I realized she was without underwear. I flicked my forefinger out like a snake's tongue and felt hair and soft wet labia (we knew the terminology). Her groan showed I was on the right lines. I slid my finger all the way in, feeling no obstruction. This girl was definitely experienced.

"Come," she said, stepping back and leading me to the tarpaulin that covered a stack of logs. She unclipped her bra, a front loader, then pulled up her skirt with a saucy smile. Then she leaned forward, undid my belt and popped the button on my trousers.

"*Mon Dieu*," she whispered, when she put her hand down my shorts. "You are very big, Samit."

I bit my lip as she extracted my organ and scrotum. My pubic hair was thick and black, and she ran her fingers through it. As soon as she clenched my balls, I spurted uncontrollably, the semen landing on her skirt and that dense triangle. Drops hung on the hair like twists of cream on a chocolate cake.

"I knew you would finish quickly," she said, smiling. "First time, yes?"

I nodded, both joyful and embarrassed.

"It's OK." Christine put my hands on her tits. "Now the good things really start."

She was right about that. I drew her nipples out and they turned a burning shade of pink. Then she took one hand and pushed it to her groin, directing my finger to a lump above the labia. Hail, clitoris!

Christine showed me how to rub it and soon she was bucking and gasping. I used my tongue on her tits and that drove her even crazier. Finally she shuddered and clenched, her eyes wide and crazy.

"You learn fast, Samit," she breathed. "Are you ready to come inside me?"

My cock was at half-mast, but a few strokes from her changed that.

"Let me," she said, taking a foil wrapper from the pocket of her now crumpled skirt. She shook out the condom and smoothed it over my dick. It felt constricting.

"I know," Christine said, taking in my expression. "But you'll get used to it."

Actually, I never did, but the world has enough babies. She guided me in and then ground herself against me, frowning and blowing.

"There is a place in me," she gasped.

I let her do the work, aware that if I made any rapid movements I would fill the bobble at the end of the sheath.

"Aaaaaaah!" she cried, and seconds later I came too. The sky exploded and I felt myself cartwheel through the universe, every nerve in my body reacting, chain reacting and connecting me to something at the heart of creation.

"Fuck!" I said.

"*Mais oui*," she replied, laughing.

I withdrew slowly and let her strip the condom off. The tip was bulging with my seed.

"Tomorrow, same time?" Christine said, after kissing me with her lips and tongue.

I nodded, breathless, then saw Morag's face at the window above. She looked like a cattle prod had been applied to her "airse", as my Scottish friends said.

It was raining the next day – a year-round hazard in the Athens of the North – but that turned out not to be a problem. Christine was waiting for me with Morag, who had the key to the big shed. None of us said anything as she opened the padlock and I shoved the door enough to allow us entry.

"So, my friends," Christine said, a sweet smile on her lips. "Here is how it goes. Samit, Morag would like you to initiate her to the mysteries of love."

I stared at her.

"Don't worry," Christine said, squeezing my hand. "I will help."

I looked at the housemaster's daughter. She was breathing heavily, her plain face red all over. She was taller than average, though shorter than me, and there weren't any protrusions to speak of under the cheesecloth blouse she was wearing.

But Christine's touch had fired me up. She undid Morag's buttons, took off her friend's blouse and then lifted the vest she was wearing – no bra – over her head. I gaped. Her breasts were small, but the areolae were dark and extensive. Suddenly there was a bulge in my pants.

"Touch," Christine commanded.

I tweaked Morag's nipples and they hardened, provoking a loud intake of breath. Meanwhile, Christine had undone Morag's jeans and pulled them down. Her knickers were white and large, which initially put me off. Then her lower half was bared and I took in sparse brown hair, plump lips protruding.

Christine fingered Morag and nodded to me. I slid my forefinger in and the housemaster's daughter fell back against the door, panting. I kissed her tits, running my tongue over the tiny bumps on the dark pigmentation. Then I felt hands on my waist. I looked down and saw Christine's hands undoing my belt, button and zipper, then easing my cock out.

"Look, Morag," she said teasingly. "Big and black and all for you. Take it."

Her friend did as she was told. At first her touch was tentative, but then she got interested, bending down as she moved her hand up and down the shaft.

"Wait, I'm . . ."

My spunk shot out, hitting Morag on the face, tits and belly. She pulled back, then saw Christine's smile. After a moment, her tongue appeared and moved to the nearest spatter. She drew it back and tasted my gift. It seemed she liked it.

"Very good, *mes amis*," said Christine. "Now the second course." She took off her clothes and leaned against the wall beside Morag. "Samit, you know what to do."

I stepped forward, applying one forefinger to Christine's clit and the other to Morag's – it was large, like a little boy's cock, and it grew rapidly. The sight of it made me harden again. I sucked their nipples, darting my tongue from one to other. Christine came first, her head banging against the wall. Morag was panting, but she hadn't climaxed. I wasn't sure what to do. Christine was.

She pushed my head down and took over the stimulation of her friend's nipples. I pulled the large clit in and out of my mouth, and Morag's thighs closed tight around my head. Then I nipped her with my teeth, only lightly, provoking a stifled scream. I thought my head was going to be shaken off, but finally the legs parted and I was able to withdraw.

"You've never done it, have you?" Christine said, kissing Morag on the lips. "Not even to yourself."

The housemaster's daughter shook her head, looking down.

"No, *ma chère*, there is nothing to be ashamed for." Christine glanced at my dick. "Besides, now comes the third course."

I gulped, unsure if I'd be able to satisfy them both. I needn't have worried. Christine called the shots perfectly.

"Put your finger in," she said to me, indicating Morag's slit.

I did as I was told. Although wet, it was much tighter than the French girl's. Morag quivered, her eyes away from mine.

"Are you sure you want this?" I asked.

She nodded, then smiled to reassure me.

"Of course she does," Christine said. "But we must lie down. There is a blanket over there."

I went to get the green tartan object. It had some holes, but seemed clean enough. I spread it on the earthen floor.

"Now, *ma chère*, lie down and make yourself comfortable." Christine pushed Morag's knees apart. Then she took out a condom and ran it over my cock. "Ready to go? I will help you enter."

And she did, with a degree of dexterity that made me sure she'd done this before. Morag blinked and I stopped, then she nodded and I moved on slowly.

"Is it all right?" I whispered.

This time her nods were avid, at least in part because Christine was sucking her nipples. I reached a barrier and pressed ahead gently. Morag took a deep breath, then let out a squeak and grabbed my buttocks, pulling me deeper. She began to groan as I juddered against her, then I let out a similar noise. Christine had her fingers round my balls and was squeezing.

Morag's face was red and covered in sweat.

"I have a finger for you," Christine said in my ear.

I jerked forwards as the said digit was pressed into my arse. I was close to orgasm, I couldn't hold back, whatever state Morag was in. I reared up and buried myself in her, the whole of my midriff exploding. I hoped the condom had held.

After I pulled slowly out, Christine tugged it off. There was a little blood on the outside, but nothing too disturbing. Morag lay back, panting, then sat bolt upright, as if she'd suddenly become aware of where she was and what had happened. She gathered up her clothes, pulled them on and went to the door.

"I will lock it," Christine said.

Morag nodded, gave me a shy smile and was gone. It was only then that I realized she hadn't said a word from beginning to end.

"And now, *mon ami*," Christine said, tearing open another foil pack, "it is my turn."

I groaned, but it wasn't long before I was back in the saddle.

The matron was a fearsome figure, known throughout the school as Battle Axe. There were countless tales of her abrupt and usually painful execution of the doctor's orders. Both of them assumed all boys were malingerers, though nothing could have been further from the truth. You were let off chapel to attend the surgery. I had a bad case of athlete's foot and had no option but to see the doctor after the housemaster spotted me scratching obsessively in the dorm. I imagined there was an ointment or special talc, but the Axe had other ideas.

"In here, boy," she said, pointing me to the treatment room. "Take your trousers and socks off and sit on the table."

It was as I completed those actions that I caught the look in her eye. It was one I'd grown familiar with. She was on her knees, taking what looked like a toothbrush from a stainless steel tray. Beside it was a bottle of dark-coloured liquid.

"This will sting a bit," she said, with relish.

That was an understatement. As I blinked back tears, she scrubbed away the skin till my toes and the gaps between them were raw. I looked down and saw that the top button of her uniform was undone. The Axe must have been in her fifties and her face was definitely not for the faint-hearted, but her body wasn't too bad. Her bosom was nicely inflated and I could see the pale flesh over the top of an industrially constructed bra. The pain in my feet increased and, to my shock, I felt my traitor cock begin to stir.

The Axe looked up and smiled hungrily. I was helpless as my shorts began to protrude. She stopped painting the hideous liquid on my feet and grabbed my calves.

"What are you waiting for, boy? Take it out."

I was so surprised that I hesitated.

"Take it out."

I did as I was told, then reached down for her.

"No touching," she ordered. She pulled herself up until her head was level with my rampant tool. Then she started to exhale warm air over it. That lightest of pressures was enough to get me going. She saw that and moved on to her next trick, which involved running the very tip of her tongue from my balls and up the vein to the bulb and eye.

"I . . ."

"Wait," the Axe demanded. She got higher and put her lips over the head, touching it very gently.

"I . . ."

"Don't you dare, boy!" Then she closed her lips around me and started a series of small movements.

"Nurse . . ."

"Mmm mmm."

I took that as another warning not to explode, but I didn't know how to delay. I could pull away, but the thought of what the Axe's teeth could do to my knob killed that plan.

Then she took her mouth off and looked up.

"Very well, you've proved yourself, Patel. Let me have it now." She reapplied her mouth.

My heart was thundering and the usual galaxy-upending nerve connections had started. I gasped and then shot my load, or rather loads, the Axe's thick fingers clawing my thighs. Her head jerked back as if she was taking bullets to the throat. Eventually I was drained and collapsed back onto the bed.

The nurse got to her feet, her lips closed. There was an incongruous dreamy look on her face, then she leaned over me, caught my eye and swallowed very deliberately, several times.

"Right, boy," she said, wiping her lips with the back of her hand. "Get dressed. The solution should work within a week." Then her lips formed into her version of a smile. "Of course, it'll have to be redone every morning."

There was a band at the time called Head, Hands and Feet. I became an instant fan.

When I was sixteen, I entered the sixth form. Or, to be more accurate, I entered several female members of that august body. By then, there were thirty female pupils, most in the first year sixth like me. Christine was long gone, but Morag was doing the Oxbridge exams. She'd come out of herself and had a steady boyfriend in her year. I can only imagine that she had spread the word about my cocksmanship. I didn't exactly have to fight the girls off – they formed an orderly queue, each having me for a fortnight. Most of my male contemporaries hated my guts, but they couldn't argue with my results. I fucked or gushed behind the sports pavilion, in the girls' common room, in chapel, in the bushes and in a bunker on the golf course. Some little bastard landed a ball on my naked arse. The girl didn't notice: she was too busy getting sand out of her slit. We repaired to the changing rooms, where I applied the shower head in ways that got me back in her good books.

And then came the school play. That year, whether by accident or design, it was *Othello*. I suppose I'd have been called to audition even if I didn't have a commanding voice and reasonable thespian skills: I was the only even partially dark boy in the school. I got the part, probably because I'd become an expert at dissembling before, during and after my erotic adventures. Amazingly, I'd never been caught slipping in and out of the house or other buildings, let alone in flagrante. That made me daring, which was not necessarily a good thing. I was deep in a girl called Alison between the rear stacks of the library when the headmaster came in. Fortunately I saw him through the gap between the shelves and managed to disengage. Alison curled up under the table and he wandered away after giving me a vague nod. I almost burst out laughing, then joined her and finished the job to our mutual satisfaction.

The play was a challenge on several fronts. Although it had been abridged, there were still plenty of lines to learn. The director, one of the junior teachers, was keen to impress and took that out on the cast. He also fancied Desdemona to the extent that he had to lick his lips non-stop when she was on stage. And there was my biggest challenge. I too wanted to get between Aminta Forbes-Ker's succulent thighs, but she was one of the few sixth form girls immune to my charms. The rehearsals brought us into close proximity, but she managed to preserve an invisible membrane between us. This only made me more frustrated. She was the second most stunning girl in the school – I'd had the most stunning and she turned out to have the sex drive of a sloth. Aminta's hair was thick and blonde, her face a neat triangle with pouting lips, and her body, though she was below average height, a garden of delights. Big tits on a small woman always got me going. Then there was the way she looked at me – almost contemptuous, as if I was a lesser being.

The director succeeded, with difficulty, in getting Aminta to tone down her sultriness on stage, but close up I felt it pulsing around her. It was all I could do to restrain myself from tearing open her temptingly low-cut costume.

We got to the dress rehearsal and I decided to ignore her, giving my scenes with Iago and Cassio more power. That irritated Aminta, I could see, so I kept it up. The director was irritated and kept telling me to put more emotion into Othello's relationship with Desdemona.

There was a shared dressing room, overseen by one of the housemaster's wives, who took pleasure in watching me change. Aminta got close enough to me to whisper, "Tomorrow night. Lean close when you smother me."

That was an order I'd never expected to hear. I was used to the Axe, to whom I still went to every few weeks and who had moved on to applying a toothbrush to my scrotum as I came in her mouth – she still wouldn't let me touch her with my hands. I tried to ignore it as I prepared for the first of the two performances. In fact, I lost myself in the role so much that I reached Act 5, scene 2 without remembering Aminta's words. But when she started to speak, eyes flashing and lips brightly painted, then it came back to me.

"Will you come to bed, my lord?" she asked, with cod innocence.

I got into my stride, telling her she was to die and ranting about the fateful handkerchief. "Down, strumpet!" I commanded sternly.

"Kill me tomorrow, let me live tonight!" was her riposte, eyes beseeching and hands extended.

I leaned over her, my cock suddenly rigid as a flagpole, pressing against her right tit. She moved against me, in full view of 250 people.

"It is too late!" I cried, as I came against her. Fortunately I was wearing a codpiece, so I was able to finish the scene without bringing the house down.

"A guiltless death I die," said Desdemona, her gaze catching mine. I'd never seen anyone look less innocent. My spirit caught fire.

I raced through the rest of the scene, giving extra weight to the lines: "Behold, I have a weapon;/A better never did itself sustain/ Upon a soldier's thigh . . ."

Aminta was off stage by then, but I was sure I heard her laugh. I was in a hurry to end Othello's life and show the minx a thing or two.

"I took by th' throat the circumcisèd dog/And smote him – thus."

Which was inaccurate: I had not been circumcised, as plenty of girls in the audience could attest. I stabbed myself and waited, prone, till Lodovico finished the play – "Look on the tragic loading of this bed," and so on. Then I took my bow, holding the temptress's hand. Several bows, in fact. They liked me – or us.

"Behind the swimming pool," I whispered to her, as the curtain came down. "If you dare."

"Sirrah, my father he doth wait for me," Aminta said, with a slick-lipped smile.

I thought quickly. "When do you have free periods tomorrow?"

For a few moments I thought she was going to ignore me.

"Fifth."

The one before lunch. I had it for personal study too. "Below the dining room."

Aminta walked away with her head in the air, then dropped her handkerchief. I picked it up. I had plans for it.

It was a risk, going to the dining room out of hours, but I'd acquired a taste for breaking the rules. Anyway, my blood was up after the school play and I wanted Aminta more than I had any other girl. I went down the steps and into the cloakroom, a large area with hooks along the walls. No sign of her. Of course, she wouldn't have been in the boys' place. I went back out and pushed open the door of the girls' cloakroom, a much smaller space. That was a serious infraction that could get me expelled, but my blood and cock were up. No one. I went to the toilet cubicles at the far end. All the doors were open. Fuck. Or rather, not.

Then the main door crashed open. I turned and got the rear view of an unusually tall and fleshy woman. She was carrying a bucket and mop, which she let drop with a clang to the tiled floor. Then she swivelled, light on her feet, and saw me.

"Hullo, son. Wha' are you doin' here?"

Even after four years, I struggled with the local dialect.

"Em, a friend of mine left an essay for me."

"Oh aye." The woman came closer.

I'd seen her many times. She was one of the few cleaning staff that bore a second glance. Her face wasn't as pinched as the others and her body a lot softer, even in the unflattering overalls they had to wear. Recently I'd ignored her in the dining room when she wheeled the food trolleys around, but when I was younger I'd spilled my seed at night on her soft mounds and cushioned thighs – in my imagination.

"You ken what?"

I shrugged, unsure how to respond.

"Ah've never had a black cock."

I understood that. But what about Aminta? I looked at my watch. She was ten minutes late.

She – I think her name was Janice – led me to one of the cubicles.

"Naw, leave the door open. We can close it if anyone comes."

"Anyone except us," I quipped.

She grinned, displaying uneven and nicotine-stained teeth, and started to undo her overalls and the blouse beneath. What had been undefined globes now took shape in an old grey bra with holes in it. This woman was seriously well stacked. She pulled her skirt down and I saw knickers that would soon be pensionable, the fabric off-white and the elastic slack.

"Hurry up!" she said, her voice hoarse.

I got my trousers open and let my cock hang loose.

"Jesus, what a monster!" She grabbed it, running calloused hands over the straining skin.

I got her breasts out and rubbed the nipples. They were inverted and stayed that way.

"I like it like this," Janice said, pulling down her underwear and turning her backside to me. Her head was close to the toilet, her hands holding the cistern behind.

I fumbled for the condom in my jacket.

"Never mind that," she said. "Ah've got no disease."

I thought about that for about a second, then my appetite for risk took over. I laid my dick along the crack between Janice's large buttocks, pressing my balls against the hairs around her arse. Then, hands on her tits, I drew back and sent the heat-seaking head between her legs. A bristle of her pubes, then it was in. Gods, she was wet! It was like sliding into a fish's mouth, fortunately one without teeth.

"Aye! Aye! Aye!" she urged.

I drove hard, hearing squelches as my length went all the way.

I was on fire, my eyes locked on the curves of her buttocks as my stomach pushed against them and the fissure that led to her hole. I took one hand from a heavy breast, slid it in and out of my mouth and then pushed it slowly into her fundament.

Janice quivered, squeezing hard on both my digit and my dick.

"Now!" she grunted. "Gie me it now!"

I did what I was told. My climax was a blast of star-shine, of planets reeling through the void. She seemed to come too as I dug hard with both prongs. The after-jerks were many and pleasurable.

"Fuck me," Janice gasped, as I withdrew from front and rear orifices.

"Not again."

We froze as Aminta's cut-glass voice echoed off the tiled walls.

I looked over my shoulder. She was leaning against a wash-hand basin, skirt up and hand inside her floral briefs.

"You finished too soon," she complained.

"Not me, hen," Janice said, pushing me back and fussing with her clothes. "You're some boy, you," she said, kissing me on the cheek.

I gave her the handkerchief from the play.

"Thanks. Ah've got a lottae moppin'' up tae dae." She grinned as she moved away.

"Anything I can help you with," I said, holding my trousers up as I headed towards Aminta.

"You must be joking," she said. "How could you do it with that common cow?"

I raised my shoulders. "You didn't come."

"I'm trying to rectify that," she said, hand moving up and down.

"Anything I can do?"

"Stand there and watch."

Despite, or rather because of, being ordered around for years at school, I didn't take well to commands; nor did I like the way she'd referred to Janice.

Aminta used her other hand to undo her blouse and slipped it beneath the clean white bra. Her breasts were nothing like as big as Janice's, but they were well formed. I raised a hand towards them.

"No!"

Although I resented her tone, it had a positive effect on my cock. The Battle Axe effect.

Aminta looked at it, her mouth open, hand rubbing away.

I took a step closer.

"No!" she repeated.

"I can make it much better for you," I whispered. "I know—"

"Shut up!" She kept staring at my cock, her breath coming hard and fast.

I moved my face towards hers.

"Don't!" she panted, close to bringing herself off. "Filthy . . . black . . . pig!"

I waited till she blinked and exhaled, her body jolting back and forward, the back of her head almost hitting the mirror above the basin. Then I put my finger against her lips and ran it along them, taking care to avoid her teeth.

"You've got a dirty mouth," I said, doing up my trousers.

Aminta gagged after she licked her lips. I'd applied the finger that had been up Janice's backside.

"Think on thy sins," I said, Othello again, and turned on my heel.

There were more delights in my final year, more and varied, but I will regale you with only one. A surfeit of girls desperate to experience my exotic cock drove me to ponder upon more exciting ways to pleasure myself and them. Risk and rapidity were solutions. I had one girl, spotty Susan with the chainsaw voice, in the corridor between lessons, her friends forming a ring around us. I timed the exchange of fluids at just over two minutes. That set me up nicely for double physics.

But always I wanted more, and different. I did the work I was set quickly, being a brainbox, leaving me plenty of time to plan my next conquest. The object of my desire appeared quickly. In fact, she had been in my mind in varying degrees of lucidity since I was thirteen. Mrs Arkle, the head of English's wife. They were the school's trendy couple, young and clearly in love. She wore better – and tighter – clothes than the other teachers' wives and was a lot more physically attractive. Gallons of semen had been deposited on the school's sheets by desperate masturbators over the years, in part because she was completely unattainable. I needed to get close to her, make her notice me. I'd seen the feral look in her eye when she watched her husband in chapel and in the theatre, and I was pretty sure she'd pick up the waves I gave off – if only I appeared on her radar.

In the end, the easiest strategy was the best. It was summer and the annual school sports day was nigh. I had developed into a useful cricketer and had no interest in track and field. On the other hand, Jack Arkle did: he was the coach of the athletics team and would be acting as organizer and announcer all afternoon. Mrs Arkle – Lucy – would make an appearance, I remembered from previous years, and then go back to the house the couple had been allocated in the school grounds. I showed up, as we were all required to, paying no attention to the girls who were smiling and sticking their chests out at me. This time Lucy Arkle hadn't even made it to the cinder track. She was standing between two trees in the line that separated the sports fields from the school. I went to the tree at the bottom and then moved swiftly up the slope, stopping between each one. Then I took out a book and leaned against the tree beneath her. Out of the corner of her eye, I saw her head turn towards me. Contact!

After a while she said, "It's Patel, isn't it?" Her voice was high-pitched, her accent very English. She had auburn hair and freckles on her face and neck. I wondered how far down they went.

I looked up, as if I'd been distracted. "What? Oh, sorry, Mrs Arkle. Yes, I am Patel." The fact that she knew my name was a definite plus.

"Samit?"

I nodded. "How . . . how do you know that?" I hadn't been in her husband's class since the second year.

She smiled. "I like to keep up with the school's promising pupils. You're going to try for Cambridge, aren't you?"

"Yes, natural sciences."

She walked up to me. "Really? And what's your favourite subject?"

This was going better than I had dared to hope. "Biology," I lied. In fact, chemistry was much more to my taste in class, though you could say that practical biology kept me going in my spare time.

"How interesting," she said, her breath playing on my cheek. "And what experiments have you carried out recently?"

She was hooked, there was no doubt about it. I looked past the tree and took in the crowd cheering as some poor souls dragged themselves round the track.

"Human reproduction," I said, gazing into her green eyes.

"Indeed," she said, her voice low. "Give me five minutes, then come to the house."

I nodded and raised my book to deflect attention, not that I could make out any of the words. I didn't trust my watch and counted the seconds one by one. Then I walked down the line of trees and stepped quickly away. My blood coursed through me like lava and my heart was fluttering.

The front door was unlocked. I went in and immediately saw a lacy, pale yellow bra on the staircase. Further up was her blouse, then her skirt. No other underwear, but I could live with the idea of removing it.

There was a shoe on the landing and another outside one of the doors. I went towards it, my stomach clenching in anticipation.

Lucy Arkle was lying on the double bed, her arms above her head and her legs wide. She was wearing split-crotch panties the same colour as her discarded bra. Her pubic hair was a deeper shade of red than I'd expected. It acted like a magnet for my eyes and cock, which was fighting to break free. The freckles were all over her breasts.

"Come here, darling boy," she said, beckoning me forward. When I got there, she touched my distended trousers with delicate fingers, then unzipped me. I got myself naked in seconds.

"Human reproduction, eh?" Lucy said, a touch of alarm in her voice.

"Don't worry, I've got protection." I reached for my jacket.

"Not yet. I want to see everything first." She gave me a broad smile. "Boys your age recover very quickly."

So I wasn't the first. That took the wind from my spinnaker for a couple of seconds, then she began to move her fingers, soft as a butterfly's wings, up and down my rod. I got on to the bed, then lowered myself on to her belly.

"Mmmm," she groaned, as I rubbed her nipples. They were also a dark red hue and lengthened considerably.

"Mmmm," I said in return, grinding my arse against her pubic hair. "Stand . . . by . . ." Then I fountained high into the air above her, the jissom landing in splats across her face, neck, breasts and stomach.

"So much," she moaned. "I hope . . . there'll . . . be more."

I passed the time till my balls refilled giving her a good tonguing. She bucked like a drowning fish, rubbing her tits with my spunk till she came in a crescendo of screams that I was sure would be heard by the neighbours.

Soon afterwards, my tool was ready for action again. We went at it from the front, behind – she had a wonderful arse – side by side, spoons, you name it. I was all right because I needed some time. The problem was Lucy. She was squealing and barking again, panting and covered in sweat. The police would be round soon looking for a murderer. I decided to bring things to their conclusion.

I got her on her back, slipped myself in and pulled her legs over my shoulders. That way my finger could reach her backside. She struggled when I put it in, but quickly submitted. We got into a good rhythm and I could feel myself approaching climax.

"Oh my God," she said, pushing me back. "Condom!"

It was too late, I wasn't going to break off now. But I could understand her reluctance to end up with a mixed-race child. So I withdrew, spat on my finger and rubbed it around her arse, then pushed down on her and introduced my cock into her tight brown hole.

"No . . ." she said, hands on my chest again, "no . . . no . . ." Then a grin spread over her lips. "Yes . . . yes . . . YEEEEEEES!"

I emptied myself into her, the strokes more frequent because of the unaccustomed tightness. My climax seemed like it would never stop.

But, of course, it did. I got away without being arrested or spotted by a nosy neighbour. After Lucy Arkle, the remaining girls didn't do much for me, not that I denied them.

I finished school soon afterwards. But those girls and women, I've never forgotten them.

And, now, neither will you.

Exquisite Corpse

Aimee Nichols

His Feet

He finds his own feet a bit of a turn-on.

He doesn't do anything special to them, not really. He's seen other guys who paint their nails, rid themselves of all foot and toe hair. He thinks that looks nice enough, just as it does when women do it, but looking at the foot fetish websites has made him realize that he's not interested in anyone else's feet.

He's not interested in other men. He's not interested in other male body parts.

He's never said anything outright to any of his lovers. One seemed to know, and would lean backwards and stroke his feet as she rode him. Never for very long though, as the position was sadly impractical from a comfort standpoint.

But he's started doing yoga, and he's pretty pleased with how well he's progressing with the Baddha Konasana. It's only a matter of time.

My Thigh

The threads of my fishnets form slightly different patterns this far up on my thigh. Not like the girls on the packaging where it stays pretty much the same all the way up. Past my knee, the holes in my fishnets transform into hundreds of tiny mouths, gasping, caught wide in a moment of some undefined emotion. Heading to the apex where they become fraught diamonds, the place where flesh threatens to spill through.

My right leg has won this particular battle, its victory two small, strategic snappings of thread. Flesh pouts out from it, a sensitive little mound all softness and nerve endings. I stroke it and tremble; it is like finding a new clit, so close to my old one that surely I'm being greedy.

All night I keep my hand under the table, skirt rucked up, and play with my new treasure. No one at the table of National Party MPs even notices.

Her Genitals

She has always found the things not quite said to be the most interesting. Her friends laugh at jokes about budgie-smugglers, sneer at guys with their singlets and shorts too tight in summer. The idea of the male body as a thing of beauty, to be displayed and looked over, fills them with revulsion.

She feels a little bit differently. In high school photography class, her appreciation of Max Dupain's work was a little more furtive than everyone else's. Discovering beefcake photography was like finding the holy grail. She ogles the tight swimming trunks, the skimpy little swimmers, the designer underwear. She traces over the pronounced bulges with her thumbnail, biting her lip, imagining the heat and silkiness that would be present in real life. Her favourite combination is white and wet, where the skin shows through, just a little, and contours are all the more sharp.

She likes the same look on herself. She puts on high-waisted white cotton knickers, the kind her friends would call granny knickers, and watches in the mirror as she pulls them up, up until they bunch and fold and cleave, her lips pouting through them. She rests her vibrator against the cotton gusset and focuses on the warming of fabric and flesh.

His Torso

If she could burrow her way into his chest and live there, she would. She doesn't tell him this because she senses it would be a little weird to reveal her desire to be a parasite in his body.

His chest and stomach are muscle, enveloped in fat, coated thickly with hair. She understands what a bear is now; that special combination of softness and the power to tear flesh apart at the slightest whim. A fierce, wild being popularly rewritten as a cuddly companion.

She wishes she could name every hair on his chest. She runs her fingers through the forest on his stomach, up to his nipples, and squeezes.

His Hands

His hands are just as big as they need to be.

People have given him shit for them all his life. His father was a proper burly blokey bloke who took up all the space and air in every room he walked into, with big rough dirty-nailed hands with which he made his living. He never quite got over his bemusement and offence at having such a girly man for a son, smallness and soft skin and clean nails all adding up to the crime of limp-wristedness.

Many of his friends have been no better. His hands scream pampered desk job in a world that sees rugged outdoorsyness as a virtue. The world is divided about his hands, divided into camps of those who know what he can do with them and those who do not.

Now his hand is inside her, fist bunched tight. She has enveloped him, and he barely dares breathe, let alone move, as she writhes against the bed, there on the end of his arm. Her arousal flows around his hand, into the folds of his clenched fist, drips down to his wrist outside. She clenches and convulses around him, making sounds that in all his life he's never heard before, and finally he understands.

His hands are just as big as they need to be.

My Head

My brain has basically been a custom porno theatre since I was twelve years old. A few things happened that year: I got the Talk, and I saw my first nudie magazine. Compared to some of what I hear kids watch on the Internet these days, seeing a smiling, pretty young woman spreading her pussy lips with her fingers seems damned tame by comparison.

Moralists like to rant about gateways. Gateway drugs, gateways and stepping stones into various realms of vice. That magazine, pilfered from a friend's older brother, was my gateway into sexual fantasy, and into porn.

They say your brain is your biggest sexual organ and my biggest sexual organ can encompass everyone and everything. In my mind I've fucked pretty much all of the guys working in porn today, a decent proportion of the women, as well as boyfriends of girlfriends, girlfriends of boyfriends, attractive people I see on the street and around everywhere, and particularly of note the guy who works the night shift at my local 7-Eleven; we've had some damned kinky cerebral good times.

I don't see a raging pervert when I look in the mirror; I see a pretty ordinary twenty-something woman, albeit one with a knowing little smirk that never quite seems to get wiped away. Only the most trusted of lovers get to see inside to what's really there, and only if I think they can handle it.

In the outside world I am meekpolitenicegood, all these characteristics ascribed to girls like me, I play them like a virtuoso. In my head I taste and fuck the world.

Alice Before her Period

Emma Becker

Translated by Adriana Hunter

There *is* something worse than not making love to Alice, and that's doing it when she's in a bad mood. It doesn't matter what she's annoyed about; it might be something two days back or first thing that morning, it might not be about anything at all, just rooted in the unfathomable mysteries of Alice's dear heart, but she's completely consumed by it. And although taking her when she's blazing with hate like this can be a turn-on, it's a challenge not to be taken lightly, and one that encourages analysis as well as empathy. Not that you don't enjoy it yourself but you'd have to be extraordinarily stupid to believe the contortions and gesticulations she instinctively comes up with to avoid being asked too many questions. There are impressive storms lurking behind that stubborn forehead, thunderclaps to make you shudder, and it doesn't take much for them to break out; the tiniest lapse and her glaring indignation comes to roost in the crease of an eyebrow, but what was the lapse, when and why?

One afternoon Emmanuel collapses on top of her panting, having teetered on the brink of death-by-orgasm only seconds before. Because yes, it has to be said, even in a filthy mood she's still a prime receptacle, her thighs heartbreakingly soft, her muddle of blonde hair and those incisors laid bare in a half-open mouth. And counter-intuitively, counter to her wishes (*I mean, why submit to a fake communion of souls when all you have to offer are furious imprecations?*), she has quite a repertoire of hip gyrations that don't really belong to someone harbouring a glowering temper. Maybe she pushes just a teensy bit less, to sow the seeds of doubt, to make you aware there's a problem. However wily she may be, though, Alice doesn't realize that it's precisely this deliberate lethargy, this obvious grudgingness that actually makes you come. The feeling you're taking her slightly against her will is so unusual that you find you're obsessing about the escalating pleasure written on her face, and the fury this provokes in her – exactly like a rapist. She'll hold back genuine proof of delight as long as she possibly can, trotting out only the crudest signs, the sort that make you want to slap her and crucify her with your cock, and suddenly the only reliable part of her body are her ears which just can't help flushing red, unlike her shameless liar of pussy.

Legend would have it that during lovemaking a woman's parts have a life of their own, but you should see Alice's when she's made up her mind to take you for a ride – it's enough to make you really hate women and their diabolical cleverness! They very soon realize their cries aren't enough to fool you, and the bitches (and Alice is the most fascinating example of the genre) start faking the involuntary and utterly poetic contractions their insides make in the heat of battle. They imitate that indecipherable sort of Morse code, one sustained squeeze, two shorter ones, putting together the lie as if assembling a bouquet; and when the time comes *not* to reach orgasm, these paler-by-the-minute and pinker-by-the-minute, incomparable and insufferable actresses dig their nails into your arm and tighten their pussies in a single wonderful gulp that intensifies and, rather poignantly, locks tight at the end. Who can you trust then, if even the part of the body that's meant to surrender first is in on the conspiracy?

What a performance Alice puts on! What a feat of engineering, lubricated to perfection, complicated by the fact that she hates having a hump when she's got the hump. How inhuman, when you come to think of it! Lying on a bed of deliciously tangled hair, she affects the agonizing swoon of a Bernini statue, the tendons in her thighs apparently strained to breaking point, her little stomach heaving helplessly in and out, her cheeks filling angrily with breath so she looks like a cute caricature of the Greek god of the wind. Alice gasps, she has the cheek to sigh "Yes, yes!", tenses all her muscles and cavorts wildly on the mast that's impaling her. You'd think she was on the brink of overdosing and having a heart attack at the same time. This is when Emmanuel realizes that, simulated though it may be, the masquerade had him all the way, the concept that she might not be experiencing pleasure is grotesque, she's so exultant! Her half-open mouth produces throaty sort of gurglings that *just can't* be faked, every inch of her undulating body exudes an intoxicating musky sweat and you can feel a jittery engine thrumming beneath her skin, the drum roll of her heels spurring you in the buttocks, her tunnel of wonders widening then clamping its gums like a newborn, every last bit of Alice holding its breath before the final spasm when she completely loses herself . . . and at the height of all this turbulence, just as Emmanuel comes, staring at her with bulging eyes, she opens hers, her blue liar's eyes, her whore's eyes, disgustingly calm and knowing, parked implacably between her eyelashes, and – amidst all that euphoria – they speak for her, saying she didn't come, no, she didn't come and you can go to hell. It's like a bucket of cold water as he shoots his load, but there's nothing for it now except to accept that she may be a manipulative bitch and a stupid cow rolled into one but she's still just as fantastically fuckable; she can't fake that or help herself, she can't stop her little breasts bouncing or her cleft from making a slight squeal with each intrusion – whatever you do, Alice, however clever you may be, when it comes down to it you're still just a nice hot hole with pretty bits and bobs moving about around it.

That's how to redress the balance a bit: as he leans into her forehead and comes, Emmanuel thinks *and you can go to hell too*. She really does ask to be insulted, this geisha who even imitates those exhausted, post-orgasmic gasps, apparently identifying the moment when he's expelled the last drop and given the last sigh and when his anger at being conned is tussling half-heartedly with his pleasure, his undiminished pleasure.

Once the curtain has fallen, though, the audience would be wasting their breath asking for an encore. Alice furiously pulls away from the weight bearing down on her, and lies there on her back, wide-eyed. And in those eyes are all the mysteries of the world with their non-Euclidian angles and their ungodly contours, impenetrable whichever way you approach them. She risks a sideways glance with a flicker of distant contempt for having been believed – because she herself believes in her strategies, she puts enough faith in them to feel they stand up on their own. *Filthy little bitch*.

And then the miracle happens; in her efforts to heave a great sigh like a sulking child angling for consolation, Alice pushes out some of the scalding sperm that Emmanuel has resentfully surrendered to her. The sudden surprise on her face! She raises her long goat-kid legs, reaches out her hands and gently splays herself open, gliding one finger between the slippery surfaces and bringing it back out with an exasperating soft cork-like pop. Alice has forgotten her fury now, she's lost in earnest contemplation of the ravaged playground, subjecting it to a series of swift suction movements. She's like a lone little monkey at the top of a tree, fiddling with itself completely unnoticed; and just as Emmanuel, now drained of his strength, feels a fierce rage mounting, an ill-defined hatred for the girl and her fickleness, Alice throws herself back onto the pillows with a groan, grasping her petals of pink skin in both hands and – now reduced to a perfectly, intolerably bestial state – moans:

"Oh, finish me off, finish me off!"

Tourist

Angela Caperton

Sometimes in the early morning hours, Rutger insisted on fucking Julie on the stage.

"It is good for business," he told her. "Not every night, not even very often. Just now and then to keep the suckers wondering if it will happen or not. Keep them coming back."

She objected the first two times, but her resistance only enflamed the drunken crowd and after that she decided that allowing Rutger to fuck her, usually from behind, was only another form of dance.

"Everyone in Berlin is a whore, darling," Rutger told her, "but you are also an artist. It is not like I want to fuck you," he persisted. "You know I prefer men and big women, but the Mandrake Club's reputation will suffer if we do not sometimes offer things to our audience that they cannot easily see at a dozen cabarets on the street."

Julie did not bother to tell him that most of the cabarets near Friedrichstrasse offered similar fare, along with girls fucking girls, erotic flagellation, and even more exotic entertainments. Rutger knew this well, but Rutger did not really care about anything other than his own opinions.

Each night, he welcomed the denizens of Berlin and the foreigners who came to sample the city's delights. He stalked the stage in his mad clown's make-up, swollen red drunk's nose and wardrobe of wigs, introduced the girls who sang, the men who dressed as women and the women in suits. The blur of sexes and genders hardly mattered in a city where everyone fucked everyone more or less without regard for anything but the moment. Berlin sagged under the weight of the lost war, under the oppression of joblessness and crazy money, but at night, on Friedrichstrasse, escape lived in flesh, song, frivolity and unfettered sexual abundance – always for a price.

Julie danced at the Mandrake. Her name and a grotesque distortion of her image hung in a tattering poster beside the door. She had been dancing there since '22, when Papa had turned her out into the street because he could not feed her. Now she had an apartment of her own, which she shared with a shifting cast of roommates down on their luck, other dancers from the club, men who aspired to be pimps but who lacked the moral fiber, and petty black marketers in between deals.

She appreciated the relative fortune of her simple walls and furnishings but always Julie told herself, "Someday my luck will change. Someday I will have more."

The night she met Paul, she began to believe the stories she told herself. Paul strode into the Mandrake like a champion, head level, eyes sharp and determined, his very presence shivering Julie's soul unlike anyone she'd ever met. He wore his blond hair short, stiff in a funny way, and it smelled good with a hint of something exotic. He looked like money. He wore an expensive suit that he told her later was real silk. He had the most perfect teeth she had ever seen, gleaming white in the stage light when he sat at the front table and watched her.

"Pretty Julie," he crooned with sincerity. "If you will come with me tonight, I will make you a duchess." He barely looked at Rutger before giving the wicked clown a handful of gold coins.

"I don't care if you don't bring her back," Rutger chuckled as he winked and smiled at Julie. "Good luck. Have fun."

Paul walked out with her, his arm around her waist, possessive and endearing in his hold. He took her to the Paradise and Inferno nightclub, and Julie swallowed hard, awed and worried that she was not dressed well enough. A bony doorman dressed as St Peter looked them over. "We want to go to heaven," Paul told him. "Only heaven is good enough for my Julie."

Julie smiled as the doorman's scorn melted away when Paul gave him a generous fold of marks, and then they were inside the most infamous club in Berlin. A nearly naked Cupid led them to a booth on the left side of the stage, shrouded in shadows but sometimes washed by red light from the spotlights and flood-lights that danced across the stage. She tried not to stare at the dancing sparkle of diamonds and satin flash when the stage light-ing splashed sometimes over the women in the audience. As Julie looked around the cabaret, she wondered, what did it feel like to wear a ring that cost more than food for a year? A gauzy white curtain bisected the theater. On the other side of it, Julie knew from stories, Hell's patrons sat in equal splendor attended by handsome devils and almost-nude lady demons.

Satan, his muscular chest bare and painted red, paraded on the stage addressing the audience. Julie grinned, wondering if the obvious bulge in the tight black pants he wore was real or a stuffed prosthetic. Regardless, the illusion gave many in the audience reason to twitter approval. "So, Berliners, welcome to Hell," he said to the half of the audience hidden from Julie by the white curtain, before he turned to Julie and Paul's side of the room. "Our friends over in Heaven, don't worry! We delight in showing you—" he chuckled with low, wicked delight "—what it is you're missing!"

Paul sat beside her in the booth, his light laughter a hymn beyond the other merriment in the club. She glanced at him as they both faced the stage and smiled, delighted by his obvious enjoyment. Then he slid his warm hand under Julie's skirt and stroked her slit through the black lace of her panties. She remembered her price tag, but she also grew wet under his touch, her heart pounding. The giddy wonder of his forwardness surprised her even as a touch of disappointment dimmed the glow of the evening. He stopped after only a moment and leaned to her, pressing trembling lips to her ear. "Remove your panties, Julie," he commanded with a whisper that rippled through her soul. She started to stand, to find shadows or a powder room, but he traced his hand down her wrist and locked it in a grip that claimed, took, breathed, and promised. "No," he corrected her. "Remove them here."

She shifted and adjusted, reaching up and behind and under, unfastened her garter and slowly squirmed out of the soft cotton panties. Anyone in the club who looked at her would surely know what she was doing, but perhaps the shadows concealed her. She surrendered her underpants to Paul and looked at him, waiting.

Paul curled his fingers into the white material, his thumb stroking the prim edge, then at Paul's commanding nod and curt order, the waiter brought a strong brandy and a bottle of good wine. On the stage, a thin woman, entirely nude, pale as ivory, danced in smoky light, a study in white and black, milky skin, black-ringed eyes, the whipping mane of her raven hair, and the thick tangle of silken black between her legs. Sinuous, precise, she fought with the smoke and made love to it, a teasing undulation of flesh and dreams.

Paul took Julie's hand and rested it on his hardening cock. She pressed through the smooth material of his trousers, her fingers expert from many nights in the Mandrake. She brought him to full, impressive erection, just as the dancer on the stage twirled one final time and vanished into the billowing smoke.

Everyone applauded. Julie smelled opium and hashish. The smoke and the brandy turned her mind golden and she relaxed against Paul, opening his trousers and reaching in to touch the bare heat of his cock. She smiled and stroked down its pulsing length with one testing finger.

The silky bead at the tip delighted her, the slippery warmth of it, the affirmation of Paul's desire. She smeared the bead and relished his quickened breath.

The stage stayed dark for a long moment, then a clown dressed as an angel appeared and began to tell stories and make dirty jokes about politicians and Socialists, Frenchmen and Russians. Paul put his hand over Julie's, his fingertips almost tickling the back of her hand as she slowly pumped him. "Wait," he whispered, and she stopped, but he didn't move her hand, allowing her to hold the hard, responsive flesh.

He poured wine for her and she drank. "You are an American?" she asked him casually as she tightened her grip a moment, then relaxed her hand.

"Yes I am," he answered with a little smile. "Have you ever been in this place before?"

"No. Have you?"

Paul shook his head. "I've heard a great deal about it – read books about it."

"Are you a teacher?" she asked him.

"No. Only a tourist, Julie. Like so many in Berlin."

"Why did you come here?" Julie leaned toward him, her stomach tightening pleasantly as they talked. Not only was Paul handsome and his cock seemingly full of promise, but his eyes glowed with the mellow light of kindness and thoughtfulness. The discomfort of moments ago melted with his patience, his quiet answers, his indulgence. She liked him. Maybe that would be a mistake, but Julie accepted the risk. It wouldn't be her first, or her last.

He sighed thoughtfully, watching the clown as though he might have been observing a squirrel in the park, with only casual interest. "Because in . . . America . . . it is not easy to do the things I wish to do. The possibilities here are so much richer."

"It doesn't always seem good to me here," she said, "but I do like the freedom we have, and I am glad you are here with me now."

The clown finished on stage, bowing with a flourish to a parade of beauties who streamed from the wings clad in gossamer white and feathers, angels with bared breasts and red lips. Paul's cock jumped under her hand and she began to stroke him again.

The women on stage danced with each other, the gossamer costumes floating like wings about them, hands busy on arched backs and long pale legs, round buttocks, a flash of pussy here and there, calculated to arouse. The audience made noises of appreciation and Paul's hand stroked hers, then stopped her motion again. He waved to the nearest Cupid and said to him, "A round of drinks for everyone here and a little something for yourself." He handed the waiter a stack of bills and the waiter bowed.

"Anything you wish, sir," the Cupid said with a cherubic chuckle.

Paul turned back to Julie, his eyes bright with wickedness. "Sit in my lap," he told her.

She giggled, thrilled but also uncertain. Then she obeyed him, gathered her short skirt in nervous fingers, settled her bare bottom against the smooth silken texture of his trousers. He reached under her and freed his cock so that it rose like a rod of precious, warm jade between her legs, the round shaft parting the moist lips of her pussy. He did not penetrate her, but held her, one hand stroking her breast through her blouse and chemise, the other stroking her sex, lingering at the bud of her clit, until she began to pant.

On the stage, the angels danced.

Julie's cheeks heated as she glimpsed some of the patrons around them watching her writhing body, admiration shining in their eyes. They sipped the drinks the waiter brought them, but soon Julie realized their interest in her and Paul's private show barely aroused them. She closed her eyes a moment, enjoying the build of shocking pleasure in her pussy as she accepted that such sights were not uncommon, though here in a club of some repu-tation it added to the excitement that their brazen public display was not ordinary. Blood boiling, her pussy pulsing with need, Julie rose from Paul's lap a little and he maneuvered his prick beneath her so that when she settled, he filled her in one long, thick slide, a slow and tight possession that stole the air from her lungs.

She began to moan and rock on him, shifting her hips to increase her stimulation. His practiced touch delighted her and she hardly believed how truly wonderful he felt inside her. She forgot her surroundings, the crowd, the dancers; the stage and lights only distant hums and blotches of blurred colors. She began to push against the table as he countered her motion, bucking slowly under her, their goal the same, to touch the golden tip of bliss.

His fingers moved with relentless precision on her clit and the blast of pleasure that shattered inside her overwhelmed her senses. She came hard, clutching the table, moaning louder than the music. His body pulsed inside her, his arms around her banded her middle with thick heat. The deep thrust swelled against her electrified pussy as he climaxed, and the wet gush inside her turned her knees to butter. They came together, hot and united. His hands continued to stroke her, the nipple between his fingers rock hard and her slit soaked but greedy, and, without warning, another orgasm rocketed through her. She sagged in his lap, her head falling back onto his strong shoulder. Sweat trickled down her back and between her breasts while he murmured incoherently in her ear and the angels took a bow, some of them – the ones on the left side of the stage – giggling at Julie and Paul, their eyes shining in the footlights' glare.

Paul's lips found the raw nerve at the base of her neck and her whole body clenched with exhausted ecstasy. "Thank you, Julie," Paul said to her, his kiss lush and true. "You have made my dream come true."

The next night Julie stared at herself in the mirror of the Mandrake dressing room. "I liked Paul very much," she said to Rutger before swirling her make-up brush in the chipped bowl of face paint. "Do you think he will come back?" Rutger, stripped to the waist, worked on his make-up as well. Julie, costumed as a harlequin for the first number of the night, watched him through the reflection.

"Who knows?" Rutger answered with disinterest. "He's a tourist, Julie, and he probably spent a great deal to come here. If you made him happy, maybe he will come back."

"How much did he pay you?" she asked. "You should give me some of it."

Rutger barely shrugged, but then handed her a handful of marks.

Julie counted them and smiled. "That's generous but I saw he paid you in coins."

"Mind your business, Julie, and you will be happier. Just because you liked his cock and he took you to Paradise doesn't make him anything special."

She rubbed rouge into her cheeks. "I think he is in love with me."

Rutger laughed. "Love isn't real. If life in Berlin teaches you anything, it should teach you that. Your good fortune is making you crazy. If it were not for me, you would just be another *chonte*, fucking sailors for pennies. I've made you a real table-lady now and you had better keep your head on and be grateful for what you have. Don't do anything stupid. Go out there and be a good little dancer tonight and I will try to find you another man who loves you. Best you forget your American because I am sure he will forget you."

But a week later, Rutger came to Julie backstage, his grin not reflected in his eyes. "Your lover is back and he wants something really special tonight."

Julie's heart beat as hard as a street drummer. She stood, smoothing the folds of her short skirt with nervous strokes. She didn't dare tell Rutger, but, as far as she was concerned, Paul didn't need to pay her a thing. She had thought of no one but him in the time since they had gone to the Paradise and Inferno together, and the ache his absence had burned into her drove home her need to just be with him, regardless of the circumstances. She waited for Rutger to speak, not trusting her own voice yet.

"Tonight, in the last performance, your tourist wants to make love to you on the stage wearing a mask. He is a wild one."

She nodded, her emotions and thoughts tangling so much she only managed one word. "OK."

Rutger caged her with his gaze. He paced in front of her like a predator. "I told him it would cost him – that there was great risk from the police, bribes to be paid, and so forth, and he did not even hesitate. He also wants your company until then. Go with him. Be good to him. I don't think that will be difficult for you." Rutger looked her over from head to toe, his expression one of uncertain awareness. "Come back here at three o'clock, maybe four, he'll have his mask and his fun. We are really going to be lucky now, you and me," Rutger stressed, as if his words could brand her. He smiled at her, his made-up face pale and ghastly as a movie vampire, but Julie barely registered his implied claim. Her ears still rang with the only words she cared about.

Paul waited for her.

In the dim light of the little club, she did not see him at first and he called to her. The tone in his voice might have been joy and she tried to control her steps so that she did not appear too eager as she wove among the tables and patrons to reach him.

He rose and took her hands, holding them tight between warm fingers and all concern that he might not feel as she did faded from her heart.

"It's been so long, Julie," he exclaimed, pulling her lightly into the seat beside him, his gaze devouring her with a hunger and a reverence that made her heart pound.

She studied him through the dim light of the club and a thin sheen of tears and her stomach clenched, cold. Small lines creased across Paul's forehead, and his hair looked just as short and spiky, but not as vibrant and not as thick. He looked worn, older – more so than she thought even a week on the hardest streets of Berlin could cost a man. "Are you all right?" she asked, trying to keep her voice light and clear of worry as she gently traced the small line at the corner of his mouth.

"I am now," he said, his smile taking the edge from her fear. "I returned as soon as I could."

"I have thought a lot about you," she said. "I liked our last date very much."

"I hope you are not just saying that because you want me to believe you," he laughed and poured her schnapps.

She relaxed in the chair beside him, returning the pressure of the hand that still had not released hers. How was it that just seeing him, just feeling his touch again should lift her spirits so high, should flood her vision with images of home and family, tree-lined lanes and every good thing? Giddy. That was the word for it, that feeling of an ever-present giggle of happiness within one's chest. That was how she felt. That was how Paul made her feel just seeing him.

He leaned over and kissed her, a tentative press at first, then a light stroke of his tongue against hers, just a taste. Her mind reeled as her body honed to him. As he pulled away, Julie inhaled his scent and smiled. He smelled like some incense she could not place, a manly spice that sweetened the air.

"Did Rutger tell you what I want to do tonight?" he asked her and she nodded, feeling her cheeks burn with more modesty than she would have thought herself capable of.

"I will do anything for you," she said. "Anything."

They drank their schnapps quickly, in silence, and then he led her out of the Mandrake around a corner and down Friedrichstrasse, past the noisy little crowds at the doors of the restaurants and clubs. She imagined that the street girls watched her with envy as she passed them, on the arm of her handsome Paul, and she pretended that she was his mistress, silently wishing it true.

Arm in arm, they walked past the last of the clubs, out of the garish light and into darkness, the next light ahead of them marking the entrance to a little park with a lime-bleached statue. A rising wind blew papers against the iron fence and Paul put his arm around her. She huddled close to him. Many times she had walked with dates to this park and they had found a bench where she would use her mouth or hands on them. More than once, the man with her had been robbed here.

"Paul, I want to go with you, but this park is not so safe."

He laughed. "It will be all right," he said. "I want a quiet place we can talk without being heard."

She let him lead her through the open gate and to a bench just beyond the statue. He held her close, his hand gentle on her breast, finding the nipple through the wisp of her blouse and the cotton of her brassiere. She loved his touch, loved that it was different from all the others she had known. She kissed him openly, giving him more than she had given any man in a long time.

Beyond the golden sphere of his embrace, she heard footsteps in the last moment of approach. Paul pulled back from her and turned toward the sound.

Julie knew one of the men as Red Maik, quick with his knife and fond of pain. The other one she had seen, though she did not know his name. He looked like a white-faced monkey with little, mean eyes.

"Lovers," Red Maik crooned with contempt. "So sweet. You can go back to your kisses when you have given us what we want."

Paul glanced at her with a crooked, sheepish smile. "You

warned me," he whispered, then turned to the men. "You want money?" he asked them, a trace of amusement in his tone.

"Leave him alone, Red," Julie said. "Please."

"Give us enough—" Red Maik ignored her "—and we'll let you keep your pretty clothes."

"All right," Paul said calmly, as if he was buying bread, then he reached into his pocket. His hand came out with something no bigger than a cigarette lighter. It made a popping sound and both of the thugs dropped to the ground like puppets with cut strings, not even twitching, still as death.

Paul bent over them a moment, pressing fingers to their necks.

Julie stared, stunned. "Are they . . . ?"

"No. They'll be fine in an hour," Paul said as he rose. "Probably won't even remember what happened."

"What did . . . ?"

"I stunned their nervous systems for a moment."

"But how?"

He put his arm around her and led her back out of the park and toward the lights with long strides that carried them away from the scene quickly. "It is very important that I did not hurt them. Julie . . ." he started and the tone of his voice held the weight of dire importance. "How old do you think I am?"

Forty, she thought. "Thirty-five? Maybe a little older?"

"Close enough," he said, then released a long breath. "In another sense, Julie, I am no age at all. I have not yet even been born."

Julie's steps slowed. "A joke? I don't understand."

"I don't suppose you've ever heard of a man called H. G. Wells?"

She shook her head against his shoulder, a veneer of ice slowly sliding down her spine.

"You know how a ship travels on the ocean, yes? I am from a place where men have learned to voyage like that across years, centuries."

Paul tightened his hold on her shoulders, pulling her lightly back against his side. "All my life, I have read about Berlin . . . here, this year, this street, and I have wanted to come here."

They reached the narrow front of a café between two clubs. He led her in and paid the waiter for a private booth in the back. Paul ordered wine and looked around carefully before he spoke more.

"We can travel backwards in time, but such travel is stringently monitored and restricted because a person who goes into the past can cause great harm with even an action of kindness."

She watched him, listening to his words and tone, wanting to believe him.

"Just like here in Berlin where everything has a price, where I am from there are those who sell such trips for enormous fortunes in spite of such travel being against the law. I have . . . I had . . . I will have a great deal of money and influence, but I had nothing I cared about in my world, so I paid men for this illegal travel and I came here."

He was quiet for a moment while the waiter brought the wine and poured it.

"I came here to be with you."

"You knew about me?" she asked, again wanting very much to believe him.

"'I knew about Berlin, about this time, what it was like. I didn't know about you until I saw you . . . was it only last week?"

She nodded.

"For me, almost three years have passed. It took me that long to arrange a second trip. I have given nearly everything I owned to come back to you." He took her chilled hand and raised it to his lips, the light kiss giving back some warmth.

"What did you mean when you said it was important that you not hurt Red . . . those men?"

"Anyone who travels back in time must be very careful. I am told that little actions show no harmful effects. The scientists argue details, but most agree, time is like the ocean, it fills in what is moved or taken away . . . but a big action can cause huge changes in the future. There are men – like policemen – who stand . . . outside of time and watch for such things. If I had killed Red or his friend, I would be in very serious trouble."

She drank her wine and thought about all he said. Her decision didn't trumpet or flash, it simply settled like satin on skin, and for that, Julie trusted it. If Paul was mad, it didn't matter. She loved him. "Making love on a stage is not a big action?" she asked with a small smile.

"No. I won't leave anything behind me but a memory of a man in a mask enjoying the greatest of pleasures with a beautiful woman. Telling you all I have told you is far more risky."

"Why do you want to make love to me on the stage?"

"Where I am from, we are watched always, but rarely ever seen. That will be hard for you to understand. You are often on a stage. Men want you. For me, there is no more exciting thought than to be on that stage with you, sharing a human, intimate act, and being watched by strangers, and knowing that those who watch us will be aroused, and knowing too, some might think it offensive and wrong – but won't turn away. That is what I paid for."

She looked down, sad and disappointed. He touched her chin, raised her face to meet his gaze. "Before I came here," he said. "It could have been with any woman and I would have been happy. But, after I met you, after what we shared in Paradise, it can only be you. In all of time. In every place that has ever been."

Her smile bloomed like a white rose on a perfect summer day. She was twenty-six years old, and had never been so happy in all her life.

The Mandrake was packed with men and women, every table filled, some of the crowd drunken or sedated with opium and hashish, some manic from cocaine. The air swelled, alive, and as Julie stepped onto the stage, she gazed upon a show palace that seemed as vast as Germany, so much bigger than the little club had ever seemed before. The tiny band played American jazz, wild and free flowing, and Julie danced around a velvet lounge that had been placed at center stage.

She wore a set of scarves that fell away from her like petals, five misty veils, not seven, each of them the color of pearl, shining and translucent. By the time she had shed three of them, her body shone beneath the filmy silk. Beauty and divinity radiated through her, into her. She was a temptress, a depraved saint, a goddess, a woman. She didn't dread what awaited her, not this time. She anticipated with growing excitement the act that had always before seemed sadly necessary, horribly sordid and somehow pathetic.

Rutger watched from the left wing, his evil clown face grinning, but his eyes hard as black glass.

Paul emerged from the right, masked in a luminous white satin mask and clothed in a thick red velvet robe. He moved with grace, the steps of his dance naive but beautiful, rising to the music's spell like a cobra to a charmer. Julie saw the crowd's attention focus upon him and she saw his excitement, understood something of what he wanted here, a rite of affirmation she wanted now as much as he did.

She cast the last two veils away and sat on the couch, spreading her legs in a manner that would have been lewd had she not been in the throes of the spell she shared with Paul. She wanted him to see her, open and wet, and she wanted the crowd to know she glistened there for him, anticipating the glory of his cock.

Paul dropped his robe and his beautiful member stood out like a pole, the scepter of a priest, of a god-king, eager for union with his goddess. Julie's hands ran over her body, offering herself to him, to the watchers, inviting them into the act, to share the sacrament of union. She leaned and licked down a thick cock vein, and cupped his balls in her hand. She smeared the glistening tip on her painted lips, then parted them and took him in. She savored the salt, the musk, the mysterious smoky spice that was uniquely him. She worshipped him, filling her mouth, sliding him into her open, greedy throat, then flickering her tongue as she pulled away. Rapture fell like fog over her, and she sensed the same spell upon the crowd. She leaned back to let a line of saliva between her lips and the swollen head of his prick shine silver in the footlights.

The crowd stilled.

She sucked him, oblivious then to the men and women who watched, though she basked in the power of their watching eyes, their breathing that matched hers and Paul's. Looking up at him, at the smooth, white mask he wore, she grinned, realizing he could be any man under it, but the reality, the truth that pounded in her bones and muscles, her veins and skin, was that this was Paul, and he was there for her. This moment was his.

And hers.

He pushed her head back, disengaging his stone-hard prick from between her lips. He stroked her cheek, leaned to kiss her with deep passion, and then moved to mount her, his left hand under her right thigh, his right hand opening her pussy to him, testing her and finding her wetter than she had ever been.

She surrendered to him, reverent and wholly focused on what they shared. No performance, no lines, no music beyond what hummed in her blood and breath. This was life as it was meant to be led, daring and bold, heedless of everything except the instant, the future not even a concept, certainly not a real place or time.

He penetrated her with slow fervor, thick and long, sliding deep, beyond past lovers and even her dreams. His tender touch was that of a seducer taking a virgin, confident and strong, yet infinitely careful as he began to fuck her with masterful strokes.

Julie moved with him, shameless and defiant of anyone to condemn her for this act, this glorious union. They moved together, the music and the band matching their rhythm as they quickened, Paul's cock sliding almost out of her and then deliciously back in. He gripped her hips and kissed her breasts as he rocked them both toward paradise.

She fell, endless and otherworldly toward the rush of orgasm, the timeless oblivion of a really good come bright as diamonds before her closed eyes. She clutched at him, her nails raking across his shoulders as he threw back his head, grimaced, perspiration at the edges of his mask glistening, and then he emptied his heat into her, lost in a gush of blinding joy. She tightened around him, fighting the need to cry out. Then she rejected the last shred of modesty and gave her bliss voice. Her scream rose, a hymn of ecstasy to soar above the celebrant jazz of the band.

Paul held her, sweating, his arms tight around her as the audience applauded, whistled, and uproariously called for encores.

Close to her ear, so close no one could possibly hear him, Paul christened her soul, saying "I love you, Julie."

"Paul, my Paul," she whispered back, tears pushing at the gate of her lashes. "I love you too."

Later, Paul and Julie sat in the small cook's garden behind the Mandrake Club. Two big white moths fluttered around a smoky light of the oil lamp Julie had set in the middle of the crude wooden table they shared. Pending sunrise dulled the stars and seeped red like distant fire. Rutger swaggered through the kitchen door, a bottle of schnapps and three glasses in his hands. He pulled up a crate and sat, his clown face smeared in a painted snarl.

"To you, Paul," Rutger said, raising a glass of schnapps. "You've made me a wealthy man."

Paul still wore the white mask. "I should stay here," he said, his tone almost serious. "Make us both wealthy men."

Rutger drained his glass with a hoot of laughter. He wiped his mouth on his sleeve. "You know you can't do that."

Julie leveled her gaze on Rutger, hating him for that one statement. She held Paul's hand in a death grip.

"I do not think I will ever come back," Paul said, and Julie saw a trace of tears in his eyes behind the mask. Her heart splintered as Paul's hand clenched her fingers, hard and determined as stone.

"Oh, you will be back, brother," Rutger said again as he poured another generous shot. He smiled lopsided and strange, and lifted his glass to Paul. "I will see you in just a few weeks. You will find a way."

They sat quietly. Julie hated Rutger more for not going away and leaving her alone with Paul. After a while, dawn turned the garden rosy and banished the moths. Paul hugged and kissed Julie, his lips warm and alive, the tender contact conveying more than words. Rutger paused in his cleaning, grinned drunkenly, and gave a curt nod as Paul released her and slipped into the grey morning. She watched him as he walked up Zimmerstrasse, vanishing into the pale light all too soon. Gone.

For the entire month of July, Julie waited for him. She disappointed many men by politely declining their company, always giving them very good reasons, but in her heart, she knew Paul would walk back into the Mandrake, and back into her life.

Julie believed with all her soul that she and Paul belonged together, and she clung to the simple hope they could be together. The desire became a steel thread that sewed her life to meaning.

One morning in early August, Julie wove her way through Saturday morning crowds toward her apartment, carrying a small straw shopping bag filled with bread, cheese, and beer. A shabby beggar watched the crowds from the narrow doorway of a closed bakery, and after she passed him, she heard shambling steps behind her. She glanced back to see the ragged man following her. Her heart danced nervously as she picked up her pace, then looked back again, hoping to assess her odds should she need to fight him off.

The handles of the straw bag slid down her arm to the ground as she recognized her follower. The beggar, Paul, thinner and harder, dressed in rags, closed the distance in two measured strides.

Her pulse blasted in her ears and her breath would not fill her lungs. She panted on the verge of keening, tears springing to her eyes and a million questions on her lips.

Paul shushed her before she could speak, then asked her for money. She stared at him, shock and a moment of insanity brushing against her cheek. She shook her head and he walked away from her, not glancing back. She looked up and down the street, picked up her bag and followed him toward her apartment, still many blocks away. She lost sight of him sometimes, but then he would reappear, begging coins from a tourist, loitering against a wall. When Julie reached her apartment building, Paul materialized at the door and slipped in.

Hidden from the crowds, he caught her in a heated embrace. "I had to," he said, kissing her hard, hungry. "I had to return."

"I know," she managed before nipping his lower lip and closing her arms around him like iron bands.

"Will you go with me?" His eyes probed hers. She saw more lines around his eyes, the cuts of cruel time at the corners of his mouth, but love, unbound and courageous, shone on his face.

"Anywhere," she told him.

"Nowhere," he answered her. "We must go somewhere no one sees us, somewhere safe."

"Anywhere," she repeated.

"Listen," he said, his rough fingers caressing her cheek. "I know so much more than I did before. Someday, darling, I will tell you all the things I have done to come to . . . now, here. I cannot go back. I have committed so many crimes. You and I, Julie." He swallowed hard. "We must disappear."

Julie saw beyond the years that must have passed for him, saw how his time away had tempered him like metal. She hugged him hard, unwilling to trust her voice with her feelings.

"Here's what we must do," he said into her hair. "You must do exactly what I say."

Julie listened and held Paul tight. She would never let him go again.

Never.

Rutger smiled like a man who had found a golden coin.

"You want to buy her?" he asked Paul, Rutger's glance at Julie contemptuous.

"Her contract or whatever arrangement she has with you," Paul explained. "And what can I pay you to forget you ever knew her?"

Rutger had not yet donned his clown face. Without the greasepaint pallor, his ruddiness gave him a mean glow, and now he grew redder by the moment. "More than you've got, *mein herr*," he sneered. "It is time to stop pretending, yes? Time to show you my real face."

"I don't understand," Paul said, and Julie saw him glance at her, the question in his eyes, *Are you ready?*

She thought about what he had told her, that there were moments when time might be changed, when all the things that seemed ordained might be undone. She didn't know about that, didn't know if she believed in ordained time, but she believed in Paul.

"I know who you are," Rutger said, drawing a little pistol and pointing it at him. "I know where you are from. The men from— what do you call it? The Chrono Bureau? I have worked with them for a long time. Many tourists come to the Mandrake Club and you are not the first who has tried to stay here. Let me see your hands."

"What will you do to me?" Paul asked, raising his hands. "And to her?"

"To her? Nothing. It's bad you've told her so much, but I am assured that her life will mean nothing. She will live as she is meant to. You, I will hold here until they come for you.'"

"You should get away too," Paul told him. "You know what will happen to this city in a few years? To Germany?"

"'I know. I am told that I will prosper under the new government, that I will be an officer in the Party and an official in London after we have conquered it. It's all history to you, isn't it? They've told me everything that will happen to me. I will die in bed in America when I am an old man."

"Of course that's what they told you. Did you think they'd tell you an unpleasant story?" Paul shook his head. "Let me and Julie go," Paul said. "I will give you more gold than you can imagine. We will go away where no one will ever see us, where our lives will make no difference."

"It's no good," Rutger said with a cruel laugh. "All of this is already written. They told me you would come here. They told me what you would say. You will fail because you have already failed."

Paul nodded to Julie. She drew the little device that looked like a cigarette lighter from her dress pocket and pressed its side the way Paul had showed her. Rutger jumped as though he had been shocked. He collapsed, the gun falling with a clatter to the floor.

Paul checked Rutger's pulse, then turned to Julie, and nodded. "We need to go, now. I don't know when the Chronos will come, but we've got to be far from here when they do."

He took the device from her, made an adjustment to it, and pressed it to Rutger's pale forehead. Rutger jerked and lay still. Julie knew Paul had killed him.

"Paul! What about . . . big actions?"

Paul shrugged. "Any future where he does not live will be a better world."

Julie struggled to understand. "What he said . . . that he knew you would fail. How did you know what to do?"

He smiled at her and she saw pride and cleverness in his eyes, a kind of certainty. "I knew, Julie, because I have done this before . . . and failed. I knew what to do this time. Now, we must hurry. There will be dangerous men here in less than ten minutes."

They ran together from the Mandrake Club, down Friedrichstrasse. Paul had more gold. He gave her coins they could change into marks later. She flagged down a taxi and paid the driver to take them to the edge of town, to the place Paul told her. Outside an *imbiss*, the two bicycles waited.

As they maneuvered the bikes down a packed lane between two bright yellow fields, Paul reached over and squeezed her hand. "We just need to lay low for a while, then make our way to the port, then on to Costa Rica."

Julie smiled at him, fear and excitement turning her blood to liquid gold. Together they would do what he had told Rutger. They would go across the sea, live somewhere no one could find them, where they would leave no trace to be read in any book in the future.

As they pedaled, a thought came to her.

"Paul. What happens now? You have changed what Rutger said was written."

He stopped his bike and she hers, her feet light on the packed dirt path. He reached over and lifted her chin, kissing her with a fervor she'd not tasted before. His touch and his kiss filled her with hope and a sense of infinite possibilities.

"Does it matter?" he asked her. "To you and me? Does it matter at all? I came to Berlin to experience my greatest fantasy – to be watched making love to a woman. I spent a fortune for the hope of that fantasy. I wanted to be seen, Julie. I didn't expect anything more than my few minutes of spotlight and sexual fulfillment." He brushed a hand over her hair and smiled, the deep lines around his mouth beautiful in the late afternoon sun. "Many of the people I knew, they paid fortunes to experience their fantasies over and over again. I thought I'd be one of them. I'd pay again and again to fuck for an audience, but I didn't just fuck some *chonte*. I had the most intense experience of my life with the woman I love." He kissed her forehead, his thumb brushing aside the tear that slid down her cheek.

"That moment will be ours forever, Julie. Now there can be no more stages. We will live in shadows and cast none of our own, and it will be all right. Everything shines now, Julie. For us, maybe for the world, from this moment, everything is new." He kissed her lightly and smiled before sitting back on the bicycle.

"We will travel together into the new future.

"One day at a time."

Here There be Dragons

Ashley Lister

"Dragonmeister?"

Georgianna of Roxburghshire stopped moving. She snapped her head back toward the sound of the voice that had summoned her. Her heartbeat quickened. Above the stench of subterranean earth and dung, her nostrils caught the harsh stink of the burning tar.

Mercifully, the burning-tar was unlit.

The night down here was as lightless as the tomb of a forgotten pilgrim. But the smell was assuredly the burning tar and that was a substance that had no place in the eastern catacombs.

"No," she whispered.

It was as much as she dared to say.

She was patrolling the catacombs, a thrice daily chore for the dragonmeister of Gatekeeper Island, and inwardly cataloguing her stock. Here in the easternmost catacombs she kept a weyr of orientals that included three-toed Japanese dragons and five-clawed Chinese dragons.

The orientals were the most ferocious and dangerous members of the island's livestock. Maintaining their successful husbandry was an achievement that had won her shields of honor from Caleb the wolf slayer, laird of her fiefdom. But the husbandry of the orientals had never been a chore that George took lightly. It was a perilous job and she insisted there were rules that needed to be followed.

"Dragonmeister? Are you their mistress Georgianna?"

After the question came the sound of flint striking stone.

George clenched her teeth and shook her head.

Her eyes grew wide in the darkness.

It was one of the apprentice hostlers. She recognized the adolescent squeak of his voice. He was one of a cadre that had

arrived earlier that year at summer's end. In any of the other catacombs his ignorant mistake would merit little more than a stern
reprimand.

But this was the easternmost catacombs.

This environment was not forgiving.

In the western catacombs, where she kept the European dragons, the apprentice hostlers were known to fly the beasts in
tournaments and race them for pleasure or for daring or for
gambling. The western catacombs were larger than their eastern
counterparts and hosted a range of dragons that made her laird's
fiefdom the envy of every baron beyond Gatekeeper Island. The
western catacombs held Portuguese caco, Polish smok and
Catalonian víbria.

And every one of those creatures was controllable and trainable.

The víbria were amongst her favorite beasts because they took
pleasure and satisfaction from helping humans. The víbria lit
fires for summer barbecues. The víbria gave gentle rides to small
children. And a blazing torch of the burning-tar would not
present a problem in the lair of the víbria.

Snakes of unease writhed in George's belly. She held her
breath and silently prayed to the gods of the golden temples that
they would not need the sacrifice of a death this night. Sensing
the carnage that was about to take place, she strongly suspected
that her prayers would pass unheeded.

Above the catacombs, guarding the golden temples of Gatekeeper Island, there was a family of wyverns: two-legged,
long-tailed dragons. The wyverns were responsible for protecting
the doorways from the temple to the catacombs. They were also
guardians to the fiefdom's vault of treasure. George was slowly
learning the language of the wyverns just as the creatures learnt
hers in an exchange of wisdom and culture. It was a fascinating
area of study and she had already begun to fall in love with the
rhythmic cadence of wyvern poetry.

And, as dragonmeister of Gatekeeper Island, George knew
that the combined danger posed by every caco, smok, víbria and
wyvern was not as menacing as the threat that came from a single
oriental.

"Dragonmeister?"

There was another scratching crack as the flint struck stone.
The stink of the burning tar struck her nostrils with renewed
force. George heard something growl with barely suppressed

hunger. And she breathed a sigh of relief when the flint refused to spark for a second time. If the apprentice hostler survived this night she would flay him until sunrise so he could act as a warning to the rest of her subordinates.

"Are you there, Mistress Georgianna?"

George insisted that there were three rules for working with the orientals. If she had maintained her needlework studies from when she was a strapling she would have stitched those rules onto a tapestry and hung the framed needlework in the golden temple on the doorway above the easternmost catacomb.

The dragonmeister always patrols the eastern catacombs alone.

The dragonmeister always patrols the eastern catacombs in silence.

The dragonmeister always patrols the eastern catacombs in absolute darkness.

She had thought those three rules were made known to everyone who lived on the island. But clearly this apprentice hostler wasn't aware of them. Or, if he was aware of them, he was too dunderheaded to heed rules.

Either way it was going to prove fatal.

There was another growl from the darkness. This one was heavier. And George did not need the gift of presentiment that came from working with dragons to know that it was now too late for the hostler.

"Dragonmeister?"

There was another scratching crack as the flint struck stone.

This time the spark erupted into flame. It caught the burning tar. The catacomb was immediately flooded with liquid yellow light. George could see she had been right: it was one of the apprentice hostlers. She recognized him from the ginger hair on his head and the hessian tunic he wore. His name had been Bob, or Rob or something like that.

And he had entered the last minute of life.

"Dragonmeister?"

Bob or Rob peered toward her but he was clearly bright-blind from the flare of the torch he carried. If he had been able to see anything at all he would have noticed the dragons, three Japanese and two Chinese, circling around him.

"Are you there, Mistress Georgianna? The island has visitors. We're called on by the esteemed Thane Vortigern of Merioneth who comes he—"

He didn't get to complete the sentence.

A Japanese exhaled. Its breath caught the flame from the torch and ignited. The fire seared the ginger hair from the hostler's head. Before he could properly start to scream a second Japanese dragon had acted quickly and ripped his tunic away.

The sound of aged and leathery wings flapped indolently in the shadows.

The dragons looked lemony-white in the glow of their own burning breath. The scene was ghoulishly played out for George as a brightly lit testimony to hostler stupidity.

Momentarily she stood riveted as the dragons snatched at him and nipped at him.

The Chinese clawed.

The Japanese snorted fire.

The hostler was naked and bleeding and weeping and screaming. His hands flailed in a pathetic attempt to keep the beasts away. His sobs were mercifully inarticulate. If he had called for her by name George would have felt guilty for abandoning him. A Chinese slashed at him with five-clawed talons. Black-red lines opened across his abdomen.

And then the hostler's screaming ended.

George turned away and fled.

The hostler had been beyond help before the dragons attacked. Going in to save him would only have ended her own life. Even if her work did not necessitate the gift of second sight, she would have known that much from having worked with orientals through her adult life.

As she burst through the temple doorway from the catacomb, she was adamant that someone would tell her how a mistake like this had happened. And she was adamant that the person responsible would pay.

"Dragonmeister Georgianna of Roxburghshire?"

The man was tall and handsome. A pair of wyvern glowered down at him with characteristic suspicion.

George motioned for the dragons to stand at ease.

Obedient, the beasts relented from their stiff posture. They continued to strike a menacing pose but neither looked likely to eviscerate the visitor.

The stranger was dressed in the polished silver armor of a lowland warrior. His shield was decorated with the emblem of a blood red snake. Because he stood a head taller than her, George felt a little threatened and intimidated.

Defiantly, she threw back her shoulders. She met the challenge of his leering stare. Whether she was dealing with a truculent caco or a visiting warrior, she knew the secret to remaining in control was with a display of confidence.

Of course, it didn't help that she was near-naked.

Save for the leather thong she wore whilst working in the catacombs George was unclothed. Any other type of garment could have likely given away her presence to the vicious oriental dragons. They would have heard the rustle of hessian skirts or the scratch of denim trousers on her thighs. They would have smelled the feral memories of animal stink on full leathers or protective furs.

Hostlers were used to seeing George's bare-breasted presence on the island. When she was escaping the catacombs she looked no more undressed than the temple prostitutes. But she was aware that there were circumstances when her state of near-nudity could sometimes send out the wrong message to the island's occasional visitors.

And this was clearly one of those circumstances.

"How enchanting," the stranger breathed. He stepped closer and cupped her right breast with his left hand. His fingers were warm against her cool flesh. His thumb absently stroked the nipple.

She was jolted by a sting of unwanted pleasure.

As the treacherous bead of flesh grew stiff she slapped his hand away.

He looked hurt. His eyes flared. There was a curl to his upper lip that turned his appearance from attractive to cruel. She noticed the narrowing of his brow.

"Vortigern?" she asked, raising an eyebrow. It was the name the hostler had used in the easternmost catacomb. "Is that who you are?"

He looked perplexed by the informality of her address.

If he was Thane Vortigern of Merioneth then the rules of cordiality dictated that she should address him with the full honorifics of his status. He was titled gentry and she was only a lowly dragonmeister. But George was still angry at having witnessed the unnecessary death of the apprentice hostler. And she strongly suspected that Vortigern was responsible for the tragedy.

"Thane Vortigern of Merioneth," he corrected.

"Are you the shit-for-brains that sent a hostler down to summon me from my duties in the catacombs?"

Vortigern's lips thinned. He looked as though he had been slapped.

"I am Thane Vortigern of Merioneth," he told her. "I sent your hostler down to summon you from your duties, dragonmeister. But you're being visited by a nobleman and his attendant retinue. I think that the civilities of ceremony and greeting are a little more important than counting livestock and sweeping dung."

She bit back the response she wanted to make. The apprentice hostler's life had been far more important than any demonstration of ceremony. But a gnawing sense of danger tingled at the back of her neck. Having worked with dragons long enough to have developed the gift of second sight, she trusted such instincts.

"What business do you have here, Vortigern?" she asked coldly.

He extended a hand.

It was the same hand that had stroked her breast.

"I have been sent by your laird, Caleb the wolf slayer. He has granted permission for me to visit here and oversee an exchange of treasures." Vortigern paused. His eyes sparkled. "Aboard my ship I hold Y Ddraig Goch, the red dragon."

George muttered a squeak of delight. She strained to look past Vortigern's shoulder in the hope she would be able to see down to the harbor and catch a glimpse of his ship.

"The red dragon?" she breathed. "The Welsh dragon?"

Without thinking, she took hold of his hand.

The moment's prophecy flashed at the back of her eyes.

Vortigern had killed Caleb the wolf slayer. She could see the lowland warrior decapitating her laird with a single stroke from a steel broadsword. Vortigern's men had pillaged Roxburghshire. All that remained were smoldering huts and a handful of bewildered womenfolk and children. In her mind's eye she could see the charred buildings with smoke spiraling up from their remnants. And now Vortigern was here to inveigle his way past the wyvern and plunder the treasures from Caleb's fiefdom.

Her heartbeat quickened.

She could sense that Vortigern had said something but she had no idea what. It struck her that she needed to keep her newfound knowledge from the warrior. If Vortigern learnt that she knew he had murdered Caleb and destroyed the fiefdom, he would not bother with the pretense of cordiality. And, George knew, it was only a pretense of cordiality that would allow her to survive this encounter.

"Y Ddraig Goch," she said carefully. She forced herself to smile for him. "That is the Welsh dragon, isn't it? The red dragon?"

"The very same." Vortigern smiled. "It's a gift from my people to Caleb. He said you would be able to make better use of it here.'"

"It's a very generous gift," George told him. "Thane Vortigern of Merioneth is clearly a man of immeasurable generosity."'

For a moment she thought his frown was skeptical. She wondered if she had overdone the praise for his generosity and if he knew that she suspected his treachery. Then the expression of suspicion had disappeared. He was smiling at her bared breasts again with lecherous approval.

"I'm not a man of immeasurable generosity," he admitted. "In return for the gift of Y Ddraig Goch, your laird said I could expect two things."

"Two things?" George raised an eyebrow. She still held Vortigern's hand and noticed that it grew warm in hers. The sensation was pleasant. Disquietingly arousing. "What might those two things be?" she asked.

"Caleb said my men could retrieve gold to the weight of Y Ddraig Goch to fill my ship's hold."

George nodded.

There was no way the wyvern would allow Vortigern to plunder the vaults of the treasury and he clearly knew as much. But, if George granted him and his retinue permission to take gifts, the lowland warrior would be able to steal whatever he pleased. Knowing that she had to play this carefully if she wanted to survive the encounter, George asked, "What is the other thing that Caleb promised you?"

Vortigern stared poignantly at her bare breasts. "He promised your hospitality."

The words hung between them like a challenge.

"The pleasure of bestowing that gift will be all mine," she told him.

Stepping closer to the thane, pressing her nearly naked body against him, she stood on toes to get her mouth close to his. The polished silver of his armor was cool against her bare body. Yet, when she shivered, she knew the response was coming from arousal rather than cold.

Being dragonmeister of Gatekeeper Island was a lonely existence. Aside from the annual visit from Caleb, there was no one with whom she could have a relationship. The apprentice hostlers were young boys – unable to satisfy the needs and demands of a woman's body. The temple prostitutes made for interesting distractions, but the experiences they provided were more spiritual than physical. And there were times when George yearned for something that was purely physical.

Vortigern, male, powerful and domineering, offered the prospect of something that was physically satisfying.

His hand had returned to her breast. As they kissed she felt his tongue slide serpent-like into her mouth. She raised one leg, smoothing her thigh against his hip and urging herself close to him as she savored his arousal.

The thrust of his manliness jutted from the crotch of his pants.

"Thane Vortigern," she murmured. Her voice had fallen to a husky whisper. "It feels like you're ready to welcome my hospitality."

"You're comfortable with us fucking in a temple?"

She stroked the bulge of his excitement through his pants, enjoying the heat that radiated from him. He sounded doubtful about the prospect of sex in a temple but she supposed some of the lowland religions had strange attitudes about acceptable communion in plain view of the deities. She knew there were some churches that condemned sex as immoral, and others that deemed ecumenical orgies a necessity for proper worship.

Her personal belief was that sex was a gift from the gods. It didn't matter where it took place so long as the experience was enjoyed by everyone involved.

"Follow me to the altar," she insisted. She led him by the hand. "We'll be more comfortable there."

He unbuckled the harness that held his chest armor in place and then removed his hauberk. Beneath she saw his flesh was clean-shaven and glossy with manly perspiration. The sight made her inner muscles clench with greedy sexual hunger. When he removed his helmet, and brushed a hand through his sweat-moistened curls, her need for him intensified.

He glanced up toward the golden architecture.

The walls were lined with stone dragons. The altar was guarded by two wyvern who stepped aside as George led Vortigern past them.

"I've never fucked in a temple before," he grunted.

She pushed him onto the altar and then tugged the pants from his legs. Exposed, his length was as formidable as she had hoped it would be. He possessed a broadsword of an erection that was long and thick and looked like it would be a fearsome weapon for the battle she intended.

Unable to resist the impulse, George leant close to him and drew her tongue against his exposed skin. He tasted of salt and desire. The smell of him filled her nostrils with animal hunger.

"*Rhyfeddol*," he gasped.

She chuckled. She didn't know the word but she could guess it was a term of approval. Placing her mouth around him she sucked on his swollen end for a moment until his eyes were wide and his grin was broad.

Then she climbed on top of him.

It was a slow journey. She made sure her bare breasts caressed his body as she moved. He had clearly been admiring them when she appeared from the catacombs. She suspected that he would enjoy having them stroke against his bare skin.

But she could see that he was also interested in her nether regions. Tugging the crotch of her thong to one side she exposed the bare lips for him and moved closer to straddling his manliness.

"*Prydferth*," he said, reaching out to touch her.

His fingers fell into the crease of her need-oily skin. One broad digit disappeared into her warmth. Another slipped beside it, stretching her wide. A fat thumb stroked against the nub of flesh that she considered the root of all sensation.

Her breath quickened.

She regarded Vortigern with new esteem. The explosion of sensation he inspired was more profound than anything she had enjoyed with any man previously.

She reached for the base of his length and clutched him tight. His fingers sparked bolts of delicious magic from the lips of her sex. She had expected their union would be perfunctory – a civic formality of dominance and acquiescence. But it seemed that Vortigern was one of those rare men who believed in the benefits of shared pleasure. Unable to resist the unspoken invitation of his lips, she pressed her mouth over his and kissed.

Slowly, they worked their bodies together.

She held his length and guided it toward the sopping need of her sex.

His fingers stretched her lightly, preparing her for the broad girth of his manliness. And, when he finally entered her, they both sighed heavily with the satisfaction of bliss. Vortigern allowed her to sit adrift his length as he toyed with the swell of one breast. His finger and thumb squeezed and rolled at an acutely responsive nipple.

"Dragonmeister," he sighed. "You should give up your position here. You should come and live with me in the lowlands. You could care for my estates. I could rehome your livestock in my catacombs. And we could play like this whenever it suited your desires."

"Sex talk," she laughed softly. She knew a man would say whatever he believed a woman wanted to hear whilst she was straddling him.

Vortigern shook his head.

He continued to tease her nipple with one hand. His other hand slipped to her rump. His fingers smoothed over her rear and slipped saucily close to the union of their bodies. She could feel the syrupy lips of her sex bristling to the light caress of his touch.

"It's a serious invitation," he promised.

She was pleased to hear that his breath was ragged with passion. Despite the import of his words, the pleasure she inspired was having an obvious effect. It was a testament to her skills in the womanly art of lovemaking that she was able to distract a thane from his purpose.

"Rescind your loyalty to Caleb," he suggested. "Pledge fealty to Merioneth and I'll install you as the fiefdom's dragonmeister."

George raised and lowered her hips. Sliding her sex along his length took her close to the impending eruption. She caught a breath and held it as the waves of excitement flooded through her flesh.

And she tried not to be tempted by the offer he presented.

The gift of second sight was showing her the future he promised. If she did as Vortigern asked she would be installed in the scenic splendor of a lowland country estate. There would be catacombs for her to patrol and countless weyrs of wyvern, víbría, and Y Ddraig Goch. She would spend her days with dragons and her nights with Vortigern. The sun's pleasures would only be outshone by the intensity of the night's passions.

All it would take was for her to renege on the loyalty she had once pledged to a man who had been her lover and was now dead. A tear trailed down her cheek.

The ripple of pleasure flooded through her body. She bit back a scream, knowing the gods of the temple did not approve of such demonstrations of satisfaction. Vortigern's length erupted inside her. The copious rush of his molten seed flooded her womb.

Another surge of raw delight rushed through her flesh. This time, uncaring as to whether or not the gods approved, George screamed.

Trembling, she peeled herself away from Vortigern. She gave his spent length a kiss of gratitude. He tasted of their mingled pleasures. It was a flavor she savored as she licked her lips. And she knew she had already made her decision in response to his invitation.

It was an easy decision to make.

"There is the temple doorway to the fiefdom treasures of Caleb the wolf slayer," she said, pointing. "Take your retinue with you to collect your gold," she added quickly. "Carry as much as you can. Break your men's backs with the weight of the gold they carry because the wyvern will only allow safe passage the once."

Vortigern nodded as he dressed. First he donned his pants. Then his boots. Then the hauberk and finally his armor.

"Your honesty is appreciated," he admitted. "And my offer to you is an honest one. If you pledge fealty to Merioneth, you can reside as dragonmeister in my fiefdom. Your skills would be appreciated and well rewarded."

And I would be whoring my skills to the man who slew my lover and the laird who trusted me with the safekeep of his dragons, she thought bitterly. Aloud, she asked, "May I consider the generosity of your offer whilst you're retrieving your gold?"

His retinue approached. They held torches dripping with the burning tar.

"Consider the offer and know I'll stay true to my word." He strode to the doorway she had indicated. It was barred by a pair of wyvern.

George gestured for the wyvern to stand down.

Obedient, the beasts relented from their stiff posture.

His retinue started toward the doorway but Vortigern stopped them. He fixed her with a warning finger. "I get the impression you've lied to me."

She shook her head. "We've lain together, Thane Vortigern of Merioneth. You'd know if I'd lied to you. I can place my hand on my heart and say I haven't lied to you once."

He considered this and then seemed appeased. Brushing her cheek with an apologetic kiss he motioned for his retinue to continue. A true leader, he snatched a torch of burning tar and led the way.

George watched him hasten into the shadows.

A sad smile played on her lips. She hadn't lied to him once. She had lied to him at least three times.

She had lied when she said the wyverns would only allow safe passage once. That had simply been a ruse to ensure that Vortigern and his entire retinue followed her instructions and went through the doorway.

She had lied when she said she would consider his offer. Her loyalty would always be to Caleb the wolf slayer, even though the laird was now dead and his fiefdom destroyed.

But, most importantly for Vortigern, she had lied by sending him to retrieve treasure through that particular doorway. There was no treasure in the easternmost catacombs where he was now headed. In the easternmost catacombs there was only the mortal danger of the orientals. It was a mortal danger that, she knew, neither Vortigern nor his retinue would survive.

Suffer for Me

Teresa Noelle Roberts

Martin said, "I want to suffer for you."

I smiled. I tried to make it an aloof, catlike one, but my heart ached with a combination of tenderness and lust and I'm sure it showed on my face. "You're such a good boy," I said, continuing to stroke his long brown hair. "And so beautiful. Why would I want to make you suffer?"

He was sitting at my feet, his head in my lap. He looked up at me, his eyes huge and lost, almost tragic. "Please . . . I want to be worthy of you, ma'am. I want to suffer for you."

Martin was younger than me and new to admitting his own submissive nature. The admission had released a streak of dark romanticism, abetted by much erotica read with too little grounding in reality. I could chuckle about it, remembering my own early, fantasy-fueled explorations ten years ago – and yet his leather- and hemp- scented romantic fancies, his yearning devotion, had swept me off my feet just as much as my firm but sensual control had swept him off his. Now we were trying to figure out where to go from here. I was the experienced one, and I had definite ideas where I *wanted* things to go with my beautiful, biddable Martin – but a responsible domme finds a balance between her own needs and those of her sub. This is especially important at Martin's delicate exploratory stage, where a wrong move could sour his fascination not just with me but with kink.

I tangled my fingers in his hair, tugging cruelly. "If you weren't worthy of me, you wouldn't be here," I said, dropping my voice to a low, ominous register. "Do you question my judgement, or my taste?"

"No . . . I . . . I . . . I'm sorry." He froze, his entire body rigid with tension. I was sure his cock was rigid as well, caught up in imagining the painful punishment he was sure was on its way, half dreaded, half longed for. "I just thought . . ." His voice dropped off and he almost whispered the end of the sentence, "I thought maybe you wanted me to beg for it, ma'am. I mean, you control me, and you tease me, and you make me take care of you in different ways, but you've never really hurt me and I thought . . ."

"That's your problem, Martin. You think too much. I'll make you suffer when I want to – in my way, in my own time. Meanwhile, sweet boy, put that tongue of yours to better use than saying silly things out of bad porn." I lifted his head off my lap long enough to raise my skirt. He didn't need further encouragement, and whether or not the delightful alchemy between his tongue and my clit stopped him from thinking, it stopped me.

But not before I'd come up with an idea. He wanted to suffer for me, and a delightful, obedient, clever-tongued morsel like Martin deserved to get what he wanted. I wasn't that fond of inflicting serious pain, though – too much work for too little enjoyment on my end. It was only worthwhile for me if a boy really craved pain, needed it to be fulfilled, and my gut instinct was that Martin didn't. He just thought he should, based on the one-size-fits-all lesson of porn.

But there was more than one way of making a man suffer exquisitely. And the way I had in mind we would both *enjoy* exquisitely – in the end.

"You look so good like that," I purred, running my nails lightly across Martin's straining abs. I surprised myself with the husky, lusty quality of my voice, but he took my breath away. I was no mistress of intricate shibari, and the way I'd tied him to the bed wouldn't earn any prizes for beauty or elegance. The way his body looked, spreadeagled and taut with desire, was another story. He was so gorgeous in his helplessness, yet at the same time, he didn't seem helpless at all. Martin had gentle hands and a quiet demeanor, at least around me, but he also had muscles, and the way I'd positioned him made those muscles stand out. He looked like a bound, tattooed young god who'd chosen to be exactly where he was for mysterious reasons of his own.

Maybe not so mysterious. The straining cock was a pretty good clue. But he looked no less divine for his obvious desires. Hell, he looked more so.

I couldn't keep my hands off Martin, but luckily I didn't have to.

That was the whole point of this exercise, the whole point of having my beautiful boy tied so securely to the bed – to touch him, to tease him past what he thought he could bear and prove to him that he could bear it, and to make it end in pleasure that was also almost past bearing.

I began with his nipple.

When I caught it in one hand between my long red fingernails, he braced himself for a twist, a cruel pinch. I could see in his wide, entreating eyes that he both feared and hoped for it.

Instead, I caressed first one then the other with all the delicacy I could muster, applying just enough pressure that it pleasured rather than tickled. Then I took one into my mouth, licking and sucking and teasing the little nub, nipping down enough to vary the kind of pleasure he experienced, but not enough to push it over into real pain.

It occurred to me as I did that I'd never played with his nipples this way. I'd bitten them, put clothes pins on them, dribbled a bit of hot wax on them, but never simply caressed them. In fact, it had been a long time since it had occurred to me to do this to a man, and I was surprised by how much I was enjoying it.

"Ma'am . . ." he said, something in his tone sounding like the beginning of a protest, as if he didn't think it was right I lick and kiss his body.

I shut him up with a kiss. "I don't want to gag you," I explained as I pulled away from his luscious lips. "Not today. But I swear I will if you if you say something stupid, like you're not worthy of this kind of attention."

He shut up, confirming my suspicions of what was going through his silly subby head.

And once he was quiet, I went back to work on his nipples until he wasn't quiet anymore. Soft moaning, though, was a perfectly acceptable noise – a delicious noise – in fact, the very reason I hadn't wanted to gag him.

I raised my lips from a nipple now swollen from suckling and red from my lipstick.

"Sweet music, Martin," I murmured.

Then I started kissing my way down his body.

When my lips reached somewhere around mid-belly, he jumped as best he could in his bonds.

When my lips brushed the tight dark curls of his pubes, while entirely avoiding his straining cock, he let out a stifled noise that might have been a bitten-off curse. I chuckled, and continued kissing and stroking down one muscular thigh, nipping and running my fingernails lightly down the more sensitive skin of his inner thigh until he shivered against his bonds. When I reached his bound ankle, I outlined the rope with my tongue. He shivered at that and sighed. I told him rather than asked him, "I bet you'd forgotten that I might be gentle with you, but you're still at my mercy."

"No, ma'am," he said, a plea I couldn't quite understand in his voice. "I don't forget that. But I'd almost forgotten the rope. Thank you for reminding me."

"Remember that you're thanking me now," I said. "You'll probably curse me later. Then you'll thank me again."

Then I worked my way back, blowing on his cock and balls in passing but not touching them, and repeated my performance on his other straining leg.

By the time I made my leisurely, teasing way back, poor Martin's face was as red and straining as his untouched dick. His muscles were even more defined now, tense with need.

I took a long, deliberate moment to admire my handiwork, no contact with him but a hand resting lightly on his thigh. "Beautiful boy," I breathed. "Beautiful, beautiful boy. Be good and don't go anywhere. Oh, wait. You can't anyway." I smiled as I said it.

"Curse you, ma'am," he said in a small, yet happy voice. "Curse you and bless you. I couldn't take this if I wasn't bound."

I leaned in close, cupped his face. "Yes you could," I whispered, surprising myself with the intensity in my voice, "if I wanted you to. But I'm being kind this time."

I turned away long enough to grab the lube.

Martin winced at the slight coolness of the slick substance as I coated over his cock – or maybe the wince was simply because he was that sensitive. That thought made me grin.

The grin turned into an outright laugh when he sighed with pleasure and thanked me. "Don't thank me yet, sweet boy. You said you wanted to suffer for me, and suffer you will."

And I proceeded to give my boy the most teasingly drawn-out hand job in the long history of hand jobs.

I watched his face as I stroked him, listened to the subtleties of his breathing, checked how his muscles tensed, how his hands clenched and strained against the ropes, how his feet tried and failed to move. Whenever his breath caught in his throat too much, or I saw his ab muscles start to twitch, I backed off, resting my hand on his hip bone, stroking that smooth, hot skin lightly, until his breathing regularized.

By the third time I did this, he was thrashing against the ropes so hard I'd have feared for my bed if it weren't a sturdy Mission frame. His skin was glazed lightly with sweat, making him look all that more beautiful. His eyes were all pupil, and he stared fixedly, frantically, as though he was seeing through time and space and seeing the face of the divine in me. His lips moved in a silent litany. I could guess what he was saying, or at least the gist of it, but nevertheless I demanded, "Speak up, Martin. I can't hear you."

"Please," he begged, his voice still barely audible. "Please, ma'am. Please."

I knew what he was pleading for, of course, but I wanted to hear him say the words. "Please what, dear?" I stroked his rigid length idly – only it wasn't idly at all, but carefully calculated, just enough pressure to keep him hard and aching with the need to explode, but not enough to bring him any closer.

"Please . . ." It was clearly an effort to make his brain form a coherent thought. "Please let me come, ma'am. Please."

"Doesn't it feel good?" I was stroking more forcefully now, cupping his balls.

I bent down and ran my tongue over the head of his cock, just once. My mouth had never gotten anywhere near his cock before.

He arched up off the bed with a harsh cry. Without the ropes, I swear he might have levitated until the ceiling stopped him. "Hell yes, but . . . almost . . . too . . . sensitive. Almost hurts." His voice was strained almost to breaking.

"Should I stop?" I sat up, withdrew my hand. Withdrew all contact from him except my hip brushing his flank, because he was flying way too high for me to pull away altogether. That would be too cruel in a game that ultimately I hoped he too would enjoy.

"No, please. But please, please . . . let me come!"

"In time, sweet boy. In time." I kissed him almost chastely, though he tried to make it deeper. "Right now it's making me wet and hot to torment you, to see you suffer." He made a sweet, tortured noise that made me wetter yet.

I slipped my hand under my skirt and ran my fingers between lips almost as sensitized and needy as his cock must be. I showed him the glistening evidence, then ran it over his lips.

He desperately sucked my fingers as if that might bring him relief.

"I need you to suffer for me a little longer, Martin, because it's making me feel so good. Can you do that?"

He replied with a muffled, but enthusiastic, "Yes, ma'am" around my fingers.

With his consent I returned to my teasing work. And as he did, I talked softly. "You look so gorgeous right now, Martin, all flushed and messed up and sweaty. You're going to have lovely rope marks on your wrists and ankles because you can't stop yourself from struggling. But at the same time you want to give yourself to me, to take whatever I give you. Right?"

He nodded tightly.

"And even though this is hard to handle in some ways, I bet it's also pleasurable. Exciting. You're just so sensitized now that the pleasure's also painful, like pain can be pleasurable.'"

Another tight nod.

"Remember how this feels, Martin. Remember it with every cell in your body." I timed the movement of my hands to the cadence of my words, letting both become slow, relentless, hypnotic. Between extremes of pleasure, enforced obedience, and bondage, Martin was already so far into sub-space I was dealing with an altered state of consciousness. If I remembered my college psych classes – and the erotic hypnosis demo our local BDSM community had arranged – I might be able to slip a suggestion, at least a fun one that he'd want to obey, into his wide-open brain. "Remember every detail, because even though you feel like you're suffering now, you're going to want to relive this afternoon over and over again. You're going to want to remember this peak of arousal and the powerful orgasm that follows. Aren't you, Martin?"

A very small voice replied, "Yes, ma'am."

"Do you still want to come, Martin?"

"No, ma'am." He hesitated, then added, "Well, yes, of course . . . but when you want me to. This is awful and wonderful, and I know when you let me come, it'll be amazing."

"And what if I don't let you come, if after all this teasing I deny you?"

I could see in his face how he was struggling to answer me both honestly and respectfully. After what seemed like a very long time, which I punctuated with a series of excruciatingly slow strokes on his cock, he replied, more coherently than I would have expected, though in a shaky voice that sounded like he was holding himself together by sheer will, "I really hope you wouldn't do that, ma'am, please. But it's your choice. And no one's ever died from not coming – though right now I feel like I might."

I thrilled to the message there, the way his wish to obey and please struggled with his body's by now urgent demands and conquered those demands for my sake. "You are such a good boy, Martin, such a wonderful, good boy," I said, and I meant every word. "You've pleased me very much. And I think right now it would please me to have you come for me. Come for me, Martin, and remember how it feels. Let it burn into your brain and your body. Come for me *now*."

I didn't change what I was doing, but the words, the permission, set loose a freight train of an orgasm that engulfed his whole body. His face reddened and screwed up so that he was almost unrecognizable, and his eyes rolled back into his head. His abs contracted and rolled like a particularly ambitious belly dancer's. The ropes groaned against the bedposts. His cock danced wildly, spurting come everywhere. He bit his lip, but it didn't stifle the roar of fulfillment.

So hot. So hot I came myself watching him. The orgasm was quick and shimmering, like hands-free ones usually were, but it was followed by a second wave of pleasure warm as sunlight. Not a physical orgasm, but a blend of pride and delight and tenderness as heady as coming and far more dangerous, because it meant that my heart was snared by Martin's beautiful submission as tightly as his body was by my ropes.

And just for that, just because looking at him caught in pleasure so strong it was almost pain made me want to slap a collar on his neck and hell, maybe a ring on his finger, I didn't relent, as I often would after a good come had softened me.

When his struggles subsided and his face slackened but his dick had't, I rested my palm on his come-slick belly. "You remember how that felt, the build-up and the orgasm?"

He nodded, his eyes so spacey I expected to see stars in their depths.

"Good boy. Relive it for me now and come. Come again, Martin."

I wasn't sure it would work. I hadn't formally hypnotized him, after all, just tried to slip in a suggestion when his brain was out to lunch.

A look of awe and astonishment overtook him as his abs began to contract under my hand. His cock twitched, though there was nothing left to explode out.

This time he didn't even try to hold back his cries.

When the cries faded to something more like sobs, I untied him quickly. Then I curled up on his come-splattered chest. "You're safe, sweet Martin," I murmured. "You're safe and you're brave and you've pleased me wonderfully."

"Thank you. I didn't think . . ." His voice was shaky, almost inaudible, but I could tell now that the tears were tears of release, nothing bad. "I didn't think that was possible. Thank you so much, ma'am. Thank you."

"After suffering for me, you deserved a treat." I thought for a second before adding, "And you know something, sweet Martin? I wasn't sure it would work either. But I'm so glad it did."

Might as well admit I didn't know everything, I thought, lightly kissing his sweaty chest. Being a clever boy, he'd figure it out on his own eventually. After all, I wasn't planning on letting him go.

No, I wanted to keep this one around to suffer for me – and come so prettily for me – for as long as I could. Maybe, just maybe, forever.

The Horniest Girl in San Francisco

Charles Gatewood

Last October I was invited to read at Litquake, San Francisco's famous spoken word festival. I decided to read, "I Got Laid at the Anarchist Book Fair," a real-life story with lots of spice and flashes of local color. I figured my goofy tale would be a hit with the hipster crowd – and I hoped I would meet a groupie or two.

The crowd at Café Laszlo liked my story and gave me a nice round of applause. Afterward, a very flirty woman chatted me up – I mean she was all over me.

Shazam was an unemployed lawyer, a pleasingly plump sexpot in her mid-thirties. She had thick auburn hair, big rascal eyes, and a let's-go grin. Shazam was obviously a problem drinker – she had a scar over one eyebrow and a nose that had kissed the sidewalk a time or two – but so what?

"Two years ago," said Shazam, "my whole life fell apart. I crashed and burned, big time. I lost my husband, I lost my job. Now I sleep on my ex-husband's couch and do phone sex for money. I also review sex toys for Carnal Nation, and write a sex blog called Random Rim Jobs."

"My first rim job," I said, "was from Annie Sprinkle – over thirty years ago."

"Really?" said Shazam. "Wanna try it again?"

I felt a stiffening in my jeans. "Are you highly skilled?"

"Honey," said Shazam, "I am sensational. I give the best blow jobs, too. I have a serious cock addiction. I adore thick, meaty cocks. I like having my hair pulled, and I like having big meaty cocks rammed down my throat."

Whoa. I'd only known Shazam for a minute and a half, and she was telling me she liked big meaty cocks rammed down her throat.

"Do you live in the Mission district?"

"I live at Bryant and 24th," said Shazam, "in my ex-hubby's loft. How about you?"

"I live in Bernal Heights, just minutes from you."

"Well, whadda ya know," said Shazam, flashing a grin. "We're neighbors, babe. Let's get together."

Back home, I checked out Random Rim Jobs, Shazam's sex blog. One thing was clear – the crazy girl wasn't kidding. Her real-life sex stories were tough, raw, and gritty. She was an anything-that-moves kinda gal, hot to party with anyone in sight. Me, I play with six or eight girls every year. Shazam, the naughty slut, has six or eight erotic encounters *every week*.

I don't want a relationship right now, said one of her recent blog entries. *I just want a good hard pounding.*

I found the stories on Shazam's blog truly amazing. The "Random Encounters" ads she ran on Craigslist attracted hordes of "horny net geeks." Shazam fucked them all, even the pasty-faced slobs and dorky nerds who smelled like cheap cologne.

Craigslist, Adult Friend Finder, OK Cupid, Fetlife, Twitter – Shazam found sex everywhere. Some of her contact ads were especially clever. *Here's a good trick,* said one blog entry. *A single bisexual woman trolling for threesomes is so rare we're called "unicorns." My unicorn ads get good results. Mostly I meet couples in their twenties or thirties who want to experiment and fool around.*

One of Shazam's wildest stories was about closing time at the Makeout Room, how she stood in the street outside, rowdy drunk, yelling, *Will somebody please FUCK ME?*

Oh my. Even at my neediest, I was never this hungry. Shazam was a very horny girl. A few days later, I sent Shazam an email. *Hey Crazo, wanna play? Come see me on Sunday!*

So we hooked up – the horny Mission nympho and the bizarre fetish photographer. Shazam showed up at my place with two bags of groceries and three bottles of white wine. When I told her I never touch alcohol, Shazam said, "Good – more for me." She drained the first bottle of wine in about ten minutes, and immediately popped the cork on the second. "Maybe I'll quit drinking one day," she said. "But I do love it so – getting high, getting buzzed, feeling just the right amount of drunk."

"I want to write a story about you," I said. "Tell me some juicy tales."

"I do phone sex for money," said Shazam. "That's pretty entertaining."

"What's it like?"

"Well, I make fifty cents a minute. The agency has certain rules, like no age play, no animals, no incest, no talking about poop or golden showers. But sometimes I break the rules. Like last night, I pretended to be a horny teen having sex with my little brother. That's two taboo subjects at once – age play and incest. It's cool as long as nobody complains."

After finishing her second bottle of wine, Shazam was ready for sex.

"Get naked," I said, "and I'll buzz you with my vibrator."

"Oh boy," said Shazam.

Shazam stripped naked, lay on my living room futon, and spread her chubby legs. I pulled a condom over the head of my Panasonic vibrator and began buzzing Shazam's close-clipped mound, *buzzzzzzzzzzzz*.

Shazam squirmed and moaned with delight as orgasm after orgasm shook her fleshy body. I pleasured Shazam with the buzzing vibrator for the longest time, buzz-buzz-buzz until she begged for mercy. Now it was my turn to be pleasured. What followed was one of the most unusual blow jobs of my life. I sat on the couch, pants down, legs spread wide. Shazam started off slow and easy, licking and nuzzling my glistening shaft, oh my goodness. Her lick-and-slurp technique had a soft, jazzy rhythm – pure heaven. Suddenly, without warning, Shazam began ramming my cock down her throat, hard, harder, harder, Lord have mercy, jerking her head and growling like a dog as she deep-throated my cock.

"Hey," I said, "take it easy—"

Shazam popped my cock from her mouth. Her eyes were wild, her expression ecstatic. "You love it," she said.

Shazam grabbed my cock again and swallowed it whole. What a wild and crazy suck it was. A bit rough, perhaps – but who was complaining? I came like gangbusters, and collapsed in Shazam's arms.

We lay together in sweet afterglow.

"You're amazing," I said.

"You're pretty hot for a geezer," said Shazam.

I enjoyed five or six hot dates with Shazam, each wilder and crazier than the last. The girl wasn't kidding – she was insatiable. And so, to end the year with a bang, I invited Shazam to spend Christmas day with me.

"You're a gourmet cook. Why don't you make us a big Christmas dinner? I'll pay for everything."

"That sounds great," said Shazam. "I'll make beef short ribs and my special risotto. We'll need butternut squash, balsamic vinegar, soy sauce, cornstarch, cream sherry, beef broth—"

"Whoa," I said. "That sounds like a big expensive production. Let's keep it simple. How about a juicy steak, scalloped potatoes, and a tossed salad?"

"On one condition," she said.

"What's that?"

"I'll make you Christmas dinner," said Shazam, "if I can suck your cock for dessert."

"Done deal!"

Since she was bringing food, and since public transportation is notoriously unreliable on Christmas Day, I offered Shazam a ride to my place.

"Great," said Shazam. "I'll have everything all ready."

When I drove to her pick up, however, a tipsy Shazam said she had no food at all. "I didn't have money to shop."

Oh, for godsake. It was mid-afternoon on Christmas Day, and Safeway was about to close. Shazam was half drunk, and when she told me she had another date later in the evening, I got annoyed. Another date?

"Calm down," said Shazam. "Her name is Sugar, and she's a real hottie. We met on Craigslist Casual Encounters last month. Sugar is a sex worker who calls herself an 'adventuresome bisexual.' Maybe we'll have a hot threesome."

So, I lightened up. I bought a big juicy steak, a bag of Idaho potatoes, a hunk of sharp cheddar, a head of iceberg lettuce – and a quart of vodka for the girls.

At my place, I served pot brownies while Shazam mixed a strong vodka drink. We smoked a joint, nibbled a brownie, and began preparing our Christmas feast.

As we peeled potatoes, I asked Shazam to tell me more about Sugar.

"Oh my," she said. "Sugar is a trippy girl. It was actually her husband who saw my ad and suggested we hook up. Sugar is an escort who charges her male clients $350 an hour. She's my favorite fuck-buddy. Let's send her a text – maybe she'll join us."

I put scalloped potatoes in the oven, made a big salad, and prepared the steak for broiling. After that, I asked Shazam if she would like to see the manuscript of *Dirty Old Man*, my recently completed memoir.

We looked at my memoir, and I read Shazam part of the first chapter. But Shazam seemed restless. "Can we look at your book later? she asked. "Right now, I want to suck your cock."

Whoa!

I wasn't disappointed. I flew into magic space as I watched the hungry wench devour my meat. The pleasure went on and on with me urging Shazam to *slow down, make it last . . .*

But Shazam sucked me hard and fast. Just as I popped – *ahhh- hhhh* – the kitchen timer went *Ding!* The scalloped potatoes were ready. It was time to toss the salad and broil the steak.

I was plenty high from my world-class blow job, and the pot brownies were coming on strong. And when Shazam received a text message from Sugar saying she would join us, I felt a warm golden glow.

Christmas dinner was perfect. The scalloped potatoes were excellent, the salad was tasty, and I broiled Shazam's steak "bloody," just the way she liked it. *Bing-Bong.* The doorbell rang. It was Sugar! I was surprised – Sugar looked a hundred per cent *straight*, like the girl next door. Who would guess Sugar was a high-priced call girl? She was in her late twenties, tall and leggy, short brown hair, nice breasts, pleasing face. "Hi Charles," she said. "I brought you some tequila."

I poured Sugar a drink and took her on a tour of my studio. When she saw my nude pin-up photographs, Sugar said, "Could you take some photos of me? I need new pictures for my website."

"Sure," I said.

"Just don't show my face," said Sugar. "My mother would have a cow." Minutes later, Shazam started kissing Sugar, woo hoo. I watched the girls strip naked and curl up in the white leather chair near the fire. Shazam gave Sugar lots more kisses as Sugar fingered Shazam's pussy.

"Can I take photos?" I asked.

Sugar pulled away from Shazam, laughing. "Here, take my keys. My red Honda is parked in your driveway. There's a bag in the front seat – with a harlequin mask inside."

I ran downstairs, zoom zoom, unlocked the Honda, found Sugar's bag, ran back upstairs, pant pant, totally out of breath. I found Shazam and Sugar sprawled on my living room futon, kissing and hugging and fingering each other. I loved watching their mad passion and the way their bodies glowed under the colored Christmas lights. I sat close, a few feet away. The naughty girls, flying high, were deep in the pleasure zone. By the time they stopped to catch their breath, my penis was standing at full mast.

I showed the sex-crazed girls my magnificent Viagra erection, and moments later I had the joy of watching two naked girls pleasuring me at once. The girls took turns licking and sucking my cock, just like a porn movie.

"Click," I said, taking a mental snapshot.

"Oh, you can take photos," said Sugar. "Look in my bag for the mask. And can you bring us some lube?"

Sugar called it her "whore bag." It contained tricks of the trade – colored foil condoms, chrome nipple clips, a leather paddle, a black leather blindfold, a Gillette razor, shaving gel, a vial of lube, a strap-on dildo, and a novelty vibrator shaped like a banana.

I gave Sugar the harlequin mask, and she slipped it on. And so it happened – I flashed photos as the girls took turns sucking my cock, point-of-view dream shots for sure. After she kissed Shazam some more, Sugar finished me off with a sweet, passionate suck that couldn't be beat. I came like a champ in her pouty red mouth. I was drained, but the girls were just warming up. They kissed and nuzzled and fingered each other for the longest time.

Shazam, crazy-drunk now, started screaming, *"Yaaaaaaa-aaaaaaa!"* "Keep it quiet," I said. "My landlord lives downstairs—"

"Ha-ha," said the naughty girls.

Shazam flashed a drunken grin. "Charles," she said, "how would you like to fuck Sugar? You want to?"

I looked at Sugar. She was smiling. "Let's do it," she said.

What thrilled me about this delightful scene was not just the crazy, spontaneous fun, but the real honest-to-goodness passion we shared. This wasn't a play-for-pay deal, or one of those carefully negotiated fantasy role-play "scenes." This was the real deal – dripping with feeling and wham-bam excitement. It was my hottest sex in weeks – my best Christmas *ever*. And it all happened because I met Shazam – the horniest girl in San Francisco.

Coucou

Mia More

I love stripping on stage. I have the audience in the palm of my hand and I'm playing with them, slowly teasing them with the power of suggestion: an item of clothing shed here, a flash of skin there, the hint of a curve revealed, a coquettish smile over a bare shoulder – and I have them hooked. It's an art, Burlesque, if you do it right, and I do it so right that people come back for more. When I scan the tables and make eye contact with my spectators, I see men exhale the breaths they've been unconsciously holding in, and I know women are instinctively and involuntarily squirming in their seats. Oh yes, I'm bloody good at my job – in fact I'm famous for it. "Coucou . . ." I tantalizingly beckon in French with a finger. "Coucou!" And there isn't a person out there who doesn't want to follow me as I leave the stage clad only in my ostrich feathers.

Last night was no different, except for one thing: in the audience I saw someone. Someone who had a certain something about them – that sexual allure you can pinpoint a mile off, that animal magnetism you couldn't bottle if you tried. He was suited and booted like the rest of the upmarket crowd before me, but whilst the others on his table were sitting taut and engrossed, he was relaxed and attentive, and his smile was generous and true. I knew in that way you know that he would be mine before the night was out.

And then there he was backstage, this man: not tall, not short, which suited my five foot seven in heels perfectly. My sister Annie introduced us: "Coucou, this is Benjamin Dax—"

"Call me Ben" he interrupted. Suddenly I was looking into a pair of brown eyes sparkling with intelligence and humour. I liked what I saw.

"Ben then, nice to meet you," I smiled and held out a hand. Ben took it in his, so that my fist was embraced in his palm and his fingers were around my wrist. The pressure was so subtle as to be almost imperceptible, yet somehow it felt electric. My professionalism escaped me: my legs went weak and I could only smile goofily like a teenager. Annie noticed and grinned imperceptibly.

"Drink?" Ben offered. "I think you've earned it tonight. You were sensational up there."

"Thank you – I'd love one. But not here," I replied, recovered. "I feel as if I'm still onstage. It's like the eyes of the world are still upon me!" And indeed they were: all carefully selected heads present were surreptitiously turned our way, wondering what the handsome, well-dressed stranger was doing backstage with their star, their Coucou.

"I know a great little place," Ben suggested, "a short hop away. I'm sure you could manage it – even in your heels."

"Take me, I'm yours," I acquiesced, throwing on my fake fur coat over my glamorous offstage outfit. Ben nodded approvingly. That's the thing about being a star – people expect you to be dressed like a "somebody" when you're not working, and I do hate to disappoint my audience, even during my time off.

With a casual wave to Annie and the others I followed Ben out of the door. This was no longer my usual way of doing things, so I was slightly nervous. But, true to his word, Ben's "great little place" was just around the corner, and he was a real gentleman the whole stroll there: taking my arm, he walked on the outer part of the pavement, sheltering me from passing vehicles, whilst on the pedestrian side he answered any questioning glances from passers-by with "No, it's not . . . she gets that all the time", turning to me with, "Honey, you really should change your hair, people are confusing you with Coucou again!"

I could actually feel myself relaxing in Ben's confident and charming company, and as we walked into the bar I took the strong hand he offered as he helped me up the stairs, and I deliberately didn't let it go until we were sat in our private booth. Ben smiled at me over the table as the pretty waitress took my order, his eyes never straying from my face. "I'll have the same," he said. "Mojitos for both of us."

Over the next few hours we chatted and laughed in our secluded sanctuary. I felt elated: here was this perfect stranger sat opposite me, unafraid of my fame – my face – and yet still perfectly attuned to my body, my womanliness, but without the

cachet of celebrity. I was impressed – and entertained. I felt reck-
lessly intoxicated: the feel of Ben's knee pressed against my leg
was driving me crazy, and as his hand massaged my thigh I felt
like some kind of glamorous courtesan, dressed up to the nines
with my stockinged feet in his lap. I was flirting like a demon and
loving every moment of it. And so it was that my professional
mask slipped bit by bit, so that by the end of the evening I was no
longer Coucou but Elizabeth once more – I was me. And I was
having a hell of a lot of fun again.

As the bar closed, we called a cab – to Ben's. "No chauffeur,
I'm afraid." He smiled ruefully. "A refreshing change," I beamed
at him in response. As per our historic family rules (although it
had been a long time), I sent my sister Annie a "safe" text to let
her know where I was headed and with whom, and I stifled a
smirk at the thought that since she was probably tucked up in bed
she would read it in the morning – which is when a barrage of
return texts would be coming back my way begging me to tell all.
This evening I really was being the old me again – how wonderfully invigorating!

I felt all dizzy with joy at the thought of truly shedding the
stage for a night. But not, it has to be said, as dizzy as when in the
back of the taxi Ben stroked the hollow at the back of my knee,
both reassuring and exciting me at the same time. I turned to him
as the street lights flashed by, looking up at his face to get the
measure of him. "Yup, I'm still here," Ben laughed, now squeezing my leg with his hand. I placed my own over the top. "Me too."
I smiled. Ben's eyes danced, and his grip tightened, but he made
no move to kiss me.

Soon enough we drew up outside a smart block of flats. The
building was Art Deco in design, and as Ben helped me out of the
cab I read the words "Underwood Mansions" inscribed over the
grand entrance. "I'm on the third floor," he said, showing me into
the old ornate lift. Holding my hand, he surveyed me in the
mirrors, drinking in the sight of me.

I couldn't help it: "What do you see?" I asked, pouting my
famous lips, my elegant reflection echoed back to me in multiple
by the fabulous gilt-edged mirrors surrounding us.

"I see a beautiful woman who needs to stop working so hard,"
Ben smiled.

"Just as well I'm making the most of my time off right now
then, isn't it?" I batted back with a wink of my stage lashes.

I noticed Ben's even teeth under the ornamental light, the beautiful curve of his mouth, and the softness of his skin. I wanted to touch his face, but didn't quite have the courage, so I did the next best thing and took his other hand in mine so that we stood face to face. Despite the warmth of my fur coat, the hungry look in his eyes gave me goose bumps, and I trembled slightly in anticipation, my very essence vibrating with desire at his touch. I was eager for him too.

The bell announced the third floor, breaking our reverie, and as though in a dream I tottered along the corridor to Ben's place, my arm threaded through his. I could feel the strong muscles on his forearm and smell his fresh masculine aftershave. I was under his spell, and my body hummed in recognition.

The flat was small but functional. As Ben fetched me a drink of water, I looked around the living room. It was very male, very clean, and very, very comfortable.

I yawned. "If you're not careful I'll be crashing right here, Ben!" I called through to the kitchen.

"Would that be such a bad thing?" he asked as he came in and passed me my drink.

"Cheers." I smiled in response, clinking my glass with his, not quite daring to meet his eyes.

Ben took the drink from my fingers and placed it on the coffee table. This was the moment we'd been building up to all night, I could feel it. We were about to flip from flirtation into fact, and the tension was palpable. The butterflies in my stomach stretched their delicate wings and took flight, and my heart beat faster in my chest, as though trying to keep pace. Ben kissed me, and I melted. It was as though I were no longer made of skin and bone, but of molten glass, flowing and ebbing. I was liquid on fire, and I wanted more.

"Ben . . ." I breathed. His reply was a tongue dipped delicately into my mouth, searching, wanting, his lips increasing the pressure on mine as with the power of his kiss he drew me ever closer into him.

Grabbing my handbag for that all-essential condom I habitually carried, I kicked off my heels as Ben led me to the bedroom. Pulling me to him, he knelt in front of me, and buried his face in my silk dress. I groaned as he lifted my skirt and pushed his nose to my slit, tonguing me through my lace panties. I took his hair in my fists, and as his arms reached up and encircled my waist, I moved in front of him, helping his mouth find my hot spot. It had been so long, and I was so ready to feel his breath on my skin that I couldn't shed my underwear fast enough. "God you're wet," Ben panted, "and you taste delicious." His hands went round my thighs, and his fingers separated, searched and explored my petals from behind.

I was speared from the front and the back, and at that I lost what remained of my inhibitions. I couldn't help but grind my pelvis into Ben's face, and as his tongue and his fingers buried deep inside me and I moved ever closer to him, I could only throw my head back and emit a guttural groan as I came – hard. I had lost Coucou, and I was so caught up in the glory of pure physical sensation that for a moment I even lost Elizabeth.

Once the waves had subsided and my head was mine again, I brought Ben back to his feet and took charge: Coucou was back and she wasn't taking "no" for an answer. After pushing him backwards onto the bed, I made to unbutton his shirt. Like me he was breathing heavily, and as I pinned his wrists back with my body weight, he lifted his head to explore me with one of his magic kisses.

"Christ, you're good at that," I shuddered, breathless.

He answered the compliment with another long tonguing, taking the back of my head in his hands and planting my lips ever firmer on his. I traced my breasts over his chest, and teasingly placed a nipple in his mouth. Ben growled and tilted his head to take as much of me as he could into his mouth. This was pure heaven, but the star in me wanted yet more recognition of my beauty and allure, and the heat emanating from Ben told that he needed to let loose too. I wanted to prove so irresistible as to give him his own release – and more. So, taking charge, I straddled him and began to undo his shirt, nuzzling his neck as the top buttons parted under pressure.

"Stop," Ben panted, and then more firmly: "Stop – please." He pushed me backwards gently, so that he was sitting upright on the side of the bed, my legs wrapped around his back. "This is amazing as it is – you're just amazing," he whispered. I wriggled in his lap, trying to gauge a reaction, wanting him to want me more. I craved this hot, sexy man before me, and I yearned for him to lose control and to take me fully.

Ben pressed his face to my chest, holding me, tracing my full curves with his mouth. I was slick with desire, my body already wet with sex sweat. Ben looked up at me, and his troubled expression stopped my heart in its tracks. "What is it?" I asked. "What's wrong?" I could've kicked myself as the teenage girl still somewhere deep inside me blurted out, "Don't you fancy me?"

"More than you know," was his gritted response.

"Then what is it? Something's bothering you," I persisted. I was not used to not getting my own way, and flushed from our passion I certainly wasn't ready to stop there. "Are you OK? Can I do anything? Drink of water? Do you want me to call a cab? Do you want me to go?"

"No, absolutely not," Ben answered vehemently, "I want you to stay!"

Unhearing, I blathered on, unaccustomed to feeling insecure and anxious: "Are you too hot? And I don't mean this in the chat-up line sense, but would it help to take some clothes off? I'm semi-naked here, and I'm burning up!"

"I know, and I'm loving it," Ben grinned, his spark reignited. He lay back on the bed again, his hands around my waist, his thumbs circling lazily against my stomach. Relieved, I pitched forward and leant my head on his chest. I could hear Ben's heart beating like crazy, and the heat coming from him was so intense that I slid my fingers beneath the remaining buttons and set them loose, blowing cool air on his skin as I went. I could feel him tense, but this time he didn't stop me from removing his shirt.

I kissed the hollow of Ben's neck, and lovingly worked down between his pectorals, licking and biting softly as I went. Upon reaching his chest I stopped. I felt Ben stiffen and hold his breath.

Early morning had come, and the room was bathed in a cool light. "Is this what you were trying to hide?" I chided gently. Still straddling Ben I sat up and took his face in my hands. He met my gaze, albeit reluctantly. With his eyes upon me I dipped my head down to the two horizontal scars beneath his chest and kissed them tenderly. Ben sighed a long, languid sigh and his whole being noticeably relaxed from deep within. He stretched back so that his torso was flexed and his stomach muscles convex. I could see the tight hairs furled over his belt, and I wanted to pleasure him. Reaching down to his pelvis I hesitated. "Is this OK?" I asked.

"If it's OK with you?" Ben counter-questioned, his eyes locked with mine, scanning me searchingly.

My reaction was to undo Ben's belt and slowly pull his trousers and then his boxers off, kissing his abdomen all the while. He held his breath as I caressed his hip bones and then dropped to his inner thighs.

"Are you all right with me penetrating you?" I asked Ben. I wanted to make this handsome man feel as sexually celebrated as I had been.

"If I'm completely honest, it's been so long that I'm really not sure . . ." Ben blushed. "You're the first person I've let close to me in a very long time."

"I'm honoured," I smiled. And I meant it: I was bowled over by Ben, and I was touched that he clearly felt the same as me. It might sound weird, but although I work in the erotic arts, I rarely really fancy people: maybe it's the fame, maybe it's because I'm always working, but it takes a rare person to get me interested enough to pursue a few dates, let alone get sexually involved. So I wanted Ben more than I'd wanted anyone in years. And I wanted him to want me too.

So, flipping into seduction mode I looked up at my new lover from under my exaggerated lashes and drew my mouth along his pubic area. Ben groaned, and tensed as I lowered my tongue to his pussy. His clit was significantly larger than mine – from all the male hormones I guessed – and I hoped this meant he was extra responsive. I licked carefully as I didn't want to hurt him, trying to gauge his sensitivity.

"God that feels so good," Ben moaned. I smiled inwardly: no problems there, then! I took his hardened clit into my mouth and sucked it like a dick. This sensation at least I could give him, and it seemed like he enjoyed it – below me I could see his toes curl. I licked Ben vertically, tracing the folds of his labia, and tentatively traced my tongue to his hot opening. He was wet, and I knew he wanted me – I felt myself become moist in response. "You're gorgeous, Ben!" I exhaled into his depths.

"I think I might be OK with—" Ben gasped, too turned on to finish.

I quickly slipped a finger inside him, gently, insistently. As he bucked against me I slid another finger in, and then a third. With my mouth on his clit I licked a finger from my other hand and pressed it against his dark opening. I paused, waiting to see if Ben was happy with this. Like most men, of course he was – what he may have lacked in physicality he more than made up for in mentality. I heard a positive growl in response, and felt him press his arse hard against me. I needed no more encouragement and, lubricating my finger once again, I teased his body's coy resistance until it offered itself up to me. Suddenly I was able to slide my finger in, and at that moment Ben was full of me. With my mouth on his clit too, it was only moments until I had him writhing in my hands, impaling himself on my fingers. It had clearly been as long for him as it had been for me: soon I could feel his cunt tense around my fingers, and as if from far away I heard and felt a sonorous rumble . . .

"Uhhh!" Ben roared.

"Hooo!" I breathed on his clit, as a warm fountain of wetness hit me on the chin. Not only had Ben come, but he'd actually squirted!

"Hangover from the old days," Ben panted. "Sorry!"

"No need to apologize," I blew back. I'd been so focused on Ben's pleasure that I'd hardly taken a full breath myself, and suddenly I was desperate for oxygen. I collapsed on top of him, feeling our hearts beat hard in unison, our fresh sweat sweet and slick on our chests, my head nestled in the safe warm space between his jaw and his shoulder as I shielded my eyes from the daylight.

"Wow, that was more than worth waiting for!" I heard my lover say. I could hear the true contentment in these words and feel the happiness fit to burst from his chest beneath me. I knew he could hear the smile in my voice as I enthusiastically agreed: "I needed that too!"

We sat up so that we could see one another more clearly, our fingers embracing, our faces beaming with a joy so genuine that I knew that our night together had been unexpectedly special for both of us.

"You're really something else, you know that?" Ben murmured as his mouth tenderly nuzzled the sensitive spot below my ear.

My whole body quivered in response. "You're really something else too," I said.

From the depths of my handbag I heard a text come through on my phone. I smiled as I turned back to Ben. My sister would have to wait . . .

Marks

Rachel Kramer Bussel

"Stop it!" Emma squealed as Russell's blows with the belt went from slaps with more noise than sting to ones that seared her skin, ones that would surely leave marks all over her pale backside. Normally she loved knowing that he wasn't just spanking her in the moment, but was giving her a parting gift as well, something she tucked into her panties and skirts as she went to work or was reminded of as she sat down at a restaurant for lunch with a friend.

The tinge of afterglow combined with being able to admire her ass were added bonuses to the thrill she got from being spanked, the rush of delicious sensation that she could rarely get enough of. Even on her most off days, when the world seemed askew, a spanking from Russell could set her mind at ease, could right her world. As wonderfully painful as they were, she balked, sitting up and shifting so she was sitting on the hotel bed. "They're all going to know." Yes, even at an alternative venue, Emma wanted to be liked and not judged, to fit in. She was all too used to feeling like the odd woman out for liking things like being spanked, slapped, tied up, choked and verbally degraded. She'd found a community of like-minded people who gave her the support she needed, who understood that after a long day she liked to come home and sometimes wear nothing but a collar. This was a new adventure for Emma and Russell, a welcome pleasure after eight years together.

"Know that you like to be spanked? Honey, I'm sure they can tell just by looking at you," Russell coaxed her. The idea of being "found out" in non-kinky company had always been something they'd talked about in bed, but now it wasn't having its usual arousing effect on her. "And besides, so what? We're adults and we're at an adult resort. The point is to do whatever we want. And I know you want a spanking." He was right; she did, very much so, and she knew he wasn't talking about a simple over-the-knee hand spanking, but the kind of blistering session that made them both breathless, the type of spanking that fueled their relationship and, Emma thought, kept it solid and secure.

Spanking was something they could always turn to – and did. But showing off her ass after a full round of Russell at his most vicious wasn't on her agenda. The bruises and welts he tended to leave on her pale ass were special to her, marks of her endurance she treasured with pride, but they were for her to see in the mirror or him to admire around the house. She'd wanted to come here, but she was still feeling out the crowd, and didn't want to jinx herself and be seen as separate because of her spanking predilection. Sure, most of these people maybe engaged in a few slaps before and during sex, but Emma liked it hard and rough.

"Well, it's fine for them to suspect, but I can't walk around in a nudist hotel the way I normally do, with marks and bruises all over me. It's one thing if I show off my tattoos or maybe bend too low and they see a bruise or a few lines so quickly they could almost think they imagined it, but what would these people think if they saw exactly how red you make my ass? They're exhibitionists, sure, but that doesn't mean they're kinky. I don't want to scare them." Still, even as she said the word, the idea of scaring them filled her with a sense of excitement, a sense of power. She was an exhibitionist, but she was also a perfectionist and competitive at everything she did, from her job as a party planner to finding the best-tasting coffee in town.

If she was going to do something, she wanted to be the best, and if you're at a nude resort, the goal is not so much to have the mythical "perfect" body as to score the most attention. If Emma hadn't known that when they walked in, she'd have figured it out from the parade of people, classically beautiful and not, strolling through the hotel in their altogether. The truth was, to really stand out in a place like this, you'd have to not just wear clothes but dress like Lady Gaga. Emma liked her size-ten body, liked the way it felt when she draped herself across Russell's lap, liked how her large breasts bobbed as she walked around topless, as she had last night, their first at the resort. She'd been too nervous to go bottomless, but eating dinner in public with her tits hanging out had been freeing, and exciting, and they'd both enjoyed seeing so much naked flesh, whether they were interested in touching it or not. Russell had moved his seat next to Emma's so they could whisper and discuss their fellow diners, and who they'd want to kiss or spank or fuck.

"Fine, for tonight. No marks. But I'm not letting you go to dinner until I've enjoyed your ass, one way or another. What'll it be, Em?" He was asking her if she wanted to get spanked or have him spread her cheeks and shove his cock deep into the hole he opened up there. She liked both of them, though spanking was her favorite. She'd never been spanked before meeting him save for a few light smacks, and those hadn't done what his smacks did for her. Russell's spankings were a work of art, from the way he teased her to the way he made her ass feel like it was coming alive under his hand.

When she didn't answer, he took her silence to mean she was letting him decide, and he bent her over the hotel bed, first stroking her pussy, then slapping her sweet spot, where her cheeks met. Emma used to make noise when he spanked her, thinking, based on previous experience, that that was what all men wanted, that that was what a true sub did. She'd thought that until Russell had ordered her to be quiet or he'd make her be quiet, and she'd realized that the act of suppressing her noises turned her on as much as holding off on coming when ordered to. She wasn't just a spanking slut, but a glutton for being ordered around, told what to do, made to obey automatically. Even thinking about having to ask a question, knowing Russell would get to decide the answer, made her pussy clench whether she was in line at the drugstore or just waking up.

So she stayed quiet as his hand swiftly beat her bottom, faster and faster, harder and harder. No matter how many times Russell did it, Emma found something new to enjoy about his smacks, and at that moment, if he'd dared to ask her, she'd have been so far gone in the pleasure of what he was doing she wouldn't have cared about the marks. But Russell was true to his word, and he merely left her ass burning with heat that made its way to her cunt. He ignored that, telling her she'd get fucked when he was allowed to mark her. She smiled, an ironic, secret kind of smile, the kind only a fellow submissive or intuitive dominant would understand. It was a smile of delighted denial, a smile that promised her pleasure for obeying, or the pleasure of pain for disobeying. She sucked his cock on her knees, her heels pressed against her warm buttocks, knowing they wouldn't last the whole vacation without her being marked.

*　　*　　*

And then they ventured out into their first morning at the resort. Many of the guests at this hour were wearing swimsuits or some light form of clothing, fluttering white dresses blowing in the breeze, thong bikinis nestled between tight bottoms. Emma gasped when she saw a stunningly gorgeous woman, statuesque and curvy, with a mane of glossy, beautiful honey-blonde curls tumbling over her breasts. But it was when the woman turned around that Emma's heart started to beat faster, because her ass looked like what Emma's looked like after a particularly rough spanking session. There were dark stripes of red set against an overall paler shade of pink, as if the woman had gotten sunburned and then spanked, but the otherwise pale skin surrounding the redness told Emma otherwise.

As they made their way to the buffet table, a tingle of excitement swept through Emma. There was something about being around so many naked people that made exhibitionism a whole different ball game. It was one thing to playfully flirt with having a wardrobe malfunction while on the subway, or to be the girl getting beaten the loudest and longest at a kinky play party, but when nudity was simply the norm, it made you notice all sorts of other things about people. Emma had trouble selecting from the sumptuous feast in front of them because she was so excited about having spied the woman. She didn't consider herself bisexual exactly, but there'd been a few times in her life when the sight of a stunningly gorgeous woman had made her reconsider the label, or at least made her want to drop everything and immerse herself in the woman in question.

Emma and Russell had agreed that, while they were mostly monogamous, and had only indulged with one other partner each in the time they'd been together, this vacation was their chance to be free, unfettered from their daily lives, including the constraint of monogamy. As long as they told each other what they were doing, they were free to indulge. So as Emma spooned some macaroni and cheese and salad onto her plate, she was already cooking up opening lines. She scanned the room for the woman, who was seated next to an older man with a bushy salt-and-pepper beard. "Let's sit over there," she said to Russell, who was a few steps behind her.

"Is this seat taken?" Emma asked, knowing it clearly wasn't. The couple introduced themselves as Janet and Paul, and they chatted easily, as if they weren't all sitting there topless. When Emma's hand reached for Russell's beneath the table, she also felt how hard he was, and that intimate knowledge made her squirm. She picked at her food and tried to sound intelligent as she patiently waited until there was an appropriate moment to ask Janet about the state of her ass. For all the flesh on display, it wasn't like they were at an orgy, and the chatter around her was on much more mundane topics than belts versus paddles.

Finally, they'd finished eating and Janet suggested she and Emma head over to the women's spa and soak in the hot tub for a while. "You'll be all right on your own, won't you, honey?" asked Emma. At Russell's nod, she went off with Janet, feeling her skin tingle before they'd even stripped down and planted themselves in the almost-scalding water. Emma couldn't help but ask, "This doesn't bother you? I mean, I noticed your marks . . ." She trailed off, hoping she hadn't said too much.

"Oh, those?" Janet said, laughing as her hair fell into the bubbling water. "Doesn't hurt any more than it did getting them."

Emma let that sink in before saying, "I like it, too. Spanking. Getting spanked, I mean." She laughed nervously. "I was actually worried about being too marked here. I didn't know how kinky a place this was. I've been to a few swingers events, and every time, kink was definitely frowned upon. I didn't want to be the odd girl out, and I actually stopped Russell from using anything too heavy this morning. And then I saw you . . ."

Janet stood and thrust her ass out toward Emma for her to admire. They were the only ones in the spa, and when Janet said, "Go ahead, you can touch it." Emma did, finding the woman's skin warm to the touch. She cupped her palm around Janet's perfectly lush curve, smiling as she saw up close exactly what Janet's welts looked like.

"I can take a lot," she said. "I mean, I pay for it when I sit down, but it's worth it. What about you?" Janet was as casual as if they were talking about knitting.

"Me, too. We tend to only play to our limits on the weekends, when there's some downtime to recover."

"What about here?" Janet asked, floating across the water so she was right in front of Emma, her lower lip jutting out and her lips parting in a way that even not-so-bi Emma could read as desire. "Did you come prepared?"

"Yes," Emma said, the word catching in her throat. "We have some equipment." She swallowed, suddenly light-headed, her pussy throbbing.

"Do you only play together, or does he ever loan you out?" The way she asked made Emma's whole body tingle with the assumption that Russell owned her.

"We're allowed extracurricular activities, though mostly I'm just with him. It's so intense that . . . well, most other people don't tempt me. But that doesn't mean I wouldn't."

"Wouldn't what?" Janet asked as she leaned in and before Emma could even think of an answer she was kissing her, her tongue sliding easily between her lips, hot and seeking. Janet pressed herself right up against Emma, mashing her into the edge of the hot tub. Emma gave herself over to the kiss, and to Janet's knee pressing against her pussy.

"Wouldn't . . . I don't even know, actually."

"Wouldn't let me spank you?" Janet's words hung in the air. "Just because I can take a lot doesn't mean I can't dish it out. I don't top too often but this ass—" she reached down to grab it "—would be an honor to spank."

Emma smiled at her, still stunned at how fast this was moving. "I'd like that. A lot," she said, realizing that in all her time with Russell, no one else had given her anything more than a light slap on the ass. And she'd never played like that with a woman. Emma was a good eight inches shorter than Janet, petite to Janet's tall, commanding presence. From the way Janet leaned down and sucked on her lower lip, then shifted to her neck, sinking her teeth in, Emma had a feeling Janet would rival Russell in her spanking ability.

They made it out of the hot tub, drying off with the sumptuous extra-large towels. When Emma reached for a robe, Janet tugged it out of her hand. "You don't need it here," she said, then squeezed Emma's cheek. That pressure alone was enough to make her twitch.

Emma thought about calling Russell on their way back to the room, but she removed her hand from the phone she clutched. She wanted Janet for herself, wanted to see what it was like to be spanked by this aggressive, sexy woman, before sharing her with Russell. The idea of Russell watching was exciting, but she didn't want to feel like she was putting on a show, the way she sometimes did at the play parties they attended. She liked showing off, but only under the right circumstances.

Emma shivered as they walked, noticing the envious stares, from men as well as women, when Janet put her arm around her,

her hand resting on Emma's hip. Emma's fingers trembled as she inserted the key in the lock, and she took deep breaths to center herself. "Relax," Janet whispered in her ear. "I'd say I don't want to hurt you but, well . . . you know. I want to make you happy, though. I want to give you what you need, what you deserve, Emma. Why don't you show me your toys?"

Janet's voice was calm but inviting, almost soothing. Emma pulled out their toy box and showed Janet a fraction of the kinky implements they owned; the ones that offered the most bang for the buck and were easy to travel with. Janet held up a wooden paddle with holes in it as well as a shiny red-leather slapper and the old standby, a solid hairbrush that Emma had never used on her hair. "Do you want to get over my knee?" Janet asked, her tone respectful but, Emma sensed, not for much longer.

"Yes," Emma said, caught somewhere between nerves and confidence. She wasn't scared that she wouldn't be able to take what Janet dished out, or that she wouldn't like it. Her fears were more amorphous, more about opening this Pandora's box.

"It's going to hurt, Emma, and it's going to mark you. You have to be ready for that," Janet said as Emma settled herself across the naked woman's lap, her hair draping down toward the ground, her legs sticking out in the air. "Your safe word is *spa.*" Emma committed the word to memory, testing out the start of it, the hissing of the *sp* against her lips, making sure it was nestled somewhere at the back of her mind in case she needed to call it forth. She settled herself until she got comfortable, murmuring a confirmation. And then there was the first blow, rougher than Russell usually started out with, one that startled her into paying full attention. There was no Russell, no concern about what any of the guests would think, not even, except remotely, concern about what she herself would think. Emma's focus was on Janet, on making sure she was good for her.

And that was clearly Janet's focus, too, as she praised her with "Good girl," before using her right hand to deliver loud, stinging slaps, and then turning to the hairbrush. The blows were brisk and stern; Emma realized quickly that Janet was stronger than she looked. She wasn't tasked with counting, the way Russell often made her, and she sank into the sensation of the spanking, the feel of every blow on her skin, which was still just tender enough from earlier to feel the sensation doubly.

Emma was quiet, her quaking silent and internal, until she couldn't keep it in anymore. "Ow," she cried out, receiving a harder blow next. Her next cries weren't words, merely screams, ones that made the smacks feel even better, helping her get through them in the same way she grunted when lifting a heavy weight at the gym. When Janet cupped her hand again against Emma's hot ass and dug her long, sharp nails briefly into her skin, Emma whimpered. Janet picked up the paddle and smacked her on the border where her upper thigh met her ass. Emma knew she was getting wet, but she was too focused on her ass to care.

The next blows were even fiercer, and Emma felt tears starting to fall as stuttering moans left her lips. "Do you want me to stop, Emma?" Janet asked, pausing in her ministrations to stroke Emma's upper back. "Or should I get something else out of your toy box?"

"Something else," Emma said, her face heating up as she admitted that she wanted more.

Janet lifted Emma and placed her face down on the bed, then slid her red silk eye mask over her eyes. "You just lie there and wait for me. Actually, spread those legs enough so I can see your pussy." Just as Emma was obeying her, she heard a fumbling at the door. If she hadn't had the blindfold on, she'd have given Janet a stricken look, but Janet simply pushed her head down and said, "Stay there, or your spanking ends. In fact, spread your legs even wider. I think Russell will want to see how pretty your lips look."

Emma sucked in a deep breath and did spread her legs. Janet moved toward the door and she heard only whispers before Janet laughed and said, "Come in, come in, you guys are just in time."

So Paul was still with Russell. "You don't mind waiting until I'm done, do you? Honey, Emma was admiring my ass – very good job, sweetie – and apparently decided she needed to match me. Beautiful, isn't she?" Janet said and, as she did so, Emma felt a blow from the riding crop greet her ass. They'd shifted from the wider heads to this crop, with its smaller, and therefore more stinging tip, one that Janet took full advantage of. The blows were more concentrated, striking one small section of Emma's ass and making her bite her lip before moving on to another equally tender spot. "Don't clench your cheeks, Emma; you won't get to really feel it that way, and I know you like to feel it. Doesn't she, Russell?"

"Oh, yes," he said, and she could hear the grin in his voice. Janet kept on striking her, occasionally making forays to her upper thighs and once or twice tapping at her pussy, which made more of the squeaking whimpers escape Emma's lips. "Want a turn?" Janet asked, handing the crop to one of the men. Emma wasn't sure which, even when the first very strong blow landed. She was too busy sucking the two fingers Janet had inserted into her mouth, pulling them as deep as she could, trying not to bite as the blows got harder and harder, ones she knew were leaving behind reminders on her skin that would be there throughout the trip. Emma sucked harder and harder on Janet's fingers as the crop kept going and going, until finally she felt it ease away from her ass, the leather meandering down one leg, tickling the ball of a foot, then pressing against her pussy in a way that made her throb.

"What do you think, Russell?" Janet asked as she eased her fingers out of Emma's mouth. Emma was grateful for the eye mask, because she wasn't sure she could handle seeing her husband and the man and woman they'd just met that afternoon seeing her in such a state.

"Stunning. My Emma's such a good girl, isn't she? I hope you don't mind, but I think I can take over from here."

"Not at all," Janet said, and Emma wondered if he was going to keep spanking her, and wondered if she could take it.

In moments, he was on top of her, his skin warm from the sun as he whispered in her ear. "You're amazing, do you know that? I had no idea you had that in you. I'm going to reward you now, baby," he said and then just like that, he was sliding his cock inside her. She didn't care that Janet and Paul were watching, not after what they'd just seen. Well, she did care, actually, she found out as she heard them kissing. She cared enough to get even wetter as Russell shifted them so she was on top and he held her ass cheeks, pulling them in a way that surely bared her asshole, not to mention made her hot cheeks even hotter. He kissed her fiercely, like they'd been apart for weeks rather than hours. Emma whimpered some more as she came, the intensity hitting her all at once. Russell, who wasn't usually one to make much noise at the moment of climax, let out a roar in Emma's ear. When he went to remove the eye mask, she shook her head, keeping it on as she nestled into him, curling her body toward him as she breathed into the pillow and a few stray tears trickled down her face.

After Emma had had some time to recover, they decided to head out for cocktails at the bar. The air was bordering on cool, but still pleasant enough that they could go in their birthday suits, which is precisely what they did. Emma had to resist the urge to keep reaching for her ass, feeling the raised skin, the heat that had stayed with her, stroking her flesh like it was a kinky kind of Braille she could use to read how much of a pain slut she was.

The marks were something she could carry with her, claim utterly and completely as hers. They branded her as a woman who could take a mean spanking, whether she liked it or not. Emma liked that they invited speculation, and now that she'd gotten used to it, she welcomed the stares. It was like having a particularly bold tattoo, or, in her case, five, the kind people can't look away from, yet more powerful. Their eyes, even in such a sensual setting, were drawn her way and instead of the judgement she'd expected, there was desire, admiration, respect and curiosity. She could see the questions as they were being raised on people's faces, and she liked having the power to answer them, or not answer and just let them guess.

Walking hand in hand between Janet and Russell, with Paul on Janet's other side, Emma knew they were attracting attention, all of them nude, the women with matching red bottoms. And this time she stood tall, claiming every marker of who she was, what she wanted. If anything, maybe she could be a kind of spanking ambassador and inspire some other attendees to bend over themselves. Either way, she was looking forward to the rest of the stay, and the marks she'd take with her on her way home.

Halloween in the Castro

Donna George Storey

"What should I be? A witch or a slut?"

Those seemed to be my only two choices. All the costumes in the "adult women's" section were either black gowns with scalloped sleeves, leopard-skin hooker dresses or naughty schoolgirl uniforms.

Julian smiled. The lucky bastard already had his costume picked out – an Albert Einstein wig and a fake white mustache. Halloween stores definitely provided a wider selection of alter egos for men.

"How about a slutty witch?" he offered.

It wasn't a bad idea. All I had to do was grab spider web stockings and a pointed hat to go with a slinky black minidress I pulled from the rack. No one expected dazzle from a couple of tourists from New Jersey. Julian and I were going to the famous Halloween party in the Castro to sightsee, not be seen.

Still, I was happy to note the lustful flicker in my husband's eyes when I stepped out of the dressing room to model my outfit. Even the plastic skeletons leered down from the walls.

"I guess it took a trip to San Francisco to bring out my true nature," I said, noticing in the mirror that the hem of the dress barely covered my buttocks. "You don't think this is too provocative, do you?"

Julian stepped up behind me and leaned in close. "I love seeing this new side of you. Besides, all the other guys there will be gay. I'll have you all to myself."

He reached out and gave my ass a quick squeeze.

I giggled.

It was the last time that gesture would ever be so innocent.

The rest of the day followed the ritual we'd established during our week in the City by the Bay. We explored yet another charming neighborhood and ended up at a restaurant that was recommended by our friends Chuck and Michelle. This time we ate dim sum at Pearl City where we feasted on plate after plate of barbecued pork buns, shrimp-and-cilantro dumplings and sticky rice steamed in bamboo leaves – all for less than twenty bucks total. Afterwards we headed back to our hosts' Noe Valley town-house for an afternoon tumble on the guest room futon. In honor of the holiday, Julian asked me to put on the witch dress while I "rode his broomstick." Once he had me flying high, he started whispering that I really was a witch, because the dress made me look so hot he'd wanted to hike it up over my hips and fuck me right in front of everyone in the store.

I came almost immediately.

Later that evening, I wore the dress again to go up to the Castro. Fortunately the night was warm for San Francisco, because I was showing a lot of flesh. Not that I was alone. The streets were teeming with partiers in lingerie and seriously dangerous fetish wear.

"Chuck sure seemed anxious to get us out of the house," Julian laughed, taking my hand as we strolled along among the Grim Reapers and naughty nurses. "He was talking up Halloween in the Castro all week – *it'll be a night to remember* – then suddenly they have to stay home to hand out candy. At 10 p.m.?"

"They probably started humping the minute we left. There must be something in the fog here that turns everyone into a sex fiend."

"I know." His gaze slid over my clingy costume. "Actually, I can see us moving here some day. Then we can be sex fiends all the time."

"It works for me. I'd transfer to Schwab's office here, and I'm sure you could find something pretty quickly, Einstein. Every-one's interested in a good physicist."

"E equals mc squared! Love your costume." This from a burly, bearded man dressed as Dorothy from *The Wizard of Oz*. I tried not to stare, but there was something oddly compelling about thick, hairy legs coupled with a blue gingham skirt and ruby slippers.

A skinny scarecrow in the same group winked at Julian. "I wish I had your brain, honey."

I waited until they walked ahead to tease him. "See, everyone *is* interested in a good physicist."

Julian gave my butt a smack. "Watch yourself, or I'll have to punish you later."

Yes, something about San Francisco definitely brought out our wild sides.

By now the streets were bustling. We passed more Dorothys, lots of Marilyns, a whole squad of beaming nuns, all in drag. Mixed in with the locals were college kids, obviously drunk, some carrying rubber masks of famous actors or politicians, others not even bothering with a "Cheap Ass Halloween Costume" T-shirt. Soon the crowd was so dense, we were shuffling rather than walking.

Julian wrapped an arm around me. "Hey, I think that's the parade up there."

I followed his gaze. I couldn't see much but the head and shoulders of a tall, beefy man in a green sequined evening gown. Perched on his head was a huge golden crown decorated with filigreed towers and terraces like a south-east Asian temple. Shimmying to a throbbing drumbeat, the Halloween Queen wound his way through a roped-off passage in the center of the street. Several other buff guys in bright sequined dresses danced behind him, a fitting court of honor.

The music was almost deafening, and I was about to shout to Julian that maybe we should go back, but we were already hemmed in by bodies on all sides. The crowd pushed us forward, and Julian's arm slipped from my shoulder. He wedged himself in behind me.

The *Oz* group we'd seen earlier had joined in the conga line. A man dressed as Toto lifted his leg and pretended to relieve himself on the onlookers. He actually used a squirt gun for the gag, and the crowd roared, lurching back and throwing me against Julian's body. Fortunately he caught me, cupping my bottom and tipping me back on my feet. His hand lingered for a moment, steady and reassuring, then pulled away.

But apparently, he couldn't resist my charms for long. A moment later I felt his fingers brushing my cheeks, gently, but with enough confidence to send prickles of pleasure straight to my pussy.

My eyes widened in surprise, but I quickly adjusted my expression to a neutral stare. Why not let my husband feel me up in public? He probably just wanted to reassert his heterosexuality after being ogled by the hairy Dorothy. Besides, the

way he was touching me – as if the illicitness made him appreciate every sweet inch of my ass in a whole new way – was
incredibly arousing.

Maybe I *was* turning into a slut?

I rocked back against him, a secret signal to carry on. If the
tent pole in his jeans was any indication, he was enjoying this as
much as I was.

That's when Julian began to caress me in earnest, raking his
fingertips in slow circles over my flesh until my buttocks were
melting with pleasure. Other parts of me responded, too. My
breasts felt heavy and sensitive. My clit ached for his touch. And
my cunt was a faucet, soaking my panties with hot juices.

I lolled my head back a little to let him know I liked it.

His breath quickened, but oddly, he seemed content with the
teasing caresses.

I felt a flicker of annoyance. He could talk a good game in bed,
but when we actually had a real chance to do something in public,
he lost his nerve. No one was watching us. A straight couple
dressed in cheap costumes from the Spirit Store was the height of
boring in this part of the world.

Little did they know.

Suppressing a wicked smile, I grabbed the hem of my skirt and
inched it up over my hips. Now there was nothing between my
ass and that warm, grasping hand but a pair of fishnet hose.
Spreading my legs, I tilted forward from the waist, boldly offering
myself – just in case he had any doubt of my desires.

I half hoped he might force his way through the pantyhose and
finger-fuck me on the spot, but Julian just kept rubbing my fleshy
cheeks. He used both hands now, kneading and squeezing, as if
enchanted by the heft, the softness. Not that his new devotion to
my butt wasn't flattering, but I needed more. I swiveled my hips
discreetly, nudging his hand along until his fingers slipped into
my furrow.

The hand paused. I held my breath, my pulse throbbing
between my legs. If he didn't touch my wet pink parts soon, I
might well pass out from frustration. After one unbearable
moment, his forefinger finally snaked down into my cleft and
tapped my asshole lightly.

Electric jolts sizzled through my body, and a moan spilled
from my lips. It would certainly be a night to remember if Julian
made me come in the middle of the Castro Halloween Parade.

Suddenly a college kid, reeking of beer, stumbled into me from left. "Hey, let me through. I bought front-row seats, ya know."

Staggering behind him, his buddy smacked straight into my body, hurtling me forward through the crowd as easily as a cock glides into a well-lubricated vagina. Murmuring embarrassed apologies to the people around me, I quickly yanked down my dress and turned to find my husband.

The drunk kids had pushed him far over to my right. His Einstein wig was awry, and I saw my panic mirrored in his face. When I caught his eye, he jerked his head back the way we came. I nodded and began to push my way toward him. After all, we could carry on with the evening's real entertainment back in our bedroom.

We didn't have the chance to talk until we were back on Jersey Street.

"That wasn't a night to remember," Julian grumbled, "that was a fucking zoo."

He was right, but his sudden grumpiness surprised me.

"Come on, sweetie, you were enjoying yourself."

"Not really."

"No? You didn't like feeling me up back there?"

Julian stopped in his tracks.

I should have caught on then, but I was still giddy from the lingering effects of that tap-dancing finger. I leaned toward him and whispered, "Don't worry, I won't tell anyone you were fondling my ass in public."

He frowned at me, eyes narrowed. "What the fuck are you talking about?"

Suddenly I did get it. My jaw – and my stomach – immediately crashed to the sidewalk.

"OK, what happened back there?"

"Nothing." I started walking. Fast.

Julian kept pace with me. "It wasn't nothing. Someone was touching your ass."

"Let's talk about this later." My face was on fire, but the whole lower half of my body was cold and numb. Someone – I'd never know who – was indeed touching my ass.

"No, not later. I have a right to know exactly what happened right now."

Did he? I gritted my teeth. Did the real Einstein ever act like such a possessive jerk? And wasn't *I* the victim here?

Julian wouldn't be put off. "What did he do to you?"

"It could have been a 'she'," I shot back, although I knew, of course, that it wasn't.

"Sandra, I think you need to tell me."

His voice was gentler, and I slowed my steps.

"I thought it was you, OK? And nothing really happened. He just patted me a couple of times. It was . . . friendly."

Julian made a *humph* sound as if he knew I was lying.

Which I was.

We walked the rest of the way in silence.

When we got back to the house, we found Chuck and Michelle in the living room, sharing a bottle of wine and watching *Halloween*. They invited us to join them, but Julian muttered something about having a headache and retreated to our bedroom.

Stalling for time, I sat down and polished off a glass of cabernet in three swallows.

"How was it?" Chuck asked, his smile so mellow, I knew the two of them had indeed gone at it the minute we left.

"The crowd scene was pretty intense." I wasn't really in the mood to go into detail.

"Every year the party gets crazier, although I hear nothing too out of hand happens until after midnight. There's even talk about canceling it completely one of these years," Michelle said.

"Good thing you got your chance tonight. I'll bet you never forget this experience," Chuck insisted.

"You're right about that." I stood up wearily. "Well, I'd better get to bed."

"By the way, Sandra?" Chuck called after me.

I turned.

He wiggled his eyebrows. "That dress really shows off your assets."

Michelle jabbed him in the ribs.

I gave them a crooked smile and crept back to the guest room, which now felt more like some haunted house for wayward wives – the Lair of the Demon Husband.

The room was completely dark. I eased the door closed, just in case Julian was actually asleep.

A voice floated up from the bed, low but determined. "Sandra, we have to talk."

My pulse jumped. It was time for my punishment. "I know." I peeled off my costume, vowing to toss the cursed thing in the garbage the next morning. Then I crawled under the blankets, keeping a careful distance from Julian's body.

"I'm not mad at you," he said gruffly.

"You could have fooled me." Marriage manuals always warned you not to go to bed angry with your spouse, but I'd definitely be doing that if we didn't clear the air. "Look, I'm sure we both have lots of confused feelings, but for the record, I thought it was you and there was no, uh, penetration at all. I hope if we talk about this honestly, we can put it behind us."

Without a word, Julian rolled toward me and took me in his arms.

He was hard. Rock hard. And huge, as if he'd downed one of those cock-enhancing potions they sell on the Internet.

"What's this?" I blurted out – as if the answer wasn't obvious.

"Are you sure you want an honest answer?" Suddenly Julian sounded like the guilty one.

I swallowed. "Of course, I do."

"Well, I'm totally pissed off at that creep for taking advantage of you. If he was here right now, I'd break off every one of his fingers and then do the same to his dick."

I laughed uncomfortably, although his rough chivalry touched me.

"But . . ." he faltered.

"But what?"

"The thought of a stranger touching you like that is kind of . . . exciting."

Now it was my turn to give the little *humph*.

"What are you thinking, babe?" His voice was almost a whisper.

Was *he* ready for honesty? Because, in fact, his confession had conjured a spirit I'd been trying very hard to put out of my mind – that faceless man who'd so gently caressed, even savored, my ass. Would *he* remember the night he met an unknown female so horny she let him rub and squeeze her cheeks, even hiked up her own skirt and practically forced him to finger her cleft? Was he thinking about it now, his fist wrapped around his cock as he sniffed his musky finger, his own special Halloween treat?

Julian's arm tightened around me. "Sandra, you can tell me the truth."

"OK, but I really don't know what else there is to say. It happened. It's over."

He took a deep breath. "Did you like it?"

I froze, unsure how to respond. There was no doubt I'd enjoyed it at the time. But later, on the way home, I felt tricked and violated, not just by the wily stranger but by the accusation in Julian's voice: *slut, whore*.

And now?

My belly clenched, a sharp spasm that lingered on as a throbbing ache. I couldn't help picturing that anonymous hand kneading my cheeks while Julian watched, his monster cock straining against his zipper. Perverse as it was, it excited me, too. I felt like a sorceress, reveling in my dark power to seduce men, bewitch them, bring them to their knees.

"Yes," I admitted, "I liked it."

We lay together for a few moments without speaking. Julian cleared his throat.

"What did he do to you?"

It was the same question he'd asked me before, but this time his voice was soft with need. He wanted a different answer.

And I realized, at that moment, that I wanted to give it to him.

I wasn't sure I could actually say the words, the truth, out loud. But to my surprise, when I started to speak, my voice came out low and silky like an incantation.

"It all seems so strange now. I was just standing there, and the person in front of me stumbled back and I lost my balance. I didn't think anything of it when you – he – put his hand on my butt to steady me. He acted like he had a right to do it."

"Then what?" Julian whispered.

"Then he started stroking me, drawing circles on the cheeks with his fingertips. It wasn't at all like some pervert grabbing what he could get. He was slow and careful. I thought it was you teasing me, daring me to want it in front of all those people. Soon my whole butt was tingling. I could feel it in other parts of my body, too."

Julian's hand reached around to cup my ass. His fingers began to trace circles on the bare flesh.

"After a while, I got so horny I hiked my skirt up to my waist and pressed myself against him."

At this Julian let out a whimper, but his fingers kept stroking and circling.

"I wanted him to put his hand between my legs to feel how wet I was, but he just kept rubbing my cheeks, like he was mesmerized by them. I was going absolutely crazy, so I wiggled around until he . . ." My voice caught in my throat.

"What did he do?"

"His finger slipped into my crack and he . . . touched . . ."

Julian inhaled sharply. "Yeah?"

"He touched my asshole. Very lightly – *tap, tap, tap*."

My husband made a strange sound in his throat as if he were in pain.

I clearly had him under my spell, but the words had hypnotized me, too. I was right back on Castro Street, my pussy throbbing and drooling in my underpants, desperate for release.

"Can I fuck you now, Jules? I've been thinking about it all night."

Beyond speech, he simply grunted and rolled on his back.

I swung my leg over his hips and sank right onto him.

"Your cock's so big and hard," I breathed. "Just like his."

He made that funny new sound again, a twisted cry of yearning.

I wanted to make him do it again.

I started to ride him slowly, grinding my clit against his belly. "Did you like hearing about the things he did to me? Be honest now."

He choked out a quavering "Yes."

"Then you tell me. Tell me what it's like to be married to a slut who wants it so bad, she lets total strangers rub her ass in the street."

"Oh, God . . ." He arched back on the bed and gave me another sweet, strangled moan.

"Now stick your finger in my crack like he did."

Julian was panting, his mouth opening and closing like a fish, but he dutifully licked his finger and slid it down my crack. Then, just like the stranger, he touched me – t*ap, tap, tap* – right on my puckered hole.

My orgasm shot through me, up from my ass and straight to my skull, where it exploded in a blizzard of sequins glittering and dancing before my eyes.

I don't know what Julian saw when he shot his load a few seconds later. But I could tell it was pure magic.

Of course, I didn't throw the dress away the next day. I took it home with me and brought it back again when we moved to San Francisco a year later. Somewhere along the way they did cancel the famous street party. There were too many unruly incidents, too many arrests.

Still it is an unforgettable part of the city's history – and of ours. Every now and then we like to keep Halloween in the Castro alive. I put on the dress and ask my husband, "What should I be tonight? A witch or a slut?"

Spar

Kij Johnson

In the tiny lifeboat, she and the alien fuck endlessly, relentlessly.

They each have Ins and Outs. Her Ins are the usual, eyes ears nostrils mouth cunt ass. Her Outs are also the common ones: fingers and hands and feet and tongue. Arms. Legs. Things that can be thrust into other things.

The alien is not humanoid. It is not bipedal. It has cilia. It has no bones, or perhaps it does and she cannot feel them. Its muscles, or what might be muscles, are rings and not strands. Its skin is the color of dusk and covered with a clear thin slime that tastes of snot. It makes no sounds. She thinks it smells like wet leaves in winter, but after a time she cannot remember that smell, or leaves, or winter.

Its Ins and Outs change. There are dark slashes and permanent knobs that sometimes distend, but it is always growing new Outs, hollowing new Ins. It cleaves easily in both senses.

It penetrates her a thousand ways. She penetrates it, as well.

The lifeboat is not for humans. The air is too warm, the light too dim. It is too small. There are no screens, no books, no warning labels, no voices, no bed or chair or table or control board or toilet or telltale lights or clocks. The ship's hum is steady. Nothing changes.

There is no room. They cannot help but touch. They breathe each other's breath – if it breathes; she cannot tell. There is always an Out in an In, something wrapped around another thing, flesh coiling and uncoiling inside, outside. Making spaces. Making space.

She is always wet. She cannot tell whether this is the slime from its skin, the oil and sweat from hers, her exhaled breath, the lifeboat's air. Or come.

Her body seeps. When she can, she pulls her mind away. But there is nothing else, and when her mind is disengaged she thinks too much. Which is: at all. Fucking the alien is less horrible.

She does not remember the first time. It is safest to think it forced her.

The wreck was random: a mid-space collision between their ship and the alien's, simultaneously a statistical impossibility and a fact. She and Gary just had time to start the emergency beacon and claw into their suits before their ship was cut in half. Their lifeboat spun out of reach. Her magnetic boots clung to part of the wreck. His did not. The two of them fell apart.

A piece of debris slashed through the leg of Gary's suit to the bone, through the bone. She screamed. He did not. Blood and fat and muscle swelled from his suit into vacuum. Out.

The alien's vessel also broke into pieces, its lifeboat kicking free and the waldos reaching out, pulling her through the airlock. In.

Why did it save her? The mariner's code? She does not think it knows she is alive. If it did it would try to establish communication. It is quite possible that she is not a rescued castaway. She is salvage, or flotsam.

She sucks her nourishment from one of the two hard intrusions in the featureless lifeboat, a rigid tube. She uses the other, a second tube, for whatever comes from her, her shit and piss and vomit. Not her come, which slicks her thighs to her knees.

She gags a lot. It has no sense of the depth of her throat. Ins and Outs.

There is a time when she screams so hard that her throat bleeds.

She tries to teach it words. "Breast," she says. "Finger. Cunt." Her vocabulary options are limited here.

"Listen to me," she says. "Listen. To. Me." Does it even have ears?

The fucking never gets better or worse. It learns no lessons about pleasing her. She does not learn anything about pleasing it either: would not if she could. And why? How do you please grass and why should you? She suddenly remembers grass, the bright smell of it and its perfect green, its cool clean soft feel beneath her bare hands.

She finds herself aroused by the thought of grass against her hands, because it is the only thing that she has thought of for a long time that is not the alien or Gary or the Ins and Outs. But perhaps its soft blades against her fingers would feel like the alien's cilia. Her ability to compare anything with anything else is slipping from her, because there is nothing to compare.

She feels it inside everywhere, tendrils moving in her nostrils, thrusting against her eardrums, coiled beside the corners of her eyes. And she sheathes herself in it.

When an Out crawls inside her and touches her in certain places, she tips her head back and moans and pretends it is more than accident. It is Gary, he loves me, it loves me, it is a He. It is not.

Communication is key, she thinks.

She cannot communicate, but she tries to make sense of its actions.

What is she to it? Is she a sex toy, a houseplant? A shipwrecked Norwegian sharing a spar with a monolingual Portuguese? A companion? A habit, like nail biting or compulsive masturbation? Perhaps the sex is communication and she just doesn't understand the language yet.

Or perhaps there is no It. It is not that they cannot communicate, that she is incapable; it is that the alien has no consciousness to communicate with. It is a sex toy, a houseplant, a habit.

On the starship with the name she cannot recall, Gary would read aloud to her. Science fiction, Melville, poetry. Her mind cannot access the plots, the words. All she can remember is a few lines from a sonnet, "Let me not to the marriage of true minds admit impediments" – something something something – "an ever-fixèd mark that looks on tempests and is never shaken; it is the star to every wand'ring bark . . ."

She recites the words, an anodyne that numbs her for a time until they lose their meaning. She has worn them treadless, and they no longer gain any traction in her mind. Eventually she cannot even remember the sounds of them.

If she ever remembers another line, she promises herself she will not wear it out. She will hoard it. She may have promised this before, and forgotten.

She cannot remember Gary's voice. Fuck Gary, anyway. He is dead and she is here with an alien pressed against her cervix.

It is covered with slime. She thinks that, as with toads, the slime may be a mild psychotropic drug. How would she know if she were hallucinating? In this world, what would that look like? Like sunflowers on a desk, like Gary leaning across a picnic basket to place fresh bread in her mouth. The bread is the first thing she has tasted that feels clean in her mouth, and it's not even real.

Gary feeding her bread and laughing. After a time, the taste of bread becomes "the taste of bread" and then the words become mere sounds and stop meaning anything.

On the off chance that this will change things, she drives her tongue through its cilia, pulls them into her mouth and sucks them clean. She has no idea whether it makes a difference. She has lived forever in the endless reeking fucking now.

Was there someone else on the alien's ship? Was there a Gary, lost now to space? Is it grieving? Does it fuck her to forget, or because it has forgotten? Or to punish itself for surviving? Or the other, for not?

Or is this her?

When she does not have enough Ins for its Outs, it makes new ones. She bleeds for a time and then heals. She pretends that this is a rape. Rape at least she could understand. Rape is an interaction. It requires intention. It would imply that it hates or fears or wants. Rape would mean she is more than a wine glass it fills.

This goes both ways. She forces it. Her hands are blades that tear new Ins. Her anger pounds at it until she feels its depths grow soft under her fist, as though bones or muscle or cartilage have disassembled and turned to something else.

And when she forces her hands into the alien? If intent counts, then what she does, at least, is a rape – or would be if the alien felt anything, responded in any fashion. Mostly it's like punching a wall.

* * *

She puts her fingers in herself, because she at least knows what her intentions are.

Sometimes she watches it fuck her, the strange coiling of its Outs like a shock wave thrusting into her body, and this excites her and horrifies her; but at least it is not Gary. Gary, who left her here with this, who left her here, who left.

One time she feels something break loose inside the alien, but it is immediately drawn out of reach. When she reaches farther in to grasp the broken piece, a sphincter snaps shut on her wrist. Her arm is forced out. There is a bruise like a bracelet around her wrist for what might be a week or two.

She cannot stop touching the bruise. The alien has had the ability to stop her fist inside it, at any time. Which means it has made a choice not to stop her, even when she batters things inside it until they grow soft.

This is the only time she has ever gotten a reaction she understands. Stimulus: response. She tries many times to get another. She rams her hands into it, kicks it, tries to tear its cilia free with her teeth, claws its skin with her ragged, filthy fingernails. But there is never again the broken thing inside, and never the bracelet.

For a while, she measures time by bruises she gives herself. She slams her shin against the feeding tube, and when the bruise is gone she does it again. She estimates it takes twelve days for a bruise to heal. She stops after a time because she cannot remember how many bruises there have been.

She dreams of rescue, but doesn't know what that looks like. Gary, miraculously alive pulling her free, eyes bright with tears, I love you, he says, his lips on her eyelids and his kiss his tongue in her mouth inside her hands inside him. But that's the alien. Gary is dead. He got Out.

Sometimes she thinks that rescue looks like her opening the lifeboat to the deep vacuum, but she cannot figure out the airlock.

Her anger is endless, relentless.

Gary brought her here, and then he went away and left her with this thing that will not speak, or cannot, or does not care enough to, or does not see her as something to talk to.

On their third date, she and Gary went to an empty park: wine, cheese, fresh bread in a basket. Bright sun and cool air, grass and a cloth to lie on. He brought Shakespeare. "You'll love this," he said, and read to her.

She stopped him with a kiss. "Let's talk," she said, "about anything."

"But we are talking," he said.

"No, you're reading," she said. "I'm sorry, I don't really like poetry."

"That's because you've never had it read to you," he said.

She stopped him at last by taking the book from his hands and pushing him back, her palms in the grass; and he entered her. Later, he read to her anyway.

If it had just been that.

They were not even his words and now they mean nothing, are not even sounds in her mind. And now there is this thing that cannot hear her or does not choose to listen, until she gives up trying to reach it and only reaches into it, and bludgeons it and herself, seeking a reaction, any reaction.

"I fucking hate you," she says. "I hate fucking you."

The lifeboat decelerates. Metal clashes on metal. Gaskets seal.

The airlock opens overhead. There is light. Her eyes water helplessly and everything becomes glare and indistinct dark shapes. The air is dry and cold. She recoils.

The alien does not react to the light, the hard air. It remains inside her and around her. They are wrapped. They penetrate one another a thousand ways. She is warm here, or at any rate not cold: half lost in its flesh, wet from her Ins, its Outs. In here it is not too bright.

A dark something stands outlined in the portal. It is bipedal. It makes sounds that are words. Is it human? Is she? Does she still have bones, a voice? She has not used them for so long.

The alien is hers; she is its. Nothing changes.

But. She pulls herself free of its tendrils and climbs. Out.

Romanesque

O'Neil De Noux

Just as I finished snapping a picture of the Romanesque statue of the three nymphs just inside the rear archway of the Arena, a woman walked through the archway, into Verona's ancient Roman coliseum. Suddenly, the naked bodies of the buxom nymphs looked like pudgy boys to me.

The woman moved smoothly, catlike, her long black hair swirling behind in the northern Italian breeze. Her low-cut minidress did little to hide a beautifully sculptured body – tall and thin with oversized breasts that took my breath away.

As she walked past me, her short red dress rose and I saw she wasn't wearing panties. I almost fell off the steps where I stood, my trusty Nikon in hand.

As she walked to the concrete steps that led up to the Arena's time-worn seating section, a voice called out behind me. I turned as a man came through the archway where the woman had entered. Two cameras dangling around his neck, the man called out, much to my surprise, in English.

"Slow down," he said as he hurried to keep up.

The woman slowed, looked back over her shoulder and smiled wickedly. She looked to be about five ten. The man trailing her was about three inches shorter, a lot heavier and wore glasses. He looked around, noticed me and nodded. Looking back at the woman, he pointed up the steps to the seating area. He hurried past her and led the way up.

As the woman ascended the steps, she looked at me for the first time and flashed a warm smile. I took the smile as an invitation to follow those sleek legs and that nice round ass up the steps to where her photographer had set up.

She stopped and turned and the breeze lifted her skirt again. I saw her neatly trimmed bush and felt a tug in my crotch.

"Stand right there," her photographer said as he bent at the knees and took a picture.

The woman raised her hands and put them behind her head and I could see up her dress clearly as I snapped a quick picture. The man turned to me, and I asked, "Is it OK if I take a picture?"

He looked back at the woman and she said, "Sure. It's nice to meet another American here." Then, incredibly, she pulled the straps off her shoulders and bared those luscious breasts, her dress dropping to her waist.

I focused on her breasts, on those small nipples and pink areolae and took several pictures. I was mesmerized, staring at the perfectly matched pair. Heavy and wide, they seemed huge against her thin frame. I was breathing heavily.

She giggled and sat on the stone arena seat and pulled her feet up next to her, her knees high. She posed for both of us. I scrambled to get her ass and bush and those incredible breasts in the picture. I made sure to also capture that gorgeous face – deep red lipstick on full, pouty lips, dark brown eyes. She threw her head back and, as if on cue, the breeze took her long hair.

She brought her knees even higher and opened her feet slightly. I could see her pink slit. My crotch throbbed as I carefully focused and snapped another shot.

The man turned suddenly and introduced himself as Lee and told me the woman was Carrie, his wife. Nodding at her, he said, "Not bad, huh?"

"She's gorgeous!"

Carrie dropped her left knee, giving us a clear view of her pussy. We both took several shots. She laughed a deep, sexy laugh, then moved again, sitting cross-legged. A mischievous smile on her face, she reached down and lifted her dress to her waist to expose her pussy completely. She leaned back and turned her face to the bright sun.

"Take your time," Lee said as he noticed me hurrying my shots. "She's not going anywhere."

"Yes," she agreed, "I'm not going anywhere." Her voice dropped an octave. "I may come, but I won't go."

Lee told me they were from St Louis. I told them I was from New Orleans and Carrie said they went to Mardi Gras last year. She flashed her breasts all day on Bourbon Street.

Her husband looked around and said, "OK. Let's go for it."

Carrie stood and reached back and unzipped her dress. She climbed out of it and tossed it to her husband. Looking right into my camera lens, she posed for me – naked, except for her red high heels. I saw Lee move around to get us both in his camera. So that's what he was up to, getting pictures of a strange man taking nude pictures of his wife. OK. Who was I to complain?

I controlled my heavy breathing as best I could as Carrie moved slowly, raising her hands, then reaching down to cup her magnificent breasts, then reaching down to brush her bush, then turning and reaching around to cradle her fine ass as she bent over.

I kept refocusing and shooting, the flash of my fill-in light bathing the beautiful naked woman as she posed in the ancient Roman amphitheater. Built in the first century AD, the Arena is the largest Roman arena, after the Coliseum in Rome. At least that's what the tour guide told me before disappearing because it was siesta time.

He told me how Christians-and-lions spectacles were held in the infield below, how the wide pit was filled with crocodiles so Christians could be thrown to them. Now the Arena was the site of spectacular night-time operas and concerts.

It smelled of old brick and dust. Towering above the tilted tile roofs of old Verona, it was an architectural spectacle – witnessing another spectacle, Carrie. I wonder, as Carrie sat again, if the Romans ever held orgies here.

Carrie sat cross-legged again, leaning back, her elbows up on the seat above. I snapped another photo. And slowly, she uncrossed her legs and opened them for me and her husband. Then she raised her knees to give us a better view of her pink slit. I could see it was wet.

I love a hairy pussy and Carrie's was particularly hairy. I especially like those soft, silky hairs around the base of the pussy, just above the asshole. Carrie's looked so delicate. I had an erection that could slice steel. I moved in and took another picture, an even closer view of her breasts. I noticed small beads of perspiration on them and saw them rise with her breath.

I don't know why I was nervous. I guess I just didn't want it to end. I must say, looking back at her husband, as he photographed his wife, I felt admiration for a man who would share such a beauty.

Lee nodded to his wife and said, "OK. OK."

Carrie rolled to her side and laid down on her back on the seat, opening her legs and arms, spreadeagled. I stepped above her and shot more pictures. Carrie, really getting into it, began to move her shoulders and hips around. She rubbed her breasts, squeezed her nipples, then moved her hands down to her pussy.

None of us spotted the cop until he spoke.

Standing below us, a uniformed *carabiniere* pointed a white-gloved hand at us and said, "No. No." Then he rattled off several hurried sentences in Italian.

Carrie stood up and brushed off her ass, then moved slowly down to the cop, who was still chattering. She stepped up to him, leaned forward and kissed him on the mouth. He stopped talking. She grabbed his crotch and started pulling him back to the first seating row. I had to shoot a picture. He was slack-jawed, staring at the naked woman pulling him by the crotch.

Tall, the *carabiniere* must have been six foot three. He pulled off his hat, a Napoleon-looking hat, and wiped his brow with a white glove. He had slicked-back black hair. Carrie unfastened his belt, unzipped his pants and reached in. The cop looked around as Lee and I took pictures.

Carrie pulled out his swollen cock. Pointed skyward, it was ready. She kissed its tip as I took a photo, then licked it, then sank her mouth on it and started bobbing her head up and down.

The cop moaned and closed his eyes. His uniform pants at his feet, the *carabiniere* fanned himself with his hat and started pumping his ass to Carrie's sucking. I took more pictures and suddenly Lee said, "Stop. I gotta reload."

Carrie stopped moving. The cop looked around incredulously as Carrie's husband started reloading his cameras. I snapped another picture and hurried to reload my camera too. Carrie pulled her mouth off the cop's wet cock and started slowly stroking it with her hand.

The cop moaned again and, just as I finished reloading, reached down and pulled Carrie up. He grabbed her breasts and pressed his open mouth again hers. They French-kissed each other, their tongues probing as the man continued squeezing her breasts. Then he pushed her back slowly, on the seat, and moved between her legs. Carrie lifted her ass slightly, reached down and guided his cock to her pussy.

The cop still had a hold of her breasts as his cock slipped into her. And as we took more pictures, they fucked right here in the

Arena, groaning and moaning, gyrating their pelvises, crying out in pleasure.

"Oh, God!" Carrie cried as the cop worked his cock in her.

The cop called out in Italian, something about his mama. I photographed Carrie's breasts moving back and forth with the humping.

"Good, huh, baby?" Lee asked her as he took another picture.

"Yes," she gasped. "Come on. Fuck me. Fuck me good!" She reached around and grabbed the cop's ass.

They pumped away, grinding against one another. Carrie cried out again as the cop pounded her like a pile driver. Then the cop grunted as he came, his ass jerking in spasms. I moved in for a closer view and could see semen leaking from the sides of Carrie's pussy. Finally, they both eased up and caught their breaths.

Carrie's husband started to reload his cameras again. I looked down and saw I had only one shot left. I took it of the two lovers, still pressed together, then hurriedly reloaded.

When I finished reloading, I move back to Carrie, as the cop backed away and started pulling up his pants. Carrie lay there as I took a close-up of her wet pussy, her legs still wide open.

When I looked up at those big brown eyes, she smiled and said, "You're just going to take pictures, or what?"

Lee bumped into me and reached for my camera. I passed it to him and unzipped my jeans. Carrie was still breathing heavily, her gorgeous breasts moving up and down as she looked at me in expectation. I dropped my pants and climbed out of my jockeys. My cock was up like a flagpole and she smiled at it. She reached for it as I leaned forward.

I went directly for her breasts and squeezed them, then kissed each nipple, rolling my tongue around each areolae. They tasted sweet and wet from perspiration. I sucked her nipples, then opened my mouth as wide as I could, filling it with tit. Carrie guided my cock to her wet pussy and I slipped inside.

Her pussy was slick and hot and tight and grabbed my cock as we began to rock and fuck. I heard Lee clicking away, saw my fill-light flash as he took pictures with my camera too. Moving from breasts to breast I continued sucking as we fucked. Finally, I came up for air.

Carrie's face was flushed and her hair damp with sweat. I smelled semen and her sweet pussy juice. My God, she was knock-out stunning as she rocked back and forth to my fucking.

Carrie was one great loving, sexy fuck. She seemed to tune everything else out but me as we screwed. Craning her neck up, she kissed my lips and tongued me. We Frenched long and hard as I rode her until she cried and shuddered and I cried out and popped inside her.

When I climbed off, Lee was already out of his pants. I eased off and picked up the cameras and shot more fuck shots. The *carabiniere* was dressed and looking around as Lee fucked his wife and I took pictures.

When Lee climbed off, I moved in for more close-ups of Carrie lying with her legs open. I focused on the thick cum oozing out of her sopping pussy. She smiled weakly at me.

The cop started chattering again, stepped forward and helped Carrie up. She kissed him on the cheek. Her legs were rubbery. The big cop deftly scooped her in his arms and carried her back to the arched entrance, to a well-hidden bathroom. They went inside, while Lee headed back for Carrie's dress.

Later, Carrie peeked out and asked Lee for her dress. Stepping out in a few minutes, she looked radiant. Lee took her hand and the cop led the way out. I followed, wondering if I should ask where they were staying.

As they turned a corner ahead of me, I heard the *carabiniere* start arguing with someone. Rounding the corner, I saw two more *carabinieri*, each nearly as tall and good-looking.

Carrie pulled away from Lee, pushed her way in between the cops and kissed each of the newcomers on the mouth. The first *carabiniere* took a step back. Lee focused his camera and I followed suit. Carrie wrapped her arms around the waists of the two new cops and they all turned toward the cameras. After the picture, Carrie pulled her hands away and pointed her back to one of the *carabiniere*.

It took a few seconds for him to realize she wanted him to unzip her dress. The man's eyes lit up as he did. Carrie stepped out of her dress and tossed it again to her husband. And she posed naked with the cops.

The cops chattered a lot until Carrie started grabbing their crotches. The men responded and sandwiched Carrie between them. There I took some of the best pictures of those luscious breasts as each cop sucked a nipple, their hands feeling up Carrie, rubbing her ass and fingering her pussy.

It was there I took the best picture of the lot, a shot of Carrie's rapturous face with a *carabiniere* on each breast, both men looking up at her face as they sucked her nipples.

It took a while for the new *carabinieri* to climb out of their pants. They turned Carrie around and one slipped his cock into her pussy, doggie style, while she took the other in her mouth. Lee and I snapped away.

The three rocked back and forth in unison. The two men came together. As soon as they finished, the first cop stepped up, moved Carrie to the stone wall and fucked her standing against it. It was a long, grinding fuck that went on and on and Carrie was wonderful in the noises she made, little cries and gasps, along with the sound of her ass slapping against the wall.

When they were done, the *carabinieri* kissed Carrie gently and dressed her.

They waved and left Carrie still trying to catch her breath.

Lee and I helped Carrie walk out to a taxi parked against the curb of the Piazza Bra.

I had to ask, "Where are y'all staying?"

Carrie leaned forward and gently kissed my lips. She smiled and said, "Goodbye."

She waved as the taxi pulled away to disappear in the heavy traffic of the piazza.

Turning back to the Arena, I passed through the gate and the statue of the three nymphs. I looked at each face, which seemed caught in rapture, and wondered if they indeed had had an orgy as they posed.

If so, they couldn't have had the time we had under the warm Italian sun. Romeo and Juliet's Verona will never be the same for me. It's Carrie's Verona now, and those magnificent breasts and silky pussy.

And I've got pictures to prove it.

Fleshpot

Lisabet Sarai

Cas was right. It's a disease. She was right to cut the ties, when she found me in the garden shed with sweet Susan the babysitter, in flagrante. I offer no excuse.

It doesn't feel like a disease, though, when I'm in the throes, my senses drenched in the seashore scent of my latest conquest. It feels like I'm on the edge of a revelation, like this is the fuck I've been seeking all my life, the one that will make everything clear, new, beautiful and real. When I burrow into that mysterious place between her thighs, I'm not just looking for pleasure. I'm seeking some kind of truth, or at least that's how it seems, like this is the time that I'll break through that barrier. I catch tantalizing glimpses of brilliance, just out of reach, shining like the grail in some celibate knight's vision. That's me, on a quest for the ultimate knowledge. Except of course, I'm not celibate.

When the papers came from her lawyer, my transgressions sucked dry by legal language ("extramarital liaisons"), my kids stolen by some judge's whim, I took off. My business – electronics OEM – can always provide an excuse for a trip to Asia. My meetings in Bangkok consumed a day and a half. Since then I've been here in this sleazy coastal resort town two hours from the capital.

I've done it all, in the past two weeks, tried everything. The lithe Thai beauties who twine like snakes around the poles, in all the bars and clubs along the Walking Street. The buxom, pushy Russian girls, with their milky complexions and succulent nipples, ripe to the point of bursting, eager to empty both my cock and my wallet. The ladyboys, as slender and graceful as their sisters, even more feminine, in fact, the prick erupting from their hairless, perfumed loins as much a shock to them as to me. I've sampled the exotica on sale here, the dwarfs and the cripples, the grossly obese young woman who nearly smothered me in her lush, unutterably soft flesh. I've been whipped and returned the favor. So far I've managed to resist the fifteen-year-old boys, but just last night a youth of terrifying beauty who claimed to be nineteen drained me in the men's room of one of the go-go places. An acrid mixture of urine and camphor stung my nostrils as I pumped my come into his agile mouth. And in that transcendent instant, as always, I felt myself on the verge of understanding.

I'm taking a break from the throbbing music and naked skin of the indoor clubs. I perch on a bar stool at the edge of the pavement, watching the parade of tourists and touts ambling by.

I'm tired. The twins I fucked earlier, in a red-lit, windowless room above one of the bars, drained me with their convincing enthusiasm for my body. Nee and Nu were indistinguishable, two toffee-skinned tarts who claimed to be eighteen but might have been anywhere from fourteen to thirty. One sat on my face, the other on my cock. Nee (or was it Nu?) made short work of my hard-on; I exploded into the condom with just a few minutes of massage by her muscular pussy. Nu, though (or maybe Nee?), humored me, letting me lick her bare twat and breathe her low-tide scent for as long as I wanted – until I hardened again, earning laughter and admiration from my two playmates.

Sitting here, I can smell the exposed mud flats beyond the row of rickety buildings that shield the Walking Street from the sea. Fifty years ago, I've heard, this was a quiet fishing village. The men harvested the bounty of the gulf. Their wives raised children, prayed to the Buddha, left flowers and rice for the older gods. Then came the soldiers, with their insatiable hunger for flesh, looking for that brief instant of communion to erase their pain – the little death that helped them forget the constant threat of annihilation. Bars and brothels mushroomed, appearing like magic. The Thais are an accommodating people.

The soldiers are gone now, but the hunger remains. Men from a dozen countries stroll along the pavement like sunburned, hairy ghosts. And I've become one of them.

My beer drools with condensation. A headache tickles behind my eyes. I lift the amber glass to my forehead and get a moment's relief from the relentless heat. Tilting my head back, I swallow the last few gulps of yeasty brew. The brief chill soothes my parched throat. Before I even set the bottle on the bar, there's a girl at my elbow.

"You want more beer, sir?" Her eyelids are crusted with purple glitter. A gold amulet nestles in the hollow between her succulent breasts. Her smile is bright enough to make me dizzy.

"No, thank you."

"You buy drink for me?" Her hand creeps up my thigh, heading for my crotch. She doesn't look down. Instead she gazes into my face in a winsome appeal that's hard to resist. But she knows I'm hard, that I've been hard since the first whiff of her perfumed sweat.

Pavlov's dog, that's what I am.

"Please, sir." Her palm cups me through my jeans. "I have room, next soi . . ."

Why not? She's pretty, in a plump, robust way. In the past, I've read, Thai women were all delicate as sylphs, but these days they come in all shapes and sizes. It's true – I know from personal experience. I look at the girl teetering next to me on her four-inch heels and I know already how my fingers will sink into her pillowy breasts, how I'll mark her ripe ass with my nails as I pound into her cunt. I can picture it all, right up to the moment when I shoot my load and launch myself into the ether, vainly seeking enlightenment.

Why bother?

"Sorry, no – I've got to get back to my hotel." Her hopeful expression turns sullen. I slip five-hundred baht into the bamboo tube that holds my check – three times the cost of my beer. "*Mai pen rai,*" I tell her. "Keep the change."

Her scowl evaporates. "*Khorp khun ka!* Thank you, sir!" I watch her butt jiggle in her tiny shorts as she weaves her way to the register, then lever myself off the stool and join the wandering crowd.

I'm a bit off balance, but not really drunk. You have to shell out for a beer each place you visit, but then you can sit as long as you like, enjoying the "entertainment" – girls in bikinis, girls in lingerie, girls wearing nothing at all – writhing to the music, spreading their legs, cupping their tits, kissing one another in a pantomime of lesbian lust that's arousing despite its silliness.

The other men drift around me like specters. I see only the women. A busty pair of Swedish girls saunter by, easily six feet tall, blonde hair gleaming on their tanned shoulders. A diminutive black woman in a multi-hued African print laughs and points at a tame monkey in the middle of the road. Even the Arab women, shrouded in black, make my balls ache. *What the hell are they doing in this fleshpot?* They walk behind their spouses, staring with a mixture of shock and fascination at the many varieties of sin surrounding them. Their luminous, accusing eyes meet mine, then skitter away. I imagine stripping away their protective garments to probe the mysteries beneath, and know that I'm damned.

"Hey, mister. What you looking for?" The voice is like rusted chains being dragged along the ground. I try to focus on its source. A hand clutches my T-shirt.

"You want something special?" The wizened man at my side offers a toothless grin. "Got something special, very special. Sex like nothing else in the world."

A dull blanket of despair settles over me. It's suddenly hard to breathe. Am I that transparent?

"Leave me alone!" I try to shake him off, but he's like a tick on a dog.

"Look, look. Very special. Most beautiful girl in world." He pulls a tattered photo from the pocket of his shorts. I can't help myself. "Look."

The image is dark, the background indistinct, but in the center a woman's face shines like the moon. Her skin's so pale it's iridescent. Her tangled hair is snow white, touched with silvery highlights. It tumbles in tangled ringlets over her shoulders and onto her chest, half-hiding luscious, ripe breasts. Erect, plum-hued nipples peek through the platinum tresses.

Her body is a wet dream, but it's her perfect face that holds me breathless. Silver brows arch over bottomless black eyes. She has high cheekbones streaked with violet shadows, a delicate nose and purplish lips so full they look bruised. She does not smile. Although her features are those of young girl of twenty, maybe less, there's a terrible, ageless wisdom in her expression that makes my chest hurt and my cock swell to impossible hardness.

"You like?" I hear triumph in the aged procurer's voice. He knows I'm hooked. "Only five-thousand baht."

"Who is she?" I tear my eyes from her solemn gaze. "Your daughter? Your granddaughter? You selling your own flesh and blood for a few baht, old man?"

"No, no, she not family." He clutches the amulet hanging around his scrawny neck in a strange, superstitious gesture, then grins up at me. "Just a lost woman – work for me – she work for you, mister, believe me. Make you so hot, so hard . . ."

"If she's just a woman, I don't need her. I can get lots of women." Something contrary makes me argue, though in truth I'm dying to meet this exquisite creature.

"Not like Nangloy. Nangloy special. Only one like her . . ."

He shoves the photo in my face. I want to look away – her loveliness only sharpens my anguish – but I can't resist another glance. I imagine those pale, rounded arms twining around me. I wonder about the taste of that lush dark mouth. She snags me with her cold eyes, not pleading like the other girls, but challenging me. Do I dare take her?

How can I refuse? Perhaps this is it, at last – what I've been looking for.

"Three thousand," I say finally. I don't want him to know how eager I truly am.

"Cannot, cannot! Must feed her, take care of her . . ."

"Never mind then." I shrug and stride away.

"Wait, wait!" He scampers like a crab, trying to keep up with me. "Three thousand five hundred."

"Three thousand." He's as desperate as I am, for some reason.

"No . . . Cannot. Nangloy special, cost a lot . . ."

"Then find some other sucker who'll pay for something so 'special'." I stop walking and fold my arms across my chest. I'll let the universe decide. If the geezer will drop his price to my level, that'll be a sign. Otherwise, I'll find some other flesh to console me. "Three thousand or nothing."

"OK, OK. Three thousand. But you come now, OK, mister? Nangloy, she waiting for you."

What better time than now? I'm hard and ready. Meanwhile, a ray of unlikely hope dispels a bit of my gloom. I can tell by her face Nangloy is like no one I've met before. Maybe – just maybe – she's what I need.

"Come on," the skinny old man urges. He leads me down a narrow corridor floored with scarred planks, between two seafood restaurants. I hear sports announcers and rock music, then clattering plates and hissing oil. There are still a few diners loitering on the wooden balconies overlooking the bay. Kerosene torches smoke in the limp air. The half moon above us is blurred. Lights from the luxury hotels on the cape to the south twinkle like distant stars in the mist.

The path becomes a rickety wharf, stretching out into the sea.

"Careful, careful," the old man warns. "Some missing boards. Watch out."

"Nangloy is out here?" The tide has turned. Murky water laps at the piles ten feet below.

"Yes, yes. Just a little way."

The pier ends in a wooden shack. The old man unfastens a rusty padlock then pulls open the door. The place stinks of stale beer and rotten fish. Dread crawls up my spine.

"Never mind. I'm going back."

My guide grabs my wrist with surprising strength. "No, no! She waiting you. Don't be chicken shit *farang*."

"This place looks dangerous."

"Sure, Nangloy dangerous. Most beautiful girl in the world – of course she dangerous. Everyone want her." He lowers his voice, as though telling me a secret.

"Tonight, she yours."

He flips a switch – I'm surprised to discover the hut is electrified – and a bare bulb in the ceiling throws the rough space into sharp relief. A table and two chairs – a wooden platform with a thin, stained mattress – some shelves holding a bottle of Thai whiskey and a couple of smeared glasses. A rectangular hole in the far wall offers a view of the bay.

Such a lonely, desolate place . . . if I scream no one will hear.

The twinge of fear banishes any residual drunkenness. All my senses are on high gain. The rising tide splashes below us. The briny smell is almost overwhelming, but now, I'm starting to find it pleasant. It reminds me of the woman I am about to meet.

"Where is she, grandpa?"

"She down there." He points to a trap door in the floor. "Leave your clothes on bed. Then you go down."

I follow his instructions. I feel him staring at my cock as I remove my jeans. I am iron-hard. I wonder how I can be so clear-headed, with all that blood swelling my penis. Nangloy's pimp had opened the flap in the floor while I was undressing. I head for the aperture, eager to meet my fate.

"Wait, wait. You pay first."

"OK, whatever." I extract the wallet from my pants pocket and flip three bills in his direction. I only have a few hundred more, so I don't worry about him robbing me while I'm with his special whore. He tucks the money into his shirt.

"You go now." In the glare from above, his wrinkled, grinning face looks skeletal. "Enjoy."

I start to clamber down the metal ladder, but something stops me. A last shred of rationality, perhaps. A whiff of fear, as insubstantial as the mist veiling the moon. "Wait a minute, gramps. You come too. Introduce me to your protégée."

"No, no – you go alone. She wait for you. I come later, when you finish."

I decide not to argue. In truth, I'm too eager to see what awaits me below. I descend the rusty steps into another chamber, filled with a dim, greenish light. The sound of waves is all around me. I must be barely above water level.

The room appears empty. The wooden floor is damp and slimy under my bare feet. As my eyes adjust to the dimness, I realize there's a big iron tub in the far corner. In that tub, her eyes fixed on my naked body, sits Nangloy.

In person, she's even more astonishing than in the photo. Her pearlescent skin gleams from within. Her hair cascades like liquid light over her perfect breasts. The tub's full of water, up to her waist, so I can't see her hips, her buttocks or her pussy, but if they're anything like her upper half . . .

She regards me gravely. She doesn't smile, doesn't speak, but she holds out her arms in a graceful gesture of welcome. I take a step forward, my fingers itching to stroke that iridescent skin, run my fingers through that silken silver hair.

My pulse pounds in my temples. I want to rush to her side. At the same time, I want to stretch out this unique moment, contemplating her incredible, bizarre beauty. Who – what – is she?

Finally I'm standing by the side of the tub. She twines her delicate fingers around my raging erection. A chill seizes me. At the same time, my cock stings, as though her skin were secreting acid. The slight pain only makes me want her more. She ripples her hand down my length, milking me. My balls tighten. *Not yet, not yet!* The sensations she kindles are like nothing I've experienced, simultaneously languorous and urgent.

I reach for her, capturing both nipples between fingers and thumbs. They're tough and rubbery. When I twist them, her eyes grow wider, but she still makes no sound, just strokes, strokes, strokes my cock, trailing fire along the shaft.

I bend over, kneading her breasts, burying my face in her hair. She smells of seaweed and stone, pearls and foam. I brush her purple lips with mine. They're icy cold, yet the same strange fire burns my mouth in the aftermath of contact. She won't open to my tongue. I finally give up and try to pull her to a standing position.

"Let me see you, Nangloy – all of you. I want to taste your pussy."

She doesn't exactly resist but I can't budge her from her sitting position. Her expert touch has me on the edge of coming. I want to do the same for her, yet she barely reacts to my caresses.

I crouch beside the tub and plunge my hand into the water, seeking her cunt. I find a slick, slippery, muscular slit that grips my probing fingers. Her fist tightens around my cock when I drive into that hot, wet space. I hover on the edge of climax, struggling for control.

Finally, I think I've moved her. Her inky eyes close for an instant, as if in ecstasy, and her pussy flutters around my hand under the surface.

"I want to fuck you," I tell her, though I'm pretty sure by now she doesn't understand. "If you won't come out of the tub, I'll have to get in." I pry her fingers from around my organ. The taut skin tingles as I step over the rim into the water.

Something slithers past my calf, then clamps around my ankle.

"What the hell?" I teeter on one foot. *What kind of kinky crap is this?* My leg's caught in some kind of slippery rope that's pulling me sideways, slowly but inexorably. I lose my balance and tumble into the tub, onto my ass, sending a wave crashing over the rim onto the floor.

A second rope, or cable, or whatever, encircles my other ankle. My thighs are pulled apart. Nangloy leans forward to pinch my nipples with her fiery fingers as something round, smooth and slick spirals around my cock and then squeezes.

I groan. The cum races up my shaft. Nangloy grabs my wrists. I fight for control.

A million fingers dance over my submerged prick. The water's murky. I can't see what's happening, but God, I can feel it! The pleasure's unbearable, unbelievable. I should be horrified but my wildly sparking nerves smother any rational thought.

Another appendage tickles my anus. I clamp down against the invasion. The sensations are too exquisite to resist. The fleshy stalk prods my sphincter, circling, tickling, coaxing me open. I struggle in Nangloy's iron grip. The probe slides into my rectum and I come, thrashing against the fleshy bonds pinning me under the water.

Globs of semen float on the surface. Nangloy still holds me fast, her beautiful face pale and impassive. There's a stirring under the water, more stroking and probing. I start to get hard again.

A fat purple tentacle rises from below, hovering like a blind snake. It flutters across my nipples, then grazes my lips.

When I scream, it slips inside my mouth. I choke as it slithers halfway down my throat.

Finally, terror overwhelms my stupid lust.

I bite down and the tentacle retreats to explore my ear. "Help! Help me!" My weak, thin cries are almost drowned by the sound of waves. Another more slender, column emerges from the murk. It winds round my neck, then enters my nostrils.

"God, somebody! Help me!'" I rage against the implacable grip of Nangloy's appendages. I don't succeed in freeing myself, but I manage to eject most of the water from the tub. Now I can see my lower body, buried in a writhing nest of purple and green tentacles. They all flow from Nangloy's hips, like some obscene hula skirt. Some are as thick as my arm. Others are thin as spaghetti. And in the center, where the strands radiate out, where her cunt should have been, sits a raw, gaping mouth, making ghastly sucking noises as it contracts and expands. I remember the slick, muscular orifice I'd explored earlier, and shudder.

There's a rustle from above. The old man scrambles down the ladder like a crooked-limbed monkey. His grin drives a new spike of panic into my chest.

"Now look – you damn *farang*, you get water all over floor. Nangloy needs water. Got to fill her tub again."

He opens a port in one wall and tosses out a bucket.

"Get me out of here, damn you!" I realize that anger won't help my cause and change my tone. "Please – please – get her off me. I'll give you money. Lots of money. Ten thousand. Twenty."

Nangloy's keeper pours seawater into the tub. "No want money. Need to feed Nangloy." He returns to refill his bucket from the ocean below the floor. "My son found her in his net, long long time ago. He couldn't stay away though. Nangloy, she pretty special. Most beautiful girl in the world."

He dumps in two more buckets, ignoring my entreaties, then climbs back up the ladder. The water level rises. I can't see Nangloy's lower parts anymore. But I can feel them.

I'm mostly immobilized now. Tentacles wreathe my thighs and circle my shoulders, slowly pulling me under. Strands of Nangloy's flesh are embedded in my ears, my throat, my nostrils. That same acid burn follows wherever she touches me.

She still watches, as I finally relax and accept the inevitable. Her eyes are bottomless, ancient and wise. She doesn't need her hands to hold me anymore. Instead she palms her breasts and circles her nipples with her thumbs, as though offering them to me. Below, she captures my still hard cock and squeezes tight. A massive probe breaches my loosened anus and burrows up into my intestines.

The slick walls of her cunt-mouth engulf my cock. I can no longer distinguish pleasure from pain. As she sucks me deeper into her cavernous body, as my flesh starts to dissolve, one last climax shakes me. In that searing explosion of pure sensation, I think that, finally, I understand.

The Pick-Up Artist

Alison Tyler

Valentine's Day at a singles bar. Life doesn't get much lonelier than that. Flirty paper hearts were stuck to the mirror on the back of the bar. Shiny Cupids dangled on fishing wire overhead. Keith eyed the girls in their frippery and finery – so much scarlet, fuchsia, and pink. The bartender was pouring carnation-colored Cosmos and cardinal-hued Sea Breezes – anything with a bit of cranberry juice or grenadine. Keith asked for vodka – clear, not pink – and scanned the room.

Oh, look. There. The brunette with her hair piled high on her head.

God, she was pretty. In that soft cashmere twinset sort of way. He gazed at her, sitting there at the end of the bar, one of her black patent-leather high heels dangling loosely as she rocked her foot up and down. He wasn't the only one watching. He could feel the palpable interest of several other men in the dimly lit room. This is why he moved first, trying not to startle her when he came up at her side. She caught his eye in the mirror behind the bar. He could see from the look on her face that she wasn't the type to startle easily.

"What are you drinking?" he asked, thinking, *Thank God it's not pink*.

"Why do you want to know?"

"Curiosity."

"You know what they say about curiosity."

"Sure, but I'm not a cat."

She tilted her head, seemed to take him in fully. "No, you're not."

He picked up her drink, took a sip. Then he slid his own to her.

"Kettle One," they said together, and then they both laughed. It was a good start.

"No Valentine?" he asked.

She made a face. He hoped she wouldn't begin that rant about how Valentine's Day was created by the blowhards at Hallmark. He steeled himself, just in case, but she simply said, "Not this year."

That was good. She wasn't whiny. She wasn't kicked-to-the-curb depressed. Who'd kick *her* to the curb, anyway? She also wasn't desperate. All qualities he could appreciate. They sipped together and didn't say much, a few words here and there. But he could feel her heat, feel that she was moving her body slightly closer to his whenever she could. He put money on the bar and turned toward the door. He heard her shoes on the hardwood floor, and her hand on his arm stopped him. She couldn't see the smile on his face.

No pat line. No, "Your place or mine?" No, "Where to, big guy?" She held him in place with her hand on his arm, and then stood at his side, like they were already a couple.

Valentine's Day will do that to you.

She followed him to his apartment. There was one light on in the office, a golden glow through the papery curtains. Keith waited for her to park, and then went to the side of the car and opened the door for her. When had he last picked up a girl at a bar? That one was easy enough to answer.

He watched her step onto the pavement. His eyes did that tour of her body again – top to toe – and he smiled. He knew how to choose the right kind of girls.

She took his hand when they reached the front door, gave his hand a squeeze. For reassurance? Maybe. But reassurance for him or for her? He didn't bother asking. He slid in the key, opened the lock, and pushed the door open. He had heard that once you lived in a place for a certain period of time, you no longer could appreciate the smells. Could she? Did she notice anything?

She didn't seem to. He led her into the kitchen and poured each of them a fresh drink. Kettle One he had on hand. He was aware they weren't talking much. Not even that nervous chit-chat of getting to know each other. He was glad that the place was so clean – almost monastic. He appreciated good lines, strong angles, no knick-knacks, no clutter. She sipped. He sipped. She laughed. "So this is Valentine's Day when you're single."

"New to you?"

She touched the spot on her ring finger, and he saw the white band in the skin.

"How long?"

"Long enough," she said. He touched the spot she'd touched. He saw her shiver, and he bent and kissed the dip of her neck. She leaned her head back and sighed. That was all they needed. One kiss against the kitchen counter, and both were primed. He took her drink, set both vodkas on the counter, and lifted her in his arms.

He carried her down the hall, past the sleek modern art on the walls. No photographs. He'd always collected the work of local artists, loved living amidst their colors. In the bedroom, he hesitated. Put her on the bed right away, or let her walk to the mattress herself. He didn't generally hesitate. She grinned at him and said, "Are you thinking face up or face down?" and he placed her on the mattress. He didn't bother closing the door.

She undressed at the same time he did. Speedily. He had on black jeans and a black shirt. She was in a skirt and sweater. They were both nude in a heartbeat, and then he was on her, kissing exactly where he had in the kitchen – but the sensation was different now that they were naked.

"I didn't want to be alone," she said when he began to work down her body. "I couldn't be alone."

He didn't think she needed a response. Not more than his mouth on the insides of her thighs, his fingertips on her cunt. He licked her skin but not her pussy. With his thumbs, he spread her lips apart and ran circles around her clit. She was the opposite of alone right now, wasn't she?

"Valentine's Day never meant much to me before," she said, and he thought for an instant that he'd been wrong. She was going to launch on the commercialization and all that shit. But she didn't. "When you're part of a pair, you take it or leave it. When you're all by yourself, every red heart is like a smack in the fucking face."

He nibbled at her inner thighs, and then he rolled her over. While she arched, he reached for a condom. Second drawer on the right. He had it on before she could muster a whimper.

Getting in from behind for the first time was always delicious. He slid his cock in deep from the start. He hoped he'd guessed right about this girl. She'd looked as if she would . . .

"Oh, God . . ."

Yeah. He had. She was noisy. That was good. As he slid into her, she bucked and moaned. Her dark hair, so artfully arranged at the bar, was coming loose from the complicated style. Tendrils this way and that. He would have gripped onto a handful if he'd known her better. As it was, he held her hips and moved her to his speed.

"Oh, Jesus," the girl groaned. "That feels so fucking good."

He wanted to make her feel even better. He slid one hand around her waist so he could rest his fingertips on her clit. She shivered all over when he stroked her very lightly. She was sensitive. He liked that.

He didn't pay much attention to his own pleasure. This round was for her. He drove in as deep as he could, and then slowly pulled out. He got her teetering on the edge of pleasure until she had stopped moving completely – trusting him solely to bring her where she so desperately needed to go. As long as she kept making those noises, he was happy. He moved inside her, tickled her clit, caressed her skin, and then he began to do all those things faster. And faster. Her voice grew louder. Her moans extended. She came in a burst of rapid contractions, but his cock didn't respond. He had enough training to stay hard.

That didn't mean he couldn't put on an act. As she was sliding into sublime, he echoed her moans, "Christ," fucking her as if he'd come, play-acting that shy turn when he pulled out and removed the condom – unsoiled by his spend.

She looked pleased. She looked cat-who-ate-the-canary satisfied. Rolling over, basking. She looked . . . confused. He was dressing, handing her over her clothes. His attitude had changed dramatically. No rhyme. No reason. She fumbled, pulling her sweater on backwards, slipping the cashmere around to face front. Skirt giving her trouble, when it had behaved perfectly on the reverse. Finding her knickers and grabbing them in her fist. Shoes on. *What had changed?* her eyes seemed to ask him, but he was business now. No more pleasure.

He saw when she decided not to worry. They'd fucked. Fucked away loneliness on Valentine's Day. He didn't give her a kiss. He didn't ask for her number. He listened to her let herself out, then walked down the hall and locked the door behind her. He washed both vodka glasses – looked around the kitchen. Nothing of her remained.

Then he headed down the hall to the office.

"Honey," he said as later he entered the room that was right across from the bedroom. He breathed in deep. The room smelled of mandarins and honeysuckle. He always wondered why they never knew. A woman lived here. It was clear to him.

There she was – the girl of his dreams – tied and gagged on the futon. Her dark brown eyes were huge. He came toward her, bent on his knees, felt her pussy. So wet. So fucking wet. He didn't bother taking her into their bedroom. He pulled her off the sofa and spread her out on the soft rug, her bound wrists over her head. He undid the leather thongs that held her ankles together. He needed access and fast.

Her pussy was so sweet. He pressed his face against her and licked until she came. Once. Hard. She'd earned that, hadn't she? He wanted to hear her tell him what she'd felt like. But that wasn't the game. Not yet. She had to be gagged for this part, had to feel his naked cock in her knowing that he'd been inside another woman only moments before.

Now he could finally get his. He moved up her body and thrust inside of her. His cock, so well trained, seemed to know that bliss was imminent. He fucked her while she moaned against the gag, fucked her while tears streaked her face. He was hers. Always. Forever. Hers. He showed that to her in the way he manhandled her, in the way he touched her. In the way that he only came when he was with her.

Like now, as he pulled out and climaxed on her belly, using his palm to spread the spend into her skin.

He didn't know why she needed this. She couldn't understand it herself.

But *she* was the girl of his dreams. And *her* dreams were to hear him fuck another woman – a lay he'd pick up for only a single night – and to do so while she waited in the other room, listening. Bound so she couldn't possibly get free. Gagged so that she couldn't cry out.

This was her fantasy.

"Happy Valentine's Day, baby," he said, as he set her free.

Come Inside

Mathew Klickstein

I cannot help asking, whether we do not, in that very heat of extreme gratification when the generative fluid is ejected, feel that somewhat of our soul has gone from us?

Tertullian

As Balzac said, "There goes another novel!"

Woody Allen

Chanel's pint-sized butt pokes up into the misty, brisk black night beach air. Each champagne-colored, pearl-shaped cheek bubbles outward under a delightful patina of gritty, flaxen sand.

Chanel is at attention like a good doggy. Hands and knees. Me on my knees behind her. She jutting away from my groin pointing toward her ass.

Minutes earlier, Chanel had been lying naked on her back. This explains the butterfly-shaped coating of sand ornamenting her perfect, tanned buttocks.

So perfect, in fact, I bow downward to bite her left cheek where she's spotted with a black, strawberry-shaped birthmark. Something about this makes her ever the more adorable and I bite again, harder.

Chanel winces, but does not turn around to stop my nibbling her fleshy morsel.

She knows better than that.

The waves of the black frothing ocean ooze up the beachhead twenty feet from where we're enjoying our nocturnal assignation. Over this calming sound of the sea, I do hear Chanel's winsome, "Careful . . ."

She's still not turning around as I nosh on her drum-skinned, burnished buttock with growing fervor. "Quiet!" I demand between breathless bites.

I want only to tear through her skin with my teeth as one would the silky tenderness of a boiled chicken breast. But I'm lustfully hardened by twee Chanel's beatifically repressed whimper and – cocksure – I can wait no longer to arise, driving my swelling erection peeking out of my unzipped, sandy denim jeans into that warm-moist aperture betwixt her two champagne pearls.

The moon's celestial luminance coruscates the sand on Chanel's opalescent ass, as she deeply sucks in the cool mist that encysts us on this vacant plot of beach belonging only to us.

I shuffle my knees imposingly closer to her body, thrusting myself deeper into her crevice, clutching her flank with my right hand and slipping my left arm underneath and across her tight washboard stomach.

I lower myself against her fey body, allowing my scratchy red flannel shirt to gently scrape across her maple-colored back.

She's quiet like a good girl. Gasps once or twice as I pump myself back and forth, slow and steady, so deep inside her. The warmth of her inner body comforts and excites my nascent penis pressing onward within.

The rest of my clothed body is cold, clammy, and sweaty as it slides up and down her naked and fit soccer-player frame.

The roiling waves continue to bat against the shore with a faint susurrations. A seagull squawks in the unseen distance of night. And the sand beneath our entangled bodies churns as my penis plunges the depths of her, me tightening my arm's grip on her belly.

My hand stealthily smears up her flank to her fist-sized hard ball of a breast.

I squeeze tight – too tight, or perhaps just tight enough – and Chanel moans, craning her head backwards. My cold-sweat face is now diving into her redolent, bronze French twist of a downy soft hairdo.

"I love you," I whisper not so much to her but to the pelagic air . . . and she knows this heralds what will come next.

"Wait . . ." she tries. But it's of no use.

Strengthening my grip even now on her flat-hard stomach and crushing her tennis-ball tit with all my might, I clamp my dressed body to her denuded one and . . .

. . . groan a prolonged release, relieving myself of the impossible tension at once, pressing through her, squirting the hot spurts

of gooey garlands within her. Quick fragments of the semen fusil-
lade paint the inside of her with my effervescent essence.

Chanel seizes wildly – but only momentarily – with me still
sealed to her like a stamp to an envelope.

Tremulously, Chanel blurts out, "Oh . . . my goodness . . .'
Her puritanical reserve makes me giggle, and I slip out of her,
rolling off her back and onto the ice-chilled granola sand crunch-
ing beneath me.

I extend both arms outward like Christ or the wings of the
chimerical seagull out there squawking. The painfully refreshing
sea air I'm quickly sucking into the back of my throat is salty and
sweet.

I stare up to what almost seems to be an artificial glow of the
moon looming over us, perfectly round like Chanel's perky backside.

Respiring, I roll over to my left side and playfully spank her ass
cheek. Chanel collapses onto the sand belly-first with a hot-
winded "Whoof" characteristic of the position in which we just
made feral love.

"Did I do good?" she asks, chin in the sand and facing away
from me to the ocean beyond her nose. The waves shimmying
against the shoreline, Chanel's bronze French twist – somewhat
tousled now, of course – all but in my face.

I fall again onto my back and gaze up to the low, glaucous
moon. My penis – sticky with her body's inner workings – shrinks
back into itself for the frigidity of the wet night air.

I zip up. "Did I do *well*," I correct Chanel.

"Oh. Right," she says without a hint of derision.

There's a pregnant silence then but for the repetitive stretches
of the bustling ocean. I hear the sand shift beneath her and I roll
onto my left side once more, my fingers interlocked atop my
head.

Chanel turns to me: naked, resplendent, delectable. I could
easily fuck her again, and at twenty-three – the perfect age for a
girl, being both sophisticated and easily subdued – she could
probably keep up with me if I suggested it. Her large, almond-
shaped bluest eyes glimmer inquisitively in the creamy moonlight.

Her long dark-brown eyelashes flutter, and she dislodges a
grain of sand from her left eye (or right? I can't quite remember).
She's staring at me. Gazing, really.

"What?" I grin.

She does not answer. Only gawks.

"*What?*" I laugh this time.

"Before . . . You said . . ."

Oh, Christ. Here it comes.

". . . You said you loved me."

"I know," I say. "I'm sorry."

"Why'd you say it, then?" she asks, really wanting to know. As though it were her first time – *Oh, at last!* – that someone had deigned to confer the proclamation upon *she* of all people.

Chanel scratches her button-bunny nose tinged with a faint spray of reddish brown freckles.

"Look," I say. "You feel *really* good when I'm inside you, and . . ."

But before I can sigh and resign myself to the mess unfolding, she says something uncannily unpredictable. Particularly uncanny for a twenty-three-year-old who confuses "good" with "well."

"Is it because you . . ." she stammers, ". . . you see something in me that is . . . more than myself?"

What?!

"What?!" I exclaim.

She furrows her brow. "Is it . . . the *objet petit a* you see in me when we're . . . making love?"

I huff – somehow through my nose – and smirk. "What have you been reading lately?"

Chanel shrugs, shaking her goofy head. "Nothing. I dunno. Tumblr's 'n' stuff. The usual. Whatever, you know?"

"And, what, you're reading Lacan's posthumous blog or something?"

"Who's *that*?" she asks.

"*Exactly*," I conclude.

"Gosh," Chanel rejoins in that puritanical way of hers that both delights and exasperates me now. "I suddenly feel like I know what I'm talking about here. You love not *me* but rather instead that part of me that is *more* than me. The incomplete gap between the me you perceive as a symbol of me and the me that exists beyond your, my, or anyone else's subjective parallax view of me."

I'm shocked. And so is she, apparently. Only, she's grinning . . . and I'm *not*.

"Wow," she says.

"Here," I say as epilogue to Chanel's short dissertation. "Open."

Leaning on my left elbow into her, I snatch at her chubby-cheeked dimpled chipmunk face, squeezing until she does as commanded, and unzip my pants. I pull out my erect cock – peremptorily jerking it with punishing celerity – and pull her face toward the reddening beast so that I can jam the girth of its flesh into her fucking childlike maw.

I keep her olive-shaped head against my groin and hold it there, staring up at the green-glowing moon. There is no blow job here. No back and forth movement on her or my part. I have a load to release into this irritating smart-mouth, and she's gonna take it.

It happens . . . and I grunt, a beast myself now discharging into her throat.

Perspiring relief washes over me, as I look down to Chanel's wide-open bunny blue eyes. Ejecting gobs of goop into her warm fleshy-moist mouth.

She gags with me still inside her face, and I quickly clamp her nose shut – *No, no: you take it all, little girl.*

Chanel's eyes shut tightly and she's resisting my pressing her nose to my crotch. My fingers keep her nostrils shut; a little choking'll do her good.

She finally pulls away – I allow it – and I fall backward drenched by droplets of greasy sweat.

Chanel breathes fast, slurping up the excess semen streams sliming down her lips to the right side of her chin, and wipes her nose with the back of her caramel-colored, velutinous arm.

Both of us still on the ground, Chanel smiles and lunges at me lapping up my face with her tiny tongue. "Mmm," she says. "You taste like butterscotch."

"I do?" I say, incredulous.

She tilts her head to the side, questioningly, as though hitting upon another mysterious epiphany. "No. Actually . . . you taste like . . . like *you*. But the you that is more than you."

Oh, fuck.

"I gotta write all this down," Chanel says, bolting up, and pitter-pattering across the sand on her bare feet toward her clothes a few yards away. She quickly pulls on her frilly pink underwear, tight black jeans, and red woolen sweater.

"Come on!" she calls out to me. "I just gotta write!"

*   *   *

Me, I can't write at all lately.

I've been trying to finish like a fiend this piece I've been doing for *The Coast* – funnily enough, about Lacan and the *objet petit a*. But nothing has been coming.

Certainly not since my beachfront tryst with Chanel.

To cope with the strain of my first-ever bout of writer's block, I've instead been watching that new cable show *Some Young Broads*. The plots and dialogue are the worst kind of puerile flummery, and when I first tried to watch it, all I could think of was, *Yup: this is definitely the work of "some young broad."*

But something about the main young broad – the show creator, of course – sickeningly gets me every time. Trini Dobowitz, with her stocky tree-trunk stems characteristically enveloped in white schoolgirl leggings, and those billowy polka-dot dresses of hers affectively widening her already generous waistline.

That haggard, droopy face. Her bobbed brown hair that'd look so damn good if Trini Dobowitz weren't so damn ugly.

There I'd be, naked on my GoodWill orange-peel couch in the near-darkness of my compact studio apartment. Mercilessly jacking off to the corpulent image of Trini on the intermittently glowing television before me. The corduroy ridges of the couch slicing into my bare behind. Keeping my T-shirt on (as always) even while masturbating to the boob tube.

Jacking it to that dumb dame with a flare for thirties fashion and twenty-first century technology, with pathetically small flabby pancake tits she so loves exhibiting to the public, to the camera, to me . . . and the millions out there glued to their sets and basking in the static-electric warmth of TV's glass teat.

Me, pulling and tugging at my circumcised six inches bobbed at the tip (like Trini's bobbed hair that in this scene is festooned with an O'Keeffeian purple rose).

She's lying on her bed. Her deadened brown eyes peering up into those of the infantile series' interchangeable svelte, five-o-clock shadowed Semitic boyfriend always named "Dave" or "Jonathan." He lumbering over her bare, neotenous chest. The boys on this show always on the verge of tears; the gal always the man of the show . . .

. . . And I'm maniacally shucking my shaft in the flickering glare of the TV screen. Harder and faster, practically peeling off the cob's irritated skin.

No moisturizer for me – I crave the friction and grit my teeth.

I bite down on my bottom lip, close my eyes, hear only the sound of Dave–Jonathan and Trini on the screen making sloppy, silent white-people love.

I think the fellow is really crying now and I hear Trini cackling on screen between moaning and slapping Dave–Jonathan's behind. He cries out and she laughs more with that mannish guffaw of hers.

But my eyes are shut, and all is a consuming void less the twisting and turning of my erect penis puffing larger, thicker in my right hand. I can feel it, the thickness swelling and the snake's skin pushing upward.

I should loosen my grip and let the thing breathe, but instead tighten my grasp – along with my eyes that are clenched to the point of "seeing" before me a reddish kind of white light that comes to me always before sleep.

I gulp the excess saliva in my mouth that I've forgotten to swallow and listen as the creaky bed on the TV screen squeaks up and down with the continued banging of the broad and her boy.

I'm blowing out hot air through my clamped lips, intermittently squeezing my cock while violently stroking the bastard, and my nose forcefully expels my air like I'm a frantic bull, before . . .

. . . I open my eyes to see Dave–Jonathan leaning down to gently kiss the flappy flapjack tits of his porcine paramour, licking circles round the pointy, bright-red, sweaty nipples poking out from her brown areolae. She looking hopelessly into his whiny epicene eyes . . .

. . . And . . . *Fuck her*! I let loose the font of sticky-white spray, still ripping at the steamy skin of my erection handful.

I stand up and rush over to the TV, letting the last gasp of semen spittle pelt the screen. Right at Trini's fucking face. Right as the purple rose falls from out of her antique hair, onto the remarkably well-kept carpet of her unrealistically large New York apartment.

I stand, trembling. Spent.

My penis strained and stingy. My fingers and wrist stiff with arthritic exhaustion. There's one more squeeze of juice in me and I shoot it out at her dumbfounded face, frustrated now at the unsatisfying technique of her lover *du jour* who resembles all the others in her TV life.

I let go of my penis, already shriveling back from the seeming fluorescence of the TV. Standing, balling my hands into fists.

No!

Ejaculating to that corpulent cunt? Christ! Fuck her. Fuck *her*! Me, feverishly jerking off to her mounds of gluttonous glob – *purely out of spite, mind you!* – and she gets picture deals and book deals and TV shows and her own fucking cereal . . . All of this: the shows and the success – just like Chanel, I realize – coming from *my* essence. These broads taking *my* essence and flourishing . . .

And that *is* what's been going on! It all flashes before me at once!

There was even that one girl who became a poet. What was her name?

Let's call her . . . Amy. Soft, simple, subtle, supple. Amy. Yes, "Amy": the perfect name for this girl with messily cropped plucky pixie highlighter pink hair (did it glitter? can't recall) and bright alabaster-skinned face that never shined as though the whole of her physiognomy was nothing more than a matte photograph.

Pearly, smiley teeth and, just . . . You get it: adorable. A gentle swan of a girl working at the coffee shop across the street from me. Silvery barrettes in her pink-pixie hair and those emerald-green eyes bursting out of her alabaster face in vividly vivacious 3D.

She'd have on a too-tight, pedomorphic rainbow-striped eighties retro polo that would really flaunt those size-B boobs of hers, poking out of the horizontal Skittle lines of her shirt. Her short sleeves would reveal the treasured tattoo on her right arm of a puckish fairy-child (not unlike Amy herself) enmeshed in a baroque network of faded-grey ivy.

Oh, and those black-and-white striped referee shorts she'd wear over her ultra-firm, nearly non-existent butt, all of which was then covered from waist to knees by her green cotton coffee-shop apron that domesticated this fallen angel in a way that made it ever-the-more inviting when she would come to you from the coffee maker to the register before saying, "Any room for cream?"

That night, I'm opening the door to my apartment with Amy on the other side of me. Her back to the door now nearly ajar. Me mashing up against her face to face, mouth to mouth, tongue to tongue. Forehead to forehead.

Pushing her the rest of the way through the opening door with one hand; my face and body against hers. Closing the door with a reverse mule kick and shuffling her across the stained grey carpet toward the orange-peel Good Will corduroy couch.

Amy unwraps her bright-red home-made knit-yarn scarf in the infinitesimal space between our two bodies even now smashed against one other.

We do not stop with the mindless kissing, and Amy falls against the back of the couch, allowing me to collapse atop her.

The scarf now off and thrown to the floor.

With the same catlike dexterity – and without failing to continue consuming my mouth with hers – she unbuttons her black pleather jacket and tosses it too to the floor beyond us while I unzip my jeans and hold the side of her head with my other hand.

We're making out like we're sixth-graders in the back of the baseball field – full and vital, lustful and unfettered, sloppy and slippery, slobbering and great.

She says between panting and kisses – with her eyes closed and frenzied octopus hands all over my face and body now – "So how's the cheese book coming along?"

I stand up, my pants in a heap around my shoes, my bare shins against the couch, the arrowhead knob of my erection protruding through the dark brown plaid of my boxers, right toward Amy's head resting against the back of the couch.

Slowly, I pull her rainbow polo up and over her head. Amy's raising her pale, silky-smooth doll arms (there's the tattoo) in subservience to my touch, which I feel rings a quiver down her now . . .

. . . and – bending toward her body – I slowly, slowly suckle her ripe, pointy, salmon-colored nipple that caps her pastel-pink areola a thumb's length round in circumference.

Amy's whole body sinks back into the couch – arms still sprouting above her head, allowing me to do as I please – and I hear the crinkle-creasing of the corduroy as the only sound in the humid apartment.

I nurse on her tit so small and proud. I am satisfied that Amy feels no need for a bra.

I'm on my knees now, buttressed by hers.

Amy's black-and-white striped ref shorts lead to her opaque black leggings that scratch a bit when I gently caress one, but look too damn good on this little swain to complain.

I'm licking her nipple, lapping up crystalline sweat droplets with my oversized, puppy-dog, raspberry-skinned tongue. Play-fully, quietly squeezing the breast itself with my right hand.

My left hand continues to caress Amy's scratchy legging filled with her leg before me.

I stop for a breath to answer, "Oh. You know, cheese is cheese."

But what Amy did *not* know – while I retracted my hand from her leg in order to guide my arrow-point penis from out of the plaid boxers through the slit in front, gripping its head and stroking; she taking the cue to bring her arms down and pull down her leggings to the floor, followed by those referee shorts of hers – was that the "cheese book" would never be finished.

I had stopped working on it and in fact had to return the advance from the publisher (not an easy task in this tough economy of ours, I can tell you!).

It was my second bout of writer's block. A block of big, fat, stinky Limburger cheese.

Not knowing this (or probably not much caring, anyway), Amy slowly raised her white ceramic leg past the side of my head with the skillful grace of the ballerina she once most likely was as a fragile young thing.

I reached out to her foot just above my head and folded it down, popping a green-nailed big toe into my mouth, bobbing it as one would a tasty sucker; my right hand now playing again with her left tit whose nipple was unbelievably firm against the cautious swirls of my thumb.

Thinking to myself all the while, *if only you knew* . . .

All those faggoty years of fantasizing about being a poet! The modern-day laureate! *No* one does that anymore . . . but for a few sad, suicidal goth girls and rich, effete androgynes living in Park Slope. *I* would bring back the Bukowski, the Miller, the Kinski.

Hence, no more cheese book.

These things came to mind to the new soundtrack: the faint flesh-petting of Amy's soft meringue of shaved pussy. Masturbating with her leg still vertically held against me.

Bending her foot further toward my face and gleefully feasting on her big toe, I selfishly decide to shove the entire size-6 into my grateful gob.

Taking the moment to climb spryly into her lap – folding her leg back into her; foot still in my mouth (further proof of those years of ballet flexibility) – and mounting her. My thickening, hot-blooded meat finding purchase in her gaping creaminess of crack.

I'm pushing myself forward, against her body, against the back of the corduroy couch. Pressing myself up inside her malleable innards with a soft groan from her closed-eye fairy face framed by sweat-lined strands of lithe pixie-pink hair.

No, in lieu of confessing my longing to be a poet, I held her small head with both hands, thumbing her baby elf ear. I leaned in to nuzzle her cheek to cheek, hearing the sound of the couch keening (almost as though it were that creaky bed of Trini's; _Get it out of your mind!_).

Breathing out of my nose and rocking myself back and forth – gently but true – against and inside Amy's small body. I could feel my back straining. My spine tingled as I did burrow myself deeper inside her, pulling her impossibly close to me, jowl to jowl, and eyes closed.

Amy's chapped pink lips popped open, exposing the silver ball piercing her kitten tongue and then (no, I did not tell her) . . . _it came_. A long, prolonged stream of hot viscosity bursting forth from out of my body and into hers. The arrowhead shaft of my penis purging itself, flushing her insides with _me_; she digging her short-nailed fingers into my back and shoulders, pulling me even – yes – _closer_.

Clinging to me, inviting my sperm to enter her, wanting it, needing it.

I'm now drawing _her_ closer, all but crushing her skull between my bear claws, mashing the side of my face into hers, pumping and pumping my hot load up into her warm, creamy crevice; filling her fey, frail body whose eyes suddenly bolted open.

"Wait," Amy said, as though shocked back to life.

_Uh, oh . . ._

Amy's surprisingly iron grip on my back and shoulders loosened and she pulled away from me. I had heard it all before and knew it was coming. _Here we go . . ._

. . . But, no. Instead of _How dare you_, it was, "I suddenly have . . . thee . . . best . . . idea . . . for a poem . . . _ever!_"

Navigating around my body, Amy stood up off the couch, tugged up her leggings and shorts, and was out the door and from my life for good. Out of the coffee shop, even.

About a year later, her two-volume poetry collection (_Before the Storm_ and _After the Wake_) were bestsellers, single-handedly revitalizing the fledgling poetry industry. Meanwhile, I . . . I couldn't write _line one_ of my grand poetry opus.

Not after that evening with this bright new star.

You may have heard of her, in fact. They call her " Anaïs" Annie. Actually . . . Yes! That was her name. Annie. Not Amy. *Annie.*

The memory flashed to *finito* and I was left vacantly flipping through the TV channels in my otherwise dark studio apartment with one hand holding my emptied, limp dick. Literally marinating in my own juices of failure.

And what followed was yet another rerun of *Some Young Broads* (now on three channels, as you may know; one of the runs dubbed for Spanish-speaking audiences, which finally makes me laugh in a way that the English version never could).

So these fucking bitches keep stealing my ideas. My energy. My power. My . . . *me.*

Whether I'm pumping into her twat, face, or even TV image, it doesn't matter. Off they go to become bigger, bolder, better than I could ever imagine (and if I *could* imagine, *they* would steal that from me, too! Whores!).

You don't believe me?

I tell you, the more I jerk it to this Trini Dobowitz slut – to her fat fucking face – the more powerful and successful she becomes. It's happened all year. OK? The same fame and power that then eludes *me.*

It's *mine.* There inside me, percolating inside my loins, incubating and ready to rock and/or roll . . . then POW: a simple lapse of judgement and I flush it all out of me and into *HER.* Whomever *SHE* may be at the moment of too-tantalizing temptation.

But . . . *wait!* Why *hadn't* I realized it before? (Christ: the latest promo for *Some Young Broads* says Trini has been nominated for an Award for Brilliance in Women . . .)

And, more importantly, why hadn't I done something about it? How could I have been so foolish? So weak? So cowardly to face the all-consuming fait accompli of the thing: *Each time I come for a girl, she absorbs my ideas!*

Really, it's not even my fault. Or *their* fault. Like Chanel. Poor thing is (was?) so scatterbrained, I was always a bit surprised when she actually remembered to remove her tampon before our getting down to business. Then, suddenly, she's deconstructing the double negations of Hegel through the perspective of Lacan's *Seminar III*? Becoming some kind of grand poobah in the psychoanalytical Academic Circle that continues to shun *me*?

Clearly, this was happening all along.

I knew now what I needed to do. This would be the thing. This would be the one that would bring me to that next level of my career. The elusive "loose fish" mariners tried to best in the stories told by *Moby Dick*'s faithful crew.

Here it was. I couldn't *believe* my luck once it all came together in my mind: I possess some weird "reverse" magic power, if you will, and now I can write about it. Do a stand-up act! Sure! Who's doing stand-up these days? A bunch of hipster kids talking about their troubles with social media? Bah. I could do better!

I could wrap an entire set around this wacky story!

All I needed to do was *write* the Christing motherfucker!

My palms were sweaty with exhilarated anticipation. Oh, how fun it would be to write! Oh, the exuberant joy of seeing my story told. And how – oh, yes! – how amazing it would be to at long last land myself in the coveted Victor's Throne!

And I was off!

Off to the bar calling me with clarion siren's song. (I needed a snifter of potvaliancy here before taking on that most formidable of all foes: the white-blank page.)

Three shots of Wild Turkey 101 and two bottles of Sam Adams later and my arm's around the short shoulders/neck of the utterly ravishing, dark and brooding June sitting on the barstool next to me.

I'm laughing my sick fucking ass off, and June's trying her best to smile with a crooked, placating grin, revealing her baby Chiclet teeth all adorably misshapen. Her pillows of red-red ruby lips glint in the dun-colored gas-lamp lighting of the Degas-blurry bar scene. And her blackest Snow White hair is topped by a purple-and-white polka-dot hairband affixed just so.

Just so *for me*. Just so for this night of revelation, excitation, and celebration. I will be writing all the wrongs of my life and finally . . .

. . . But, first: two more shots. And June.

June with the shockingly penetrating onyx eyes. Eyes that are pupils only. Somehow. June with the bashful button nose that crinkles when she continues to placate me with her custom crooked grin. June with the baby powder pale skin wrapped tightly around her baby-doll frame.

June in the flickering, fluorescent light of the drip-drop, claustrophobic box of the wet-floored, tile-floored bar bathroom.

There we are together. And she's about five foot four, making her the perfect height to be spun around (bathroom door click-locked), and my two lesbo fingers – middle and ring – dig up and into her slippery, slick-wet cunt from behind.

We're both standing, but that does *not* stop me from drilling her sweet vagina with these fingers, pounding her and all but scraping her bulbous clitoris along the way.

Over and over, fingers diving deeply into her gut, palm of my hand slapping against her supple white ass enshrouded in shadow for the moments of darkness from the flickering, erratically humming low light above us.

In the scratched, broken mirror before us, we can see through the layer of rust-brown dirt to our muddy reflections.

June's eyes shut as I continue to finger-ram her remorselessly, gritting my teeth and letting go of any inhibition, allowing the alcohol to take over and make my hand a machine pelting her ass and forcing my fingers up and into her, over and over, without stopping, doing all I can to rip her whole goddamn petite body apart.

She's loving it – I think – and I can barely see in the mirrored reflection that her closed eyelids are painted with a light lavender hue.

There's that crooked smirk of hers again, both of us hearing only the on-again/off-again buzz of the low light above and the quickening, gooshy flesh-slapping of my pile-driving fingers penetrating her body endlessly.

The fingers of my left hand knowingly wrap around her left ribs to clasp her flat stomach beneath her tight black leather biker jacket whose jangling, kitschy chains assure me she's no motorcycle rider.

Holding her in place grants me purchase to really go to work here, forcing her to climax. My brow folds with sweaty, deliberate dedication. I want her to come and she will do it, and she will do it from my fingers alone.

Up and in, again and again, these two of my hand's strongest fingers, ruthlessly excavating her slimy-lipped slit; her warm and welcoming body taking each thrust, almost inhaling the entirety of my hand.

June is soundless, licks her lips slowly, and I can then hear her deep breathing; each exhale long and quivering. Each inhale quick and strong as though her last.

"Harder," she whispers as I quicken. "*Harder!*"

And I oblige, even faster still, pummeling her wet dripping vagina oozing with excitement and sweat.

With each rapid thrust pumping her insides, I feel the cold firm skin of her buttock against the palm of my perspiring hand. I notice a small brownish-black bruise just underneath the back of her knee and something about it turns me on in a way few other things could.

I'm really railing her now, banging her with my one hand, clutching her stomach with the other and literally pulling her into each advance of my fingers inside of her, all but breaking her spine in the process.

No sound from her at all, as I open my eyes to look into our shared reflection in the grimy mirror and see her eyes – pupils, as I've reported already – and her lips mouthing the word, "Please . . ."

She whispers it now: "Please."

And I stop, losing my balance a bit, and with both hands (my right fingers sticky and warm from her insides) I unfasten my belt, unzip my black slacks, and drop them to the floor.

I spin June around to face me.

Her body trembles as I drag my sticky-wet hand up and down her tight-crack vagina sprayed with a black peppering of prickly hair, and injudiciously ram myself home (a trick, to be sure, in my besotted state; but, still . . .).

And her eyes bolt wider than I'd ever dreamed and her breath expels a galaxy of cool spritz motes in my face.

I lean into her face, bite her lip, let her go, and birl her around again, shoving her up against the mirror with a crash and a grunt from June.

I spread her ass cheeks apart, draw back spittle in my throat, and shoot it out at her puckered spiral of an asshole practically winking at me.

"Wait," she says. But I'm not listening. Clutching her pert size-Cs (impossible for her tiny frame, but not my prerogative) from behind, I bash myself up and into her, driving home and boring her tender, fleshy asshole.

The slimy flop of entrails' mucous skin encase my cock as I pump her faster and harder, jabbing her with all the power in my back and body, hanging on to her firm breasts underneath her leather jacket (jangling chains).

Her onyx marble pupils always open in the reflection of the mirror against which her head is banging with each crash of myself into her cold, fleshy cheeks.

It is in that reflection that I see her agog at me as though in disbelief, still making not a noise – petrified perhaps – and my right hand slithers down her belly button to her black-peppered, bristly twat whose lips I strum, impossibly speeding up my cadence of savage ass-fucking.

Our inhales/exhales are in perfect syncopated sync, both of us clammy and sweating through the same jouissance and pain. June being torn from within, me tensing my back muscles and feeling the hot sting of my penis teeming with volatile sperm ready to engage.

Then I hear it once again: "Please, please, please."

I let her know: "I'm gonna . . ."

"All of it," she says. "Please. All of it. I want it. Oh, God! Please . . ."

And I feel it. Starting in my belly, hot and bothered like the whiskey's gonna come back up – but it's not – and I clench her left leathered tit with one hand, playing with the top of her lady-finger pussy with the other; she screeching in pain as I squirt and let loose, draining my juice up and into her guck-ey mash of fenny flesh and breathing out quickly as I finish releasing deep within her asshole.

And I pull out, wipe the excess cum on her left buttock (just above the enticing bruise), place my hand on the mirror beside her face, and lean against it to catch my breath.

I expel a loud sigh and almost laugh.

June turns around, exhausted and pouring sweat. She stares into my eyes as she pulls up the black skirt that had been on the ground round her white, filthy tennis shoes.

She pivots round to her reflection. Fixes her hair, makes sure her polka-dotted hairband is just so once more.

I grip my cramped side in pain and breathe hard, a little wobbly from the booze still violating my system.

"Well," June says. "Thanks."

I nod my head. Then she breaks out into the loudest belt of laughter.

"What?" I ask.

"Oh, nothing," she says.

"No, what? Tell me."

She tilts her head now, and it's the first time I sense a semblance of sentience in her otherwise expressionless, robotic face. She's no longer placating me with a crooked grin. This is her. This is she. This is June. And she just figured it out.

"I just thought of something . . . sooooo funny."

I'm suddenly sobered. *Oh, no.*

Wait, what was I gonna do after this . . . ? What was the idea again?

"Wait!" I call out to her; but June's already unlocked the door and is out of the bathroom. I see the back of her fake biker jacket – "Sorry! I really gotta go!" – as she's out of my presence forevermore.

I'm alone. Spent. With an absentee mind.

Blank.

And I know I'm too drunk to remember June.

Until a few months later, that is.

There she is. On the TV. On *cable*. It's a clip from an upcoming episode of *Some Young Broads*. They're talking about the season premiere.

And it's June. Doing stand-up at a club on the show. *I remember her!*

I found her first! I . . . . . . came in her ass! I came in her. And now she's doing stand-up. On *Some Young Broads*. There she is: "Hey, girls. Does your guy ever do something that just . . . *totally* gets on your nerves? He's demanding anal, and meanwhile you're all like, 'Uh, no thanks!'" Laughter in the crowd (fake? real?).

June finishes, "Just remember next time, when you're feeling guilty about it: *It's not 'complaining'; it's 'explaining what bothers you!'*" The audience (fake? real? Almost all females, that's for sure) goes crazy for it.

And now Trini Fuckin' Dobowitz is discussing the clip and how she found June at a nightclub a few months back doing this bit about "complaining" and how it *tohhhhhhtally* gelled with her "aesthetic" and . . . etc., etc., etc.

Trini then explains that she and June are *sooooo* gelled in their "aesthetic," in fact, that she will be executive producing June's own series on NBC next year . . .

And I'm in my shitty little studio apartment. Wondering how I'm gonna pay next month's rent. No food in the fridge. No ideas in my head. In the dark. Alone. And with nothing.

I can only look at the camera deadpan and say the line.

"FUCK."

And I swear I can hear canned laughter and applause as the credits roll . . .

Risk Reduction

Madeline Moore

Nikki wanted sex. All night long she'd dreamt of sex with strangers and she'd awakened with the female equivalent of a hard-on. Unfortunately, since she'd slept through the alarm, there'd been no time to slip her hand between her thighs and stroke her buzzing clit to climax.

Work had been busy, at least. And the "sublimate your sexual energy" approach she'd been taught by Dr McConnelly had worked. She'd rocked her job. But busy meant lunch at her desk and coffee on the run. No time to duck into a cubicle in the lady's room and soothe her snatch with some three-finger thrusts and a thumb diddle, never mind indulge in a little daydreaming about lunching *under* the gorgeous new CEO's desk, he of the six-pack abs and guns that bulged when he shot his cuffs.

Dr McConnelly allowed her fantasy as a form of risk reduction. He and Nikki were almost but not entirely sure that, disinhibited though she may be, she'd learnt her lesson at her previous job. It still made her blush and cringe and, admittedly, laugh to think about it.

Nikki hadn't been on the sales team for the San Francisco-based firm very long when the Holiday Season hit. What a party the company she'd worked for had provided! Being very young (this had been a few years ago) she'd drunk way too much champagne and decided to blow the boss.

He was cute and married so she'd likely have gotten away with the fast and dirty cock-sucking she'd performed in the men's room. But they'd been caught by a co-worker so nothing would do but that she blow him, too. And another, and another, and soon guys were telling other guys, "Betty's giving holiday blow jobs in the men's room!" It'd been glorious, really: down on her knees, not caring about the ladders in her stockings or the stains on her crimson satin party dress; the smell of sex and sweat and cologne surrounding her; all those hard cocks coming at her; cream running down her chin; the groans of the one coming in her mouth mingled with the cheers and moans of those already spent or waiting their turn. Mm.

But she'd been terminated before the hangover had worn off. Never again, Nikki.

Never again would she drink so much or sink to her knees for even one workmate, let alone a dozen or more. She'd moved from the west coast to the east and started using her middle name as her first. And she'd gone into therapy with the marvellous, patient, brilliant and adorably Irish Dr McConnelly.

Nikki left work early, as she had one Friday a month for the three years she'd been with her present firm, to meet with him. They were winding down their sessions. He was taking early retirement and she'd learnt plenty about boundaries, which was what he'd decided she needed after she told him her version of a Christmas story.

Boundaries. First, she'd learnt what they were. Then she'd established some of her own. Then she'd learnt to respect the boundaries of others. Nikki'd come a long way in therapy, but she wasn't looking forward to the day when she was released by Dr McConnelly and unleashed, solo, upon the world.

Nikki rose from the Metro at the proper station and tip tapped along the sidewalk in her high heels. She wore heels the way other women wore crocs. Her straight cut black hair just brushed the collar of her stylish charcoal jacket. The matching short skirt showed off mile-long legs that were sheathed in dark stockings and then those killer black leather heels. If she attracted a few glances from the men and returned them with appreciative glances of her own, that was OK, right?

Maybe she'd talk to Dr McConnelly about it.

What she really wanted to do was kiss Dr McConnelly.

They'd worked through her "transference" period where she'd been desperately in love with him and terrified he'd find out. It'd been embarrassing, stupid even, but it was long over. He'd promised that someday she'd come to regard him with indifference but that day hadn't arrived and now that he was taking early retirement it likely wouldn't. Nikki no longer fantasized endlessly about fucking Dr McConnelly, but she still had to battle a desire to flash him while crossing her legs, or brush her breasts against him when he took her coat, or just touch his hand as he wrote out their next appointment in his looping script.

"How are you?" Dr McConnelly's pale blue eyes were focused on her, his position in the leather wingback chair relaxed but alert. God, he was good at his job.

"The truth is I've been sexually needy all day."

He blushed, as he always did when they discussed sex. She'd seen him blush many times over the years. They both ignored it now. "Have you contacted your 'friends'?"

"I''ve been texting all day. No luck. But it's Friday. Even for friends with benefits it's a little late."

"Masturbation?"

"There wasn't time this morning. I suppose that'll have to do tonight, but as you know after a certain point it just makes me blue. And I've reached that point."

"Hmmm. Shall we go over the list of things you *aren't* going to do?"

Nikki ticked off the items on her fingers as she recited them out loud. "I'm not going to approach any of my girlfriends' husbands, even though Janet's away for the weekend and her husband Graham clearly lusts after me."

"Good."

"I'm not going to pick up a strange man in a bar."

"Good."

"And I'm not going to order a male prostitute. Although I still don't see what's so terribly wrong with it."

"Shall we go over it again?"

"Nah. I'll take your word for it. Anyway, I promised to meet Paula for dinner."

"She's the depressed friend who complains constantly?"

"Yes. Maybe I should fuck her?"

"But you've always said—"

"That I'm not into women. But I'm thinking if I'm horny enough it won't matter. They say a lot of the guys who give lap dances in gay clubs are straight. Just super-sexed. At a certain point they'll do it with another guy, just to get off. Maybe it'd be like that for me. What do you think?'"

"We're all on the spectrum somewhere, with heterosexuality at one end and homosexuality at the other," he shrugged. "I'm not suggesting it but I'm not vetoing it, either."

"I don't think I could do Paula." Nikki shuddered. "She's too . . . lumpy. But there's that new club in town, what's it called? Velvet? Velvet and Iron? Maybe I should check that out?"

"It's Velvet Plus Iron. I believe it's members only. For couples who swing."

Nikki flashed him a sexy smile. "In my experience, a super-sexy single woman is always welcome."

"Tell me about this dinner with Paula. Will it be interminable?"

The rest of the session unfolded smoothly. Nikki compart-mentalized her desire for the good doctor by promising herself that, at the conclusion of their final fifty minutes together, which would be soon, she'd kiss his thin, ascetic lips if he didn't kiss her lush, pretty painted lips first. It probably wouldn't happen but it soothed her to think that it might.

"I'll see you next month," he said as he wrote down their next appointment date and time.

"Great," she said.

"Keep trying, every day, to spend a wee bit of time in reflection."

Nikki shivered. She adored his Irish accent, never more so than when he said "wee".

"Chilly?"

"No. I just like the way you say "wee". She batted her lashes. Maybe they'd kiss right now and consider it the end of her therapy?

Dr McConnelly blushed again. It gave her a rush even as it silently admonished her. He handed her the appointment card and their fingertips touched. She shivered again.

He turned away.

Nikki steered herself out the door and onto the street. God fucking damn she wanted him. Instead, she faced dinner with Prozac Paula and her lengthy list of woes. Fuck.

For the first half of the meal Nikki practically squirmed in her seat, she was so overdue for a good orgasm. She kept her cell-phone on the table, where it passed the evening as it had passed the day – silent. Paula droned on about her mother and her job and her dieting woes. Nikki felt like screaming.

Midway, Nikki abruptly switched gears. It was either that or go mad. Instantly, it was on the tip of her tongue to say, "Look, Paula, let's just go to your place and make out." She'd never been with a woman, not even a gorgeous one, so it was a good measure of her desperation that she'd even consider popping her girl/girl cherry with Paula. Nikki easily practised restraint until she could escape.

Good fuck. Good fuck. Good fuck. Nikki's heels tapped out a rhythm to the single phrase that thudded in her head and pulsed in her pussy. She was walking home, too impatient to descend to the subway or try to snag a cab. It was true that she had a rampant libido and that she was disinhibited. But it was also true that she needed a good fuck.

It was easy to understand why she wasn't to fuck any more of her friends' husbands. Harder to understand, really, why she mustn't pick up a stranger. After all, he wouldn't be a stranger for long, would he? Almost impossible to get what was wrong with ordering up a male prostitute. But Dr McConnelly said no. Dr Mc Connelly said—

The penny dropped. In fact it dropped with such force that, had it been a real penny it would've been as flat as if it'd been run over by a train. Dr McConnelly said the club was called Velvet Plus Iron. Dr McConnelly said the club was for *members only*. Now how on earth did her dear old Doctor know that?

Nikki slid onto a stool at the polished mahogany bar of Velvet Plus Iron. She let her skirt ride up until the tops of her black stay-ups were exposed. She'd undone the top three buttons of her crisp white dress shirt and hung up her jacket. Now she hooked one heel over the foot rail on the bar and smiled at the barkeep. "A glass of chardonnay," she said.

When it arrived she was surprised at the way her hand shook when she picked it up. She was excited, she knew that much. Her pulse was pounding in her ears and her cheeks were hot to the touch. But so excited her hands shook? Perhaps she'd obeyed the dictates of her boundaries for entirely too long. After all, a girl's got to have some fun.

She glanced around from beneath half-closed lids. The club was dark, the tables lit with little lamps and the dance floor illuminated only by spot lights. It was crowded with couples, most of them making out madly. Fuck. It'd been easy to get in but what if she really wasn't welcome here without a mate to swap? What if *he* wasn't here? She'd been so sure he would be she hadn't actually considered . . .

"Hi." A tiny, voluptuous redhead leant on the bar, too close for politeness, which suited Nikki just fine.

"Hi. Um – I don't have a mate so I'm just wondering if it's OK for me to be here."

"It's certainly OK with me. My name's Amy." The woman held out her hand.

"I'm um . . ." Nikki took her hand with her own. The other woman's palm was small and fleshy in hers.

"You don't have to use your name if you don't want to," Amy grinned. "That's my husband over there." She jerked her head towards a dark corner. The man could be – he leant into the light to wave. It *was* him.

A wave of relief washed over Nikki, leaving in its wake a desperate desire in her loins, so deep it was almost hard.

Dr McConnelly smiled and mouthed. "Hi."

"He's quite a bit older than you," said Nikki.

"Is that a problem?"

"Not at all."

"Let's dance."

Nikki allowed Amy to lead her to the dance floor. The smaller woman took the lead, steering Nikki around with practised ease. Nikki was a bit wooden at first but she relaxed quickly. It was fun.

When Dr McConnelly joined them he kissed his wife on the mouth, then took over her position, dipped Nikki, and kissed her, too.

Nikki was so excited she moaned when their mouths met. Their electricity, connected at last, zapped swiftly through their bodies, leaving her breathless.

"Shall I go up to the room?" Amy asked her husband.

He nodded. "We'll join you shortly."

"Yes, Sir," said Amy.

Sir? Doc-tor! Nikki melted into his arms. He pressed her close to his chest and bent his head to nibble her ear lobes and neck at his whim, all the while leading her in a series of dances that included the rumba, the cha-cha and a waltz that was a whirl around and around the dance floor that left her panting. Fun!

"Enough foreplay," he said. "Come on."

He led her from the dance floor to an elevator at the far end of the bar.

"What do I call you?" Nikki snagged her jacket from the rack as they rushed past.

"Jack." He pressed the button and the elevator doors opened. "Or Sir. Depends."

"Has my therapy officially ended?" Nikki followed him into the car.

"Oh yes." As the doors closed he was already gathering her into his arms for another long, breathtaking kiss.

She'd been walking in high heels ever since she'd hit her teens, but as soon as they were inside the hotel room she kicked hers off.

"It's either that or you stop kissing me," she said apologetically to Jack. "I'm weak in the knees."

In response he picked her up and carried her to the king-sized bed, where Amy already reclined, stripped down to her pink bustier and hose. Nikki squealed in genuine surprise, once when Jack had effortlessly swooped her off her feet and again when she tumbled onto the bed beside Amy.

"I've never kissed a woman before," Nikki managed to blurt out before it was no longer true. Amy's mouth was soft on hers and Nikki willingly parted her lips when a curious little tongue tip invited her to. This kiss was familiar in a way, lips on lips, tongue teases and touches, and yet completely opposite to the kisses she'd just enjoyed with Dr— with Jack. Whereas he had possessed her with his mouth, sending shock waves throughout her body, Amy's kiss was a light, delightful sensation, more sensual than sexy, warming Nikki as a comforter might, rather than scorching her from the inside out.

Masculine hands relieved Nikki of her blouse, skirt, bra and panties while feminine caresses kept her distracted. Amy's lips had travelled down her neck and were following her fingers to Nikki's breasts when she felt a strong, lean, decidedly male body press against her from behind.

"Relax," whispered Jack. "Lean into me." He slid his arm under hers and cupped her breast, presenting it to Amy's eager mouth. He hooked his other hand under one of her knees and gently parted her legs, then slid his fingers up her inner thigh until they were pressed against her mound.

Amy nipped and sucked her nipple until it was as hard and pink as the eraser on a pencil. Nikki arched back against Jack, trapping his erection in the cleft of her bum, the tip bumping wetly against the base of her spine.

Jack tortured her with his fingers by gently stroking her pelt without dipping more than the pad of one finger into the slit, making her labia stay furled when Nikki was desperate for them to be splayed.

"Please . . ." she whispered, "help me."

Jack crooned in her ear. "You're doing just fine. Be patient."

"I can't stand it."

"You can." He spoke more firmly, in a stern manner she'd never heard before. "You will."

"Yes . . . Sir," she whispered. The subservience of it sent a thrill through her, instantly replaced by a fierce desire to find out what disobedience would incite.

"Amy, gorgeous Amy, please suck my clit just exactly as you've sucked my nipple, I need to . . ."

Amy's surprised look blurred as Nikki was swiftly tilted to expose her ass to the air. Before she could draw a breath the hand that had caressed her pussy with infinite care came down hard on one cheek and then the other, the sound as surprising and sharp as the pain.

"Wait! I'm not ready!" Nikki struggled against his other arm, now firmly pressed against her chest so that her upper back was pinned to his chest while her bottom was left free to wiggle and blush with each blow.

"You're way past ready, girl," he muttered. He raised his hand higher, which resulted in a harder, louder smack.

Nikki didn't struggle long; it was pointless and the blows that missed their mark due to her movement hurt more than the ones that landed on the plumpest part of her ass. Besides, she found she couldn't catch her breath and when she finally did she started to moan, because by then her ass was on fire and the heat had somehow ignited a flame in her clit.

"Are you going to behave?" Jack still spanked her, as strong and steady as ever.

"Yes. Yes!"

"Do what you're told?"

"I promise!"

Still the spanking continued. Nikki soared completely past pain to pleasure . . . then back to pain. The salty taste of tears wet her lips.

Amy leant in to lick them from her cheeks. "Sir," she whispered.

"I promise to be good, Sir!" Nikki shrieked.

"All right then," he said. The beating stopped as abruptly as it had begun. Jack released Nikki and she collapsed back against him once more.

"Amy, why don't you lick this little slave's pussy?" Once again, Jack parted Nikki's knees with his hand. This time, instead of a maddening little stroke, Nikki felt the tip of Amy's tongue circle the circumference once, twice, three times before it started lapping at her clit.

"Oh God, oh thank you, Sir," mumbled Nikki. She ground her fiery ass against his rigid length, not caring, in fact enjoying, the pain it caused. She was desperate. Not for cock, but for *his* cock.

Jack hitched up behind her and a moment later the rubbery head nudged her slick pussy lips apart. He jerked up hard, sinking the first few inches of his manhood into her aching hole.

Instantly, she began to moan.

The second thrust introduced another few inches. With each subsequent stroke Jack's cock travelled further up her tunnel, stretching it to fit. And Amy's tongue still circled her clit, her lips now wrapped around it like a second sheath.

It was good, so good to have her cunt perfectly attended to at last. Of course it would take two people, one sucking her clit and one fucking her hole, to do it right. Of course one should be a girl, same as her, non-threatening, helpful even, and the other should be a man, a stern, hard man with a firm hand to make a girl behave. Of course.

Nikki's pussy was as hot, now, as her punished bum. Her need for release reached boiling point. The orgasm rushed like steam through her body, scorching her nerves and making her shriek. It would kill her before it made good its escape!

"Stop!" She didn't mean it as an order; it was a plea. But it was ignored by her two new lovers. The woman in front kept lapping at her clit while the man behind thrust faster and deeper, fucking her through the scary, scalding part of the orgasm and into the part where it gentled to a rolling boil.

Finally, when Nikki was little more than a limp, occasionally shuddering shape on the bed, they relented and withdrew.

She watched as Jack's cock disappeared between the cheeks of his curvy wife's undulating ass. It didn't shock her that he smacked Amy's bum a dozen times, plundering it all the while, before he reached around to make her climax. She was a little surprised at how loud he was when he came, not at all surprised at the extent of Amy's ecstasy.

"Now for a wee nap," Jack said. "When we wake up, you'll

return Amy's gift of oral sex and give me one of your infamous blow jobs."

"Yes, Sir," said Nikki.

"If everything works out," he said, "Amy and I just might keep you."

"Oh?" Now this was a big surprise.

"Uh huh," said Amy. "We're done with swapping, Nikki. We'd like a third to share with each other and some of our good friends." She gave Nikki a big wet kiss and cuddled up against her. Jack spooned her from behind.

It should have felt strange, but, as Nikki drifted into a dreamless sleep, she felt right at home.

Flesh and Stone

Sacchi Green

A scarlet-crested helmet shadowed the face above me. To have seen even that much could provoke beating, if the prospective buyer took offense; I cast my eyes downward and willed my body to the stillness of any inanimate work of art.

"What price for this one?" The voice was low, husky – and female. Something close to hope rippled across my skin. Even in my former master's secluded villa, and more so while shackled in the slave market, I had heard of the woman champion. The very air of the capital vibrated with more tales of her than could possibly be true.

The trader, shaken, stumbled over his recitation of my virtues. "A . . . a rare golden pearl, Lady, from the house of the late epicure Mendelas, well known in the south. Young, beautiful, trained in all the arts of pleasure, skilled enough to satisfy any . . . ah . . . any desires, adaptable to any taste."

I dared raise my eyes for an instant and met amusement in hers. His desperate attempt to avoid saying "any man's desires" had not been lost on her.

"Girl."

I raised my eyes again, looking into hers deeply enough to draw out some hint of her mood.

"Can you cook?"

"Yes, Lady, but only simply."

"Can you mend cloth and leather?"

"I was taught as a child, Lady, before . . ." The slaver's grip tightened. I hoped he would not forget that bruises lowered my value. "Yes, Lady. I was raised in the horse tribes."

"Then you know something of handling horses, as well."

The trader sidled in front of me. "If it is a maidservant your eminence wishes, I have others less costly."

"Than this 'rare pearl'?" Impatience edged her voice. "What price for her?"

Rattled, he named a sum scarcely larger than he hoped to get, and she disdained to haggle. I let myself breathe again. I knew already that I would follow this mistress anywhere, do any task, be anything she desired. I did not read in her eyes the sort of interest he assumed, but in time . . . who could tell? The trader had not exaggerated my skills.

"Have you belongings?" Not that a slave could possess anything, but a craftsman's tools might be assumed to be included in the bargain. My "tools" were bits of exotic clothing and jewelry and jars of unguents in a small woven bag, and tucked beneath them a few more arcane objects rolled in a length of embroidered silk.

I hid my joy and followed my new mistress meekly. The woman champion! A princess, some said, from a mountain kingdom to the north. A sorceress, others muttered, who could turn men to stone. I neither believed nor cared. All that mattered was that she was strong and skilled and brave, nothing like those coarse women brought into the Emperor's games as titillation for a jaded court.

She swung me up easily onto her horse and mounted behind me. I clutched my bag and concentrated on balancing, since my narrow skirt kept me from riding astride. I longed to lean against her bound breasts, to tune myself by touch to the resonance of her thoughts and desires, but tried instead to show that I had not lied about my ability to sit a horse.

"Have you a name, girl?" The cool voice made me tremble.

"My master called me Gazelle."

"What did your mother call you?"

"Shebbah, Mistress." Mistress. The word was full and sweet in my mouth.

"Well, Shebbah, I will be in disgrace when we get home. You are not quite what I had in mind, but no doubt something can be arranged."

I did lean against her then, searching through her body toward her emotions. Did she not intend to keep me? Why then had she purchased me? But her mind was bound as tightly as her breasts.

She swung me down before a modest house. An ageing man-at-arms limped out to take the horse; he frowned, but the lady forestalled him. "I know, Rafen, I know. Hecanthe will give me a tongue-flogging. The sooner you get the horse stabled the less of it you'll miss."

The room seemed dim after bright daylight. A lamp beside a low couch lit the sharp features of the woman lying there. Some other presence loomed in the shadows to my left, and I would have turned that way if her snapping black eyes had not gripped me.

"What's this?" But she knew already exactly what I was. "You go for a strong wench to cook and clean, and come back with this . . . this little yellow-haired 'bird of paradise?'"

Despite her servant's garb it was clear enough who ruled this household. I knelt and looked full into her keen old eyes, hiding nothing of myself. "I am stronger than I look, Grandmother, and my skills are not only those of the harem."

"Indeed." She too could reach out with her mind, and recognized what she found. "You might do, after all." Then, more loudly and a bit harshly, "Did you think to distract the Emperor, Domande, with this little sweetmeat?"

"If only it were that easy." My lady's voice was weary. "The Emperor desires my humiliation, not my flesh. Even *his* taste is more refined than that!" The note of buried pain spoke more than she herself knew. "Offering a more appealing bedmate would be pointless. He has ordered me to attend him tomorrow night; I will slay him if I go to him; therefore I must leave."

She had shed the cloak and the helmet with its champion's crest. In tunic and clinging hose she had the strength and grace of a lioness; when she stretched and ran her fingers through her short hair, I could not believe that anyone, of any sex, would fail to take pleasure in the touch of that smooth, taut body.

Bronze curls clung damply above amber-green eyes. Her finely sculpted face could have topped the statue of a young god; or as easily, softened by flowing hair, a seductive goddess.

"What then?" Hecanthe asked sharply. "A gift to placate that one, since you imagine you have wronged him?" Her eyes flicked toward the shadows. "If ever he returns to matters of the flesh!"

A presence seemed to advance from the darkness, but there had been, could be, no movement. The man was made all of grey stone.

It was no statue, no creation of any carver, but a naked, crouching figure of muscle and bone frozen in the moment of rising from a fall.

I looked wildly from Lady Domande to the old woman. Whose power had wrought such a curse? Hecanthe smiled grimly, but her mistress forgot us both as she contemplated the stone face.

"This is the young man's own doing," the old woman assured me. "It was triggered by yet another attempt on the Emperor's part to humiliate her. She blames herself, but that is mere foolishness."

"I could have let him win," my lady muttered without shifting her gaze. "For Nyal the stake was freedom. For me the prize was only his servitude, which he might have known I would refuse. We had often talked, in the training fields, of our far-off homes; I knew how hotly he burned for his liberty."

"You never in your life 'let' someone win," the old woman said caustically.

"He should have won! He is stronger, with skill close enough to my own; there was a moment when he had me, and loosed his grip for fear, I think, of hurting me, and I took advantage of the lapse. It was ill done."

"It was ill done to let the Emperor goad you into wrestling naked in the first place!"

Lady Domande shrugged dismissively. "If I claim right to compete with men on equal terms I have no right to refuse such a match, which was known in ancient times. And besides, I expected Nyal to win, to gain the freedom the Emperor dangled before him. I was prepared to be beaten – but when it came to the point I couldn't just *let* it happen!"

"Oh, gods forbid!" The old woman's voice was brittle with irony. "Girl! You, girl!"

I struggled to attend her, my mind still pulsing with images of those two magnificent bodies coupled in naked combat.

"Is it too much to hope that you might teach our lady something of a woman's proper weapons? And of what may be won with them?"

"One may always hope," I answered meekly, but Lady Domande swung around toward us.

"Shebbah will have little chance for such lessons, since I leave before daybreak, and she stays to care for you, Hecanthe."

"No, my lady, she goes with you."

"Impossible! Who . . ."

"Leave Rafen to care for me until my hip is mended. Surely you would not part us after all these years!" There was a gleam of mockery in her eyes as the old man limped in from the stable yard. "Your delicate flower will, I think, do well enough for you. Girl!" And her hand flashed upward with a glint of steel.

I caught the spinning dagger in the air. So long ago . . . But the reflexes were still there. My fingers' dexterity and strength had only increased in six years of plucking harp strings and drawing melodies of sensuality from human flesh.

"What can you do with that toy, girl?"

"I can gut fish, fowl, or man. I can chop meat, bring down a hare, or carve secrets slowly out of an enemy." I fell to my knees before my lady. "I can serve and protect to the last flicker of my life, if you will only accept my loyalty. Please, Mistress, take me with you!"

"Well." She was disconcerted at such a display of obeisance. "More to the point, perhaps, is whether you and I together can lift that stubborn lump of stone. I will not leave him here for the Emperor's mages to probe, however much he may deserve it."

She stood surveying the rigid figure. "I would not have kept him slave!" Her voice was low and rough with pain. "What did he think I would require, that being stone seemed less terrible?"

With a mixture of longing and reluctance she put her hands on his broad shoulders and gestured with her head toward his loins. "You grasp him there below. A pretty little thing like you may lure him out of his sulking!" It was a joke, but a bitter one.

As I touched the cool, hard curve of his buttocks I felt something more than stone. He was aware. Aware, at least, of my mistress; an unmistakable current flowed between them.

He was not truly as heavy as stone; we lifted him without much difficulty. Indeed, I think she could have done it alone, though he was broader and slightly taller than she. I noted that before he had hardened into stone one part of him had already hardened in the flesh, and most impressively.

Wrestling in the public glare of the arena with my gloriously naked mistress – could embarrassment turn a man to stone? I was tempted to try whether skillful stroking could turn that great stone cock back to flesh, but the undercurrents in my lady's emotions deterred me.

I sighed. My dreams of a mistress who would demand the pleasures I could give, whose strong body would press mine into breathless submission, needed some adjustment. Matters promised to be more complex than that.

We left, as she had said, before dawn, Nyal wrapped and bundled awkwardly onto the packhorse. We bound other gear around him to obscure his form, but the arrangement was unwieldy at best.

"If there is pursuit, Domande, you must leave him behind. Shebbah, I charge you to be sure of that." Hecanthe transferred to me some of her scolding authority.

"If there is pursuit, it will be your fault for not persuading the Emperor's minions that I keep to my rooms with a fever."

"They will think that your 'fever' is fueled by dalliance with your new little love slave," Hecanthe said wickedly. "The tale of your purchase will doubtless spread to the Emperor's ears, and both infuriate and inflame him. Was that what you had in mind?"

A flush rose from my lady's smooth, strong throat to her face as she glanced not at me but at the laden packhorse. I sighed again.

"Go on now," the old woman said, relenting. "I know why Shebbah caught your eye. She looks very like the portrait of your mother."

"Yes . . ." My lady looked at me as though she had not really seen me before. "You may be right. She is the beauty I should have been."

I stifled a moan of anguish as my fantasies retreated further. Her mother! My horse pranced nervously and I concentrated on keeping my seat.

We traveled for more than a week at a pace painful after six years of soft living. Even my mistress showed strain, more from weariness of thought than of body. She was wary of pursuit, and, after we had left the well-traveled highways, not always sure of our route.

"Have you been to this place we seek, Mistress?" With no one else for conversation, she had come to treat me more as companion than slave, but her deeper emotions remained as closed to me as though she too had been stone.

"I was conceived there, if that counts." Her smile was wry. "Perhaps it does, because I have a growing sense that this is the right valley at last, and the right river, and that just around the bend where the forest comes close to the water we may find our refuge."

And so we did, though "refuge" might have been too grand a word. It had once been a nobleman's hunting lodge, but even so long ago as my lady's conception it must have been a ruin.

The main hall had barely enough roof to shelter the horses, and only the kitchen offered any hope of habitability. I set to work at once to clean and sweep and unpack our meager supplies while my mistress set off with her bow and quiver.

There was, at least, a store of dry wood, and the chimney was not too plugged to draw. The place had once been well furnished; I found and scoured a huge kettle and a copper bathing tub and had water heating when my lady returned with a brace of hares.

The room had warmed by the time our meal was done, its unaccustomed comfort as mellowing as wine. "What do you think, Shebbah, should we unbind our companion?"

The question was rhetorical. Now that her mind was on him she would not be distracted.

"Will we be here long, my lady? You had spoken of a messenger."

"It could be forever." Her expression made me wish I had kept silent. "I sent to discover whether . . . whether my father the King," she gave a grim half-smile, "would grant me asylum from the Emperor."

"Surely . . ."

"Nothing is sure, except that my father the General will do his best to persuade the King, and may well succeed." Her greenish eyes held a glint of bitter humor. "Besides devotion to the king-dom, they share a weakness for delicate blonde women. Like you. Like my mother. If I had grown to look like her . . . But she died while I was a babe, and even in his grief the King could not be blind to how little I resembled him. He did not cast me out, he merely turned his back."

"And the General?"

"He took pity, when I grew tall and awkward and lonely, and trained me as he would a son. He is proud of me now, I think, and loves me in his way, but he will be angered that I did not handle the Emperor more adroitly."

She was beginning to droop now with weariness and the weight of painful memories. I could not bear to see that beautiful, proud head bowed in sorrow.

"Come, Mistress, I will unbind your stone gladiator, and then you must let me unbind you, and bathe you, and ease you."

"You must be as tired as I, Shebbah."

"Please, Mistress, your ease will be my ease." She couldn't comprehend how truly I meant that. Longings suppressed by the hardships of travel were rising in me now. If only she had inherited her sire's weakness for small blonde women!

I sensed deep-buried tremors of longing in her, too, but as I unwound Nyal's wrappings the heat of her gaze brushed past me to his cold form and I marveled that he did not melt under it.

She watched him broodingly while I filled the tub. I sprinkled in some herbs from my precious silk-wrapped store, and thought, as I inhaled the sensuous musk, that even stone might be stirred by such a mist.

"Come now, my lady, let me slip off your tunic." She raised her arms, unresisting. "And unbind your breasts . . . ah, Mistress, how can you be so cruel to such beautiful flesh?" I stroked the creased skin under her arms, then, very lightly, the silky curves of full breasts freed at last from confinement. Her nipples tautened, and so did mine.

"Legend says that women warriors used to cut them off, the better to wield their weapons. At least I have stopped short of that."

"I am very, very glad," I murmured, drawing her toward the bath. I intended to make her very, very glad, as well.

She stood before the fire and pulled off her hose. I ached to do it for her.

Her body in the firelight was golden, and so beautiful I could scarcely breathe. I felt a pulsing emanation from the stone figure in the corner; he too was aware, and aroused, and I wondered how long he would hold his rigid form, or whether indeed it was under his control.

"What herbs are these?" She bent over the tub, breathing in the vapors. The long lines of smoothly muscled legs flared into taut, rounded buttocks, firm as any athlete's but just full enough to be unmistakably a woman's.

"A secret blend, my lady, with special soothing powers." I slipped out of my own clothes and set them aside.

"Soothing? Are you sure?" She sounded doubtful, but stepped in, and sat with bent knees as I poured more water and watched it sheet over her strong shoulders and swirl around the curves of her lovely breasts. The herbs were, in fact, more stimulant than relaxant, and I too felt their effect, but it hardly needed that to make my own breasts swell and a sweet ache build in my loins.

I had to close my eyes and struggle to focus, to remember my art and my role. To give pleasure, to seek out my mistress's longings and fulfill them, to show her joys she had never imagined; to be slave to her desires, even those she scarcely knew herself.

"Let me massage your neck, Mistress, and your back, to rub away the tension." She leaned forward compliantly. Short bronze curls wrapped around my fingers as I kneaded the stress out of nape and scalp. My hands moved over shoulders and then upper back, and as I worked my fingers into the firm muscles there I could feel the heavy pull of her breasts against the skin.

"Does that ease you, Mistress?"

"Mmmn. Don't stop." But I knew already what she felt. At last she had opened to that sensual link that was my greatest skill, and I felt with her the stirrings of her pleasure.

My breasts pressed against her wet flesh as I reached farther down, and she arched against the pressure of my hands on her lower back. Then gently, slowly, I stroked her sides and around to her belly and below and let my fingers tangle lightly in dark-honey curls.

"Do you call this easing?" My head was against her back now, and her voice vibrated through her body into mine, but there was no anger in it.

"The wilder the journey, the greater the ease at the end," I murmured. "If you will just let me show you the way, Mistress."

She tensed slightly, then grasped my arm and drew me around to face her.

"Do you think me so untouched, Shebbah?" Her look was a challenge. I met her gaze and said nothing, and after a moment she glanced away. "I was as curious as any other, but the 'journey' was always brief and disappointing. I found better use for my body in feats of arms."

"Let me show you, Mistress, how much more it can be."

She leaned back, and now her eyes were deep amber pools reflecting the fire. "Why not? Why should I not know what it is to be a woman?" She let one sidelong glance stray toward the stone figure. I could sense its mounting tension. Soon there would come a shattering, or eruption; but not, I hoped, too soon.

"Not just 'a woman,'" I said, slipping into the water and kneeling astride her thighs, "but a transcendently beautiful woman, indescribably desirable. Yes, it is true," as she started to shake her head, "and you must feel your own beauty to let your pleasure flow."

It was all I could do to keep from rubbing my throbbing ache against her wet thighs; only my training kept my focus on her sensations, not my own. I longed to kiss her full lips, but her head was tilted back and I knew she was open not to intimacy but to pure erotic stimulation. Even so, the mind is the body's most sensuous organ.

"Such beautiful breasts." I cupped and gently pressed them and flicked my thumbs across the nipples. "So swollen with pleasure, yearning, aching for more and more."

She thrust against my hands, head still back, eyes closed, breath fast and uneven. I kept my touch light, tantalizing, making her reach for it.

"Open your eyes, Mistress, watch, see what your body does. See how full and round, how hard and pointed, how straining toward my touch. Feel the pull, feel what you need, feel . . ." I licked with feather-light tongue one nipple and then the other, again and again, as her hands clenched on the copper rim and shuddering sighs tore from her throat. At last, just when I could not have borne it an instant longer, she grasped my head and forced my mouth hard onto her flesh and I sucked and bit at one nipple and then the other until her pleasure verged too closely onto pain.

I caught her hand and slid it down her belly and below, into the water. "Feel there, how beautiful, how tight and full." I gently pushed her fingers aside and stroked her myself, just as lightly, then just as firmly, as her mounting need demanded.

"And here, lower, deeper, so deep, so pulsing." I slid a finger between her nether lips and gently into her clinging heat and thought of raising her hips out of the water so that my tongue could probe her sweetness, but she was arching and thrusting against my hand with such hunger that I dared not withdraw it.

My mind melded into the pleasure-core of hers, touching her in the very ways and places that most filled and drove her need. I felt a flood of power greater than desire, as the strong body that could break me without effort writhed in unspoken pleading for what I could give. I slipped in another finger, and one more, and pressed my thumb against her as my fingers moved in the slippery depths.

"So beautiful a body," I breathed against her mouth, leaning my breasts into hers. "So strong and sweet and surging with pleasure." And so tuned was I now to her sensations that I rode the wave with her, gripping her wet thighs with mine as she arched her hips out of the bath in her driving need to be probed ever deeper and harder. If my hands were not enough I had other means in my silk-wrapped roll of "tools," but it seemed impossible to move away long enough to reach for them.

Then her ragged moans resolved into a full-throated cry, and my own sobs of release began to rise, and the deeper roar that swept over us seemed only a part of the ecstatic whole – until the world crashed sideways, water swirled and metal clanged on wood, and we were spilled out onto the floor.

Nyal stood over us, all fury and solid flesh, pain twisting his face even as lust engorged his loins.

"You!" he bellowed at Domande. "You . . ." But words were too frail to bear his rage. He dragged her up, and she was too dazed (I dared not hope too wise) to resist.

I was not quite so dazed as to forget my little dagger, but what surged between these two they must resolve alone. Even when he slammed her against the wall I made no move to stop him.

Nor did she. He bound her wrists above her head with her own belt, looping it tightly over an iron game hook so that her feet barely touched the floor, and still she hung unresisting. He shoved his body roughly against hers, and I began to throb anew at the thought of his hardness pressing into her belly, but she was silent and the only cry came from his own raw throat.

"You!" He gasped for words. "The ice princess, the unmoved, the untouchable! But not so untouchable after all, not so cool."

He wrenched himself away and turned his back to her. His gladiator's body shone with sweat and the swollen head of his shaft gleamed even slicker than the rest.

"Nyal!" At last she found a voice. "You are free! I am defeated. I do not hold you, you may do as you will."

He should have turned, should have let her see in his face that he would never be free of her. But instead he lurched toward me and twisted his hand in my hair and forced me to my knees.

"Ease me, girl," he grated. He may have thought to punish me and her, but he had stabbed her deeper than he knew. I could not tell him what a fool he was; a slave's training runs too deeply. And what pressed against my face was too full and throbbing.

I took him into my mouth and teased his slippery tip with my tongue as I reached to stroke between his thighs, using all my skills at the game of stimulation and prolongation. He struck my hand away. "Just ease me, slut, quickly!"

He had been hard, after all, one way or another, for more than a fortnight. I brought him swiftly over the edge. His spending burst hot and metallic into my mouth and all the way down my throat.

The silence following his final gasp might have been seconds, or minutes, or hours. He slumped against the wall, head down. When finally I looked to my mistress she seemed at first immobile; but her long smooth muscles were tensed and I saw that she tested the strength of the wall-hook holding her.

I ran with my knife to cut her down, but her blazing eyes held me off. "Get away! And you," she spat at Nyal, "take your freedom while you may!" She began to arch her body in rhythmic convulsions, and the wood around the hook started to splinter.

"Why so slow to run?" she taunted, panting slightly from her exertion. "Hiding in stone again?" And indeed he seemed frozen, watching her strong, beautiful body strain at its bonds. "For her you are all eager flesh, but for me only stone! Such a Gorgon as I must be!"

"No!" He sounded strangled. "It is a curse in the blood! My grandsire had the skill to wield it as a defense, but I had not known it was in me until . . ."

"Until what?" she challenged. A final lurch brought the iron hook tearing from the wall, and Nyal ducked as it shot past just over his head. I dared to dart forward to cut the belt still bound around my lady's wrists, but neither of them paid me any heed.

A slow smile lit Nyal's face. Only then, I think, did the last of the stone leave his system. "Until I was tormented past bearing by a rival and comrade who seemed untouched by the fire she lit in me."

"Did you think me so untouched?" Rage abruptly gone, she let the whisper of a smile curve her lips. "Try me."

Her wrestling stance would have horrified Hecanthe, who had wanted me to teach her "a woman's proper weapons," but the two gleaming bodies testing and striving against each other understood far better than I the erotic tension of strength on strength.

They began with classic wrestling moves, scarcely stirring for long moments as flesh strained against taut flesh. Nyal's shoulders were broader, but Domande's lithe dexterity countered his strength so that they were evenly matched.

He was instantly, magnificently aroused, despite his recent release. This might have given my lady the advantage, but her own tasting of her body's hungers had served only to increase them. She put her mouth to sweaty muscles straining to break her hold, brushed hard-swollen nipples against his heaving chest, then turned to clasp his probing shaft between tensed buttocks before a swivel and thrust of her hip sent him to his knees.

Any resemblance to formal wrestling crumbled then. He grasped her hips and pressed his mouth into her belly, and she pushed his head downward toward the dark-honey curls between her thighs, and though my link to her was fading I knew by her gasps just where his tongue and hands caressed her.

When he pulled her off balance and pinned her shoulders to the floor she resisted only enough to savor the friction. His hardness stroked and probed her slippery tenderness until she raised her hips for him to plunge in all the deeper and gripped his thrusting buttocks with her long, strong legs.

Her moans grew rougher and more demanding. Suddenly, with a great heave, she flipped him to his back. He cried out, but she covered his mouth with her own, then raised upright until she was riding him hard astride, and his groans came between clenched teeth as he fought to hold on until at last her head went back and a cry of triumph tore from her throat.

My link was gone. Just the sight and sound of them made me wild with longing. I could not have told which of them I would rather hold, which rather be, but there was no one to ease me now, and I did not know how to bear it. Slavery had never been such agony.

I picked up my cloak and slipped out through the ruined hall, past the horses, and into the night. With no clear goal I made my way along the overgrown road as quickly as moonlight would allow, mind and body in such turmoil that I nearly stumbled into a horse and rider coming toward me.

"Riette!" Eyes wide with shock stared down at me from a bearded face. I turned and ran, and the deep voice rumbled again, cracking in pain, "Riette, come back!"

I reached the lodge just ahead of him and burst into the kitchen. "Mistress! Someone comes!"

Nyal leaped to his feet and grabbed my lady's sword, but she stayed him with a gesture. The giant figure looming in the doorway fixed his eyes on me as though I were a ghost, until the firelight revealed that mine was not quite the face in his dreams. His great head bowed for a moment; then he shook off past sorrow and turned to my mistress.

"You are looking very fit, Domande." His tone was dry as he glanced from her naked flesh to Nyal's.

"Never better, Father." She grinned like an urchin, and his answering smile was a mirror of hers. His hair was a darker, grizzled version of her bronze curls, and his eyes beneath heavy brows glinted with the same green-amber flame.

He moved as though to embrace her, but suddenly drew back and lowered himself to his knees. "Lady Domande." His tone was now measured and formal. "Your father the King is dead. The Council entreats you to return to lead your people."

Her face turned pale and set. "Do you think I would renounce my father the General?"

He rose wearily to his feet, leather armor creaking over massive shoulders. "No need of that. The people are not deceived, but they judge that your blood-claim through Queen Riette is sufficient. Your strength is needed to resist the encroachment of the Empire; backed, of course, by my strength and the loyalty of my troops."

"And mine." Nyal laid his arm across her shoulders; when she did not shake it off he tightened it into an embrace. The General cocked an enquiring brow.

"Then so it shall be." Domande's face was serene with assurance and fulfillment. "Shebbah." She turned to me, and I felt the General's weary eyes on me as well. "There are no slaves in my country, and there are none here. But it would be good of you to help the General to remove his armor and bathe away the dust of travel. Will you give him ease while Nyal and I go to view the river by moonlight?"

"I will, Lady." It was hard not to call her mistress. As I took the older man's callused hand it jerked and then tightened on mine, and I felt the link take hold. I knew, now, who would give me ease, whose great strong body would press mine into submission, who would demand all I could give and fill me with all I desired.

Or almost all. I let one lingering glance caress Domande's smoothly muscled form as she went through the door, then turned my full heart and mind toward the Master whose need was greatest.

Against the Wall

Catherine Paulssen

The humming of a building crane and monotonous strike of a distant hammer beat heavily through the idleness of the summer afternoon as Annie let her eyes wander over the groups of soldiers lingering across from her perch on the watchtower – the men from the 8th Infantry Division on her side of the barbwire and slabs of concrete, the Russian soldiers gathering with members of the East German police corps on the other.

None of them seemed to have anything particular to do. They looked as calm as the air that hung leaden over the city. But she knew the soldiers on West Berlin ground had a sharp eye on what was happening on the other side of the border, which would soon be manifested with a wall much taller than a man's height. They were watching the enemy, on the lookout for even the slightest commotion that could be a sign of people trying to escape to freedom.

The Soviet soldiers that guarded the construction site on the eastern side were looking for the exact same thing.

Two weeks ago, they had started to build the wall, and ever since that day, fugitives had been fleeing the eastern part of the city. Officially, the US troops and the Allied forces stationed around them didn't interfere. But it was an open secret that they would help anyone who made an attempt to choose their side.

Annie sighed a little. Even though the soldiers appeared to have hardly anything to do, she would trade her work as a cryptographer any time for their tasks. She had never been one for staying inside, and she would happily exchange her uniform and pumps for her male comrades' boots and fatigues. She scratched her neck, slightly sticky with a sheen of sweat. At least the skirt was a welcome relief for the summer, one of the hottest that Europe had seen in decades.

She reached for a field glass and let her gaze wander over the Soviet soldiers leaning against a fence. To her, they all looked the same. Tall and pale-skinned, but with red cheeks and a slightly defiant, proud expression around their lips. One, though, stood out from the crowd. His stout figure gave him an angular appearance, but his gestures when he talked weren't stodgy or gruff at all. His face was round and open.

She would sometimes catch sight of him on her strolls outside the command post, and her heart would always beat a bit faster, though she couldn't exactly figure out why. He wasn't supposed to make her feel that way, after all. She was a county commissioner's daughter from the Midwest, she believed in the Apollo mission, Elvis Presley and the New York Yankees.

He was a captain serving a Communist regime.

Now he took off his cap and wiped his forehead. She adjusted the binocular to take a closer look. His light blond hair was just a bit too long. Not so much that it would get him into trouble with regulations, but enough for her to see that any further inch could. She imagined him losing himself in tunes played by forbidden radio stations as soon as his daily duty was over.

"Second Lieutenant McMillan," came a voice behind her. She turned and saluted the First Lieutenant. "Keeping a close watch on the enemy?"

"I . . ."

"You know you're not supposed to be up here," he said. His voice was stern, but she could see an amused glimmer in his eyes.

"I'm sorry, sir. But I'm off duty," she hurried to add.

"Even more reason," he said good-naturedly.

"Yes, sir."

That night, when she went to bed in her cabin, sleep didn't find her for hours. She blamed the sticky air, but the true culprit, she knew deep down, must have been the Soviet soldier.

"You can't go out there now!" Mae protested. "Look!" She pointed at the window, where towering grey clouds had darkened the sky so much that the late afternoon looked more like evening. Thunder was rolling in the distance.

"I have to. My mother gave me that watch before I left for Europe!" Annie grabbed her garrison cap and gave her friend a look that sought her understanding. "I know where I must have lost it. I'll be back before the storm gets here."

Before Mae could further object, Annie ran out of the office building that hosted their command post and headed straight for the construction line. When she reached the deserted no man's land, the first drops of rain began to fall. Heavy, thick blobs soon speckled the dusty ground with dark spots. She threw a glance at the clouds being chased by the wind. No way would she return now, even if the price to pay was getting soaked to the bone. She'd probably lost her watch while strolling here during lunch break today, and she silently cursed herself for not having replaced its threadbare strap earlier.

Through an opening where the barbed wire hadn't already been replaced with cement slabs, she could see some workers running into a shed and the lights being turned on in the Russian barracks. The machines stood still, and all she could hear was the thunder's glowering rumble. She passed a pile of cobblestones that smelled as only stones could in the middle of a city when the summer rain made their smooth surface shine.

Careful not to come too close to the fence while keeping her eyes on the ground, she startled when a glaring bolt of lightning tore through the gloom. Thunder followed a moment later; hard and striking, it pierced the air with its force. As if on command, the raindrops multiplied. Soon enough, her cord jacket was soggy, and she could feel the wetness nibbling at her shirt. She turned up the collar of the jacket to prevent streaks of water from trickling down her wet hair onto her neck.

Big puddles formed on the ground. She hadn't expected them to cover the site that quickly, but suddenly, she found herself in the middle of a vast lake with only a few islands of mud scattered across it. The raindrops bounced off the surface of the water like shiny little pearls glistening whenever a flash of light hit them. She stuffed her cap into the pocket of her jacket and started to jump from mud speck to mud speck, unable to see much ahead of her, so thick was the curtain of water lashing down. Realizing she had come quite close to the wall, she paused and looked for a place to wait for the thunderstorm to pass. Suddenly, she felt a hand grabbing her shoulder. She shrieked and turned to find the bear-like Soviet soldier standing right next to her.

"*Nje*," he said, making a gesture with his fingers, then pointing to where they were standing. She looked at him with wide eyes, and he added the word "*Gefahr*", his voice loud to drown out the rushing of the wind and water.

She thought she knew the meaning of that German word. "You mean it's dangerous to be here?"

He nodded. "Dangerous."

His accent was hard, but it was softened by the concern in his voice. She ducked her head as another flash of lightning darted from above. "But there's no one around, and I know the area."

Did she see his mouth twitch in the dazzling white light? He said something in Russian, then shook his head. "Woman *nje* out. Dangerous."

"I'm not a woman. I'm a second lieutenant in the Women's Army Corps of the United States of America." She raised her chin and tried her best not to blink as the raindrops hit her eyes.

For a moment, he frowned, and she wondered if he suddenly realized that she was, after all, the enemy. But then he broke out in loud laughter, a laughter so hearty, it couldn't be swallowed even by the grumbling thunder. "Come," he said curtly.

He grabbed her arm and rushed her across the open space to a place where concrete slabs were piled high. As she tried to keep up with his long steps, she wondered if it was wise to follow a Soviet soldier she knew nothing about, with no one else to turn to and nobody in her unit knowing where she was. And yet, this was more a curious feeling than real fear.

At one side of the piled slabs stood a small stand where cigarette stubs swam in big pools of rainwater. He dragged her behind it to a narrow passageway where the stand's roof met the stacked slabs. It was dry, and the cement had even stored some of the day's heat.

Annie leaned against the back of the shelter and panted. She smiled at him. "Thank you."

He returned the smile. After some moments, he pointed to his chest. "Sergei."

Her smile became bigger. "I'm Annie."

He nodded formally, and she couldn't help but find him incredibly endearing.

Now, no longer running or concentrating on her way, she became aware of how the water had crept into every layer of her clothing and how chilly she was growing. Sergei tilted his head and narrowed his eyes. Then, he took off the raincoat he was wearing. He folded it, carefully laid it on the floor and took off his jacket as well. Another thunderbolt lightened the darkness for a few seconds, and she could see that he had not been affected much by the rain apart from a few dark patches on his shoulders. He made a step towards her and motioned her to take off her jacket. She could feel his eyes on her face as she unbuttoned it, and it made the blood rush to her cheeks. Her fingers trembled, and she fumbled with the buttons. He waited patiently, then took the damp cord suit from her hands and placed it on top of his coat. As he reached around her to put his jacket over her shoulders, she could smell his body and the rain on it. In the mingling scents of wet cord, gabardine, rain-soaked mud and his soap, she felt strangely comforted and safe. He closed the top button of the jacket, and Annie could feel the goose bumps vanishing from her cold skin.

"Thank you," she said once more and cleared her throat as she heard her own voice croaky and strange.

"*Spahseeba*," he said, and his breath touched her face. It tasted of tea and some fruit, dark and sweet.

"*Spahseeba*?"

"Thank you. *Russki*."

"Oh." She blushed and tugged the coat a bit closer around her. He didn't retreat; instead, he propped one of his huge hands against the wall and continued to watch her.

Annie raised her head a bit and looked directly into his face. "*Spahseeba*," she whispered, and the next moment, the fruity smell of his breath touched her lips, followed by his warm mouth on hers. Another flash of light streaked through the passageway and by the time the thunder roared, he had pressed her against the shelter's wall. She grabbed his arms, and they felt just as strong as she'd imagined they would.

He lifted her up a little while he kissed her and, for a moment, she could feel how excited he was through her skirt and his uniform slacks. They broke the kiss, both catching their breath, and even in the shadows she could see the quizzical look on his face.

She bit her bottom lip and took off his cap. His hands didn't let go of her waist, and they radiated warmth to her skin even through her damp shirt. He stood completely still, and her heart turned towards him.

She ran her fingers through the blond hair and down his temple. His skin felt soft from the rain. When he didn't show any reaction, she moved the tip of her finger to trace the shape of his

ips. He opened them, and she ran her fingers farther down his
chin, over his neck, to the hollow above his collarbone. She
pressed herself a little closer against him and placed a kiss on his
mouth.

The force with which he answered and deepened her kiss left
no doubt that he had just been waiting for her cue. The tenderness of his hands as they crept underneath her shirt to explore
her skin revealed that it hadn't been a lack of experience or
shyness holding him back. A shiver ran through her body as his
rough fingers ran down her spine and trailed the rim of her skirt.
Their touch felt so warm, and when his fingernail grazed her hips
and traced the line of her curves up to her arms, she moaned
softly into his mouth.

He smiled against her lips and next thing she knew, his hand
was cupping her breast and caressing it so givingly, it made her
forget about the bra that lay between his skin and hers.

Another flash crashed down from above, and she noticed that
it took a while until the thunder followed. The rain was still pouring, but she couldn't help feeling anxious – anxious that the
workers would return, anxious that someone might catch them
red-handed. She fumbled with the buttons of his pants, and he
stepped back a bit. While she opened his slacks, he watched her
face, his gaze unwavering.

"*U teebiya krahseeviyeh glahza,*" he muttered. The admiration
in his eyes told her something about the meaning of the mysterious words, and when his thumb ran over her brow and down her
cheek, she assumed he had made a compliment about her looks.

She gave him a smile, and the high that rushed through her
body at the thought of what she was about to do thrilled her. She
found her way into his shorts and fondled his wiry curls. It
aroused her almost as much as it did him. So much time had
passed since she had last felt a man's touch, and it was even more
special now because he was making her feel simply good. His
cock bobbed against her hand, and she curled her fingers around
it. He closed his eyes and groaned. Very softly, she began stroking
him up and down, and he let her do as she pleased for some
moments. Then, with the next rumble that rolled through the
skies, Annie found herself pinned against the walls of the shelter.
Maybe he was realizing that the thunderstorm wouldn't last
much longer; maybe her caress had become too much.

Maybe he had wanted her all along.

He shoved up her skirt and yanked down her panties. A strangled moan escaped his lips as his fingers stroked her pussy, and the surprise she thought she heard left her embarrassed at the moist sensation he must certainly be feeling, a dead giveaway of how turned on she was. She lowered her gaze. Sergei lifted up her chin. The look in his eyes was sincere, and the kiss he gave her made her abandon any feelings of shame.

He took the hand that was still rubbing his cock and put it around his neck. He held her tight as he entered her, very carefully, but when she responded to his first deliberate strokes, he grew more daring. Her fingers dug into his shoulder and a surge of warmth flooded her body as he completely abandoned his restraint. Annie buried her face in his chest as he rocked her with heavy thrusts; locked in his embrace, she let him carry her away.

Their moans mixed with the sound of raindrops tumbling on the roof and the hauling of the wind around their retreat. A bolt of light flashed through the clouds and as the thunder died in the distance, they leaned against each other, gasping. Her head resting against Sergei's heaving chest, Annie drank in his scent.

He didn't break away immediately, but rocked her a little bit back and forth in his arms, as if he were dancing to a tune playing in his head.

"Sergei . . ." she whispered, and he smiled. He placed two fingers on her mouth, then moved them to his mouth and kissed the tips that had just touched her lips.

After he had redone his clothes, he bent down and picked up her jacket. In a silent gesture, he held it out to her, but instead of taking it, she wrapped her arms around him and remained in his embrace until the rain's intensity was no more than a soft thrum on the roof.

"If I stay for much longer, I won't be able to leave," she whispered, and she knew he understood because his arms held her even tighter, and he buried his face in her hair.

She took her jacket from his hands, removed his coat and reached around him to drape it around his shoulders. "*Spahseeba*," she whispered and quickly kissed him.

She hopped through the muddy pools back to her command post, not noticing the water that splashed across her legs or how the construction site was once again filling up with workers

Only when she reached the security booth did she throw a quick glance back.

Her watch would be forever gone. But she had found something else while searching for it.

A few days later, as she was on her way out of the office, Annie passed a group of fellow soldiers from her unit talking about the Russian troops. She bent over the water fountain to listen.

"I heard it is some sick sort of sport to them, like a . . . a hunt," she overheard one of the women saying.

"And afterwards, they brag about how they seduced the enemy," another woman said.

Annie choked on the water she was about to swallow and ran towards the bathrooms where she threw up. Panting, she looked at her face in the mirror. Her eyes had a reddish brim, and she hadn't looked that pale in a long time.

Whatever Sergei had complimented her on, he surely would change his mind if he saw her like this.

So maybe he was one of those? No, he couldn't be. He had treated her with such respect and consideration. She rinsed her mouth to get rid of the sickening taste.

But he hadn't really hesitated to sleep with her. And he had seemed experienced.

The doubts didn't leave her all day, and they continued to haunt her deep into the night.

By lunch break the next day, she had decided she would take the risk of climbing up the watchtower again. She wasn't sure what she expected to see or if it even mattered at all.

She saluted the guard on duty and, when he didn't pay her much attention, rushed past him towards the side of the tower facing the border.

There he was – Sergei, standing in a group of soldiers patrolling the construction site. She watched him turn to a private and strike up a chat. Something the private said must have been funny because soon Sergei was laughing. As she watched his open mouth, she remembered the sound of his laughter, deep and genuine. The other soldier walked away, and Sergei turned his head towards where she was standing. For some reason, she had the feeling it wasn't the first time he had peeked over to the US watchtower.

He squinted and stood completely still.

With bated breath, she watched him cast a quick glance at his surroundings before looking back right at her. His face crinkled into a broad smile and for the blink of a second, he tipped his hat.

In the bright midday sun, she beamed back at him.

What Vacations Are For

Thomas S. Roche

As she looked at the famous bridge illuminated in its breathtaking journey across the rocky mouth of the bay, Heather felt Clint's hand sliding up her thigh.

"Darling," she said. Her voice was musical – flirty but a little reluctant. "What are you doing?"

"Not a thing," he answered, his voice dark, his mouth close to her ear. "Not a damn thing, remember? I'm on vacation."

His arms were around her, clutching her close, and his big hand was firm and hard and knew what it was doing. Before she realized what was happening, it was thrust between her legs, rubbing her pussy through her very tight jeans. They were stretchy, made of very thin fabric; they, together with the flimsy excuse for panties she was wearing, didn't make much of a barrier against her husband's insistent fondle.

Clint stroked her sex through her jeans. Heather's clit surged. He started rubbing her rhythmically and Heather gasped.

She whined, "Clint, baby, you shouldn't . . . people might see us."

"I'm counting on it," growled her husband into her ear, his breath all to against her skin.

"You wanna get arrested?" Heather snarked with a nervous purr.

"If that's what it comes to," said Clint. "Hey, what are vacations for?"

He pressed in harder and Heather whimpered, involuntarily rubbing her ass against his cock. He was wearing a coat, so she couldn't feel it, but she knew he was hard, or getting there. She tried to squirm away, but there was nowhere to go; he had her pinned against the railing, which was how he liked it. And to be fair, Heather really didn't try very hard.

"Clint!" Heather gulped, trying not to pivot her hips and rub her pussy against his hand. She reached back and tried to push on him, but he wasn't budging. "People will see. And besides, I'm cold . . ."

She definitely was; she hadn't worn a jacket, thinking, *It's California in August. How cold can it be?*

The answer was "very cold." Heather was shivering before she even got a decent look at that fucking pompous bridge. Her nipples jutted painfully through her light sweater – and that was before her husband shoved his hand between her legs. The wind felt like it was biting into her flesh, and Heather's teeth were practically chattering.

"Honey, I'm *cold*," she repeated.

"So I'll make you hot," said Clint. Then he did something *nasty*. He seemed to have planned this part. He took his hand from between his wife's legs. He reached up and seized her wrists – both of them, all at once. He had something in his hand – something hard and firm and metal, with a short chain that rattled.

Before Heather knew what was happening, her husband had snapped the handcuffs around her wrists and handcuffed her to the railing.

Clint knew how to handcuff a girl with terrifying efficiency – a thing Heather found out with some regularity, though only occasionally in public. Heather squealed and tried to get away, but there was nothing for it. With an easy, smooth gesture, Clint unbuttoned his overcoat and pulled it around her and shoved the edges into her hands. Clint's overcoat was big on him, and his slender wife fit easily inside it. She clutched her hands to the railing with the ends of the coat gripped tightly – and her body temperature began to rise.

"Warmed up yet, baby?"

Heather spat bitterly, "No! I'm still fucking cold. And if you think I'm going to—"

That's when all of it stopped – her protests, and the world.

It was eleven o'clock at night, and the observation deck was practically empty because of the wind and the cold. But Heather knew that only made Clint's dirty mind work overtime. And as cold as she was, she knew she'd give in – like she *always* gave in when he pulled this shit. She knew she *needed* to give in, and Clint knew it, too – maybe more than Heather knew it herself.

He did something to her, then. He did the one thing he knew would make her stop protesting and want it so bad she couldn't control herself.

He knew how to make her forget all human language; with his hands and his lips, he knew just where to touch her. Even when she got scared and embarrassed, she could never remember what the fuck she was supposed to do if she got *too* scared and embarrassed.

And she liked it that way. She liked the way he made her brain go all fuzzy – made her pre-verbal when he did those *things* . . . right here in public.

He did "those things" now – three of them all at once. He undid her belt with the skill of an expert. He put his hand in her hair and gripped it lightly, tipping her head forward, making her feel all submissive.

And, perhaps most importantly, he kissed her on *that spot* – the spot that made her crazy. He did it gently at first with tongue and teeth barely grazing her flesh . . . and then harder as she surged and writhed against him.

That spot was the place on the back of Heather's neck that only her husband could find. Other men had tried – both before and since the wedding, the latter inspiring many fights and a series of tearful apologies on her part.

That was all before she realized there was no man on Earth who was ever going to find *that spot* with the virulent ease with which her husband did it; the guys who had tried had proven disappointments. Clint knew how to find that spot, wake it up, bring it to the point where her mind and her body were totally incapable of functioning in any capacity that didn't involve getting fucked very hard from behind, and maybe spanked and tied up for good measure.

Now, his hands were quite busy – one was unzipping her very tight jeans; the other was gripping her hair to keep her head in just the right position to expose what he wanted. So it was Clint's perfect mouth, with his full strong lips and his wet, surging tongue, that awakened her *spot* – packing a year's worth of love-making into a soft slow slurp across the back of her neck, his tongue caressing his flesh between gentle bites . . . and sometimes harder ones.

Heather's mind spun. Her eyes rolled back in her head. She tried not to moan. She moaned anyway.

Heather gripped the railing as Clint pulled her tight jeans halfway down her thighs, exposing her sex.

Her legs were not quite together, but not quite apart. With a
pair of smooth hard kicks, he nudged them open wider so he
could get at her more easily. Heather barely knew what was
happening as he forcibly spread her legs; she was simply in
heaven. He drove her crazy with his mouth – expanding the
"spot" by working his lips and his tongue from the spar between
her shoulders to the soft spot between her spine and her jaw. She
was reeling.

Then Clint's hand went up into her slit, and Heather's mouth
dropped open. She shuddered and gasped out a cry of desperate
pleasure into the wind.

She could feel the frigid air pouring off the ocean and hitting
the back of her throat. As she rode her husband's fingers, Heather
felt pinned between her man and the ocean, his glorious right
hand and his gorgeous, cruel mouth. Clint's left hand was out of
its sleeve now; only her husband's broad shoulders and Heather's
grip on the railing kept the coat in place now. He reached between
them and unzipped his pants. His cock came out; Heather felt it
against her bare, smooth ass, trailing smears of pre-cum that
seemed alternately sticky and slick, warm and chilled.

Then she was lost in sensation again, as her husband's big left
hand slid easily up under Heather's snug sweater and down into
the cups of her bra. He took hold of her nipples one at a time and
pinched and rolled them. Sensation flooded Heather's body. She
loved it when he did that. She loved it even more when he did that
with his other hand on her clit, his mouth on the back of her neck
and his hard cock rubbing up insistently between her smooth ass
cheeks.

Heather surged and undulated between Clint's hands, Clint's
mouth, Clint's cock. She trembled and shivered and bit her lip,
trying not to scream. She couldn't stand it anymore. She needed
to be fucked.

If there was one thing she could count on her husband knowing, it was that. He knew when she needed to be fucked, sometimes
when she didn't even really totally know it herself. When he'd
kissed her and held her just before they left the car, she'd felt
ripples going through her – ripples Clint had felt, or detected, or
something. While Heather had felt more than content to daydream
about their warm hotel bed and how hungrily she was going to

suck her man's cock – in fifteen minutes, twenty, thirty, maybe an hour – Clint knew Heather would be happy if she didn't have to wait.

Bastard, she thought, clutching the coat and the cuffs and the railing. *Smug fucking bastard*.

She wanted him in her.

Swaying, Heather bent forward, leaning hard against the railing. Her body reacted instinctively, as if on some evolutionary level. She felt as if her craving had turned her into an animal. She knew how to mate without conscious thought. She presented her sex to her husband, wanting him more than she'd ever wanted anything. She felt the handcuffs scraping the metal railing and tugging at her wrists as she desperately clutched the ends of the coat in her fingers, afraid she would lose her grip in her pleasure and let the whole world see him take her.

Bent over, Heather lifted her ass as high as she could. She was very much shorter than him, so that just barely put her sex within reach of her husband's glorious cock – which only meant he'd fuck her at a downward angle, she knew. From her experience, that could only mean good things.

Still, Clint was so much taller than her that he still had to stoop a little to get it in her. As he did, he paused to take a brief glance over his shoulder before he took his wife up against the railing.

The coast must have been clear. With his right hand, now slippery with Heather's cunt, Clint reached back between her legs and guided his cock to her entrance. He penetrated his wife with agonizing slowness; she wanted him in her, but he took his time. All told, it probably took half a minute . . . but to Heather, pinned against the rail and feeling helpless, it seemed an eternity. Clint was torturing her.

He got what he wanted; Heather gave in. She finally shoved herself onto him, moaning into the icy wind as she did. She started fucking back onto him, and if anyone was watching, there would no longer be any doubt about what they were doing. Clint's right hand had returned to her clit, his left to her tits, his lips to that spot on the back of her neck. He fucked her and stroked her and pinched her nipples, and sent cascading electric tingles through her body as his tongue swirled against her flesh between gentle bites – and hard ones, sometimes, as she got closer and closer.

She'd been right; the angle was perfect.

306 *Thomas S. Roche*

Heather tried to stifle her cry of pleasure, but it was hopeless. She let it all out.

Heather howled into the wind, coming hard on her husband's cock. She had to stop fucking herself back onto him, and just sort of spasmed there, helpless, suspended between his cock and the railing.

He took up the slack and drove deep inside her as he felt her sex spasm around him.

He let himself go deeper inside her.

Heather felt the soft wet surge of her husband's seed in warm, rolling spurts in her pussy, and if anything she came harder as she held as still as possible so as not to lose it.

As Clint's cock spent itself inside her, he leaned forward and kissed Heather's "spot" with one last tender, wet slurp of his tongue and hard bite of his teeth. It sent a sharp rush of pleasure through her body, and Heather pulled hard at the handcuffs, feeling very out of control. She felt the wind at the back of her throat again, and realized she was moaning at the top of her lungs. She didn't even care if people could see her.

Heather trembled all over, and not from the cold. Without unlocking the handcuffs, Clint pulled up Heather's jeans, zipped her pants and his own, buckled them both up and righted her bra cups. He pulled her sweater back down over her tits. His hand dipped into his pants and came out with his keys; they jangled against the railing as he unlocked her.

He didn't put his arms back in his sleeves; rather, he swept the coat off of his shoulders and wrapped it around his shivering wife. He walked her to the car with his arm around her shoulder. Her teeth were chattering, but the walk helped her focus and turned up the heat. It raised her body temperature just enough that she felt warm as Clint held open the door and helped her into the car.

That's what she loved about her husband, Heather thought, as she buried her face in his coat and took a deep draught of his scent. One of the many things. Always such a gentleman . . . even when he'd just handcuffed his wife over an observation deck railing and fucked her from behind.

Always a gentleman; that was her husband.

Clint started the car and pulled onto the onramp.

As he merged, Heather's thoughts returned to the warm hotel bed. She remembered what she'd been thinking of doing when Clint had kissed her and held her and sensed her need. She'd been thinking about getting into the warm hotel bed and sliding down under the covers and sucking her husband's perfect cock with the kind of vacation-sex gusto that comes once a year, at best.

She was still gonna do it, she decided. Maybe she'd even filch those handcuffs and see if she could cuff him to the bed when he wasn't looking so he couldn't try to sixty-nine her like he usually did when she sucked his cock. She'd make that smug bastard spread wide and take some pleasure, the way he'd just done to her.

She'd rock his world, and he'd thank her for it. Isn't that what vacations are for?

La Belle Mort

Zander Vyne

"Young woman, you do realize if you could be with child you may plead your belly?" The judge had tired eyes.

Eliza remained quiet, and the audience tittered.

"Very well. Lady Elizabeth Jane Morton, you are sentenced to be taken hence to the prison in which you were last confined where, after three Sundays have passed, you will be hanged by the neck until dead. May the Lord God have mercy upon your soul."

Gypsy . . . succubus . . . witch – murmurs, as she was led away.

Had they looked beyond the snow-white skin, wild black curls, and eerie calm, they would have seen the bones of her knuckles shining through her skin; she held her hands clenched painfully tight to keep from lashing out at all of them and going absolutely mad.

A cell to myself at the end of a narrow, gloomy hall. Dank, always cold. Oozing drips stain the walls rust brown. Insanity – cackles, moans and screams. Fleas, mice and slithering sounds in the darkness. A cot and rough blanket. A long bench to sit upon. Small comforts from Charity Ladies, mercifully none familiar to me. They bring gifts, the smell of perfume, and pity.

I accept them all. Today's treasures – ink, quill pens and paper. Solace found.

Eliza fought slumber; it crawled with dark dreams and beckoned with greedy fingers. Hours, long and black, were spent struggling to cling to awareness, her life dwindling away. Regrets stung. Time was short, and peace was as elusive as life. Insanity promised everlasting oblivion, and she was tempted to succumb as so many had around her. Writing gave her temporary respite. There was no one to write, so she wrote for herself; poems, thoughts, lists and letters she would never send.

Dear Lord Dover,

Do you sleep peacefully? Do your children fare well without their nursemaid in their nursery?

Despite what you have done, my prayers are with their poor little souls.

I wonder where you hid the necklace and if it calls to you in your dreams. Will it haunt you, as surely I will if there is a God and he grants wishes?

My life is forfeit, and still I would rather this death than your wrinkled hands upon me.

Lady Elizabeth Jane Morton

She folded scribbled-upon paper into tiny birds and sailed them into the courtyard. Sometimes, they landed in the shadows of the gallows themselves, but usually the wind caught them and carried them away to join the plentiful refuse littering London's streets.

GOOD THINGS
Father
Mayfair House
London
Carriages
Ball gowns
The Waltz
Flirting
James
The Dover children
BAD THINGS
This place
A "new" dress – bodice too tight, tattered skirt. A string to tie my hair off my neck – blessed relief. Small things mean so much now.

She documented everything, writing furiously, clinging to sanity.

A hanging – crowd swelling, sudden and boisterous, fathers lifting children upon their shoulders, vendors selling meat-pies and posies. It was like a country fair, everyone smiling, fun in the air.

Her mind screamed, "Don't! Look away!" But she was compelled to watch. They led the prisoner out. His head was down, but Eliza saw the glistening tears on his death-pale flesh.

Placed under the gallows, his feet centered atop the wooden trapdoor, he wept openly. His legs were pinioned, to prevent his soon-to-be flailing feet from finding purchase on the brick-lined walls of the famous Long Drop below. The noose was fitted; a large knot of rope adjusted to rest, just so, beneath his left ear.

The hangman – cloaked in black – the very specter of death. The prisoner wailed – a high-pitched whine – when the hood was placed over his head. Did he open his eyes then, when the cloth covered his face? Did his lashes catch on the fabric, and did he take it in his mouth, dry and musky as he gulped air, grunting and snorting? Did each prisoner have a new hood, or did that frantic man, about to die, smell the deaths that had come before his, lingering in the cloth? Ghastly snapping sound ringing out of the pit. Imagined? Surely so; the crowd had cheered when the man fell out of sight. Life passes too slowly, too quickly. What prayer will save me from this fate?

Eliza was sleeping the first time he came, at dusk.

"Do not be afraid."

She was – trapped in here, weak from lack of real food and sunshine; she was helpless.

The man sat on the narrow bench. He was rather fine looking, his face somewhat stern and his clothing somber.

A cleric, Eliza decided, calming.

"Has that much time passed? It must have, for them to send you."

"I want to help you."

She held back a bitter reply; no one could help her. "I do not believe in God."

"I am the only one you need believe in." He spread his hands wide as if to dare her to argue that he was anything less than flesh and blood.

Eliza remained silent, and he reached into his pocket, pulling out a square of paper. He read, "Life passes too slowly, too quickly. What prayer will save me from this fate?"

"That is mine!" Eliza bolted from the cot.

Too slow. He tucked the note into the folds of his coat. "Yes, I know." He handed her another scrap of paper, his fingertips brushing her wrist as it changed hands.

Her cheeks flooded with color, and she escaped his gaze, reading the words on the page.

Proud beauty, angel amidst foul circumstance.
I hear you calling,
and know you weep.
Let me guide you in your dark journey,
and give you peace in this dread.
In your ruin, find faith in me.

What manner of cleric was this? "I told you, I do not have faith."

"And I told you, have faith in *me*."

"I do not understand."

He lifted his hand, tracing the path a tear made down her cheek.

Eliza held very still, quivering under his fingertips.

"You do not have to understand, Lizalamb."

She blinked. He'd called her Lizalamb, just like her father had a lifetime ago.

How odd.

"I'm afraid."

"Of course you are, but you can conquer your fears and all will be well. This I promise. Have *faith*."

He freed the string she had used to tie her hair back, and reached into his pocket once more.

Red ribbons, bows that give girlish pleasure. His voice gruff as he gifted them. What a strange, fascinating man.

Eliza nibbled her bottom lip, the treasures clutched in her hand, red ends trailing from her fist. "Will they let me keep them?"

"Yes, Liza. No one will bother you anymore."

"Thank you."

A pail of warm water, beside it – wrapped with care – a whole bar of jasmine-scented soap.

Eliza plaited the scarlet ribbons into her hair. She waited, writing.

A stranger, in my darkest hour,
offering peace for my faith,
scarlet ribbons to tie my hair.
My fate is unchangeable, measured in rope and wood,
the dozen yards to my doom.
Rise above, fall below.
The silent clock keeps ticking.

Yet, something about him – sanctuary;
already, I am anxious for his return,
to feel as I did in those brief moments,
when his hands held mine.
Hopeful.

Finally, he came.

It was night. She was sleeping.

"Close your eyes." He placed his hand over them.

Eliza struggled, pushing him away.

He let her go, holding up his lantern.

More handsome than remembered. A trick of light or a young girl's heart finding something of desire's fancy in these last days? Lust, peace, comfort. His voice – an anchor in the night.

"You can control your reaction to fear if you control your mind. You need not face the unknown at all if you have a place within yourself of peace and serenity, and a means to find it. Change what you *think,* and you change what you feel." He opened the little door in the lantern and blew out the flame within. "Close your eyes."

This time she obeyed.

Days, hours and precious little life left. What is the harm in doing as he asks?

His fingers skimmed her hair. She whimpered but did not move away.

"Think of a place, familiar, happy and safe. Go there in your mind. Picture it, smell it, feel it."

Mayfair House – Father, servants, old wood and lemon oil, laughter, parties and endless possibilities. Death, ruin, empty, sold, gone.

"I have no safe places."

She had struggled, in this place, to find tranquility as memories crashed in on her, and she wanted more than anything to think of something else. Anything else.

"Then make believe. Tell me where you would be, if you could be anywhere you desired."

His smell – crisply clean, manly under soap. A sudden image – him, standing in a lake, surrounded by a meadow dotted with tansies, forget-me-nots and lemon balm. The sky above is endless, blue. His hair is loose, dark. He is naked.

"Ahhh," she sighed.

"Tell me."

"No!"

"Why not?"

"Because!"

"This I definitely wish to hear. Tell me." His voice held a new, teasing note that sent prickles down her arms.

"Well," she said, clearing her throat. "I saw a meadow of wildflowers and a lake, bluer than the sky."

"And?"

"You were there."

"Me? What was I doing?"

"You were in the lake."

"Drowning?"

He was not old, but he was not young either. A cleric, surely he had heard lustful thoughts before.

"No, bathing I think."

"Naked?"

"Of course! Clothing would be silly indeed if one were bathing."

"What were you doing, besides watching me?"

"That was all I was doing!"

"No picnic, no flower gathering or cloud watching?"

"Oh, yes! We supped on steak and kidney pies, Devonshire cheeses, and exotic fruit sent in from India." She laughed.

"What eclectic tastes you have! Did I kiss you?"

"Oh, my . . . yes. We kissed and kissed," she said, her voice dreamy and girlish to her ears.

"And, were you joyful then, Lizalove?"

"Yes. Yes, I was," she answered, faintly surprised.

The next time he came, he carried a rope. "Is this one of the things you fear?"

"Yes." Her gaze darted to the coil of twine.

He placed it on her lap, the ends snaking to the ground. Her fingers shrunk away.

"Tell me what you fear."

"The way it will feel. The weight of it, the roughness of it, the finality of it."

"Do you trust me?"

What is it about him? I am girlish and hopeful, excited to greet the day because he might fill it. Be he cleric or devil, man or beast, in these last days he gives things believed lost forever. I am drowning, willingly.

"Yes."

He took the rope from her, his fingers lingering over hers. Her flesh tingled, from his hand to her belly, and between her legs.

He made a loop of the rope and hung it around her neck.

She did not move.

He bunched up her skirt with one hand and held the rope with the other. She met his gaze and spread her legs wider. She wanted his touch, no matter what that made her, or him.

His hand slid up the rope until his knuckles brushed the skin under her chin. His other hand curled around her inner thigh, fingers walking a silken path. He pinched her and petted her, and she did not move.

"In fear can be found pleasure, just as in darkness can be found light."

Eliza felt the truth of his words as the rope around her neck tightened, the hemp scratchy. Like whiskers, they licked her. She no longer cared about the rope because of what his other fingers did. Her head lolled back against the wall.

"Do you feel it?" His breath kissed her cheek.

Eliza jutted her hips to his hand. "Yesss." She watched him lick his lips as he slid his fingers into the hot clutch of her body.

"Yes, Lizalove. You feel it." His eyes were obsidian darkness.

Torture – spread wide for him, still, not flinging myself upon him. He gave what was needed yet held back. I know there is more. Twin sighs as fingers pushed inward, curling within. He did not ask about the lack of barrier.

"Is the rope a concern now?"

"Nooo . . ."

Languid, craving the pleasure – forbidden delights. His lips curving against mine, tongue slipping between. Suckling him, an arm looped around his neck, fingers winding in the tangle of his dark hair.

"You can find this place too, anytime you wish. Squeeze your cunnie around my fingers."

Cunnie – a startling word, naughty. I like it and think, had I the time, I might find that I am a very, very bad girl after all.

Her flesh gripped his fingers, and new pleasures bloomed.

His thumb nudged high in her cleft, burning.

"Oh, God . . . please."

"Yes indeed, Eliza. Soon, soon." He withdrew his fingers.

She started to pull her thighs together, but he stopped her, tightening the rope around her throat.

"Not yet."

She shuddered and stayed spread wide.

"Do you touch yourself in the night, Lizalove? Right there?"

His hand cupped her yearning flesh again.

"Yesss."

"What do you think of?"

"Youuu . . ." She could not lie to him.

He removed the loop of rope from her neck. "Think of the darkness, think of the rope, think of my cock," he said.

"Ohhh."

When she opened her eyes, he was gone.

She went straight to bed.

Losing track of time, sun and moon changing places. He has not returned. Found out? Had all he wanted? Maybe something has happened to him. I do not even know his name.

Wondrous gift. A note from him:

> *How can this be?*
> *I mourn what is not yet gone!*
> *Emptied by the future that does not hold you.*
> *Do I risk hell for a heaven here and now?*
> *Dare I tempt the rope?*
> *I find you guilty of only one thing, angelic thief;*
> *you have taken my heart, and wherever you are,*
> *I know, there shall my heart be too.*
> *Fear not the darkness – I am the dark,*
> *and you are my secret, eternal.*
> *I will set you free.*
> *Give all to me.*

Still, the Cleric does not come.

A new visitor. Why am I so afraid when they tell me?

No formal visiting rooms here; Charity Ladies, physicians, clerics and visitors all came to the condemned's cell when audience was desired.

Nothing to tidy, no mirror to check, knowing she had never been dirtier or more ashamed, she stood with her cheek pressed to the bars so she could see whom the guard led to her.

James Thomas, Lord Dover's gardener and her erstwhile suitor.

Her knees went weak. She crumpled to the dusty floor; the only thing keeping her from falling was her grip on the metal doors.

Shouldn't she at least be allowed a choice? She was to die. Should she not be given the right to refuse a visitor? She only wished to see the Cleric.

She closed her eyes and, only because she refused to be found by anyone groveling in the dirt, she lifted herself up and was standing when the doors opened.

"James." She wished she had it in her to tell him to leave. Leave now and never come back, never think of her again like this. It would be easier for them both.

James

Sweet, sweet boy.

"Eliza, I came as soon as they would allow it!"

He did not offer his hand or a hug, and that was not surprising. His courtship had been most proper. It was not in his nature to be overly demonstrative. James Thomas had an innocence about him that still tugged at Eliza's heartstrings, though she was not in love with him. On the Dover estates, their paths had crossed often. She had spent much of her time out of doors with the children, and James was always to be found rallying the score of servants who attended to Lord Dover's expansive gardens wherever the family was in residence.

She had gently rebuffed his overtures, her heart still wounded over her father's death and the sudden changes in her life without him, though a part of her had started to warm. James was so sweet, good and kindly. He would make someone a very fine husband, she had started to think.

"You should not have come." She started to say more, but realized that was all there really was to say. Anything they might have had was best forgotten. He should go. She turned away from him.

"I had to come! They have not found Lady Dover's necklace. Lord Dover says if you wish to return home, you know what to do. I guess he means tell them where you hid it, but you cannot have done what they say. Not you. You're a good person, Eliza, I just know it." His brown eyes softened, though worry bracketed them with a thicket of frown lines.

Lord Dover had sent him. Sent James to tell her to acquiesce to his demands. For that was what his coded message meant. *Sleep with me. Be my mistress and all will be forgotten. You can come home again.*

Could he really do that? she wondered. Have the Court reverse her sentence? Yes. She supposed a man as powerful as Lord Dover, who had managed to get her convicted of theft without any evidence, could do that. All she would have to do was sleep with him. Not just once, for that she may have been able to stomach, but many times, for as long as he desired her. She would have to let the old man do anything he wished with her, anything at all, or it would be back to prison.

When her father died, and Lord Dover had offered her the post as nursemaid to his brood, he had seemed so kindly, her father's old friend, sympathetic to her loss and change of status. With nowhere else to turn, she had gratefully accepted the position. Very soon, it became apparent that the old man had motives other than kindliness. His pursuit of her had been relentless. After he'd tried to sneak into her chambers one night, despite having nowhere to go, Eliza had been on the verge of fleeing when he had sprung the theft trap, and had her arrested.

He had made her the same offer before the authorities arrived to take her away. *Sleep with me. Be my mistress, and all will be forgotten.*

"James, you may tell Lord Dover I did not take the necklace." She would still rather die than be his plaything. Maybe she had gone insane after all in this place.

"Eliza! There must be a way to stop this nonsense. You cannot hang for something you did not do!" Emotion seemed to overcome him, and he reached for her hand, which she allowed him to hold for a moment before gently pulling away.

"Please, just go."

"I wanted us to marry, you know." His voice broke.

"James, you barely know me. You need to forget about me."

"How can I? I love you." He made to reach for her again, and she moved away, unable to face the pain in his gentle brown eyes.

Once she had dreamed of love, and marriage. Back then, she would have rebuffed this boy's advances, preferring to dally with the affections of older, richer men. The daughter of a lord, she had her pick of powerful, handsome suitors, and had been sure she had plenty of time to settle on the right match.

"James, I do not love you. You are a gardener. Nothing changes that. You and I were never meant to be together. Had my circumstance been different, I would not have deigned even to speak with you." Harsh words, meant to hurt, and not entirely true, for she had always been nice to everyone. They were words designed to send him away, to make him think of her no more.

"How can you say that? You were always so kind. So nice. I could tell you liked me too." His look of bemused hurt almost made her stop.

"Like I told you before, you never really knew me at all. Now, go. Please. Deliver my message to Lord Dover and forget all about me."

"Eliza!"

"Guard! He's ready to leave." She did not watch as he was taken away and would not have seen even had she looked. Tears flooded her vision and choked her breathing.

Though she had not loved James, in him she had glimpsed the possibility of a future, of a life without her father that, while different, would be liveable. Sending him away, she finally allowed herself to mourn all of her losses. Her tears did not stop for days. More than once, she was tempted to give in to Lord Dover's demands so that she might live.

And still, the Cleric did not return.

I would give him anything. My dreams are filled with images of him, naked in the darkness. He is all I have left. He is all I desire.

A pail of warm water, beside it – wrapped with care – a whole bar of jasmine-scented soap.

He's coming.

When she woke the moon was high, and he was there. He stood near the window. Beyond him, she saw falling snowflakes.

She moved to one side of the cot, telling him in the action exactly what she wanted from him.

He was upon her before she could let out a breath. He pulled up her skirt and they crashed together. Their mouths clung, and their hands clutched. His whiskers abraded her skin. She arched into the pain of it, needing him with a violence that was frightening.

He ran his hands slowly over her body. Eliza thought he meant to be tender then, and she did not want his kindness. She wrapped her fingers around his arms, her torn nails ripping into his flesh, dragging him down to her.

He fisted his hands in her hair and yanked her into place beneath him. She spread her legs wide, welcoming him like the whore she had been called.

He devoured her mouth, leaving it only to lick his way to her nipples, biting and suckling them through the bodice of her dress until she moaned, forcing him to clasp his hand over her mouth. He undid his trousers. She felt the heat of him slide into her. There was no pain, only a sense of fullness and pleasure.

He rose over her, propping himself up upon his hands. She opened her mouth to lick a corded muscle in his arm. A droplet of sweat seeped from his skin, and she savored its salt on her tongue.

She came, in a flood – sudden, harsh and sweet – and then so did he, lifting himself out of her, stroking his cock as he knelt between her thighs, shooting his seed onto her belly.

"Lizalove." He kissed the bruises his passion had left upon her.

"I do not even know your name." She rubbed his release into her flesh.

"William."

"Thank you, William."

Another day.

"There is one more thing, Liza."

She nodded.

I will give him anything he wishes for, and not ask a single question. I will do anything he wants; this is all I will ever have.

He wrapped his fingers around her throat, his other hand delving between her thighs.

"Hold your breath, Lizalove. Do not breathe for as long as you can, until you grow dizzy."

William kissed her, pushing his breath into her mouth, showing her how to breathe, slowly and deeply. She took his breath into her body, holding it when he squeezed her throat.

It was difficult, not gasping for air, not panting with lust, but she looked into his eyes, and found euphoria in the control he showed her. She went with him to the place he had shown her, the peaceful meadow. His fingers worked magic, and her body opened for his bunched, fucking fingers.

Before it was over, he pushed his cock into her, choking her as he took her. He came flooding into her body just as she was overtaken by darkness.

"Breathe," he said, giving her his own breath until hers returned to normal.

He held her. "I wish I could do more," he said as she closed her eyes to shut out everything but him. "Just remember, there is always light, after the darkness. *Always.*"

And, for the first time, Eliza believed.

They came for her later, the hangman's assistant and the warden.

They tied her hands behind her back and led her into the morning sun. Her feet made clumsy imprints in the blanket of blinding white snow. The air was crisp and cold. Eliza saw her breath – a warm fog of life she walked through before she closed her eyes.

The crowd cheered, but she was far away, at a pristine lake, with a man who loved her. Flowers bloomed all around them and she wore red ribbons in her hair.

Under the gallows, she breathed deeply, calmly until peace flooded her. She opened her eyes again when the hangman placed his hand upon her shoulder.

Eliza looked into his eyes – death's eyes, the hangman's eyes, William's eyes.

"Have *faith*," she heard him whisper.

Then there was only darkness.

Suite 1226

Michèle Larue

Translated by Adriana Hunter

The Cathay Pacific Boeing 727 was gliding in across blue Eastern skies towards Bangkok. Relaxing in the front row of the forward section, Veronica's endless legs stretched out into the aisle. From time to time her eyes left her laptop and strayed to the blue curtain leading to the cockpit past the toilets and the metallic row of fridges and microwaves. She was starving. At long last a red-jacketed stewardess wheeling the meal trays down the aisle. Veronica pulled back her legs, popped up her seat and flashed a smile at her, another at the Chinese man sitting next to her and opted for the Thai curry menu.

She devoured her chicken, tapping her feet to the strains of Baxter Dury in her headphones and went back to her reading: a report on the refugee camp where she was to spend the next two months, on a mission for a Hong Kong-based NGO. Once again, her long legs stretched into the aisle. The music in her ears made the statistics scrolling down the pink screen seem a lot less boring.

As she finished reviewing the first part of the report, Veronica sensed she was being watched. The chief pilot's tanned hand was holding back the blue curtain and his hefty body was framed in the opening. Their gazes met briefly. Heavy-set in his uniform, the man was staring at Veronica's bare feet, plainly manicured, slender and pale in their beige sandals. The pilot's eyes slanted towards his temples and his prominent cheekbones were like those of South American Indians. His face would have been handsome were it not for those teenage acne pockmarks, Veronica thought to herself as she resumed her reading, determined to finish in time to have two free days in Bangkok before being enrolled into camp routine. When she raised her eyes again, the curtain was back in place. She had scarcely shut down her laptop when the "fasten seat belts" sign went on.

Veronica strode through wide airport hallways and collected her backpack from the baggage carousel. The chief pilot with his tan was standing next to the glass door opening onto the metal foot-bridge that led to the taxi ranks. He approached her with the faintest of smiles.

"I have a company car. I can drop you off in town. Where are you staying?"

"That hotel near the bus station."

"The Rex?"

Having leafed through a guidebook in Hong Kong, Veronica knew there were dozens of hotels in that vicinity. Tourists spent the night there before taking a bus to one of the southern beaches, Khao Lak, Phuket or Pattaya. But she didn't know the name of a single one, she'd planned to explore the area around the station on foot and psych out a decent accommodation for her two nights in Bangkok. So she decided to bluff.

"That's right, the Rex."

"Me too, I can drop you there, if you like."

She followed him to the company car and climbed on the back seat beside him. He introduced himself as Bernardo but didn't bother to shake hands: he was from the Philippines and didn't know a soul in Bangkok, despite his countless stopovers between Manila and the Middle East. As the car sped down the highway, his eyes dwelled on her feet.

"What's your shoe size?"

"Seven and a half."

"Small feet for your height. How tall are you?"

"Five feet ten."

"No fooling, we're exactly the same height!"

The coincidence brought smiles to their lips. This was the first Filipino Veronica had met. She sensed in Bernardo a man who'd risen out of poverty, culturally illiterate, and she took the best-seller she was reading out of her backpack to test him.

"Awesome, Douglas Kennedy's last book. Have you read it?"

"I don't read much. I am a movie fan, thrillers mostly."

In the lobby of the Rex she laid her passport on the front desk while Bernardo parleyed with the clerk in his own language, Tagalog, or was it Thai? Veronica didn't speak either one. He turned to her.

"There's a luxury suite on the top floor. We could share it. Separate bedrooms with a sitting room in the middle. My airline will pick up the tab."

He took Veronica's silence for assent, made the arrangements and handed her a key card. In the lift, Veronica suddenly felt giddy. Why had she accepted this? She was a practising psychologist, accustomed to settling other people's conflicts and who rarely lost her composure on the job. Nor had she ever entered into an affair without weighing at length the pros and the cons. But the uniform preceding her down the corridor was reassuring: after all, Bernardo was a chief airline pilot. A man of confidence, responsible for the safety of his passengers. She'd never heard of any jet-crew member accused of rape.

Behind their crimson portières, the two bedrooms were spacious, each with its own double bed. On the coffee table in the sitting room, a boat made of coconut shells and filled with fresh mangoes, pineapples and mangosteens had pride of place. The man pointed up to the high bay window, long and narrow like a movie screen.

A tangle of electric wires was visible with thousands of starlings perched upon them.

"Those'd make a nice fricassée! Ever tasted ortolans?"

"No, never."

"They're delicious. Some restaurants in Manila still serve them."

Perhaps that was meant to be tit for tat, so to speak: a plate of ortolans against Douglas Kennedy. Almost everyone has heard of Douglas Kennedy, his paperbacks are on sale in every airport, but who has any idea what ortolans taste like? Veronica's ethnological instincts were aroused, her curiosity about this roommate became more appreciative. They retired to their respective bedrooms. Veronica heard the spattering of Bernardo's shower. She stepped into her own bathroom and revelled in the warm jet. Then, wrapped in a bath sheet, she lay on the sofa by the boat of fruit, wondering what came next.

Bernardo had a bath sheet around his waist when he joined her in the sitting room. His torso was covered with tattoos, a dark green jungle crawling with serpents and dragons dotted with symbols that meant nothing to Veronica. *Yakuza*, she thought while he was seating himself cross-legged at her feet on the thick wall-to-wall carpet with its leafy design. Without thinking, she held out her legs to him, impulsively stretching her arms and toes, yawning discreetly. Bernardo took her foot and pressed it to his lips, then looked up to see how she reacted. With any other man, Veronica would already have pulled her foot away, but her ethnological curiosity got the better of her: she let him suck her toes, and was soon surprised by the way the feel of his tongue affected her: warm and damp, it was both firm and tender, alternating rough swipes and exciting little licks, sawing back and forth between her toes. Bernardo's tongue seemed as long as a hand. It curled around her toes with uncommon agility; huge and red, obscene as the tongue of a dromedary when the animal sticks it all the way out, it trailed along the side of her foot without even tickling. Instead of revolting her, the sight of such an unusual proportion of that organ actually aroused her further. A wave of pleasure rose to her knees then flashed up the inside of her thighs and straight to her groin. Her sex was as wet as an oyster between contractions. She knew she lacked the willpower to deny him the follow-up. She was wetter than wet and losing patience, when suddenly her head swam. She came, and her juices swamped Bernardo's face. He lapped them up quickly and without even a pause to catch his breath, began licking her vulva, descending from clit to anus and back. Scarcely had a few minutes gone by when Veronica shuddered with another orgasm, which left her empty sex throbbing. Her back arched, her ass went tight as another wave swept her high on a deserted shore.

When she became aware of her surroundings again, Bernardo's tattooed chest was bending over her. He must have been watching her when she came. She was dying for more. She spread her sex wide, buttocks relaxed, thighs akimbo. Bernardo was ready for a repeat performance. The tongue climbed quickly to the zenith and down again, zeroing in on a point near the entrance, at twelve o'clock, the fount of all sensations.

When Veronica returned to earth after another moment of oblivion, Bernardo was standing by the minibar downing a two-shot bottle of whisky. He then lay on the sofa, modestly draped in the bathsheet. He must have put on a condom before entering her. His cock slithered through a mire of her juices, yet Veronica felt nothing. Bernardo, who didn't seem too well hung, came quickly and returned to his bedroom without a word.

Veronica took a mango to bed with her and peeled it with the switchblade Buck knife a colleague had brought her from a trek-king trip in Utah. She always carried it in her suitcase whenever she went on a mission, the way other people might take a Swiss army knife.

Bernardo knocked on her bedroom door.

They chatted while she savoured her fruit.

"Where did you learn that thing with your tongue?" she asked.

"In Manila, when I was a kid, we used to drink sodas sticking our tongue as deep into the glass as it would go. The one who lapped up the last drop was the winner. It was a kind of initiation for us street kids. Tora-tora, the tongue massage, was invented in the Philippines when the Americans were fighting the Japanese for control of the Pacific islands. There are still women in massage parlours who provide it."

He lay down on the bed next to Veronica. She ate a slice of mango, drowsily answered his questions about the camp and fell sound asleep.

When she woke, her cellphone screen read 6 a.m. The shape of Bernardo's body was still visible on the sheet. She leapt out of bed. The pilot's bedroom was empty. The case he'd been carrying was gone too. Not a single personal effect in the bathroom. Veronica ran to her backpack and leafed through her pocketbook: nothing was missing. Her passport was in its side pocket. None of her possessions were gone . . . except the knife. She searched through the fruit basket, under the pillows, even under the bed. She felt muted anger rising. When you came right down to it, the man had taken advantage of her, and then made off with her knife like a thief!

In the lobby, the desk clerk confirmed that the bill had been paid. There was no message for her. Suddenly she wasn't angry any longer. She put her pack in the room where tourists left some of their luggage while they did their sightseeing and took a taxi to the airport.

The Cathay Pacific flight for Manila was posted. She glimpsed the backs of the uniformed crew and caught up with them at their exit gate. When Bernardo turned and saw her, he didn't seem the least surprised.

"Give me back my knife, please," said Veronica.

"I hid it in the sitting room," said Bernardo. "Behind the mini-bar. In my country, a woman with a knife is a dangerous woman."

He went through the gate without looking back. Veronica was pensive as she walked to the taxi rank.

At the Rex, the desk clerk informed her that the suite had just been let to some other foreigners. He offered her a small ground floor room for her remaining night. Veronica settled in with her backpack and collapsed onto a small bed with soiled sheets for a couple of hours of sleep. When she woke, she went up to the penthouse suite and rang the bell. A tall fair-haired man, a German or a Scandinavian, opened the door. The sitting room was a mess, a scene of debauchery. Empty liquor and beer bottles, Thai girls in bikinis, guys as fair as the one now holding Veronica in his arms, calling her "a gift from heaven". Veronica let herself be kissed. The man offered her a drink. While he rummaged in the minibar, Veronica leaned forward and felt behind the fridge. Her fingers came into contact with the closed blade. She extracted the knife from its hiding place and slipped it into her pocket. The man kissed her again and led her to the sofa where she'd had such powerful sex the night before. She let him have his way and thought back on her adventure. Once again she could see the chief pilot's tattoos and his huge red tongue. She pulled away gently and stood up, claiming an urgent appointment.

The next day, in the refugee camp, her predecessor was about to leave for the airport. He was going on vacation. Veronica was here to replace him.

"So how were those two days in Bangkok?" he asked.

"Wonderful! I visited the Royal Palace and saw the reclining Buddha."

"Isn't it extraordinary! Even the Buddha's toes are covered with gold foil!"

Veronica smiled. Children dragged her to a hand-operated merry-go-round. She started to turn the crank: the machinery must have dated back to the sixties, just like that game the street kids played in Manila, sticking their tongues into glasses. She turned the crank as hard as she could, relishing the physical activity. The Thai children spun faster and faster around her.

Lessons Learned

Jade Melisande

"He says he wants you to teach him how to tie a girl up and spank her," Sabine told Julian. Julian was in the middle of a complicated tie, holding Sabine's arms firmly behind her back as he secured them in place. He gave the rope a firm tug and spun her around to face him.

"Down on the floor," he said.

With his hand on her arms to steady her, she sank to her knees obediently, and then, at his direction, further down, so that she was laying flat on her belly with her chest on the floor. For a moment he held her head down, preventing her from looking up: all she could see was the front of his booted feet and the floor beyond. She loved the sensation of being bound, of the strict rope biting into her flesh, of the feel of his hands on her, holding her in place. He moved behind her and bent her legs at the knees to bring them over her back. With a few deft movements, he wrapped her ankles tightly and secured them, heels against her ass, to her wrists. Next he pulled her hair back into the tie, arching her neck and back into a bow and exposing the long line of her throat.

He stepped back and admired his handiwork for a moment, then moved out of her line of sight. A second later she heard the click of his camera as he immortalized his vision on film. She could just see him out of the corner of her eye, stepping in closer and then moving further back, the camera clicking away the whole time. He finally came back into her field of vision to stand in front of her. She strained to look up at him where he loomed over her, but the ropes restricted her movement and finally she just closed her eyes, forcing herself to relax into the tie, and felt herself begin to drift.

"You'd like that, wouldn't you?" she heard him say.

"Hmm?" she murmured, eyes still closed, still in that half-dreaming state that rope so often put her. It'd been so long since either of them had spoken that she'd lost the thread of their earlier conversation.

"This," he said, and delivered two stinging slaps to her backside. She yelped, her eyes popped open and she jerked against the ropes in surprise. Her lover did not favor a subtle approach. "You'd – like – me – to – teach – Rick – how – to – do – this." Each word punctuated by another *smack!* of his hand against her backside. As his hands, small for a man's, but meaty and dense, connected with her bare skin, Sabine felt a familiar warmth spreading through her. As her ass warmed to his touch, so did the rest of her.

Julian paused and ran his hand over the curve of her ass, soothing, or perhaps only admiring, the heat in her tender skin. The hog-tie did not allow for much movement, but what she could do, she did, wriggling her butt at him in what she hoped was a suggestive manner. The suggestion being: "Spank me! Spank me more!"

He seemed to understand her body's unspoken language perfectly. First, though, he reached down and loosened her hair from the tie, allowing her to drop her head to the floor so that she could catch her breath. Then he crouched next to her and started in again.

This time he did start slow, patting her round, full ass from the curve where it met her thighs to the dip in her lower back and down again, striking every inch of flesh that the hog-tie left exposed. He slapped the skin on her thighs and hips and what he could reach of her calves, warming every bit of her. She sighed in pleasure, giving herself over to the feel of his hands on her flesh, to the rhythmic rat-a-tat-tat and the heat it was generating. Without changing the tempo, he began to ratchet up the intensity, smacking her harder, the pats becoming slaps and then deep, steady blows that threatened to take her breath away. She grunted as each strike connected, her body jerking involuntarily, and felt her cunt begin to throb in time to his slaps. Soon she was panting and moaning beneath his hands, writhing helplessly in the ropes on the floor, alternately trying to wriggle away and to expose more of herself to him, to open herself up from within the ropes even as her body flinched, even as she felt the blows reverberating throughout her entire body. She was no longer sure if she wanted him to continue or to stop.

He stopped, and without a word slid a hand between her legs. She gasped as he pushed two fingers against the opening he found there. The folds of her cunt opened easily for him and she felt her wetness drenching his fingers as her body spread wide, like a greedy mouth, to accommodate him. She pushed back against his hand, moaning softly, fighting the ropes that kept her immobilized, wanting so much more.

He laughed and pulled away. Standing abruptly, he looked down at her. She struggled to steady her breathing. He leaned down and put his fingers into her mouth, letting her taste her own excitement.

"Oh yeah," he said, "I think you'd like that a lot." And then, "Set it up."

A week later Sabine perched on a barstool at her favorite wine bar, tapping her foot nervously as she waited for Rick to arrive. She checked her cellphone for what seemed like the tenth time. He was only five minutes late. She sipped her wine and told herself to be still.

A moment later Rick walked in. She waved at him as he came in the door and he hurried over. "Sorry I'm late," he said, giving her a somewhat awkward hug. She hadn't seen him in a month or more, and she looked at him curiously, trying to figure out what was different about him.

He saw her looking at him curiously. "Contacts," he said, pointing to his face.

"Aha!" she said. They both laughed, their initial awkwardness broken.

While he ordered a beer, she discreetly gave him the once-over. A handsome man with blond hair and startlingly green eyes (she wondered how she could have missed their color before, even behind glasses), he towered over her own five feet two by at least a foot. She had never felt intimidated by his size before, however, and wasn't now. She felt comfortable with him, even knowing that within the hour she would most likely be naked and bound before him. Her gaze dropped to his hands, which were large and long-fingered; thinking about what those hands would surely be doing to her soon, Sabine shuddered delicately.

They'd met several months before at, of all things, a book discussion group. The book they'd been discussing had had some oblique references to a D/s relationship, and Sabine had felt compelled to correct some of the group's misconceptions about the lifestyle of which she was a part. She had noticed Rick's rapt attention as she spoke (as well as several others' obvious disapproval) but she had only exchanged pleasantries with him in the months since.

That is, until he had emailed her and asked her to tell him more about what she and Julian did. She had known instinctively that his enquiry wasn't for wank material but that there was a genuine interest there, and they had exchanged several long emails before he had finally asked her if she and Julian would be willing to meet him in person to give him a "lesson."

BDSM 101.

"When did you get interested in spanking?" she asked, when his beer arrived.

He took a sip and looked thoughtful. "To be honest, it was your description of your relationship with Julian that intrigued me," he said. "What he does to you, what you share, is so unique. So powerful. I haven't stopped thinking about it since. And now . . . well, I've met someone. A woman who says she wants me to tie her up and spank her. It's like a dream come true! Except . . ." He spread his hands wide and shrugged helplessly. "I don't know how to do any of the things she wants." He actually blushed as he said it, and Sabine felt her stomach do a little flip-flop. She remembered, now, how quiet and reserved he had always been in their book group and she found it both amazing and endearing that he had worked up the nerve to do this.

She placed a hand on his arm. "We all had to start someplace," she said.

That someplace was Julian's house a little less than an hour later. Sabine stood in the center of the room in only panties and a chemise, while Julian demonstrated different rope techniques on her. First he would tie a limb or other body part, then he would have Rick do the same to her. Rick was a fast learner, and although the setting was not in and of itself erotic, Sabine couldn't help reacting to the feel of his and Julian's hands on her, to the feeling of being a life-size doll, put there only to be moved around like an inanimate object, turned this way and that and maneuvered between them by their hands and the rope. She felt a slickness between her thighs, her pussy ached to be touched, and the room was redolent with the scent of her arousal.

If either man noticed, they weren't letting on.

Occasionally though, as she was spun around or moved from one position to another, her arm or hip, or even, once, her cheek, brushed against a groin, and she felt an erection there, both Julian's and Rick's.

You're not as unaffected as you seem, she thought with a gleeful inner smirk.

Finally Rick asked Julian about the "correct" way to give a good spanking. Sabine listened quietly as Julian went over the basic techniques for a "safe but effective" spanking. As he talked he re-coiled the rope and tossed it aside. Standing off to the side a little, Sabine stifled a yawn. She was much more a hands-on kind of girl. She sighed, shifted from one foot to the other, and wondered if he was ever going to actually *show* Rick how to spank her.

Suddenly, and with no warning, Julian grabbed her by a handful of hair. Sabine let out a startled yip as he dragged her unceremoniously over to the spanking bench that he had set up in the middle of the room. Ignoring her protests, he pushed her roughly down across the bench and pinned her there with one hand.

Sabine gasped as he landed the first blow across her ass, but when she jerked instinctively away he held her down more firmly and said, his voice cracking as sharply as his hand had across her ass, "Don't move, slut!" He continued slapping her ass with his other hand, striking heavy blows on first one cheek and then the other with a ferocity that made her flinch and struggle futilely against his hold on her.

"Julian!" she finally managed between gasps and grunts. "Please!"

He stopped. "What?" he asked. "You want more?"

She swallowed, still panting. Her backside was on fire, and her mind reeled, but the truth of the matter was that yes, she did want more. Yes, she liked a good long, warming-up-to-full-on spanking, but she also loved this too, this balls-out aggression that Julian exhibited at times. But the thing was, she knew that Rick was looking for something else. He'd told her about the talks he'd had with his new love-interest, and it didn't sound to her like this was exactly the sort of spanking she was looking for. Something more . . . civilized . . . was in order.

She looked back over her shoulder at Julian, with Rick standing right next to him, his mouth hanging open. She knew that with her legs spread like this over the spanking bench, both men could see very well how wet she was; how much the spanking had excited her.

"Yes," she said, because there was no sense in lying, "I do want more. But . . ."

She had a sudden inspiration. An inspiration and a conviction that had been growing in her since she had sat next to Rick at the bar and watched him blush when he talked about what it was that he wanted.

Straightening up from the bench, she turned around to face the two men and cocked her head. "I have an idea," she said, rubbing her tender ass. "May I show him something, Julian?"

Julian looked from her over to Rick and back again. "Sure," he said.

Sabine took Rick by the hand. "I like what Julian was doing, don't get me wrong," she said. "But . . . there's another way I like it too. Can I show you?" She tugged on his hand to lead him toward a chair that stood in the corner. He hesitated a moment, then followed her. Eagerly, she thought.

There was a mixture of anticipation and trepidation on his face that she recognized – she knew she'd worn just that expression, had had just that wonderful mix of conflicting feelings, herself. And inside herself she felt something unfurling in her chest, something waking up in answer to the hesitant, excited look in his eyes.

She stepped close to him and slipped her hands inside the waistband of his shorts, caught the bottom of his shirt and tugged it gently out. "I want to feel you," she said, her voice a husky murmur. She stood on tiptoe, allowing her breasts to brush against the springy blond curls on his chest, sliding her hands from his belly to his shoulders as she pulled his shirt up and over his head. Out of the corner of her eye she caught Julian watching them closely.

"This will work so much better if you can feel it against your skin," she said. *And*, she thought, *if I can feel it against your skin.* She was shocked at how much the idea of spanking him was turning her on. She reached for the waistband of his shorts again, noting how his breath caught as her fingernails grazed his belly. She looked up at him as she unbuttoned his fly and felt a tug, low in her belly, as she saw the beginnings of a smile cross his lips. Delighting in his reaction, she pulled his shorts and underwear down. His cock sprang out from the confines of his shorts as though seeking her mouth, but she only chuckled and shook her head. She saw a slight flush creeping over his chest and up his neck, and looked into his beautiful, green, inquisitive eyes, seeking an answer there.

And found it. Never taking her eyes off his, she stepped forward again, drawn toward him as though pulled by a wire thrumming taut between them.

A breath away from him, she stopped and placed a hand against his chest, lightly, so lightly. Face tilted up to his, they stood that way for a moment and simply breathed together. Then, putting a hand on his shoulder, she turned him around. Taking his wrists, she guided them to the arms of the wooden chair so that he was bent slightly at the waist. She trailed a hand down his back and over his haunches.

God, his skin felt so good. Warm and surprisingly silky, with soft, downy hairs that tickled the palms of her hands. A sigh bubbled through her. She heard him take a tremulous breath as though in answer. She stroked a hand across his ass, cupping the roundness of it, admiring its firmness beneath her fingers, before lightly patting first one cheek and then the other. She lay herself against his bent back, stroked the skin of his ass and the backs of his thighs, and just breathed in the strong, male scent of him.

When she felt him relax beneath her, she straightened and began to spank him.

She started with pats, just testing the water, and loved the way her hand sprang back with each blow, the way he sighed and submitted to her, all the tension seeming to drain away from him. His ass was firm and round, but not too hard. Just the way an ass should feel, she thought. She spanked him harder, slow and steady, and harder still, deeper, until she was delivering sharp stinging blows, over and over across both cheeks. His ass began to glow, warm and pink. His breathing quickened, became a panting that matched the timing of her hand. She relished the sting in her palm, the crack of sound that her hand made each time it connected with his backside. She wanted to go deeper yet, but wasn't sure if either of them was ready for that. She paused, taking a breath, then slapped him sharply once more, and felt him flinch. She liked the way his muscles tensed as she drew her hand back again, liked the way he seemed to be holding his breath, liked the way she could see his testicles between his legs, swinging back and forth as he moaned and swayed slightly.

Instead of the smack he was expecting, that she wanted to deliver, she brought her hand down softly and stroked his heated flesh, then, simply, held her hands against his hot, red, tender skin.

She stood that way for a time while their breathing slowed. After a moment she felt Julian's hand on the back of her neck, his lips on the top of her head. She leaned into Rick, slipping her arms around his waist, feeling the heat from his skin against her belly, and Julian leaned against her, wrapping his arms around her just as hers were wrapped around Rick. The three of them stood that way for a long time, while Sabine's and Rick's breathing slowed. Finally, she pulled away and turned Rick around to face her.

The wonder she felt was reflected in his face.

"I think," she said, touching a hand to his cheek and then to his lips, touching the smile that hovered there, "that that concludes Lesson One. For both of us."

The Graffiti Artist

Amanda Earl

On nights when the heat won't let her sleep, Mariah is prone to wandering. When the humidity of the city is so oppressive, the walls are closing in on her, she hefts her bag of spray cans, paints, rags, brushes and turpentine onto her shoulder and climbs down the fire escape to the alley below and into the empty streets, in search of whatever trouble she may find.

It is July. The weather has been unbearable for days. Mariah's night prowling is becoming a habit. She returns to the scene of her most recent crime, a billboard advertisement by a brewery with ties to arms dealers.

Mariah knows her work is ephemeral. But then again, so is life. When her grandmother died, leaving her penniless and alone, she learned that lesson. She used to dream about becoming a real artist with her work displayed in galleries and purchased by collectors.

When she was twenty, after Mariah had spent a couple of years being bored out of her mind in a general arts programme in college, her grandmother paid for her tuition to a local fine art school with an excellent reputation. She believed Mariah had true talent.

Initially Mariah loved being there. She'd always sketched and painted, ever since she was a little girl, but being able to study the greats like Van Gogh, work with live models, talk to the working artists who were her professors and gain their advice, was thrilling.

One instructor in particular, Professor Josef Markoviz, became her mentor. He was the most striking man she had ever seen, with his flashing eyes, dark beard threaded with silver, thick shoulder-length hair, and an Eastern European accent, which caused her body to shiver with desire and her mind to conjure up fantasies. He was originally from Poland, but had left in his late teens to lose himself in the exuberance of art, as he explained to the students on the first day of lectures.

He introduced the class to abstract expressionism, to the energy and beauty of Mark Rothko's work, the geometric precision of Barnett Newman. He strayed off topic to the antics of the New York School, the jazz, the poetry, the dance theatres, the unbridled sex. The latter was a subject not breached until after class with a group of adoring young disciples, of which Mariah was one.

He took the group to openings where they met other artists. They went to bars and discussed art, sex, death and beauty. To start with Mariah was enthralled, but every time she looked into Josef's dark eyes, all she wanted was to be alone with him. Everything about him mesmerized her: the way he held his cup to his lips, the way his fingers brushed over hers when no one was looking. Soon it was clear they both wanted to be away from the crowd and alone together.

At first, she resisted his attempts to see him in private, but that didn't deter Josef. They continued to meet in public at a local bar, a smoky dive that played jazz and served moonshine after hours. They talked all night. He told her stories about Paris, about Modigliani's tragic lover who killed herself after his death, about Jean Cocteau's back-room parties in an opium den. She wished she was a decadent bohemian living in Paris between the wars. She wished she wasn't so conservative, so staid and bourgeois.

Her grandmother wasn't pleased. During Mariah's teenage years, her grandmother had insisted that she not associate with boys throughout school. Warned her to focus on her studies. Mariah's mother had slept with a fellow high school student and ended up pregnant with Mariah. When her lover discovered she was going to have his baby, he left town and never looked back. Mariah's mother worked multiple jobs to take care of her child and died young from exhaustion and overwork. To Mariah's grandmother, it felt like Mariah had forgotten all this and was heading down the same path. They had words over it. But Mariah assured her grandmother that she wasn't going to sleep with Josef.

When she wasn't with the professor, she worked in the studio her grandmother had set up for her, painting rough seas, layering coat after coat of dark blue, green, turquoise, gold, orange, violet, red, silver, brown and black, transfixed by colour. She had stopped going to class entirely, and never spent time with her grandmother. Her grandmother grew increasingly concerned, but there was nothing she could do.

One night Josef finally succeeded in convincing Mariah to go home with him. Perhaps he took advantage of her naivety, or his constant teasing of her bourgeois values had the desired effect. Perhaps Mariah succumbed to the little voice inside her head that told her she was being uptight. After all, none of her art school friends were virgins. Technically neither was she, having lost her virginity through the usual means of self-exploration as a teen; however, she'd never slept with a man. When he offered to take her to his place for a taste of Sliwowica, a Polish drink made from vodka and plums, she acquiesced. He insisted it would set her creative juices flowing and it did. All over him.

Imagine our young Mariah, innocent, wide-eyed and pliant, entering the lair of a sophisticated Svengali. When they kissed for the first time at his bedroom door, he tasted of plums. Mariah let herself fall into his arms. He picked her up and tossed her on his bed.

This was the first time she had ever been alone with a man in his bedroom. Mariah knew she was ignoring every piece of advice her grandmother had given her. Don't drink too much when you're with a man; don't let him get you alone; don't let him touch you . . .

Mariah's brief pang of guilt was dispersed with kisses on her ear, her neck, her lips. Josef took her lower lip between his teeth and sucked it. Mariah's heart caught in her throat. Her pulse raced. She shut her eyes as Josef's hands grasped her breasts through her thin blouse, pinched her nipples until they were stiff and erect beneath the flimsy white garment. He ran his teeth along her neck, sending shivers through her. He tore the thin fabric off to reveal her naked breasts, so firm and untouched. It was thrilling and frightening. Never had a man looked at her like this, with such a burning need in his eyes. Never had her body felt such yearning in response.

She'd craved to be touched like this, to have a man's dark head bent over her nipples, licking, sucking, teasing her tits with his tongue and lips. He probed her mouth with his tongue, grabbed her head and pressed her against him. The muscles of her stomach tightened as her arousal grew.

Josef's hand yanked at the shredded material of her blouse. Remnants of silk fell to the floor. He lifted up her long peasant skirt and put his hands on her cotton-panty-covered mound.

"You're wet, girl," he said, "so wet and ready."

He yanked the panties down and placed his thumb against her aching cunt. She rubbed herself against his hands as he parted her lower lips and found her clit. The first man to touch her nipples and stroke them into erectness, to put his hands on her body, her aching cunt. She'd wanted this for so long.

Mariah froze. She tensed up as she felt a finger pushing into her.

"Sssh, little one, it'll be all right."

He slid his hot, trembling hands along her thighs. Spread them wide, dipped his head down and pressed his lips against the soft skin of her naked cunt. Mariah grew more aroused, rocked against his face, took more of the finger inside her.

"That's right, baby, open up for me, let me in."

She put her hand on his head and pushed it toward her body, thrilling at the feel of his cool lips against her cunt. He licked along her labia, put his tongue against her clit and held it there. Mariah writhed and moaned.

"Keep still, let me fuck you," he said.

She tried not to move. The tension in her body mounted, the feeling of his tongue on her cunt made her greedy, she never wanted it to end. The pressure built. She felt taut, like a wire being pulled tighter and tighter. His fingers thrummed her clit. She couldn't hold it any more. She had to let go. Mariah lifted her hips and cried out as the orgasm coursed through her body. For one brief moment she was all cunt, that part of her body was all she felt. So good, so right. Josef had licked her to orgasm, her first orgasm with a man. Better than any she'd ever had on her own.

Josef rose from the bed, his lips wet with her juices. He removed his clothing. For the first time, Mariah saw his naked cock, strong and thick. She wanted a taste, so she rose up on her elbows, but he pushed her back.

She lay back on the bed, wide-eyed and naked, her legs parted, wanting to please him. She looked up at him. Her legs trembled as he parted them roughly and lowered himself onto her body.

She felt the weight of a man's body on hers for the first time. Warm, unyielding and pressing her down into the mattress. She was afraid, but she wanted this.

He grabbed a condom from the nightstand by the bed. A flash of how many women he'd likely had on this bed went through Mariah's mind, but she shook it away and focused on the aroused man above her.

His eyes were closed, he shoved his cock inside her quickly and humped into her. She cried out. He was so brutal she thought she'd break in two. The pain caused her to bear down on his cock. He groaned as he came.

After he climaxed, he wasn't interested in more sex; he fell asleep and soon began to snore into his pillow. Mariah was shocked. She thought he'd want to touch her more, to lick and caress her, give her another orgasm, take her more gently. This wasn't what she'd imagined when she read romance novels as a teen.

The fireplace was full of ashes. The dull varnish of the black cherry wood of the four poster bed looked like it hadn't been polished in ages. The room stank of sweat and semen. The ashtray on the nightstand was full of cigar butts. The cold aftermath of reality dulled Mariah's bright eyes. She looked down at the snoring professor and saw a washed-out has-been, a lousy lover, a desperate man, old enough to be her father. She was disgusted with herself.

She grabbed one of his T-shirts from the pile of laundry on the floor, since her blouse had been ruined, quickly rinsed off in the bathroom, straightened up and left.

She chided herself for being such a fool. A cliché. She couldn't believe that was all there was to it. Everybody had talked about losing virginity as a remarkable act, and the pain of it certainly was remarkable, but not the least bit fulfilling. It wasn't losing her virginity that had set Mariah on fire, it was the way his mouth and hands had felt on her skin, on her lips, on her clit. The desire in his eyes before he fucked her, the pent-up feeling of wanting him for so long.

She went back to attending classes but never returned to Josef's bed again, despite his pleas. Instead she explored her desires further with other men, satisfied her appetite with students her own age.

After leaving art school, she continued to paint, but when her grandmother died, so did her ambition to have work shown in galleries. She knew her grandmother would have been disappointed, but Josef and his pretentious peers had demonstrated to her that it was all bullshit. The real reason those guys wanted young ingénues was to get into their pants.

Mariah was heartbroken. She felt guilty for not spending any time with her dear grandmother, for wasting time with the lascivious Josef instead of devoting her attention to her classes.

After selling her grandmother's treasured art collection, she had some money but it didn't last long. All that her grandmother loved was so easily traded for a pittance. She took only what she could carry on her back in a large backpack, a big duffel bag and a suitcase of her grandmother's and found shelter wherever she could, rooming houses, the occasional couch of a well-meaning stranger, and occasionally an abandoned house.

To paint over this particular beer ad, overflowing with hulky masculinity and testosterone, Mariah sketches a naked woman standing in the middle of lush greenery, breasts and sex covered by leaves, the portrait inspired by Gaugin's Tahiti primitive, exotic abstractions. Just looking at it makes Mariah feel cooler, more at ease. The woman's eyes are daring, the kind of fuck-you look Mariah often sees in her own eyes when she looks in the mirror.

Mariah paints self-portraits on office walls and billboards. Illegal and unsanctioned by the authorities. There'd even been a brief write-up about graffiti in the city and her work was mentioned. No name given of course. She'd never been caught by the police.

She's always on the move. She squats in various abandoned houses, often having to leave due to their demolition. She likes this way of life, but it means she doesn't keep many friends, or lovers.

Of course there are still men, from time to time. A desirable and insatiable young woman like Mariah with her caramel-coloured skin, soft brown hair and penetrating black eyes can have men anytime she wants. And she often wants.

Most of the time she tries not to draw attention to herself. Wears thick plaid shirts, ball caps, men's baggy cargo pants. She travels incognito.

The art on the billboard is still intact. She makes a few touch-ups, packs up and climbs back down. That's when she feels a hand on her back. Her heart hammers hard against her chest. She ries to run, but the guy has her. Damn, it's some security guard. She stomps on his foot and makes a run for it.

There are several places she can hide. The rent-a-cop doesn't make enough money to bother giving chase. He'll likely call the police, who will file a report. They're too busy with drug busts and domestic violence cases to allocate any resources to chasing down graffiti artists and taggers, but if they catch her red-handed, she's doomed. Or at least she'll be fined and she has no money.

Once she loses the security guard, she heads over to an all-night diner where her old friend Pedro, the line cook, works early mornings. She opens the kitchen door, and he hands her a plate of fried mashed potatoes and eggs with salsa. She grabs some milk from the refrigerator, pours herself a big glass, and sits as far away from the grill as she can in the hot, greasy kitchen. They don't talk. She eats; he cooks. They've known each other for years. He's one of the rare people who Mariah keeps in her life. He never makes a pass at her, is excited by her graffiti and never judges the way she lives her life.

Once her belly's full, she burps and Pedro lets out a throaty guffaw.

"You're not exactly refined, are you, babe?"

She sticks out her tongue at him and wipes the milk off her upper lip.

"Some dude in a suit asked about you last night, Mariah."

He sits down in the chair opposite her. There aren't many orders this early in the morning, thankfully. He can rest his feet.

Mariah wipes the salsa off her mouth and looks up at him in alarm. "What man?"

"Don't worry. He didn't know your name, and I told him nada, just that sometimes you eat here. He wanted to talk about your graffiti. Gave me a card to give to you."

Mariah reads the card. "Alessandro Aleguera," it reads, but there's nothing other than an email and telephone number. Seems suspicious to her. She crumples it up.

"Could be a trick, the beer company or cops or something."

"Relax, hon, if anybody wanted to have you arrested, you'd probably be in jail already. He seemed interested in your art, your training, that kind of shit."

Mariah drinks the rest of her milk in silence while Pedro cooks up a batch of grilled cheese sandwiches for some construction workers.

Amanda Earl

As she walks back to the current squat passed on to her when a fellow street artist moved out, she thinks about the suited guy hounding her in the diner. Wonders if it's time she moves again, maybe to another city this time. She's got too many memories here though, of her grandmother and their life together. In the back of her mind, there's this flicker of a memory, more like a memoryette, of a woman singing to her, rocking her in the cradle. Her mother. She'll take gladioli to her grave again soon. Her grandmother said it was her mother's favourite flower, the tall stalks with their bright bursts of colour. Her mother loved colour. Mariah inherited that love.

Another night of restlessness drives Mariah back to the streets at dawn. She's out earlier than the garbage collectors and the street cleaners. She loves having the city to herself, calling it her own. It's just barely light enough to paint, but Mariah has good eyesight and is used to working in the wee small hours.

On a chain supermarket wall, she's started a new painting in the style of one of Georgia O'Keeffe's erotic flowers. Inside the store they sell dying and neglected plants which haven't seen sunshine or been tended by a loving hand in their lives. This orchid will have a brief life, but it will be full of sunshine. She's concentrating hard on her work. For Mariah, painting is like caressing a body, stroking the blank canvas into an ecstasy of colour, bringing out its beauty by cherishing it . She's so absorbed by what she's doing she doesn't notice the man standing across the street and smoking as the sun finally rises, as he watches the splendour of her work take shape before his eyes.

Alessandro Aleguera is overjoyed. He's finally found her, the graffiti artist responsible for all the bold and compelling outsider art he's been seeing around the city since he moved there to curate the local art gallery a few months ago. She's incredible. She's not a typical graffiti artist, she's trained, influenced by the great masters, driven by passion. She's using acrylic paint in addition to the usual aerosol spray cans and markers.

He wonders how she can wear such thick clothing in the heat? She must be so dedicated she doesn't even notice. She leans down to pick up a rag and he manages to discern a fine, round bottom in the ragged cargo pants. His cock stirs.

"*Che sei bella da morire,*" an old Italian pop song goes through his head, "You're so beautiful, I might die." He doesn't want to make her skittish again. Since he left his card, he hasn't heard a peep out of her or seen any more of her work. This is a breakthrough. She's going to have to return to finish the piece. He'll take his time, not rush her. It's her art he's interested in, or perhaps more than just her art.

He comes back for the next few days, but she doesn't show up. He wonders what's happened to her. Why is this woman so damned elusive?

Mariah scores a gig teaching teens to make art and even makes a bit of money. Is too tired at the end of the day to return to the orchid, her work-in-progress. She finds it rewarding to spend time with the kids at the local community centre, with a budget for paint and craft paper. She relates to their shyness and reticence to show their attempts, but she works right along beside them and establishes a great camaraderie. Once they are comfortable, the teens exhibit unbridled creativity. Her supervisor is so impressed with their paintings he suggests they have a show and contacts the local art gallery. The curator is receptive.

The night of the opening, Mariah's nervous. At the last minute, she's included a painting of hers. She doesn't know why. She leaves it unsigned. She doesn't own fancy clothes to wear to the opening, but she's kept just a few of her grandmother's things. Inside her grandmother's suitcase is a lacy yellow chiffon sleeveless dress with a flower on one of the shoulders and some shoes. She feels like Cinderella. The dress and shoes fit perfectly, as if they were made for her. It dawns on her that maybe the dress and shoes belonged to her mother or maybe her grandmother. They're vintage, they'd say today. Evocative of the Roaring Twenties.

She wonders if the dress is too elaborate, too fancy for the opening. But it feels like she's wearing a costume. Like the dress of one of the daring women in Paris, off to meet Picasso or Dali at a ball. She's in a decadent and dreamy state when she arrives at the gallery. The place is packed with parents, friends and family of the teens.

She stands off to one side as she watches a suited dark-haired man appraising her painting. He lingers for a long time. Her supervisor whispers in his ear and he looks around. She realizes he's looking for her, the artist. She takes a deep breath and walks towards him.

He smiles and takes her hand. "I know you," he says.

Mariah is confused. Wonders if it's some cheesy pick-up line.

She blushes and turns to go, but he holds on to her hand. She feels a spark of desire as she looks into his eyes, which are gazing into hers with a burning intensity.

"I've seen your work, all around the city, on store walls, billboards, in back alleys."

Mariah doesn't know what to say. Has this guy been stalking her? Is he going to report her to the police?

Her supervisor introduces the two and wisely leaves them alone. Mariah can't believe this guy is the curator of the gallery. He seems too young and even though he's wearing a suit, he has kind eyes, doesn't seem like some boring business type at all.

"Look, I have to stay until we close tonight, but can we meet for coffee so I can talk to you more about your art? It's too good not to share with the world, Mariah."

Mariah trembles a bit. Remembers Josef and how he flattered her to get her to sleep with him.

"Uh, thanks. Maybe some other time. I have to go now," she says and rushes away.

Alessandro doesn't let her get far. He rushes out the door, thinking to hell with the opening.

Mariah can't run very fast in the high-heeled shoes she's wearing. It doesn't take too long for him to catch up.

He doesn't think, he just steps up to her and kisses her.

She slaps him, hard. "What the hell do you think you're doing you asshole. Get your hands off me."

"God, I'm sorry, Mariah, I'm so sorry. I'm just so damn thrilled by you, have been for months. It's your work, so erotic, so unleashed . . . but you're a difficult woman to get hold of. Why are you so goddamn . . . ? Hell, I'm babbling. Can we please just go grab some coffee and talk for five minutes?"

Mariah starts to laugh. She has been skittish, it's true. Sitting for a few minutes with this guy in a café isn't going to kill her. Clearly he's not going to have her arrested. He calls his associate on his cell, lets him know he's had to leave the show early and asks him to put away the crackers and cheese, show the guests out and stack the wine crates in the fridge.

"Now we have all the time in the world," he says to Mariah, as he turns to her.

A spark. She feels it. Has this urge to kiss him, but resists.

They find a café that isn't crowded.

"Do you want a coffee?" he asks.

She twirls her hair in her fingers and notices the way his eyes follow adoringly. She puts her hands on the table and smiles. "I don't really like coffee."

They both laugh.

"They make a great chai here; shall I get us a pot?"

She nods. He takes off his jacket and lays it on the chair. She studies him while he's at the cash. Tall, well built, strong shoulders and muscular legs. She remembers the feel of his hand in hers, his fingers were lightly calloused, not smooth like some desk jockey. She runs her fingers over the lapels of his jacket, which gives off a subtle scent of wood smoke with a hint of musk. Mariah wonders what it might be like to leave his bed, the scent of that musk and wood smoke still on her body. She imagines caressing his naked back. She licks her lips.

"Hi," Alessandro says as he returns to the table, the tea spilling as he puts the pot down. "Oh, damn, sorry," he says, his voice breaking.

Mariah realizes she's flustered him. She blushes and they both laugh. It's awkward but a good kind of awkward. They talk for ages. It turns out he usually spends his summers at a kids' camp as a counsellor and has taken over the gallery for a change of scene. He used to paint, but gave it up, took a business management course, got bored, has been kind of lost ever since but is enjoying this stint at the gallery.

"Especially now," he says.

She winks at him. Before they know it, the hours have passed and the café manager asks them to leave.

"We're probably the only art nerds in town who manage to shut down a café and not a bar," he says, causing her to laugh again.

Mariah's enjoying herself so much, she doesn't want the night to end. She surprises herself by inviting him back to her place to see more of her work.

"I hope you're spry," she says, and shimmies up the fire escape to her current room in an abandoned old house. He follows right behind her.

"Haven't done that for years," he says, but he's not out of breath.

"The place is chaotic, I'm afraid . . . it's just temporary . . . I'm moving out soon."

Mariah holds her breath while Alessandro gets his bearings He doesn't seem to notice all the junk piled up on the floor or the hotplate in the corner. He makes a beeline for the unrolled canvas stretched out on the mattress with its bright blue triangles, star-shaped silvers, flecks of gold.

"I've been working on some abstracts since I started working with the teenagers," Mariah says.

"It's gorgeous. There's a melancholy tone to it. I love it Mariah."

His eyes hold hers for a moment. She wants to lose herself in them.

Alessandro smiles at her. "Do you have more?"

Mariah gulps. Realizes she was standing there completely still gazing into his eyes. "Sorry," she says and blushes.

Her hands tremble as she opens her duffel bag. She's never shown this work to anyone. She pulls out a series of small paint-ings.

"These are just roughed-in pieces, ideas for graffiti. I can't make anything big because I don't stay in one place long enough . . ." Her voice trails off as he sits on the mattress and looks at the art.

"These are really fine, Mariah. You've got a keen eye for detail."

He asks her a question about the work, and she sits down on the bed near him to answer. Their legs touch.

She examines his face. Thinks he's a work of art himself, those long eyelashes, the dimple in his chin, the warm brown eyes. She turns towards him and they kiss, a long, lingering kiss.

He gets up and gently takes the art off the mattress and asks her where to put it. She walks over to the duffel bag and he passes the paintings to her. Their hands touch. The art falls to the floor as they embrace. His body feels hot against hers. She kisses his lips, his chin, his Adam's apple. He removes his jacket and lets it fall. She undoes the buttons of his shirt and kisses his chest. His fingers trail along her shoulder, he lifts up a curl and twirls it.

"I've wanted to do that since I saw you playing with your hair in the café," he says. He kisses the side of her neck. "You have beautiful skin, it glows."

He kisses her naked shoulders, slides his hands over her shoul-der blades and down her back, pressing her against him. She feels his erection through their clothes and moans.

She reaches for his belt buckle. He takes her hand away, presses it against his lips, kisses each finger and down her arm, then down the other arm. He turns her around and unhooks the clasp at the top of her dress, caresses the nape of her neck, and slides the zipper all the way down. He kneels and kisses the base of her spine.

Mariah feels warm and languid. This man is in no hurry. He takes her hand and she steps out of the dress. The floor is covered in yellow lace. They step around it. She removes her bra and panties.

Mariah is naked except for the black high heels.

"You're a vision. Just like in those self-portraits you've made, which drove me crazy, you know. Portraits of sexy little Mariah scattered all over the city in the nude but impossible to find. I should punish you."

Mariah grimaces, but he winks. Takes a nipple between his fingers and caresses it gently, languidly until it is a hard, puckered peak of desire. He bends down to kiss it while rolling the other nipple between his thumb and index finger.

He touches her as if she's made of marble. Light feather kisses that tease her gently into arousal. When she can't stand the wait any longer, she asks him to remove his pants.

He gives her a wink. "Sit down on the bed, *cara mia*."

Mariah sits as Alessandro does a sexy striptease before her eyes. He unbuttons his belt, undoes the button on his pants, stands there with his hand at the zipper.

"Don't make me beg," Mariah says. He smiles at her and lowers the zipper millimetre by infinitesimal millimetre. A long shiver of desire runs through her body. She wants this man. She moves closer to the edge of the bed. She needs to taste him.

Alessandro lets his pants fall to the floor. Beneath his briefs there's a significant bulge. Mariah wants it. She wants to feel that cock inside her.

He pulls the briefs off one hip and then the other, turns to show her his sexy ass. It's tight. She'd love to lick it. The briefs fall to the floor. He walks towards her. She can no longer resist and presses her face against his erect cock, licks the underside of his balls, along the shaft, around the rim, then takes the cock into her mouth.

Alessandro groans as she sucks. He places his hand on her cheeks, strokes the spot where his cock bulges. Mariah feels desire in every part of her body from her cunt to her breasts to the base of her spine.

"I want you," he whispers.

She pulls out a condom from beneath the mattress and slides it down onto his hard cock. He lies on the bed and she climbs on top of him, slowly lowering herself down, hovering above his cock.

"Now it's your turn to wait," she says.

"You're an evil woman," Alessandro says, and they both smile then groan as he pulls her close and enters her.

They kiss and keep kissing as they writhe against one another, trying to get more of his cock inside her, trying to go as deep as possible. They hold hands while they fuck. She watches his eyes darken, his pupils widening.

There's more to this than a fuck and they both know it, can feel it in the beating of their hearts, which is in sync, the way they keep holding hands after they orgasm, their legs curled around one another. The way their breath slows down and they fall asleep in each other's arms.

Mariah wakes up at dawn, Alessandro still in her bed, lightly snoring. He's so beautiful, like an angel. She doesn't want to wake up, but she needs to paint. She puts on some clothes and, quiet as she can, climbs down the fire escape.

He finds her later by her orchid and hands her a cup of chai. She doesn't run away.

You Belong to Me

C. Sanchez-Garcia

When he can breathe again he looks up into the torrent of freezing rain pouring in through the open skylight. The converted mortuary table suspended high above in the leaping lightning of the sky sways dangerously in the gale, threatening to tip over on one end. One of the high cabled kites has caught fire and is falling like a meteor.

It was this last bolt that had struck close enough to shake the stone walls, rattle and crack the thick glass jars of chemicals and preserved homunculi, and raise erect the coarse hairs of his immense arms. The thunder crash was close enough to blot out his cold objectivity and fill him with an animal urge to cower and hide.

He takes up a dry wooden rod and cautiously bats down the circuit breaker lever on the wall. The lights die and glow like altar candles. Leaning all his great weight against the heavy chain hanging from the suspended block and tackle, he curses for it to move but it refuses. Grunting, hunched, he gives the chain a violent shake that sends waves of rage to the sky. Now wrapping the chain around his huge shoulders, bowing his head, he throws himself hard against it until it surrenders to his will. The table spins halfway around in the high wind as the pulley catches and the assembly begins to descend.

It occurs to him, as he labors at the chain, that he is not prepared for what to do if he succeeds. He'd been practiced only in steeling himself against disappointment but not how to endure hope.

Catching a lightning storm with any reliability in the spring or summer when they abounded was in itself almost impossible. The indifferent things of nature performed when they would; unlike the things of man they could not be stolen or bullied while his labor dissolved into rot.

In the beginning he had studied the mysteries of his own body and despaired of the depth of the difficulties ahead of him. The single legacy his god had passed on to him here, in this very place, was his savage birth on the same table dangling above. As he grew to appreciate this accomplishment first hand he began to develop a grudging respect that was almost enough to give him a heart to forgive his creator for the crime of bringing him into this world. But he could not.

There was only a very short window between the winter's murderous but preserving cold and the spring's life-giving storms where he could hastily cut, cauterize, and stitch each muscle and vein before they turned sour and stinking. Each storm season he'd grimly pushed his harvest of foraged human flesh into the boiling clouds. Always the cruel lightning refused the ghoulish bundles of tailored carcasses he offered to it. Until tonight.

The table suspended at a crazy angle on its chains at last rattles into view, but there are pillars of smoke rising from the bandaged body there. Forcing himself to look away, swallowing his panic, he forces himself to think only of pulling the chains of the tackle with tender patience until he hears the rails of the table slop down into the swamp of mud. For two minutes he can't bring himself to raise his eyes from his shoes.

"She's roasted."

Liberated from the throes of hope, he sullenly turns and goes to the hulk mired in the mud. But the rain-soaked band-aged tape is uncharred and the clean clouds that rise have the cheerful lightness of new birth. This is only steam. Without touching the body he unfastens the half-dozen mule chains that hold it in place. The hot steel lightning-kissed links sizzle his fingers. He pushes the table into a dry place and leaves it only long enough to light torches. The storm is sailing far away now, stars are out and the workroom is silent but for the beating of his heart.

He holds his breath. He clenches his fists. Under the soft patter of the receding rain – the sound of gentle wheezing. There.

Frantically fumbling through a toolbox he finds the greasy meat shears when he stabs his finger on them in the dark. At the table he watches the rumpled bandages gently rise and fall, rise and fall. Shaking like a terrified bridegroom, he has no idea where to begin.

*   *   *

Once upon a time, not so long after he had been driven by his remorseful maker from the cells and smashed laboratory of the abandoned monastery where he had been given life, the giant patchwork puzzle man had sought out people and been hounded away until he fled from them all, finally defeated.

Hiding in the mountains, he had come across a small house of stone and straw in which a woman lived alone. He first saw her as she went to her chicken coop with a basket, walking with one hand held out. She was craggy faced and middle-aged, with shining black hair shot with thick shocks of silver grey, like a skunk. He was about to break in and rob her of food but a young man and woman came to visit her just then, carrying a baby. The baby fascinated him. His presence was unknown to them; he could have simply burst in and massacred them, but seeing the baby even from a distance stopped him. He had the heart of an orphan and could not bear to make an orphan of another.

At night when the windows glowed, he listened outside at the glass with the senses his maker had made better than human. It was the only time he felt afraid and monstrous. As he watched her waving hands, and the way she paced the room, and the way she lived in the indifferent dark after the family left, he understood she was blind.

During the time her family stayed with her he learned language by listening to their endless arguments, which seemed to rouse violent memories of another life like shards of a broken mirror. He mouthed her angry words and speech began to awaken in his tongue. Flocks of words and ideas came back to him in a fury, not learned but rediscovered. He came to understand that the son had left her before, rejected her, and now had returned, demanding that she should move in with him and his family and submit herself to his authority. It wasn't safe out here alone, it wasn't decent, and how people talked of him, leaving his sightless mother to fumble for herself among the trees and ravenous wild beasts. It was hurting his business trade. It was only right for her son to look after her in her old age.

But she wanted no husband or son to rule over her, and most of the time no company at all. She was done with all men. Now that she had been tossed out alone, she had learned solitude. She was as confident and self-contained as a wasp. Listening with his ear at the window glass, the patchwork man understood about solitude. He understood about being done with all men. He adored her strength, her ferocity.

He slept in the outhouse and ate his foraged meals there, because it was out of the rain, and the closed walls gave him a sense of how it would be to have a home. He imagined life in the outhouse with the blind woman and a child, both sitting on his knees snug in the small drafty space with the spiders that lived under the seat holes. When caught by surprise, hearing her approach, he would hide in the pool below under the seat, where he lurked as she shat on his head.

He progressed from her outhouse to her bed in stages.

Please, please.

The shears snag on the bandages until he sees he's stabbing at them in his panic and fever. At last he sets them down, turns his back to the table and sits on it.

Gentle now, gentle. This moment will never come again, because if I fail this time my soul will die. I can wait a little. This moment is mine. This creation is mine. Something new. Something defiant. My raised fist against God.

He listens to the rhythm of the steady breathing from behind and it soothes him. Calmer now, he takes up the shears again and begins cutting. First up the arms because it's the easiest and straightest, the simplest place to begin. As the bandages drop away the flesh shows through and the sight of it makes him dizzy.

Is this how he felt when he saw me? When he saw me for the first time did he feel this excruciating thrill? How did we ever learn to hate each other so terribly?

The skin showing under the bandages looks different than before, pinker, but it's so hard to tell by the torchlight which makes everything pink. His runs his finger along the hot skin and it feels tough and resilient. It feels like his. He snips his way up the bandages above the elbow, revealing thick and complex sutures he'd made only the day before from long study of the illustrated notebooks; the scarred map lines of his own body, and the endless apprenticeship of stitching the battalions of bodies that had all gone bad and been thrown in a reeking pit where animals came at night to feed. He snips across the bandages of the chest and breasts. The two breasts are mismatched, one larger, one smaller because they come from different women.

From her collarbones down between her breasts she has been burned. Her skin bears a winding feather of bright bleeding crimson, with delicate branchings as if a daguerreotype of the bolt that had given birth to her had been cruelly branded into her skin, a permanent locket image of her cloud mother. He has the same special burn covering his own heart like the mark of Cain, the secret sign of their kind, the lightning children, born not of woman but of some inferior storm goddess.

He snips up the shoulders, the neck, the face. When he draws the bandages away the amazed windows of her soul are looking at him with wonder. The gusting torches make her skin glow so that it seems to him she's the only source of light.

He touches a hand to her cheek and feels her temperature. Her eyes are rolling wildly in her head and finally settle again on his face. Her spectral hand trailing bandages, reaches up and caresses the long faded mountain range of scars that cross his troubled forehead and travel behind his ears and down his neck where a man he had left for dead had once sewn his face onto his skull in this very room. Her fingers smelling of scorched roses and of the sky play over his lips and he kisses them. He permits his heart to heave and fall in love.

The blind woman became gradually aware of him as a malodorous curve in space at the edge of her intuition. She felt his presence come and go leaving the scent of old shit and piss in the air like a nasty comet tail but he would never answer her shouts. Then the presents began. Strangled rabbits and throttled pheasants left on the doorstep for her to stumble over. Then forest fruit and pine nuts. Then he himself when he was caught kneeling in the act of leaving wild flowers for her. She opened the door suddenly, grabbed him by the top of his hair and yelled "Who the shit are you?"

Because he wouldn't answer and remained sensibly on his knees she invited him inside. He crouched by the fire like a whipped dog, and she sensed in the air beyond his fecal stench and beyond the shadow of a doubt that he was a harmless, maybe not very bright man, who needed a friend. She undressed him and made him a hot bath, the very first of his life. With lye soap and a kitchen brush she stripped layers of grime and filth from his strange carcass. He allowed her to help herself to the exploration of his body as she scrubbed him.

Her hands told her he was a huge man, with broad, powerful shoulders and large warm hands. His brows were thick and she imagined what his eyes might look like, because she had only become blind after she'd been stricken with measles. His waist was narrow and his belly hard and flat. But most mysterious were the coarse stitches that covered his huge male carcass, as if he had been tailored from rags.

He didn't know how to respond to her curious maternal hands as they scoured his hide. Three times she changed the bath water and pushed him back in. She washed his feet and thighs and when she reached to wash his balls she found his penis standing up as thick and hard as a rolling pin. She felt him squirm and heard him sigh deeply as she soaped it. She set down the soap and caressed him there playfully until his stentorian breathing stopped suddenly and he bent over laughing haw-haw-haw and she felt his penis pulse languorously inside her fist like a mighty thrumming heartbeat, and a warm thickness spread over her wrist.

When he laid his head on her shoulder and abjectly wept she realized she was holding the fine and useful phallus of the loneliest being in the world.

His fierce tears on her neck sent a dull sagacious pain to that exact spot between her legs which had gone silent, now awakened ferociously to clamor for that pain and know herself as a woman again. She felt a great heat radiating from her hips and he seemed to sense it too. She dropped her clothes on the floor and joined him in the tub.

Like a mammoth doll with the beautiful breath of a boy and the musk of a mountain goat, he proved to be perfectly malleable and ignorant and eminently trainable to make love correctly from a woman's view. She wrapped herself in his solitude and maleness until his tumescence filled her with infinite possibilities. He surrendered to her caresses utterly as she determined his thorough seduction and domestication.

She burned his clothes, aired out the house and made him a hot dinner served with corn whisky which they ate together in the nude. It was the first time he had experienced happiness. The mysterious feeling frightened him. He didn't know what to do. He felt he wanted desperately to touch her with tenderness but didn't know how, never having been tenderly touched himself. He sat mutely watching her gnaw a turnip, with the moist eyes of a grateful animal.

She gave him the first male name that came to mind, "Jonah", because he had washed up on her doorstep smelling as though he had been vomited out by a whale. She fed him, owned him, loved him and led him docilely to her bed to commence the exertions of his education.

Having shed her clothes to share his bath she never felt the need for them again. They wandered through the house and the forest as boldly naked as frogs. The cool air and his caresses revived her youth. His towering nudity and infinite vigor made him available to her as often in a day as she desired him. They lived like cats as the summer drifted by. Soon the days shortened and chilled. She began sewing him suits of clothes to stay warm outside where she couldn't warm him with her impatient body.

Her ultimate conquest of him was the patient releasing of the undertow of pain that caring for her so terribly invoked in him. Their first tentative couplings revealed to her his fear of happiness, so that she laid siege to him all the more violently with her body, coaxing his heart open, not by sex alone which he joined in easily, but by the wild darkness of her passion which convinced him he would be permitted at long last to feel joy.

In his eyes she was not a blind ageing woman. He wanted to protect her and maybe shut her away so that no man would suspect that he alone possessed the most beautiful woman in all the world.

He brushes his face against hers and breathes the ripe storm scent of her hair. After a moment he whispers in her ear, "Can you speak yet?" Her chest wheezes and he feels her throat struggle.

He looks away, worried, and sighs. His thoughts run over the interior work he crafted on her throat and yes, he's sure it's all been done right. But there was no way to know until now. Her lips move and sounds come out, but no words. He can't help himself, he has to touch her. There is no question of waiting. He is starving to caress her everywhere. He passes his hand over her cheek and touches her ear with his fingertips. The ears are not on the same level. That will have to be adjusted sometime when she's gotten her strength.

"Soon you'll remember how to speak," he says. "It won't take long. Don't worry; I can fix anything that doesn't work. Once you hear voices it all comes back very quickly, you'll see. I'll talk to

you and read books to you and sing to you. I'll whisper in your
ear how beautiful you are."

Her eyes fix on his face and he holds his breath, waiting to see
if she screams and turns away. She only goes on watching him
and she's not afraid. There is a movement on the other end of the
table and he sees she's wiggling her toes under the bandages. Her
hair is still covered by bandage tape. Without the shears, he draws
it gently back so he can see all of her. There are bright shocks of
hair like rivers of silver that run back from her temples where the
magnetic conductor plates had been placed.

"You look so much like her," he whispers.

On an early winter evening with snow falling, and the night
clouds glowing from a hidden light, she is sewing him a warm
pair of moleskin trousers, sitting naked on a blanket by the fire, in
pinkly girlish health since his arrival in her life.

She feels him as an insect would, creeping up silently behind
her; the stealthy descent of his hot iron hands, which tickle the air,
close around her neck – and squeeze.

"Oh, you," she whispers and lowers her sewing, the needle
impaled in the cloth in mid-stroke.

The fingers, which have snapped the heads off grey wolves to
save her, pick up soft handfuls of her neck and shoulders, knead
them delicately and let them fall, pick them up, let them fall, as
though hypnotizing her with his gentle rhythm. He is secretly
searching her shoulders to see if the buds of angel wings have
begun to sprout. She leans forward a little, offering her back to
rub. He wraps his arms around her shoulders and bear hugs her
carefully, holding her snug with his lips at her ear. "Are you my
woman?" he whispers into her hair.

She rocks a little in his huge arms.

He releases her and brings his hands back to her shoulders and
kneads and squeezes carefully, her neck, her shoulders, moving a
little down her back, gentling her baby bird bones in his hands.
Her odd litany of ceremonies which have invented themselves
from coupling after coupling draw him to her. He feels her
tension melting under his firm caresses like icicles. She lifts her
elbows a little and he passes his hands under her arms, circles her
ribs until he finds her large, downward-looking pear-shaped
breasts. He hefts them in his palms and warms them, begins
moving his hands lightly back and forth under them, letting their

weight rest against his moving palms, touching her chest, stroking forward towards her nipples, retreating and stroking, petting
her breasts from below, breathing her, taking her into himself. If
he strokes her breasts just right, the scar ridges of his sewn wrists
will make an intolerable tickling pressure behind her big red
nipples.

He palms her smooth under-breasts until he feels her start to
wiggle with cat-heat, lifting her ass as if crouching for him. A
relaxing rhythm on tired muscles, shoulders and spine, mesmer-
izing her until he feels her start to sag. His feather-light caresses
under her breasts blow up her tickling, tormenting fires until he
feels her struggling to push her nipples into his hands for relief;
he denies her and goes back to the gentling massage.

"Are you my woman?"

Her nipples are pointed and hard now the way he wants them.
Between thumbs and fingers a tenacious pinch, held hard, pressed
tight for a few seconds and he releases her with a gasp. All these
things she has taught him perfectly.

"Say it."

He draws her body back, holding her against his chest, rocking
her and taking the moment in silent space to cherish.

She reaches her hand up into his hair.

"You have to say it."

He lifts her arm, dips down his head and buries his nose in her
ripe armpit. She has not washed for a day and he holds his nose
in the oily onion dampness breathing her in, filling his senses with
her. The flavors of her kisses, the strong odors of her body
torment his rapacious senses beyond endurance. It takes an effort
not to crush her bones. She has taught him how to touch a woman
by placing baby chicks in his hands.

He licks and nuzzles her armpit. His lips move across her chest
like a nibbling pair of caterpillars to the swell of her right breast.
He does not kiss her breast, but lets his lips linger just at the edge
of her skin, so she can barely feel him but without receiving him.
He hovers and lightly licks the sweat from her skin. He brushes
his lips in a circle over her breast. She tries to raise her nipple to
his mouth but he eludes her. He moves instead to run his tongue
over the depression at the base of her throat, licking it like a bowl.

It is the space between their skins, the hair skin space of expectation and anticipation of touch that he dwells in like an amorous
ghost between worlds, moving his hands as lightly as butterflies

over her, exploring hands, gentling, warming, caressing and lingering. He reaches both his hands together under her little pot belly and hefts it. "This is mine," he says, gently rolling her belly in his huge fingers. He scratches his fingernails lightly over the skin and down below, brushing the hair between her thighs and feels her thighs move apart for more. He brings his hands up instead and passes them around the rolls and curves of her breasts. "These are mine." Her lips brush his face. He presses his mouth to her tensed lips and sucks her roaming tongue.

She pushes him away; her fingertips travel over his face, linger at his lips. "This is mine," she whispers back, runs her hands over his body for a moment and slides down his massive arms. She stretches herself supine on the floor. She bends her old knees and lets them fall open.

He lays down between her legs, as he must, he knows exactly how, draws her knees apart and sees how wide her pink rose has blossomed under his caresses. Pausing, he calms himself and lets the blood pound in his head. He brushes the inside of her thigh with his lips. His right hand moves above her rose and feels there, her wiry hair. She opens her legs more, rolls her hips up inviting, but he puts his face in her hair and lets himself rest there. There's no hurry. Breathing the musky smell of her, gloriously unwashed and odorous after a long day of laundry, letting it inside of him to harden his cock. Now snuggling his face into her belly; she gently closes her legs around his neck.

He draws back a little and stretches out his tongue, the great lavender tongue that came from somewhere and presses it flat against the lips of her vagina, presses it tight and holds it there, breathing hot steam. He hears her grunt up above. Her hips wriggle as if trying to escape and suddenly push back hard against his tongue.

"Jonah!"

She's making strangling noises and now her hips are thrusting wildly like a boy. Her frantic hands are searching for him. He holds his tongue pressed hard as she grinds herself against it, and then draws back and he sucks her bud between lip and tongue, pinches it gently as she grabs his hands and puts them on her breasts and presses her hips into him. He finds her nipples, all the time pinching her, then sucking, then pinching, then sucking as if he would suck the juice out of her. His hands move over her breasts, softly, barely touching, making her come to him so that in her exasperation she pushes her breasts at him and the frantic thrusting goes on below. With thumbs and fingers he pinch-pulls her nipples, lip pinches her clit, and her thrusting goes on and on.

He narrows his thick hot tongue and pushes it deep into her cunt, which seems to stun her motionless for a second and then the thrusting takes up again more ferocious than before. He holds his tongue still as she slides the wet length of her cunt back and forth over it. She reaches down and grabs him furiously by the hair in both fists and rides his tongue, bucking against it with her cunt. He reaches up and caresses her face, touches her lips. His excitement recedes and returns in waves, so that he forgets where he is or what is happening. The world has gone away, and there is nothing he is thinking of except her. She is all that exists in this moment for him forever.

He is a man who has lived with losing. To have something precious snatched away is so natural for him that he has brought this into his lovemaking. When he feels the rising tremblers of her pleasure shake the air around them, rather than chase after her slippery orgasm which he cherishes vastly more than his own – he stops.

He takes his tongue away from her shivering cunt and lifts up on his arms, and begins a slow pilgrimage up the length of her body, kissing and lingering in her wet cunt hair, kissing her belly, moving up and laying his lips on each breast, taking in a stiff nipple, then mouthing all the breast, a kiss of the throat, a nuzzle at the ticklish spot behind her ear and finally pressing his tensed lips to her mouth, taking her lower lip between his and sucking on it as his fingernails lightly scratch up and down the length of her belly, and then coming from behind to caress the nape of her neck. His mouth is still glazed from her cunt and she tastes her essence from him.

He begins the return journey, kissing her face, kissing her ear and her neck, kissing each breast, then her belly, then points his tongue and pushes in again. Her body unleashed, convulses instantly.

"No . . . no . . . no . . . no!"

She fucks his tongue in and out. He has all the time in the world because the world has gone away. In and out. In and out.

She falls limp and still. She will not stir.

Ah.

He plunges his tongue deep inside.

Her cunt tightens like a fist and she sits up suddenly – "No!" and her belly is shaking under his face. Her body is shaking and her tight scrunched face has turned bright red. ". . . . Oh goddamn . . . goddamn . . . goddamn you . . ."

She drops down limply, and her chest is heaving. His tongue has slipped out but he is ready to take it up again if that is what she wants. He will do anything for her. She rolls onto her side, grinning and gasping.

He climbs up from between her thighs triumphantly and kneels beside her and seizes a hank of hair loosely in his fist. "My woman."

"Says who? You?"

He slips his arms under her shoulder and under her ass and easily lifts her from the floor. She snuggles against his chest.

He brings her to the bed and lays her down delicately and for a moment holds her wrists over her head, pinning her shoulders, and he looms over her stretched-out body, not touching, only looking. He looks down at her black and white-streaked hair fanned out over the bed, her face, her lips, the peaks of her audacious breasts, the color of her nipples, the valley between her breasts, the fine wrinkles of her belly. "All this is mine," he says.

She pretends to struggle a little with her arms pinned above her head and crosses her legs. "No." She is giggling. She's gone silly. She kicks at him a little.

He lets go of her wrists and drags her by the hips close to him until her ass is positioned on the edge of the bed; stands with his feet on the floor beside, looming over her and his cock is starting to drip impatiently. He grasps an ankle in each hand and pulls her legs apart and holds her feet up high as though he might split her in half.

The knob of his cock touches her cunt lips and gives the gentlest of thrusts. He gives her just the tip. No more. He looks down because he loves to see the way it looks when it's just touching inside her. He wishes she could see it too. She wiggles her hips trying to get all of it in but he holds himself back. "You have to say it."

"I'm your woman."

"Yes!"

He slips inside her with a grunt of pleasure, the huge stiffened length of him, her receiving him in and in as her mouth falls open, until he feels the hair of their groins press. This first moment of slipping it into her is the most precious moment, feeling her holding him all around fatly and wetly. For a minute he stands quietly, feeling it snug inside the easeful depth, feeling welcome and whole and healed of all rage. This is the moment and the place in all the world where he feels most perfectly like a man. He lifts her ankles up higher over her head, pressing her down and he begins his motion. He's pistoning the great thick length of his cock in her now, and there's no holding back, he's going to let it all pour into her.

Moving the slickened length in and out, feeling himself move in her, enormously, plunging deep, pressing his weight on top of her, his lightning-filled body rejoicing with the raw rapture of his male vigor. "My woman," he says. "I love my woman." He looks down and watches his glistening wet penis vanishing in and out.

On the other side of the room the door swings open and the snow blows in; it's her cheerful son and daughter-in-law, holding the baby and a basket with a warm holiday dinner and the son carrying a shotgun. There are screams from the door. Though she is blind, she looks up from under his deep cock strokes swaying the big bed; he glances up from the horizontal bobble of her breasts with such a look of puzzled despair, peering out over her pleasure-curled toes at the people in the door, just as the barrels of the shotgun explode.

The storm is thundering far away and a damp breeze is blowing, making everything cool and vibrant. He looks down at her mismatched breasts. She knows no self-consciousness or shame. The sylphy girl no more cares about her nakedness than a new baby. He runs an exploratory hand down his creation's breasts, first one and then the other.

"They can't take you from me," he says, and kisses the delicate lightning burn between the swell of her breasts, which makes her wince. "You'll be my woman. Yes."

Bending down, he kisses her lips exactly as he has been taught. Her mouth does something, trying to smile or maybe grimace, but it's impossible yet to tell.

Into the Baptismal

Peggy Munson

Kay was the one who broke my virginity pledge, when I was just fifteen.

Barreling through the country in a bus, I stroke myself as I think about seeing her again. My pussy is a glistening nightlight beneath my old brown coat, guiding my frantically rubbing hand. Across the aisle, a curdled man chews his floppy lip in sleep. Through the windows, the taffy of headlights stretches between mile marker signs. We near a leaning, eavesdropping barn as I jiggle my clit to come. *Oh God*, I moan into the travel pillow fluff. The barn listens to a clothesline of flapping shirts that flirt with midnight sylphs.

We were naive at fifteen, grappling for our own religion. A pair of plaster prayer hands sat on the dresser, as small as elm leaves. Midway through a languid summer of walking beside lanky corn, we bull rode the old propane tank on sunny days, hot metal against our cotton underwear, trying to feel sensations down there. Kay's dad had been a rodeo clown, and we still pretended to be cowgirls. Some nights we threw Kay's sister's Barbie clothes in gas can-fueled fires and made "polyester pyrotechnics," as Kay liked to say. She had flint eyes that promised a hot meal on a ship-wrecked island.

Our hormones were rising, mercury-like in the hot tube of summertime. "Dare you to moon the moon," she said one night, when the moon – as my aunt used to say – was in estrus. So full you want to jab it with a stick.

"You're on," I replied, and dropped my pants to my knees. I thrust my butt up and shook it. That's when Kay ran her finger up my crack and said, "Check out your furry caterpillar crack," and made my asshole shiver.

It was my first inkling that I liked my cousin Kay. I had never felt that kind of want – the kind that leaves you trembling.

But we had signed virginity pledges with Faith Baptist Church, and we were also big recruiters. We used to troll through school and find some limp-haired Mary and wax hellfire and brimstone until she contracted her body to Christ. Still, things had shifted in Davis City, and our best recruiting happened before the paper screens came to town – before the car plant rose amongst the cornfields and Japanese businessmen demanded restaurants with shoji screens. The first time I tasted raw fish, I watched a boy punch his fist through the shoji paper and saw how much disdain boys have for flimsy white contracts. The sushi chefs circled the boy with choppy words but what did they expect? The puppetry of shadows made boys stiff with rage. Boys spent hours *tocking* lampshades, wishing they could punch their way through skirts. Girls needed more armor than pulp and ink.

"Feel mine," said Kay. "Seriously. It's a wooly caterpillar." She took my hand and thrust it down her back end. "Tell me if you think I'm revoltingly hairy."

It was a sinful invitation. There were too many potential butterflies down there. Then, my hand slipped down her crack to her wettest spot. "It's not worth pissing yourself over," I teased, yanking out my fingers. I pushed her away with so much freaked-out force she fell against the clothesline and grabbed a pair of shirtsleeves to steady her body. I dove after her, giggling. Before I knew it, we were wrestling the phantasmal shirt on the ground, playing sumo with thread ghosts instead of shoving the men of the cloth from our minds. At one point, Kay slipped her hand under my waistband. She tickled my badlands. Her finger flitted against a nerve that shot through me like a diamond blade, and I couldn't help but gasp – her hand down there felt amazing. The sun surrounded her molasses skin and tight braids. I thought about dunking her in the swimming hole, and making her translucent so I could see all the way through. I reached for her face. I leaned close like I was going to kiss her.

Then the screen door banged. "Kay? Ally? What are you two goofing about?" It was her dad. He still resembled a rodeo clown. He knew there were bulls that needed the distraction of hyperbole. He squinted at us on the lawn, the shirt and our bodies all akimbo. "The shirt attacked us," said Kay hastily. "It was an ambush, Dad."

"Stop your tomboy roughhousing and run it through the wash," he chided. "I need that shirt for church tomorrow." Then his eyes crossed from Kay to me, and I saw his shoulders buckle, the invisible oxbow of insight bearing down on him. I hated watching men go limp. It was easier to see their rage, the way they punched their hands through the veneering of thin signatures, goading girls along. That night I curled up next to Kay in Grandma's spare bed, rubbing on a pillow between my legs as she slept. I felt the heavenly spirit light up my groin. I wanted Kay to watch me.

In the morning, Kay and I zipped up our desire in Sunday clothes. Church was a reminder that we didn't believe in the literal body and literal blood. We didn't think Jesus inhabited stale crackers the way Catholics did. Instead, we put our faith in symbolism. In the hard pews, our bodies were sterile Mason jars of seductive fruit, in cellars for times of famine. We let hunger build in us until tornadoes pushed us down into places of relief. We waited until the funnel clouds unleashed their angry cunts on tiny houses that fell like paper screens. Then we still ate bland casseroles.

In spite of our lawn wrestling – and whatever he thought he saw – Kay's dad was kind to us. Kay had washed and ironed and starched his shirt and laid it out that morning. She made him Sunday breakfast of sausage and eggs and orange juice and milk. She put triangles of toast on four points of the plate, like black tabs that hold yellowed photographs. A sweet man, he knew the world was made of bulls and cowboys, and one could only stave off the bulls for so long. He sensed the way things were moving, and he directed the flow then scurried over fences, so as not to be gored. He let Kay go her own way. After church, he wiped his brow and said, "This is some lunatic heat. You girls ought to head to the swimming hole."

"You think?" Kay said giddily. On Sunday, we always helped our aunts with chores – sorting Amway goods, mashing potatoes, snapping the ends off of beans. Although the city was sprawling, and our church had a brochure in Japanese, life on the farms hadn't changed much. Kay and I liked the routine, the old houses dotting the landscape and the mores that held us safe and still.

"When your folks were young, it was a veritable tradition," he said to me. "Swimming after service. They called it 'into the baptismal.' I used to go with them too, before I ran off with the rodeo."

I found it peculiar that Kay and I were still modest enough to turn our backs when we changed into swimsuits. Hadn't I touched

her wet spot the day before? Her father was right about the lunatic heat. Thinking of how I touched Kay made me feel a psychotic
hunger in my crotch. I turned my back and stuck my legs through
my swimsuit, looking at the prayer hands. When I straightened up
and spun around, Kay was gawking. She looked flustered. She
gathered her clothes and towel and said, "Your boobs look huge
in that, you know."

I hadn't noticed but she was right. Our bodies were filling out.
I couldn't remember a time in life when I didn't feel watched, and
yet, the awareness that Kay had ogled me made me unduly shy.
We walked on the grass beside the road to avoid hot asphalt but
then got scratched by weeds and a few disorderly corn stalks. At
the swimming hole, Kay grabbed the rope and swung into the
water with a splash. "Come on, cowgirl," she said, grinning. It
was too early for the gossipy crickets, and the pond was as smooth
as a rolled crust. I was self-conscious about the way my boobs
jiggled as I flew through the air and splashed in next to her.

"You'd better be careful at the city pool," said Kay. "If you dive
in that suit, those melons will pop out." She wouldn't stop talking
about tits. She was leading me into a corral of wild horses with
her. "How come yours are so much bigger, anyway? It's not fair."
She grabbed one of her own while she spun her legs underwater
like an eggbeater being slowly hand-cranked.

"No, yours are nicer," I said, a little too rhapsodically. "They're
so even. They're like halves of a whole."

"A whole what? A whole ping-pong ball?" she replied. She
created a fury of water, pushing it up into high feathers with her
hollow palm. "Water fight!" I yelled. I lunged for her swimsuit to
pull her under. And then one of her perky tits popped right out,
and my hand accidentally scooped around it. Buoyancy directed
everything, and I felt out of control, like I hadn't even guided my
own hand until it was feeling her up. Kay looked stunned, staring
at my fingers. I felt her nipple harden and I rubbed some friction
against it with my palm. "Are you crazy?" she said angrily, and
shoved me away.

But it was obvious that my hand and her breast belonged
together, the way certain eggshells once held hard-boiled eggs.
She was my cousin but was adopted, so the fit did not feel familial. Her skin was as black as night-burned country asphalt, and
mine was pale as flour: nobody mistook us for blood kin. I wasn't
hurt by her rebuff. I felt calm right then. Kay was kicking to the

side of the pond, her tits tucked properly back in her suit. Until that contact, I had felt the uneasiness of being lost. It was what I often felt when I rode my bike along unmarked roads through the uniformity of cornfields, and then suddenly, saw the sun pass the crest of the sky and fall west, so that west was a definite direction. I always knew to turn west then, even if I didn't know which road I was on, and the turning made the journey more enjoyable, better than one without the scramble and fear.

On the bank, the weeping willow did not look sad any more. It was a cabaret wig of leaves. I wanted to touch Kay's hair but she looked delicate and mad. She was carving roughly into the dirt with a stick. Her suit clung to the rounds of her stomach. The sun flitted through the leaves to cover her in confetti of dappled light. I knew I shouldn't talk or comfort her but the silence was awkward. Normally, I would have put an arm around her shoulder, but now I stood several feet away and yanked leaves off of branches, making them bow backwards and snap. "Did you hate it?" she finally asked.

"Hate what?" I answered dumbly, ready to blame it on buoyancy.

"Did you hate my breast? Is anyone ever going to want to touch it?" She looked anguished.

"I told you it was nice," I said, distantly. I didn't want to squabble.

"Nice is not much of a word," she answered. "Sometimes I don't want to be the obedient Christian. Sometimes I don't want to recruit virgins. I mean, what if I'm boring, down to the boobs?"

"You certainly aren't that," I said, softening my tone. Kay was staring at her chest. "Close your eyes for a second."

Skeptically, she sank into my instructions. Her lids shut. I grabbed her hand and smoothed her palm around my boob. I lifted my hand and put it on her breast. Kay squeezed her eyes at that moment, and her breathing changed. Aside from that, we were completely quiet, like deer that trance hunters with their eyes. I worked her nipple with my thumb the way I might work the edge of dough, then just held my palm there and breathed. Touching her tit was like holding my hand over a globe as it was spinning and taking me to new hemispheres. Kay made whimpering noises that sent a tingle down my spine. "You see?" I said knowingly. "They're both nice and not boring at all." I didn't dare move her hand anywhere else, even though her touch was too light and I wanted more. My boob filled it out completely. I felt naive for not knowing how much I had wanted it there. We'd talked a lot about the evidentiary, such as broken hymen and blood on a sheet, but we couldn't pretend that this was meaningless.

Her eyes popped open. "Ally," she said seriously. "This is not what nice girls do." She yanked her hand away and started putting her clothes back on over her suit, even though it was still wet. It left two ovals where her butt was and it was soaking through her shirt. She looked ridiculous. I followed her lead and put my clothes on, and we headed quietly back to the house. I moved a stick along corn stalks as if they were pickets. "You think it's going to storm?" I asked, as if this was the reason for her hurry. "I'm not a meteorologist," she replied tersely. The clouds were so unfettered that they grew to celestial proportions, casting huge shadows. I began to shiver, and Kay sped up so fast I could barely keep up. Right before we got to the house, she spun around. I almost slammed into her. "If this is what you are, I want to know," she said. "If you're some kind of a lesbian, you better tell me now."

"Come on, Kay," I dodged, and tried to weave around her but she stuck her arm out, stopping me. She raised one finger up and pointed it at me. She was really pissed off now.

"You said you'd only give it up for God," she said. "You *signed.*" Her voice was trying to squeeze itself into a fevered whisper.

"Nothing is broken yet," I answered sharply. "We're still intact. Good Lord!" Before we could go further, the sky broke open and it rained. I smelled the scent of rain on new cement because her dad had poured a patio last month. We bolted for the house, trying to squeeze past each other. Then the screen door slammed behind our dripping bodies as we hurried in.

What we did seemed innocent enough, nothing a doctor wouldn't do. I closed my eyes and rubbed my lower lip against my palm, to feel its strange pink texture. Even that made me feel so amazing, especially if I thought of kissing Kay. The days were like notes held too long by a soprano in a house of clear glass.

Grandma loved hawking Amway in the rain, because more people were home, and they were grateful for any company. Plus, being industrious in poor weather earned good standing with

God. "You poor girls are rained in and reined in," she said cheer-
fully as she bustled out the door. We should have been miserable
to be cooped up in the trailer but we weren't. Kay had softened
toward me, though we avoided talking about our outburst of lust
while we read magazines on the bed. Kay methodically studied
an article on how to pluck eyebrows. "The family's chicken
pluckers from way back," I assured her. "It's our legacy." Every
time one of our legs got lazy, our calves or feet banged together,
then we pulled away, electrified. I imagined myself stroking the
cocoa skin of her thighs and kissing her elegant collarbones. Kay
sprung up and paced around the room nervously. She held
Grandma's costume necklaces to her neck and put them down.
She fiddled with some decorative bells. Finally, she picked up the
prayer hands.

"Maybe we should test your faith," said Kay, mischievously.
"Do some kind of trial-by-fire."

"Like what?" I answered neutrally, my body stiffening. I hoped
her game was some spin-the-prayer-hands that involved groping
and tongues.

She smacked the prayer hands into her palm. "These are small
enough, and one of us should know how it feels," she said.

"How what feels?"

"It, Ally. *It*," Kay said patronizingly. "How many its are there?
Don't make me spell it out."

"As previously noted, I've got meeself two big 'its," I said,
trying to break her with a stupid joke. But Kay wasn't having it.

"Be serious," she said. "I am."

She shoved the magazine to the ground so it was flapping like
a bird held by its feet. Chickens are slaughtered that way: inverted
and desperate. Minutes earlier, Kay and I had been savoring girl
talk about make-up and celebrities, chattering in a parlor of easy
commonality. Now, she had assumed a different posture, slinking
low toward the chicken coop. She got right up on top of me.
"We'll just see if you like it," she said. "OK?" She tucked the
prayer hands into the elastic of my shorts, so they pressed cool
and firm on my waist. "It's better to try these things with someone you know, so you'll be ready when the big day comes. Who
do you know better than me?"

"Not even myself," I replied, terrified of her sudden assertive-
ness. Kay began rubbing the prayer hands lightly against my skin,
which made me tingly. Then she set them on the bed.

"Come on, Ally," she soothed. "Don't be chickenshit. You're the brave one. Someone's got to try it. They say not to sign a contract unless you understand the terms. How can we be good virgins if we know nothing of the alternatives?"

"That doesn't make sense," I answered. I felt a powerful convection heat cooking me from the inside out. I wanted her so bad.

Then she kissed me on the cheek and assumed the pragmatic planting and sowing tone we'd learned from our family. "I know what to do," she whispered authoritatively. "I've been reading magazines all day." One hand reached down and opened up my shorts. I couldn't believe what was happening. My brain floated on top of me like a doomed dirigible. Her fingers slid beneath my underpants, into the gasping canyon that had formed slowly from an unheralded stream. "Does this feel good?" she asked timidly, as she was tracing patterns with her fingers, looking for a place to put them in.

God, it felt incredible. I didn't want her to stop. I thought about my stretched-out, cheap underwear that had come in a three-pack. We always bought it in quantity, the way one might send bundles of dry goods to Africa, and I loved its pragmatic and distant spiritual insurance. Kay wore the exact same kind, and there was something seductive and sexy-librarian like about its plainness. She acted like she had swerved around that familiar stitching a thousand times. Kay's lips were parted and swollen with red, hungry. I felt one finger slip inside of me and I gasped. "Oh wow," I said.

"Don't you ever masturbate?" she asked. Clearly, *she* did.

"Where would I do it? In the shed? I'm never alone." I didn't tell her about my pillow grinding.

Kay moved her finger in and out, then started widening my hole with it by circling right inside the opening. "Concentric circles, nesting rings," she said. "Just look at it – you're beautiful. And why not in the shed?" I wished that I could kiss her but I knew I might break the spell if I moved. Kay had more sense than this usually. "I guess you must like boys a little bit," she commented. "You like having something inside." I didn't point out the flaw in her reasoning, that the thing inside of me wasn't a dick, but *her*, and nothing else felt so good. She pulled my shorts down off my feet. She yanked my matronly underpants away. "Let's get on with it," she said feverishly, and I thought *hallelujah, yes*. I looked at my coils of pubic hair and then, above, her saintly face. The scent of me wafted through the room, an aromatic telegram, and I was scared the trailer doors would not contain the news. We panted in the tentative stillness. "Now spread your legs," said Kay. "Relax."

We'd never done the Passion Play or Stations of the Cross, but Kay seemed to know something about sacrificing virgins. My toes grazed the footboard as I spread my legs apart. Spreading them so wide felt amazing, and my thighs grew hot. I felt a teasing breeze from somewhere but the windows were all closed. Kay ran one finger up and down my wet pussy, parting the seas. "OK, it will hurt at first and then feel good," said Kay. "If the sex books are correct. I think I'm competent. Try to relax." She slid the diminutive fingers of the prayer hands into me. Their coolness made my muscles clench. I felt the sweetest pleasure bubbling through my groin as she eased the hands in.

"Oh, Kay," I exclaimed, despite myself. "That's nice. Please don't stop."

"Don't worry, Ally Cat," she said. "I've got to find your soul in here to save it."

She slid the plaster further into me until I crawled backwards a little bit. Then her slender fingers stroked my body, coaxing me, letting me know it was OK. I felt myself spreading for her. She tweaked the spot above my hole, so she could slide the hands further in. "I found your magic button," she grinned. She massaged around my opening, while I let out little moans. "That's it, relax for me," she said. My saggy underwear hung on the foot post of the bed. She rocked the prayer hands in, and suddenly, I felt a rapturous explosion, right from the plaster fingertips. "Oh!" I said, and Kay slammed one hand over my mouth.

"Be quiet," she said. "People will kill us. Did you come?"

"I think I did," I said. She looked angelic with her hair glowing in the lamplight. It was my first orgasm.

It kept pulsing in me, like the glow of a star, while Kay set the prayer hands back on the dresser.

Years later, I wonder if that star still guides her, as it does me. I walk toward the address her father has given me, down a battered asphalt road. I don't know if Kay has ever fucked another girl.

Kay's kin are the only ones who want to see me since I came out as a dyke. They are serpent handlers, or Sign Followers – as

queer to my other scripture-strict relatives as I am. They split off
with the family and fled Indiana after taking up with snakes, and
it has been six years since I last saw Kay. At twenty-five, I still feel
like an awkward teenager when I walk toward the house. The
congregants haul metal chairs for tomorrow's service. Aunt May
shucks corn by the round hood of my uncle's truck. Like the
others, Kay wears nondescript garb, her hair smoothed back, but
her arms are buffed out and sexy from the Army. She Frisbee-
tosses a paper plate my way and squeals, "You made it!"' Aunt
May strides up and kisses me right on the lips, and I back away,
surprised. "It's our faith tradition," explains Kay. "Second Corin-
thians tells us to greet those of our own sex with a 'Holy kiss' and
we kiss like that." She gives me a sly glance.

The landscape is lush with suggestive underbrush. I am tense
about what slithers beneath the obvious. How could they accept
me when they believe the Bible asks them to drink poison and
wrestle deadly snakes? Still, they have invited me here, knowing
what they know. I wonder where her dad keeps the box of
copperheads. He rises from the porch and drags his bad leg
with his good leg, then hugs me with one arm and says,
"Welcome to Tennessee, darlin'. You're always family hear." I
almost cry to hear him say this, since I've felt so shunned by the
rest of the family. Before I can offer to help set up, he seizes my
duffel bag and sticks a limp pillowcase in my hand. "What's this
for?" I ask.

"We're going hunting," announces Kay. "Before sundown."
She grabs a long stick with a metal hook on the end. "You girls
catch a lively one," says her dad, and grins.

Kay is silent and doesn't snap a single twig as she steers me
through the woods. We don't talk about my coming-out process,
her escapades in the barracks, the rickety railroad bridge between
our lives. I feel nervous. I wonder if she judges me, or if she still
dates men. Over time, our letters grew polite and petered out.
Her solemn brow twists like a point of wind turmoil on a grassy
field, and I remember my first orgasm like it was yesterday. It
makes my clit throb to have our bodies so close. She rattles along
with the snake stick, and I watch the rhythm of her shoulder
blades. Kay might have had a hard time as a black kid in a white
family, but people always kowtowed to her. Like those sturdy
farm structures that just won't fall, Kay has an effortless way of
making the wind bend around her skin. My pussy still

remembers how she slid it open. At twenty-five, she looks like something decadent and tasty only adults get to eat.

Kay plods down the overgrown trail, pointing out poison oak so I don't step on it. "Shhh. Be still," she orders, holding out her arm. Before I can ask what's she doing, Kay slides quietly to the left and scoops the snake stick down into a leaf-dappled area beside the trail. She lifts the thick, twisting body of a timber rattlesnake with the metal end. I hadn't even noticed its cryptic yellow and brown colors hiding there. She grabs the viper by the head while I jerk back. My heart rifles with adrenaline. "So you like to fuck girls?" she asks dispassionately, pointing the rattler's fangs at me.

"Hold on—" I protest. Then Kay bursts out laughing. "I need the pillowcase, fool," she says. "I'm not going to kill you for being a dyke." She rope-ties the end of the bag and the viper thrashes inside then goes still. "They call me 'charmer' now." She says proudly. "I flush the serpents out." I nod and respond, "I can see how you'd be good at that." Her eyes run over my serpentine curves. Her tone hooks a slight drawl and softens. "We've got time to kill now," she says. "So why don't I show you my favorite spot?" Then she takes me to a tiny shack in the woods, pulls the vine-covered door and leads me in. She plops the snake bag on the plank floor, "It's an old hunting squat," she says. "Don't you love it?" The timber rattlesnake squirms and I try to move away, but Kay suddenly herds me near it, pressing me against the dirty wall with her whole body, keeping me scared. I'm trapped. She is thrillingly present, her arms holding me there. "One thing I've learned about the power of venom," she says, "is that you should keep it in the family." Then she grins. She puts her fingers through my hair and breathes heavy on my neck, flushing me out. What is she doing to me? I moan a little. Kay is so intense up close.

The serpent rustles and our eyes shoot to the bag, then we giggle. "I bet it's the pillowcase I used to hump when I thought of you," I confess, reaching out to stroke her cornsilk-soft cheeks, to let her know I want her too. She brushes my hand away, like it's just a pesky fly, letting me know she's in charge. She leans forward: she has a hot rock to warm my cold blood. She thrusts her hips a little bit, so I feel the lump in them against my body. "You feel what I've got?" she asks.

"Is that—?" I ask.

"It's a viper," she cuts in. "It'll kill you quick." She grabs my hand and rubs it over the lumpy curves in her jeans, then blocks me from touching it again. I can't believe Kay is packing a dick. "Oh God Kay," I marvel. "I want to feel it."

"You just wait," she orders. "Wait for it." Then she shakes her hips until I hear a rattling sound. I don't know if it's a rattlesnake or gourd or can of dimes. I don't know if it's a dick at all. I scrunch my brow. "Is that a real snake in your pants?" I ask, perplexed, and Kay pins me tighter. "Yeah, it's a serpent I caught for you," Kay says calmly, and puts my hand back on the lumpy mound that really does seem to wriggle. "Don't make me pin you face first and give it to you *Deliverance* style." I hear the rattle growing louder, faster, as she grinds her hips against my pubic bone. I try to back away, to ascertain what's slithering in her pants, but she squeezes me against its cotton case. I get irrationally scared but Kay calmly holds my wrists in one hand. She unzips and pushes down my pants. "Can you handle the serpent?" she asks fiercely. "Are you a child of God? Are you holy and willing to prove it?"

She shoves me hard against the wall. I gulp.

Then I feel the venom, the quietude, Kay's sweet cock sinking in.

The rattle comes from so far down, I cannot tell its origin. It rises up inside the room. It seizes me. It clutches Kay. My muscles knead themselves into a wild delirium. Kay rocks her hips and pushes deeper into me. "Oh yeah," I groan, and try to pull her further in. But then Kay slides out her cock and makes me look. I tug at her to call her back. "First take a peek," she says. Her dick is jutting out, and where the balls should be, there are the curving lumps of keratin: she's fixed a rattlesnake rattle there. "Some fiddlers put these rattles in their violins because they think it makes the instrument more masculine," she says. "Or that it sings along. I harvested this rattle from a tire track rattlesnake. Good luck for me, but not the snake." She runs her fingers down my chest. "See, you can kill the body, but not rhythm. Rhythm lives. That's why the serpent handlers rise up off their seats to praise." She starts to move her hips, and pierces me. I grab at her and feel her sinking in. "I'm going to make you come so hard," she says. "For all the years I've held it in." And then my hot, adopted cousin fucks me good. I'm baptized in her sinuous religion.

Balancing the Books

Lucy Felthouse

A bead of sweat ran down the side of Philip's head and trickled into his hairline. He'd been lying flat on his back on the cold parquet floor for what felt like hours. Realistically, it probably hadn't even been one hour, but because he'd been trying so hard not to move a muscle for fear of toppling the stack of hardback books resting on his abdomen, every single minute was torture.

And yet, at the same time, it was complete and utter bliss. Giovanna was sitting on a wooden chair, the legs of which were either side of his hips – as were hers – and she was using the pile of books as a table. She idly flipped the pages of the weighty tome she was pretending to read, and studiously ignored Philip, as though he really were nothing but a table.

Philip's cock had never been so hard. He was torn. Part of him wanted the books to fall so Giovanna's beautiful eyes would flash with anger and she would punish him the very best way she knew how. The other part wanted to please her, in the hope that she might let him bury his face between her thighs and lick her delicious pussy to orgasm, and maybe, just maybe, be allowed to come himself.

Another droplet of sweat followed the first one into his rapidly dampening hair. Philip's erection strained beneath his clothes, and he decided to try and distract himself by thinking of something else. *Trees. Taxes. Tridents.*

It didn't work. Instead, his mind wandered to how he'd gotten into this predicament in the first place.

Giovanna was Philip's boss – in the usual employment sense, as well as the mistress and slave sense. Just a few short weeks back, he'd been wandering the high street of the town he lived in, and had come across an amazing-looking bookshop. He'd peered through the window, fascinated. The slightly gloomy interior was all dark wood and spiral staircases, and was a book lover's wet dream. And Philip was a book lover. Turning, he made for the door. As he reached it, he noticed a sign stuck to the pane of glass in its centre.

EXPERIENCED BOOKKEEPER WANTED.
COMPETITIVE RATES.
APPLY WITHIN.

Philip didn't need a job. He was, in fact, a highly qualified accountant, and some of the past investments he'd made had come good and meant that he could live very comfortably off the profits. In fact, it wasn't worth his time to work, as the taxman would pinch even more of his pennies.

Philip didn't need any books, either. His custom-built home library was fully stocked with an abundance of fiction and non-fiction, and he really needed to read and get rid of some of them before he started purchasing more.

He peered through the door, catching sight of a voluptuous bespectacled woman standing behind the till, writing in a note-book. She sure was easy on the eye, with her long dark hair pulled up into a high ponytail, and the hint of ample cleavage peeking out of the top of her blouse. She must have caught sight of him out of the corner of her eye because her head snapped up from what she was doing and she looked straight at him. Peering over the top of her glasses, she continued to gaze at him, unsmilingly. Many people would have found her demeanour cold, unapproachable.

Philip pushed open the door and walked in. Before he knew what he was doing he'd walked straight up the counter and the aloof woman behind it, and said,

"I'm interested in the job."

She put down her pen and raised an eyebrow. "And what are your qualifications?"

He was, in fact, vastly overqualified for the job she was offering. He could do the paperwork for the bookshop standing on his head. With one hand tied behind his back. However, the cool, unimpressed stare the woman gave him made him *want* to impress her – and so he gave her the full whammy of his qualifications and experience.

The woman's face remained impassive.

"It sounds as though you're used to much bigger accounts than you'd be dealing with here. Why on earth are you interested in *this* job?"

Because I want to fuck you.

"Because I live off the profits of some wise investments and don't need to work, but I *do* need something to fill my time, before I go stir-crazy. There's only so much golf a man can play. I figure you can pay me in—" he'd been going to say books, but as he tore his gaze away from her steely one and onto the tantalizing curves of her body, his brain substituted the word for a much more inappropriate one, "—kind."

The bookseller's eyebrows shot almost into her hairline.

Philip gulped. *Stupid idiot, what did you say that for? She'll have you done for sexual harassment!*

Narrowing her eyes, the woman paused for a few seconds, then asked coolly, "What's your name?"

Unable to cope with the intense glare he was being subjected to, Philip lowered his eyes to the counter between them and mumbled his name. He also pulled in his shoulders protectively, fully expecting her to flip her lid and give him a tongue-lashing before throwing him unceremoniously out of her shop.

"Well, Philip, I *do* need someone to balance my books. And—" she looked him up and down "—it certainly seems as though you're more than up to the job."

She thrust out a hand. "I'm Giovanna. And you're hired."

Philip took her hand and shook it. It was cool and dry, much like her demeanour.

And that had been the start of their relationship. Giovanna had taken charge immediately, leading Philip into the tiny room behind the counter and showing him where everything he needed could be found. He'd followed that rotund, swaying arse willingly and decided there and then that he'd follow her anywhere.

She'd watched him as he'd leafed through paperwork and tried to make sense of it – she'd obviously not been doing any book-keeping at all until he'd shown up. There were bits of paper, scribbled notes, receipts and invoices shoved randomly into box files; and although Philip was exasperated at the amount of work he would have to do to even get the stuff in order, let alone balance the books, he was also secretly pleased. It meant more time spent in the company of the divine Giovanna. He was already so besotted that he'd happily watch paint dry, if it meant being with her.

Hopefully she'd be so grateful that he'd sorted out her paper-work nightmare that she'd deliver on the promise her eyes had given as they'd looked him up and down.

Under Giovanna's watchful gaze, Philip continued his job with renewed vigour.

Later that day, Giovanna had indeed paid Philip in kind. When he'd padded out of the office to where she was dusting the banis-ter of the gorgeous spiral staircase, she'd peered at him over her glasses, her cold blue gaze pinning him to the spot.

"Done?" she said curtly.

Philip nodded meekly. "Yes. I've got everything pretty much sorted out, but I'll come back tomorrow with a proper ledger to get everything recorded so its easy for you to refer back to, if you ever need to."

"Yes what?" Giovanna asked.

"P-pardon?"

"You said yes, when I asked if you were done. And I'm now asking you, yes what?"

It took Philip a good few seconds to understand what she was getting at, but as those piercing blue eyes continued to burn into him, he suddenly understood. Or at least he hoped he did.

"Yes, Mistress."

Giovanna gave a satisfied nod. "That's better. Now finish cleaning this, and then you can go."

She tossed the duster at him, and Philip immediately set to his task. Giovanna climbed the staircase, giving him a tantalizing view of her rump as she did. Then, just as she reached the top and he was about to silently lament the loss of the spectacular view, she turned and sat on the top step.

Philip's already semi-hard cock sprung to full attention. Giovanna had positioned herself so that anyone looking up at her from below would be able to see right up her skirt. This would have been enough to drive Philip to distraction, but Giovanna had taken it one step further. She wore no underwear, and her bare pussy was completely on display. Philip had no idea if he was supposed to look at her or not, but he couldn't tear his gaze away. Licking his lips, he eventually clawed back the presence of mind to turn his eyes to Giovanna's face, which wore a smug grin.

"Like what you see?"

Philip's throat was suddenly so dry that he opened his mouth to respond, but couldn't make the words come out. Instead, he nodded vigorously, desperate to palm his cock and enjoy some temporary relief, but instinctively knowing that would be the wrong thing to do.

Not without permission.

Where had that come from? Since when did Philip, the big-shot wealthy accountant, wait for permission?

Giovanna's grin widened, and she pulled the hem of her skirt up, parting her generous thighs at the same time. Philip's attention immediately snapped back to the beautiful pussy that was being displayed before him; the splayed and swollen labia, the sheen of juices, and the nubbin of sensitive flesh that resided at its apex. He wanted to eat her; pleasure her delicious cunt until she came all over his face.

"Want a closer look?"

Now, her smile was as wide as the Cheshire cat's. An arched eyebrow seemed to punctuate her ridiculous question. Ridiculous because the answer was so obvious that the question may as well have been rhetorical.

Eager for Giovanna to allow the very thing she was asking, Philip swallowed, and forced the response from his mouth. "Yes, please, Mistress."

Her slick pussy was so tempting that it took all of his willpower not to dash up the stairs, grab those luscious thighs in his hands, and eat it for all he was worth. Instead, he waited patiently for her response. His cock, however, wasn't so well behaved. It strained against his clothes, making every movement both painful and incredibly stimulating at the same time.

Giovanna said nothing, and the two of them stared silently at one another for a good few minutes, until eventually, she said, "Come."

Philip would have liked nothing more than to come, but he knew that wasn't what she meant. He dropped the cloth in his hand and scrambled eagerly up the stairs until he was two steps down from Giovanna, which, when kneeling, brought his face almost level with her cunt. Still, he waited, resisting the urge to rub his swollen crotch against the edge of the step in front of him. She'd know exactly what he was doing, and he was damn sure she wouldn't approve. He wasn't going to risk pissing her off because there was no way she'd let him lick her pussy then. And he really, *really* wanted to taste her.

His good behaviour was rewarded when Giovanna finally uttered the words he'd been longing to hear. "Make me come."

"Yes, Mistress."

Philip didn't need telling twice. As soon as the words left his mouth, he shuffled forwards, slipped his hands beneath her creamy fleshy thighs and lowered his head to the prize between them. As his tongue touched her heated, swollen cunt, his cock leapt. She was *delicious,* but then, somehow he'd known she would be. How could such a woman be anything else?

He ate her pussy the best way he knew how, enthusiastically licking and nibbling at her labia, dipping his tongue into her saturated channel, and sucking her engorged clit. Giovanna spoke no words of encouragement, and not so much as a moan or a sigh issued from those perfect lips, but the occasional involuntary twitch or thrust of her hips told Philip all he needed to know. Plus, he felt sure that if he was doing something wrong, she'd soon let him know. Giovanna wasn't exactly backwards in coming forwards, which is how he'd ended up eating her out on a spiral staircase in her shop, having met her only a few hours previously.

In all of his previous sexual encounters, Philip had found that when going down on a woman, the noises she made were important to help him gauge how he was doing. The absence of any sounds from Giovanna, however, just made him try harder. If he could wrench even the tiniest moan from her, he'd be thrilled.

A titbit of delight was thrown to him when, rather than making a noise, Giovanna moved her hands from where she'd been leaning back on them, and tangled them into his hair and pulled him more tightly to her crotch. He took that as a sign that she was close to coming, and, remembering that her order had been "make me come" with no specifics as to how, he shifted his right hand from where it had been gripping her ample thigh and slipped two long fingers up inside her pussy. Manoeuvring so he was stimulating her G-spot, Philip was hugely gratified when he heard a sharp intake of breath from Giovanna.

He decided there and then he was going to get a noise out of her, even if it killed him. Capturing her clit between his lips once more, he began to suckle and nibble it, as he stroked the soft pad of flesh deep inside her cunt. The walls of Giovanna's pussy clenched tightly, and he felt a fresh surge of blood to his dick as he imagined how it would feel to have his shaft buried deep inside her instead of his fingers. He wondered if he would ever find out. He really hoped so.

Soon, the rippling of Giovanna's pussy made him forget all about fucking her, and concentrate solely on giving her the orgasm of her life. He worked his fingers roughly against her sweet spot, and flicked at her clit with his tongue until his jaw ached. Suddenly, Giovanna's grip on his hair tightened, and he heard a series of tiny grunts before she let go and her orgasm washed over her.

Philip whipped his fingers from her cunt and replaced them with his mouth, so he could taste the delicious juices that trickled from her. Tart, and yet somehow sweet at the same time, Philip couldn't help the groan that came from his own lips as he suckled at her lower ones while she bucked against his face.

Giovanna's movements slowed as her climax waned, and Philip felt the feeling come back into his scalp as she released her hold on his hair. As Giovanna then leaned back on her hands for a few seconds as she got her breath back, Philip expected her to recline on the steps for a little while. But no, she was made of tougher stuff than that.

Suddenly, she stood and snatched her skirt back into place, before looking down at where Philip still crouched on the step. He paused, wondering what she would do next. A curt nod, perhaps?

Giovanna managed to surprise him again. She leaned down and patted him on the head, not unlike the way you'd pat a dog, and said, "Very good."

Heat rushed to Philip's face. He'd pleased her, and that pleased him. He still had a raging hard-on, but somehow, he didn't care. Making Giovanna happy was more important, and he suspected that he'd get rewarded at some point.

Several weeks later, and he was still waiting. Giovanna was really making him work hard for his reward, which is why he was flat on his back being used as a human book rest. Sure, over time she'd given him little rewards, like more pats on the head, and even allowing him to rest his head in her lap, but she hadn't yet allowed him to come. She'd even forbidden him from masturbating, claiming she would know if he did it when he wasn't with her. Philip was too frightened to take the risk.

He wasn't miserable, though. Far from it, in fact. From the moment he'd set eyes on her, Giovanna had awoken the submissive inside him that he never knew was there. Every time he was allowed to feast on her tits, her pussy, rub her feet and lick her shoes was a reward to him. He adored her. Worshipped her, even.

Back in the present, Giovanna had obviously realized that Philip's mind had wandered. She slammed the book she was reading closed, causing the pile of books beneath it to teeter dangerously. Philip scarcely dared breathe, in case the movement turned the teeter into a topple. He didn't want to let her down. Not now. Not ever.

Quietly, she asked, "What were you thinking about?"

"You, Mistress. How we met, the things we've done . . ."

He tailed off. He daren't confess how much he wanted to come because if she knew how much he desired it, she might just make him wait even longer. And at this rate, his balls would soon drag on the floor when he walked.

"Hmm."

Philip wasn't sure if she believed him, or whether she wondered what he was going to say before he stopped himself.

"You have done very well in the time that we've been together. Especially for a novice."

"Thank you, Mistress. I just want to make you happy."

A curt nod acknowledged his words. Then she stared into the middle distance for a few minutes before snapping her attention back to the pile of books in front of her, and the man beneath them. She stood carefully, then pulled the chair from its position across Philip's body.

Philip's heart thumped hard in his chest as he wondered what she was going to do next. He worried that the thump-thump-thump would dislodge the books, but as Giovanna straddled his lower legs, he knew that there was no way he could calm his thundering pulse.

When Giovanna reached for his belt, Philip knew the books were done for. It was just a matter of time. She undid his belt and fly, then eased his straining prick out of his boxers.

Philip gulped, and stared at the pile of books as though he could pin them into place with his gaze. Adding to his torment was the fact that the books being there meant he couldn't see what Giovanna was doing. And she was a seriously unpredictable woman. The last few weeks had proven that.

A gasp escaped his lips as Giovanna's hand wrapped around his swollen shaft and began to stroke it. Slowly at first, then faster until Philip felt his orgasm hurtling towards him at an alarming speed. The books swayed dangerously as his lungs pulled in the air he so desperately needed. He sent a silent prayer to any deity that might be listening to just keep those books upright until he'd come. Once he'd come he could deal with anything, including any punishment Giovanna might see fit to dish out after allowing those goddamn hardbacks to hit the floor.

As it happened, the acts were simultaneous. As Giovanna's expert fingers teased a climax out of him, the resulting jolt from his body sent the books tumbling. Luckily, the heavy tomes went off to one side, rather than hitting either of them. Even luckier for Philip, Giovanna didn't stop touching him. In fact, she continued to work his cock until she'd milked every last drop of spunk out of him and he was spent and gasping like a man starved of oxygen.

As he struggled to get some semblance of normality back to his breathing and demeanour, Giovanna stood and stalked away. Philip frowned. He hadn't exactly been expecting a cuddle, but to walk away without a word? His unasked questions were answered as she returned with a tea towel from the kitchen and dropped it into his lap with a smile – the first he'd ever seen from her.

"Clean yourself up," she said, her eyes twinkling. "It's month end. You've got some more books to balance."

Hina, the Hawaiian Helen

J. D. Munro

Molokai, twelfth century

Hina combs her short hair as thousands of men breathe their last in the thundering surf below. A red waterfall spills between the steep cliffs. Crashing whitewater at the gorge's base churns the flowing blood. The ocean's frothy fingertips grasp the bodies littering the rocks and sand, carrying dead warriors out to sea for the shark god's feast. Hungry waves dash themselves against the mountain crags, demanding more kills to chew and swallow. Booming breakers echo the dull thuds of war-clubs on flesh and bone. Dying shouts choke and burble into silence, and even the sea rests in quiet for a moment, licking its salty lips.

Hina waits. Eighteen years a prisoner behind these fortress walls, abducted when she had already borne two children to another island's chief, and still Hina is the most beautiful woman in all of Polynesia. Her fierce lover, Koa, defeats vast battalions in protection of her. Koa will come to her soon, exhausted but inflamed by war. Hina will purify him – she is a trickling brook. Since Koa first gazed upon her bathing in her mountain stream all those years ago, Hina has been as slick as the smooth and slippery rocks clattering in the streambed, chattering as Koa stole her away.

She refused to cover her nude body when he interrupted her bath a lifetime ago, her thighs spread for the water goddess's cool tongue of current to wash away a desire that the aged chief, her husband, couldn't arouse nor slake. Resting back on her elbows in the shallow water, head tipped back, she watched Koa splash upstream, upside down. Her black hair, which brushed the ground when she stood, flowed like seaweed. She waited, hair tugging at her scalp like her clamoring thoughts. This stream was taboo, a death curse on anyone other than the royal *ali'i* rulers who touched its water. Pele, the volcano goddess, would turn this intruder to stone for his sacrilege. But no molten lava scorched and manacled the stranger. He stared down at her, his *malo* fluttering in the trade wind. Far from being struck dead for breaking sacred law, the scant swatch of loincloth emphasized his continued pulse of life.

Hina stood and faced him, tall and naked, knowing no shame in her expansive beauty. She kicked at her wet hair tangling around her ankles in the swirling water. Gentle ripples trickled around his shark-tooth anklets, their fierce rattle and the pebbles clacking the only sound as the pair stared at each other.

He dropped to his knees, skinning them on the rocks, stunned by the truth of her fabled loveliness. Tales of her beauty had teased him for years, but he set out to capture his enemy's prize property only to provoke war. He, busy rebel with rival lands to attack and conquer, had no time for love.

A scout shouted in the distance, spotting Koa's infamous red-sailed canoe. Koa seized her. Hina didn't resist. Her husband could barely balance on these slippery rocks, but Koa ran downstream despite her opulent weight. Draped across his shoulder, her wet breasts pressed to his back, her bare *okole* nestled against his cheek.

Koa could have taken brutal possession of his stolen property, could have slaked his lust and simultaneously punished her husband, the chief who sailed here from Tahiti with his imported gods and oppressive religion of restrictions and curses. He could have tossed her to his warriors for leftovers, then fed her to the shark god. This was the way of their people; her husband would have done the same with one of Koa's women. Instead, he set her down in the back of the twin-hulled warship, away from the men's stares. His godlike body towered over them. He covered her with the soft folds of a *kapa* cloth blanket and helped his men paddle home.

Untied and unobserved, she sat behind him as they skimmed across the sea. He pulled back against the oars, his shoulder-length hair brushing her lap. His muscles danced under his skin. Like the simple human figures her people carved in rock, his broad shoulders narrowed to a slender waist. His bare haunches gripped the wood plank seat under his *malo*. The loincloth covered only the seam of his body. Where her husband's *okole* spread and jiggled, this man's dense muscle rippled, square and solid as stone. The sheen of sweat sparkled on fine brown skin as constellations guided their way through darkness.

He glanced only once over his shoulder at her during the long voyage away from the only land she had known, towards what she knew not. As he paused, his oar dripped. The quiet splash sang to her over crashing waves and grunts of the men. That plink of water began to wear down her heart, as a waterfall erodes crevasses out of cliffs, carving a gaping chasm of desire.

The steep cliffs of Molokai stabbed the skyline of her new home. Koa carried Hina up a narrow ravine, root-brambled and rocky, the only oceanfront access to his impenetrable fortress, hidden above on a high plateau. He slung her over his shoulder again. She rested her hands at the small of his back to steady herself, and felt his shifting muscle and bone. He wrapped his arm around her thighs, his hand gripping her hip. His opposite hand rested at the back of her knees. Her hair whipped his face in the wind that chased them up the mountainside, but he knew the secret path's twists and turns like the crooks of his own body – like he would soon know hers. A sheer drop-off fell behind them, but his footing was sure, his breath even, his hold strong despite her significant weight. The ocean receded far below them. No one would be able to rescue her from this place.

He entered the smooth-floored compound, placing her gently on her feet when he crossed the threshold of a private room. They stood facing each other, alone. His chest rose and fell after the exertion of carrying her.

Hina stood poised and regal. She'd seen what happened to the women her clan captured and enslaved. Because of the blood afterwards, the new slaves were banished to the menstrual hut, where the tribe's women must wait out their monthly flow out of men's sight. As if a woman's blood would contaminate them, Hina thought, these men who made the shedding of blood their daily business. It wasn't a monthly flow that trickled down the prisoners' thighs but battle wounds, man's war carved out on the bodies of women.

Knowing this, Hina wondered that she felt so little, not even fear. She had felt nothing as they paddled away from her husband, children, mother. She didn't look back over her shoulder at the island of her birth, didn't regret the lack of pursuing boats. This nothing wasn't so different from the nothing that was her life – no choices, given to an old man at her first blood. The ageing chief had chafed during her adolescence, waiting for proof of her womanhood, salivating for the rupturing of her virginity, more blood so soon after her first blood, then no blood, then the blood of childbirth. Then war. It all came back to blood. Though why the old chief had been so anxious to heave and grunt over her she couldn't say; it seemed more toil to him than satisfaction. As his bulk loomed over her, his rapidity was the only thing that saved her from crushing suffocation. Sometimes he didn't even make it inside her. He thrust at the magnificent fullness of her thighs before she could open them, flooding her legs and the *kapa* mat.

She dropped the blanket and turned her back to Koa. Let him take her like the dog that she was to these men who leashed her. She lowered herself to the floor, graceful within her glorious size. She waited on her haunches, her hair spread on the floor around her. After pain and fury would come the relief of death, not so different from the boredom that defined her life

Koa sat behind her, his legs spread to scissor her girth. His inner thighs pressed against her outer calves. The flap of his *malo* tickled the bottoms of her upturned feet, curled under her *okole*. He gathered her hair at the nape of her neck. Even his large fist couldn't encompass it all. He tugged, needling her scalp, then let go.

Then – he combed her hair. This mammoth task took her slaves hours every morning. Now the muddy tangles would grow worse when matted with her blood. He started at the ends, using his fingers. Hina tensed. This soft subservience was beneath the dignity of royal *ali'i* such as himself. As he worked, he hummed. Though they'd been together for hours now, she hadn't yet heard his voice. He commanded his army through actions, not words. He had not sent a soldier for her capture but had kidnapped her himself. His rich-timbred voice was as smooth as polished calabash bowls. Her toes, tucked up between his legs, now and then wriggled – his answering, insistent pressure against them never faltered.

He switched to a whalebone comb. She relaxed as he combed this hair that shackled her – a chain made of her own body. She passed her days lying down to take the oppressive weight off her scalp. The chief refused her request to cut the black mantle to the waist-length of the common girls.

She dozed while Koa combed. She awoke to a dry kiss on her shoulder and the rustle of his leaving.

The next day, she watched from her hut as the fortress came to life. Women pounded *poi* in the courtyard, breasts swaying as they beat the taro root. Men sharpened their weapons and practiced for battle. Hina made out the hut of the slave girls – some would be from her own clan.

Laughter at ribald jokes rippled through the compound. She found the camaraderie between men and women unusual. Still, unease ran through the camp, on account of her. Koa should never have brought such precious cargo here. Alert sentries paced at the walls. The wars would never cease now. Her husband would never stop looking for her. Many warring chiefs divided the island chain, but her loss would unite separate factions against Koa's rebel forces – who fought in defense of his people's old ways against these foreign usurpers, who had sailed here from a different island chain with their tyrannical gods in tow.

She didn't see Koa. His people numbered in the thousands, a great responsibility.

In the evening, a magnificent *luau* feast celebrated the successful raid. Hina refused to attend, though the roasting *kalua* pig tempted her. Nobody forced her. She watched from the shadows. The men and women ate together, and the women ate everything the men did, even ate out of the same calabash bowls. More broken taboos. Her gods forbade the two sexes from eating together, and women couldn't eat the fruits and meats reserved for men – not bananas, coconuts, pig, shark, turtles, fowl . . . just about everything but taro, *kapu* even to her, the queen.

Like Koa standing in the *kapu* stream, nothing happened to the blasphemous infidels. Hina paced inside her hut. Her hair irritated her, heavy on her scalp, hot on her neck. Koa took no precautions against her. Amidst the rare, colored skirts and finery he provided for her lay several weapons, decorative but still functional. Hina picked up a coral knife. Foolish man, she could murder him in the night.

So, this barbaric invader loved her hair. She sawed at her thick locks with the knife, cutting at the nape of her neck. Let the gods strike her dead on the spot. Anything was better than living death under the weight of this shroud. The hair coiled at her ankles.

Koa, carrying a tray laden with food, kicked back the *kapa* cloth that covered her doorway and stepped inside. The *kukui* nut oil lamp illuminated her dark room, filling it with warm fragrance. Dressed in his royal finery, a red and yellow feather cape was draped across his broad shoulders, tied at the hollow of his throat. A helmet of the same color fit his head, arching over his face like a curved beak. His *malo*, again of rare yellow feathers plucked from thousands of birds, rode low on his hips. The golden garments accentuated his brown skin. The soft plumage caressed his hard, punished body.

She tossed the knife on the floor between them. She shook her head, bobbed hair brushing her bare shoulders.

Koa set the tray down and circled her. He stepped close. She flinched, expecting the beating that she incited, but he bent down to his knees before her, again. He gathered up the shorn hair until he held one long, thick strand in his triumphant fist. As he worked, he brushed against her, his breath hot on her calf. She refused to step away. Koa tied off the ends.

Koa sat cross-legged before the dinner tray. He motioned for her to sit. Confused, she sank down. What did he want of her? To humiliate her by flaunting her religious laws? To laugh at her weakness when she broke down and broke them? She'd never eaten in front of a man, never seen a man eat. He smiled at her as he chewed, eyes crinkling, motioning for her to eat the *kapu* foods denied her, like bananas and coconut cake. How fitting that her first sight of him was upside down, because he turned her world over. He held a slice of *haupia* to her lips. The thick white cake jiggled like her breasts. He eased it into her mouth, fearless of her teeth so near to his fingers. She closed her eyes, savoring every second of this bite that would be her last before the gods blasted her into oblivion. Serve him right to go through all this trouble to kidnap her and be left with nothing but a smoking heap of ash. The firm pudding melted on her tongue, sweet ambrosia of gods and men.

Nothing happened. She swallowed. Opened her eyes. Koa watched her, his eyebrows a question mark. She didn't wait for him to feed her again, but devoured another slice, adding a banana for good measure. He brushed a crumb from the corner of her lips and tucked her hair behind her ears. He leaned back on the floor, hands behind his neck. Satiated, she, too, lay back. Again, he left her half asleep, the rope of her hair draped across his shoulders. Intending to deliver the ominous present to Hina's husband the next day, he found he couldn't part with it.

Nearly two decades later, he would be buried with Hina's long braid.

On his third night of wooing, Koa taught Hina to dance. Hula was man's dance, serious invocation to the gods in preparation for war. They chanted *meles* and stomped ritual steps. Women merely watched. But today Hina observed Koa's women dancing in the courtyard. That they weren't turned to stone no longer shocked her. She turned in unison. She felt light. Koa came to her that night dressed in a *ti* leaf skirt. He wore a crown of *maile* leaves low on his forehead, with matching bracelets and anklets. A simple shark-tooth necklace dangled on his bare chest. He sang and danced for her. The skirt rustled as he crouched low on his thighs. His bare feet murmured a susurrus across the woven *kapa* mat, like trade winds whispering through the sandalwood trees. Koa sang of the creation of his land, of his gods, and of the mythological beauty of Hina who called to him across the seas. His pure voice flowed smooth as water, touching a chord deep within her just as the rippling brook had. Koa motioned her to join him. She took tentative steps, copying him, graceful hands mimicking the movement of breezes, of waves, of the blooming of rainbows, of the birth of love.

Silent loneliness descended when he left, the door curtain falling closed behind him.

On the fourth night of Hina's captivity, Koa fell asleep. He lay down upon her mat and closed his eyes. His breathing shifted to the deep slumber of an exhausted man. His *malo*'s waistband shifted as he slept, revealing a lighter shade of untanned skin across his hips and belly. Light mahogany striped a deeper bronze, like the varying hues of brown on a polished tortoise shell, like the light flecks in his dark eyes. So, too, was his belly carved like the turtle's back, the interlocking muscles hard and square. She knelt beside him and fingered the scabbed knees where he fell when he first saw her, insignificant additions to his many scars. His pelvic bones and ribcage reminded her that he was breakable, a mortal shell for a superhuman spirit. His weapons rested alongside him, so easy to kill him. Instead, he awoke to find her sleeping beside him, the spear tucked between them like the eternal war that would someday, finally, tear them apart.

Hina awoke. Once more, this strange king knelt before her – crouching, his mouth between her legs, finishing what he had interrupted at the brook. She thought this, her first climax, was her death, punishment for the broken *kapus*. At the cresting of this bursting pleasure, she expected to see her toes turning to rock. She had swallowed Pele whole, her body heaving like Mauna Kea erupting. She'd seen men sucked out to sea by the riptides, becoming specks in the distance. Like the merciless undertow, Koa's mouth sucked the soul out of her, leaving her limp and empty.

He looked up over her soft belly and spoke his first words to her: "I'll take you back to your home."

"You don't want me?"

"If you leave, I'll let your husband kill me. But I won't keep you here against your will. The choice is yours."

Hina didn't pause. "I'll stay. For a while."

Koa rose up from his knees and kissed her, smelling of the sandalwood forest. He shed his *malo*, straddling her. A slow trickle between her legs started, and she wondered if she had wet herself in fear. But she wasn't afraid, and this moisture wasn't urine or her menses. Perhaps this humiliation was part of the curse, of her punishment. She would disgust this new conqueror, this handsome warrior, and he would toss her out like rancid meat. But Koa only smiled at her body's invitation. Her understanding blossomed. Like her climax, this was a gift the goddess had withheld from her up until now, like so much else her people's religion falsely denied her. This smoothing of the way for him was like soft flower petals between her fingers as she strung them together. When he joined with her, at last, it wasn't like her husband chafing her brittle dryness, but a slow and gentle fullness. Not a scorched friction as with the old chief's thrashing, but a blending of heat – not like the rubbing of dry wood together to create a fire, but like the *kukui* lamp, flame and oil burning slick and hot together, and one died if the other ran out.

And so it's been every night for eighteen years. Until finding her, he'd been like the rare driftwood timber that kind gods spit onto the beach. Enormous pines that traveled from distant, unknown lands, these prized logs lay unused until another matching tree beached itself, perhaps years later, so they could be lashed together to traverse the seas as true mates.

She has named him her Koa, not calling him by the long name he is known by in legend. Koa, her tree that would stand through storms for her, that she could cling to in the buffeting wind, his body like the changeable koa wood out of which they carved bowls and weapons. Like the giant koa tree that towered over all others in the forest, its massive crown a protection for all who sheltered beneath it, its gnarled wood could yet be polished into smooth works of beauty. Scarred and scabbed, yet striated with softness like the koa's varying hues, Koa's colors changed in her presence. Not a monarch, not a warrior, but a lover.

For two decades he defends her. Her liberation symbolized everything he fought for. But tomorrow he'll be ripped from her as roots from earth in a hurricane. Her own two sons have grown to adulthood and will reclaim her at last. They've discovered and converged upon his hidden compound. It would seem that Hina is powerless, but she listens to the screams of the dying men and understands her power. The fate of great men, great nations, great religions, revolves around her. She won't fight her destiny. But tonight is hers, her last to repay Koa for the gift of love he has given her, for his protection during her years of captivity, which were really her years of freedom.

The sky opens up and weeps in grief for tomorrow's separation of the two lovers, cleansing Koa of the day's blood and gore. He sheds his soiled garments outside her hut and steps inside, naked. For the first and only time, his body betrays no desire for her. Water catches the lamp flame and dances in his hair like the setting sun on ocean waves. Hina falls to her knees before him, arms wrapped around his legs, face pressed to the center of his being, this sacred part that locks their bodies together. A fine shivering dances through his body, as his muscles tic with exhaustion. Rival forces outnumbered him ten to one today, and enemy gods decreed his defeat, yet still he stands. He drops to his knees beside her.

She moves behind him and runs the whalebone comb through his hair, now the color of silvery dawn but still thick and curly. He collapses back against her, and she cradles him to her breast. He falls asleep there, though he fights slumber, not wanting to waste a precious last moment. She stares down at him as she did that night so long ago, when she could have killed him but chose to love him instead. Despite the passing of years, he's still supple and muscular. More scars decorate his body, inevitable tattoos of war. Deep lines along his eyes have been carved not by the sun, but by his smile. She prays to Pele to give him dreams of her love, rather than ghastly visions born of battle carnage, and the volcano goddess answers. Passion rises during his brief nap, and he wakes with his hard *ule* in her fist. Even in this, when death awaits to distract him, he won't fail her. She straddles him. Tomorrow she'll dry up, an old streambed choked with rocks and weeds, to be entered again by nobody. But tonight she's mossy and slick, and she rides him like the waves. Koa has taught her to surf. She often paddled her redwood board far out to sea to greet him on his return voyages, his red sail parting the distant sky like a sunrise.

Long ago, when he had first flipped her over halfway through lovemaking, she perched on top of him like a startled turtle on a log. Once more he'd turned her world upside down. She stared down at him from the dizzying height of this new perspective, her body controlling his as he lay beneath her. He reached down, his thumb nestled into the part in her body, and she moved against his hand, against his body, invoking Pele's eruption inside her.

But tonight, when he lays beneath her, too weary to move, she staves off the finality of pleasure. The wind outside howls and tattoos a furious beat against the walls, protesting the lovers' parting. His hands reach up to her breasts, and tears trickle down his cheeks. She leans down to kiss him, and he tastes like the sea.

In the end, it is love, not man, not the gods, that sends Koa to the dark underworld of *Po*. Nothing less could kill one so great. The next day, Hina's lover of two decades comes face to face with Kana, sprung from Hina's own womb. Koa cannot bring himself to kill his lover's son. Hina's own beloved features are carved into this boy's face. Both men stand with spears raised. Koa's advantage is clear. Kana is barely a man, an unformed pup with fear in his eyes, weapon shaking. Hina still had milk in her breast for this child when Koa stole her away. Koa lowers his arm and drops his spear. Kana deals the glorious death blow to the unbeaten king.

As Hina sails away, she looks back over her shoulder. Flames rising from Koa's temple lick the heavens, sending his spirit to decorate the night sky. The shark god's statue stands headless on the cliff. In her lap she carries the whalebone comb. She works her fingers along the teeth, imagining that she massages the knotty ridges of Koa's spine when he returns from battle. The comb's teeth have caught strands of their hair – his silver, hers still black – as they themselves were caught in the tide of history and legend.

The mother that Kana carries triumphantly home is not the

ious and still woman that Koa abducted long ago. They say
ears of captivity cracked her mind. She openly breaks taboo by
ating forbidden fruits and dancing. She hacks off her hair and
ides the ocean waves. She prays to a constellation in the sky that
10 one else sees. The gods don't strike her down, for she can't
1elp her unhinged mind. Though she's crazy as an *o'o*, she's more
ovely than the day she left, as graceful as a breeze that fails to
hase away the sorrow in her eyes.

Hold

Adam Berlin

When I fuck, I hold my sperm.

I feel whatever body is against me, watch whatever eyes are
there, some open, some closed, some rolling into the back of their
heads, shark-like. I listen to whatever sounds they make. And I
plug in, into their heads, into their bodies, pressing into their
rhythms until they're raw and done. Women say they feel damaged
after sex, after the kind of sex I do best, hard one-night sex, but
pity the men. Once our load is spent, the emptiness comes in. It
enters even before the last spurt exits. The rest of the day, all
those hours to get through, seems too, too long.

So I fuck. And I hold it. And when they ask why I don't come
I tell them. I have things to do. For me the fucking is enough. And
after I fuck, I run. Literally run. I run through city streets to prove
I can go on if I have to.

And that's what I'm doing. I'm running. Down the steep hill
where West End Avenue coasts into 96th Street before it turns up
again, past the doormen standing outside luxury buildings, waiting for elevators to come down so they can open doors, hail cabs,
see the rich off safely and soundly. My running shoes are Nike,
black stripes on the side. My running shorts are sidewalk grey but
light, material made for breathing. My shirt's a simple white T.
The music pressed against my ears has hard beats that keep me
running hard.

My breathing is even. My legs feel mighty. My balls are full. I
turn and run back, fast, faster. When I reach my apartment I stop
and stretch for a few seconds, hands against a fire hydrant, feet
on the curb. Then I open my building door and run up the five
flights of stairs. Off the street, the music's louder in my ears.

I open the door, 5F, and the floor's wood slats move my eyes
straight to the single window that's all the way open, my view of

Broadway's uptown lights so unlike the downtown Broadway lights they sing about.

And sitting in my desk chair, her ankle cuffed to the radiator, a ball gag in her mouth, is C, the name I've given her. I met C three nights ago coming out of a downtown club. I was walking by, she was walking out and I didn't have to say a word. Her too-tight leather, her breasts squeezed together, constricted in black, her heavy blue mascara, the whole costume I knew too well, was all I needed to see. I looked straight at her for a long time and she didn't move her eyes. I said I needed money. She reached into her bag and made sure I saw the cuffs, the ball-gag, the clothes pins, the dildos, the vibrator. Then she opened her wallet and counted out ten one-hundred-dollar bills, half a month's rent.

"For what?" I said.

C showed me three fingers, fingernails painted black.

"Three nights?" I said.

She nodded.

"And three days?"

She nodded again.

We took a cab uptown where I handcuffed her, ball-gagged her, fucked her, didn't come.

Three full days.

Seventy-two hours.

And this is what we do: I fuck her and then I leave. To go to work. To complete a chore. To take a run. To hit a bar for a late-night drink. To do whatever I wish. I keep her waiting for me, my awaited entrance a thrilling expectation – maybe I'll show up soon, maybe I'll show up never. The waiting makes C's pussy drip.

In one hour the seventy-two hours are done.

On the desk is a bowl of dry cereal and a glass of water. I leave her something so she won't starve if I don't return for a while. The longest I've been gone is eleven hours. After eleven hours, my cock slipped right in.

I take off my sweaty T. I take off my running shoes and shorts. I don't even look at C. I go into the bathroom to shower. I soap my body and my cock. I wash my hair. This is the last time I'll fuck C and I want her to remember me, remember the way I fucked her. I hold my sperm. I want them to hold me in their heads, the way I fucked them tattooed against their brains, so on

empty nights they'll touch themselves and think of me. It's the
only power I have. My work is mundane. My studio apartment is
small. I have no ambition anymore and really no goals. I can fuck.
I can hold my sperm. I can run.

I towel myself dry and walk along the wood floor, barefoot,
naked, my cock half hard. I stop in front of C. Her eyes are on my
eyes. I take the ball-gag from her mouth and put my cock in. She
sucks on it, needy, makes it rock.

"Last one," I say.

She doesn't say a word.

"Last one and then you leave."

I unchain her ankle. Grab the back of her hair. Move her to my
bed.

We've done everything there is to do, used her ropes and cuffs,
used her dildos and vibrator, used her clothes pins and electric
clamps, and I've fucked her everywhere, every way.

So as something different I do the most conservative thing in
the world. I get on top of her. I put her legs around my waist. And
I fuck her hard. I listen to her come and come and come and she's
still wet when I take my cock out.

The hour's done and C is good about standing up, getting her
things together, putting them back in her bag. She puts on her
clothes, the clothes she wore when I met her coming out of the
club. I'm in bed, naked, watching. She looks like she looked three
days ago, a cartoon of a woman dressed for painful pleasure, but
it's late enough that her costume won't be so absurdly conspicu-
ous. Manhattan at night is big enough to take in everyone without
evoking more than a glance or two.

"Have you done this before?"

I've never heard C speak and her voice is soft, softer than I'd
expected. I've only heard her come.

"Have I done what before? Gotten paid to fuck, or played this
little BDSM fantasy game before?"

I haven't talked to her either, except to tell her what I was
going to do, or what I was doing while I did it, so my voice, I'm
guessing, sounds different to her too. She takes me in. Her eyes
are the oldest part of her. Her body is still firm and her skin is
mostly tight, but there are fine lines around her eyes and her
irises, more than black, show she's been around.

"Either one," C finally says.

"I have. I've done the one. I've been paid. And I did the other when I was married. I was married for a short time. She was a famous dominatrix. I thought her life was a joke."

"That must have made her happy."

"We were married for less than a year. If she remembers me at all, there's not much happiness attached to it. We jumped in. We jumped out."

"Why did you think her life was a joke?"

"It's a game."

"'You could say everything's a game."

"I could. And I could say, Look at you. Look what you're wearing. Those aren't clothes. That's a costume. You have toys in your pocketbook. You want to be controlled. You want someone to threaten you with pain at all times. That's a child's position. It's all Dungeons and Dragons with a little bit of hurt."

"Look at you," she says.

I look myself over. My body looks perfect. My cock looks perfect. My balls, full and tight and round, look perfect.

"Look at me," I say. "I have nothing to hide."

"That's your game. Not a care in the world. But you're very good at playing the game you call a child's game. That says something."

"Want me to be crass?"

"Let's hear it."

"For a thousand bucks, I can be good at most things."

"That's too easy," she says and the word kicks me between the legs. Too easy is what my wife always said. When I laughed at her. When I threatened her, bragging I could walk away in a second and never come back. When I told her she would remember me more than I'd remember her.

"Good," I say. "Then I'm easy."

"I didn't say *you* were easy. If you were easy I wouldn't have gone home with you."

"So you knew I was hard? You knew I was difficult?" The smirk's in my voice even if it's not turning up my mouth.

"Look at you," she says again, no smirk at all, her voice soft, calm, patient, an adult talking to a kid, not the other way around. I pull the sheet over me. It just happens. I'm aware of everything, but I hadn't been aware of that until my hand lifted the sheet, covered my cock. I pull the sheet off me and laugh a fake laugh. C's not fooled. Her eyes keep taking me in.

"Look at me," I say. "But I thought we already did that."

"When I saw you, when I saw you on the street walking past, I thought you were handsome, of course, I thought you were sexy, of course, but handsome and sexy is all over this city. I saw your eyes and they were empty. That's why I let you take me home. You needed something and maybe this is what you needed."

"I needed the money."

"I wasn't sure what you needed until now. Maybe you needed your wife."

One night, I was out drinking with drinking friends and we passed the Limelight where they held the Black and Blue Ball, one of the big BDSM events. My wife was inside the club and my friends and I, by chance, walked by the line in front. It looked like a Halloween party for lost kids and out-of-shape adults. Everyone was dressed in their best black and blue costumes. There were lots of piercings, lots of tattoos, lots of leather and latex. The guys I was with laughed at these people. I laughed at these people. I didn't tell them my wife was inside. When my wife and I fought, which was constantly, fights the whole year we were together, she accused me of having a problem with what she did. I had no real problem and that was the problem. Men paid big money to worship her, but to me, she was just my wife. And that's what I'd tell her. It was the word just that pissed her off. It was the word "easy" that pissed me off.

"I divorced my wife."

"So you said, but maybe you needed something a child needs."

C stands there. She walks over to me. She lies down next to me. She puts her hand on my cock. I take her wrist in my hand, but she keeps her hand on my cock and I let her. She starts to stroke me, slow.

"I don't need anything," I say.

"We all need something. I know what I need, so it's easy for me to get. Easy can be good too. I saw your pupils dilate when I said that word. I saw the flash of anger."

"You didn't see anything."

She doesn't answer that. She just strokes my cock.

Then she stops.

Then she stands.

C takes off her clothes and gets back into bed with me. Her skin against my skin is warm. When my wife and I fought, when the screaming was done and her crying was done, sobs that turned to heavy breaths that turned quiet, I'd go to the bakery on the corner and buy her a piece of carrot cake. She loved their carrot cake, loved the coconut they put on the frosting. She loved the word "coconut". She'd say "Co-co-nut," stretching out all three syllables, and she'd smile and finish her cake and fall asleep.

C puts her hand back on my cock.

"Can you do this?" she says.

Now it's my turn not to answer.

"Do you want to do this?" she says.

I turn her over. I put my cock in her and look in her eyes. I move as slowly as she stroked my cock. It's a pantomime of making love, an expression I hate. Fucking is fucking even when it means something. When my wife was in bed with me, her state-of-the-art BDSM studio with its cage and chains and whips and canes many subway stops downtown, her work far from the door-way of our home, our apartment so close to Riverside Park we smelled the leaves turning in fall, that's what we did. We fucked. We fucked more gentle than rough, more soft than hard, and after she came and then curled next to me, she really was a kid, a sweet kid, naked, costume-less, my wife. That's how I fuck C. I fuck her slow and slow and slow, watching her eyes, kissing her mouth, her neck, her shoulders, her breasts, moving steady and slow, and when she's about to come I tell her to wait and she waits, and when she's about to come I tell her to hold it and she holds it, and I move and move until she says she can't hold it anymore.

I stop fucking her.

"You can't, can you?" she says.

"I can come on a dime."

"You know what I mean."

"I'm pretending."

"I know," she says.

"You're not my wife."

"Did you pretend with your wife?"

"I pretended a lot of things. I pretended our marriage was real. Sometimes I even pretended our marriage would last."

"Pretend some more."

"My marriage is done."

"With me. Pretend with me. If you pretend hard enough, it won't be pretend anymore."

"You're wrong," I say. "I'm a pro."

"I know. I paid you."

"No. I'm a real pro. I don't mistake any of this for what it isn't. All you BDSM fakes think you're living on the edge, that your games make you unique, that you're plugged into something, connected to something the rest of the boring, homogenized population doesn't understand, but you're just like everyone else. That's why your game's so sad. That's why it's so fake. I never pretend. It's just fucking. It's no different from eating or taking a shit. Dress it up all you want. It's just fucking. And that's why everything fades. Show me one married couple that says their sex has improved with time and I'll show you two liars. And if they start talking about love, I'll show you two people who've stopped wanting to fuck."

"You're empty," C says.

"Look at me," I say.

"Yes. Look at you."

I put my hand around my balls and hold them. "Look. I'm full. They're full. And as long as they're full, I'm mighty. I'm connected. I'm interested in you. I could stick my cock in your cunt in a second. But as soon as they empty, I'll be empty. And I'll think of my ex. And I'll think of every woman I thought I loved. And I'll know it was all pretend. And I'll be colder than I am right now."

"What if you weren't?"

"Cold?"

"What if you came and you weren't cold."

"I'm not a child anymore. I told you, I don't pretend."

I get out of bed. I stand there and look down at her. She looks warm and open and I keep my eyes on her eyes until I don't care.

"Go on," I say.

She doesn't say anything

"Go on."

She breathes heavy, a long inhale and exhale that's almost a sigh.

"Go on," I say. "You don't need me. Go on."

She moves her hand from between her breasts to her stomach to between her legs and I watch. I watch her move her fingers from the top of her cunt to the bottom then up to the top again. I watch her press her fingers against her clit. I watch her move her fingers, slow at first, back and forth, then a little faster, pressing her fingers in, moving her fingers faster. I'm watching her, but she's in bed alone. I'm watching her, but she's touching herself. A sound comes from her mouth then another and her fingers are moving faster, faster. Her eyes close and she's all alone. Her fingers. Her cunt. Her. And whatever she's thinking, and I've always wanted it to be about me, a tattoo of me, remember me, but even if it is me, me in her head, it's just pretend. What's real is her, her body, alone on the bed.

I put on my running shorts. I put on my running shoes. There's a poem about pros, about pro-fuckers, who approach sex like running, who never mistake, and that's the word, who never mistake fucking for love. The poem ends with the image of a runner.

It isn't just an image. Not for me. I'm a runner. I run with full balls.

C has been in my apartment for three days, much of it alone. I'm leaving her alone again, but this time, when I return, she'll be gone.

I leave my apartment, go down the stairs, go out the door. It's officially fall, but I don't smell any leaves.

I start to run.

I run fast, faster.

Fast running.

Hard running.

My balls full with sperm.

I'm running and I want to cry, but I hold it, hold it, hold it and make my eyes empty and run.

Golden Hand

K. L. Gillespie

Rush hour was well under way and Molly had already picked two pockets by the time she arrived at Victoria Station. She worked the main concourse for twenty minutes before jumping into a black cab and heading over to the city where the richest pickings were to be had. She always took taxis, unless she was following a mark, because the public transport system was full of criminals.

Molly had been dipping professionally since she was fifteen and she had it down to a fine art. She'd honed her skills on the Paris Metro where she was known locally as *"la main d'or"* until she had her heart broken by a French Lothario and moved back to London.

Meanwhile, on the other side of town, Nicholas was running for his train. There were no seats left so he leaned against the door and closed his eyes while the train cut through London.

Molly was speeding along the Embankment in the back of a hackney cab. She didn't look like a pickpocket. Her clothes reeked of money, they had to, they were a tool of the trade, allowing her to melt seamlessly into the crowds of commuters that she worked five days a week. They were also her "get-out-of-jail card" because on the rare occasion that she did get caught what overworked, stressed, ex-public schoolboy could resist her five-inch Louboutins and seamed stockings. None so far, that's for sure.

Nicholas spent his journey drifting in and out of a waking dream where he was tied to a bed by a beautiful woman, naked bar silk stockings and stilettos. It was only when the train pulled into the station and the doors jolted open that he woke up with a start. His dream was long gone but a throbbing erection in his pants was there to remind him as he was herded onto the platform by a wave of commuters.

London Bridge was still heaving when Molly arrived, just the way she liked it, overcrowded and anonymous, perfect pickpocketing territory. She had a good feeling about today as she positioned herself under the announcement board, eyes peeled.

Molly scanned the station and within seconds she had found her mark. Experience told her that he would be an easy lift – tall, mid-thirties, well dressed, just Molly"s type. She watched his every move with the eyes of a hunter.

Nicholas checked his watch, time was getting on so he picked up his pace and headed into the Tube.

Molly watched him disappear into the underground and instinct told her to follow him but she had to move fast so she trotted across the station in her heels and tailgated him down the escalator and into the surreal depths of the Northern Line. A sea of heads stretched out in front of her but she was focused and never lost sight of his dark brown hair bobbing above the crowd. She felt at home weaving through the subterranean network of tunnels that connected London. The Tube was her favourite hunting ground; it did half the work for you because people expected to be bustled, so her deft hand could easily go unnoticed as it slipped in and out of unsuspecting men's pockets.

Nicholas squeezed through the crowds on the platform and waited. Fleeting glimpses of his dream kept infiltrating his mind's eye and his cock was stirring again.

As Molly entered the platform a train pulled in and she squeezed into the carriage behind her mark. She fanned him without anyone noticing, locating his wallet in his front-left trouser pocket.

The doors closed and as the carriage jerked off she tipped forward onto her toes and jutted her breasts into his back. She felt his feet adjust, strengthening his balance and he leaned back into her, increasing the pressure between her nipples and his shoulder blades. First contact had been made and in five seconds he would be used to the pressure of her body against his.

Nicholas was oblivious to the young woman pressing up against him, he was used to being jostled every morning. Besides, he was too busy wishing he were somewhere else, somewhere private where he could give his erection the attention it demanded, to notice anything happening around him.

As they entered the tunnel and darkness swamped the train Molly's hand entered his left trouser pocket. Her touch was light and she was sure that he hadn't felt a thing. She had expected her polished, carmine fingertips to find his wallet straight away and whip it out in a split second but she was momentarily thrown when they rested on his erect penis. She knew she had to be professional about this but his cock was throbbing hypnotically beneath her fingertips and there was no way that he could have failed to notice her hand cupping the tip of his erection, but he hadn't even flinched.

Nicholas froze. He knew he should have turned round and confronted them but the touch was so charged that he succumbed to the thrill.

When Molly sensed his submission it set her pulse racing. She gently squeezed him and when his breathing deepened she realized she had complete control. With this free rein, Molly started to run her nails over his cock; the lining of his trousers was as thin as silk and she could feel every ridge and vein as she probed deeper into his pocket.

Nicholas had always fantasized about an anonymous encounter like this and now his dreams were coming true.

Molly had him in the palm of her hand and she basked in the power. It was electrifying and she could feel her cunt throbbing against the lace of her pants. She squeezed her thighs together putting gentle pressure on her vulva and worked her hand up and down the length of his cock. She allowed her blood-red nails to play over the marshmallow softness of his glans as it strained against his trousers and she dragged at the inside of his pocket with her £100 manicure, desperate to feel his naked flesh.

Nicholas wanted to see who was touching him but he was scared that if he turned round she would stop. He strained his eyes to the side as far as he could and caught a glimpse of her shoes and stockings reflected in the door. It was enough to send his libido hurtling into orbit and he lifted his briefcase up, providing her with a shield to work behind as she pushed his foreskin to and fro with energetic relish.

Molly pulled him towards her and picked up the pace. She pushed herself into his back, forcing her pudendum into his gyrating arse as it buffeted backwards and forwards. She gritted her teeth and wave after wave of unrestrained pleasure started to swamp her body.

Nicholas could feel her thrusting against him and the more she thrust the more disengaged he became with the world around him. His heart was pounding against his chest as he swayed his hips in time with her strokes. Rapid, rhythmic contractions swirled round the base of his penis, and his pelvis contracted. He had reached ejaculatory inevitability and there was no going back now.

Molly too was unable to control herself any longer and she slipped her fingers into her pants and cupped her cunt tightly in her hand. She was already slick and needed only the slightest pressure, expertly applied, to tease out an orgasm. She came easily, without missing a stroke and as the train hurtled through the tunnel her mark hurtled towards his orgasm.

Nicholas felt his whole body tense in anticipation and lost himself in the moment. The last thing he remembered before he was hurled into the vortex of his own climax was her body spasming against his and, as the train pulled into the station, he came, and came, and came.

Molly felt his warm cum as it seeped through his pocket and she silently withdrew her hand. The train came to a standstill and Molly slipped out quietly as soon as the doors opened.

Nicholas was spent. His heart was pounding and his mind was racing. He couldn't make sense of anything that had happened but it had been exhilarating and he was addicted. He wanted more, to follow her, to thank her, to see her again perhaps, but she had already disappeared into the crowds and he knew it was over.

Molly opened her bag on the escalator and took the wallet out. She stroked it before opening it up and checking his cards. Nicholas Sackworth, he had a name now. There was a photo too and for some reason she couldn't put it down. She stared at it all the way up the escalator, desperately looking for clues to his life but it was just a passport photo and it told her nothing. Nevertheless she kept it and the eighty quid that she had found, but she threw the rest away in the nearest bin before hailing a taxi.

Stella

Saskia Walker

Even when she was totally naked Stella was a lady. Even when she was getting herself splendidly fucked there was something quintessentially ladylike about her. I'm not sure if it was breeding, or money – although she did come from an aristocratic family – but it was an enduring quality, and given that Stella was naked rather a lot that was quite a skill to maintain. Stella was the most outstanding woman in our year at university, and it was because of Stella that I began to identify as a bisexual woman.

I'd noticed her long before she spoke to me, of course, but we actually met on this one sunny day when I was walking up the library steps with a couple of others from my seminar group. Stella was holding court halfway up the steps. As we approached her that day she waved to one of my companions. "Pete, please say you'll come to my party."

There was laughter in her eyes as she asked the question. As if anyone would say no to an invitation from Stella. I stared at her. I couldn't help myself. A secret smile lingered around her mouth. She was wearing black ski pants and a soft pink sweater that barely clung to her. It hung off her shoulders. She was Nordic looking, and always seemed to wear clothes that looked as if they were painted on, or about to fall off. As I stood there watching her in awe I noticed that she wasn't wearing a bra and her nipples stood out under the soft wool. I could imagine how good that felt, and secretly admired her for being so clever.

She noticed me staring, and some sort of recognition flickered through her eyes.

Pete was speaking. She replied to whatever he said and Pete grinned. "And bring your girlfriend, won't you."

She was looking at me. My breath caught in my throat.

Pete looked awkward.

"We're not," I blurted. "I mean, we're just friends, we've been in a seminar together."

My response seemed to bait her interest even more. She stepped closer. "That doesn't matter. Come to my party, pretty please."

It was almost as if she had forgotten all about Pete and was totally focused on me. I nodded. I was so thrilled that I couldn't manage to respond verbally, but I was smiling. Looking back on it, I wondered if she spotted something in me right then. She walked away, but glanced back over her shoulder, right at me. That was enough. I was hooked.

In the days leading up to the party I couldn't stop thinking about her. Was it just her star-like quality, or was there another reason why she made my pulse tick faster? I couldn't deny that it turned me on. Even thinking about her made my hands clench and between my legs an eager pulse tripped higher and higher, like a time bomb close to detonation. I wanted to drink in that unique quality she had in her sexuality: ultra feminine, confident, powerful, and yet somehow fragile and beautiful all at once, the quintessential blonde bombshell. It was like watching some Hollywood goddess from the fifties walking through a movie set.

I liked having sex with men, so this strange fascination with Stella made me think about my sexuality and question it, especially because I was so excited by her personal invitation. It was more than just admiring her. I was definitely sexually aroused. Did that mean I was bisexual? It was something I'd never considered before. I'd never had to because I'd never felt like this before. She definitely turned me on, I couldn't deny that. Stella made me want to touch myself while I was thinking about her. I wanted to savor her, like a fine wine. I wanted to watch and absorb her, enjoy every moment and every sensual response I felt. That's why her invitation triggered a massive sense of expectation and arousal in me. Not only would I see her again, and soon. I would get to observe the lioness stalking in her own territory.

The house Stella lived in was large and well furnished – no student dive. I sipped wine and passed the time until I saw her moving through the rooms chatting with her guests. She was wearing a slip of a dress the color of ruby red port. It shifted over her breasts when she moved and looked as if one touch would have it dropping to the floor. That sent a shiver of arousal through me, because I automatically pictured myself nudging that strap free from her shoulder, initiating the undressing of Stella.

"I'm so glad you could come," she said as she approached me, eyeing me with that half-smile as if she knew why I was there better than I did.

Heat flared in my face. "Thank you for inviting me."

"Come on, I'll get you another drink." She urged me into the kitchen, one hand possessively against my back between my shoulder blades, as if we'd known each other forever. Was she coming on to me? We chatted a while, mostly about which courses we were taking the following term. The usual stuff you did when you first meet a student you don't know very well. Then someone called her away and I went back to my own crowd, but I felt somehow enriched, as if I had a secret.

The next time I saw her it was past midnight and I was looking for the bathroom. "Here," she beckoned, her eyes filled with humor, "you can use my bathroom."

She led me into a bedroom littered with discarded garments, which made me chuckle. Always getting naked? I wondered. A bedside lamp covered with a red shade gave the otherwise gloomy room a sensual glow. The bed was stacked with cushions and throws and looked as if it had been unmade forever.

Stella nodded over at one of two doors on the far wall. "Help yourself," she said.

Then she was gone. The door closed behind her. I was left alone in her lair. I breathed in her scent. My gaze was drawn back to the bed. The sheets would smell of her, the pillows too. After I'd used the bathroom, I got curious about the other door. Surely it wouldn't do any harm to have a peep in there before I left?

There was a light switch on the wall, but I didn't want to take the risk of turning it on. As I got accustomed to the gloom I could see it was a wardrobe of the walk-in variety, and it was packed with shelves and racks of clothes. I wandered in and ran my hand over them. Stella's clothes, the things she wore against her skin. I trailed my fingers over various items on coat hangers, thinking about them being against her skin and imagining how that felt.

Before I had a chance to think about it any more I heard laughter and the sound of a door opening. Dismayed, I glanced back into the bedroom. It was Stella, and she had a man with her. A sense of panic quickly rose inside me. She must have forgotten I was in there or assumed I had already gone. Mercifully, she kept the guy at the door until she'd scoped the room. Then she grabbed him by the hand and pulled him in after her, shut the door behind him, and turned the key in the lock. Next thing I knew, she was backing him toward my hiding place.

That's when I realized it would have been better if she'd seen me. I could have made an excuse and hurriedly left. Now I was trapped. I was locked in her private space with them, and by the looks of it they were about to indulge in some hot bed action. I had to announce myself, and quickly. But just before I got the words out, Stella embraced the man and looked over his shoulder, making direct eye contact with me. She lifted one finger to her lips and winked at me.

It began to dawn on me – she'd obviously set this up on purpose. Stella was an exhibitionist. My mind and body buzzed in response to that sudden realization, the heady rush it unleashed unlike anything I'd ever experienced before. I tried to steady my erratic breathing. I had to get a grip on myself. She obviously didn't want her companion to know, because she kept him standing with his back to me as she undressed him and went about measuring his chest with her hands and whispering things to him as she went, making him grin with pleasure. Did she just like an audience, I wondered, or was she bi and this was her opener?

The guy she'd brought to her bedroom was well built, and I recognized him as one of the university football team, a real stud who could have his pick of the women. It didn't surprise me that he was quite willing to be Stella's plaything. However, when I looked at the way she handled him, I wondered if he was just a prop for what else was going on here – the silent link between us, our shared secret. Or was I the prop? Either way, she was getting off on it. Oh, the thrill! I'd already been turned on, and my recognition of the true nature of the set-up made my arousal flare wildly. The skin on my neck prickled with heat, my center tightening with anticipation as I watched.

"Jesus, you really are horny," the guy commented as Stella made short work of undressing him.

She laughed aloud and tugged his belt from his jeans, casting it aside before popping the button and wrenching down the zipper. "You better believe it."

She backed him toward the bed with her hand flat against his bare chest then pushed him down onto it. With a sexy purr of a laugh, she quickly removed his shoes and tugged off his jeans.

From time to time Stella smiled in my direction. When she tucked down his jockey shorts, he growled and try to snatch at her, but she ducked and escaped his clutches, determined, it seemed, to stay in charge of the situation.

His cock bounced up, long and hard and ready. He groaned and pushed his head back into the pillow, quieting down while she examined him. She traced the length of his shaft up and down with one elegant finger, making his cock twitch.

"You're tormenting me," he whispered from between gritted teeth.

"Not for long." She kicked off her heels and reached for the hem of her dress.

He watched while she lifted the fabric up and off, shimmying out of that slip of a garment. "Get over here now," he urged.

His response didn't surprise me; she was magnificent.

She wasn't wearing underwear, yet she looked as if she were instantly more comfortable in her naked self, her hands running over her body as she moved toward the man on the bed. She opened a bedside drawer, reached inside and then stroked his upright cock with one hand as she held aloft a condom in the other.

He snatched it from her raised hand, tore it open and rolled on the condom, holding the base of his cock with both hands after it was on, as if he didn't trust his cock not to leap at her of its own accord. Seeing his erect cock sheathed and ready made my core clench.

Once again Stella smiled my way, and she did it as she strad-dled his hips. My emotions grew tangled. What was she doing to me? I was aroused to the point of distraction, unable to look away, and yet her blatant glances made me feel so unbearably awkward. To top it all, the confined space of the wardrobe was growing increasingly hot, my own levels of arousal making the air stifling. But I quickly forgot my own discomfort, enthralled as I was by her blatant actions.

The guy muttered something that I couldn't catch then reached for her hips. Stella reached into the drawer by the bed, pulled out a pair of metal handcuffs and dangled them in front of his face.

"Oh, fuck," the guy said, "you kinky bitch."

I shook my head at his graceless comment. It wasn't regal enough for our Nordic dominatrix. Stella chuckled and tugged his wrists together, weaving the handcuffs between the metal uprights on her headboard before locking the second cuff into place. I was in awe. How easily she took charge of him – how easily she had taken charge of both of us, in fact. In the space of a few minutes she'd managed to arrange both of us exactly where she wanted us. Still I wondered why. Was she tormenting me, not him, was she laughing at me? Did she just like an audience and I was a convenient onlooker? I hoped not, I wanted more.

"Don't be cheeky," Stella said as she guided his sheathed cock and mounted it.

The guy grunted with pleasure. Leaning back, she put her hands on the bed behind her and rocked her hips, working herself on his rigid cock. Her body bowed exquisitely, everything on display. My hand went to my crotch and I squeezed myself through my jeans for relief, my core clutching as I watched. I could feel it all, Stella's gorgeous body, milking him off, and the rock hard cock she had inside her. The guy was completely gone on being ridden by Stella, his chest arched up to her, his head rolling against the pillows.

She looked like a goddess. It was her glorious abandonment to her pleasure that was so fascinating, her sheer hedonism. I wanted to be the one lying under her, her sex slave, having her ride my fingers, or better still a strap-on. As the desire ran through me, turning me to liquid heat, her hips moved faster, her mouth opening as she took her pleasure from the man beneath her.

Oh, to be giving her that pleasure, I wished. Oh, to be fucking Stella.

Burning up inside, I forced myself to face up to it. Before I saw Stella, I was a woman who wanted men. I'd admired other women before. I'd wondered what they were like in bed, but never before had I felt this need, this desperate craving. I had to consider the fact that I was bisexual, and it was because of Stella that I'd found out. The worst of it was that this revelation made me hornier still. The need to come was overwhelming. My hand was wrapped around the seam of my jeans, applying pressure to my throbbing clit, but as she stirred her hips and turned her head to brazenly meet my stare, it suddenly wasn't enough. Stella was naked and performing in front of me, and I had to find release. I plucked open my button and shoved my hand inside my pants, my fingers centering quickly on my hot, swollen clit. I rubbed fast, nipping and pinching, chasing relief.

Stella knew, and approval shone in her eyes. Then she planted her hands flat to the bed either side of him, the lioness crouched over her man. He groaned, his hips pushing up into hers. She worked faster on him, lifting and plunging. He was about to come, and so was she. Her eyelids lowered, her eyes narrowing into slits and her mouth opening. Oh yes, she was about to come. And still she looked like such a lady, a totally decadent lady. It made me smile. I bit my lower lip as I locked my clit between two fingers, squeezing until I flooded. I staggered against the shelves of clothing, closing my eyes a moment. Not for long, once I heard her make a sound I was watching again. When she recovered she laughed gleefully and lifted her arms. Her fingers ran through her hair as she gave an ecstatic post-coital stretch.

"Come on, let me touch you," her lover demanded.

She made him wait. No one could order Stella around – that much was obvious.

She climbed off him and stroked her slit languidly. I knew what she was doing, capturing the wave, making herself come again while she was still right there on the edge, claiming every ounce of pleasure and not giving a damn. In that moment, I loved her for being everything I wanted to be, and more.

Eventually she undid the handcuffs and threw them aside. The man beneath her grabbed her and rolled her over, but he couldn't hold Stella down. She was on her feet and stepping back into her high heels, pacing her bedroom naked, smiling secretly to herself. As he attempted to look cool and tug on his jeans, she slapped him on his bare arse before it was covered up. "Get me a drink and I'll join you out there in a few minutes, when I've freshened up."

Once again, my pulse went out of whack. She was trying to get rid of him, and she was staying behind. I felt the sudden urge to flee my hiding place, to flee the building and hide myself somewhere. But there was no way out. Stella had made sure of that.

He'd barely left the room when she made her way to my hiding place. My heart thumped hard in my chest and my mouth went dry. She pushed the door wide open, and flicked on the light. I blinked, trying desperately to meet her gaze and not stare at the rest of her, glorious as she was in her regal nakedness, deliciously enhanced as it was by her post-coital glow. Nerves assailed me.

"Sorry." I blurted the word out, unsure of myself.

"Don't be." She stepped closer. "I did it on purpose."

"Why?"

"I like you." She paused, as if to let that sink in. "And I like my female lovers to be into men as well, as I am."

My lips parted, but I couldn't speak, because I couldn't find the words to respond to that. She'd said so much in that simple statement.

Stella laughed softly and stroked my hair back from my cheek. "Did it turn you on?"

The mischievous look in her eyes made me hot all over again. I nodded.

"I'd like to be sure." Swift and deliberate, her hand dived inside my jeans and panties, where mine had been moments earlier. I nearly passed out when she touched me that way. Then her nimble fingers parted my folds and moved over my sensitive clit. "Oh yes, you really did like it, didn't you?"

There was a growl in her throat and I could see how much she enjoyed the fact I was wet because of what I'd witnessed. The evidence was right there in her shining eyes and the deliciously peaked tips of her erect nipples. Meanwhile her touch was unrelenting, one eager digit sliding inside me while the palm of her hand settled over my clit.

"Yes, I did." I steadied myself by putting one hand on her upper arm. It was an excuse to touch her, and a moment later I ran my fingers around the outline of her breast, my thumb stroking over her nipple. "Did you want me to . . . to be . . . turned on by watching you?"

"Of course I did, but this is the best part." She pushed her finger deeper, moving it around in my wet heat. "Knowing what it did to you . . . that's so good."

Her pupils were dilated, and there was no doubting that she was aroused.

"You liked me watching?"

She nodded. "I'd have liked it even better if you'd been in the bed too."

A moan of pleasure escaped me. My hips began moving of their own accord, rocking in time with the thrust of her fingers, the nudge of her palm against my tender clit making me gasp aloud. Driven by lust, and knowing for sure that having me there had obviously made her hot, made me bold. My hands roved over her, reveling in the way she felt. Stella moved closer still, responding.

"Mmm, yes," she murmured encouragingly.

I moved my hand lower, to her bare pussy, and stroked my knuckles over the plump cushion of her mons. When she didn't pull away I acted quickly, finding my way into her slick niche to the bump of her clit. Our eyes locked and it sank in that we were there together, each with a hand wrapped around the other's pussy, about to jack each other off. Then sheer physical need took over.

Pumping and grinding we worked each other hard and fast, our bodies shunting together. Elbows and hips hit the shelves and clothing fell to the floor. The storage unit creaked loudly as we worked each other to a mutual peak up against it. My earlier orgasm had been quick, furtive and desperate, but this was so wild and hot and mutual, and my body was practically singing as she drove me into ecstasy. It barreled through me, stealing my breath away and making my legs weak. It was the most marvelous thing ever, because I had never come that way before. I could feel Stella's core clamping on my fingers and her juices running into my hand. It made my chest burn with pride.

When she leveled, Stella laughed joyously, and her smile lit something in my chest. I was smiling too. Sweat broke out on my skin and my crotch was drenched, my cunt pounding with release. She kissed me then, tentatively, then more insistent and seductively, her tongue teasing between my lips. She was so soft yet so strong and decadent, and I wanted her badly.

Meshing her fingers with mine, she kissed me along the jaw and when she reached my ear whispered to me. "Come on, I'll get dressed then we can go back into the party together."

She squeezed my hand, meaningfully.

That surprised me because she had arranged to meet her male lover. "But he'll know I was in here."

She shrugged and mischief shone in her eyes. "He won't be sure, and it'll drive him mad. Don't worry, he knows I'm bi. I'm sure he'll be pleased to meet you."

She kissed me again, long and hard, and it meant something. It held a million promises. She drew back, and looked me in the eyes, all serious. "Are you willing?"

How could I resist? I grinned, and nodded. "Willing and able."

Make Your Own Miracles

Nikki Magennis

Violet takes a steamcab to the dirty end of town. She suspects
the driver is taking her a tortuous, inventive route, but she
doesn't mind as much as she should. She likes these dark narrow
streets, the pockets of decrepit and dangerous buildings popu-
lated by fiends and outlaws. In addition, she herself is up to
much the same kind of farrago. This whole trip, in fact, is part
of a tortuous, inventive route to increase her personal gain. Her
very personal gain.

She raps on the ceiling.

"Here will do," she calls, over the hissing of the pistons. The
wheels grind to a halt against the cobbles. She's on the corner
of Trongate, could almost be visiting a hat shop, looking for a
suitable frippery to wear to her next afternoon garden party
– if she weren't dressed, that is, in rather unusually sombre
clothing and if she were not draped with a dark, voluminous
cloak of thick velvet.

"Tenner," said the driver, turning to spit into the gutter.

"That's outrageous," she said.

"My usual rate for such a precious cargo. Sir Catter wouldn't
like to think his daughter were bein' carried round by some fly-
by-night villain, now would he? 'Specially in these parts of town.
A woman needs lookin' after round here, don't she?"

He leered at her with a mouth full of broken teeth.

Violet passed him the note, her fingertips feeling greasy
although she didn't touch his grubby mittens.

Once the cab had spluttered along the street and was lost
among the afternoon traffic, Violet slid down the alley between
the bakers and the music hall. The smell of hot bread made her
mouth water, as it always did. Or perhaps it was anticipation of
another sort.

The door was heavy, but Violet had learned the trick. With one sharp kick of her leather boot, it sprang in the hinges and gave enough that she could tug it open. She lifted the cape to cover her face. The smells down here were of the nightsoil variety – thick enough to make you retch.

The lift was a fearsome cage – rusted so thick that it appeared to be made of dried mud. Flakes of old paint came away on her glove when she closed the doors behind her. She swallowed her fear. Four floors, she said to herself, pulling the lever to raise the lift upwards. The higher she rose, the more light-headed she felt. Her palms were damp, and she rubbed them against the soft fur of the cape.

He knew she was coming. Of course he knew. Would he be waiting for her? Automatically, she reached to her face, buried her hand in the wild black frizz of her hair. She drew her shoulders back and watched the floors roll slowly past outside the criss-cross lift bars. Something clicked as she rose higher. A cog complaining of the strain. Cables stretched to breaking point.

Violet closed her eyes.

The lift drew to a halt. She got out and arranged her skirts before ringing the bell.

"Hello," he said, pulling open the studio door.

"You were expecting me."

"Of course." He stood watching her. His – she didn't know exactly what to call it – his machine hand, the prosthesis, gripped the doorframe.

"It is cold out here, sir."

"Come in, come in." At once, he flung open the door and turned to the dim chaos of his studio. Violet followed with as much dignity as she could muster, even though her knees felt horribly like they were not connected to the rest of her. As if she were cobbled together, like Gustav, a broken person who'd been remade and was now something other than entirely human.

"Care for a drink?" He threw the question over his shoulder.

"Yes." She needed something sharp.

Gustav lived like a wild animal. His workshop was also his home. Violet had been shocked, on her first visit, to see a heap of blankets and animal skins tumbled in a corner, dishevelled and obviously recently slept in. Women like her were not raised to visit the sleeping quarters of males. The sight of Gustav's bed sheets was enough to make her cheeks burn. But Gustav laughed when she blushed, and now, after two subsequent trips out here to Hell's western outpost, she had taught herself to ignore the depraved manner in which the man chose to live.

"I've made some modifications," Gustav said as he reappeared and handed her a shot glass. "I think you'll be pleased."

"I know what I want."

"And you are all the more admirable for it," Gustav said. He raised his glass to her. When he threw back his drink, Violet's treacherous gaze hooked onto his throat, the jut of his Adam's apple. Her eyes slid inexorably down, towards the second, more shadowy jut, the slight protruberance at his crotch. It wasn't the first time she'd been secretly fascinated by the workings of a man's body. Only Gustav's seemed, somehow, so much more . . . vivid than those of other men.

"Unusual," Gustav said.

Violet's eyes jerked up to meet his. She swallowed, and tasted the fumes of whatever potcheen he'd just served her. "What is?" she asked.

"A woman who has the gall to demand what she wants. But then, you are born to a family that is used to doing whatever it pleases."

"I'd be grateful if you would not mention my family," Violet said. "While I'm here, I'm your employer, not anybody's daughter. Is that clear?"

Gustav stared at her.

"You've been amply rewarded for your compliance," Violet continued. "It would be wise not to forget that."

"And it would be wise of you to learn not to try to buy someone's loyalty," Gustav said, his voice low.

"I beg your pardon?" Violet clutched her glass. Somehow, it was empty. Her mouth was burning dry.

Gustav didn't answer. Instead, he set his glass down with a click and moved towards the bench in the centre of his studio. The table was strewn with detritus, piled high with spanners and cutters and hammers and glass tubes, all discarded over scribbled plans and intricate drawings. Gustav abandoned projects when his attention was drawn to something else, the newest, ever more exciting inventions that his brilliant, darting mind came up with. Here and there among the rubble, there were tiny marvels. Violet noticed a clockwork bird, its feathers minutely engraved and its one wing perfectly constructed. She knew without asking that it was a working model, that it would fly if it was ever finished.

Because Gustav was a genius. It was how she'd heard of him, all those stories the servants retold in back rooms when they thought none of the gentry were listening. The outraged claims of her married lady friends, the hotly whispered secrets. What she'd overheard. How he'd fought as a young man, in the Clockwork Revolution, nearly been killed. And how he'd rebuilt himself. A firebrand beholden to no one, living on the edge of society, building his awful toys for the idle rich.

"I think you'll find it still fulfils your demands," Gustav said. His voice was flat now, like any servant's. His face turned away, Gustav pulled the tarpaulin from the lurking shape in the centre of the room.

The chair was a beautiful piece of craftsmanship. Anyone would be taken with the skill of the carving, the finely wrought detail on the headrest, the way the wooden spindles virtually melted into the metal. The seams were invisible. It looked almost as though it were something alive. Violet's mouth watered as she ran her eyes over the curves of it. In particular, she lingered on the special additions, the hidden components that made the "fainting chair" such a very special piece of art.

"Rather wonderful, isn't it?" Gustav said. His hand stroked the undulating backrest, as if it were the shoulder of a friend. "I've grown quite attached." With this, he held out his hand – not the flesh and blood hand, but the other one, his wire and steel simulacrum.

Violet hesitated for a fraction of a second. Long enough for a shadow to pass over his eyes.

"It won't hurt you, you know," he said, voice full of spite. "I do control it."

He reached for her hand and took it, his grip surprisingly warm, as though the metal fingertips had a pulse, and the smooth battered leather of the palm were still living skin. Still Violet flinched.

"I'm sorry," she said, shrinking back.

"You? Sorry?" Gustav raised an eyebrow. "A Catter, apologizing to a miscreant and a rebel?"

"Don't," she said, tugging at her hand. But his grip was firm. Of course it was. It wasn't entirely human. He probably couldn't read her signals, Violet thought, trying to stop herself from panicking. Couldn't feel her try to shake him loose. There was no feeling in his arm, after all.

"Oh, come now," Gustav said, almost whispering. He smiled at her. "We have to try out your machine, after all."

"No!"

"No? It was a very expensive commission, my lady. Surely you wish to satisfy yourself that it works?"

"I trust you," she said, hopelessly. His hand held her wrist casually, belying the strength of his hold on her.

"Do you?" he said. "Do you really?"

Their eyes met. His were a deep, dangerous brown, like metal that had rusted, been tempered by time and experience. Violet was no weak, simpering girl. But she wasn't used to meeting people as forthright as Gustav. The men in her circle were powerful, buoyed up by riches and inherited empires. They put on a good show of force and bravado.

Gustav was different. He had virtually nothing, yet he carried himself with the ease of a prince. With his rough, ragged shirtsleeves and his wild, shoulder-length hair he managed to wear the look of a man beautiful enough not to need polished boots and well-cut clothes. It was the way he moved, Violet supposed. The way he held himself. The way he . . . touched her.

She was silent as he pulled her towards the centre of the room.

"You want me to sit?" she asked, obedience coming far more naturally than usual.

It was, in fact, a fainting couch, he'd told her. Not for sitting in. She would lie prone over it. Face down. The thought did indeed make her feel faint.

"First things first."

His voice was as low and quiet as an idling engine. "Remove your clothes, please."

Violet felt the blood drain from her face. "How dare you."

Gustav merely inclined his head. "Violet." It was the first time he'd used her name. "Remember the measurements I asked for?"

Though she thought it impossible, she blushed harder. Her face must be as beetroot red as a scolded child's. She gave a hard nod. How could she forget? Sharing her intimate details with a stranger – it had been the most intrusive and excruciatingly embarrassing conversation. Well, almost. Asking for the machine itself should surely have been her worst nightmare. That first visit, that exhilarating leap into the unknown. She had felt herself on the edge of life, that day, ready to scream or swallow the muzzle of a gas gun. Desperate enough to do something insanely reckless. You're hysterical, she'd told herself, and then she'd gone out to find a steamcab.

She had found herself in Gustav's infernal den, and met the man with a bravado and daring to match his own. "For my health," she'd said, almost smirking. "As my dear friend Amelia was advised by her own physician."

Of course, she wasn't married. But meeting Gustav, she was certain that this detail would not bother him. Not with a purse full of coins and not with a customer as formidable as the daughter of Lord Catter himself. She'd almost felt dizzy as she stood in front of Gustav's laughing, bold brown gaze. For once, the idea struck her that she might use her power for her own satisfaction, rather than let it use her.

At the same time, she had felt herself so overtaken by rising sensation that she had barely trusted herself to stay upright. As though her body might swoon with the rushing tides of pulse and breath, as though she might lose control at any moment.

The feeling had returned.

"Measure twice. Cut once," he said. "I cannot check the fit through thirty layers of lace."

"This is necessary?" she said.

"It is, if you wish your commission well made," Gustav said reasonably. "And I did warn you this would be an intimate process."

"Your threats have not been forgotten!"

"I merely reminded you of the need for discretion. A project like this is not without risks, as you know. Sensitive information must be kept under wraps, for protection."

"Whose protection? I think you care not for my honour, sir! If my father knew what you were doing . . ."

"He'd disown you," Gustav said mildly, refilling his glass and taking a leisurely swallow. "You'd be cut off with nothing. Milady."

Violet trembled. But it was rage, not fear, that spurred her onwards.

"You would not emerge unscathed," she said. "Remember that."

"No. But I think of the two of us, you have more to lose." He came close, then, and the smell of whisky on his breath swept over her. "Far more at stake than your inhibitions, don't you think?"

"You're enjoying this," she said, reaching for the button at her throat. "You want to see me broken."

"Not broken," he said. "Merely – undone."

She shrugged. "I am not afraid of your scorn," she said.

Then there was no sound, only the muffled pop of her buttons and the swish of silk as she pulled her bodice apart. She would not let him see her cowed.

"I have defied men greater than you, sir."

"Yes. But I bet you never let them see your underwear," he said, idly, walking round his machine as if he'd lost interest in Violet's striptease already.

She barked a laugh at him.

"Don't fret, madam." He eyed her gravely. "Remember, I am doing this for your pleasure."

"Pleasure. You make it sound like a mere whim."

"Were it not for the whims of the rich, I'd be a pauper."

"It's more than idle fancy!"

"How so?"

"I am not married, sir."

"I had noticed," Gustav said.

"Unmarried ladies are not greatly popular, you know. Even if they have chosen to be so. If I wish to live alone, I must—"

"Oh, what would you understand about it? Having your whole life mapped out already. Having to fight for every scrap of independence."

"Perhaps more than you think."

Gustav was bent over the machine, adjusting a strap. Violet looked at his false fingers, noticed how delicate they were, how skilled the movements. As she watched, a calm came over her. Like a draught of cold air after a thunderstorm. She dropped her arms. Her heart fluttered in her breast, like a bird trying to escape a calico cage. Violet removed her dress in silence, only the rustle of fabric disturbing the air in the studio. Outside, there were shouts in the street and the whistle of steamships passing, floating into the Upperspace where they would circle above the smog and bustle of the city.

"Good," Gustav said lightly. "Now, here." He touched her arm more gently than she'd thought he could, with his warm, flesh and blood hand, and motioned for her to lie, face down. With as much grace as she could muster, Violet kneeled on the padded leather and slid down until her body was nestled against the curves of the chair.

"Part your legs, this way," Gustav murmured, touching her

calves very gently. He circled her, making small adjustments to her position, checking that she could reach the levers and handles. Lying prone, with her cheek against the cushion, Violet noticed a curious sensation. Despite her agitation, the chair invited her body to unwind. It supported her, like the body of a lover, she imagined – it was firm, generous, enveloping. Rising to meet her between her legs, with dips and hollows at her breasts, chin and knees, it moulded to her shape perfectly.

The leather warmed and softened under her, and she felt herself melt into the chair – had she ever felt this cared for, this mellow? A fleeting word tickled the back of her thoughts. Was this how it felt, she wondered, to be loved?

"Ridiculous," she murmured.

"Beg your pardon?"

"It fits," she replied, "very well."

"Of course," Gustav said. "But we need to test the working of it. Here, let me."

Violet bit her lip. Gustav's hand had fallen on her thigh. He dragged her legs apart, not roughly, but as though she were a doll to be posed and adjusted according to his whim.

"Ready?"

Violet murmured her assent. Gustav bent down low so that his mouth tickled her ear.

"Don't struggle, now. This will be easier if you hold yourself still."

He took her left hand, led it to the polished wooden handle.

"Just very easy, now, pull this back."

Violet did as she was told. Underneath her, cogs ground against each other. A pulley creaked. There was a loud sigh, as steam escaped, and an insistent hum as the power ran from the central steampillar and entered the machine. And she felt pressure rise against her pubis, the chair extend and curl upwards, as though a large stiff tongue were pushing against her, digging between her legs. The chair shook and hummed, as though the tongue were singing to her, a song so unbelievably warm and expansive it terrified her.

She pressed her mouth tightly closed.

"Good. A little more," Gustav said, his voice tight. She felt his hand burrow into her drawers, and let out a gasp.

"'Shh,'" he said, laying his other, mechanical hand on the small of her back. "I'm just checking."

It was enough, she thought, to be lying half undressed in the crepuscular, squalid studio. Enough that she had shared her most shameful and abominable desires with him, and found herself trapped in a cage of her own making. That he would now lay his hands on her—

"Stop," she said, suddenly. With no little difficulty, she pulled herself upright. Her bodice was awry and her clothes crumpled. Yet her defilement had not made her a mewling wreck, at least. A hot coal burned in her breast. This feeling was familiar. Violet was angry.

"Sir," she said. "This has gone far enough. I cannot tolerate you mocking me any longer."

Gustav stood, his face a mask. "I do not mock," he said.

"I came here," Violet said, standing and pulling at her clothes, trying vainly to cover herself though everything seemed to be slipping. "I came here because I needed something from you."

"And I have made it," Gustav said. "Haven't I fulfilled the brief?"

Violet looked down at the chair, which was still buzzing, gently. Its curves suddenly seemed treacherous, its embrace just another cage that sought to trap her.

"You don't understand," she said. "How could I have thought you ever would?"

To her fury, tears rose up to accompany the words, spilling generously from her eyes. She turned her head away.

Gustav sighed. "I believed I was providing you with a machine to service your needs, my lady."

"No. More than that." Violet fixed her eyes on the closed doors of the furnace, behind which burned the engines that kept the buildings running.

She had never fully understood the exact workings of the city, the giant burning columns that provided the power harnessed from the steam, the railways that criss-crossed the streets, carrying coal and wood, the curious and complicated machinery that converted that power into useful apparatus – she knew only that when she needed something, it appeared.

Her every wish, dream or fancy instantly fulfilled – just so long as it was approved by her mother, father, the gentlemen of the court, and the unwritten and unbendable rules of etiquette that governed her everyday life and it seemed, by some unarguable and inexplicable logic, kept the world running smoothly.

"I needed something to sate my wants," she said, her voice flat and dim. "A machine that would assuage my frustrations . . ." She bit her lip. "The inner life of a lady, sir, is not as peaceful as you may imagine."

Gustav laughed. "I do believe you're admitting it at last."

"Sir?"

He stood and approached, scratching his stubble with his machine-hand. Violet had an inkling that he knew it frightened her. She suspected he enjoyed the shiver that she could not quite suppress.

"That underneath all that fine lace, you have what everyone else has."

Violet narrowed her eyes. "Could you stop yourself from being coarse for once? Do you even have it in you?"

"I'm not talking about your body's natural appetites." Gustav nodded at her. "That's your own imagining, my lady. I'm talking about—" he laid a hand on her chest, where the shelf of her bosom rose and fell faster than it ought to "—your heart."

His hand was warm. He kept it there. Nestled in the valley of her breasts, she was surprised to find it comforting rather than threatening. She looked up at him. For once, there was no rusty fire in his eyes. Only a deep and quiet warmth.

"I do not need to love," she said.

"Or to be loved? Forgive me, but I do not believe you."

She pulled away, but he tugged her back, replaced his hand.

"It beats," he said, softly. "I can feel it."

"Yes, it beats. Whether I wish it or not."

Violet raised her chin. "When I lie abed, alone in the darkness, I am at last able to let go of the damned smile I must wear day in day out, the cursed, cultivated, ladylike mouth that I paint on in the morning and loathe from the moment I wake until the hour I retire. I jam my hand between my legs. I stroke myself. I induce such paroxysms that I could scream."

Gustav did not let his eyes drop. "And yet it is not enough," he said. "Is it?"

Violet stepped forward. She kissed him hard. Hard enough that his stubble scraped her cheek. At first, her tongue darted into his mouth as fast as a flickering flame. Then, as they sank against each other and his warmth flowed into her body, she let it meander a little, over his lips, to taste the salt there, the fire of the whisky.

He broke away, breathing hard.

"My lady," he said, "Violet."

"Quiet," she said. "I am not paying you to talk."

"I trust you are not paying me to make love to you, either."

Violet held his face in her hands. "I have spent my life paying people to do what I wish. I have never wanted for anything. Why should I stop now?"

"Because what you want can't be bought."

They stood with their faces inches apart, so that their hot breaths met and swirled together. Violet felt again the grip of his metal hand and this time she wanted him with a violence that almost overwhelmed her.

"What do you want?" she whispered. "What is your price?"

"Everything," he said. "Everything you own."

She searched his eyes. "You think I'll give up all that, to soothe the lust in my heart?"

"Not lust. The one thing you are really afraid to admit."

"Which is?"

"Love," he said, simply. "To live here, with me. As a free woman."

Violet laughed. "It seems a veritable bargain."

Gustav didn't laugh back. Instead, he held on to her with his machine hand and started, with the other, to loosen her corset. The lacing pulled from the eyes with a little ripping sound.

"Give up your life," he said, "and you will win me."

"My flat?"

"Abandon it." He tugged at the laces around her waist. As they came free, she exhaled noisily.

"Thirty servants. A steamtrap and driver."

"Set them free."

He pulled the shell of her corset away in two halves, as though he were removing the shell from some sea creature. Underneath, her bare skin was marked with lines where her underclothes had bitten into her skin.

"A place at court. Invitations to the very best parties."

Gustav raised an eyebrow. He took hold of her petticoat and ripped it apart, tearing it from her waist to her knees. Violet shrugged, and stepped out of the ruined skirt. She laughed as though she had breathed in for the very first time.

"The proceeds of my trust?"

Gustav paused. "How much?"

"More than I need."

He nodded. Traced a line from her chin, down her collar-bone, to the gentle curve of her breast, where he circled, as if entranced. Her eyes dropped to the twitching fingers of his metal hand.

"How did you lose it?" she asked.

"I was impatient," he said, lifting his wooden-tipped fingers, as if to surrender. "I wanted to master the world. Be the greatest inventor that ever lived. And I refused to listen to anybody."

"Sounds familiar."

She took the hand and examined it. He held it still, not flexing the spring-loaded joints, not curling the delicate beaten-tin fingers.

"I built it myself," he said.

"That must have been difficult."

"Yes. But now – it works. It is part of me," he said at last.

Violet looked up at him, then bent to kiss the worn leather of the machine palm. She drew the hand down, to her drawers, and placed it between her legs, pressing against it through the slit in the cotton.

"It works?" she said.

Gustav nodded. He pulled her towards him, crushing the awkward metal of his hybrid hand between them, making her moan.

"Like any man, my body is weak," he said. "Only I have been blessed with a hand of my own devising." He interspersed each sentence with caresses, raining kisses down on her bare neck and shoulders like molten lava. "With it, I can create miracles."

The blunt tips of his fingers pressed and pushed at her, the polished wood hard but curiously supple too, so that it felt he was making love to her with a wondrous mix of urgency and tenderness, the sensation circling, rising and dipping to some intricate pattern of his own creation. Violet felt a scream build in her belly, low and urgent, as though her voice was not her own.

With his other hand, Gustav had freed his cock from his trousers, and now he pushed her against the couch, lifting her buttocks so they perched on the curve of the headrest.

His first thrust was almost desperate, rushing her hard and

deep so that she cried out involuntarily. At the sound, he lunged again, and bit down hard on his lip.

"Forgive me," he started to say.

"Never," she replied, and pulled him to her. This was what she had been seeking, she realized, as he sank into her, meeting the rock of her hips with the jut of his own. This unbearable proximity, this suffocating closeness. To be filled with him, to swallow him up. This was the prison she would never wish to leave.

He ground against her, and his mechanical fingers drummed a fantastic tattoo around her sex, thrumming there on the most sensitive part, the little screw that held it all together, as she thought of it.

They beat against each other as if locked in a struggle, both reaching, clutching hold, writhing as if climbing the ladder of each other's bodies. She felt herself rise, and grow furiously dizzy, calling out to him as she did so, slamming against him as if she could join their flesh by violence.

As the sensations grew ever more urgent, she dug her fingernails into the flesh of his back. He moaned and bit down on her neck. That moment, she wanted to be marked by him, wanted them to both be changed, irrevocably changed. As she milked his cock and wrung a climax out of his heated, struggling body, his mechanical hand worked at her and she felt herself tumble, a wound-up machine gone wild, spun out of control, overtaken by the exquisite and miraculous machinery of the body itself, fuelled by blood and spit and desire, attracted irresistibly to this man by some inexplicable force, both damned and redeemed by this fabulous creation, this wonderful cage, this beautiful trap that she found herself, for once, glad to be contained in.

Their ecstasy split the moment in two, and they collapsed onto the couch, knocking levers and bruising themselves on protruding parts. Violet lay across her incredible machine, overtaken by waves of laughter as Gustav rose and disentangled himself, reached for the bottle and returned to lie with her in glorious, foolish disarray.

"May we live long and never leave each other," he said, his dark eyes locked on hers as he took a swig from the open bottle.

"And cherish our freedom," she said, taking the bottle from him. "Us penniless outlaws." She spilled whisky and he leaned forward to lick it from her arm, sending a fresh wave of laughter rippling through her.

"May we make our own miracles," she said.

"And recognize them when we find them," he said, bending to kiss the whisky from her lips.

Statues in the Snow

Steve Finn

The shuttered apartment was so warm I didn't want to leave. The food was good, the conversation lively. The host was an American film critic, and I was young and ambitious and I wanted to get him onside so that maybe he would give me some freelance work writing about the movies. I was the last to leave, and we talked into the small hours. He was gay, but I knew he wouldn't make a move on me. He offered to call me a cab, but I told him the streets around his apartment in the Faubourg Montmartre were always full of them: I would have no problems.

Neither of us was aware, cocooned in that warm flat, that while we coffee-housed, six inches of snow had suddenly fallen on Paris. As the outside door slapped shut behind me, I took in a sight I had never seen before: Paris, empty. There was no sign that a human being had ever visited this outlandish white place. There were no people, no cars, certainly no taxis. There wasn't even any sound. I pondered whether I should ring the bell again and explain my predicament, but then the enchantment of what was before me took over. I had a long walk ahead of me, right across the ancient heart of Paris to my tiny garret on the Left Bank, but it was a walk I knew I would never have a chance to experience again.

So suddenly there was noise in this silent city: the grainy crunch of rather too-thin shoes on fresh snow; the warm laboured breath of the determined pedestrian; the soft expletives of wonder as each turn revealed something new, something refreshed and redefined. Thankfully it is always warmer when it snows, and my spirited walking made up for my lack of a hat or scarf, though I was glad of the lined leather gloves my girlfriend had given me when last I saw her in London.

The wonders of the newly naked city took me out of my direct route home. The distant green and gold and now white of the Opéra drew me down the Boulevard des Italiens, way off my southerly course, and then the prospect of the severe Madeleine softened by snow kept me tramping and crepitating on my south-westerly route. A good hour, perhaps, I had been walking, and staring at the church where Bel-Ami had prospered made me think of the warmth of my bed. Not being a fan of the desolation of Place de la Concorde, I wound my way through the side streets onto the rue des Pyramides, passing without a glance the gilt statue of the ancestor of my future, as yet unmet, wife and crossed the deserted rue de Rivoli into the Jardins des Tuileries.

My thoughts had been full of the growing dampness of my feet and the ache of limbs unused to the effort of walking through snow. But as I crossed the Tuileries a realization grew that now, finally, I could have my moment of consummation with my favourite Parisienne, and the prospect warmed me and quickened my steps.

From the courtyard of the Louvre down to Place de la Concorde ran the formal gardens of the Kings and Queens of France, the Tuileries. I am not fond of formal gardens and usually the Tuileries are packed with tourists waiting to visit the Louvre or recovering from said visit. But scattered about the gardens are the wonderful statues by Aristide Maillol: life-size bronzes of nude women in arresting and unusual poses. One in particular I adored: a naked girl, resting on her right hip, which was the only contact statue made with pedestal, her strong, shapely legs straight, toes pointed; her torso cocked upwards, her left arm held straight out along her line of sight, the fingers cupped strangely so that she might be sighting something through them, or holding (and contemplating) something invisible within them.

She lay, as though roughly thrown, just above a sunken part of the gardens, and my steps grew more hurried as I got nearer, realizing that I could now, in this *hivernal* emptiness, finally touch those strident out-thrust legs, those tempting nates, that deliciously carved back without anyone officiously telling me not to.

She was delicately iced with snow along her length, but even so she looked both serious and coquettish at the same time. I slowly approached her, pulling off one glove to reach a bare hand to her no doubt frigid bronze flesh.

"Elle est belle, n'est-ce pas?"

I must have choked some recognizable expletive as I turned to see the figure behind me.

"I'm so sorry, I startled you," she said, in heavily accented English. A woman, in a long black coat over boots, a fur hat on her head and a heavy scarf draped around her. "You are American?"

"English," I managed to say, trying to recover from my hour-long solitude, so instantly ruptured.

"And you also like *l'oeuvre de* M. Maillol?"

"I admire his work, yes, but I have always loved this statue."

The woman came closer to me. "She looks cold lying naked in the snow, doesn't she?"

I had recovered enough from my shock to think that perhaps I ought to hold an end up in this conversation. "She looks, as ever, impervious I think."

She turned to look at me. I saw that she was much older than my twenty-five, perhaps twice that, but handsome still. She looked down at my bare hand and smiled.

"I think I interrupted you. You wanted this chance to touch her, *non*? *Sans les gardiens et les touristes*?"

I felt embarrassed that she had read my mind so easily, and she must have read that easily too.

"*Allons-y.*" She took my arm in her gloved hand and led me closer to the statue. "Dina won't mind."

I looked at her, wondering what she meant.

"Dina is the model for this statue you love so much. She's an art dealer now. We say hello now and then. Of course, she was very young when she sat for this. Can't you tell . . ."

She startled me anew by taking my ungloved hand and placing it square on one of the statues high, pert breasts.

". . . these are the tits of a young woman."

And they were. And they were icy cold.

"They were warmer then."

The nipples, though sculpted in detumescence, were nevertheless hard against my palm.

"Her breasts are what we French call 'an honest man's hand-ful' – just enough, you understand!"

And she laughed, a shocking sound in that muffled silence: and her laugh had that little ragged edge that spoke of a smoker. Her hand then took mine lower, down the gentle contours of an adolescent belly and up onto the proud haunch of a woman unafraid of work and along the calf of a woman with the strength to keep going, and down to the toes that I had always thought would look so beautiful splayed in orgasmic bliss.

I thought her hand would continue with mine on this erotic excursion around this beautiful form. Instead she pulled me back, and then around to the head with its peaceful yet puzzling expression.

"What are you thinking, young man?"

Her voice was suddenly sharper.

"Do you think she is ready to fuck? Do you think she is opening her legs for her lover? That her enigmatic hand is grasping the cock that she seeks to pull into her wet mouth? Well?"

I must have looked like a goldfish, my mouth opening and closing as I searched for an answer to her aggressive questions, for suddenly she was laughing that rough laugh again.

"I'm sorry, I'm sorry. Forgive me, I'm only teasing you. Put your glove back on, your hand is frozen."

And it was, from that sensual glissade along Dina's body. I hurriedly put my glove back on.

"But what I said is what I hear, most days, from louts and perverts who hang around here and whisper the foulest things about her: about what they would do to her, about what she would do with them. About how she is a tart who spreads her legs for the world to see."

A mute young Englishman watched a tear start in the eye of this strange Frenchwoman, swathed in black.

"But I knew her you see, know her still. She was a sweet and innocent young girl who happened to have no shame in her naked body, and he was an honourable old man whose art was dead and she brought it alive again. Please don't sully her with your fantasies."

"I didn't mean to . . . I just love the statue."

She looked at me then, and sighed a great cloud of breath.

"I wish her story could have been mine."

Puzzled, I began to speak, but she stopped me with her cold gloved hand on mine.

"I need a hot drink. If you would like one too, my apartment is not far."

We walked in silence within the greater silence of the city, her arm crooked in mine, across the Pont des Arts and up into the Left Bank streets. She lived not far from where Oscar Wilde died bemoaning the bad taste of the wallpaper, on the fifth floor (no lift, of course). The place seemed warm but poky when she switched on the lights, but then I realized the room we were in was cramped by heaped piles against each wall, covered in heavy cloths. It pushed the furniture into a small area in the centre of the room, like a wagon-train besieged by Indians. The kitchen area was curtained off with an expensive-looking drape, which she swept aside and hooked up. I could hear the sounds of a kettle filling, a match struck, gas igniting.

She came back in, unbuttoning her coat, which she threw, along with her hat, gloves and scarf, onto one of the formless piles against the wall.

"I am having a tisane. What would you like?"

"A coffee, if you have any?"

"I can reheat some. I think I have some whisky too. You like?"

She didn't wait for an answer, but swept back into the kitchen nook. Another pan was set on another ring and the bitter smell of coffee soon filled the flat, vying with the herby aromas of her tisane.

"I was also a model, like Dina."

She was curled in one of the big armchairs, her tisane in its outsize cup steaming away on one arm while she took a sip of her whisky. Her dress was black and shapeless: a large piece of freckled amber hung from a gold chain on her breast.

"I grew up in Normandy, near the sea. I was a good student, and was sent to the *Lycée* in Caen. It was a long walk from the bus stop home and the buses were irregular, so my parents were used to me being home late. The walk took me past a large dilapidated house, an old *gentilhommière*. I had heard that an artist lived there, but no one seemed to know much about him, which was a shame as the idea of an artist living close by certainly piqued my adolescent interest.

"I had seen no sign of life there until one day in the spring of my final year. I was early, for once, dawdling on a nice afternoon when I heard this voice. 'You girl, come here.' I saw this big, shambling . . . well, mountain of a man coming down from the hitherto empty house. I remember he had on this loose white shirt over blue trousers, both dirty and stained, and his hair and beard were wild and straggly. He looked a mess, frankly, but if this was the artist, well . . . wasn't that how they were supposed to look?

"As he came closer to me, I could see he was looking me up and down in the rudest way. If it had been one of the Caen boys, always trying to look up our skirts, I would have said something. I had a sharp tongue. I was known for it. Not now. 'You'll do,' he said, and grabbing my arm pulled me towards the house. 'There's money in it, if you're good.'

"Why didn't I fight? Why did I let him drag me into his house like a goose? I didn't know then, and I don't know now. He pulled me along a dark corridor into a back room suddenly full of light and the appalling mess of a painter in mid-flow. A large easel, canvases stacked everywhere, paint over all, every surface streaked and dirty, and an old brass bed in front of the windows covered with a greasy-looking spread.

"'Get undressed,' he said, leaving me suddenly marooned mid-room. I stood there in my drab school uniform as he grabbed a sketchpad and charcoal. He saw I hadn't moved. "Get undressed!" My hands trembled as I obeyed him, but the first man I stripped naked for never even looked. As I hastily removed my knickers he threw the charcoal into a corner and started instead to sharpen a fat pencil. Horribly aware of my nudity, I waited until he was satisfied with his preparations. Only then did he look at me.

"'You young girls don't eat enough,' he said quietly as he came up to me. There was a smell about him that . . . it made me wrinkle my nose, but . . . More whisky?"

I must have goldfished again. She chuckled and produced a half-crushed packet of cigarettes and a tiny lighter from somewhere in her dress. She lit up and exhaled a perfect cloud of smoke in the still air.

"Help yourself to more. He briefly felt my small tits, my nipples puckering madly as he handled them, then he stepped back to look down at the dark hair at my groin. His hand gripped my shoulder to twist me so he could see my bum. He handled me like meat. I was eighteen and had kneed a boy in the balls for touching my bum at last year's St Jean. Why did I let him treat me like meat?

"'Lie on the bed, on your back, arms above your head, crook your left knee open.' I did as he told me, and he sketched: quickly, violently, a page finished and ripped off the pad and thrown to one side. 'Pull your knees to your chin.' 'Hold your tits.' 'Rub your slit.' 'On all fours.' 'Dip your back and push your arse out.'

"I did all that and more as the sketches fluttered down until the floor was littered with them. I was embarrassed and ashamed – *quelle honte*. But I was also aroused and soiled, and I didn't know what my poor heart was going to feel next. I was face down, holding my buttocks open, when I felt his huge hand on me again. He pulled me upright, sitting on the edge of the bed. I felt like I was coming out of a cloud. He was fiddling under his shirt, and suddenly produced his penis. I know now that it wasn't prodigious, but it seemed so to me then.

"'Are you a virgin?' I managed to nod. 'Open your mouth . . . and use your tongue.'

"I went home with a promise to return, an old 100-franc note and the taste of sperm in my mouth. Does my story discomfort you?"

"No . . . not at all." I was hotter than the flat, but I couldn't say so.

"You haven't refilled your glass. Let me."

She had the grace of a cat as she unfolded from the armchair, grasped the bottle and leant over to refill my glass. Her scent, and the warm fragrance of tobacco, enveloped me.

"I should have been disgusted. His cock smelt rank, unwashed, sweaty, and I had sucked it. His sperm was heavy and tasted bad, but that night in bed my tongue teased behind my teeth in case a sense of him had survived the *potage* and the pork. I slept badly, remembering the thickness of his cock between my lips, how it bruised them as he fucked my virgin mouth. His filthy smell remained in my nostrils and made me ashamed and wet."

She sank bank into her chair and fumbled for another cigarette.

"Of course, I went back next day. I can't explain why. He didn't even have to tell me to strip. He just gestured to the bed, and there I was – naked and spread for him. I was young and limber and he had me take positions I never knew could exist, and I could feel the dampness in my loins as I opened my body to his uncaring eye. I was in a world of my own lust when he pulled me roughly off the bed onto my knees. My mouth was already opening before I even saw his penis. He ejaculated on my face, told me to sit still and sketched me as I knelt there, bespattered and oddly elated.

"I played with the drying flakes of his sperm as I walked home, peeling them from my face and putting them in my mouth. There was an old *lavoir* at the edge of the village, and it was only there, within sight of my house, that I washed my face clean.

"Every week day, I was a model student at school and a model whore for him. As we worked he told me all the dirty words for the body and what could be done with it. After a week or so he no longer needed to fuck my mouth: I would avidly kneel to suck his cock the moment his fumbling at his flies told me our session was over. He taught me how to touch myself as I writhed for him, and I learnt to come under his implacable gaze.

"The weekends were too full of chores for me to get away, and I found myself longing for that riot of exhibition, and for the taste and torture of his smelly, unwashed flesh.

"The third week, he made me take longer poses, and spent longer on his sketches. His favourite was me on my knees, shoulders on the bed, back arched, buttocks spread. It was a particularly shameful position for me, knowing that my vagina and anus were so intimately exposed for him. It was humiliating and jaggedly exciting. I was posed thus, one day, when I felt his hand between my shoulder blades holding me firmly down. He hardly ever touched me, and I bucked against his hand.

"'Keep still. I won't hurt you.' I obeyed, even when I felt his other hand, cold and greasy, move over my bum. His callused finger hurt me, despite the grease, when he prised me open. I whimpered and tensed. 'Relax yourself, *ma petite*. It will hurt less, and you'll still be a virgin.'"

I found my breath was held tight as she was speaking. Perhaps she saw it. She took a sip of her tisane and the cup clanked against the saucer, allowing my breath to escape unnoticed.

"That was a different walk home, I can tell you! The whole lower half of my body ached, and each step seemed a torment. My anus felt as if it would never close again, and the oily trickle from it only added to my shame and the hot blush of disgusted excitement. I couldn't wash that part of me at the *lavoir*!

"I told my mother I needed a bath before supper. While it ran, I inspected my bottom in the mirror, bending over at a ridiculous angle. My anus was a little red, that's all. I couldn't help touching it. My fingertip opened me easily enough. I can't remember how I ended up on the floor, fingers wildly fucking each of my holes as I bit down on a towel to stem my screams.

"I could barely sleep. The thought of doing such a dirty thing with a man, having his penis in my bowels, feeling him ejaculate there – I couldn't stop masturbating at the thoughts that crowded and clashed in my head, and I couldn't stop coming.

"He didn't bugger me that often. My mouth and face gladly took his offerings, but I often found myself half hoping he would pull me onto all fours and inflict that exquisite torment on my arse.

"And then he died."

She studied my face a moment as she took another sip of her tisane.

"It was the Easter holidays and I couldn't get away that much. My body throbbed for his filthy embrace. Easter Monday I managed to slip away for a while. I walked down the road thinking of what he would do to me. I was wet with anticipation. At the gate was a large black van, a couple of men leaning against the back of it smoking. I slowed down, suddenly afraid. An older man came out of the house. One of the van men offered him a smoke. They all seemed unconcerned, enjoying the spring sunshine, enjoying their Gitanes.

"I couldn't hear much of what the older man said. '. . . a pigsty . . . no, alone . . . heart attack probably'. They were grinding their cigarettes out and opening the van. I slipped through a gate into the field and took the long way home. I cried all the way."

She drank her tisane in silence for a while, sunk in her memory. I felt I had to show I had been listening, that I cared – and not just about the solid erection which had been paining me throughout her story.

"I'm sorry, that must have been awful for you. What did you do then?"

She gave me a look that chilled me.

"What do you think I did? Go into mourning for my dead lover? Tch! I threw myself into my studies, talked to teachers about universities, tried to keep my thoughts away from what we had done in that studio and my hands out of my privates. I passed my Bac. My family were pleased with me. And then . . .

"One of the last days of school, a lovely summer evening, I walked past the closed-up house without looking, as usual. I heard a creak behind me and a voice calling, '*Mademoiselle.*' My heart was pounding as I turned. There was a very well-dressed middle-aged man standing in the open doorway, gesturing for me to come closer. He looked very dapper, very out of place in the countryside. 'I knew I would recognize you,' he said as he held the door open for me. 'Please come in. I have something for you.'

"The studio looked no different. A bit more dust on the dust I'd breathed every day. I stood in the middle of the room as the man made space for his briefcase on one of the cluttered tables. He was very . . . businesslike. 'My name is Marcel Gijon and I was poor Henri's agent and am now his executor.' Did I know his name was Henri? Had he ever said his name to me, or I to him? I couldn't remember. 'Henri rang me several times before he died, raving about the young model he had found locally – a model who was so free and open with her body that it had given his painting a new lease of life. Artists often say things like that – they do like to exaggerate! So I had no great hopes when I came down here to make an inventory.

"'Imagine my surprise when I saw his work – saw your work! 'Why do you think it was me, *Monsieur*? It could have been any of the local girls.' He grinned at me and turned to pull a sheaf of drawings from a folder, handing them to me one by one. Oh, it was me all right. Me, naked, in all manner of obscene poses: my breasts, my vagina, my anus all drawn with marvellous energy. The last drawing was of my face. It was a very good likeness right down to the thick gouts of sperm that adorned me.

"I shivered as I looked at that picture. I felt shame that this man had seen how defiled I had been, how sluttish. And yet I was also proud of how I looked, and newly aroused by the memories of those evenings. Henri had never shown me anything of the drawings he had made of me. Looking at them for the first time I understood that there had also been something special going on amidst the dirt and squalor and lust. We had created something.

"'They are very beautiful, these sketches, and very arousing. Don't you agree, *Mademoiselle*?' 'Yes, they are.' 'And you must see some of the paintings he made from them. He must have finished this one just before he died.'

"Marcel crossed to the easel where a large canvas was shrouded with a dust sheet. I followed as he pulled it away and there I was on my knees and elbows, my back arched, the really beautifully caught sheen of sweat on my widespread buttocks and the dizzyingly erotic trickle of semen from my slightly dilated anus. 'So wonderful. Henri was truly a gifted artist. And he's left all of these gems to you.'

"I turned to look at Marcel. He could read my disbelief. 'Oh yes, he updated his will not long ago. And I am a loyal executor of that will and I am here to see that you get what is now yours.' He gave me a moment to take this in. 'But, *Mademoiselle*, I am also his loyal agent and if I may I would like to make you a proposition.' And I heard the sound of the zip on his trousers being unfastened. He asked a question with his eyes to which he already knew the answer. Demurely, I knelt before him and accepted his penis in my mouth. He talked as I sucked. I was happy with his proposition, and his cum tasted sweet after my long drought.

"So I didn't go to university. I came here to Paris with Marcel, as principal model and muse to the group of artists of which Henri had once been a part. You won't find the work of the group in galleries: we make erotic art to private commission. There are other models, of course, but I have always been their favourite since the day I arrived fresh-faced from the countryside. I work with them individually, but sometimes they get together for some particular project, and that can be quite tiring. A woman has only so many orifices."

I must have blushed as the meaning of this sank in. She laughed throatily.

"I enjoy my work, *Monsieur*. I've enjoyed it ever since that day Henri hauled me off the dusty road and had me strip in his studio. It took me a while to accept my enjoyment, that is all. Come here."

She stood and moved to one of the covered piles that I had noticed when we had arrived. I understood now what they were.

"I've kept most of Henri's work, for . . . sentimental reasons. I am well paid by the group, but if I need a little extra, Marcel sells one for me. They fetch good prices. And I have had some outrageous offers for this one."

She pulled the sacking back, and there was the painting she had described: a beautiful young girl exhibiting her anal defloration. It was truly breathtaking, and my tumescent penis leapt anew at it. But what does an aroused man understand about anything? I bent to look closer at the painting.

"And the other model . . . Dora? Did she ever work with you, or was she . . . ?"

"I think you should leave now, *Monsieur*."

"I'm sorry, I . . ."

"Please leave now. It is late and I have work to do later."

I gathered my warm clothes in the sudden chill of the apartment. She was silent until I stepped out onto the landing.

"Her name is Dina, not Dora, and I told you that she was and is a good woman. The first time we met she saw straight through me. I blushed as if she could see me on my knees sucking men's cocks. But then she smiled at me, and that unjudgemental smile bit deep. We were both models, yes, but everything I have posed for is hidden and out of sight as if it were shameful, and she adorns the Tuileries like a modern goddess.

"Was what you have seen and heard shameful, *Monsieur*?"

I had no idea what to say. Her lips gave a little twitch. It might have been half a smile.

"Goodnight, *Monsieur*."

As the door closed the timer on the landing light went out and I realized that there was a faint glimmer from the window above. Outside, dawn was breaking. In the hours I had listened to the story, Paris had woken up and got on with life – snow notwithstanding. As I walked along the river towards my room, buses and lorries were churning up the streets. People were everywhere, walking carefully amidst the slush.

Paris was the same again, just whiter and dirtier.

My Ass is Your Ass is My Ass

Kristina Lloyd

So, there he is with his cock in my ass, and I'm biting the pillow, making all sorts of groans. At least, that's how it looks on the outside. Not that anyone's watching. We're in my bedroom and very alone together, the way you are when someone's fucking your ass. Very alone together.

So that's the outside view: kinda porny and inadequate. On the inside, I'm floating in a space nebula, and star clusters of silver are pulsing bright and dark. I'm about to go supernova, when Tony asks a breathless question. "You've got to save one thing for me," he says. "Your ass or your throat."

He could be speaking a foreign language. Slow colorbursts spread across my mind like intergalactic ink stains: electric blue and peacock green with halos of neon pink and gold. My ass is so stretched and full of his big, beautiful dick.

"What is it, huh?" he says. "I'm giving you a choice here. You gotta make up your mind. Anal or deep-throating?"

I wail and whimper. The question's too difficult. It's like he asked me to explain string theory.

"Come on," he urges. "I know you fuck other guys. No need to be shy. I know you're a slut but you're *my* slut, see?" His fingers grip below my hips. "So you got to put up a 'reserved' sign on one part of your body. 'Only for Tony.' What's it to be? Ass or throat?"

I want to work through the question employing all my faculties of reason. I want to write a list of pros and cons and give due consideration to the implications of this decision, both for myself, for my relationship with Tony and with the others. But I can't. So I reach into deep space and pluck a word from a distant constellation, a single syllable burning bright and white.

"Ass. My ass."

Tony groans and holds himself deep. "Good girl," he murmurs. Whenever he says that, I go loose with lust. "What am I doing right now?" he asks.

My words are tangled up with stars. "Fucking me."

"Where's my cock?"

"In my ass."

"Whose ass?" He slides away and in again, slow and controlled. "Whose ass is it really?"

I'm spiraling toward a whirlpool of blackness and I fight the pull, knowing gravity wants to steal my words.

"It's your ass," I say. "My ass is your ass."

"That's right," he breathes.

"Is my ass," I gasp. When I come, I fall through nights of liquid velvet, lights prickling as ageless galaxies die across the dark skies of my mind.

That was five months ago. I've been with half a dozen other guys since then and I've kept my word. Well, more or less. The trouble is, Tony and I never discussed how this would work. We didn't establish rules or boundaries. If I keep my ass for Tony, does that mean no one else can touch, lick or penetrate me there? Or simply that no one else can fuck me?

I'm too scared to ask in case Tony wants to – 'scuse the pun – ring-fence my ring. And then we might have to call the whole thing off because that's too great a sacrifice for me. I like having my ass played with. But Tony's ownership of my ass turns me on so, instead of fine-tuning the small print of our deal and risking disagreement, I've been making it up as I go along.

"Did he fuck your ass?" Tony asks on the phone whenever I tell him about a recent encounter.

"'Course not," I say. "Only you get to fuck me there."

He never asks for more detail so I never go into any. But there's a lot to tell.

I meet most of these other guys online, on dating websites and chat forums. Occasionally, I pick someone up at a party or nightclub; and a couple of times (OK, four), I've gone home with a guy who's been drinking in the pub where I work. That's how I first met Tony.

"A large bourbon and one for yourself," he said.

"We're not supposed to drink on duty," I replied, primly flirtatious.

He looked at his watch. "When are you off duty?"

I get a lot of guys hitting on me at work, not because I'm outstandingly beautiful but because they're too drunk to distinguish between the goods for sale and the person selling them. Frankly, it bugs. And they never seem to appreciate I'm not their type. I'm an art-school dropout who still dreams of traveling the world and having a studio to paint in. I buy my clothes from thrift stores and stay up late listening to old jazz on vinyl. I don't know what to do with my life but I've always felt there are colors beneath my skin. Scratch me and I'll bleed you a rainbow.

The guys who chat me up in the pub want someone conventional in stockings and heels. I can see it in their eyes. They only make a pass at me because I'm there. But I could tell immediately that Tony was different, and damn, he was a looker. Rangy and inked, he had this air of louche confidence that existed on the right side of sleazy, but only just. He wore his hair in a soft rockabilly quiff, jet-black curls licking at his collar, neat sideburns by his ears. His jeans were narrow, his shoes pointed and his smile filthy. When he talked, a silver front tooth flashed like a warning light. My mother would have hated him.

"Midnight, and the name's Coral," I said, sliding his drink onto the counter.

"After the reef?" he asked.

"No, the bookie's."

We were great together that night. For several crazy hours, we lost ourselves in a loop of sex, talk, laughter and sex, both of us eaten up with curiosity for the other. We smoked a lot of weed and at five in the morning, we lay across the bed, stoned, fucked and comfortably smug, listening to Chet Baker and lazily comparing tattoos, trying to ignore the gold dawn light filtering into the room. A lyric from Chet curled like smoke around my mind: "flirting with this disaster".

But we're doing OK, me and Tony. One fuck led to another and now we're seeing each other in a committed but non-monogamous kind of way. He's not exactly Mr Reliable but unpredictability is part of his charm. Hook-ups don't always pan out so well and that's why it's best not to fuck the customers. It gets awkward if they're still interested and you're not, and you have to serve them beer and act like you never sucked their cock or begged for it harder. Regular dating is far more sensible.

As well as Tony, I'm seeing a guy called Stedman Snowdon. I find it hard to say his first name without his last. Stedman Snowdon. The words roll off your tongue and it's hard to put the brakes on after Stedman. By way of a compromise, or maybe it's laziness, I refer to him as Snowy. It suits him. He has Nordic and Chinese blood in his veins. His eyes are steel blue and sloping, his nose is tiny, and his ice-blond hair frames his face, straight as a helmet. He'd always known Tony was my main squeeze and Snowy has a serious girlfriend so we just get together for occasional fuck-buddy fun. When I told him we needed to start having less fun – i.e. my ass was now off limits – he rolled his eyes and said, "Oh, Coral. You've just made me want to fuck your butt even more!" He said he wished he'd known our last time was the last time, and tried to persuade me into having a final session where he could kiss my ass goodbye. He said "kiss" but he meant "fuck".

I said no, and ever since then, Snowy's been pushing at the new limit, trying to seduce me into reneging on my deal. And I've been close, so close. Having to say "no" when my body's crying "yes" is a real test of my willpower and devotion to Tony. It's cruel of Snowy to tease and tempt me, and that's why he does it; he knows I like to suffer.

All the guys I fuck respond differently. Some respect my request and leave my ass in peace. Some play lightly with the rule while others push hard.

"Is this allowed?" asked one before flicking his tongue over my rim.

"He only means fucking your ass," said another more assertively as we got frisky behind the hotdog stand at the funfair. "He won't mind me doing this to you." And with that, as the Ferris wheel's gaudy lights turned in the corner of my eye, he slipped his hand down my skirt and stuck a moistened finger in my butt.

"Hey," I said. "I think *I* mind that." Because it's not too pleasant when you're still tight and together, and someone goes in cold.

The times I'm horny with Snowy and my body is melting are my weak points. His head is between my thighs, his mouth and my cunt feeling like a single, slippery, wet entity. He shoves his fingers inside me, works me hard, and when I'm flailing in bliss, I hardly notice a thumb sliding gently into my ass. Then I do notice, and I like it and try not to whimper for more. But he gives it to me anyway, getting off on my predicament. He bought a toy especially for me, a butt plug with a sweet, silly pony tail in lurid, fuchsia pink. On my hands and knees, I allowed him to ease the plug inside me.

"There we are," he said. "My little pony! Don't you look lovely? I'm sure Tony would be so proud."

That's when I began to wonder if Stedman Snowdon had started seeing Tony as a rival or a threat to our relationship (small "r"). I soon suspected a small war was being played out between my sheets, my ass as the battle zone, their hard cocks as weapons. Even the thought of it was enough to set my pulses thumping. But I knew Snowy wouldn't invade by force. He wanted to make me hand over the territory of my own free will, humiliating Tony and myself while relishing his victory.

I didn't trust my powers of resistance and began to worry about letting Tony down. Plus, I really missed having Snowy in my ass. I wasn't sure which direction this might go in or how to fix my minor issues until one evening Tony strolled into the pub, all quiffed and shabbily cool, and my little brain went "Eureka!"

"Tony," I said, leaning close as I slid him his regular bourbon. "If my ass is your ass and so on, and if you've put up a 'no entry' sign, does that mean you get to take it down and invite someone else in?"

He downed his drink in one and said, "Another please, Coral. And one for yourself." I did as told. It's my job after all, and the manager wasn't in so I got myself a double. "What exactly are you saying here?" asked Tony.

He swirled his drink around the glass, the soft spotlights above the bar gleaming on the shark's tooth pendant around his neck. Outside, it was a gray, grim evening. Rain trickled down the frosted windows of the pub, and the tatty, crimson interior was as cozy as it was desolate. Few people had ventured out, opting for the colors of TV over the dull, silty puddles on the streets. I can't say I blame them. I'd have stayed home myself if I hadn"t been getting paid for it. When Tony appeared, the tattoos on his arms were like TV to me, lighting up my night.

"Tony, I mean a threesome," I said.

"With another guy," he said, nodding thoughtfully. It wasn't a question, more a statement of the obvious and an expression of indifference or maybe disappointment.

"That's right. With Stedman Snowdon."

Tony grinned, flashing his mouth-metal. "What kind of fucking name is that?"

"Snowy," I said.

"Oh him. Sure, if that's what you want. I figure I could get into it." He tapped a beer mat on the counter, turning it in his hand. "So, what kind of scenario do you have in mind, Coral?"

I sketched out a few ideas, having to break off at one point to serve a couple of women who had yoga mats strapped to their backpacks. They clinked their glasses together, chimed, "Om shanti" then hooted with laughter.

Tony listened closely to my ideas. "Coral," he said. "I am so fucking hard right now I can't stand up. Another bourbon, please, and one for yourself."

Snowy was keen. I knew he would be. Sexually, his range is as broad as his chest and he likes to experiment whereas Tony's a pervert in a very specific way. When Snowy tops me it's partly because he knows I like it, while Tony tops me as if he has no choice; as if he's driven solely by a desire to get something out of his system, and I don't mean a sacful of jizz. I was hoping their different motivations would prove a good combination, free of egos bumping up against each other.

We arranged an evening at my place. Tony turned up late with a bottle of Jim Beam wrapped in green tissue paper and a cigarette tucked behind his ear. Snowy was in the bedroom, shoes and socks off at the ready. Fairy lights looped around the head of my bed pricked the dimness with spots of color and, when I returned to the room, Snowy seemed suddenly incongruous, a Scandinavian prince in a crack whore's boudoir. He stood to greet Tony and the two men clasped hands, shaking warmly.

"So," said Tony, "you want to fuck her in the ass?"

"Yup, just like I used to," replied Snowy.

Weirdly, one plus one seemed to equal much more than two. My poky apartment felt packed with men, and when Tony went to hang his jacket on the back of my chair as per usual, he couldn't because Snowy's jacket was there. So he hooked the jacket on the corner of the kitchen door when he went fetch glasses, spreading masculinity across my home.

We stood by the bed and drank a toast: "To Coral's ass!" Clink. "And to Tony's ownership of it!"

We knocked back our drinks, then Tony, always quick to get in role, wrapped my hair around his fist and pulled tight at the nape of my neck. He smelled of whiskey and weed. He made my cunt ache. Snowy stepped in front of me, scooping his hand between my thighs.

"Why are we here, Coral?" asked Tony.

I hate it when he makes me say it. "So Snowy can fuck my ass," I said, wincing in embarrassment.

"Who owns your ass?"

"You do," I whispered. "My ass is your ass."

"That's right," said Tony. "So I get to decide who goes in there. I decide who makes you scream. But your friend here, he seems a nice guy, so I'm going to lend you out to him. Once I've prepared you, that is."

Snowy lifted my skirt and stroked me through the cotton of my underwear, making me moan.

"You like that?" asked Tony.

Snowy chuckled and slipped his fingers past my frillies, rubbing my smooth folds. Tony tipped my head back onto his shoulder, caressing my breasts through my clothes, while Snowy shoved his fingers high and hard, latching onto my sweet spot immediately. He pounded me there, making my cries rise as pleasure swelled inside me then spilled like a waterfall.

"She's wet already," said Snowy. "Seriously wet."

Tony murmured words of approval in my ear. "My dirty little whore."

Being sandwiched between them was glorious. With Tony behind me, all sleazy and mean, and Snowy before me, all crisp and cool, I was locked in an embrace of lust. We were co-conspirators, hell-bent on making nasty magic, and I was seeing stars, my legs soon becoming too weak for me to stand. Tony, ever attentive, lowered me to my knees and Snowy moved with me, his fingers still rubbing.

Tony unbuckled and when his cock sprang out I reached for him with my mouth, clasping his skinny hips to steady myself. I closed my eyes and started off the way he likes it, slow and wet with lots of focus on his end. Snowy moved and when I opened my eyes, his cock was there too, angling for my assistance. In the colored half-light of my room, his pale pubes were a tangle of filaments and fireflies, tinted with a hint of pink.

I sloshed my tongue around Snowy's tip. "That's it, good girl," cooed Tony, watching me. "Show us what you're made of."

Snowy gripped me either side of my head, drawing me on to his length. He was too fast. I tapped his thigh and, recognizing the signal, he released me. Again, I licked and sucked, taking him deeper until I was ready to open my throat to him. I dipped down, tilting my head back, and steadied my breathing. When I felt him at the back of my mouth, I went with the flow, relaxing my throat and welcoming the heft of him lodged deep and tight. He groaned loudly, and I knew I'd got him. When I pulled back, my saliva was slippery and easy, and my eyes were fogged with tears. I wanted to feel him again so went back for another hit, riding the wave of tranquility that rises when I'm deep-throating.

"Such a greedy little cocksucker," said Tony.

"Man, that feels good," breathed Snowy. "Oh, man."

"I gave her a choice," said Tony. "Told her she had to save one thing for me, ass or deep-throating. I let her choose. I'm good like that, the generous sort. She made the right choice?"

I moved from Snowy's cock to Tony's.

"I miss her ass," said Snowy. "But that mouth is something else. So yeah, good call, Coral."

Tony gripped my head and drove himself at my throat, making me gag and splutter. "You hear that?" he snarled. "Everyone wants to fuck your mouth." He went in deep and stayed there. I almost tapped his thigh. "Take it," he warned. "Take it."

Tears spilled down my face and, when he freed me, I was breathless, messy and stunned. He slapped me hard across one cheek. I love it when Tony does that. I started to slip into that zone where I feel slutty and used, where the pull to surrender grows increasingly strong.

"Get undressed, Coral," said Tony. He pulled his skull T-shirt over his head and we all undressed, momentarily awkward as we put horniness on hold and dealt with the prosaic. I felt I didn't have enough hands and eyes. Two men in such close proximity induced sensory overload. Their differing bodies complemented each other perfectly. Snowy's straight platinum-blond hair was at the opposite end of the spectrum to Tony's jet-black quiff. Where Tony was wiry, inked and thickly haired, Snowy was softly muscled, clean-skinned and scattered with gold. They might have been good and evil personified, except I knew they were both bad, and so was I.

"You want to hold her while I fuck her?" suggested Tony.

Snowy responded swiftly, hooking his arms under mine and

positioning me so I was half on the bed, half off, propped against his big, sturdy chest. "That good?" he asked Tony.

Tony rubbered up, grabbed my thigh and pushed back so I was wide open to him. "Perfect."

I protested and wriggled, acting as if I didn't want it. The two men held me tighter, exactly as I'd hoped.

"No," I whimpered.

"Oh yes," said Tony, concentrating on his angle. With a groan, he sank into me and delivered a series of slow, teasing thrusts. I knew he was trying to make me beg for it and before long, I was doing. "More, Tony. Harder, please."

He held back, getting off on hearing me plead. Snowy cupped my breast, one hand kneading me, the other scooting over my stomach. "Please," I gasped.

"Like this?" sneered Tony. He started ramming into me, fast and furious. I squeezed my eyes shut. In my mind, colors bloomed and coalesced into a shifting mosaic of honey-yellows and brown. Every jolt took me higher, pressure swelling in my cunt. Snowy made a V with his fingers around my clit, rubbing steadily as Tony fucked.

"That's right," said Tony. "Make her come. Get her nice and relaxed so we can fuck that little ass."

Seconds later, I was coming hard, waves of bliss clutching over and over. The muddy mosaic dissolved into slow fireworks, sparks of brightness streaming and swirling. Images surfaced from nowhere and I saw, with hallucinogenic clarity, a red-jacketed fox hunter, a vivid blue birdcage, a kumquat whose color, on the cusp of gold and orange, was briefly, brilliantly ethereal and precious. I wanted to catch its dimpled skin but couldn't. It had gone.

And I swear I wasn't stoned. Sometimes I just see things.

"Good girl," said Tony as my cries faded.

Without prompting, Snowy released me as Tony withdrew. "On the bed," said Tony, chivying me along with a slap on the butt. "Hands and knees, that's right."

I leaned forwards on my arms, post-orgasmically weak. Tony's lubed up fingers slid easily into my asshole. He drove in with a twisting motion, back and forth, knuckles bumping at my opening. He was eager and I was ready to yield. But even so, when his cock pressed at my rim, I wailed at the invasion. My body resisted him. He pressed harder. I wailed louder.

"Stick your dick in her mouth," urged Tony. "It'll help with the pain."

Snowy was there like a shot. I gasped around his length, barely able to suck him as Tony persisted. Then, with a flash of heat, Tony was inside me, just an inch or so of cock. He moved slowly, letting me get used to him. My ass was crammed with his hard flesh, my muscles gripping, my cries fluttering around Snowy's thick shaft. Tony held my hips, giving a long groan of satisfaction as he glided in deeper. "There we go," he breathed when he was entirely inside me.

He paused before starting to slide in and out, my ass becoming wider and easier the more he fucked me.

"How does she feel?" asked Snowy.

"Tight," replied Tony. "But I'm opening her up for you, making her good and ready. I don't want the bitch complaining."

He kept at me, adding more lube to keep me moist. When he pulled out, I was slippery and greedy for more. "Your turn, bro," said Tony.

"You sure?" asked Snowy.

"Go right ahead. Stick it in there. Take whatever you want."

As Snowy moved behind me and fumbled with a rubber, Tony flung himself alongside me, his mouth by my ear. "Whose ass is it?" he asked.

"Yours," I panted, locking on to his soft, brown eyes.

Snowy began to penetrate me, filling me up fast.

"Who's fucking it?"

"Snowy. Snowy is."

"Why?" asked Tony.

"Because . . . because you said he could."

"Nope," said Tony. "It's because you're a dirty little cockslut, a whore who can't get enough. I could pass you round my friends, let them all have a go at you, and you'd still be desperate for more dick. Wouldn't you, huh?"

Clearly, it was a rhetorical question because Tony scrambled to sit in front of me, his legs spread, knees to the ceiling. He lowered my head onto his cock. I slurped up and down as Snowy hammered me toward ecstasy, the two men's groans making filthy music with my own. When I opened my eyes, the roaring panther tattoo on Tony's stomach, purplish in the hue of my fairy lights, jumped before me. When I closed my eyes, a crimson sun haloed with blue radiance burned in my mind. I reached back for my clit, rocking and rolling until I was at my peak.

"She's going to come," wheezed Snowy. "And so am I, so . . ."

I was first, my orgasm wringing me out as the crimson sun became a ruby sky swimming with shoals of blue stars. Snowy groaned intermittently, a sound close to pain, then he shuddered inside me and roared as if he too were seeing stars. Tony outlasted us by a few more minutes. He made me lie on my back then straddled my exhausted body, jerking off by my lips. When he came, I drank, and he tasted like the essence of sex: dark, bitter and secretive.

"Jeez."

"Wow."

"Oh man."

The three of us lay across the bed, breathless and sticky with sweat. I swear, the fairy lights were glowing more vividly than before, casting patches of color on our damp, gleaming skin: yellow, green, red and blue. We are Tokyo in the rain at night, I thought. Tokyo made flesh.

Tony sighed contentedly. "I've got a great ass," he said, and the three of us laughed until it hurt because it sounded strange and stupid, yet in our bubble of intimacy, the statement made sense. And though I didn't say anything, I thought they'd understand if I told them there were galaxies behind my eyes and rainbows beneath my skin.

Appointment Tee Vee

Victoria Janssen

Tuesday nights are their television nights. When they meet, Sven hasn't seen Martha's favorite show, on the air for only three episodes. Martha is already in love with the tweedy mentor character, Knightley. She and Sven fuck for the first time after Knightley's big episode, number nine, in which his risqué youth is revealed due to a magic spell and she gets to see Knightley onscreen in a skintight T-shirt.

She and Sven lie in a sticky tangle on her carpet afterwards. Martha asks him if he had a risqué youth.

His youth was her childhood. He gives her a significant look. Martha tweaks his nipple. He says, "Does doing it in the back of a pickup count?" He pauses, hand stroking the rounded bit just below her navel. He adds, "It was a parade."

A lot of the time the funny things he says aren't meant to be jokes, his mind just works that way. Martha loves that about him. Also how he looks when she finally gets him unbuttoned from his suits and ties.

She imagines naked Sven humping some beauty queen of the Flyover Dairy Cows while the beauty queen tosses candy to a screaming crowd. Martha has a bizarre imagination. She pokes him in the stomach.

"After the parade," he explains. "Me and Karen Hazilik. Crêpe paper is nasty when it dries on you. Do people even decorate with crêpe paper any more?"

"Let's do it in a pickup," Martha says. "Up at Steamy Point. We'll pretend we're teenagers, making out." This is a test. She wants to know if he's willing to play along with her weirder inspirations.

"We can't take all our clothes off. That'd be cheating," he leers. "I'll be your naughty teacher."

"Let's go Friday. Wear a tight T-shirt."

Their trip to the Point works out really well and soon they are seeing each other several times a week. Sven comes over every Tuesday around seven so they have time for pizza and beer before Martha's show comes on. Sven starts to like it, too, but he likes different characters: the fraternity brothers who are telepathic, but only with each other, because of a ritual and a lightning strike, and a family of cheerleader witches. They can see ghostly images of murder.

Martha thinks the college guys are totally doing it, and tells him so while she's getting his boxers off.

"They are not!" Sven chokes out. Then he whimpers when she kisses the end of his cock.

Martha points out, "Two men can't have children, so you don't have to worry about their mutant babies." She doesn't care if imaginary men have sex or not, but she's curious what Sven thinks. He's also adorable when he blushes. She licks the crease at the top of his leg and nuzzles around the base of his cock.

Sven is breathing faster. "Are you . . . would you want to watch them fuck? Two men? Like men like watching two women."

Martha doesn't have to think about that. "Definitely. They're both hot." She thinks about it a minute, then adds, "They could make a Knightley sandwich."

Sven blushes some more. "You know people write these stories. On the Internet." He combs his fingers through her hair; it's short and dark and curly, a bit like one of the guys on their show.

Martha is fascinated with what he's just revealed but she's busy right now. She licks around the head of his cock in teasing circles and watches his face change. "We'll Google when we're done," she suggests, and starts sucking his cock in earnest.

Sven's head falls against the back of the couch. "Oh, God, Martha, don't stop."

She pumps his lower shaft with her hand and takes time to lick his balls, enjoying the soft buzz of furry skin against her tongue and the way his belly tightens and twitches. She smooths her free hand over his abs, which aren't cut but are nice and solid.

"Push down," he begs.

He likes it when she strokes and presses around his cock while she's sucking him. She's figured out that shifting the compression of her hand diverts sensation from his cock, and helps him to last longer. She loves experimenting with him to make him feel good.

He's been trying the same thing when he goes down on her, mostly using the heel of his hand or the ball of his thumb in unexpected places. She thinks of it as "pleasure pinball."

They never get around to Googling that night but on Saturday they find stories where the college buddies are doing it with Samantha, the show's only female character. In one story, they've all been turned into vampires, and in another, they're all writers living in Paris in the twenties. Sven bookmarks those. Then Martha finds the ones (there are lots) where the guys are doing it with each other, no girl in sight. Also a story where both guys do it with Knightley, which she bookmarks, and another one where Knightley makes them wear neon nylon dog collars and put lipstick on each other using only their mouths, and fuck each other with dildos and a bunch of other kinky things. The blond one cries a lot but it doesn't stop him from having a giant woody the whole time. It turns out Knightley is doing it all because he's pregnant from a magic spell and not allowed to have sex himself for eleven months.

Martha reads the last story aloud while Sven rolls on the carpet, moaning, begging her to stop because it's so awful, a thousand times worse than any student paper he's ever read, even in his introductory classes. It's true the dialogue is terrible, and there's too much repetitive description, but Martha thinks it's hilarious, and every time she puts on Knightley's English accent giving commands, Sven laughs so hard he can't breathe and bangs his head on the floor.

Martha finally takes pity on him and stops. She decides to go back later to see if she can find some better threesome ones where Knightley is not magically pregnant. Then Sven streams some gay porn for her, which Martha thinks is really hot. She picks out which guys in the movie look most like the telepathic guys. Sven eventually gets into it a little bit because she likes it, even though he says all the naked men make him think of locker rooms instead of sex. Also, he can't believe their cocks are really that big. Maybe it's the camera angles.

They make out on and off through the whole thing, and Martha decides tonight is the night she wants to try anal sex together. That needs the bed, so they switch off the porn and find the lube.

It turns out Sven hasn't done anal before. Martha gets a thrill out of that and takes over as teacher. Sven's a little scared and cautious, so they spend a long time on foreplay. Sven massages her from shoulders to feet before he starts working on her ass.

She convinces him to rim her – she's never had anyone do that for her before, so it seems fair as well as unspeakably hot – and he figures out the best techniques on his own, sliding his hand between her legs while he tongues her hole. The sensations are delicate and fluttery and prickly all at once. She forgets everything except how good it feels. After she comes, pulsing hard around Sven's fingers, she murmurs, "Prep time."

Sven points out that the guys in the movie just went right to it. She reaches into a drawer and brandishes one of her dildos. "You want to try it?"

Sven gets a funny look on his face. "Maybe?"

That's intriguing. Martha squirts lube onto his fingers. "Tonight I want *you* to fuck *me*."

She flinches after he slips a fingertip into her, because she's so sensitive from the rimming. Sven jerks back. "No, no," she says. "It's OK. I'm just twitchy."

He makes her turn over and look at him. "You're sure." He doesn't sound nervous any more, probably because of the way he just made her come, wailing, and Martha gets a little thrill because he's hardly ever like this in bed, in charge, unless they're playing a game like naughty teacher.

"Do it," she says. "I want your cock in my hole."

His eyes get even darker at the way she says it, and he shoves her back onto her stomach. She probably shouldn't be getting him this excited when anal needs patience, but she's eager and this isn't her first time. She's sure she can take him comfortably.

Martha relaxes into his delicate massage as he works in more fingers one at a time, getting her ready for his cock. She breathes deep, relaxing, shivering at how good it feels when he shifts the position of his fingers. Finally, she says she's ready. Actually, she looks over her shoulder and says, "Take me, Knightley!"

Sven swats her ass. He's hard as a rock. "Condom," he demands. Martha grins and puts it on him with her mouth. Then he takes her from behind, not at all tentative, his cock a steady stretch, shoving the breath out of her in a long moan. Sven gets partway inside her and stops, panting. "I still don't believe they're doing it," he says, and thrusts home.

Martha is laughing, which moves his cock inside her in ways

that make her shake and clench. "I'll show you evidence next week," she gasps out. "Now fuck me."

Sven doesn't last all that long but neither does she. It's messy and sweaty and feels sensational. Afterwards, they cuddle up, sticky as they are, and talk quietly in the weird yellow light of a street lamp outside Martha's window.

Sven says a couple of the other soccer players on his college team were gay; they were together, but always said they weren't a couple. Once in a while they'd tell him how incredible gay sex was and let him know that if he was ever curious, he could stop by their place and get educated. They were kidding, sort of. But if he'd ever stopped by, he thinks they would have done what they said. Sometimes he wonders what would have happened. It would never happen in real life. They finally admitted they were in love, moved to Toronto, and got married. He says, softer than before, that he thinks about them sometimes when he masturbates.

Martha tells him what it was like growing up with her three brothers. She always wished she was a boy, too. She didn't understand girls and why they liked dresses and Disney princesses when she liked *Star Wars* and lightsaber fights. All her friends at school were boys. When they hit puberty, suddenly all her friends wanted to be her boyfriend. That weirded her out because she thought she was one of them, not one of those girls that sneak off into hallways to let a boy stick his tongue in her mouth. That's when she got curious for the first time about what boys could do together. She went to the bookstore and read a bunch of gay erotica. It was the first time she'd read anything sexy like that.

Sven asks her if she ever imagines she's a man while she's fantasizing, and she says yes. She tells him one or two scenarios. Then she sits up and rests her hand in the middle of his chest, right over his heart. She tells him that she didn't do that while he was rimming her, or while he was fucking her. Then, she was just Martha and Sven was fucking her. She can be herself with him. That's why she loves him.

Sven tells her, like it's a secret, that he loves her.

The next Tuesday, they cuddle up on the couch under a big comforter. It's fall sweeps on TV, and the temperature outside dropped unexpectedly yesterday. Martha likes fondling Sven's thigh underneath the blanket; it feels dirtier than doing it out in the open like usual. Whenever the college buddies come on screen, she points out to Sven how close they're standing.

"They're standing really close to Samantha, too," he points out.

"They're not looking at her," she says. "Look how Jamie touches Ben all the time."

"They're friends." Sven kisses her neck. "Besides, Knightley's always touching Ben, too."

"Ben is the fuck bunny on this show," Martha says.

Sven starts laughing into her neck. He nips her behind her ear, where she likes it, and she slides her hand higher up on his thigh. He says, "Do you want me as much as you want Knightley?"

"You wouldn't mind, would you?" she says. "If he came over. We could have a threesome. I wouldn't make you touch his dick if you didn't want to." She kisses his cheek, a big smacking one. "You know *you're* my Knightley."

They end up wrestling for possession of Sven's cock under the comforter, and getting all tangled in it, so they almost miss the big scene where Samantha kisses Jamie, and Jamie rejects her.

"Shit!" Martha says. "I was right! He is doing Ben! How else could he ignore those knockers?!"

"Let's go to bed," Sven says, in a faint voice, because Martha is still stroking his cock with both hands and he's hard as a rock.

"Let's do it doggie style, so we can both watch. There's another half-hour left."

It's actually really hard to watch TV and have sex at the same time, even if you're enthusiastic. Martha keeps making Sven stop when there's important dialogue and start up again when there's a fight scene. He bitches and groans but he does it, because he's watching, too. The starting and stopping turns out to be really hot.

Samantha, it turns out, might be possessed by a demon. Or might not. It's hard to tell. Martha wonders if the demon gave her better cleavage than she'd had in the previous week's episode.

Knightley does spells while Samantha's tied up, and there's a lot of writhing and moaning. Sven asks Martha if *she's* possessed because she makes those moaning noises all the time. He asks if he can tie her up and do some spells. She can't smack him because he's behind her, his cock in her cunt.

A commercial blasts on but Martha can't reach the remote. "Fuck me, fuck me!" she yells, and Sven fucks her so fast her eyes cross. They both come by the time the commercial break is over which is a good thing, because the scene has shifted and the story is back with Jamie and Ben.

"Pay attention, it's your guys," she says. She takes the condom off him and throws it away, then sits on the back of the couch with her feet on Sven's chest. He's taking up all the room.

Sven groans. "Was that an earthquake?"

On the TV, Jamie and Ben are doing a ritual. Both of them have to contribute blood to the ingredients. Martha pokes Sven with her foot and points out how tenderly they cut each other, which wakes Sven up enough to roll on his side and watch.

"Jamie *licked* him," he says. "I'm not sure if that's hot or not."

"He didn't have to lick that blood," Martha says. "Do you think he got turned into a vampire when he was missing last week?"

The background music is swelling. Ben's crouched over his middle, rocking back and forth. Jamie has his hand on Ben's head, petting his hair, and they're both panting. It's unclear if they're trying to save Samantha from the demon, or destroy the demon and Samantha both, or if this has nothing to do with Samantha at all; they could be seeing a vision of a murder. The one from earlier in the episode that might have been committed by a possessed Samantha? Is Ben possessed? Regardless, Sven looks at Martha and says, "You were right. They're totally doing it."

There's a big flash on the screen. The scene cuts to Knightley. His eyes are glowing and he has his hands on Samantha, but he keeps repeating Ben's name.

"Uh-oh," Martha says. Knightley shrieks, and the credits roll. Cliffhanger. "Fuck!" Martha yells.

Sven wraps his hand around her ankle and hugs it. "I hope nobody gets killed off."

"They can't kill anyone off yet, it's too early in the season," Martha says. "Jamie and Ben haven't even kissed yet. They have a long way to go."

Sven drags her down on top of him and cuddles her. In a Knightley-accent he says, "So do we, love. So do we."

We Are Not What You Think We Are

Nachito

As told to Michael Hemmingson

Was rooming in a cheap hotel with Paola, one of the prettiest transsexuals in Tijuana, and whoring myself out for anything between ten and fifty bucks an hour. Told Paola not to worry her pretty head; we'd find a nicer place just as soon as we got back on our feet. Home sweet home had a bed and a window two floors up in the Hotel California.

We worried about money and the next bottle of Vicodin. Every pharmacy tech on Avenida Revolucíon knew my face.

"Hey Nachito," they'd say, "back for the usual?"

You build a tolerance. I can remember taking seven pills every four hours. Odd and funny dreams flowed seamlessly from night to day.

Tijuana presented itself as the edge of the unknown where the lines of a new history were being rearranged. The contours of ordinary objects appeared dismembered, like the paintings you see in museums, and I was holding certain delusions about the world. Thought I could unlock doors without keys, predict the future, things like that.

I am born of reasonably affluent parents, you understand. They're still married; still go to garage sales on Saturdays and church on Christmas. Someday I should write an essay about how I wound up living among the whores of Tijuana.

The front desk clerk required our names for the hotel's records. Paola took a ballpoint pen and put hers next to mine.

Nacho y Paola, it read.

We then dug a few crumpled bills from our pockets and laid

them on the desk. The clerk took our money and gave us a plastic sack with clean towels, soap, and a fresh roll of toilet paper. The words **WELCOME TO THE HOTEL CALIFORNIA** were stenciled in the window just like the lyrics to the Eagles' song.

On the street below, donkeys were painted black and white like zebras. They're called Zonkies. Tourists could put on sombreros and have their picture taken with the Zonkies. That was the idea. I thought it was funny when a Zonkie pooped because it made the little kids scream and shout, "Look! He's making *caca* in the street!"

Paola preferred to hustle at the bar downstairs of our hotel. The El Paso bar was a long, narrow affair that catered primarily to gay American men who drank Coronas and eyed the round-faced Mexican boys. These men regarded me too but that wasn't my deal. They bought me beers and I'd be friendly, drink the beer.

"See dat tranny there?" I'd say, nodding at Paola. "Ain't she purdy? How'd jew like to haf y'self a good ol' time wit her?"

Problem with drinking too much, my Texas twang comes out and I sound like a cartoon.

That worked about one out of every four tries. The other three times I had to be a total dick. "I'm no fag, buddy," I said, walking with a macho sway up the stairs with my free beer.

Sought my clients on Craigslist. Usually I received emails from husbands, straight or otherwise, wanting me to bang their wives. For a good month, I was regularly doing a flight attendant from Kentucky whose husband, an airline pilot, watched us from the loveseat. In the darkness I saw the red dot of his video camera.

The burning ember of his cigarette. These things I shall not forget. They were the bread and butter of my life in Tijuana.

The flight attendant insisted that I not wear a condom. "It's totally safe," she assured me. "My tubes are tied."

They were OK enough, those two. Paola didn't like it so much. "How do you know she's clean?" she asked.

I didn't always have all the answers. "She said she was clean," I said. "I buy it."

The husband paid upfront. No chit-chat or funny business. I don't know how he cleaned his wife up after.

* * *

First time I saw Paola was on a cool September evening. Mexican wrestling on the TV. Beer and tacos on my table. I was the only customer at the Hotel Nelson restaurant. A group of men had gathered outside the window to watch the wrestling match on a large plasma TV behind me. It looked like the men were watching me. Paola noticed these men and went to see what they were looking at on the other side of the glass. I was mid-bite when this happened. There was a body slam on the tube and the men outside hooted and hollered.

Breasts blossomed from her chest and her hair was full and black and lustrous. It's no stretch to use the feminine pronoun with Paola. I honestly thought she was a chick when I raised my hand and invited her inside to eat.

Life sure can be funny that way.

When she spoke, her voice was different: a man's voice.

"Hold it," I said. "Are you a he-she?"

"Yes," Paola said.

I'd never seen one that close before; believe me, I'm from Texas.

She ran her foot up my leg.

"Cut that out," I said. "Hey."

The waitress looked at me.

"Don't get the wrong idea," I said.

Paola curled her lip and stood.

"Wait a sec," I said. "Don't get upset. Have a seat," I told her.

She sat down.

"It's pretty cold out there," I said. "Aren't you freezing dressed like that?"

"Yes," Paola said.

"You got someplace to go? Are you staying close by?"

"No," she said. "I'm from Rosarito. I don't have money for a cab."

"Couldn't you take the bus?"

"The last one left an hour ago," she said.

I considered this as I sipped my beer.

An old lady entered the restaurant with a dozen roses wrapped in plastic. She shuffled toward us. She wanted me to buy some roses.

"No *gracias*," I said.

I noticed the whiskers on her chin. "Buy a rose for your *novia*," the old lady said.

"No."

Paola found this amusing.

"Please," she said, "*mi novio*," she said. "Please?"

"I'm already paying for dinner."

Wagged my finger at the old lady and also at Paola. But again, the old lady insisted I bought a rose and finally I caved and bought one. You'd have thought it was made of diamonds by the way Paola regarded it.

"Could I stay with you?" was the next thing she requested. "Just tonight," she said.

I didn't like the thought of her going back into the cold with those men. "All right," I said. "One night; but no monkey business."

"*Me gusta* monkeys," she said.

Brushed my teeth at the bathroom sink while Paola fixed her eyebrows in the bedroom. Then she came into the bathroom and lifted her skirt to pee standing up like it was no big deal. I, being a tad gone on pills and booze, giggled at the sight. She swatted my shoulder playfully. I said, "Ouch."

The night stretched into a week. Weeks grew to months. I liked having Paola around; (s)he was smart with money and kept our place neat. We shopped for groceries at the market and found the cheapest pharmacies in town. One afternoon, Paola and I climbed aboard a Zonkie and had our picture taken because we thought it was the funniest thing in the world. I uploaded this photo to Facebook for all my friends to scratch their heads over. I got a few comments from people wanting to know who the pretty girl was. Paola got the photo framed at Sears and kept it on the dresser.

At night, we lay on a queen-sized mattress with our pharma-suicidal buzzes, watching the ceiling fan spin.

They say you can choose your friends but not your family and sometimes I have to wonder.

I met you for breakfast at the Hotel Nelson restaurant and explained the new roommate situation.

"So she's got a dick?" you said.

"Yep."

"And breasts?"

"Estrogen hormones."

You considered this while you carved your flapjacks.

"So she's a he?"

"No," I said. "He's a she."

"A hermaphrodite."

"I wouldn't call her that. She's something else."

"Cross-dresser."

"I wouldn't call her that either."

You put your fork through the flapjacks. "Here's the question," you said. "Which restroom does she use when you're in public?"

I thought about that. "Don't know; never thought to look."

Paola and I caught a cab to Zona Norte for a late supper with you and your pregnant girl, Belén, which is Spanish for Bethlehem.

Paola was drunk on Cuervo and Vicodin and talking about the differences between men and women. She'd lived for a time as both genders, so maybe that gave her the right.

Paola said, "A man can say 'I love you' to a woman and never telephone her again. But when a woman says it, she means it always."

Belén nodded.

"I don't know," you said. "I've known women who could turn it on and off like a faucet."

Paola said, "Men always think woman are crazy. And you know what? Women think men are selfish."

"Now wait a minute," I said.

Paola nudged me because she had to use the *baño*, so I slid out the booth to let her go.

Which restroom would she use? *Damas* or *Caballeros*? The three of us turned and watched.

"Ah," you said. "Go figure."

"She's pretty," Belén said. "Are you two . . . ?"

"No," I said. "We are not what you think we are."

A fistfight broke out in front of the café. Two drunks. A few jabs were exchanged and when the men were pulled apart, everybody ran in opposite directions. Minutes later a truck of heavily armed soldiers occupied the sidewalk. We watched the soldiers, two men and two women, stand with their fingers on the triggers. They looked like they wanted to shoot somebody. Slowly they climbed in the truck and drove away.

"The cops do that to scare us," you said. "They only stand around long enough to make a point."

Belén agreed.

Paola returned and I told her about the soldiers.

"*Perros*," she said.

The nights got colder and fewer American dollars flowed into Tijuana. Needed more Vicodin; if I didn't take enough, I got the headaches and cold sweats. In my mouth the pills were sweet as honey, but as soon as I'd swallowed, they became bitter in my belly.

You paid for the entire dinner and I threw up in the toilet.

The midnight fog cleared as we strolled home to the Hotel California. Paola was wrapped in my safari jacket.

"I'll never understand women," I said. I was thinking of my ex-girlfriend in San Diego. On her Facebook page, she listed her status as "widowed."

"Do you really *want* to?"

"Yes, I do. I really do."

"*Mira*," Paola said. She pointed to the glow in the sky where the moon pierced the fog. "We change our minds as often as the moon changes her face. That's why you must listen carefully to women."

The moon was illuminating the sidewalk and reflecting in the puddles and I looked down and admired the moon shadow beneath her feet.

We climbed the narrow stairs. Paola removed her earrings, we got into bed.

I was having a bad dream and she shook me.

"What is it?" I said.

Paola said, "Wake up, Nachito, I have something to say to you."

"What's wrong?"

"Oh," she said. "I love you, Nachito. *Te amo.*"

"What?"

"I love you."

I rolled over.

She took my hand and held it and I paid her no attention.

I awoke to Blondie's "Heart of Glass" playing loudly on the juke-box downstairs. I love the eighties. I was born in that decade.

One evening in late January we stopped in at the Agua Caliente casino and put our last ten-peso coin in a slot machine. The streets were slick with rain and the cuffs of my pants were wet and cold. I watched the dials spin and spin and one by one they stopped on three watermelons.

Sirens and bells went off.

"Oh shit," I said, thinking we'd done something illegal.

The equivalent of three hundred US dollars spilled into the receptacle. To us, it was a small fortune. We scooped everything into a plastic cup.

"*Ay Dios mios*," Paola said. "Let's celebrate! Let's go dancing."

"We should put this money in the bank."

"The banks are closed, Nachito. Why don't we dance?"

"I'm not in the mood," I said.

"Oh, please," she said. "*Por favor, mi* Nachito."

The Rio Verde Club was hopping. I took some crisp bills into the *baño* and had some cocaine with the cartel boys. The waiter brought beer after beer and everything was fine. The *norteño* music was loud and spastic. Men and women whirled about the dance floor like socks in a dryer and everything popped.

Paola and I shimmied and stepped and I twirled her around like a weightless thing.

People were staring at us. They realized what she was and they didn't like it. It was the rudest thing ever. I wanted to punch somebody in the face, which is the last thing you want to do at a place like the Rio Verde club, a known cartel soldier hangout where cocaine is sold in the bathrooms.

Waiting for us outside the club was a lady cop. The cop frisked Paola and found a little cocaine in her purse and then she frisked me and found nothing.

Paola looked at me for help. What was I supposed to do? Why the hell did she buy coke in the bathroom?

I offered a bribe to the lady cop and she said I could go to jail for doing that. Police cars arrived. I was frisked again, this time by a man, and all the money we had won disappeared.

They cuffed Paola and shoved her in the back seat. A crowd of onlookers gathered and pointed. "*Mira*," they said. "The tranny is getting arrested! The tranny is going to jail!"

At the Hotel California I turned on the lights and got undressed. There, on the dresser, was the picture of us on the Zonkie. I looked at that photo for a good while.

The police were no help. They wanted a full name. I didn't know her full name, his full name.

For weeks I approached strangers at the El Ranchero Bar and asked if they'd seen or heard anything about Paola. I always got the same response: "Oh, *muchacho*, she prolly went home. Happens a lot."

"Are you sure?"

"Nobody stays in TJ forever," they said. "People go home to their old lives," they said.

I suspected Paola had simply quit dressing like a woman – you know, blended into acceptable Mexican society, maybe grown a beard. There's no telling. She could have been any Chico walking down the street.

Something Twisted this Way Comes

Kyoko Church

It was a dark time for him. And titillating. Dark and titillating.

He hadn't thought the two qualities could be so exquisitely combined. Or if he had, it was just an inkling, he'd only known somewhere in the recesses of his mind, on the edges of his fantasies. But it was there. The chocolate and peanut butter of sexual dysfunction.

He would always remember that time. Those three weeks when he couldn't do anything. Couldn't work, couldn't sleep, couldn't eat. Couldn't do anything but think about her. Looking back he realized something. What made her, what gave her power, was what she knew. That in the human psyche there is no such thing as truth, only perspective. She understood that a person can have a secret, something he thinks is ugly. So he hides it from view, tucks it away, only visits it in secret, on weekends, and then only to torture himself, like picking at a scab. But she saw the glimmer of it. So she plucked it out, dusted it off. Turned it a hair to the left. And stood back for him to see. Waited for him to realize: the thing he most hated, he could actually love.

He met her innocently enough. No, that's not true. Perhaps an outside observer could have thought it was innocent. But he was not innocent. He'd been looking at some, er, pictures, at his desk at work. So he was hard. He was hard in the elevator when she stepped on, on his way to take some pressure off, taking the elevator to a more secluded bathroom on the top floor of his office building.

She stepped on, all business, tailored suit but killer heels, auburn hair swept up in a surprisingly old-fashioned chignon in contrast to the rest of her look. She was not the kind of woman he was normally attracted to. He usually went for the more petite blonde type. She was all curves, very Marilyn Monroe, but with that hair the colour of fire. Embarrassingly the words, "va va va voom" ran through his head.

She looked at him. She assessed him. Sized him up. Her eyes scoured him up and down, everything from his average clothes, his average shoes, his slightly balding average hair. The wedding band on his finger. The bulge in the front of his pants.

He glanced again at those heels, open toed with her pretty red nails peeping out of the top. She caught him looking and he blushed. They exchanged not a single word. But then she smiled at him. A slow, sly smile. He saw a light go on in her eyes and in an instant he understood that she knew him. She saw what he was exactly.

"Email me," she said, handing him a card. Then she stepped off the elevator, and was gone.

He emailed her the next day. Was he ever not going to? She told him to come up to her office on the 42nd floor.

When he got there she was stretched out on the leather sofa beneath the large picture window that looked out high over the city. Her feet were up, her heels, different ones today, black patent, were on the floor. She was wearing dress pants but her feet were bare. Again, those red toenails.

"Have a seat," she said, indicating the sofa beside her.

He settled uncomfortably at the other end, not knowing where to look or how to position his body. She chuckled. "A little closer, silly," she said, lifting her foot up, offering it to him as he moved closer. He blushed but took it, gently. Her foot was surprisingly small and slender, the skin pale so that the red toenails stood out sharply. He began to massage slowly.

"Wait a second." He looked up. "Turn to me a little," she said. "That's right, now lift your knee up onto the couch." He did so and jumped as she placed her other foot gently but firmly against his crotch. "Keep rubbing," she commanded, gesturing at the foot in his hand. "I just want to make sure you're not getting excited." Fire exploded in his face. He looked away from her, at her foot, then looked away from that.

She laughed. "It's OK," she cooed. "I know you like my feet. And I do need a foot rub right now. So you rub them." He hesitated. "Do it," she said, not laughing now. "But I just need to make sure you're not being a disgusting pervert and getting all excited about my pretty feet. This foot rub is supposed to be for me."

He rubbed, obediently trying to clear his mind, trying to think of anything but her slim foot in his hands. But there was also the pressure of her other foot against him. And then she started making little noises. Little whimpers, groans of pleasure. "Mmm, that's right," she purred. "Ooo, right there, that feels so good." He was helpless. He sat helplessly rubbing while his cock grew with a mind of its own.

"Oh my God, what is going on?" She looked at him. "I can feel you, you know," she said, wiggling her toes against his stiffness, and only worsening matters. "God, what horny little thoughts are going through your head right now? Was it the noises I was making?" she chided. "I was only enjoying the foot rub! You weren't thinking that's what I sound like when I fuck, were you?" He stared into his lap, unable to respond. "Well, if you are going to act like a horny little dog, then that's how I'm going to have to treat you."

This is how it was that he found himself, a grown man, a professional, an architect, on all fours on the floor in front of this goddess, humping her foot like some kind of human lap dog.

And even though she didn't make it easy for him by doing things like swinging her foot away, complaining that he was going too fast, laughing, forcing him to keep all four limbs on the ground, to not use his hands, even still his little problem reared its ugly head.

He spurted, hips helplessly bucking, after two minutes.

He knelt in front of her and braced himself. He steeled himself against the familiar onslaught of feeling – frustration, anger, shame – that always raged through him like a firestorm, burning through everything in its path. But instead of the usual reactions of disappointment, pity, anger or worse, the yawning silence, pregnant with judgements and unspoken resentment, there was something different.

Giggling. Like tinsel. Like glasses chinking together, crystal laughter.

"My, my, my, we are the eager little beaver, aren't we?"

Heat rose, he could hear the blood pump through the vessels in his head.

"That's OK, sweetie," she said and she leaned over, put her lips right next to his ear, so he could feel her breath on his skin. "Mistress has all sorts of ways to deal with a horny little boy like you," she whispered.

Suddenly he realized he was hard again. Harder than he had been the first time.

There was shame. But no anger. There was humiliation. But no frustration.

Pure humiliation. Not blazing, like the white hot heat of the firestorm of his secret torment, but rolling in slowly, like molasses, covering him, turning his insides liquid, enveloping him in a mass of humility, shrinking him down, making him want to place his hard, needy little cock before her in an act of complete submission.

There it was. Just like that. Turned a hair to the left. His torment died. His kink was born.

In the first few texts and emails they exchanged she asked him questions. So many questions. He loved answering them but he could barely keep up. The questions kept coming, more and more. There were some simple ones: where, when, how often. Questions about habits with his wife, did he like this, was he turned on by that. But then came more difficult, compelling questions. Like, why? Why did he like what he did? Where did it come from? And finally, what books did he like, what TV shows did he watch, who did he vote for in the 2008 election. Her desire to learn about him was voracious, like she was eating him alive. He felt like that. Or like in answering her he was ripping himself open and laying his insides out for her to casually peruse and then choose something to examine.

He dutifully responded to it all.

And then she named him. His name was not Paul. But she named him SubPaul. He could not help but wonder if it was because it sounded like "sub par".

After lunch one day she called him in his office.

"I'm going to send you an email," she said, the sultry tones of her voice coming through the phone like ribbons of silk weaving around his body. "When you get it, don't open it. You are not allowed to open it until you are ready to go home."

The email came through. He looked at it sitting there in his Inbox, subject line "**For Your Drive**", its bold type indicating it was unread, the darkness of the lettering making it appear so much more intense than the other pathetic emails beneath it and eventually over the top of it.

He glanced at the clock: 1.35. He had almost four hours until it would be appropriate, usual for him to leave. Maybe he could squeeze it to three and a half. The hours stretched out like a long road in front of him. It was torture wondering what the message said, being semi-hard over words he hadn't even read yet. How was he going to sit for all that time without reading it? What did it say?

From: MistressD
To: SubPaul
Subject: For Your Drive
Hi! This email is for your drive home. If you have opened it before then, stop, close this up. Open it back up when you are about to drive home. Put it away. Now.

OK. Are you alone now? Good boy. Have you been thinking about me? Of course you have. You're always thinking about me, aren't you? I've taken up residence in that naughty little brain of yours.

I have to address the fact that your wife doesn't go down on you. Have you wondered why I haven't commented on that in our emails? Did you think I hadn't noticed or maybe it wasn't important to me? Oh no. No, no, no. I took very keen notice of that. I have thought about that. A LOT. Because here's something you should know about me. I LOVE to suck cock. I fucking love it. The power. I really get off on the power of it. I know that if I had my lips and tongue anywhere near your cock right now I would have complete control over you. Total.

So, Mr I-haven't-had-a-blow-job-in-twenty-years, when I get my hands on you again I'm going to strip you down, sit you on a chair, cuff your hands behind your back and start licking. That spot. You know that spot? Oh yes, the one just under your head, that sensitive spot that you told me you couldn't touch because it gets you there too quickly? Aw, poor baby. Too fucking bad. I like that spot. I would flick and tongue and kiss and suck that spot until you were a pleading, begging, weeping, sopping fucking mess. Don't you dare cum in my face. I mean, Mistress loves cum, but I don't want it yet. You fucking hold it back, slut.

Now. Put your phone away. Start your car. And think about this email the whole way home. Try subtly to get wifey to fuck you tonight. Report back to me in the morning.
Kisses!

Oh. God.
Oh God. OhGodohGodohGodohGod.
Like a zombie he turned the keys in the ignition. He started the

engine. His cock was so hard he could feel the vibrations of the motor right through his body. Her words ran through his brain. He could see himself, in her office, strapped to her chair, helpless with her tongue on his trigger and her ordering him not to explode. *Don't you dare cum in my face.* Oh God. *You fucking hold it back, slut.* Oh fuck.

His cock gave one hard pulse. And then the combination of his pants pressing down on his stiff flesh, the vibrations from the car engine and, mostly, her words whirling around in his head sent pressure through his body it was helpless to combat. He swallowed hard, let out a strangled cry and released in one large spurt.

"You *what*??" She giggled uncontrollably. "You actually came *in your pants*??"

He stood before her in her office the next day, reporting, as she requested, head down, again cheeks aflame.

"Oh my God, how old are you? You're acting like a horny teen-ager!" She walked around her desk over to him. She was more casual today, in a light grey sweater dress that clung to her curves in all the right places. Her fiery hair was down and loose, cascading in waves around her face as she smiled and tsked her disapproval at him. "I knew I had my work cut out for me with you." She lifted his chin with her finger. "But even I didn't think you were *this* bad." His heart pounded. She gently placed her hand on the side of his face and stared in his eyes like she was searching for something, like she was considering a choice or trying to solve a puzzle. Then she blinked.

"You need some extra work," she said. "Some, um, let's call it therapy. Desensitization. Yes, that's it!"

He began to say something, to protest somehow, even though he wasn't really sure what she meant. But she wouldn't let him speak. "SubPaul, this is for your own good," she chastised. "I mean, how is your wife ever going to have any pleasure if you keep coming like a horny little boy after two minutes! Or if you don't even make it into her cunt." Oh God. The wave of humilia-tion was back. He felt it in his gut, deep down, hot, big in his gut and radiating out, making the edges of his body tingle. "Coming in your pants," she sighed. "I mean, really!" She put a hand on her hip and stood back, still staring at him.

"Close the door," she commanded. He obeyed.

"So here's what we're going to do," she said. "You obviously get very excited about the idea of my mouth on your cock." She licked her lips. His heart skipped a beat.

She knelt in front of him and began unbuckling his pants. His hands flew to protect himself but her head flew back and her eyes pierced him, even from her position below.

"Don't. Fucking. Move."

He swallowed hard and obeyed, forcing his hands to hang at his sides.

When she pulled his pants and his shorts down, his cock sprang out, stiff already from just her words and her position in front of him. God. His heart continued pounding its thunderous rhythm in his head. He stared up at the ceiling, searching for a way to calm down.

"Now don't look up there, look at me," she said, "and keep looking." He nodded and complied. Her eyes were no longer teasing and giggly. Now they were stern. Serious. "Listen to what I'm telling you." He watched her mouth move. She'd painted her lips a bright red, perhaps to contrast her grey dress. She put that red mouth right next to his swollen member. "You need to stop thinking about me putting my mouth on your little dick." She kept staring in his eyes. He could feel her hot breath on him. It was crazy, so humiliating, but he could feel every puff of hot air as her words escaped her lips, each one sending waves of sensation through his cock, making it pulse and throb. "I know you never get head. Aw, that makes it difficult, doesn't it?" Suddenly her eyes changed. Soft now, sympathetic. "It's OK, sweetie. Mistress knows." His insides turned to liquid. His knees mush. "But for your own good, you need to stop, OK?" She looked at his cock. He started trembling but he didn't dare move. She made her mouth into an O and put it a sliver, a hair, away from the tip, and looked up at him again. "Unh unh," she sang. She pulled away slightly so her lips wouldn't touch him as she said, "Stop thinking about me sucking you."

Then she put out her tongue, put it on the base of his trembling cock, and licked one long soft but firm, wet lick from the base all the way up to the tip, dragging that gorgeous tongue across every horny, sensitive fibre of his being. When she got to the tip, he exploded.

She let him. She put her hands on his bucking hips and held her tongue there as his cock convulsed and gushed, pulsing out its creamy disgrace. She caught it all on her tongue and then she stood.

She put a hand on either side of his face, tilted his head back slightly and put her lips to his as if in a kiss. He obediently opened his lips to her as she deposited his still-warm come in his own mouth. She licked, pursed her lips and stepped back.

"Certainly you don't expect *me* to clean up after you." She smiled. "Swallow your own fucking come."

She turned on her heel and left.

It was not completely true to say he couldn't work. He couldn't – he sat at his desk, in his office, gazing unseeingly at his blank computer screen, a million miles away, for hours. So he couldn't. Until he could.

Until he had an idea. And his ideas, like his cock, were not controllable, would pop up at inconvenient times and demand attention. Like one night, in the wee hours, when he suddenly woke and sat straight up in bed, gasping. He could see the building, the plans, see all of the lines, curves, intersections everything before him. His brain seemed to be working on autopilot, calculating the structure, envisioning how the light would come through. He glanced at the clock – 3.32 – and at his sleeping wife and briefly considered trying to go back to sleep. He almost heard his idea, like a person, like Her, laughing at him. Just try and ignore me, it seemed to say. The voice, Her voice, propelled him out of bed.

He walked into his darkened home office, looked at his drawing board. At home he still went old school with pencil and paper. The prospect of transcribing everything from his brain to the waiting blank paper simultaneously exhausted and exhilarated him. He envisioned himself reaching for his brain, through his ear, pulling it out and pitching it at that board, splat! Then watching as all his ideas gelled into drawings, all his best stuff emerging, like wheat from chaff.

He worked feverishly until morning.

Standing on the stairs to the library entrance, he stopped, looked up at the doors and took in a deep breath. He took out his phone and reread her email. The one with the subject line: Consequences. That email was the reason he was there.

He didn't want to be there. A part of him, something in his head was screaming at him to please turn around, get back in his car and go home to his wife. But it was not a request. She was very clear. There were consequences for his failure at their first therapy session, as she referred to it. He had to learn.

So he was at the library. Her orders were: go into the library, go to the non-fiction section, go to the librarian at the information desk and ask her for help. Because apparently he needed it.

He had to ask for books on premature ejaculation.

He took one last breath. And walked in.

That's how their relationship went. Therapy. Consequences. More therapy.

Usually the therapy took place in her office. He would come in, usually in the morning, and report to her on his night, if he had masturbated, if his wife had consented to sex, if he was able to last long enough to let her have an orgasm. He would confess everything to her, head down, mumbling a bit, her naughty puppy.

She would giggle and laugh at his inadequacies, provoking that now familiar heat in his stomach, making it rumble like she was reaching in and messing with it, like the way she might tousle a naughty boy's hair.

Then the therapy would commence. The second time was the worst. And so also the best.

He presented her with the library books, demonstrating that he had completed her humiliating task. She lavished him with compliments, praised him, told him she was happy that at least he was able to do this, making up for his lack of performance in therapy.

Then she put the books aside. "I have my own methods," she said. "Come, SubPaul," She was sitting at her desk. As he walked around the desk to her she reached in a drawer and pulled out a pair of latex gloves and a bottle of lubricant.

"You don't have a latex allergy, do you?" she asked, smiling. He couldn't speak. Just shook his head, no.

The familiar crystal giggle. "Oh, that's good. Because you don't think your cock is actually worthy of my hands, do you? Maybe once you can last longer than a minute or two, then you might get my hands. But until then you only get the gloves." She looked up at him from her chair and sighed. "Pull your pants down, silly boy! Do I have to do everything for you?"

He quickly unbuckled and took his pants down to his knees.

Watching her take the bottle of lube and pour some onto her black-gloved hand stiffened his already hardening cock.

"Now remember my instructions from last time. They haven't changed. You must watch me. You must not move. You can do that, right?" He nodded. "Good boy!" She rubbed the substantial amount of lubricant between both gloves, put her hands together as if in prayer, and then slowly slid his hardness between her two slick gloved palms.

God! He swallowed hard and closed his eyes. "Eyes open, darling!" she chimed. "Forgetting the rules already? I'll let it go this time. Don't do it again."

Slowly, oh so slowly, excruciatingly slowly she pumped him two more times. Already he could feel his balls tense up, his seed beginning to simmer.

"Now, see how good I am to you? I am giving you a chance by going really slowly. I know you couldn't last a second if I went with any kind of normal speed." While she spoke she switched tactics, put one smooth gloved palm on his tightened ball sac and pumped in a twisting motion with her other hand. He obediently watched and listened to her, watched his helpless cockhead pulse with purple intensity and weep pre-come. "If you get close, you have to tell me, OK? You have to ask permission for a break. No coming without permission! That would make for some harsh consequences."

Oh God! He was going to have to stop her already. He didn't want to say it. He couldn't bear for her to know that it was already too much. But the threat of the consequences. Oh God. Oh fuck.

"Mistress, stop!" he panted. Struggled.

"Now that wasn't very polite!" she said, continuing to stroke.

"Oh God! I'm sorry, Mistress! Please stop! Please!" She continued. "Please, Mistress, may I have a break!"

She stopped.

He nearly fell over he was trembling so badly, straining so hard to stop himself.

"Now that's better," she said. "You must always remember to be polite to me. I'm trying to help you! But look at your hips. They're bucking like you're a dog or something. And what's this?" Even while she spoke without touching him he was still desperately trying to hold his come in. But as her words came out, so too did one small drop from his dick. Not clear pre-come. But white, the colour of shame.

"Oh ho! You let a little bit out!" And to his astonishment she was smiling. "Do you know what that means? You let a little bit out. You started coming a little bit. But you held it back! Good for you! I'm proud of you. Now we're making some progress." He blushed, insanely grateful for this compliment. But then her smile changed. Morphed. Then it wasn't a friendly smile. It was a little bit evil. A little bit knowing. A smile that made him tremble even more.

"But now, your little cock is going to be really horny and sensitive," she said. And when she touched it again, he found out just how right she was. And he nearly cried.

As she slowly stroked he almost wept from the sensitivity, the intensity, the conflict of the near painfully glorious feeling and trying to control his body, make it stop doing what it wanted so badly to do.

"Aw, poor baby!" she said as she continued her slow stroking. "I told you. I warned you it was going to be sensitive. That's your own body's self-imposed punishment for letting that little drop out. That's wonderful, isn't it?"

He really did cry then. Sobbed out, "Please, Mistress, may I have another break," as his hips bucked uncontrollably and his cock pulsed with need and struggle.

She stopped. "Aw, of course, sweetie. Stop crying now," she whispered gently. She looked up at him and her eyes shone brightly. "Here," she said. "Let me kiss it better." Then she took his cock with one gloved hand, cupped his balls with the other, put his whole cockhead in her glorious mouth and gave it one big, wet, passionate French kiss.

And of course. He exploded.

He knew it couldn't last forever. Somehow he just knew. And in the end three weeks was what it amounted to.

One day he sat down to his laptop, opened his email and there was one from her. The subject line was "The end cums quickly." He actually chuckled. But he knew it was done.

It had been a dark time for him. And very, intensely, insanely titillating.

But it had been more.

Because for those three weeks he had never felt more alive, never more vibrant, never more connected to the world, to the air, to the trees, to other people. He felt like he caught a glimmer of how the universe fit together, that just for a moment he could see what some people called God.

And it was because of her.

Thinking now, he changed his mind. It wasn't dark then. It was dark before. Then she came along, reached in, shuffled some things around, turned the light on and left.

New York Snow

Elissa Wald

The two men in black leather chaps appeared in the club while I was onstage. The Dollhouse was so dead at that point – it was about three in the morning – that they were like apparitions in the pink neon. We were in the midst of the kind of lull everyone dreaded: about twelve dancers working the last shift and maybe three customers left in the club, all of them bleary-eyed and long gone for broke.

The two who had just walked in charged the smoky air. They looked restless and purposeful and sharp. My three-song set on the main stage was just ending and I went over to them as fast as my five-inch heels would take me.

"Are you guys gay?" I asked. This kind of opening was a specialty of mine. I favored provocative questions that would engage almost anyone, for better or for worse.

"Are you fuckin' wasted?" This came from the tall one.

"Who else would wear leather chaps over jeans on a sweltering summer night?"

"We're *bikers*."

"Oh."

He was at least six foot four, with a long, somewhat leonine face and wavy light brown hair. His friend was of average height and had a shaved head.

"I'm Magdalene," I offered then.

"I'm Billy," he answered. "And this is Lars."

How I loved that job then. Up until that evening, it would have been hard to count the number of ways. It wasn't just the dozens of different men dealt to me like cards every night, and my license to go up to them, touch them, tease them, do whatever I felt like doing. And it went beyond the money flowing in like a rain-swollen stream, though the thrill of that tax-free cash never wore thin.

It was also the pure pleasure of dancing naked, or nearly so – out in the open, where perfect strangers could see. (When had this last been permissible? Not since the age of one or two.) It was the pleasure, even, of dancing itself – moving to music that underscored the special power of the strip joint stage. Earlier that evening, I'd raked in fifty-four singles dancing to M. C. Hammer's "U Can't Touch This".

The truth was that, though I was far from the best or most beautiful dancer, I made more money than anyone else, all night, every night. I brought a special energy to the job. I was a very young woman, and I knew that I would not always be a young woman. I had the sense of having caught a certain wave before it was too late, and riding it intoxicated me beyond reason.

The *glamour* intoxicated me, seedy and small-time as it was. Sometimes in the mirrors flanking the stage, I'd catch a glimpse of the picture I was a part of: two or three young girls on a platform, on display beneath the hot lights, bodies ablaze with youth and entitlement, men crowded at their feet in supplication. It was a sight that filled me with joy. I'd grown up loving the luminaries of burlesque – Gypsy Rose Lee, Marlene Dietrich, Mae West – and I'd longed to join the ranks of those garter-flashing, wisecracking femmes fatales. So when, with a sidelong glance, I'd see facets of this wish brought to life in the smoky glass, it never seemed like less than a miracle.

I knew that many of the other strippers did in fact aspire to be actresses, or cabaret singers, or real dancers. But I had none of these talents and never would, and so this was my only real chance. To be a dream girl. (*Dream girl*: the very phrase was like a caress. I wanted to trail it like a cloak, brandish it like a fan, have it crown me like a diadem. *U can't touch this*.)

Almost as delightful as flaunting my near-naked self was wearing the different costumes the job demanded. Dancers had to be able to embody a full range of fantasies. My outfit of the evening might be sleek and black and minimal, or it might be pink and fluffy and sweet. I could be supple as a cut switch, or like so much candy. And maybe that was the ultimate source of the job's allure: the idea that, as long as I stayed within the dress code (heels a minimum of four inches high; G-string opaque; a garter to match) I could be whomever I wanted.

No sooner had I sat down with Billy and Lars than Mona was there to enforce the two-drink minimum. Mona was a cocktail

waitress and her uniform was a black and gold bodice with fishnet stockings. All the waitresses wore the same outfit.

"What'll it be?" Coming from her, these words were more a
command than a question.

"We'll take two shots of Jack and whatever Magdalene wants,"
Billy told her.

"Just a glass of cranberry, please," I said, and watched her walk
off without another word.

I admired Mona a great deal. I liked the way she looked and
the way she carried herself. Tattooed barbed-wire bracelets encircled her upper arms and her navy-black hair was cropped short
as a boy's. In the dressing room, I would watch her cover the
tattoos with beige make-up in compliance with the house rules,
blowing lazy smoke rings at her reflection between layers. She
had a hard-bitten, don't-fuck-with-me attitude and knew how to
keep customers in line.

I was the kind of girl that a guy like Billy would want to
deflower. The kind of girl who would bring the word "deflower"
to mind, despite the unlikely surroundings he might have found
me in. Mona was probably the kind of girl he could love, had time
been given the chance to tell.

As she returned with the drinks, I remembered something that
had happened the week before, when she and I were in the Champagne Lounge at the same time.

The Champagne Lounge was the upstairs room where a
customer could pay $300 to take the dancer of his choice. This
bought an hour of private time with her, and when that hour
was up, he could sign on for another if he wanted. Occasionally,
a customer would be interested in taking a waitress to the
Lounge instead of a dancer, and if there were enough barmaids
to fill in for her, this was allowed. The house got $220 of that
hourly $300 rate, so the waitress's feelings about it were of no
consequence.

The high cost of the Lounge always made me anxious. The
"Champagne Hostess," who oversaw these transactions, would
explain to the customers beforehand that no sexual activity was
allowed in there. But I worried anyway. Even if most of the men
knew better than to try to bend the rules, it was still hard to imagine what I could do to make that hour worth so much money. It
was a bittersweet tug on my heart every time a man signed that
credit card slip. It moved me to know that someone thought my

company was worth three-hundred dollars an hour. I wanted my customers to enjoy this interlude, to consider the money well spent and to not feel taken. I was always warm and attentive, hanging on their words, laughing at their jokes, dispensing innocent caresses at every opportunity.

One evening during the week before, when I arrived in the Champagne Lounge at about midnight, Mona had already been there for a couple of hours. She and her client were in the elevated seating area, on their third bottle of champagne. The man was so drunk that when he got up to go to the men's room, he stumbled over the edge of the low platform, fell flat on his face like a cartoon, and lay on the linoleum without moving again. The sound of him hitting the floor turned nearly every head in the Lounge. There was an audible murmur from all sides, of startled alarm and concern. Mona was counting her money and didn't even look up.

"That girl," Lars was saying now. He was watching Jade on the main stage. "That girl could make me come from across the room."

I sighed in a derisive and theatrical way. "I wish someone could make *me* come from across a room."

Billy turned his grey-green gaze on me. "*I* could make you come from across a room."

I smirked at him. "That's a good one."

"I could," he said. "I know I could."

"Great," I said. "Go ahead. Go across the room and make me come."

For a second, his expression seemed to hover at the edge of consternation. Then he stood and walked to the leather sofas flanking the opposite wall. Lars grinned, enjoying his friend's predicament. Both of us waited with interest to see what he would do.

Billy sat down and, staring at the floor, took a pack of Marlboros from an inside pocket of his vest. He took his time shaking a cigarette from the pack, lighting it, and putting it between his lips. As he drew on it, he looked up and fixed me with a fierce glare. Then he exhaled through his nostrils, glowering through the smoke.

This performance made me laugh harder than I'd laughed in months. Within minutes I had two black raccoon eyes from crying mascara tears. I was still laughing when I was called to the bar stage for my final set of the night, and I had to hold on to the backs of chairs to steady myself on my way to the front of the club.

The dj was playing the kind of siren song I loved, "Bette Davis Eyes". Tired as I was at the tail end of the night, it was carrying me along.

"Can I give you a ride home?"

Billy had come up to the bar stage. Apparently he wasn't one to hold a grudge. We faced each other: he in his heavy boots, jeans, chaps and a leather vest, helmet dangling from one hand; me naked except for a G-string and heels. While I was on that platform in those heels, my eyes were just level with his.

"What, on your motorcycle?" I asked.

"On my bike," he corrected me.

"What do you drive? A Harley-Davidson?"

"Fuck no. Harleys are so fashionable right now it's sickening. I've got an Italian bike, a Ducati. Fastest thing on two wheels. It can go from zero to a hundred and ten in about two and a half seconds.'"

"I'm afraid of motorcycles," I said truthfully.

"Why?"

"Oh, maybe because they're about the most dangerous thing you can do."

"Yeah, well, they're a rush."

"It would be hard for me to get on one."

"'Look . . . it's 4 a.m.," he said. "Other drivers are the most dangerous part of the equation, and at this hour no one else'll be on the road."

"Will you go slow?"

"If you want. I guess. But you won't be getting the Ducati experience."

"I don't care about that," I told him. "I just want to get home in one piece."

"Well, look. Meet me around the corner when you get off. I'll be in the Raccoon Lodge." The Raccoon Lodge was a biker bar on the next block.

"Why there?"

"Because that's where my bike is."

"Why can't you bring your bike over here?"

"Why can't you walk a block and a half?"

"Because," I snapped, "I'm not interested in walking anywhere at four in the morning in downtown New York with all that money. And you shouldn't be asking me to."

"OK, OK. Are you always this high maintenance?"

When I emerged from the club, wearing a regular summer dress, he was standing there beside a sleek red machine. Wordlessly he held out a second helmet.

"Remember," I said as I took it. "You promised to go slow. Right?"

"Just get on the bike."

I made a show out of stopping in my tracks. "No, I'm not going to just get on the damn bike. Promise me you'll go slow or I'll get a cab."

"Take a fuckin' cab then."

I laid the helmet on the Ducati's seat and began walking away.

"Magdalene!" He shouted my stage name. I realized I hadn't even told him my real one.

I turned. "What?"

"Come on. Don't be like that. I promised you, didn't I? Why would I go back on what I said?"

"Just to fuck with me," I suggested.

"I'm not going to do that. Come on."

I went back and climbed on behind him.

It seemed to me that he went as fast as it was possible to go between close-set red lights. Not the boasted 110 miles in two and a half seconds, but much faster than necessary. Why did I do this, I had to ask myself. Why endanger my life climbing onto the back of a stranger's motorcycle? A stranger I met in a strip joint, no less. Why let him know where I lived?

Sometimes it seemed to me that getting on the back of a stranger's motorcycle was just another masquerade, another costume I was trying on. I never went all the way into anything. I held myself back while taking what I could; I asked to go slow. But now, in motion with a stranger in the driver's seat, there was no way to control the experience anymore. I leaned into the turns as he instructed. I closed my eyes and clutched him with all my might until we pulled up beside my apartment building.

"What a miracle," Billy sneered once the engine had been cut and our helmets were off. "You *made it home alive.*"

I climbed off the bike and stood in front of him on the sidewalk. I was trembling with relief and exhilaration and leftover terror. "Yes I did," I said. "And I feel lucky."

"I don't think anyone's ever clutched me so tight in my life. It's a wonder I could breathe."

"You promised me you wouldn't go fast."

"That wasn't fast! Little girl! I didn't go anywhere *near* what this baby can do."

"You went a lot faster than you had to go."

He shrugged and didn't deny it.

"You knew how I felt, so what was the point?" I asked.

He shrugged again. "Crawling's no fun."

What could I say without sounding like a little old lady? *It's all fun and games until someone loses a limb.*

"Well," I said finally. "I guess I'm home, then. Thanks for the ride.'"

He looked at me steadily with his leonine eyes. "Aren't you going to invite me upstairs?"

My apartment was a studio with a sleeping alcove. On the wall beside the entrance to this little chamber, a black riding crop hung on a nail.

Billy walked straight over and took it down from the wall.

"This," he said, striding across the room with it. "*This* – I knew there was some reason I was bothering with you. This has been part of every relationship I've ever had."

I felt the first inkling of real interest since meeting him. "Most people, when they see that, ask me if I ride."

He snorted. "I know you don't ride."

"Then they wonder if I'm a dominatrix."

He made the same dismissive sound. "Dominant? You?"

"What makes you think I'm not?"

"Come on. Don't make me laugh."

"I like switching," I said defensively.

"Yeah, you like a good switching. Come over here."

I ignored this. "How many other dancers from the Dollhouse have you taken home?"

He pulled the wooden chair out from under my writing desk and rested one booted foot on the seat. I watched the tip of the riding quirt, tapping against its steel-toed rim. There was an uncomfortable silence.

I tried again. "I haven't seen you in the club before, and I've been there almost a year."

He let long moments go by before he spoke, then repeated the last thing he'd said. "Come over here."

I went to him. I let him take me by the hair and bend me over his thigh. The pungent scent of the leather took all the resistance out of me; there was no way to stand up against that. He lifted the bottom of my dress and I felt my own riding crop slash across the back of my thighs. Not starting light, as so many play-whippings do.

"*Aahhh!!*" It was more an exhalation than a cry.

"Next time I tell you to do something," he said, his voice low beside my ear, "I'll only have to tell you once. Right?"

"Yes," I breathed.

He struck me a second time, as hard as before or harder.

"Yes, what?" he asked.

"Yes . . . *sir* . . ."

And again. "Yes, sir, what?"

I spoke in a strangled rush. "Yes, sir, you'll only have to tell me once."

"That's right. That's my promise to you. I'm going to make it real easy for you to remember that."

And here it was, one of the moments I lived for: to have the word *sir* forced from between my teeth with no hesitation, no irony. To get a good ass-whipping without even trying, pure luck like finding a hundred-dollar bill on the sidewalk or hitting some lottery jackpot. Not everyone will understand the joy this brought me, but that's precisely why it was so gratifying. It was more than gratification, it was something like arrival – something like recognition, or homecoming, or relief.

This act did not segue into sex, as many would imagine. After all, I didn't really know him.

The same intuition on Billy's part that had brought about what already happened now kept him from asking for, or demanding something he must have known I truly wasn't ready to yield.

That intuition had let him keep hitting me even when I pleaded with him to stop. At that point, the whipping had not yet made me cry. This juncture would arrive, and we were well beyond it by the time he decided it was finished. His promise to me – that I would never again make him repeat an order – had been his final words to me for the duration. It was a silent whipping, from his end of it. He neither gloated nor lectured nor made me repeat the lesson learned. I had the sense that what he wanted, more than anything, was for me to hear myself. When he was done, he laid the quirt on my desk and brought his booted foot to the floor. Still grasping my hair, he asked, "Any beer on the premises?"

I nodded without speaking.

He released me. "Get me a beer, then. And wash your face."

I moved toward the opposite side of the room, to the little tiled area with a refrigerator, some cabinets and a small square of counter space. I turned on the water and stared at my hands cupped together under the jet: were they really mine? Was all of this really happening? They were trembling when I took the cap off a cold bottle of Coors and brought it to him without a word.

"Thank you," he said. "When are you working again?"

He was a different person, now. And I was a different person. I spoke to him quietly and with deference, and hearing myself now, speaking in this different tone, was almost unbearably erotic in itself.

"Not till Saturday," I said. It was only Tuesday.

"What are you doing tomorrow night?"

"I'm – actually, I'm going to my friend's play," I told him. It killed me to have to say this. "She's the playwright," I added in a rush. "It's an off-Broadway show. Tomorrow's opening night."

"What about Thursday?"

That was no good either, I realized. "Thursday my aunt's in town. I promised I'd have dinner with her.'"

He waited a moment before speaking again. When he did, his tone was both patient and warning. "What about Friday, then?"

"Friday I'm free," I said. I wasn't, but those plans at least I could rearrange. My sister and I were supposed to see a movie. And what were sisters for, if not to understand about these things?

"I'll see you on Friday night," he said.

It wasn't a question, so I said, "All right."

And I watched from the window as the Ducati blurred to a thin red streak down Houston Street.

All day Friday I could barely imagine what to do with myself. I took a long bath, then stood naked before the full-length bathroom mirror taking anxious inventory of the body he had already marked. The welts across my backside and thighs left me breathless with longing. By this time it was mid-afternoon and I hadn't yet eaten. I had hunger pangs but couldn't seem to swallow anything. Even my coffee went cold in its cup and I ended up pouring it down the drain.

He hadn't mentioned a time, I realized. He had to be coming back to my apartment, because we hadn't talked about a place, either. I spent some overwrought energy scouring the place, buying more beer, and finding the right clothes to wear. I didn't want anything that conjured the strip joint; I wanted restrained and submissive elegance. At the back of my closet I found what I was after: a red-wine dress that laced up the front, low-cut but still somehow demure. I put a silver choker around my neck. By seven o'clock I was ready for him.

At eight, I realized that not only did I not have his phone number, but I didn't even know his last name. And he had no way to contact me either, if something had come up. I was at his mercy, again; there was nothing for me to do but wait.

By nine o'clock I was racked with anxiety. I tried to remind myself that for New Yorkers, nine o'clock was still early. Still, if I'd known our "date" was going to be on the later side, I would have found some better way of killing the early evening hours. I would have gone to a film, had a drink with a girlfriend, done anything rather than pace the apartment looking at the clock. By now it was too late to go out, even for a few minutes, without the risk of missing him. If this was his idea of an s/m game, it was a very effective one. I tried to talk myself into liking it.

So far I had been listening for the sound of a motorcycle on the street below. In downtown New York, that sound came about every minute and a half. I hadn't wanted to look out the window, didn't want him to see my watchful silhouette and know that I was in a state. Now I abandoned pride and went to the window often. I saw a lot of Harleys (and indeed, he was right: they were sickening; any motorcycle that wasn't his was sickening) and still more Hondas and Yamahas and Suzukis. I didn't see a red Ducati.

At around quarter to ten, a chill set in. It was the chill of fear. I sat on the floor beside the radiator, knees drawn up and arms wrapped around them. It seemed no other position was bearable and that only by holding myself perfectly still could I endure the minutes ticking by one after the other. I sat like that for a long time, until ten thirty or so.

Nothing takes the edge off hours like these, nothing. All attempts at distraction are futile. Reading, my most reliable comfort, was all but useless. From time to time I tried to pick up a book, but the pounding of my heart was so painful and insistent I could feel it in my fingertips as I clutched the binding. I would read the same sentence over and over again. And finally I would realize that all I was doing was ruining the book, tainting it by association with this ordeal so that the sight of it would be hateful to me forever afterward.

At eleven fifteen I started to cry. I went into the bathroom and watched myself cry in the mirror. Then I made myself stop and wash my face (even this was laden now with the pang of erotic memory) and reapply my mascara. I reasoned that it would not be at all surprising if Billy rode in at around midnight, or even later. I didn't have to know him for more than an hour or two to know that. There was still a chance that he would come.

At 1 a.m. I lay down on my bed, on top of the patchwork quilt I spread across it during the daytime. I still wore my dress, my garter belt and stockings, and even my shoes. Was this what he'd wanted – for me to feel like this? Was it part of the game? If it was, I was out of my league. I lay awake, listening to the traffic, the occasional sound of a motorcycle, no longer daring to hope.

How had this happened? How had I signed myself over to this man in the course of his twenty minutes in my apartment? The Dollhouse was a place I had been able to spin my own fantasy, cast a spell, make men grovel, make them pay. Billy had cut a swift and terrible swath through all that careful artifice; he'd taken me home and taken me down, worked me over and worn me out, and it was impossible now to believe that I'd ever found him laughable. I tried to conjure the memory of the ridicule – the *scorn* – he'd inspired, trying to make me come from across the room. Instead, it occurred to me for the first time to wonder: might not that kind of helpless laughter – involuntary, racking, with its convulsions, weakness, tears, delight – be a form of orgasm?

When I next looked at the clock and saw it was two in the morning, I reached for the life raft of sleep. I didn't open my eyes again until 7 a.m. – the sun already bright in the sky, all hope faded like the nearly full moon.

It took everything I had to drag myself to work that night. Suddenly the job seemed to be the source of misery like this. It seemed to brand me as the kind of girl against whom men sought vengeance. We were hustlers, and so we deserved no better than to be hustled once in a while – to be aroused and then left to burn, like the men burned after we'd teased them into a frenzy and emptied their pockets.

All I wanted, on this night, was to stay home. I didn't want to strip myself down in front of any more men. And what if Billy himself chose to come back in while I was working? I didn't want to remain in a state of near-nakedness for him either.

But by seven o'clock, knowing I'd be fined fifty dollars for being late and twice that for missing a shift, I was dragging myself down West Broadway, past the bistros with beautiful people at outdoor tables, mussel shells piled on plates between them, the fashionable Harleys parked in a line a few yards away.

Down, down, past Canal Street and the sparser scattering of glamorous digs, to the seedier streets, Duane and Reade, like the drugstore, Warren, like the rats' nest it suggested, to Murray where the club was.

The Dollhouse flanked the financial district, which was closed on the weekends. For this reason, Saturday nights always started slow. When I walked into the club, it was almost as dead as when I'd last walked out. There was no one in the bar area but Nikki, one of the cocktail waitresses.

"Hey," I said to her, raising a hand in a half-wave.

She looked up from the tumblers she was setting out and I saw that she had been crying.

"Magdalene," she said. The glass she was holding trembled in her grip and for a minute I forgot my own hurt.

"Nikki . . ." I moved over to the bar. "Are you OK?"

"Did you hear?" she asked me.

"Hear what?"

"About Mona?"

"No, I didn't. What about Mona?"

"She was in an accident," Nikki said. "She's fucked up."

"Oh God," I said. Mona and Nikki were tight, even outside the job. Everyone knew that. "Oh, Nikki, I'm so sorry. What kind of accident? Is she going to be all right?"

"No, she's not gonna be all right. It was a motorcycle accident. She got fuckin' *mangled*."

"Oh my *God*," I said again. "When did this happen?"

"Thursday night. Late. It was after work. I found out yesterday."

"Oh, Nikki."

Carter, the manager, emerged from his office. "All right, girls. We're at work now. I know everyone's upset about Mona – I'm upset too – but as professionals we don't let our . . . emotions spill over into the job. All right? Magdalene, you better get ready to go on at eight."

Nikki stared down at the newly washed cocktail glasses and her tears splashed onto the gleaming black surface of the bar. I reached out and touched her hand before heading downstairs.

In the dressing room, all the girls were talking about Mona. Many were as distraught as Nikki.

"She was a doll. A doll! Never pressured me to drink with a guy just so she could make money, like all the others do."

"And she was only nineteen. It wasn't like this was the end of the road for her. I mean, she was just a baby. A tough chick, yeah, but really just a baby."

"Wait a minute," I said. I was just standing there, making no move to get undressed yet. "She's alive, isn't she? Why is everyone talking like she's dead?"

"She might as well be," Sapphire said. "Her neck is broken. Blaze went to the hospital yesterday to visit her and said she's in a coma. And there's no way she's gonna come out of it, either. They say she's brain-dead.'"

"Oh *my God.*"

"You didn't know, huh, Magdalene? That's right, you haven't worked since Tuesday night."

"I didn't even know Mona had a motorcycle."

"She didn't. She was on the back of someone else's. He was taking her home."

"I'm sorry, I . . . it's true, this is the first I'm hearing of this. What actually happened?" I asked. Billy's words came back to me: *other drivers are the most dangerous part of the equation.* "I mean, does anyone know how they crashed?"

"They didn't crash. She fell off."

"She fell *off*? Fell off the back of the bike?"

"It seems like she might have had a little bit to drink. Maybe she even fell asleep, nobody knows. The guy who was driving didn't even know she was gone at first. At some point, he looked behind him and no one was there."

Mona and I had never been friends. In the ten months I had been working at the Dollhouse, we probably hadn't exchanged more than thirty words. But I felt close to her then, or at least, a little too close to the circumstances that killed her. *It could have been me,* was all I could think. On the back of someone else's motorcycle, for Christ's sake. Some guy who was taking her home.

The night went by in a daze. I managed to dance for dozens of men without really looking at any of them. I had walked in the front door of the club hurting, and I still hurt, of course, but now the hurt was tangled, complicated. Mona and her accident and my memory of Billy were twisted into a single insistent knot, and the individual strands were impossible to separate.

All night I scanned the crowd for a man who stood a head taller than anyone else. From the stage, I looked across the room for a light brown mane. I wanted to tell him the story, wanted to say, *See? Now aren't you glad that I held on to you like that?*

What might have seemed like an obvious possibility did not occur to me once all night. Not till the last minute, when the late shift was over and all the dancers were back in the locker room getting dressed. It didn't come to me until I was washing my face and when it did, I almost lost my balance, even though my stilettos were off and I was flat-footed for the first time in eight hours. I had to grab the edge of the sink to steady myself.

"Whoa, Magdalene. Had a few?" Harlowe was on my left, watching me in the mirror.

"Harlowe," I said, still dizzy though the fact was I'd had nothing to drink at all. "Harlowe, the guy Mona was with? The driver of the motorcycle. Do you know his name?"

"Uh-uh. Why?"

"Would anyone know?"

"Nikki probably would. But she left at two. Carter let her go home early. First sign I've ever seen that he's human, and I been here six years."

"Do you know anything about him? The biker, I mean."

"I think he hangs out at the Raccoon Lodge. That's the last place she was, anyway, before she got on the bike. She liked to go there after work. But it's a biker bar, so I guess that doesn't tell you too much."

Once I was dressed, I walked out the door and over to the next block. It really wasn't all that treacherous. Even in the middle of downtown New York at four in the morning with all that money in my pocket, it wasn't such a big deal after all. There weren't many people in the Raccoon Lodge at that hour. I went to the far end of the bar and took a seat.

"What can I get you?" The bartender was a young guy with a Fu Manchu and a bandanna tied around his head.

I laid a five on the bar and decided to try Billy's drink. "Just a straight shot of Jack, please."

"You comin' from work?"

"Yep." I smiled at him.

He put the shot on the bar and replaced the five with a single. I added another from the wad in my pocket. "Could I ask you about something?"

"Ask away."

"Do you know about a dancer getting hurt in a bike accident?"

"Heard about that, yes."

"Do you know the guy who drove the bike?"

"Know him like a brother. He's a great guy. And he's broken over this thing. Fuckin' broken."

"Could you tell me his name?"

He looked at me warily. "Why do you want to know?"

"I – I'm just wondering if I know him."

"Well, if you knew him, you would know. Right?"

"The thing is, I just met him." When the bartender didn't answer, I said, "Well, look, what's the big deal about telling me his name? It's not a secret, is it?"

"His friends are being very protective of him right now. I don't know if the girl was a friend of yours, but he's laid out as it is and we don't want anyone harassing him on top of that."

"I promise that's not what this is about. Some guy gave me a ride home on his bike the other night. We were supposed to get together again and I never heard from him. I figured he just blew me off, but if he was involved in this accident the night before . . . well, I'd understand why he never made it over."

Silence.

"I know it's a long shot," I went on, "but still, the coincidence of it . . ."

Again, he didn't answer.

"Look," I said. "Could you just tell me his first name? I can't do anything with that. Can't look up his number, can't figure out where he lives or works or anything. I just want to know for myself."

The bartender met my eyes. "His first name is Billy."

I stared at him.

"Is that the name of the guy who took you home?"

"I can't believe it. I didn't think it would really be him."

"You sure it was the same Billy?"

"Well . . . this guy was tall. Very tall. With longish, light brown hair."

"Rides a Ducati?"

I was so relieved that his failure to show up had nothing to do with me that I was almost elated riding home in a taxi. And *vindicated*. He had made fun of me for being afraid of his bike. He'd sneered at me when we pulled up to my building: *What a miracle. You made it home alive.* And now look.

The terrible truth was that losing him this way was less painful to me than losing him for the reasons I'd been conjuring since the night before. Reasons having to do with vengeance or indifference or a sudden change of heart.

And that was the one damper on my warped little sense of redemption: the knowledge that I had lost him, no doubt about it. After the high-handed stance I'd taken toward his motorcycle, I'd be the last person Billy would ever want to see again.

And I didn't see him again, not for five years. Not till an evening in January when I was on the L train, coming home from my office job. I stepped into the crowded subway car and saw Billy standing a few feet away. After I'd been staring at him for several minutes, he looked up and met my gaze, but almost immediately he looked away again. Neither of us spoke.

At the very next stop, he got off alone, stepped out of the car without a backward glance. I didn't blame him for that. I was probably the one person in the world who – after the accident – could have said to him, *I told you so.* And I imagine that to him, this fact had turned me into someone else, someone formidable whose shadow had only lengthened over the years. Still, I could have bolted after him. I could have waylaid him on the subway platform. The minute the doors closed behind his back, I wished I had.

And I still wish I had. I'd like to tell him that I understand why he might see me as something more than myself, but that investing a near-stranger with such power is a mistake. That after the way I felt about his part in Mona's death, I've got nothing on him. Nothing at all.

And that my real name is Melanie.